The PULPS

The PULPS

Fifty Years of *American Pop Culture*
Compiled and edited by
TONY GOODSTONE

Research Consultant: SAM MOSKOWITZ
Photography: CHRISTINE E. HAYCOCK, M.D.

BONANZA BOOKS   NEW YORK

In compiling such an ambitious project I have incurred many agreeable debts. Although a substantial portion of the book has come from my own research and collection, it was only through the patient advice and generous counsel of Sam Moskowitz that this book achieved its scope. He made his collection of some 15,000 Pulps available to me, and most of the material in the book was extracted from his collection. I doubt I could have found such expert knowledge elsewhere. Thank you Sam.

His wife, Dr. Christine Haycock photographed all the material, a painstaking job, since much of it is on the verge of disintegration.

I appreciate the advice and encouragement of my many friends: Dan Ferman, Joe Goggin, Jack Goodstein, Dick Krinsley, Richard Merkin, Joe Rubin, Terry Southern, Harold Steinberg, Jeff Steinberg, Joan Tapper, Paul Zack, and last but not least, my parents, who if they had not (like so many others) banned Pulps from the house, probably would not have inspired my doing this book. Special thanks also to Jane, who put up with a remarkable amount of debris with a minimum of flak.

Finally, I wish to express my appreciation to Andy Norman, a kindred spirit, who demonstrated tremendous feeling for the project as well as his faith in me. Thanks Andy, this one's for you.

Acknowledgment is gratefully extended to the following for permission to reprint from their works:

Paul R. Reynolds, Inc.: "The Torture Pool" by MacKinlay Kantor. Copyright 1932 by Detective Fiction Weekly.

Edgar Rice Burroughs, Inc.: "The Resurrection of Jimber-Jaw" by Edgar Rice Burroughs. Copyright 1937 by Edgar Rice Burroughs, renewed 1964 by John C. Burroughs, Joan Pierce, Hillbert Burroughs.

The Conde Nast Publications Inc.: "The Shadow Knows" from The Shadow. Copyright 1943 by Street & Smith Publications, Inc. "Voodoo Death" by Maxwell Grant. Copyright 1944 by Street & Smith Publications, Inc. "The Evil Gnome" by Kenneth Robeson. Copyright 1940 by Street & Smith Publications, Inc.; renewed 1968 by The Conde Nast Publications Inc.

Popular Publications Inc.: "Wake for the Living" by Ray Bradbury. Copyright 1947 by Popular Publications, Inc.

"From the Bleachers" by Handley Cross, in Street & Smith's Sport Story Magazine. Copyright 1934, © 1962 by Street & Smith Publications, Inc.

"Incantation" by Page Cooper, "The Green Window" by Mary Elizabeth Counselman, and "Continuity" by H. P. Lovecraft are reprinted by permission from Weird Tales. Copyright 1947, 1949, 1950 by Weird Tales.

Preface

Not everyone knew about pulp paper magazines in the nineteen twenties. I didn't. I had graduated from Princeton and taken post-graduate studies at the University of Berlin without ever coming into contact with one.

At the Berlin railroad station, preparing for an overnight trip to Paris, I purchased *Detective Story Magazine* and Conan Doyle's "The Hound of the Baskervilles" to put me in the proper mood for sleep.

Much to my surprise, but not yours, I not only didn't go to sleep, I spent the entire night finishing the two of them and stepped off the train asking myself where they had been all my life. A great deal of money could be made with that kind of material, I reasoned, and it was not long before I was at it, inventing one Pulp magazine after another, until my firm, Popular Publications, Inc., had originated over 300 of them—all of which, you might like to know, made money at one time or another.

I borrowed $5,000 from my stepfather to start the firm, so it did not require much capitalization, as you can see, and some twenty-five years later the company paid an income tax in seven figures. We commenced publication with 4 titles we created and the most we ever published in a single month were 42.

Before it was over, we had become the largest in the business. Such was the bonanza of the Pulps.

They traveled a golden rail from very bad to very excellent and they appealed to all strata and all vintages of people. The names of Harry Truman, president of the United States, and Al Capone, lowest figure in the underworld, graced our subscription lists at the same time. But no matter how action-filled or how erudite the writing might be, there was one tacit rule which, with certain very small exceptions, applied throughout. The stories must be clean and sweet-smelling. The heroines dreamed of nothing more carnal than kissing and I have no doubt that many of our readers were innocent enough to attribute the genesis of childbirth to this fictional denouement.

However, Pulps were the principal entertainment vehicle for millions of Americans. They were an unflickering, uncolored T.V. screen upon which the reader could spread the most glorious imagination he possessed. The athletes were stronger, the heroes were nobler, the girls were more beautiful and the palaces were more luxurious than any in existence and they were always there at any time of the day or night on dull, no-gloss paper that was kind to the eyes. Readers still cherish such great names as Erle Stanley Gardner (with whom I adventured in many wild and remote areas), Lord Buchan, governor-general of Canada, who wrote "The 39 Steps" for our *Adventure Magazine,* Tod Robbins, author of "The Terrible Three," later "The Unholy Three" of the movies, Frank Packard, remembered for "The Miracle Man," Harold Lamb of "The Crusades," Leonard Nason of "Three on a Match," Talbot Mundy of "Soul of a Regiment," Max Brand of "Dr. Kildare," Sax Rohmer's "Dr. Fu Manchu," Edgar Rice Burrough's "Tarzan of the Apes" and C. S. Forester's "Captain Horatio Hornblower." These and many, many more meant a lifetime of pleasure for most Americans.

But now the pocket book and the finite, often times unimaginative picture on the T.V. screen have taken over. The worst is no better than the worst of the Pulps and the best depends for comparison on the extent of your imagination.

The Pulps are dead but the heroes live on and, who can tell, perhaps they may return in subtler guise.

New York
Aug., 1970

Henry Steeger, Pres.
Popular Publications, Inc.

Contents

Foreword . . .

Someday, as is almost the case now, the art of the Beatles will seem quaint: an incongruity in a world where popular entertainment will have gone beyond electronic music and narcotism to—who knows?—direct electrical stimulation of the pleasure centers of the brain.

What, then, will the Beatles' music represent for tomorrow's elders? Pleasure symbols of lost youth? Escape from the disillusion of impending age into a nostalgic womb? And what will be the value of this "nostalgia" for the young? A cultural curiosity? "Camp" entertainment? A symbol of adult conventionality? Certainly, in future surroundings the Beatles' music will seem foreign both to those who grew up with it and to their children. And as the music of the Beatles will be tomorrow; the Pulps are today: a symbol of the problems of communication between young and old. Both groups think they understand (but disagree with) each other, and both, of course, are wrong. They may use the same language, but their understanding of each other is as misconstrued as that of the Ice Age hero and his new-found friends in the first story in this collection, "The Resurrection of Jimber-Jaw." Neither can really grasp the other's simplest thoughts, even when expressed in the most familiar words (although they delude themselves in thinking they do): *because the emotional history which defines words is different for each person alienated from another by differences in cultural background.*

Until alien groups absorb and understand each other's culture they remain naive to their emotional roots, and there can be little real communication between them. Through the examination of alien culture, however (and culture becomes alien also to oneself with the passing of time), retrospective insights emerge which open the barriers to effective communication. The Pulps are more than a "Rosetta Stone" to the past: they can help to simplify the present.

In researching and reviewing more than a century of popular American fiction, and particularly in selecting the material for this book, I was struck by two other thoughts. First, popular entertainment provides an accurate barometric record of emotional climate which reveals the anxieties of the masses. (Perhaps by taking current readings on this barometer we can "read" these anxieties—predict social trends—before they explode. It might even be possible to "program" entertainment to provide "safe" outlets on a large scale.)

Secondly, in reading at least 500 stories in order to make my selections, I discovered something about the reading of fiction of which I had not been aware. The novel, now the predominant form of entertainment reading, is really the author's guided tour of *his* imagination. In the short story, however, YOU are the story. It unfolds as *your* imagination develops the details which the author has only sketched in. Therefore, this kind of material should be read leisurely and under comfortable conditions.

In conceiving this collection my philosophy has been to present the Pulps in as close to the original format as possible, choosing paper, type and layout to recreate the "feel" of the original. For the sake of practicality pages were trimmed, layout was made more uniform, and width and length of the page was increased slightly to accommodate more material.

Rather than anthologize the best of the Pulps, my goal was to find material broadly representative of the field. Thus, works vary in degree of excellence—authors and artists vary in prominence. Finally all of the material is exciting on many levels—from studious appraisal, to unabashed nostalgia, to outright "camp."

New York City
August, 1970

Tony Goodstone

Nickel Heroes / Dime Novels

In 1896, publisher Frank Munsey, believing that a story was more important than the paper it was printed on, changed *The Argosy* from a boy's magazine to an all-fiction magazine with untrimmed, rough wood-pulp pages and measuring approximately 7 by 10 inches and half-an-inch thick. He had created the first "Pulp." Before failing circulation (and, finally, one major distributor's embargo) killed them off in 1953, the Pulps had divided, amoeba-like, into unknown hundreds of titles, and furnished inexpensive reading, escape from social oppression and hope for the future for tens of millions of Americans.

In 1970 only a handful of small digest-sized detective, western and science-fiction magazines remained—the dull residue of a once-gaudy galaxy that had given early expression to some of our finest artists and writers and inspired countless others.

Thriving on deprivation in the midst of economic and industrial expansion, the Pulps were the outgrowth of a popular fiction form which had its roots in the early 19th century.

In 1830, the United States was a vast wilderness fringed on the east by a handful of states with a population of less than 13 million. Over the next decade, as the first settlers made the pilgrimage to California, crime moved west, lured by the wealth of the new frontier and its opportunities for concealment.

A squalid New York had yet to install its first adequate water system, and danger lurked everywhere, invisible in the dim light of oil lamps and candles. Charles Dickens, visiting Manhattan's Five Points in the 1840's, commented that its "leprous houses," its "filth and wretchedness" could safely be compared to London's worst. The Fundamentalist view that the cities were hotbeds of sin was reasonably accurate, inspiring religionists to publish a torrent of small paperbacks known as "chapbooks," which were peddled by street vendors along with shoelaces and pincushions. Titles ran to such intriguing lengths as: *The Affecting History of Sally Williams; afterwards Tippling Sally. Shewing how she left her father's house to follow an officer, who seduced her; and how she took to drinking, and at last became a vile prostitute, died in a hospital and was disected by the surgeons. Tending to show the pernicious effects of dram drinking.*

The success of this pious hawking of the seamy side of the street prepared the way for the "Family Story Paper," which flourished until the turn of the century. These lurid journals were the product of competition among newspapers, which tempted their readers with new attractions, including fictional narratives about vice. Family Story Papers offered, according to one publisher, "plenty of sensation and no philosophy."

In the period of intensive immigration and industrialization following the Civil War, each major city developed a "Murderer's Row" in its rapidly burgeoning slums. Thus in 1872, when the nation's first important fictional detective, "The Old Sleuth," appeared in *The Fireside Companion,* he was acclaimed by a public appalled by rampant criminal violence. He was accepted as a real person until readers finally realized that, growing crime rate notwithstanding, three different adventures each week made for an inhuman schedule.

By this time, the telegraph linked both coasts, bringing news of the violent West into nation-wide immediacy. Trans-continental railroads were in operation, and cowboys were driving huge herds of steers along the 1,000-mile Chisholm Trail to railheads like Abilene, for shipment to Chicago. Outlaw and Indian skirmishes were frequent. Buffalo were being slaughtered *en masse* as the railroads spread, and the next great fictional hero, "Buffalo Bill" (a real person whose exploits were essentially fictional), was instantly idolized by children hungry for romance of the new frontier.

As fabulous as "Buffalo Bill's" adventures may have been, they were probably less spectacular than those of his creator, "Ned Buntline" (Edward Zane Carrol Judson). Judson had run away to sea at 11, served in the Seminole War in Florida, and got himself lynched by a jealous husband and an army of pals in Nashville (luckily, the rope broke and he escaped). Serving in the Union Army, he emerged from the Civil War as a colonel with 20 bullets in his body, went west and roamed the land with Wild Bill Hickok, Texas Jack and one William Frederick Cody. In comparison to "Buffalo Bill" Cody's exploits, however, Judson saw his own as commonplace, so he created "Buffalo Bill" for Street and Smith, publishers since 1855 of Dime Novels (actually a misnomer—most cost five cents).

By now industrialization was presenting some sharp contrasts. In Philadelphia in 1876, visitors to the Centennial Exposition gaped at powerful new steam engines and hydraulic pumps. But one year later, only 250 miles west of the Centennial's celebration of the glories of technology, Pittsburgh was rocked by a railroad strike. Thousands of workers and supporters burned the Union Depot and hundreds of railroad cars, setting a violent example for dozens of other industrial centers.

The cities were choking with a growing stream of immigrants. Chicago, founded only in 1833, had burned to the ground in 1871, leaving 300,000 people homeless. Completely rebuilt, its population would pass the million mark by 1890, less than 20 years later. That same year, in Manhattan, 43,000 disease-ridden tenements would be gorged with more than a million inhabitants. Vice and corruption abounded everywhere. Tough, specialized gangs, with such names as "Plug Uglies" and "Dead Rabbits," worked out of Five Points and the Bowery committing highly organized crimes. In his recent study, *The Tweed Ring*, A. B. Callow, Jr. claims that New York in the 1870's had some 30,000 professional thieves and 3,000 gambling dens.

Street and Smith's response to the urban violence problem was "Nick Carter," boy detective. Appearing in *New York Weekly* in a story by John Russell Coryell, titled "The Old Detective's Pupil" (an obvious filching of "The Old Sleuth"), his appeal was so great that in 1891, publisher Ormond Smith assigned Frederick van Rensselaer Dey to write *The Nick Carter Library*.

Possibly the blandest hero ever created, Nick Carter was the forerunner (and the foremost) of private eyes to come, being constantly waylaid, hit over the head, and otherwise thoroughly beaten up. He was a master of disguise, and the masthead of his weekly portrayed his clean-cut visage surrounded by "Nick Carter in various disguises"—from Chinese coolie complete with queue to monocled fop. It is not known whether these bizarre alter-images contributed to the frequency of the constant cloutings he managed to attract, but the formula of the clean-cut youth in the violent situation was established for all time.

The 1890's were a time of social extremes. Laissez-faire industrialists, living in lush Victorian opulence, championed Darwin's "survival of the fittest" and resisted all efforts at social change. Reformer journalist-photographer Jacob Riis, in his vivid descriptions of the New York slums in 1889, reported that the Children's Aid Society sheltered 300,000 "outcast, homeless and orphaned children." By 1900 the census would note that there were 79,000 children aged 10 to 13 working, plus 960,000 aged 14 and 15. The total of 1,039,000 represented a staggering increase of one million child laborers since 1870. These children worked in the streets, sweatshops, factories, and mines—and withered. Of course the figures did not include scores of thousands of children, as young as three, crowded into tenement rooms doing piecework on garments, cigars, and artificial flowers until they were "old enough" to be put out to work.

The alternative, of course, was starvation.

In the face of these awesome conditions religionists, rejecting Darwinism as opposed to the "Adam" theory of creation, re-emphasized Fundamentalist values and preached clean living and hard work. Thus the anti-Darwinists as well as the Darwinists were hostile or indifferent to social reform.

Small wonder then that the works of Horatio Alger, Jr. were such a huge success. The format was simple: poor boy plus perseverance equals fame and fortune. After all, Andrew Carnegie, at the age of 12 in 1848, had worked as a millhand for $1.20 a week. By 1900 he was ready to sell out for the staggering sum of $492 million. The Alger books presented values subscribed to by Fundamentalists and industrialists alike, and offered children hope for a better life. Alger's 118 books (or as one critic called them, "one book, written 118 times") sold an incredible 250 million copies and inspired a vast array of Dime Novels with prescriptive titles like: *Might and Main Library, Brave and Bold Weekly, Work and Win,* and even a *Wide Awake* Weekly (presumably for those children suffering from exhaustion).

With the rise of college and professional sports as a recognized avenue to better education and careers, Street and Smith produced their next great hero, "Frank Merriwell," and became the unchallenged leader in the Dime Novel field. Introduced in the 1890's by Gilbert Patten under the alias of "Burt L. Standish," Merriwell's athletic exploits as a Yale student so inspired his readers that enrollment at Yale soon zoomed by the hundreds. Standish once wrote, "I confess that my imagination was often pumped pretty dry." This from the man who wrote some 20,000 words a week, had 125 million readers, maintained the pace for twenty years, and whose total experience at Yale consisted of little more than a stroll around the campus.

As low as the literary quality of Standish's writing was, critic George Jean Nathan confessed to being a fan. He maintained that the omission of Standish's biography from American literary history was its most glaring and insupportable defect, and wrote, "For one who read Mark Twain's Huckleberry Finn or Tom Sawyer, there were 10,000 who read Frank Merriwell." As for Standish, he received $75 apiece for most of the episodes and died a ward of his children.

The furious progress of the 1880's and 90's was also to produce the "invention hero" Dime Novel, such as *Frank Reade Weekly.* Covers bristled with all manner of fantastic iron tanks, parasolled flying machines, robots puffing steam, and "electric turtles." Real life was no less fantastic. Work was well under way on the Brooklyn Bridge. Steam-driven trains were already rolling along New York's second elevated railway, over a Third Avenue brightly glowing with electric light, and such wonders as the phonograph, automobile, and roll-film camera were proliferating with such rapidity that the masses were prepared to believe anything. Thus while magazines published (and priced) for the educated and well-to-do were running socially predictive stories set years in the future, the invention Dime Novels presented their extravagant fantasies as contemporary adventures.

Startling changes were also occurring in the publishing industry. Although the Dime Novels were not to disappear altogether until 1920, by 1890 the general periodicals had shifted into high gear. And in those 30 years, the American magazine would enter and leave its Golden Age in one explosive burst of creative energy.

The Big Gold Bubble / Early Pulps

Almost overnight new typewriters and electrotype and linotype machines filled the air with chatter. The thunder of giant presses punctuated the whine of electric motors. The final products erupted everywhere, in railroad and ferry terminals, candy stores, street stands, and "kiosks," as the first nation-wide distributor, The American News Company, went into operation.

Before 1893, people with money and education read stately magazines like *Harper's, Atlantic, The Century,* and *Scribner's.* (The great masses of low-income workers, immigrants, and youngsters with meager education, read Dime Novels and sleazy paperbacks costing five or ten cents.)

Lavishly illustrated, produced on slick-coated paper, and balancing fiction and nonfiction with voluminous amounts of advertising, the "Slicks" were sponsored, for the most part, by publishers whose sly intention was to promote the sale of their books through the use of critiques and excerpts from their current titles. Circulation was low, rarely exceeding 100,000. At 25 cents an issue, they were out of reach of the masses. (A factory worker with a family earned about seven dollars for six 10- to 12-hour days in the sweatshops.)

But by 1900, the illiteracy rate would drop from 13.3 percent in 1886 to 10.7 percent —an improvement of nearly 20 percent in 14 years. For the growing middle and educated lower classes, magazines were either too expensive or too cheap and juvenile.

In 1893, however, a severe economic recession began. Taking advantage of technological advances, *McClure's,* a magazine of superb quality, dropped its price from 15 to 10 cents. The middle and educated lower classes responded enthusiastically. Other magazines soon followed suit, and circulations climbed to staggering figures. In 1896, with the population at 76 million, *Munsey's* peaked at 700,000. Frank A. Munsey was inspired by its success to transform his boy's magazine *Argosy* and the first Pulp was born. In converting *Argosy* to a Pulp, he pumped it up to 192 pages of all adult-adventure fiction. Each issue reeled out 135,000 words, unrelieved by illustrations, with 60 pages of ads (on coated stock), its thick yellow covers indicating the contents. By 1907 *Argosy* had 500,000 readers.

Other publishers hurried to cash in on the Munsey rag-paper to pulp-riches formula, and from 1905 on, periodicals of size and quality were available everywhere.

There were other factors besides price-per-copy which were responsible for the rise of the magazines after 1890. For one thing, advertisers had discovered the purchasing power of the American woman—the result of growing prosperity, urbanization, and new jobs spawned by technical advances in industry. Whereas in 1870, for example, there had been only 930 female office workers, seven of them stenographers, by 1910 there were to be almost 400,000—100,000 of them, "lady typewriters."

The impact of this can be seen in the growth of Sears, Roebuck, and Company, which, recapitalizing in 1895 at a mere $150,000, would go on to sell a billion dollars in women's fashions through the mail from 1900 to 1910, $14 million of which was for corsets alone.

But that wasn't all. Demanding equal rights, 15,000 women paraded up Fifth Avenue in 1912, as half a million onlookers cheered.

Another type of parade would occur between 1910 and 1920; Ziegfeld's lush theatrical extravaganzas "glorifying the American girl" drew a yearly average of some 15,000 would-be Follies Girls.

Last, but not least—considering the militant pressure the organization would later bring to bear against the Pulps—was the founding in 1897 of what is now the Parent-Teacher Association—ironically just one year after the new *Argosy.*

To capitalize on the shift in purchasing power, advertising agencies began placing lavish ads in the slick-paper magazines, which by 1900 were already able to reproduce photographs. These Slicks had to enlarge their format to accommodate the new 8½ x 11-inch advertising plates, and there naturally followed a trend in editorial policy favoring the female readers.

In contrast to this, the Pulps, in taking advantage of cheap production methods for their ten cent price, had to rely on circulation alone to make money, and they remained either family or male-oriented adventure magazines, appealing to the middle and educated lower classes.

The period 1890-1910 presented a picture of wealth and gentility in an age of optimism. Fables such as Lillian Russell packing away a ten-course meal and then pedalling around the park on a gold-plated, diamond-studded bicycle given to her by Diamond Jim Brady, have become legend. And matrons in $5,000 gowns attended Newport parties costing up to $100,000. The rich lived well.

The other side of the coin was not so pleasant. In 1900 half a million immigrants steamed into New York and twice that number in 1905. But living conditions and prejudice were so bad that in one year alone, 1908, 395,000 of them returned home. Disease and pestilence ruled the slums. Diphtheria, typhoid and malaria were leading causes of death. (The death rate was 162.4 per thousand persons, and the average life expectancy was 47.3 years.)

The family magazines and the Pulps offered escape to better worlds as well as social commentary in the form of the finest fiction ever published in the popular magazines. Writers included Joseph Conrad, Rudyard Kipling, Arnold Bennett, Stephen Crane, Mark Twain and H. G. Wells, even though advertising did not achieve the swankiness of the ads in the class magazines. Science-fiction of the finest quality appeared, either as critical comment of the inequality between the classes or as predictive comment on the outcome of rapid technological progress—response was enthusiastic.

Of all the new Pulps, it was Munsey's *All-Story Magazine* that had the most electric effect not only on its readers, but also on the other magazines which were to emulate it. *All-Story* followed the same format as *Argosy*, with one notable exception: its three-color covers hinted at class and sophistication. The new writers it published became household names practically overnight, and immediately were fair game for the higher-paying Slicks. And so the relentless drive for exciting new talent was always on.

This was the responsibility of one editorial giant. Robert H. Davis had held top positions at some of the leading newspapers, and is generally credited with being among the first to recognize the talent of such writers as Joseph Conrad and O. Henry. This made him a natural choice in 1905 for the position of editorial director of the Munsey Pulps, and *Argosy* and, especially, *All-Story* flourished under his leadership.

In 1912, a first novel by an unknown writer appeared in *All-Story*, its title was "Under the Moons of Mars." A complete departure from the scientific or socially prophetic type of science-fiction, it was, in fact, the first to employ a romantic theme. Response from readers was so overwhelming that it was immediately followed by another work of such far-reaching magnitude that it would go on to become one of the best-sellers of all time, and translated into every major language and dialect. Sequel after sequel was to follow. In addition, it was to become the longest-running adventure comic strip, a radio program, and the top money-making film series to come out of Hollywood. Its improbable hero was a boy raised in the jungle by apes. Its author was Edgar Rice Burroughs. The story, of course, was *Tarzan of the Apes*. Burroughs was to become the major influence on adventure-fiction, science-fiction, and related forms for at least twenty years.

In 1917 Davis was to discover another new writer, whose output would reach the epic proportions of some 30 million words. He was Frederick Faust, better known as Max Brand. Faust was responsible for changing the western story from the realism of such writers as Zane Grey to the larger-than-life mythic style predominant today.

Despite the stature *All-Story* achieved in its prime, it was no better able than most of its contemporaries to survive the sweeping cultural and economic changes of the first quarter of the twentieth century. In 1906 Edison had apologized for being behind in 2½ million orders for records, but it was to be another Edison invention which had the most dramatic impact on the publishing industry. For although he had only built his first film studio in 1893, progress and acceptance was so great that by 1910 it was estimated that some 10 million people were attending the movies weekly. The years from 1913 to 1916 saw the rise of Mack Sennett's slapstick, the debut of Chaplin's tramp, the filming of "Tarzan," and D. W. Griffith's "Birth of a Nation."

World War I paper quotas were another major shock from which the Pulps never recovered. Then the war was followed by a recession.

Even before the war, Pulp Magazines that reflected interest in specialized areas of taste such as *Ocean* and *Railroad Man's Magazine* had begun to appear. The Love Pulps had begun their development in 1912 with the appearance of such pseudo-sexy publications as *Snappy Stories* and, later, *The Parisienne,* an indication of growing sexual sophistication. In 1915 Street and Smith was to cash in on the increasing crime in the urban jungles with the publication of the first of the Detective Pulps, *Detective Story Magazine* (under the editorship of one "Nick Carter"). Finally with education on the rise, the last of the great Dime Novel heroes, the old frontier fighter himself would fade away in 1919 with the publication of a new Pulp: *Western Story Magazine—Formerly New Buffalo Bill Weekly.*

Possibly the most important of all factors affecting the magazines were the problems of labor reform created by rapid industrialization. The years between 1914 and 1917 saw some of the most violent domestic scenes in our history. In the first six months of 1916 alone, there were more than 2,000 strikes and lockouts. The old outmoded values of hard work and self-reliance were no longer enough. The turn-of-the-century optimism was gone.

Hard hit by rising prices caused by paper shortages and strikes within the industry, as well as changing social attitudes and competing entertainment forms, the magazine industry did what it could to rally.

The great *All-Story* merged with *Cavalier* (another Munsey Pulp) and then again with *Argosy,* to become *Argosy-All-Story Weekly,* while other Pulps and Slicks collapsed around them. In order to maintain its 10 cent price, *Argosy-All-Story Weekly* gradually cut its pages from 224 to 144—in a single year, 1920. Shortly after, perhaps out of sentiment, Munsey reduced the name simply to *Argosy.*

The Golden Age of magazines was over, leaving a scattering of slick magazines catering to women's purchasing habits, general adventure Pulps, and specialized Pulps whose existence was to depend on readers' idiosyncrasies.

Fragments of Sensation

With the rise of prosperity, the automobile, radio, photojournalism, and the movies during the 20's, the middle and lower classes abandoned the Family Pulps for more active forms of entertainment. The new mobility and new media generated a greater sense of immediacy and personal contact with people and events which, coupled with the release from the war tension, gave rise to faddism and hero-worship.

As each new movement sprang up it was followed by a rash of specialized Pulp Magazines: with the new idolatry of the sports heroes—and movie stars—Street and Smith issued *Sport Story Magazine* and *Love Story.* Cowboy films broke out of the studios pursued by a posse of Western Pulps. Pseudo-racy, under-the-counter titles like *Pep* and *Ginger* proliferated—in perverse proportion to the shrinking of bathing suits. As Prohibition and gangsterism hit their stride, new Pulps like *Gangster Stories* and *Racketeer Stories* hit the street with the frequency of Chicago "ride" victims. (It remained only for *F. B. I. Stories* to appear when the hoods finally started paying their dues.) Lindbergh's wheels had barely touched French soil, when a whole squadron of Aviation Pulps landed on the stands. No event was too small—no taste too obscure—to be overlooked by eager publishers: from *Husbands* and *Marriage Stories* to *Submarine Stories* and *Zeppelin Stories.*

During the Depression there was practically no margin between red and black ink. The net profit on one issue could run anywhere from $50 to $1,000. It was the practice of the shrewder publishers to wait and see how the first number of a new title sold before preparing the second, and when a magazine lost popularity they dropped it and tested a new title. The less ruthless simply added additional titles in an effort to support ailing publications and the lower the profit margins, the more titles they had in their stables.

Thus whichever policy they followed the publishers contributed hundreds of obscure and short-lived titles to the genre.

George T. Delacorte, Jr., founder of Dell Publishing Company, was a model of frugal elan. He got his first few magazines on the stands for little more than production expenses by buying cheap stories, two or three years' worth, in the London literary flea-market. Then he assigned these hand-me-downs to his rewrite men, who tailored them to fit the stateside market. Although most Pulps had risen to 20 cents, he not only maintained the 10 cent price, but with things at their worst, even managed a few bold experiments at a nickel. Among the more brilliant of his techniques was his formula for dealing with unsold issues. Instead of dating his issues, he numbered them, selling them only east of the Rockies and south of Canada. When the returns came back, he trimmed their yellow edges and promptly shipped them off to west of the Rockies and Canada, for resale.

For the writers the Pulps were a bonanza. Although fable has it that the pay was a cent a word, many Pulps were paying as high as a nickel. During the leanest years of the Depression, prolific writers like Max Brand could match incomes with Hollywood stars. Furthermore, with hundreds of specialized titles on the stands, the Pulps provided new writers with the opportunity to publish for the first time, as well as the means to develop their craft. Many writers either sold stories to the film companies or advanced (or degenerated) to writing for the movies. But above all, writers wrote for the Pulps because it was fun. In keeping with the emotional climate of the time, the stories themselves were generally fast, innocent, and violent. As much energy was packed into one 5,000 word short-short as DeMille unreeled in one of his Bible-length film epics. Themes for the most part were puritanical in value, heroic in stature, and sex was rarely even implied because a second-class mailing permit often meant the difference between profit and loss. And with all that action going on, who needed sex anyhow?

The N.R.A. eagle adorned the covers of the Pulps during the 30's, proudly proclaiming "We Do Our Part." And they did, too, as a new type of Pulp Hero, armed with superhuman powers took on all the known forces responsible for the plight of the country, and anything else that itched in the imagination, particularly "red menaces" and "yellow perils."

The rise of the Superhero occurred simultaneously with the downfall of real life idols during the Depression, as public figures and heads of households lost power to unnameable forces. Estrangement from society was followed by listlessness and apathy. The Superhero offered *youth* vicarious new roles within which *they* could assume the heroic responsibility involuntarily abandoned by their authority-figures. Finally, the Superhero always satisfied fundamental values and never disappointed expectations. The few exceptions to that rule lasted but a few issues. Satisfying as they were, the Pulp Superheroes were no match in the long run for such flashy brutes as Superman of the late 30's comic books. And when American men went overseas in World War II, comic books, being readily mailable, followed them—to help fight the Axis in four colors. Then the government introduced the Armed Forces Editions of paperback books for distribution to the troops. At home paper was again put on a quota system, and even though anything as barely literate as a Love Pulp was prime reading matter, many Pulps failed, for lack of paper, to provide adequate circulation.

Production costs soared some 70 per cent between 1944 and 1947. Then, with the end of paper quotas in 1950, the new slick male magazines and paperbacks boomed. Authors like Mickey Spillane offered the same type of fiction the Pulps had supplied, only in the form of novels costing as little as a quarter. The paperbacks' affect on book sales has been so great, that it is said that more books have been published in the 15 years since 1955, than in the whole period from the invention of moveable type to that date. But many Pulp titles were still available in 1953, when a major distributor dealt the final blow by imposing editorial requirements on the publishers and finally refused to distribute anything but the more profitable Slicks and a few digest-size fiction magazines. And so, having started off in the form of the "chapbooks" over a century ago, Pulp fiction ironically was to end up confined to much the same format.

The material that follows, then, essentially represents the 20's, 30's and 40's—that voluptuous period of sublimely decadent, middle-American glory—when new Pulp artists, authors, and titles crackled through the cultural crud with the electric thrill of lightning.

Mainstream / 1 / Adventure Pulps

Awakened interest in the lusty new frontiers of the world gave the Pulps their most powerful lure in the period after World War I. As radio, movies, automobiles, and airplanes revolutionized society, distant people, places, and events suddenly came into focus—stimulating popular interest and imagination. Adventure fiction—once confined primarily to swashbuckling historical drama—now transported readers to the danger, excitement, and intrigue which lurked in all the charted and uncharted regions of the world. New Pulps with exotic and Asiatic titles like *Jungle Stories, Tropical Adventures,* and *Far East Adventures* invaded the newsstands and excited, broadened, and distorted active American imaginations for generations.

* * *

"The Resurrection of Jimber-Jaw" (*Argosy,* 1937) not only demonstrates Edgar Rice Burroughs' use of his "scientific romance" form, but also his predilection for social satire. Burroughs pioneered by developing interpersonal relationships in science fiction beyond the minimum—as distinguished from the almost purely speculative writing that preceded it. He also added depth and appeal to his stories and novels by introducing criticism of social injustice. In fact, his treatment of the Nazis in his Tarzan books caused him to be severely censored in pre-World War II Germany.

Social criticism in Burroughs' work was perhaps the natural result of the factors— poverty and despair, not inspiration—which first caused him to begin writing, in about 1911. Burroughs had failed at a dozen diverse occupations, and direly needed money to support his family. He had read the fiction magazines of the time and decided that "if people were paid for writing rot such as I read I could write stories just as rotten . . . I knew absolutely that I could write stories just as entertaining and probably a lot more so." He studied the policies of the various fiction magazines and aimed his first try at *All-Story Magazine.* It was published there in 1912 as "Under the Moons of Mars." A short time later *All-Story* published his second novel, "Tarzan of the Apes," and Burroughs' popularity was established for all time.

* * *

English writers appeared regularly (sometimes without their consent) in such general adventure magazines as *Popular, Blue Book,* and *Adventure.* Among the foremost was Edgar Wallace, the world's all-time, best-selling mystery writer. He had only been writing a year or so when "The Greek Poropulos" was published in England in 1910. It appears here as reprinted in *The Green Book* in 1933.

* * *

"The Devil Must Pay," by Frederick C. Painton, (*Argosy,* 1937) could be described as a "most unforgettable character I ever met" story. It maintains its tension through action and character rather than intricacies of plot.

* * *

1

The "adventurer-in-trouble-in-the-Orient" story achieved the height of popularity in the 30's and 40's. The only standard element missing from William P. McGivern's "Manchu Terror" (*Mammoth Adventure,* 1946) is the smell of opium.

*   *   *

Sentimental verse was a standard feature of many Pulps. "A Nigh Side Prod," by Charles A. Freeman, appeared in *Frontier Stories* in 1934. Although the title of this magazine would seem to imply a western locale, it was dedicated to the frontiers of the world.

*   *   *

Adventure ran a Letters to the Editor column in which readers could request information on any of a variety of subjects. Foreign Legion expert and popular author George Surdez was one of many "advisors" supposedly stationed on the frontiers of the world. His "Honneur et Fidelité" appeared in "The Campfire" column in 1929.

*   *   *

An air of camaraderie and tragedy permeates "The Boomer Trail," a column taken from *Railroad* (1936). Its letters reflect the romance and the hardships of life on the railroads when they were the major form of transportation, and there is a touching sadness in their tone, as the writers recall old times. More significantly, perhaps, they reflect the upheaval and isolation that were the soul of the Depression.

The Resurrection of Jimber-Jaw

By EDGAR RICE BURROUGHS
author of "Seven Worlds to Conquer," "Tarzan," etc.

*Back from the Stone Age, from 50,000 B.C., came Jimber-Jaw the Mighty
to find his mate and battle his fate—fist and fang against our
world of science.*

CREDIT THIS story to Wild Pat Morgan, that laughing, reckless, black-haired grandson of Ireland's peat bogs. To Pat Morgan, one-time flying lieutenant of the AEF, ex-inventor, amateur boxer, and drinking companion *par excellence*.

I met Pat Morgan at the country club bar, one of those casual things. After the third highball we were calling each other by our first names. By the sixth we had·dragged the family skeletons out of the closet and were shaking the dust off them. A little later we were weeping on one another's shoulders, and that's how it began.

We got pretty well acquainted that evening, and afterwards our friendship grew. We saw a lot of each other when he brought his ship to the airport where I kept mine. His wife was dead, and he was a rather lonely figure evenings; so I used to have him up to the house for dinner often.

He had been rather young when the war broke out, but had managed to get to France and the front just before the end. I think he shot down three enemy planes, although he was just a kid. I had that from another flyer; Pat never talked about it. But he was full of flying anecdotes about other war-time pilots and about his own stunting experiences in the movies. He had followed this latter profession for several years.

All of which has nothing to do with the real story other than to explain how I became well enough acquainted with Pat Morgan to be on hand when he told the strange tale of his flight to Russia, of the scientist who mastered Time, of the man from 50,000 B.C. called Jimber-Jaw.

We were lunching together at The Vendome that day. I had been waiting for Pat at the bar, discussing with some others the disappearance of Stone, the wrestler. Everyone is familiar, of course, with Stone's meteoric rise to fame as an athlete and a high-salaried star in the movies, and his vanishing had become a minor ten-days' wonder. We were trying to decide if Stone had been kidnapped, whether the ransom letters received were the work of cranks, when Pat Morgan came in with the extra edition of the *Herald and Express* that the newsboys were hawking in the streets.

I followed Pat to our table and he spread the paper out. A glaring headline gave the meat of the story.

"So they've found him!" I exclaimed.

Pat Morgan nodded. "The police had me in on it. I've just come from Headquarters." He shrugged, frowned, and then began to talk slowly:

II

I'VE ALWAYS been inclined to putter around with inventions (Pat Morgan said), and after my wife died I tried to forget my loneliness by centering my interest on my laboratory work. It was a poor substitute for the companionship I had lost, but at that I guess it proved my salvation.

I was working on a new fuel which was much cheaper and less bulky than gasoline; but I found that it required radical changes in engine design, and I lacked the capital to put my blueprints into metal.

About this time my grandfather died and left me a considerable fortune. Quite a slice of it went into experimental engines before I finally perfected one. It was a honey.

I built a ship and installed my engine in it; then I tried to sell the patents on both engine and fuel to the Government—but something happened. When I reached a certain point in these official negotiations I ran into an invisible stone wall—I was stopped dead. I couldn't even get a permit to manufacture my engine.

I never did find out who or what stopped me, but I remembered the case of the Doble steam car. Perhaps you will recall that, also.

Then I got sore and commenced to play around with the Russians. The war-winds were already beginning

to blow again in Europe, and the comrades of the Soviet were decidedly interested in new aircraft developments. They had money to burn, and their representatives had a way with them that soothed the injured ego of a despondent inventor. They finally made me a splendid offer to take my plans and formulae to Moscow and manufacture engines and fuel for them. In addition, as a publicity and propaganda stunt, they offered a whacking bonus if I would put my new developments to the test by *flying* there.

I jumped at this chance to make monkeys out of those bureaucratic boneheads in Washington. I'd show those guys what they were missing.

During the course of these negotiations I met Dr. Stade who was also flirting with the brethren of the U.S.S.R. Professor Marvin Stade, to give him his full name and title, and he was quite a guy. A big fellow, built like an ox, with a choleric temper and the most biting pair of blue eyes I've ever gazed upon. You must have read in the papers about Stade's experiments with frozen dogs and monkeys. He used to

freeze them up solid for days and weeks, and then thaw them out and bring them alive again. He had also been conducting some unique studies in surgical hypnosis, and otherwise stepping on the toes of the constituted medical poobahs.

The S.P.C.A. and the Department of Health had thrown a monkey-wrench into Stade's program— stopped him cold—and there was fire in his eye. We were a couple of soreheads, perhaps, but I think we had a right to be. Lord knows we were both sincere in what we were trying to accomplish—he to fight disease, I to add something to the progress of aviation.

The Reds welcomed Dr. Stade with open arms. They agreed not only to let him carry his experiments as far as he liked but to finance him as well. They even promised to let him use human beings as subjects and to furnish said humans in job lots. I suppose they had a large supply of counter-revolutionists on hand.

When Stade found that I planned to fly my ship to Moscow, he asked if he might go along. He was a showman as well as a scientist, and the publicity appealed to him. I told him the risk was too great, that I didn't want to take the responsibility of any life other than my own, but he pooh-poohed every objection in that bull-bellow voice of his. Finally I shrugged and said okay.

I WON'T bore you with the details of the flight. You couldn't have read about it in the papers, of course, for the word went out through official channels that we were to get a cold shoulder. The press put a blanket of silence on us, and that was that. There were passport difficulties, refusals to certify the plane, all that sort of thing. But we managed to muddle through.

The engine functioned perfectly. So did the fuel. So did everything, including my navigation, until we were flying over the most God-forsaken terrain anyone ever saw—some place in Northern Siberia according to our maps. That's where my new-fangled carburetor chose to go haywire.

We had about ten thousand feet elevation at the time, but that wasn't much help. There was no place to land. As far as I could see there was nothing but forests and rivers—hundreds of rivers.

I went into a straight glide with a tail-wind, figuring I could cover a lot more territory that way than I could by spiralling; and every second I was keeping my eyes peeled for a spot, however small, where I might set her down without damage. We'd never get out of that endless forest, I knew, unless we flew out.

I've always liked trees—a nature-lover at heart—but as I looked down on that vast host of silent sentinels of the wilderness, I felt the chill of fear and something that was akin to hate. There was a loneliness and an emptiness inside me. There they stood—in regiments, in divisions, in armies, waiting to seize us and hold us forever; to hold our broken bodies, for when we struck them, they would crush us, tear us to pieces.

Then I saw a little patch of yellow far ahead. It was no larger than the palm of my hand, it seemed, but it was an open space—a tiny sanctuary in the very heart of the enemy's vast encampment. As we approached, it grew larger until at last it resolved itself into a few acres of reddish yellow soil devoid of trees. It was the most beautiful landscape I have ever seen.

As the ship rolled to a stop on fairly level ground, I turned and looked at Dr. Stade. He was lighting a cigarette. He paused, with the match still burning, and grinned at me. I knew then that he was regular. It's funny, but neither one of us had spoken since the motor quit. That was as it should have been; for there was nothing to say—at least nothing that would have meant anything.

We got down and looked around. Beside us, a little river ran north to empty finally into the Arctic Ocean. Our tiny patch of salvation lay in a bend on the west side of the river. On the east side was a steep cliff that rose at least three hundred feet above the river. The lowest stratum looked like dirty glass. Above that were strata of conglomerate and sedimentary rock; and, topping all, the grim forest scowled down upon us menacingly.

"Funny looking rock," I commented, pointing toward the lowest ledge.

"Ice," said Stade. "My friend, you are looking at the remnants of the late lamented glacial period that raised havoc with the passing of the Pleistocene. What are we going to use for food?"

"We got guns," I reminded him.

"Yes. It was very thoughtful of you to get permission to bring firearms and ammunition, but what are we going to shoot?"

I shrugged. "There must be something. What are all these trees for? They must have been put here for birds to sit on. In the meantime we've sandwiches and a couple of thermoses of hot coffee. I hope it's hot."

"So do I."

It wasn't. . . .

I took a shotgun and hunted up river. I got a hare—mostly fur and bones—and a brace of birds that resembled partridges. By the time I got back to camp the weather had become threatening. There was a storm north of us. We could see the lightning, and faint thunder began to growl.

We had already wheeled the plane to the west and highest part of our clearing and staked it down as close under the shelter of the forest as we could. Nothing else to do.

By the time we had cooked and eaten our supper it commenced to rain. The long, northern twilight was obliterated by angry clouds that rolled low out of the north. Thunder bombarded us. Lightning laid down a barrage of pale brilliance all about. We crawled into the cabin of the plane and spread our mattresses and blankets on the floor behind the seats.

It rained. And when I say it rained, I mean it *rained.* It could have given ancient Armenia seven-and-a-half honor tricks and set it at least three; for what it took forty days and forty nights to do in ancient Armenia, it did in one night on that nameless river somewhere in Siberia, U.S.S.R. I'll never forget that downpour.

I DON'T know how long I slept, but when I awoke it was raining not cats and dogs only, but the entire animal kingdom. I crawled out and looked through a window. The next flash of lightning showed the river swirling within a few feet of the outer wing.

I shook Dr. Stade awake and called his attention to the danger of our situation.

"The devil!" he said. "Wait till she floats." He turned over and went to sleep again. Of course it wasn't his ship, and perhaps he was a strong swimmer; I wasn't.

I lay awake most of what was left of the night. The rising flood was a foot deep around the landing gear at the worst; then she commenced to go down.

The next morning the river was running in a new channel a few yards from the ship, and the cliff had receded at least fifty feet toward the east. The face of it had fallen into the river and been washed away. The lowest stratum was pure and gleaming ice.

I called Stade's attention to the topographical changes.

"That's interesting," he said. "By any chance is there any partridge or hare left?"

There was, and we ate it. Then we got out and sloshed around in the mud. I started to work on the carburetor. Stade studied the havoc wrought by the storm.

He was down by the edge of the river looking at the new cliff face when he called to me excitedly. I had never before seen the burly professor exhibit any enthusiasm except when he was damning the S.P.C.A. and the health authorities. I went on the run.

I could see nothing to get excited about. "What's eating you?" I asked.

"Come here, you dumb Irishman, and see a man fifty thousand years old, or thereabouts." Stade was mainly Scotch and German, which may have accounted for his crazy sense of humor.

I was worried. I thought maybe it might be the heat, but there wasn't any heat. No more could it have been the altitude; so I figured it must be hereditary, and crawled down and walked over to him.

"Look!" he said. He pointed across the river at the cliff.

I looked—and there it was. Frozen into the solid ice, was the body of a man. He was clothed in furs and had a mighty beard. He lay on his side with his head resting on one arm, as though he were soundly sleeping.

Stade was awe struck. He just stood there, goggle-eyed, staring at the corpse. Finally he drew in his breath in a long sigh.

"Do you realize, Pat, that we are looking at a man who may have lived fifty thousand years ago, a survivor of the old Stone Age?"

"What a break for you, Doc," I said.

"Break for me? What do you mean?"

"You can thaw him out and bring him to life."

He looked at me in a sort of blank way, as though he didn't comprehend what I was saying. His lips moved, mumbling, then he shook his head.

"I'm afraid he's been frozen too long," he said.

"Fifty thousand years is quite a while, but wouldn't it be worth trying? Keep you busy while I'm fixing things to get us out of here."

Again he fixed his blank stare upon me. His eyes were cold and expressionless as that distant cliff of ice. "All right, Paddy me boy," he said suddenly. "But you'll have to help me."

III

MY SUGGESTION was a joke, of course, but Stade was in deadly earnest once he got started. I wasn't much help, I'm afraid, after the first couple of days, for I came down with a queer combination of chills and fever that had me light-headed most of the time. But I worked when I could.

It took us two weeks to build a rude hut of saplings and chink it with clay. It had a fireplace and a bench for the queer paraphernalia that Stade had brought along—more gadgets than you could shake a stick at. Then it took us another two weeks to chip our cave man out of the ice. We had to be careful; there was danger of breaking him.

I'm the one who gave our corpse his name. There in the ice, with his skin-clad body and his hairy face, he looked like a big lantern-jawed grizzly I'd seen one time up the Yellowstone. Jimber-Jaw had been the grizzly's name, and that's what I called our discovery. That fever had me so dizzy, I tell you, that I felt like a man on a spree most of the time.

Anyway, we worked all around our frozen subject, leaving him encased in a small block of the glacier. Then we lowered him to the ground, floated him across the river, and dragged him up to the laboratory on a crude sled we had built for that purpose.

All the time we were working on him we did a lot of thinking. I kept on treating the whole thing as a sort of joke, but Stade grew more grimly serious with every day. He worked with a furious driving energy that swept me along. Nights, by the fire, he would talk on and on about the memories that were locked in that frozen brain. What sights had those ice-cased eyes beheld in the days when the world was young? What loves, what hates had stirred that mighty breast?

Here was a creature that had lived in the days of the mammoth and the sabre-tooth and the great flying monsters. He had survived against the odds, with only a stone spear and a stone knife against a predatory world, until the cold of the great glacier had captured and overpowered him.

Stade said he had been hunting and that he had been caught in a blizzard. Numb with cold, he had at last dropped down on the chill ice, succumbing to that inevitable urge to sleep that overtakes all freezing men. For fifty thousand years he had slept on, undisturbed. (Lord, how I sometimes envied him!)

I was pretty well played out by the time the final test arrived. My temperature was well past 102°, and I walked around in a semi-delirium most of the morning. But Stade insisted that he needed me, that I had to stay on my feet. He crammed me full of quinine and whiskey and I went on a singing jag. I remembered the words to some of the old songs that I thought I'd forgotten.

That's why there are parts of that day that I remember distinctly and other parts that are only a hazy blank.

Stade built a roaring blaze in the fireplace and our laboratory-hut was oven warm. The propeller of the plane, idling, kept the air of the room in circulation, blowing wind through an opening in the wall that had been built for that purpose. I helped to prop our subject in front of the fire, then slumped back, all groggy, and left the rest to Stade. It was his picnic.

He kept turning Jimber-Jaw over—first one side then the other toward the fire—until the ice was all melted. Then the body commenced to warm.

I stopped my singing long enough to get sensible. I shook the fog out of my brain and stared at Stade. I knew perfectly well that the best we could expect was that in due course our prehistoric statue would turn blue and commence to smell, but for some reason I couldn't fight off my mounting excitement. Stade's tension had got into my blood. The big doctor was trying to be the cool and collected man-of-science and failing miserably in the attempt. His eyes blazed and his big body was taut with tension. His fingers trembled as he lit a cigarette, and the half-smile on his lips was a nervous grimace, frozen there.

I chuckled. "What if he does come to life, doc?" I asked. "You thought of that? You thought what it's going to mean to old Jimber to be fifty thousand years away from all his friends? You thought of what he may do to us?"

It was amusing to imagine that and I laughed at the notion. "What sort of people were the men of the old Stone Age?" I went on. "We named this baby after a grizzly bear and he certainly looks the part. He looks like a guy who would have definite ideas about strangers who waken people to whom they haven't been introduced—people who've been peacefully sleeping for fifty thousand years. Suppose he acts up, doc?"

Stade shrugged. Devil-fire danced in his eyes. "Do you really think he'll come to life, Pat?" he whispered.

"You ought to know—you're the doctor."

He nodded. "Well, theoretically he should. It's not impossible. . . . Come on, sit over here, Pat."

Stade bent over me, half-smiling, and his eyes burned down into mine. He didn't say anything and

neither did I. Then he practically carried me across the room and propped me in a chair.

THE REST of it is rather hazy. I saw it all clearly enough—I remember the whole scene now as vividly as on that day—but it was all like a vision through a pale gray veil. Like something seen through a spirit disembodied. Perhaps it was my fever and the whiskey; I still don't know.

First Stade gave Big Jim a blood transfusion, using me as the donor. After that he injected an adrenalin chloride solution into the belly. The doctor crouched over the slumped body and turned a tense face to stare at me. His eyes were lambent fire. Suddenly he jerked back to his patient and I heard his startled gasp.

Jimber-Jaw opened his mouth and yawned!

I felt as if all the giants in the world had slapped me across the face. My breath caught and I couldn't see for a moment. Stade peered at me as if for confirmation, and I nodded. I have never in my life felt such a weight of responsibility. Why in the devil's name hadn't the man stayed frozen—why hadn't he started to decay? Now that he had shown signs of life we *had* to go on. It would have been murder not to finish what we started. I remember thinking dizzily: It wouldn't be right to murder a man who was born fifty thousand years ago. . . .

Stade injected an ounce and a half of anterior pituitary fluid. Big Jim scowled and wiggled his fingers. He was definitely alive, and it frightened me. I almost whimpered. It was like messing around with business that belongs only to God.

Stade filled his hypodermic with posterior pituitary fluid and gave our discovery a shot of that. For a second nothing happened. Then the man of the old Stone Age turned over and tried to sit up. Stade let a yell out of him and I began to grow fainter and fainter.

As in a dream I saw Stade push him back gently and speak soothingly. I coudn't hear what he said. Then the doctor injected sex hormones from sheep and squared his shoulders triumphantly. He came toward me, eyes glowing, and about that time I passed completely out of the picture. . . .

IT WAS dark when I came to again. I had a splitting headache, my arm was sore as a boil, but otherwise I was okay again. Those fever attacks of mine have a way of vanishing swiftly. Stade was sitting at the table, shirt-sleeved, with a bottle at his elbow.

"How long have I been passed out?" I demanded.

"Three-four hours."

"What day is this?"

He frowned at me. "What's the matter, Pat? Have you gone completely haywire?"

I sat up—and then I saw the figure on the bench. It hadn't been a bad dream after all. Apparently Stade had stripped the soggy skins from Jimber-Jaw, and he was wrapped in our blankets from the ship, peacefully sleeping. I went across to him and touched the bare shoulder lightly—real flesh. I could see his chest rise and fall, could hear his breathing. Slowly I went back to my home-made chair and sank down in it. I put my face in my hands and tried to think. At last I looked up and met Stade's level stare. He shrugged and I nodded.

We had worked a miracle—and now we were stuck with it.

Big Jim was a fine specimen of a man, about six-feet-three and beautifully muscled. Beneath his beard he appeared to have good and regular features, though perhaps the jaw was a little heavy. Stade thought he might be in his twenties. He certainly was not old.

Some two hours later our guest from the past sat up and looked at us. A scowl darkened his forehead, and he looked about him quickly as though for his weapons. But they weren't there—Stade had seen to that. He tried to get up, but he was too weak.

"Take it easy, pal," I told him and he finally sprawled back. For a while he watched us from eyes that were wide and calm and animal-alert. Then he went to sleep again.

He was a pretty sick boy for a long time. We both thought he'd never pull through. All the time we nursed him like a baby and took care of him; and by the time he commenced to convalesce he seemed to have gained confidence in us. He no longer scowled or shrank away or looked for his weapons when we came around; he smiled at us now, and it was a mighty winning smile.

At first he had been delirious; he talked a lot in a strange tongue that we couldn't make head nor tail of. A soft, liquid tongue with l's and vowels flowing through it; but low, like a deep river. There was one word that he repeated often in his delirium—*lilami.* The way he said it sounded sometimes like a prayer and sometimes like a wail of anguish.

I had repaired the carburetor. There was nothing serious the matter with it—just clogged and jammed up a little. We could have gone on as soon as our flood receded but there was Jimber-Jaw—whose name we had shortened to "Jim." We couldn't leave him to die, and he was too sick to take along; so we stayed with him. We never even discussed the matter much —just took it for granted that the responsibility was ours, and stuck along.

Stade was, of course, elated by the success of this first practical demonstration of the soundness of his theory. I don't believe you could have dragged him away from Jim with an ox team. Yet as the days went on the good doctor seemed to draw farther back into a shell of reserve. The training of our charge was mainly left to my hands.

The fact that we couldn't talk with Jim irked me. There were so many questions I wanted to ask him. Just think of it! Here was a man of the old Stone Age who could have told us all about conditions in the Pleistocene, fifty thousand years ago, perhaps; and I couldn't exchange a single thought with him. But we set out to cure that.

As soon as he was strong enough, we commenced to teach him English. At first it was aggravatingly slow work; but Jim proved an apt pupil, and as soon as he had a little foundation he progressed rapidly. He had a marvelous memory. He never forgot anything—once he had a thing, he had it.

NO USE reviewing the long weeks of his convalescence and education. He recovered fully, and he learned to speak English—excellent English, for Stade was a highly cultured man and a scholar. It was just as well that Jim didn't learn his English from me— barracks and hangars are not the places to acquire academic English.

If Jim was a curiosity to us, imagine what we must have been to him. The little one-room shack we had built and in which he had convalesced was an architectural marvel beyond the limits of his imagining. He told us that his people lived in caves; and he thought that this was a strange cave that we had found, until we explained that we had built it.

Our clothing intrigued him; our weapons were a never ending source of wonderment. The first time I took him hunting with me and shot game, he was astounded. Perhaps he was frightened by the noise and the smoke and the sudden death of the quarry; but if he were, he never let on. Jim never showed fear; perhaps he never felt fear. Alone, armed only with a stone-shod spear and a stone knife, he had been hunting the great red bear when the glacier had claimed him. He told us about it.

"The day before you found me," he said, "I was hunting the great red bear. The wind blew; the snow and sleet drove against me. I could not see. I did not know in which direction I was going. I became very tired. I knew that if I lay down I should sleep and never awaken; but at last I could stand it no longer, and I lay down. If you had not come the next day, I should have died." How could we make him understand that his yesterday was fifty thousand years ago?

Eventually we succeeded in a way, though I doubt if he ever fully appreciated the tremendous lapse of time that had intervened since he started from his father's cave to hunt the great red bear.

When he first realized that he was a long way from that day and that it and his times could never be recalled, he again voiced that single word—*lilami*. It was almost a sob. I had never dreamed that so much heart-ache, so much longing could be encompassed within a single word.

I asked him what it meant.

He was a long time in answering. He seemed to be trying to control his emotions, which was unusual for Big Jim. Ordinarily he appeared never to have emotions. One day he told me why. A great warrior never let his face betray anger or pain or sorrow. You will notice that he didn't mention fear. Sometimes I think he had never learned what fear is. Before a youth was admitted to the warrior class, he was tortured to make certain that he could control his emotions.

But to get back to *lilami*:

At last he spoke: "Lilami is a girl—was a girl. She was to have been my mate when I came back with the head of the great red bear. Where is she now, Pat Morgan?"

There was a question! If we hadn't discovered Jim and thawed him out, Lilami wouldn't have been even a memory. "Try not to think about her, old man," I said. "You'll never see Lilami again—not in this world."

"Yes, I will," he replied. "If I am not dead, Lilami is not dead. I shall find her."

IV

THE PLANE was so absolutely beyond Jimber-Jaw's conception that he couldn't even ask questions about it. I think anyone else in the world, under similar circumstances, would have been terrified when we finally took off from that lonely Siberian forest. The whir of the propeller, the roar of the exhaust, the wild careening of the take-off must have had *some* effect on Jim, but he never showed it by so much as a bat of an eyelid. He had all the appearance of a blasé young man of today.

I had given him an old suit—breeches, field boots, and a leather coat. He was smooth shaven now. After watching us scrape our jowls every day, he had insisted first on being shaved and then learning to shave himself. The transformation had been most astounding—from Man Mountain Dean to Adonis with a few snips of the scissors and a few passes of the safety-razor!

When I looked at him and thought of the civilization that he was about to crash for the first time, I felt sorry for Lilami. Pretty soon she would be scarcely even a memory. But I didn't know Big Jim—then.

Well, we finally got to Moscow; and there was the devil to pay about our unexpected passenger. No one believed our story. I can scarcely blame them. But what got me sore was their insistence that we were all spies and counter-revolutionists and Nazis and Fascists and capitalists and what-have-you that is anathema in Red Russia.

Of course, Jim had no passport. We tried to explain that they weren't issuing passports in the Pleistocene, but we got nowhere. They wanted to shoot us; but the American ambassador came to our rescue, and they compromised by shooing us out of the country and telling us to stay out. That suited me. If I never see a Comrade again, that will be far too soon for Pat Morgan.

After our experience in Russia, Stade and I decided to keep our mouths shut about Jim's genesis and antecedents. This was Stade's suggestion, and I confess I was rather surprised to hear him make it. The good doctor had never been adverse to publicity, and here was the greatest chance in the world for him to beat his own drum. Think of the scientific *kudos* that would shower down on him!

But Stade wasn't interested in that, he said. He suddenly went coy on me—began to talk of the difficulties of establishing absolute scientific proof and all that rot. Suggested we'd better wait a while—allow our colossus to orient himself. He'd leave Jim in my care for a time, since important business was waiting for him in Chicago.

I shrugged and agreed.

We arrived in America shrouded in a pall of silence. As a matter of fact, we smuggled Jim into the old U.S.A., and after that we had to keep our mouths shut about him. What else could we have done? After all, there is no Pleistocene quota.

When we got home, I took him to my place in Beverly Hills; and told people he was an old friend—Jim Stone from Schenectady.

He had been greatly impressed by the large cities he had seen. He thought skyscrapers were mountains with caves in them. As intelligent as he was, he just couldn't conceive that man had built anything so colossal.

It was a treat taking him around. The movies were as real to him as death and taxes. There was a cave-man sequence in one we saw, and Jim really showed signs of life then. I knew he was having difficulty in restraining himself. He was just honing to crawl into one of those prop caves. When the heavy grabbed the leading lady by the hair and started to drag her across the scenery, Big Jim hoisted himself into the aisle and started for the screen. I grabbed him by the coat-tails, but it was a lap dissolve that saved the day.

Yep, Jim and I had fun. . . .

ONE NIGHT I took him to the wrestling matches at the Olympic. We had ring-side seats. The Lone Wolf and Tiny Sawbuck (237 pounds) were committing mayhem on one another inside the ropes. It seemed to get Jim's goat.

"Do you call those great warriors?" he inquired. Then, before I could do anything about it, he vaulted over the ropes and threw them both into the third row.

The Lone Wolf and Tiny Sawbuck were sore, but the audience and the promoter were one hundred percent plus for Jimber-Jaw. Before the evening was over, the latter had signed Jim up to meet the winner, and a week later our survivor of the Stone Age stepped into the ring with Tiny Sawbuck.

I'm still laughing. Tiny is famed as a bad hombre. He knows all the dirty tricks that the other wrestlers know and has invented quite a few of his own. But he didn't have an opportunity to try any of them on Jim. The moment they met in the center of the ring, the man who lived in the day of the mammoths, picked him up, carried him to the ropes, and threw him into the fourth row. He did that three times, and the last time Tiny stayed there. You couldn't have hired him to come back into that ring.

About the same thing happened in boxing. I had been giving Jim some preliminary instruction in the manly art of acquiring cauliflower ears. By this time he was well known as a wrestler. Every Wednesday he had gone to the Olympic and ruined a few cash customers by throwing opponents at them. That was all he ever did. He never wrestled, never made any faces, never gave the other fellow a chance. He just picked him up and threw him out of the ring, and kept on doing it until the other man decided to stay out.

The fight promoter approached me. "Can he box?" he asked.

"I don't know. He can't wrestle, but he always wins. Why don't you find out? I have one thousand bucks that says he can put any of your white hopes to sleep."

"You're on," opined the promoter.

The following Tuesday the fight came off. I cautioned Jim: "Don't forget," I admonished him, "that you're supposed to box, not wrestle."

"I hit?" Jim inquired.

"Yes, you hit—and sock him hard."

"Okey-doke," rejoined the man from the old Stone Age. "Bring 'em on!"

They shook hands and retired to their corners; then the bell rang. The white hope came charging out like the Light Brigade at Balaklava, and he got just about as far. Big Jim swung one terrific right that he must have learned from the cave-bear and the white hope was draped over the upper rope. That was the end of that fight. Others went similar ways: then the cinema moguls noticed Jimber-Jaw.

One night, while we were still negotiating for a movie contract, we went to see a preview. Lorna Downs was the star. The moment she came onto the screen, Jim sprang to his feet.

"Lilami!" he cried. "It is I, Kolani."

The heavy was insulting Lorna at the time. Jim leaped toward the screen just as Lorna made her exit into the garden. Without a moment's hesitation he tried to follow her.

It wasn't so much the damage he did to the screen as the hurt to the theater manager's pride. He made the mistake of trying to eject Jim by force. That *was* a mistake. After they had gathered the manager up from the sidewalk and carried him to his office, I managed to settle with him and keep Jim out of jail.

When we got home, I asked Jim what it was all about.

"It was Lilami," he explained.

"It was not Lilami—it was Lorna Downs. And, what you saw was not Lorna herself—just a moving picture of her."

"It was Lilami," the big fellow said gravely. "I told you that I would find her."

V

LORNA DOWNS was in the east making a personal appearance tour in connection with her latest release. Jim wanted to go after her. I explained that he had entered into a contract to make pictures and that he would have to live up to his agreement. I also told him that Lorna would be back in Hollywood in a few weeks, so he reluctantly agreed to wait. Meanwhile we moved into movie circles, and thus came a new phase in Jim's career. He suddenly became a social lion. Men liked him and women were crazy about him.

The first time he went to the Trocadero he turned to me and asked, "What kind of women are these?"

I told him that, measured by fame and wealth, they were the cream of the elect.

"They are without shame," he said. "They go almost naked before men. In my country their men would drag them home by the hair and beat them."

I had to admit that that was what some of our men would like to do.

"Of what good is a mate in your country?" he asked. "They are no different from men. The men smoke; the women smoke. The men drink; the women drink. The men swear; the women swear. They gamble—they tell dirty stories—they are out all night and cannot be fit to look after the caves and the children the next day.

They are only good for one thing, otherwise they might as well be men. One does not need to take a mate for what they can give—not here. In my country such women are killed. No one would want children from them."

The ethics, the standards, and the philosophy of the Stone Age did not fit Jim to enjoy modern society. He stopped going out evenings except to pictures and fights. He was waiting for Lilami to return.

"She is different," he said.

I felt sorry for him. I didn't know Lorna Downs, but I would have been willing to bet she was not so different.

At last Lorna came back. I was with Jim when they met. It was on a set at the studio. It was in the middle of a scene, but when he saw her he walked right off the set and up to her. Never before have I seen so much happiness and love reflected in a man's face.

"Lilami!" he said in a voice tense with emotion, and reached for her.

She shrank back. "What's the idea, big boy?" she demanded.

"Don't you know me, Lilami? I'm Kolani. Now I have found you we can go away together. I have searched for you for a long time."

She looked up at me. "Are you his keeper, mister?" she demanded. "If you are, you'd better take him back to the college and lock him up."

I sent Jim away, and then I talked to her. I didn't tell her everything, but enough so that she understood that Jim wasn't crazy, that he was a good kid, and that he really believed that she was the girl he had known in another country.

He was standing a little way off, and she sat and looked at him for a few moments before she answered; then she said she'd be nice to him.

"It ought to be good fun," she said.

After that they were together a great deal. It looked very much as though the movie belle were falling for the cave man. They went to shows together and dined in quiet places and took long drives.

Then, one afternoon she went to a cocktail party without him. She didn't tell him she was going; but he found it out, and along about seven o'clock he walked into the place.

Lorna was sitting on some bird's lap, and he had his arms around her and was kissing her. It didn't mean a thing—not to them. A girl might kiss any one at a cocktail party—that is any one except her husband.

But it meant a lot to Jimber-Jaw of 50,000 B.C.

He was across that room in two strides. He never said a word; he just grabbed Lorna by the hair and yanked her out of the man's lap; then he picked the fellow up and threw him all the way across the room. He was the original cave man then, and no mistake.

Lorna struck down his hands and slapped his face. "Get out of here, you big boob," she screamed. "You tank-town Romeo—get out and stay out. You're washed up. I'm through with you."

Jim's fingers balled into a fist but he didn't hit her. The repressed fury drained out of his face and his shoulders sagged. He turned without a word, stalked away. That was the last time any one ever saw him—until this morning.

PAT MORGAN raised his hand, signal to the waiter for another pair of highballs. He stared across the table at me without expression, shrugging.

"That's the story of Jimber-Jaw," he said. "Take it or leave it. . . . I could see by your face when I was telling it that you were thinking what I used to think: That Stade took advantage of my grogginess—maybe even hypnotized me—to make me believe that I saw something in that Siberian hut which never happened.

"That's possible. He might have picked up some wandering dumb Kulak, put the evil eye on him, drugged him up—yes, it could have happened that way. But I don't believe it."

He tapped the newspaper that told in screaming headlines of the discovery of the body of Jim Stone. The story told of Stone's quick rise to fame, of his disappearance, of the finding of him that morning, an apparent suicide.

"But the whole story isn't there," Pat Morgan said. "The police called me in to identify the corpse, and it was Big Jim all right. They found him in the frozen-meat room of a cold storage warehouse—been there for weeks, apparently. He was resting on his side, face against his arm, and I've never seen a man, alive or dead, more peaceful.

"Pinned to the lapel of his coat was a scrawled note addressed to me. The police couldn't make head nor tail of it, but as far as it was concerned it spoke volumes. It said:

"I go to find the real Lilami.
And don't thaw me out again."

THE GREEK POROPULOS

By EDGAR WALLACE

A T CAROLINA, in the Transvaal, was a store kept by a man named Lioski, who was a Polish Jew. There was an officers' clubhouse, the steward of which was a Greek sportsman named Poropulos, and this story is about these two men, and about an officer of Hampton's Scouts who took too much wine and saw a pair of boots.

I have an intense admiration for George Poropulos, and I revere his memory. I admire him for his nerve; though, for the matter of that, his nerve was no greater than mine.

Long before the war came, when the negotiations between Great Britain and the Transvaal Government were in the diplomatic stage, I drifted to Carolina from the Rand, leaving behind me in the golden city much of ambition, hope, and all the money I had brought with me from England. I came to South Africa with a young wife and £370—within a few shillings—because the doctors told me the only chance I had was in such a hot, dry climate as the highlands of Africa afforded. For my own part, there was a greater attraction in the possibility of turning those few hundreds of mine into thousands, for Johannesburg was in the delirium of a boom.

I left Johannesburg nearly penniless. I could not, at the moment, explain the reason of my failure, for the boom continued, and I had the advantage of the expert advice of Arthur Lioski, who was staying at the same boarding house as myself.

There were malicious people who warned me against Lioski. His own compatriots, sharp men of business, told me to 'ware Lioski, but I ignored the advice because I was very confident in my own judgment, and Lioski was a plausible, handsome man, a little flashy in appearance, but decidedly a beautiful animal.

He was in Johannesburg on a holiday, he said. He had stores in various parts of the country where he sold everything from broomsticks to farm wagons, and he bore the evidence of his prosperity.

He took us to the theater, or rather he took Lillian, for I was too seedy to go out much. I did not grudge Lillian the pleasure. Life was very dull for a young girl whose middle-aged husband had a spot on his lung, and Lioski was so kind and gentlemanly, so far as Lil was concerned, that the only feeling I had in the matter was one of gratitude.

He was tall and dark, broad-shouldered, with a set to his figure and a swing of carriage that excited my admiration. He was possessed of enormous physical strength, and I have seen him take two quarreling Kaffirs—men of no ordinary muscularity—and knock their heads together.

He had an easy, ready laugh, a fund of stories, some a little coarse, I thought, and a florid gallantry which must have been attractive to women. Lil always brightened up wonderfully after an evening with him.

His knowledge of mines and mining propositions was bewildering. I left all my investments in his hands, and it proves something of my trust in him, that when, day by day, he came to me for money, to "carry over" stock—whatever that means—I paid without hesitation. Not only did I lose every penny I possessed, but I found myself in debt to him to the extent of a hundred pounds.

Poor Lil! I broke the news to her of my ruin, and she took it badly; reproached, stormed, and wept in turn, but quieted down when I told her that in the kindness of his heart, Lioski had offered me a berth at his Carolina store. I was to get a £16 a month, half of which was to be paid in stores at wholesale prices and the other half in cash. I was to live rent free in a little house near the store. I was delighted with the offer. It was an immediate rise, though I foresaw that the conditions of life would be much harder than the life to which I had been accustomed in England. We traveled down the Delagoa line to Middleburg, and found a Cape cart waiting to carry us across the twenty miles of rolling veldt. The first six months in Carolina were the happiest I have ever spent. The work in the store was not particularly arduous. I found that it had the reputation of being one of the best-equipped stores in the Eastern Transvaal, and certainly we did a huge business for so small a place. It was not on the town we depended, but upon the surrounding country. Lioski did not come back with us, but after we had been installed for a week he came and took his residence in the store.

ALL WENT well for six months. He taught Lil to ride and drive, and every morning they went cantering over the veldt together. Me he treated more like a brother than an employee, and I found myself hotly resenting the uncharitable things that were said about him, for Carolina, like other small African towns, was a hotbed of gossip.

Lil was happy for that six months, and then I began to detect a change in her attitude toward me. She was snappy, easily offended, insisted upon having her own room—to which I agreed, for, although my chest was better, I still had an annoying cough at night which might have been a trial to anybody within hearing.

It was about this time that I met Poropulos. He came into the store on a hot day in January, a little man of forty-five or thereabouts. He was unusually pale, and had a straggling, weedy beard. His hair was long, his clothes were old and stained, and so much of his shirt as was revealed at his throat was sadly in need of laundering.

Yet he was cheerful and *debonair*—and singularly flippant. He stalked in the store, looked around critically, nodded to me, and smiled. Then he brought his *sjambok* down on the counter with a smack.

"Where's Shylock?" he asked easily.

I am afraid that I was irritated.

"Do you mean Mr. Lioski?"

"Shylock, I said," he repeated. "Shylockstein, the Lothario of Carolina." He smacked the counter again, still smiling.

I was saved the trouble of replying, for at that moment Lioski entered. He stopped dead and frowned when he saw the Greek.

"What do you want, you little beast," he asked harshly.

For answer, the man leaned up against the counter, ran his fingers through his straggling beard, and cocked his head.

"I want justice," he said unctuously—"the restoration of money stolen. I want to send a wreath to your funeral: I want to write your biography——"

"Clear out," shouted Lioski. His face was purple with anger, and he brought his huge fist down upon the counter with a crash that shook the wooden building.

He might have been uttering the most pleasant of compliments, for all the notice the Greek took.

Crash! went Lioski's fist on the counter.

Smash! came Poropulos's *sjambok*, and there was something mocking and derisive in his action that made Lioski mad.

With one spring he was over the counter, a stride and he had his hand on the Greek's collar—and then

he stepped back quickly with every drop of blood gone from his face, for the Greek's knife had flashed under his eyes. I thought Lioski was stabbed, but it was fear that made him white.

The Greek rested the point of the knife on the counter and twiddled it round absentmindedly, laying his palm on the hilt and spinning it with great rapidity.

"Nearly did it that time, my friend," he said, with a note of regret, "nearly did it that time—I shall be hanged for you yet."

Lioski was white and shaking.

"Come in here," he said in a low voice, and the little Greek followed him to the back parlor. They were together for about an hour; sometimes I could hear Mr. Lioski's voice raised angrily, sometimes Poropulos's little laugh. When they came out again the Greek was smiling still and smoking one of my employer's cigars.

"My last word to you," said Lioski huskily, "is this—keep your mouth closed and keep away from me."

"And my last word to you," said Poropulos, jauntily puffing at the cigar, "is this—turn honest, and enjoy a sensation."

He stepped forth from the store with the air of one who had gained a moral victory.

I never discovered what hold the Greek had over my master. I gatherered that at some time or another, Poropulos had lost money, and that he held Lioski responsible.

In some mysterious way Poropulos and I became friends. He was an adventurer of a type. He bought and sold indifferent mining propositions, took up contracts, and, I believe, was not above engaging in the Illicit Gold Buying business. His attitude to Lillian was one of complete adoration. When he was with her his eyes never left her face.

It was about this time that my great sorrow came to me. Lioski went away to Durban—to buy stock, he said—and a few days afterwards Lillian, who had become more and more exigent, demanded to be allowed to go to Cape Town for a change.

I shall remember that scene.

I was at breakfast in the store when she came in. She was white, I thought, but her pallor suited her, with her beautiful black hair and great dark eyes.

She came to the point without any preliminary. "I want to go away," she said.

I looked up in surprise.

"Go away, dear? Where?"

She was nervous. I could see that from the restless movement of her hands.

"I want to go to—to Cape Town—I know a girl there —I'm sick of this place—I hate it!"

She stamped her foot, and I thought that she was

going to break into a fit of weeping. Her lips trembled, and for a time she could not control her voice.

"I am going to be ill if you don't let me go," she said at last. "I can feel——"

"But the money, dear," I said, for it was distressing to me that I could not help her toward the holiday she wanted.

"I can find the money," she said, in an unsteady voice. "I have got a few pounds saved—the allowance you gave me for my clothes—I didn't spend it all—let me go, Charles—please, please!"

I drove her to the station, and took her ticket for Pretoria. I would have taken her to the capital, but I had the store to attend to.

"By the way, what will your address be?" I asked just as the train was moving off.

She was leaning over the gate of the car platform, looking at me strangely.

"I will wire it—I have it in my bag," she called out, and I watched the tail of the train round the curve, with an aching heart. There was something wrong; what it was I could not understand. Perhaps I was a fool. I think I was.

I think I have said that I had made friends with Poropulos. Perhaps it would be more truthful to say that he made friends with me, for he had to break down my feeling of distrust and disapproval. Then, again, I was not certain how Mr. Lioski would regard such a friendship, but, to my surprise, he took very little notice of it or, for the matter of that, of me.

Poropulos came into the store the night my wife left. Business was slack; there was war in the air, rumors of ultimatums had been persistent, and the Dutch farmers had avoided the store.

A WEEK passed, and I began to worry, for I had not heard from Lil. I had had a letter from Lioski, telling me that in view of the unsettled condition of the country he was extending his stay in Durban for a fortnight. The letter gave me the fullest instructions as to what I was to do in case war broke out, but, unfortunately, I had no opportunity of putting them into practice.

The very day I received the letter, a Boer commando rode into Carolina, and at the head of it rode the Landrost Peter du Huis, a pleasant man, whom I knew slightly. He came straight to the store, dismounted, and entered.

"Good morning, Mr. Gray," he said. "I fear that I come on unpleasant business."

"What is that?" I asked.

"I have come to commandeer your stock in the name of the Republic," he said, "and to give you the tip to clear out."

It does not sound possible, but it is nevertheless a fact that in two hours I had left Carolina, leaving Lioski's store in the hands of the Boers, and bringing with me receipts signed by the Landrost for the goods he had commandeered. In four hours I was in a cattle truck with a dozen other refugees on my way to Pretoria—for I had elected to go to Durban to inform Lioski at first hand of what had happened.

Of the journey down to the coast it is not necessary to speak. We were sixty hours *en route;* we were without food, and had little to drink. At Ladysmith I managed to get a loaf of bread and some milk; at Maritzburg I got my first decent meal. But I arrived in Durban, tired, dispirited, and hungry. Lioski was staying at the Royal, and as soon as I got to the station I hailed a *ricksha* to take me there.

There had been no chance of telegraphing. The wires were blocked with government messages. We had passed laden troop trains moving up to the frontier, and had cheered the quiet men in khaki who were going, all of them, to years of hardship and privation, many of them to death.

The vestibule of the Royal was crowded, but I made my way to the office.

"Lioski?" said the clerk. "Mr. and Mrs. Lioski, No. 84—you'll find your way to their sitting room."

I went slowly up the stairs, realizing in a flash the calamity.

I did not blame Lil; it was a hard life I had brought her to. I had been selfish, as sick men are selfish, inconsiderate.

They stood speechless, as I opened the door and entered. I closed the door behind me. Still they stood, Lil as pale as death, with terror and shame in her eyes, Lioski in a black rage.

"Well?" It was he who broke the silence.

He was defiant, shameless, and as I went on to talk about what had happened at the store, making no reference to what I had seen, his lips curled contemptuously.

But Lil, womanlike, rushed in with explanations. She had meant to go to Cape Town—the train service had been bad—she had decided to go to Durban—Mr. Lioski had been kind enough to book her a room——

I let her go on. When she had finished I handed my receipts to Lioski.

"That ends our acquaintance, I think."

"As you like," he replied with a shrug.

I turned to Lillian.

"Come, my dear," I said, but she made no move, and I saw Lioski smile again.

I lost all control over myself and leaped at him, but his big fist caught me before I could reach him, and I went down, half stunned. I was no match for him. I knew that, and if the blow did nothing else, it sobered me. I picked myself up. I was sick with misery and hate.

"Come, Lil," I said again.

She was looking at me, and I thought I saw a look of disgust in her face. I did not realize that I was bleeding, and that I must have been a most unpleasant figure. I only knew that she loathed me at that moment, and I turned on my heel and left them, my own wife and the big man who had broken me.

One forgets things in war time. I joined the Imperial Light Horse and went to the front. The doctor passed me as sound, so I suppose that all that is claimed for the climate of Africa is true.

We went into Ladysmith, and I survived the siege. I was promoted for bringing an officer out of action under fire. I earned a reputation for daring, which I did not deserve, because always I was courting swift death, and taking risks to that end.

Before Buller's force had pushed a way through the stubborn lines to our relief, I had received my commission. More wonderful to me, I found myself a perfectly healthy man, as hard as nails, as callous as the most-experienced soldier. Only, somewhere down in my heart, a little worm gnawed all the time; sleeping or waking, fighting or resting, I thought of Lillian, and wondered, wondered, wondered.

Ladysmith was relieved. We marched on toward Pretoria. I was transferred to Hampton's Horse with the rank of major, and for eighteen months I moved up and down the Eastern Transvaal chasing a will-o-the-wisp of a commandant, who was embarrassing the blockhouse lines.

Then one day I came upon Poropulos.

We were encamped outside Standerton when he rode in on a sorry-looking Burnto pony. He had been in the country during the war, he said, buying and selling horses. He did not mention Lioski's name to me, and so studiously did he avoid referring to the man, that I saw at once that he knew.

It was brought home to me by his manner that he had a liking for me that I had never guessed. In what way I had earned his regard I cannot say, but it was evident he entertained a real affection for me.

We parted after an hour's chat—he was going back to Carolina. He had a scheme for opening an officers' club in that town, where there was always a large garrison, and to which the wandering columns came from time to time to be re-equipped.

As for me, I continued the weary chase of the flying commando. Trek, trek, trek, in fierce heat, in torrential downpour, over smooth veldt and broken hills, skirmishing, sniping, and now and then a sharp engagement, with a dozen casualties on either side.

Four months passed, and the column was ordered into Carolina for a refit. I went without qualms, though I knew she was there, and Lioski was there.

We got into Carolina in a thunderstorm, and the men were glad to reach a place that bore some semblance of civilization. My brother officers, after our long and profitless trek, were overjoyed at the prospect of a decent dinner—for Poropulos's club was already famous among the columns.

My horse picked up a stone and went dead lame, so I stayed behind to doctor him, and rode to Carolina two hours after the rest of the column had arrived.

It was raining heavily as I came over a fold of the hill that showed the straggling township. There was no human being in sight save a woman who stood by the roadside, waiting, and I knew instinctively, long before I reached her, that it was Lillian. I cantered toward her. Her face was turned in my direction, and she stood motionless as I drew rein and swung myself to the ground.

She was changed, not as I expected, for sorrow and suffering had etherealized her. Her big eyes burned in a face that was paler than ever, her lips, once so red and full, were almost white.

"I have been waiting for you," she said.

"Have you, dear? You are wet."

She shook her head impatiently. I slipped off my mackintosh and put it about her.

"He has turned me out," she said.

She did not cry. I think she had not recovered from the shock. Something stirred from the thin cloak she was wearing; a feeble cry was muffled by the wrapping.

"I have got a little girl," she said, "but she is dying." She began to cry silently, the tears running down her wet face in streams.

I took her into Carolina, and found a Dutchwoman who put her and the baby to bed, and gave her some coffee.

I went up to the officers' club just after sunset and met Poropulos coming down.

He was in a terrible rage, and was muttering to himself in some tongue I could not understand.

"Oh, here you are!"—he almost spat the words in his anger—"that dog Lioski——"

He was about to say something, but checked himself. I think it was about Lillian that he intended to speak at first, but he changed the subject to another grievance. "I was brought before the magistrate and fined £100 for selling field-force tobacco. My club will be ruined—Lioski informed the police—by——"

He was incoherent in his passion. I gather that he had been engaged in some shady business, and that Lioski had detected him. He almost danced before me in the rain.

"Shylock dies tonight," he said, and waved his enemy out of the world with one sweep of his hand. "He dies tonight—I am weary of him—for eighteen—nineteen years I have known him, and he's dirt right through——"

He went out without another word. I stood on the slope of the hill watching him.

I dined at the club, and went straight back to the house where I had left my wife. She was sleeping—but the baby was dead. Poor little mortal! I owed it no grudge, but I was glad when they told me.

All the next day I sat by her bed listening to Lillian's mutterings, for she was very ill. I suffered all the tortures of a damned soul sitting there, for she spoke of Lioski—"Arthur" she called him—prayed to him for mercy—told him she loved him——

I was late for dinner at the club. There was a noisy crowd there. Young Harvey of my own regiment had had too much to drink, and I avoided his table.

My hand shook as I poured out a glass of wine, and somebody remarked on it.

I did not see Poropulos until the dinner was halfway through. Curiously enough, I looked at the clock as he came in, and the hands pointed to half past eight.

The Greek was steward of the club, and was serving the wine. He was calm, impassive, remarkably serene, I thought. He exchanged jokes with the officers who were grumbling that they had had to wait for the fulfillment of their orders.

"It was ten to eight when I ordered this," grumbled one man.

Then, suddenly, Harvey, who had been regarding Poropulos with drunken gravity, pointed downward.

"He's changed his boots," he said, and chuckled. Poropulos smiled amiably and went on serving. "He's changed his boots!" repeated Harvey, concentrating his mind upon trivialities as only a drunken man can. The men laughed. "Oh, dry up, Harvey!" said somebody.

"He's changed——"

He got no further. Through the door came a military policeman, splashed from head to foot with mud.

"District Commandant here, sir?" he demanded. "There's been a man murdered."

"Soldier?" asked a dozen voices.

"No, sir—storekeeper, name of Lioski—shot dead half an hour ago."

I do not propose to tell in detail all that happened following that. Two smart C. I. D. men came down from Johannesburg, made a few inquiries, and arrested Poropulos. He was expecting the arrest, and half an hour before the officers came he asked me to go to him.

I spent a quarter of an hour with him, and what we said is no man's business but ours. He told me something that startled me—he loved Lillian, too. I had never guessed it, but I did not doubt him. But it was finally for Lillian's sake that he made me swear an oath so dreadful that I cannot bring myself to write it down—an oath so unwholesome, and so against the grain of a man, that life after it could only be a matter of sickness and shame.

Then the police came and took him away.

Lioski had been shot dead in the store by some person who had walked in when the store was empty, at a time when there was nobody in the street. This person had shot the Jew dead and walked out again. The police theory was that Poropulos had gone straight from the club, in the very middle of dinner, had committed the murder, and returned to continue his serving, and the crowning evidence was the discovery that he had changed his boots between 7.30 and 8.30. The mud-stained boots were found in a cellar, and the chain of evidence was completed by the statement of a trooper who had seen the Greek walking from the direction of the store, at 8.10, with a revolver in his hand.

Poropulos was cheerful to the last—cheerful through the trial, through the days of waiting in the fort at Johannesburg.

"I confess nothing," he said to the Greek priest. "I hated Lioski, and I am glad that he is dead, that is all. It is true that I went down to kill him, but it was too late."

When they pinioned him he turned to me.

"I have left my money to you," he said. "There is about four thousand pounds. You will look after her."

"That is the only reason I am alive."

"Did you murder Arthur Lioski?" said the priest again.

"No," said Poropulos, and smiled as he went to his death. And what he said was true, as I know. I shot Lioski.

ARGOSY
Issued Weekly

CROSSES
OF STEEL
by Rex Parson
Author of
"Southwest of
the Law", etc.

10¢ A COPY   SEPTEMBER 13 $4.00 A YEAR

1. SMALL   1919

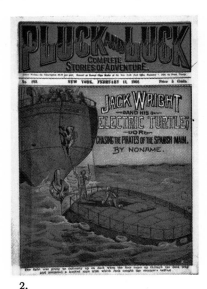

2.

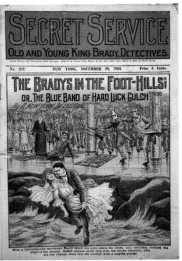

3.

4.

DIME NOVELS

Dime Novel art was rarely, if ever, signed. The Dime Novels were bound like comic-books as opposed to the thicker, bulkier Pulps which had colorfully printed edge-strips with information matching the cover logo.

Fig. 2.   1902   (#193)
Fig. 3.   1903   (#252)
Fig. 4.   1903   (# 58)

EARLY PULPS

The top illustrators of the day contributed to these Pulps, among them N. C. Wyeth, who illustrated covers for *The Popular Magazine* (Fig. 5), the only Family Pulp included in this early group of male-oriented Pulps. Of particular interest is the first publication of a "Tarzan" novel for *The All-Story Weekly* (Fig. 6).

5. N. C. WYETH   1915   (V.39 #1)

OCTOBER   THE   15 CENTS

ALL-STORY

Tarzan of the Apes

A Romance of the Jungle

CLINTON PETTEE

6. CLINTON PETTEE   1912   (V.24 #2)

PRICE 20 CENTS

JULY 1922

THE BLUE BOOK MAGAZINE

J. S. Fletcher,
Clarence Herbert New,
Bertram Atkey,
Charles Phelps Cushing,

The latest novel by
E. PHILLIPS
OPPENHEIM

H. Bedford-Jones,
Edward Mott Woolley,
Lemuel L. DeBra,
George Allan England

7. J. E. ALLEN *Darkest at Dawn* 1922 (V.35 #3)

8. ARNOLD KOHN *Manchu Terror* 1946 (V.1 #1)

9. HAROLD S. DELAY *Roman Holiday* 1938   (V.1 #1)

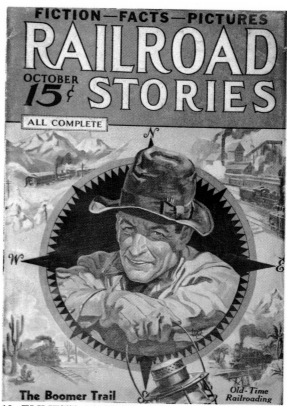

10. EMMETT WATSON   *The Boomer Trail*
1935   (V.18 #3)

THE ADVENTURE PULPS

The covers in this group reflect increasing specialization
and variety of style after the early 20's. *Mammoth
Adventure* (Fig. 8) typified in title, art, and
content the excitement of the Pulps. *Golden Fleece*
(Fig. 9) was a short-lived Historical Fiction Pulp.
Von Gelb's cover for *Oriental Stories* (Fig. 12) is a
stylistic rarity. Margaret Brundage, working in pastels,
did most of its covers and those of its successor
Magic Carpet (Fig. 14). Both publications were
owned by *Weird Tales* and lasted but a few issues each,
although overall quality was outstanding. By now,
logo design reflected editorial policy.

11. H. C. MURPHY   *Abandon Ship* 1928 (V.15 #6)

Fig. 13
CHARLES HARGENS
1923 (V.42 #2)

Fig. 14
MARGARET BRUNDAGE
1933 (V.3 #4)

Fig. 15
SIDNEY RIESENBERG
1935 (V.1 #4)

13.

14.

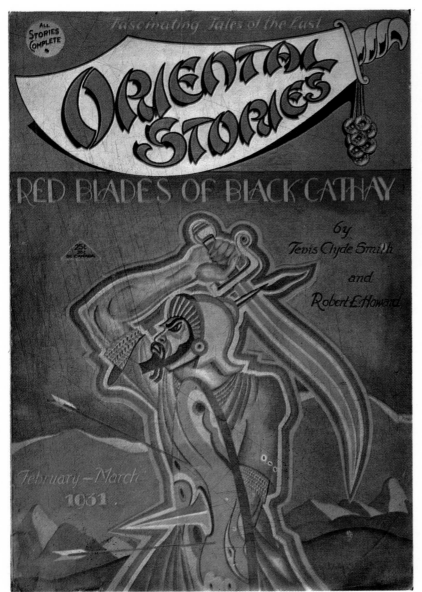

15.

12. VON GELB   1931   (V.1 #3)

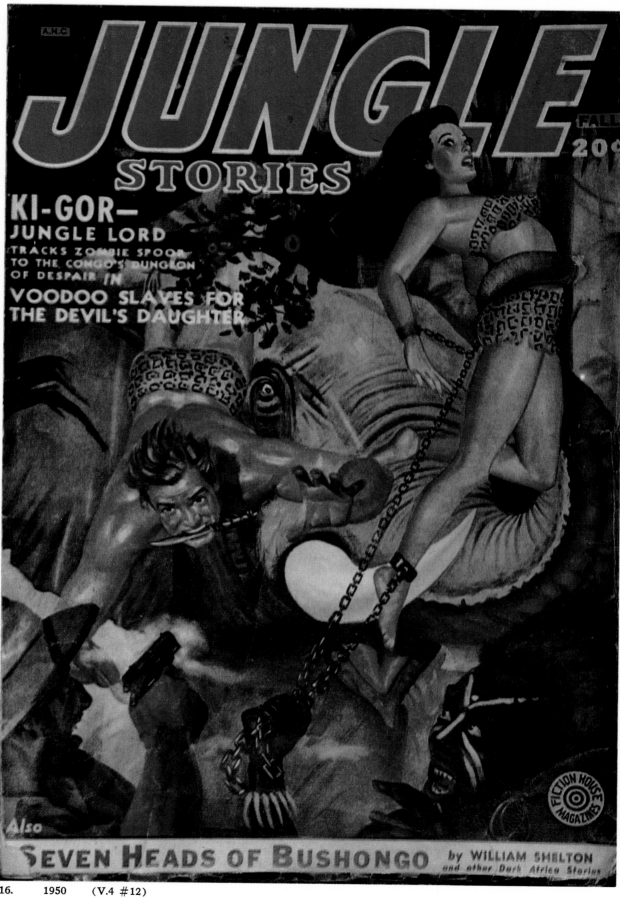

Specialization in this category extended even as far as "hare and hounds," depicted on the cover of *Sports Story* (Fig. 17). The raw style of H. C. Murphy, Jr. (Fig. 19) is as characteristic of the Sports Pulps of the 20's and 30's as the photographic style (Fig. 18, 20) is of the 40's and 50's.

Fig. 18 1944 (V. 1 #8)
Fig. 19 H. C. Murphy, Jr. 1930 (V. 2 #8)
Fig. 20 1950 (V.3 #1)

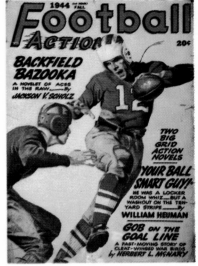

18.

17. F.A.C. 1929 (V.25 #2)

19.

20.

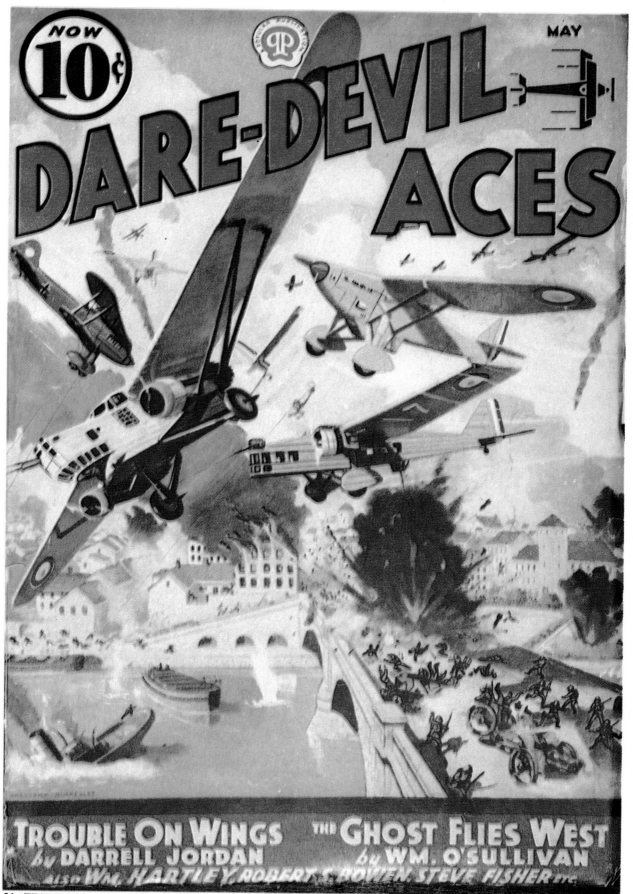

21. FREDERICK BLAKESLEE 1937 (V.16 #2)

Particular attention to factual data was a characteristic of the Aviation Pulps. The battle scene shown on the cover of *Dare-Devil Aces* (Fig. 21) depicted real aircraft and a full description of the action was provided in the contents. In some cases (Fig. 22) maneuvers were explained on the cover itself. By World War II, slickly illustrated covers predominated (Fig. 27).

22. FRANK TINSLEY   *Out-Diving the Pfalz*
1934   (V.15 #4)

23.   1930

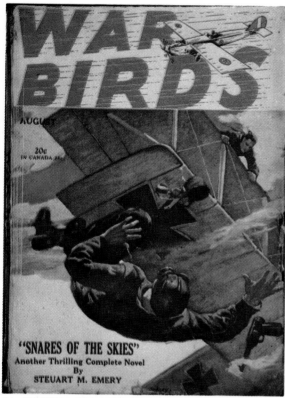

24. SIDNEY RIESENBERG   1929   (V.7 #19)

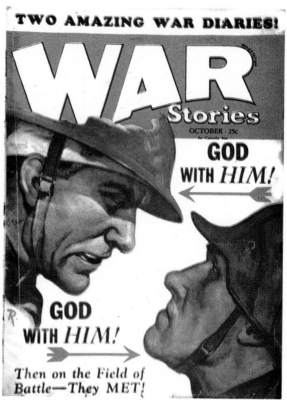

25.   1930

26. ARNOLD LORNE HICKS   1930   (V.1 #2)

27. RUDOLPH BELARSKI   1942   (V.2 #1)

FIGHTING ACES OF WAR SKIES

WINGS

A Spy Mystery Novel
by JOEL ROGERS

20c

"DEATH TRIPS
THE GUNS"
An ace novel by
a new writer
THOMAS
CARPENTER

A BIG WAR AIR NOVEL by FRANKLIN H. MARTIN
"THE GALLOPING GHOST"

28. RUDOLPH BELARSKI   1936   (V.7 #1)

29. H. W. SCOTT   *Kid Wolf's Flaming Trail* 1934   (V.83 #3)

Fig. 30 portrays the strong respect for nature which was a part of *Western Story*'s editorial policy. *Nickel Western* (Fig. 33) was a Depression experiment. By the 40's, covers were cluttered with as many elements as the cover would hold (Fig. 34).

30.   *Look Son! It's Their Country!* 1929   (V.90 #3)

31. FRED T. EVERETT *Ready For Trouble*
1928   (V.14 #1)

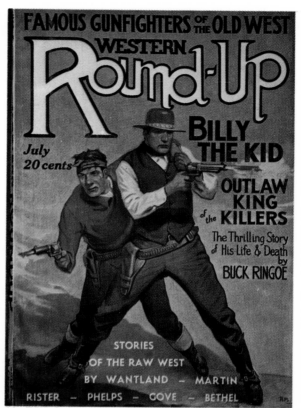

32. RUDOLPH BELARSKI *Pardners* 1934   (V.1 #1)

33. ERIC LUNDGREN   1933   (V.1 #2)

34. H. T. FISK   1942   (V.3 #3)

35.   1915   (V.1 #1)

DETECTIVE AND MYSTERY

Fig. 35 illustrates the first issue of *Detective Story Magazine;* the first significant specialized Pulp. The field changed radically through the introduction of the "hard-boiled dicks" in *Black Mask,* an early issue of which is illustrated (Fig. 36). Symbolism in cover-art appeared in the 30's (Figs. 38, 39, 43) to lure the readers as newsstands were flooded with obscure titles, two of which (Figs. 37, 41) are included. They were short-lived.

Fig. 37 W. C. BRIGHAM 1931(?) (V.1 #4)
Fig. 38 1934 (V.31 #4)
Fig. 39 FRANK TINSLEY *The Death Sentence* 1933 (V. 2 #4)
Fig. 41 W. C. BRIGHAM 1931 (V.4 #2)
Fig. 42 1935 (V.1 #1)

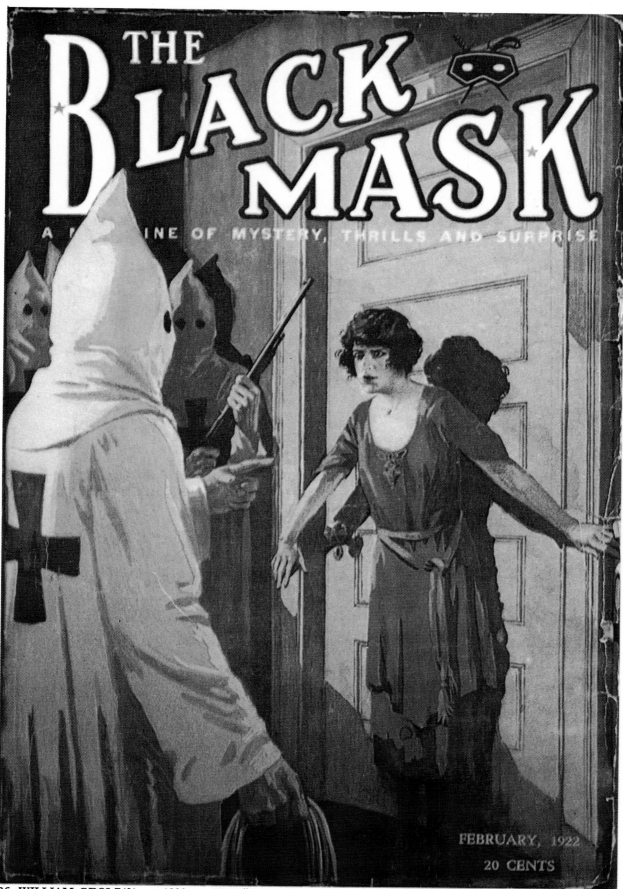

FEBRUARY, 1922
20 CENTS

36. WILLIAM GROLZ(?)   1922   (V.4 #5)

37.

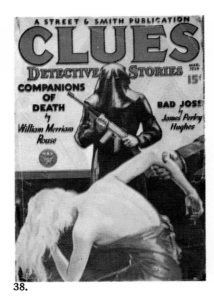

38.

39.

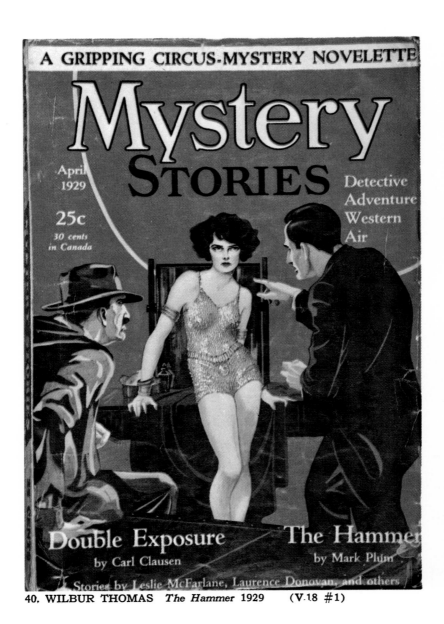

40. WILBUR THOMAS   *The Hammer* 1929   (V.18 #1)

41.

42.

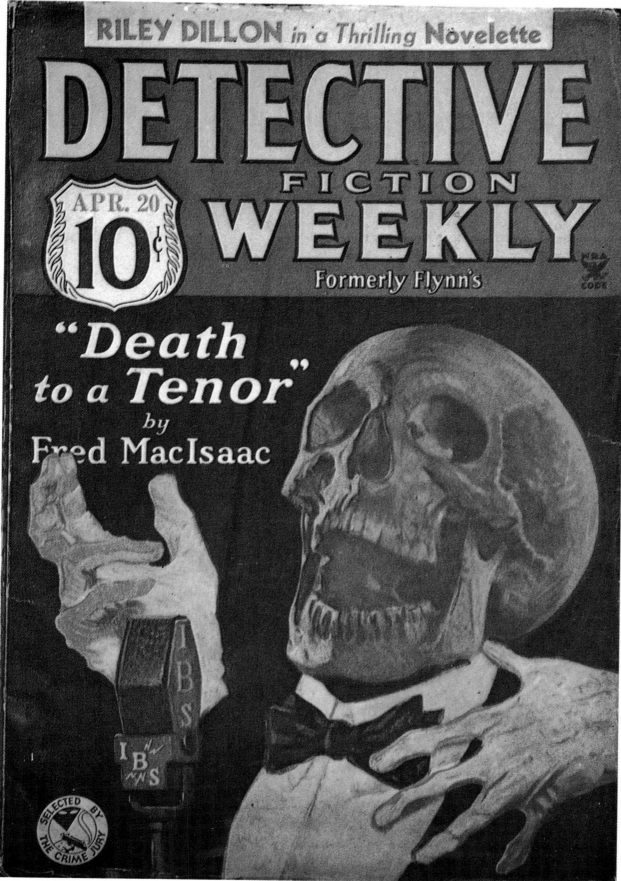

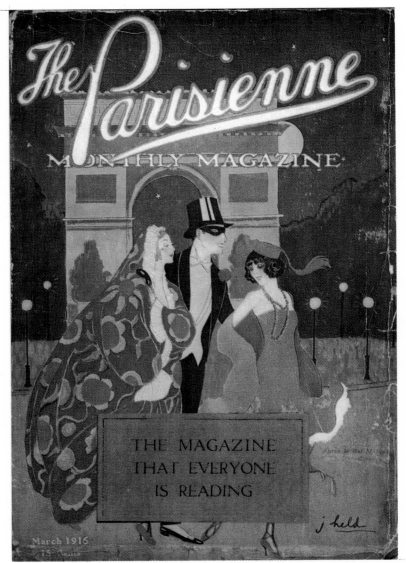

44. JOHN HELD, Jr. *Après le Bal Masque Champs-Elysées* 1916 (V.2 #3)

EXPLOITING THE GIRLS—INNOCENCE

John Held's early work is shown on this under-the-counter Pulp (Fig. 44), foreshadowing his later work for the old *Life* magazine. The *Love Pulps* (Figs. 49, 50, 51, 52,) grew out of these early illicit Pulps. Their covers reflected the purity of their contents. *Husbands* was a truly unusual experiment (Fig. 52).

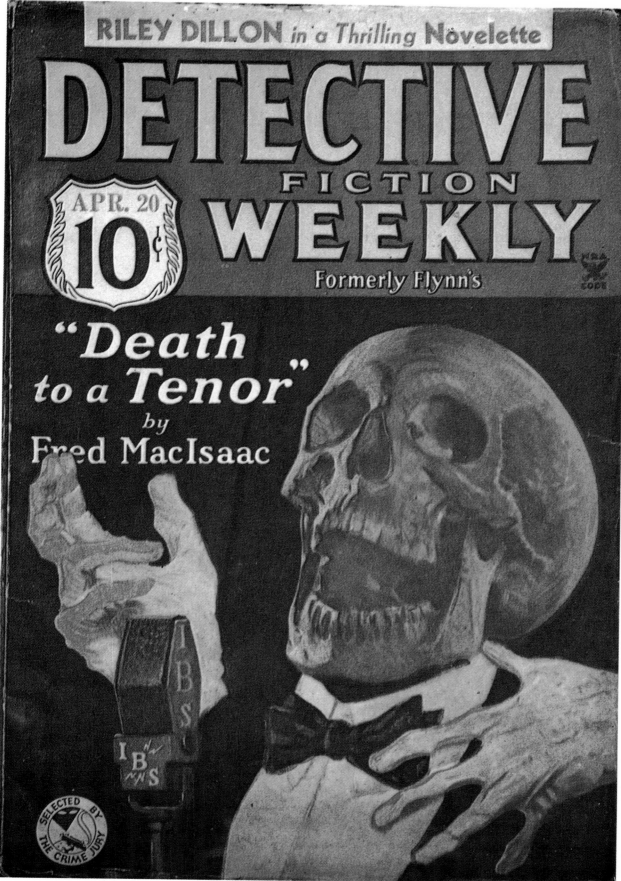

RILEY DILLON in a Thrilling Novelette

DETECTIVE
FICTION
WEEKLY

APR. 20
10¢

Formerly Flynn's

NRA CODE

"Death to a Tenor"
by
Fred MacIsaac

SELECTED BY THE CRIME JURY

44. JOHN HELD, Jr. *Après le Bal Masque Champs-Elysées* 1916 (V.2 #3)

EXPLOITING THE GIRLS—INNOCENCE

John Held's early work is shown on this under-the-counter Pulp (Fig. 44),
foreshadowing his later work for the old *Life* magazine. The *Love Pulps* (Figs.
49, 50, 51, 52,) grew out of these early illicit Pulps. Their covers reflected the
purity of their contents. *Husbands* was a truly unusual experiment (Fig. 52).

45.   1931   (V.1 #6)

46. ARDEN   1922   (V.13 #1)

47.   1929   (V.5 #5)

48.   1939   (V.52 #10)

49.

50.

51.

52.

Fig. 49 JOHN NEWTON HOWETT 1939 (V.152 #3)
Fig. 50 1926 (V.7 #2)
Fig. 51 EARLE BERGEY 1945 (V.19 #1)
Fig. 52 1936 (V.1 #1)

53. JOHN NEWTON HOWETT   1935   (V.2 #4)

54. H. J. WARD   1936   (V.5 #2)

EXPLOITING THE GIRLS— STRAIGHT-OUT SEX

Henry Steeger, president of Popular Publications, created *Horror Stories* and *Terror Tales* after seeing the Grand Guignol in Paris. But the covers of these Pulps rarely were indicative of the contents. Earlier the *Spicy* Pulps (Fig. 54, 55, 56, 57) had been introduced (under-the-counter) and had brought sex into the Pulps under the guise of lavish production. Following the success of the *Spicy* group sex was introduced into the Horror Pulps.

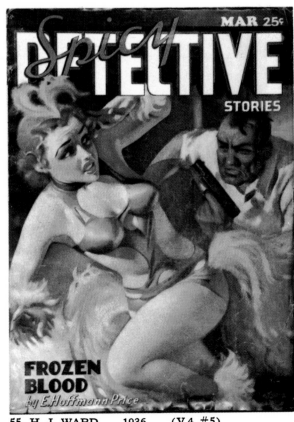

55. H. J. WARD   1936   (V.4 #5)

56. H. J. WARD   1937   (V.1 #3)

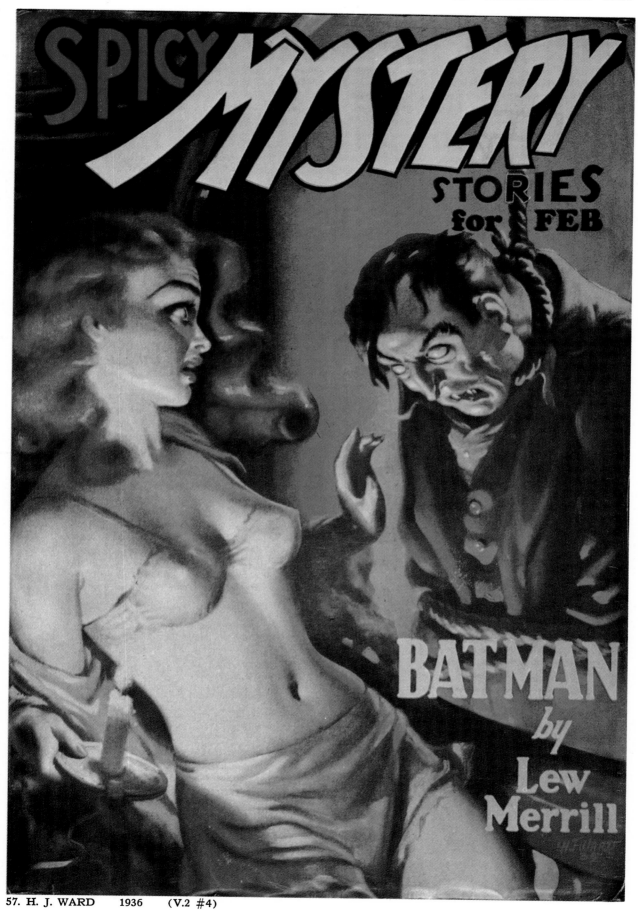

SPICY MYSTERY STORIES for FEB

BATMAN by Lew Merrill

57. H. J. WARD   1936   (V.2 #4)

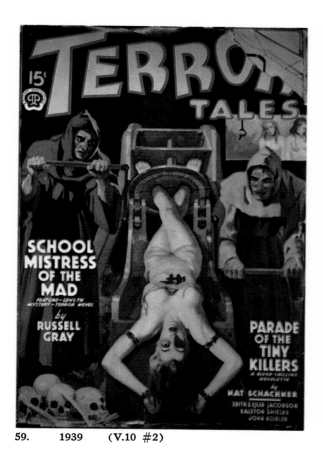

59.   1939   (V.10 #2)

60.   1938   (V.18 #3)

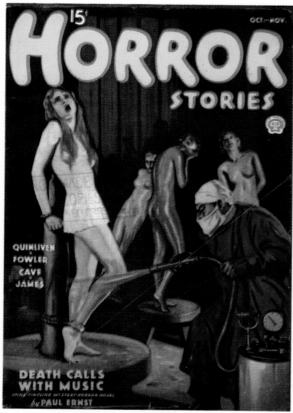

61. JOHN NEWTON HOWETT   1936   (V.4 #3)

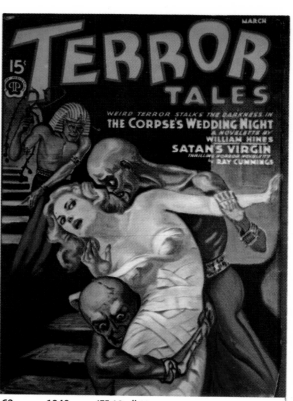

62.   1940   (V.12 #1)

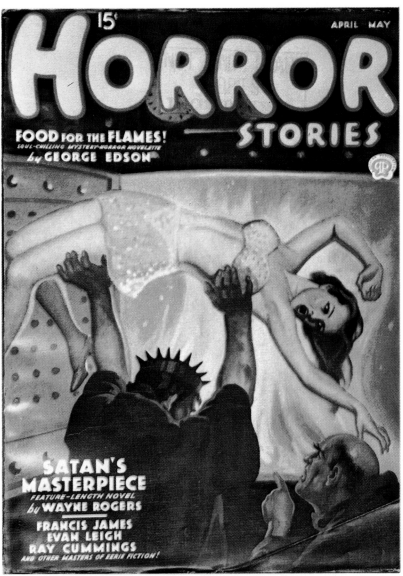

63. JOHN NEWTON HOWETT   1936   (V.3 #4)

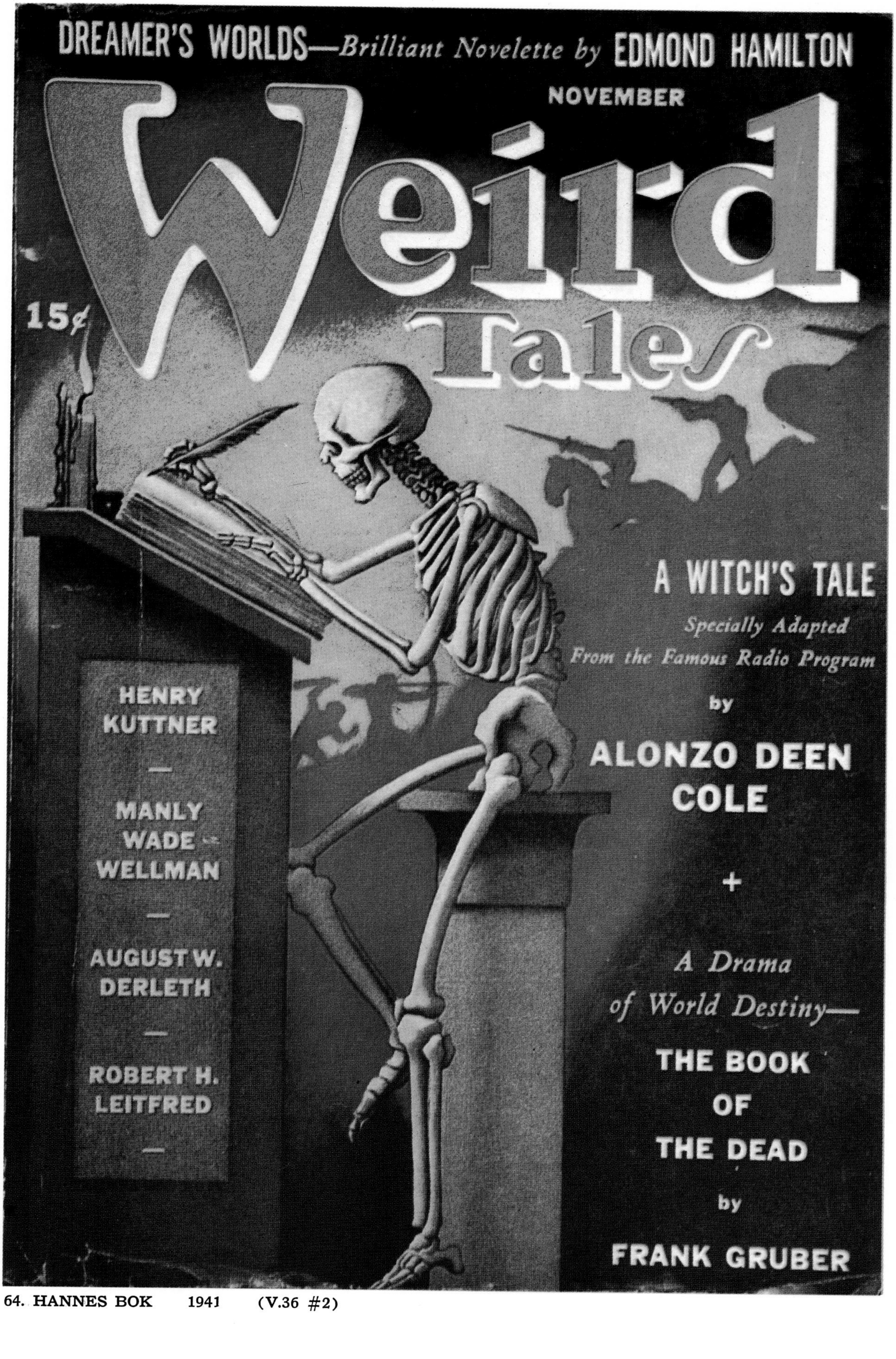

DREAMER'S WORLDS—*Brilliant Novelette by* EDMOND HAMILTON

NOVEMBER

Weird Tales

15¢

HENRY
KUTTNER

—

MANLY
WADE
WELLMAN

—

AUGUST W.
DERLETH

—

ROBERT H.
LEITFRED

—

A WITCH'S TALE

Specially Adapted
From the Famous Radio Program

by

ALONZO DEEN
COLE

+

A Drama
of World Destiny—

THE BOOK
OF
THE DEAD

by

FRANK GRUBER

64. HANNES BOK   1941   (V.36 #2)

Hannes Bok (Fig. 64) continued in the tradition of Virgil Finlay, whose black-and-white work is illustrated in the Supernatural section of the text. J. Allen St. John (Fig. 70) achieved wide recognition for his illustrations and paintings for the "Tarzan" books. His influence on the fantasy field is strong today. Margaret Brundage (Fig. 71, 72) worked in pastels. Her highly erotic covers were the subject of controversy among *Weird Tales* readers. The A. R. Tilbourne cover (Fig. 73) is one of many excellent portrayals of imagined horrors. Four other titles—which failed financially—are included (Figs. 66, 67, 68, 69).

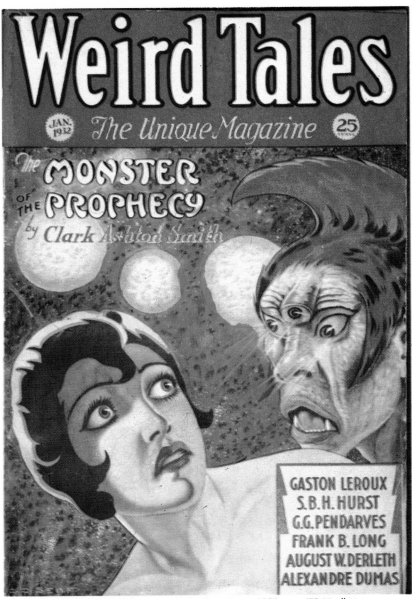

65. C. C. SENF *The Monster of the Prophecy* 1932   (V.19 #1)

66. H. W. WESSO   *The Place of the Pythons*
              1931   (V.1 #1)

67.   1919   (V.3 #1)

68. DALTON STEVENS   1930   (V.9 #1)

69. H. S. MOSKOVITZ   1931   (V.1 #6)

EDMOND HAMILTON • E. HOFFMANN PRICE • CLARK ASHTON SMITH

Weird Tales

APRIL 25¢

GOLDEN BLOOD
by Jack Williamson

70. J. ALLEN ST. JOHN *Golden Blood* 1933   (V.21 #4)

71. MARGARET BRUNDAGE *The Black God's Kiss*
1934 (V.24 #4)

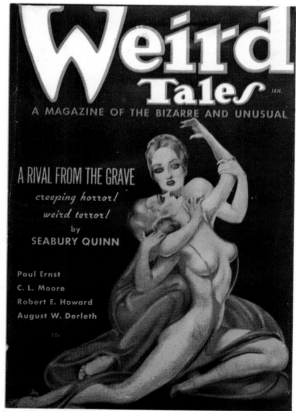

72. MARGARET BRUNDAGE 1936

73. A. R. TILBOURNE *The Hog* 1947 (V.39 #9)

74. FRANK R. PAUL *The Moon Strollers* 1929 (V.4 #2)

75. FRANK R. PAUL *War of the Worlds*
1927 (V.2 #5)

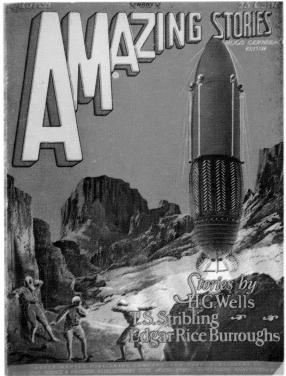

76. FRANK R. PAUL *The Green Splotches*
1927 (V.1 #12)

SCIENCE FICTION

The extraordinarily accurate "moonwalk" (Fig. 74) and the vertical take-off of a rocket ship (Fig. 76) are both the work of the imaginative genius, Frank R. Paul, the most popular of *Amazing Stories'* artists. Fig. 75 illustrates writer H. G. Wells' famous "War of the Worlds." Paul's conception of a brain transplant performed by a Martian scientist was the subject of the only *Amazing Stories Annual* (Fig. 77). The lavish detail in Paul's covers was the product of his background as a practicing architect.

77. FRANK R. PAUL   *The Master Mind of Mars* 1927   (V.1 #1)

79.

Three covers depicting BEM's (Bug-Eyed Monsters) are shown on this page (Fig. 78, 79, 80). Whereas the two by Leo Morey (Fig. 79, 80) are humorous, the BEM's of Howard V. Brown (Fig. 78) have a graceful quality not usually associated with this subject. Brown's work was typified by subtle color choice (Fig. 81) not characteristic of the field. BEM's and gaudy subjects abounded from the late 30's to the 50's. (Figs. 82, 83, 84, 85).

Fig. 79   LEO MOREY   *The Conquest of the Earth*   1931   (V. 6 #1)
Fig. 80   LEO MOREY   *The Prince of Liars*   1930   (V. 5 #7)

Fig. 82   1950   (V. 20 #3)
Fig. 83   EARLE BERGEY   *Things Pass By*   1945   (V. 27 #2)
Fig. 84   1944   (V. 2 #7)
Fig. 85   NORMAN SAUNDERS   *Avengers of Space*   1938   (V. 1 #1)

80.

78. HOWARD V. BROWN   1936   (V.17 #4)

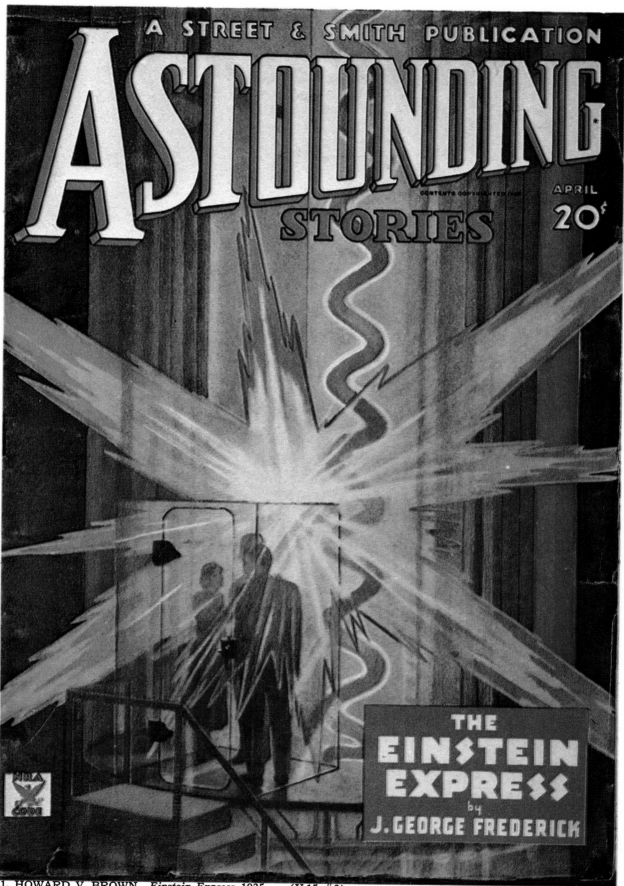

81. HOWARD V. BROWN *Einstein Express* 1935   (V.15 #2)

82.

83.

84.

85.

THE HERO PULPS ▶

No cover better represents what the Pulps meant to the masses during the Depression than that of the *Operator #5* issue, opposite (Fig. 86). The cover story's synopsis appeared on the title page:

LEGIONS OF STARVATION   By Curtis Steele

Over the whole continent, little children clung whimpering to the skirts of distraught mothers, crying piteously for food. One of the most brilliant men in America, a national figure—backed by a powerful, efficient organization —drunk on ambition and the promise of supreme power, controlled all the reserve supplies of the land. Hosts of voracious insects, bred at his command, were laying the plains waste, devouring all green things. Incendiarism and lootings daily depleted the shrinking store of government–owned food-stuffs. The Four Horsemen of the Apocalypse laughed in their saddles as they thundered their mocking call of doom—forewarning the slavery of a proud race of men. One man alone—Jimmy Christopher—can check their wild onslaught. Only he, Operator 5, can outwit the madman monarch!

Symbolism flourished in cover-art as artists searched for fresh new ways to portray the Pulp Hero who had to be depicted issue after issue (Fig. 86, 87, 89, 90, 92, 93, 98).

86. JOHN HOWITT *Legions of Starvation* 1934   (V.3 #1)

87. GRAVES GLADNEY   1940   (V.33 #4)

88.   1935   (V.5 #4)

89. RUDOLPH BELARSKI   1936   (V.15 #3)

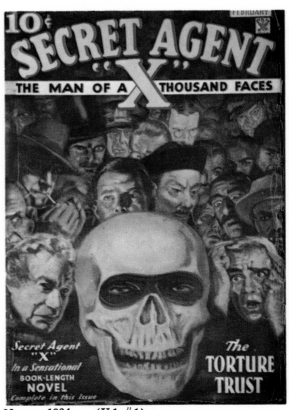

90.   1934   (V.1 #1)

91. HUBERT ROGERS   1940   (V.1 #1)

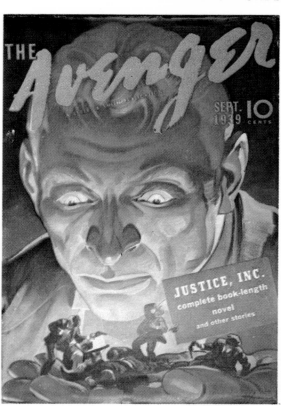

92. H. W. SCOTT   1939   (V.1 #1)

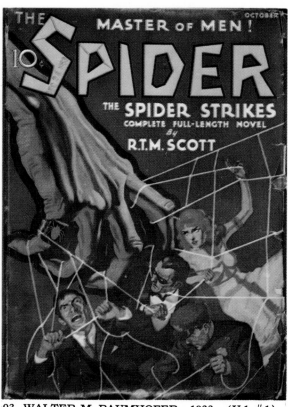

93. WALTER M. BAUMHOFER 1933 (V.1 #1)

94.   1935   (V.4 #6)

96.

95. FREDERICK BLAKESLEE   *New York was in Flames*
1934   (V.6 #2)

97.

Fig. 96
RUDOLPH BELARSKI
*Hang on when the Devil's Dread-
naught Strikes!*
1935   (#84)
Fig. 97
FRANK TINSLEY
1934   (V. 1 #1)

98. FREDERICK BLAKESLEE *He Felt the Dragon's Hot Breath* 1934   (V.3 #2)

99. JEROME ROSEN   1936   (V.2 #3)

100. RUDOLPH ZIRN   *She Shall Become a Walking*
                    Corpse!   1935   (V.1 #3)

Villains were the heroes of several Pulps, two of which are illustrated (Fig. 99, 100). They lasted but a few issues.

The trucks roared on while Gore fired

The Devil Must Pay

By FREDERICK C. PAINTON
Author of "Keepers of the Peace," "The Gods Are Jealous," etc.

FROM THE moment he saved my life I hated Satan Jack Gore. A dozen times afterward the impulse to kill him sent me blindly charging at him with groping fingers. He was evil to the core, a rascal, a crook, a beast—but see him yourself, and learn of the malign evil influence he exercised on my life.

A hot night in Marseilles with a south wind out of Africa drying the sweat on you instantly, parching your lips. I had jumped my ship, the *Exmarch*, and with fifty dollars in my pocket I had strolled down the Cannebiere and off toward the Joliette basin. I had heard that Marseilles was the most vicious city in the world. Young, hell-bent for adventure, I wanted to find out for myself. A fool? Certainly, but a man is only twenty-four once, and that is the time to stride the world with seven league boots and grin into the bright face of peril.

The alleyways stank from the filth emptied from upper floors. The darkness was filled with flitting figures. A few *bistros* gave forth feeble light where whiskered men crouched over cheap wine and schemed their schemes to gain money and food.

Girls there were who beckoned with bold provocative eyes. But I had heard of them; how they drugged a man, robbed him, threw him into the street. Lodging house keepers cried, "Sleep here the night, sailor." But I had heard of them, too, how the closets in their establishments, where you hung your clothes, had turning panels so that no matter if you locked your door you awoke in the morning penniless. *Agents de police* patrolled in pairs and ignored the jeers and curses thrown at them. Yes, Marseilles is a tough port, a fetid place where live the maggots of the world. I finally began to feel uneasy and when two soldiers in the uniform of Foreign Legionnaires warned me to turn back, I did so.

But I missed a turning and found myself in an alley scarcely the width of my shoulders, stone walls on each side. I hurried on, my breath sticking in my throat, my heart thudding. I never saw the two shadows who had crouched in the darkness of the wall on the right.

They loomed suddenly before me, taking me in front and in flank, charging with a silent ferocity that made them all the more terrible. I am six feet tall, I weigh one hundred and seventy, and I was not minded to lose everything. I met the first charge with both fists hooking to the body. But the second man jammed me to the wall.

Star glitter sheened along the edge of a naked knife.

"Now, *salopard*," growled he, "shall I slit your throat?"

I know and speak French well, so that even his Marseillaise accent did not hide the meaning of his words. While I hung between two impulses the man I had slugged rose and kicked me with the deadly toe of the Apache *savate*. I leaned against the wall, paralyzed with agony.

They knocked me down and started going through my pockets. They were talking in the *argot* among themselves.

Suddenly, however, they ceased to search me. A cry of alarm broke from one. They rose swiftly to face a huge shadow charging down upon them. By now the pain within me had subsided somewhat. I rose to help give battle.

But it was not necessary. This giant fought like a madman. His blows struck with a savage force that broke bones and numbed flesh. He of the knife tried to strike. His arm was seized in mid-air. He screamed with pain. The knife dropped; the arm hung down, twisted and broken so that the palm was *outward*. The man fled staggeringly, calling for aid. The other turned and ran past me, mewing like a cat, blood spurting from his mouth, his lower lip jammed into his teeth so that the teeth protruded through the skin.

I HAD never seen such blows struck; had never seen such a magnificent animal in action. I was speechless for a moment with excitement. My rescuer ranged alongside, cupped his hands around a match and ignited a cigarette.

So I saw his face. Deep-set eyes beneath heavy straight brows. A long nose, a powerful, almost sinister mouth. He had a great red beard that made the strong face all the more weird and powerful.

Without thinking, I spoke in English. "You saved my life. That one guy would have knifed me."

"Serve you right, too," growled the newcomer, "coming into a spot like this alone."

His accent told me he was an American.

"Well, admitting that, how about me buying a drink?"

"If you can buy a drink, you can pay off," he said. "How much money have you got?"

I listened amazed. "Fifty dollars, but I don't understand."

"Give me forty-five," he said.

A sudden fury swept me. "I see. You save me from two French thieves to rob me yourself."

"Why not?" he laughed deep in his throat. "I'm broke. Come on—kick through."

He took hold of my arm, and his grip shut off circulation, compressed muscle. "Dish it out," he insisted.

I slugged him square on the jaw with my other hand. I had all the beef of me behind it. I heard the blow explode on his jaw. I saw his head jerk to the impact. I have dropped men bigger than myself with that punch. But I didn't drop him. He slapped me so hard I shot across the alley.

I came back, crying in rage, striking wildly. He did not slap me again. He merely seized my two arms and pinned me helpless.

"You got guts," he said, "but I need the dough. If I really start on you I'll take you apart. So you'd better shell out."

I still refused, so holding me fast with one hand he slapped me again. I was half-stunned, and when he brutally fished in my pockets for my thin roll I could not stop him. He took all except five dollars which he shoved back.

"Okay," he said, "come on and I'll get you out of this hell-roost."

I followed him blindly, not to be led out, but waiting until my strength should come back. I was cursing him at every step. If I had had a gun or a knife I'd have tried to kill him then and there. As it was we finally reached the lower end of the Cannebiere.

Here at a *bistro*, occupied only by two Senegalese and a Spahi, he suddenly said, "I'm thirsty. You buy that drink."

He ordered beer. Here in the light I could see that he was close to six feet three, as broad as a house, hard-bitten, lean. And his mouth had a cruel cynical twist that was repulsive to me.

"You're a lousy crook," I flared.

He laughed, white teeth gleaming through the red beard. "Sure. So would you be if you had the guts. It's fear of the police that keep such as you slaving for nothing."

The beer came; he buried his muzzle in it, drank the glass at a draft, and wiped his red beard with the back of his hand. "Another," he said.

How can I express the feeling that gripped me then? I hated this man; I knew him for the incarnation of evil. Yet he fairly hypnotized me.

I felt his eyes studying me as he drank the second and the third beer. "You're a likely looking kid," he said. "You'd make a good man if you ever got it through your head that you could take what you wanted."

He stood up, gestured, "Pay the guy."

"You pay him," I cried hotly, "you robbed me."

It was then as if something broke inside of me. I grabbed the empty beer glass. I hurled it. I followed it up, swinging both hands, not at his jaw, but at his stomach. It was like hitting concrete. The glass didn't phase him, and with a single jerk of his arm he flung me headlong across the sidewalk to sprawl in the gutter.

I got up, sobbing again with rage. But he did not leave. He came, helped me get up.

"Come along," he said abruptly, "I've got a flop. I've got a deal on, too. Maybe I could use you."

I got control of myself. "I'll go along with you, not for your deal," I told him, "but because some day, by God, I'll knock you down and you'll stay down."

His teeth shone through his red beard.

That is how I came to meet and be a partner of Satan Jack Gore. Why did I stay with him? Certainly, not just to knock him down. That was a childish statement. I think it was because his very hellishness fascinated me.

Take the time he liked a woman's looks when we were in the Cafe d'Or. Her male escort resented Gore's remarks. He struck at Gore with an umbrella. Gore didn't half-swing and the poor devil had a broken jaw. The girl, trying to protect her man sprang at Gore, clawing, kicking. He slapped her senseless to the floor.

I had come out of my chair with a bound, every chivalrous impulse in me outraged by this act.

"You filthy swine," I was choking with fury. I pummeled at him. Strangely enough, he did not strike back. Instead he grasped my arm, hauled me out of there, me still trying to hit him.

"Some day I'll let go one at you," he growled.

"Why did you hit that woman?"

"Because she was a she-cat," he growled. "You crazy fathead, you and your gallantry give me a pain. Is every move, every thought you have directed by a lot of tradition, convention? The books tell you to bow down to women, and you do and every weak-minded man does. That's why women do so much damned harm in the world. Somebody told you not to take anything without paying for it—a law created by the weak so that the strong couldn't hurt them. You believe in that law because you're a sap. I don't."

We were on the sidewalk now. "Listen, foolish," he growled, "remember this: I'm going to get millions. How? By taking them. I'm going to have the pretty women I want. How? By taking them. I'm the strong and no weak-minded civilization will stop me."

I PASS over here the details of the deal he was working on. I merely say that he was negotiating with a Greek named Philomedes who was the biggest second hand dealer in war goods in the world. Philomedes bought all obsolete military equipment from various governments and sold it at a profit.

He had guns and machine guns, hand grenades and automatic rifles, picked up, some from Britain, some from Germany. He had sold a big shipment to an Arab sheik named Jusef ben Ali ibn Rualla. The problem was to deliver them.

The Arabs were revolting; England had declared martial law; gun boats patrolled the Palestine shores, and armored cars and airplanes spied on the desert. These munitions would increase the danger of the situation and England wanted none of that. So if we were caught, we'd be shot in the desert and reported killed while resisting arrest. Gun-runners always got that sort of treatment.

But Philomedes and Gore had a method worked out, and one morning Gore said, "We sail tonight. There's twenty thousand dollars in this if we get away with it."

"You know I hate your guts," I said. "Why do you take me with you?"

He laughed in his beard. "You won't shoot me in the back. Your stupid idea of fair play wouldn't allow you to. That's more than I can say for the other rats I'm hiring."

There is a saying that the devil looks after his brother. I began to believe it then. Off Jaffa a British gun boat took after us, dropping four-inch shells around us. A rainstorm—almost unprecedented in this clime—permitted us to escape and darkness let us reach our position off the Lebanon shores. A Syrian, a spy for either the British or French, was stealing away to report us. Gore got the man's silhouette against the sky-line and shot him dead at fifty yards.

Gore laughed in his red beard. "The devil's luck," he repeated my remark, "hell, man, some day you'll learn that the strong man *makes* his own luck. Most people are so snivelling that police and soldiers have a cinch. It is when they meet a man that doesn't fear them that they complain about *their* bad luck."

He was right.

Yet he knew, and I knew that when our convoy got under way that an armored car patrol as well as some Iraq cavalry were on our trail. Most men would have arranged to distribute the guns and ammunition there and not risk an inland trip. But not Gore.

"I know this Syrian desert like the back of my hand," he laughed, "and they'll play hell catching me." He patted the two Webleys holstered at his flanks, "and they'll find we don't take it lying down if they do come up."

He stared at me with his sea-green eyes. "But if you're yellow," he sneered, "you can turn back."

"I don't want to miss the chance of seeing you killed," I told him.

We rode through that night and all the next day and into the night again, breathless almost with the sense of pursuit; always searching the bleak brown sky-line for cavalry or steel-coated Rolls Royce. Always south, the Dead Sea, the heights of Palestine to our right.

Gore had definite arrangements to meet a detachment of Sheik Rualla's warriors at Tell Hauran, south of Er Rummel. Here the gold would pass, the guns be surrendered.

We came down the slanting *bled* just before dusk. I was in the leading truck and saw what was happening before Gore did. Pegged tents were on fire. Women were running, screaming, tearing their clothes. There, in front of a few waddled mud huts men lay crumpled in death, and a few boys, too. To the left, on the slope stood three old topless touring cars near them a *harka* of camels. Beyond this a score of Bedouins were rounding up sheep and goats and camels, ready to run them off. A Bedouin raid!

I jumped to the running board of my truck, jerking my lanyarded gun.

"Bedouin raid!" I shouted at Gore.

But he had already seen. The Syrian driver of his truck was pressing the accelerator to the floor. Gore had already prepared a Luger gun with a hollow steel detachable butt that could and did perform like a Thompson sub-machine gun.

"Get an automatic rifle," he yelled. "You can't stop them with a revolver, you fool!"

He was shouting back to the other drivers, and as we wheeled into the opened space between the mud huts and the tents, he leaped down, dropped to one knee and leveled the gun at the raiders rounding up the cattle. The distance was a hundred yards. I heard the rattlesnake rip of his gun. And saw the Arabs go over like ninepins. They scattered.

BY THEN, I had a similar Luger which had rested in the case behind the driver's seat and was busy picking off the running men. Others came dashing out of the mud huts. This I saw out of the corner of my eyes between bursts. One sight made the blood leap through me hotly.

A tall Negro, gayly bedecked, obviously a slave of the raiding sheik, had torn out of a hut at the sound of the rifle fire, and now dragged by the hair a small child, certainly no more than ten. I swiveled my gun, but saw on the instant that to cut him down I might also kill the child.

Not so Gore. He plunged across that space with a speed incredible in one so big. The Negro had turned. He had an old-fashioned gun. He pulled the trigger but it did not fire. He hurled the gun at Gore, whipped up a curved gleaming blade and slashed down with a blow that would have carved Gore from his skull to his stomach.

Gore caught that arm at the half-swing, drove his Luger muzzle against the Negro's throat and held the trigger down. The Negro's head lay in a half dozen parts yards behind the spot where his gigantic body crumpled, blood spurting from the jugular in a crimson fountain. Gore seized the girl, hurled her toward the mud hut.

He ran back to take account of the balance of the raiders. But the fight was over. The surviving Bedouins ran to their battered touring cars and with bullets chasing them from my gun as well as from the Syrians they tore off across the desert, abandoning their camels.

It was after we had parked the trucks, obtained water and settled down for food that I said to Gore, "That's the first decent thing I've ever seen you do. You saved that child's life."

"Don't be a sap," he growled. "We'll be here a few days, and this will put us in solid with the men—and the women." He grinned savagely.

Gore did not drink hard liquor often, but when he did he got drunker than fifty dollars—what you call, I think, a periodical. He started drinking that night, celebrating, I suppose, the practical conclusion of a successful job that meant plenty of money. I tried to warn him off.

"That pursuit will likely find its way here. Why don't you drop this stuff and collect later? You know Sheik Rualla's word is good."

"I'm running this," he sneered, "and I'll do it my way. Have a drink."

"I wouldn't drink with swine," I told him.

He stared at me thoughtfully. "I take a hell of a lot from you," he finally said, and tossed off a tumblerful of Scotch. "I wonder why."

Before I could reply the door opened—we were in one of the mud huts—and a woman and the child Gore had saved entered.

The woman was of the bold Bedouin type, lustrous dark eyes, hawk features yet feminine, too, a type of desert beauty that shows long breeding. Gore smacked his lips. "The good always get a break," he grinned sardonically.

"*Salaam aleykum, sitt,*" he spoke perfect Arabic in the greeting. "Comest thou to give pleasure to us who have been long without a woman's smile?"

"I came to thank thee for saving my daughter from death," she rejoined. "My daughter comes because—" she stopped speaking, for the little child broke from the restraining hand, ran to where Gore sat and knelt in an obeisance. She took Gore's big powerful hand, pressed it to her breast, her lips and her forehead.

"Thou art Allah upon whom be prayers," she said in her childish treble, "thou hast come to save us all from the *shaitans*. I bow in worship, Allah. *'La illa Allah. Mahomet er rassoul Allah.*"

I listened in stark amazement to her recite the prayer. By the Lord, she really believed that Gore was the earthly incarnation of Allah. The mother, frightened somewhat yet also superstitious, said, "The child's nurse told her that Allah was a great giant with red hair and blue eyes. So she believed. Do not take offense."

The child climbed up and kissed Gore on the forehead. "While thou protectest me and this village," she said gravely, "no 'frits nor death nor enemies may destroy me."

I WAS inclined to smile at the childish action, and scowled at Gore not to pull his usual rough stuff. He didn't hurt her. He pushed her away not unkindly and poured himself a drink. He grinned at me.

"You see," he chuckled, "now I'm God."

"Cut that," I growled. "The kid means well. You saved her life."

The child didn't understand this English, but she said in South Arabic, "Allah is huge. Allah is all-powerful. Allah slays my enemies. You are greater than all men, Allah, upon thee be peace."

I gestured to the mother to take the child and get out. But before she could drag the girl away the child kissed Gore's dust-stained boot toe. They went out and Gore watched them from the door, saw where they went. He sat down, grinning fiendishly, and drank two more snorts of liquor.

He put on his coat and went to the door. "Don't wait up for me," he grinned, "I'm liable to be late."

I scowled, but there wasn't anything I could do. I knew where he was going and why. For a few minutes after he had gone I stood there thinking; and into my mind came the picture of the little girl kneeling before him. The look of adoration in his eyes; the utter simplicity of spiritual fervor. What would she think now—a drunken, brawling brute charging into an unprotected home?

By God, I wouldn't have it. I snatched up my belt and holster, drew the gun and started on a run for the next mud hut. The door was open, a kerosene lamp burned within. And limned against it I saw Gore standing on the threshold. I could even hear what the little girl was saying.

"Allah, the Compassionate is strong, and protects the weak. He is just and upholds the poor. You may come in; my mother is ill and you will make her well."

I could see the mother. She was not ill unless absolute fright can produce a sick palsy. I could see the fearless look on the little girl's face, fearless, yet trusting and worshipful.

"I go to bed now," the little girl said distinctly, "I shall pray to you—watch over me and come to me in my dreams."

I made some sort of noise and Gore whirled, his hand streaking to his gun. He relaxed when he saw me. Then, with a sudden savage curse, he slammed the door shut in the girl's face, and strode past me and so back to the hut.

He was still drinking silently, terribly when I went to sleep. The next day I saw little of him. He left to me the task of unloading the trucks, piling cases of rifles, boxes of cartridges in the end hut. Once or twice I saw him with the little girl, walking down to the well. A Syrian told me her name was Gutner.

For the next three days Gore was tagged everywhere by Gutner. She came frequently to the hut and they talked in my presence. Once or twice Gore kidded me, "You see how the strong affects the weak."

"Never mind that," I told him, "Sheik Rualla hasn't come. He's two days overdue. How about caching this stuff and getting back to the coast? Those armored cars are moving, and a blind man could follow our trail."

Gore said, "Maybe every strong man is a god. What was Mahomet but a guy with an idea—a strong guy with the guts to make millions believe him. What was Buddha? Confucius? Strong guys. Well, I'm a strong guy. She believes I'm God."

"Well," I said, "the conventions you're always sneering at me about were laid down by men who preached God. So you'd better abide by them. And again, I repeat you'd better allay out of here or you'll be a corpse."

After the mid-day meal I was sure he was ready to go. He prowled uneasily, took a *pasear* across the hills, looking for Rualla. He came back about three and said, "We can't wait any longer."

But he had waited too long. The armored cars came over the rock rise and charged hell-bent down upon us. Two of them. One-pounders blatting, machine guns—fast-shooting Lewis weapons—rattling.

One of the Syrians fell, sieved by a lucky burst. The rest of us raced for the nearest hut. All but Gore. He wasn't around at the second, but he came up the back way about five minutes later, just when we had our guns going and had driven the British back to the protection of their armored cars. With Gore was a Bedouin—a Rualla.

GORE WAS swearing like a mad man. "Sheik Rualla is on his way—not four hours from here. We've got to hold the beggars off until he comes."

I turned from my gun. "You know what that means? If we're taken, we'll be shot against the wall."

"We won't be taken," he growled.

"They've one-pounders," I pointed out, "they'll blast us out of here. They'll—"

He raised his hand to quiet me. One of the armored car drivers was waving a white handkerchief out of a firing slit. Gore called, "Well, what do you want?"

A British subaltern, trim, natty, perfectly calm, stepped into view.

"Listen, Gore," he said distinctly, "we know you're in there. We know you've got munitions. Surrender and you'll get a prison sentence. Try to fight it out and we'll have to kill you and possibly a lot of these poor beggars who are in the village."

Gore kept silent. One of the Syrians raised his gun to blast the subaltern. Gore knocked it down.

"It's you we want, Gore," went on the officer evenly, "you're a traitorous swine, and to get you I'd blow this village to hell. You have your choice of capture and death or surrender and prison."

"Get back into your tin-foiled car," growled Gore. "If you want me come and get me."

The subaltern smiled. "I will. And thanks for not surrendering. I've been wanting to see you dead a long time. Cheerio."

The two cars had separated some so that their combined fire would rake the village from one end to the other. Gore took a look around. His eyes were bright, his mouth smiling. By the Lord, I think he joyed in the idea of this fight. Me, I saw only absolute defeat and death. Protected inside those armored cars the Tommies would blast us into hell.

But Gore had a fancy up his sleeve. The Bedouin, the Syrians and I were ordered to keep a hot fire on the steel slits. In five minutes the armored cars had enough of this. They backed off to two hundred yards where the targets were too thin for us. Here they unleashed the one pounders. Short sharp coughing explosions, the whine of the deadly little slug, then the explosion of it. By God, they were using high explosive with contact fuse. That mud hut began to fly to pieces around us, and we were all immediately wounded with the flying splinters. I had a gash in my arm that might have been made with a surgeon's scalpel.

I could see the blue flash of our ricocheting bullets. But we weren't stopping this fire—not at that distance.

But Gore was back before the hut had been half destroyed. By the Lord, he had a trench mortar, broken out of the munitions case. He also had a dozen thermite shells to lob. If one of those thermite cans hit the armored car, it would roast the poor devils inside.

"Don't," I cried. "Have you gone mad, Gore? You're making us outlaws, rebels, we'll be shot without even a trial."

"They won't get us, I tell you," he roared. "Get to hell back, or I'll slip a slug into you here and now."

He set the sights on the mortar and now he jerked the lanyard. You can see a mortar slug rise, hit the peak and drop. It detonated weakly to the right of the leading armored car, but the plash of thermite started the vegetation to burning fiercely, and the flames ran right up to the car.

The one-pounders ceased to bark.

"What did I tell you?" cried Gore laughing in his beard. "They can't take that stuff."

He lobbed another and the second car withdrew. For a while there was silence and Gore laughed wolfishly.

"Every minute plays in our hands. The Rualla will come and drive them away. We can go to Ibn Sau'd's country and escape that way. It's a cinch."

For the next hour it seemed as if Gore was right. Darkness was coming. Gore dropped no more thermite ashcans as if to say that if the one-pounders laid off, he would. And the armored cars and their subaltern withdrew over the rise of ground, out of sight and range. But I knew that subaltern wasn't quitting. He wasn't the type.

"He's going to try something," I said to Gore, "why not drop back on Sheik Rualla while we've got a chance?"

"And have them surprise us out there without protection?" growled Gore. "Don't be a fool. Here! Go find Gutner. I don't want her or her mother hurt in this."

I stole along the shadows of the huts until I found them. Gutner was playing with a doll, a home-made doll, and perfectly calm, singing in an off-key manner that contented children often use when utterly happy. Her mother was ashen, but trying to put on a front.

Gutner said, "Allah gave me this doll. It will grow into a real sister. He said so."

I nodded silently to the mother, took the child in my arms and made my way back. Things had happened in my absence. Gore had sent out a Syrian to scout the rise. The man was back, frightened.

"There are ten of them. They are going to grenade us—surprise."

The Syrians quit to a man. They had been ready to

for a long time. I said to Gore, "You can't stand that kind of attack. While they're creeping down, we can pull out, and get a good start before they learn we're gone."

"Grenades!" murmured Gore. His eyes flung a quick glance around, stopped for a second on Gutner. He laughed in his beard. "She's the only one not afraid. The rest of you will run like yellow dogs."

"The Syrians are going now," I said. "You'd better make up your mind."

Gore swore through clinched teeth. "Sheik Rualla must be close now. I'll go back on him because I can't stay here alone. But by God, I'll return with his best men. We'll get the cash for those munitions."

He swept Gutner into his arms. "Take care of the mother," he growled.

HE STOLE out into the night, the clear cold desert night where the stars pulse like naked human hearts and seem within hand's reach. By their light we could see fairly well. Unfortunately so could others and disaster struck in the space of a breath.

I heard rather than saw the thing come bouncing down to roll almost at our feet. I heard the strange sizzling sound.

A Mills hand grenade. Lying there like a striking rattlesnake. If it tore itself apart it would wipe out all of us. The Syrians gave a mad cry and ran. I drew the Arab woman behind me, a sort of instinctive gesture to civilization that saves women. My body would cover hers.

But in that split-second before the thing detonated, Satan Jack Gore acted. He hurled little Gutner into my arms.

"Run with them," he shouted.

He bent. I thought he was going to snatch up the bomb and take a chance that it would not explode before it was tossed back. That had been done, but not against experienced grenadiers who know how to jerk a pin and count properly before the thing is hurled.

No, Satan Jack Gore, the supreme egotist, hurled himself flat on the grenade, pressing it into the ground with his stomach.

I heard another sound beyond as if another pin had been jerked. I ran, ran, holding that child, dragging the woman. Yet somehow I *had* to look back. And I saw that grenade explode. Underneath Gore's body it coughed loudly, spreading a sheen of crimson that limned his body being hurled upward by the exploding force. I saw his body disintegrate, riding the hot breath of that crimson flame. Almost at the same instant another grenade, farther to the right, tore itself apart and the up-shooting spout of fire illuminated the veil of blood and raining fragments that were settling back to earth.

I sobbed in my throat, and fought my heaving stomach that bounced against my diaphragm, wanted to rid itself of the horror I had ingested. But somehow I went on, on over the rise, bearing toward the southeast. Staggering, falling, getting up and going on. The Syrians had vanished. Behind me the English Tommies had evidently rushed under cover of the bomb assault, because I heard shouts.

But the pursuit of me was not immediate. That subaltern had found Gore's remains. He had found the packed munitions. And he had hesitated long enough to bring up one of his armored cars and throw three one-pound shells into the packed cartridge, thermite, Mauser rifles.

The whole thing blazed upward like a July 4th pyrotechnical display, as I tore onward. Sheik Rualla's white camel racers came upon me before I had gone a half a league. And when I had told him that the munitions were destroyed, Gore dead, the British pressing hard, he mounted us on spare camels and turned and raced southward. Rualla was a cunning warrior, and he lost those British and headed straight for Ibn Sau'd's territory.

That night little Gutner slept, resting in my numbed arms while the camel mewed and spit and groaned as I jabbed it onward.

She awoke with the coming of the red hot sun.

She made her obeisance as best she could while the others dismounted, faced to the east and intoned the prayers of the Koran.

Then she said, "Where is Allah upon whom be peace and prayers?"

"He has gone away," I told her gently. "We shan't see him any more."

She took it calmly. "I know. He saved me and my mother and now he has gone back to heaven."

"Yes," I replied gravely, "that is so." And maybe she was right for all I know.

HE WAS quite a character. We called him Pistol Packin' Papa, which isn't particularly clever or bright, but newspapermen in China aren't clever or bright, or they wouldn't be there in the first place.

He hung around a little cafe called Yang's that we had made sort of unofficial Headquarters for the press crowd stationed in Shanghai. It was a beat-up, little joint, usually crowded, and always noisy, half of it coming from the crowd, and the other, and less bearable half, coming from a three-piece orchestra, whose members seemed to think that sheer noise would compensate any musical deficiencies.

Pistol Packin' Papa was a fat, ragged, ancient Chinaman, with tiny eyes, set in shiny folds of flesh, a scrawny mustache and just about the easiest and most profitable racket in Shanghai.

He was a beggar but he had an angle. A damn good angle.

On this night I was sitting at one of Yang's greasy tables with Ed Bartlett of Continental wire service working my way through a good rum sling, when I looked up and Pistol Packin' Papa was standing in one of the curtained doorways.

Bartlett was new to Shanghai and this was his first night in Yang's so I decided to initiate him properly. He was busy with his drink so I beckoned to Papa and indicated Bartlett with a nod of my head.

Papa got what I meant and started toward our table, shuffling slowly through the crowd, a wide innocent smile on his fat round face. When he got to our table he stopped. His hands were lost in the greasy folds of his kimona. He fixed his little porcine eyes on Bartlett and the smile on his face faded, until his features were as solemn as a Buddha.

Bartlett noticed him, and nudged me.

"What's the pitch?" he asked. He looked nervously at Papa. "This guy looks at me like he knew me before somewhere."

"Under unpleasant circumstances," I tossed in, just to help the gag along.

Bartlett is new to the East, and he's a little guy, so I don't blame him for being scared. I was too when the old gang pulled the same thing on me three years before. And I'm about twice Bartlett's size.

Papa paid no attention to me, his eyes were on Bartlett. His right hand came out of his clothes and in it was a gun that looked like a small cannon. He pointed it squarely at Bartlett.

"Stick 'em up!" he said.

Bartlett's hands shot into the air and his mouth hung open.

"Give me money!" Papa said.

"Sure," Bartlett said hoarsely. "I'll give you money."

MANCHU TERROR

Anyone who could remain calm when faced with Pistol Packin' Papa's weapon must have nerves of steel— and a heart to go with them . . . !

When I turned on the light I saw her . . .

But point that gun somewhere else."

His eyes rolled wildly toward me. Sweat was popping out on his forehead.

I couldn't help it. I started to laugh.

Then Papa started to grin again, his big foolish grin.

Bartlett looked at the two of us, and then he heard the laughter that was coming from the nearby tables. His hands came slowly down to the table.

"What's the gag?" he said weakly.

I shoved a few coins to the edge of the table and Papa scooped them up with his free hand and dropped them into his pocket. The gun disappeared.

"He 's just a beggar with a little imagination," I told Bartlet. "He's been using that stick-up gag here in Yang's for years."

Papa bowed low to us several times, grinning happily, then he shuffled off to pull his gag on someone else.

BARTLETT LOOKED after him and then took out a handkerchief and wiped his forehead.

"He fooled me," he said. "He looked like a Chinese bandit when he stopped smiling. Isn't he taking a chance that somebody will pull a gun and let him have it before he realizes it's just a joke?"

I shrugged. "Maybe he is. But he's willing to take

She had been bound by somebody who knew his business

I introduced him to Bartlett and he waved for a waiter and bought us a drink.

"Here's to peace," I said.

"An excellent toast," Yang said, with his strange little smile. "There is still work to be done but the worst is over, eh?"

We talked for a while about nothing in particular, but I got the impression Yang had something on his mind, something he wanted to talk to me about. I wasn't wrong.

He stood up to leave, shook hands with Bartlett and then, almost as an afterthought, he said to me, "Do you remember that matter we were talking about the other night, Mac?"

We hadn't been talking about anything, But I nodded and said, "Sure."

"Well," he smiled, "there's been a rather interesting development. I have the material now and if you've got a minute I'd like to show it to you. It's in my office."

"I'd be glad to," I said. I finished my drink, apologized to Bartlett, and followed Yang through the smoky cafe, down a narrow corridor to his office.

HIS OFFICE was small compact and tidy. There was a safe there, one window and a second door that led to a rear entrance. The light came from an unshaded bulb that hung from a cord in the ceiling. There were several chairs and a desk.

Yang locked the door behind him and waved me to a chair.

"Please sit down," he said. "I'll get you a drink."

"What's up?" I asked.

"This is very good," he said, pouring me a drink from a dusty bottle he'd taken from a wall cabinet. "I need your help, Mac."

I sipped the drink. "You're right, this is excellent. And what can I do to help you?"

He sat down in a chair facing me. "I am going to ask quite a lot. I want your help very badly and I can't tell you why. If you are willing to help me you must realize that it will probably be dangerous. I don't know from where the danger may come and that is another reason you are foolish even to be listening to me." He smiled and went on: "I hope you will help me. I don't have anyone else to ask."

"Well supposing you tell me just what you want me to do. Then I'll let you know if I can do you any good."

"Fair enough," Yang said. "I have a paper which must be delivered to a representative of Chiang-Kai-Shek. That representative will not be in Shanghai for another week. The information contained in the paper is highly important. I am leaving Shanghai. My usefulness here is done. I have become too well known. I must leave tonight. I want you to deliver the paper

the chance. At any rate he makes a living out of it and I suppose he figures the chance is worth it. That gun of his was probably obsolete at the time of the Boxer Rebellion. He must have found it in a junk heap and got the idea of using it on the whites here as a gag. He's harmless and everyone likes him."

We forgot about Papa and started talking shop. The situation for newspapermen in Shanghai then was worse than it had been during the war. Our copy was getting out all right, but censorship was ridiculously strict. There were a lot of Japs left in Shanghai, a lot of Russians, a lot of communists, and a few Fascist Chinese organizations and trying to play the angles in that international mess, was enough to drive a guy nuts.

We were working on another drink when Yang came over to say hello. Yang was a bland, neatly built Chinese, with pleasant friendly eyes. He wore European clothes and he always dressed sharply. I knew he was a very square guy. During the war he'd kept his place open and provided a good time for Jap officers. But how many of them got cyanide in their drinks, and how much information was collected from their drunken ramblings and forwarded to Chinese Headquarters, was something probably only Yang knew. And he never talked about it.

for me. I am asking a lot, because it is no concern of yours, but I would ask even more under the circumstances. Not for myself, but for my countrymen."

"That doesn't sound like such a tough job," I said. "I'll take a crack at it."

"It may be more difficult than you think," Yang said. "You will have to be extremely careful."

"I'll be careful," I said.

He smiled, a relieved grateful smile, and patted my arm. He got up, opened the safe and took out a plain manila envelope. He closed the door of the safe and handed me the envelope.

"The name of the man you will deliver this to is Tao Lin. You can meet him here a week from today. Any of the bar tenders can point him out to you."

I put the envelope in my inside coat pocket and said, "Tao Lin, eh? That's easy enough to remember. Don't worry, Yang. I'll take care of this."

"I won't say thank you," Yang said. "There isn't any adequate word to tell you how I feel. Let us hope we will meet again."

We shook hands and then I went back to the cafe. Bartlett was gone and I figured he'd had enough of the East for one night. I ordered another drink and drank it slowly. I don't know how much time passed before the shot sounded.

Maybe five minutes, maybe ten. I'm not sure.

THE MUSIC had stopped and the cafe was quieter than usual. I was just finishing my drink when the welcome silence was shattered by a single shot.

I was moving toward Yang's office before the echoes died away. I don't know why, I couldn't have said for sure where the sound of the shot had come from, but something like instinct started me toward Yang's office.

No one else was going anywhere definitely. Some of the people stood up, and some remained seated, and after the first instant of shocked silence, they all began babbling.

I went down the corridor to Yang's office on the run. The door was locked and I didn't waste time knocking. I hit it twice with my shoulder and the flimsy wood shattered.

The stink of cordite hit my nostrils. There was blue smoke in the room curling lazily around the bare light bulb.

Everything was about the same as when I'd left.

Except that the door of the safe was open.

And Yang was sprawled in the chair behind his desk with an ugly blue hole in his forehead!

THE CHINESE police are efficient in a ponderous fashion. The inspector from the local lock-up was a fussy little man with spectacles and no hair. The first thing he did was to chase the curious crowd out of the corridor and back to the cafe. I showed him my press card and he let me stay.

He went around the office then looking at everything. He went through the safe, looked through Yang's desk and even got down on the floor and scouted around like a beagle hound.

"What are you looking for?" I asked.

"Anything," he said, and went on looking for it.

I noticed that the second door of the room was open. It had been open when I barged in. My guess was that the killer had come in the back, surprised Yang, gone through the safe, then shot him after he'd gotten what he wanted. Or had found that what he wanted was gone.

I had a hunch the latter was correct. I had a hunch that what the killer wanted was a plain manilla envelope which at the moment was in my inner coat pocket.

I went through the second door and down a flight of steps that ended at another door. I opened this door and found myself looking into the black night.

So I went back to Yang's office. There were two more policemen there now, evidently representatives of what we'd call the coroner's office. They confirmed the fact that Yang was dead, and left.

"Are you going to close the place?" I asked the fussy little inspector.

He shook his head. "Maybe learn more by leaving it open," he said. He sounded like he'd been reading Charlie Chan. But he looked pretty smart.

I went back to the cafe and ordered a drink. The orchestra was playing again, and somethink like normalcy was coming back to the place. Drinks were being served, the waiters were busy and everyone was chattering about the murder.

I knew I didn't belong there. If the killer wanted the envelope I had then my best bet was to clear out and get back to my hotel. But I stayed.

I had liked Yang. I wanted to get whoever had pumped that bullet into his skull. I didn't have any plan, but I felt I could learn more at the cafe than I could back hiding behind a locked door at my hotel.

I FELT a light hand on my shoulder. I turned around and there was a girl standing behind me, smiling. One of her hands rested on my shoulder and the smile was meant for me alone.

"May I sit down?" she asked. Her voice was low and husky.

I nodded to the empty chair at the table. She sat down sideways on the chair, so she faced me directly, and crossed her legs. I waved for a waiter.

"The rum slings are good," I said.

"It doesn't matter."

So I ordered her a rum sling.

She was Eurasian. Probably Russian and Chinese. Her skin was pale and flawless and there was enough Mongol in her blood to give her features an interesting look without making them heavy and lifeless. She wore a tailored white suit and her bare feet were thrust into small red sandals. Her hair was dark and her eyes would be either green or blue depending on the light. Or on how she was feeling.

"A lot of excitement," I said.

"It happened before I got here," she said. "I have never been here before, but I knew Yang. It is unfortunate." She sipped her drink slowly.

"When did you know Yang?" I asked.

"Many years ago. I worked with him in Hong Kong. I learned that he was in trouble. That is why I came here tonight."

"You didn't make it in time," I said. "What kind of trouble was he in?"

She shrugged slim shoulders. "The trouble is always the same for people like us. It takes different shapes, and comes from many sides, but it is always the same kind of trouble. Did you know him well?"

"So-so," I said. "He bought me a drink when I came in as a rule. The good stuff. And we talked occasionally. That's about all."

"I thought you might have known him better than that," she said. She put her drink down and looked at me directly. Her voice was very low. "I am looking for his friends."

"You might call me a friend of his," I said. I was getting interested.

"Is there someplace we can go and talk."

I THOUGHT it over. I didn't know what this was leading to, but I'd never find out if I didn't take a chance. "Yes. That stairway in the corner of the room behind the orchestra leads up to several private rooms. The girls use them when they are entertaining their friends. We can talk there."

She looked over toward the stairway, then back at me. "I don't know this place. Will it look odd if I go upstairs?"

I shook my head. "The little girl's room is up there too, so no one will wonder about what you're going up there for. Go into the second room on the left side of the corridor and wait for me. We'd better go up separately. I'll have another drink and meet you there in about ten minutes. Okay?"

"Very well."

She left the table and I watched her slim straight back until she disappeared behind the orchestra stand. I ordered another drink and looked at my watch.

The ten minutes passed slowly. I waited another five for good measure, then sauntered toward the stairway. I stopped at the orchestra stand and glanced about the smoky room. No one seemed interested in where I was going.

I went up the steps to the second floor. The corridor was dimly lighted, there was no carpet, and the walls were dirty. I walked to the second door and knocked lightly.

There was no answer. I put my ear to the thin wooden panel but I couldn't hear anyone moving in the room. I knocked again. When a minute went by with no response I tried the knob. It turned and the door opened.

The room was dark. I couldn't hear a sound. I didn't like it. I closed the door behind me, shutting off the thin bar of light came from the corridor. Then I groped for and found the light switch.

I blinked when the light came on and then I saw the girl.

She was lying face downward on the narrow bed. Her arms were bound to her side with a triple strand of silk rope. Her ankles were bound with the same type of silken cord and the end of the rope had pulled tight and knotted about her throat, so that her legs had been bent backward. Her body was arched like a tautened bow. It was a neat way to strangle a person slowly.

I MOVED fast. When I reached her side I already had my knife out and opened. I slashed the single cord that was strangling her and then turned her on her back. Her eyes were closed and her back was flushed, but I saw that she was still breathing faintly.

Whoever had bound her had done an efficient job. One or two more minutes and I would have been too late. I cut the cords at her elbows and ankles and then felt for a pulse.

There was a beat, but it was erratic and faint. It didn't sound good to me.

Her lids fluttered open and she tried to say something, but her voice was husky and weak.

"Never mind," I said. I chafed her wrists for a minute or so and she began to look a little better. I tried the pulse in her wrist again and it was still skipping erratically.

"I didn't see anyone," she said, and I had to lean forward to catch the words. "The room was dark when I came in. I was looking for the switch when I heard someone behind me. A hand went over my mouth and then I think I passed out."

"Who wanted to kill you?" I asked.

"They didn't want to kill me," she said weakly. "They were looking for the paper Yang was to give me. They must have searched me and when they found I didn't have it they tied me and left."

I was listening and thinking. That crack about the paper Yang was to give her made me think. But the thinking didn't produce any spectacular results.

"What kind of paper was Yang to give you?" I asked.

"Please don't ask me," she whispered. "I was late. I came after he had been killed. I don't know who he gave it to."

"He gave it to me," I said. Maybe that wasn't a smart thing to say but I knew I could trust the girl. After all she'd damn near been killed by the same people who'd killed Yang.

She was looking at me as if I'd suddenly gone crazy. "You have it!" she said.

"Sure," I said. I pulled out the plain manila envelope and showed it to her. "And now I'm getting the hell out of here."

"Not right away," a voice behind me said.

I HAD the standard reactions. I've always thought it was a gag when I read about people, whose hair crawled and who felt their stomachs turning to ice. Believe me, that's not just exaggeration. It happened to me.

I turned around slowly and then I got a shock that made all the rest of the night's excitement seem uneventful by comparison.

Bartlett was standing in the open door of the closet and he had a wicked looking gun in his hand.

After the shock I felt relieved.

"If this is a gag," I said, "it's not funny."

"It's no gag," he said, and when I heard his voice I believed him. He sounded tough and cold.

"What is it, then?" I asked.

"Business," he said. "I want that envelope you've got. Give it to the girl."

I didn't have a chance to. She reached over and plucked it from my hand. She swung her legs off the bed and stood up. She slipped the envelope down the front of her dress and the glare she shot at Bartlett was green and unfriendly. But definitely.

"You damn fool," she said viciously, "you almost killed me." Her hands went to the angry welt about her throat. "That phony rope trick almost worked too well. You said I'd be able to breathe didn't you? That's good! I'd have sold my soul for a teaspoon full of air, you clumsy fool."

"You're all right now," Bartlett said impatiently. "It was the only way we could convince him you were on Yang's side. That's what made him open up. Now beat it and make it fast. I'll take care of him after you've got a decent start."

"So you two were in this together," I said. That wasn't a brilliant deduction. It wasn't meant to be, I

was just talking for time. What good time would do I didn't know.

The girl said, "So long, sucker," to me and started for the door.

I said, "You'd better get a job that's less exciting. That heart of yours isn't going to hold out much longer."

"It will last longer than yours," she said, but she looked like the idea scared her. She opened the door, looked both ways, then slipped out.

I sat down on the bed and looked at Bartlett.

"Mind if I smoke?" He didn't say anything so I lit one. "You fooled me completely. What did you do? Kill Yang after he gave me the envelope?"

He nodded. Like most people he was willing enough to talk about his own cleverness. "I knew when I went through the safe that he must have given it to you. So I had the girl pick you up afterward. I didn't want to bat you over the head until I was sure you had it. If you didn't have it I didn't want to bother you. American citizens are not the best people in the world to push around. But I've got to put you out of the way now."

"Sure," I said, but my heart wasn't in it. "So then you tied the girl up and waited in the closet. And you figured I'd feel I could trust her when I saw that she'd almost been killed by the same guy who killed Yang."

"That's it," Bartlett said.

HE RAISED the gun about an inch so that the bore of the barrel centered on a spot approximately two inches above the bridge of my nose.

When I saw his knuckles begin to whiten I knew I might just as well take the thousand-and-one chance that was all I had left.

I ducked and drove toward him as hard as I could. I heard the gun go off but I didn't feel anything, so I kept driving. My shoulder hit him just above the knees and we went down together.

He pounded me on the back of the head with the barrel of the gun, but I didn't know that until the doc looked me over. I was too busy getting my hands on his throat to feel anything.

When I did it was just about all over. He tried to get the gun into my side, but I knelt on his arm and pinioned it to the floor. And all the time I was trying my best to wring his head off his shoulders.

He made a a lot of funny noises and he squirmed and twisted like a madman, but he really didn't have a chance. Finally the noises stopped and a little later the squirming stopped. Then it was all over.

I climbed to my feet and went out the door. I didn't know which way to go, but I decided on the back way.

There was a flight of steps at the end of the corridor that connected with the flight that led from Yang's office. And they went to the same place, the door that opened out on Yang's back yard.

I went down the steps as fast as I could.

And at the bottom I found the girl. She was lying in a crumpled heap and there was a twisted, frantic expression frozen on her face, as if she'd been stricken down by a shaft of white-hot pain. She was quite dead.

MAYBE YOU'VE wondered why I took ten minutes at the start of this story to tell you about Pistol Packin' Papa.

Well here's why.

Papa was standing over the girl, with his big blunderbuss in his hand, and frightened tears were streaming down his fat cheeks.

"Missy fall down," he cried, choking and gulping over the words. "Papa make old joke with gun. Say 'stick-em-up, give me money,' and then, Missy fall down." He dropped the gun and started wringing his hands and wailing some gibberish I couldn't understand.

But I was beginning to understand what had happened.

The girl had never been to Yang's. She didn't know about Papa and his joke with the gun. And when she came running down the stairs and he suddenly popped out and stuck a gun in her side her heart just quit. The near-thing she'd had with the phony strangulation act probably hadn't done her weak heart any good, and then Papa's sudden appearance with the gun had finished the job.

She had been scared to death. Literally.

THAT'S ALL. I got Yang's paper to the right party without any difficulty. Bartlett's death was hushed up. The Shanghai division of the FBI had known about him, and they didn't want a lot of questions asked.

Pistol Packin' Papa isn't a character any more. He threw his gun away and he was so badly frightened by the whole affair that he went to work for a living.

I saw him the other day pulling a rickshaw and he looked thoroughly unhappy.

He's lost a lot of weight.

A Nigh-Side Prod

By CHARLES A. FREEMAN

JUST a rusty army spur,
  Hanging above my bunk,
Nigh-side prod, on a rotting strap,
Common trooper junk—
One of a pair they issue me
When I hit the old 'Steenth Horse:
Lanky kid in a rooky blouse,
Fresh from the farm, of course.

God, but the years roll swiftly back
When I gaze at that battered hook.
Seems as if it was yesterday
My outfit left Fort Crook;
Aprons a-flutter, and eyes tear-wet,
As we passed through Soap Suds Row,
On to Pine Ridge and Wounded Knee,
Amid the flying snow.

Sibley tents, and conical stoves,
  (If ever the wagons came;)
"Boots and Saddles" at three a.m.—
All part of the trooper's game.
Scramper of hoofs on the frozen sod,
Shots and the Sioux's wild yell,
The scream of a horse in agony,
And all the frontier's hell.

Border patrol in the sun-scorched South.
Turning a Greaser raid.
Nigh-side spur goes clink-a-clink,
'Gainst scabbarded sabre blade.
"Pop, p-r-rip, pop!"—they've struck our point!
As Foragers trumpets blare:
And once again for these old ears,
The "Charge!" rings in the air.

I seem to sense my sorrel's plunge,
The grip of down-thrust heel,
The thrill that comes to ev'ry man,
Who faces lead or steel. . . .
But, hell, boys!—'Scuse my sounding off.
We old stiffs like to jaw.
And that blamed spur just works on me,
Like whiskey on a squaw.

Frontier Stories, 1934

The CAMP-FIRE

*A free-to-all meeting place for
readers, writers and adventurers*

Honneur et Fidélité

FROM SIDI-BEL-ABBES—on the eve of Camerone Day, celebrated throughout the French Foreign Legion—Georges Surdez writes us another interesting letter. In 1863 at Camerone, Mexico, Captain Danjou's men fought against several thousand Mexicans. "There were less than sixty opposed to a whole army. Life, sooner than courage, abandoned those soldiers of France . . ." At the Sibi-bel-Abbes anniversary of Camerone Day Georges Surdez was the only outsider invited.

Night had fallen and the stars were out. Ruddy flames blazed, the torches held by Legionnaires for the torchlight parade. Spahis in red cloaks, big turbans swathing their heads, mounted on sleek horses, rode ahead and behind the Legion, sabers in hand. The red light caught the bayonets, made scintillating streaks of the cavalrymen's blades. The dust churned up by the trampling boots rose in a thin, reddish haze; the roll of drums, the blare of the bugles echoed against the houses across the Place Carnot. Green and gray shutters on the white walls; palm trees; the cool breath of the night sweeping down from the clear sky.

Unseen, but sensed, crowding the little city from street to street, from wall to wall, with their impalpable horde, marched the thousands of Legionnaires, those who died in the dunes and in the jungles, in the mountains and in the plains. Tall shakos, long blue coats crossed by white beltings, those of Algeria, Spain and Kabylia. Short, dark tunic, single pouch snug against the stomach, white gaitered, tanned under the crushed little *képi*, those who marched away to Crimea, to Italy, to Mexico, to the Army of the Loire, to the Army of the East, to the barricades of the Paris Commune.

Hundreds more, with the brand new colonial helmet forming a white pyramid on the pack, off to Dahomey, to the Soudan, to the Tonkin, to Madagascar, to China. Green epaulettes, blue *capotes*, Lebel rifles, those starting for the Great War, to Artois, Alsace, Champagne, the Somme, Picardy, Vauxail, Verdun, to Sebdul Bahr, Salonika, Macedonia.

Thinner, suppler khaki column, three abreast, off to Syria, to the Tonkin border, to the Middle Atlas, to the Riff. The Legion . . .

This year, as the bulk of the Legion usually quartered at Bel-Abbes was at Camp Bedeau for maneuvers (Bedeau is boiling at noon, freezing at night) the ceremonies were strictly private; no one not connected with the Legion could attend. Through Lieutenant Merolli, I asked Colonel Rollet's permission, nevertheless. And I received not merely permission, but a signed invitation, the only one granted. I am saving it preciously. It bears the famous scrawl that signed so many orders which made history, when Rollet commanded the March Regiment on the Western Front.

Colonel Rollet is a bearded, swarthy soldier, with gaunt cheekbones and splendid blue eyes. Providence took care to make him short of stature, that others might see the enemy over his head. His glance reaches the soul, his handshake is firm, and one is instantly, completely won. It would be easy to be brave to please him, even for one not poured in the mold of a hero. Everywhere he is called 'Le Père Rollet'— Father Rollet. And with that, the true courtesy of a real French gentleman. He was busy, surrounded by officers; there was a general present; yet he remembered me, singled me out as his guest and asked me if I had liked the show.

A good show. Songs, monologues, dancing acts, acrobats, a boxing bout—which ended in a knockout in the second round—a fencing match that drew short yells of appreciation from the expert public, sketches about the officers, a German comic artist who drew laughter and applause. From the start, when all stood to hear the "Legion's March," to the final tableau, an episode of the combat at Camerone, all was well done, perfectly carried out.

—GEORGES SURDEZ

The Boomer Trail

WANTED: Information as to whereabouts of these old-time boomer switchmen: "Old Seegram" Jerry Hart, "Hi-Pockets" Ed Frank, "Bourbon Head" Jerry O'Conner and "Gin Nose" Mike King. I worked with them on the C.G.W. and B.&O. at Chi in 1917.—JIM KERR, 1741 N. Luna Ave., Chicago.

* * *

W. G. VAN BUSKIRK, who became master mechanic of the Dutchess & Columbia Railroad (now part of the New Haven) shortly after the Civil War, began his career as a boomer engineer. One of his exploits was to run an engine into a burning freight depot at Winona, Minn., at the risk of his own life. By opening the safety valve he allowed the steam to escape with such force that it put out the flames and saved the large structure.

After he had been railroading about five years he ran into a bad month, during which his train killed four persons in four different accidents! First a farmer left his team standing in a field he was plowing and ran across the track for a drink of water. Hearing Van Buskirk's train approaching, he hurried back to calm his horses, but was hit and killed by the engine. The team was later found quietly standing still in the same spot.

The second victim was a passenger who slipped when trying to board the train in motion. The third person, like the first, was a farmer with a team; he was standing at a distant crossing, waiting for the train to pass, but for some unexplained reason he whipped up his horses as the engine approached, and man and horses met instant death.

The fourth victim in that month, like the second, had crossed the track to get a drink, but at a saloon instead of a brook. Returning in an effort to catch the train, he grabbed a hand railing on the rear coach and was killed by being flung against a pile of wood which was kept at the station for the wood-burning engines.

Early the following month, one of his facetious friends inquired: "Well, Van, have you killed anyone today?" Van Buskirk muttered something in answer. The question was put in a hotel. The proprietor then asked the engineer if he had kept a record of the number he had killed altogether.

"I don't know exactly," said Van Buskirk. "After it reached sixteen or seventeen I stopped counting."

In one corner of the room, sat a white-necktied gentleman listening intently. At that point he arose, crying: "Monster! Monster! Landlord, I am a minister of the Gospel from Arkansas. I have heard of the crimes and atrocities of the West, but I am dumfounded. Little did I think I would meet such monsters as this man. Get my baggage! I must go at once, and seek some Christian gentleman who will harbor me over night. In the morning I will leave this town where such monsters are tolerated."

The next morning, when Van Buskirk was at the throttle of his engine, despite his utmost care, he had the bad fortune to hit a wagon in which were two men pulled by what appeared to be an ungovernable horse. One of the men and the horse was killed, the other man crippled for life. To the engineer's horror he recognized the dead man as the clergyman, who had hired a team to take him to his destination in order to avoid patronizing a railroad company which employed such "killers" as Van Buskirk. Terrified, Van resigned and got a job on an Eastern road, leaving his jinx behind.

* * *

WANTED: Address of Chas. P. Brown, author of book "Brownie the Boomer," born in 1879 at Lamar, Mo., lost his legs while trying to set hand brakes in a Wyoming blizzard in 1913; last heard from at 1418 S. McBride Ave., Los Angeles. Send information to Freeman H. Hubbard, Editor, Railroad Stories, 280 Broadway, New York City.

* * *

ANYONE who knew Fred Barner—he used to run out of Pueblo on the D. & R.G.—please write to me. Fred was discharged on account of a wreck in 1909 that I want to know about. Two weeks afterward he was killed by a thug when he joined the Pueblo police.

I live five blocks from the old South Park Line, half a block from the C. & S., the Santa Fe and the Rio Grande lines to Colorado Springs. I know a little about these roads and would gladly answer questions.—BILL MATHEWS, 1422 S. Cherokee St., Denver, Colo.

* * *

WHERE is my brother, Norman J. Russell? Last heard from Oct., 1928, working for the Erie at Cleveland. Norman has always followed the railroad, so one of your readers may know him. Mother is worried.—W. J. RUSSELL, 43 Geneva St., Ottawa, Canada.

* * *

OLD friends would do well to write to Guy Goodlander, late of the Santa Fe, and Jack Glasco, formerly of the Rock Island, both at Alhambra, Calif. They are ill and in need of a cheery word.—"MAC."

* * *

COLORADO MIDLAND (Aug. issue) said Frank McCammon was killed in a head-on collision. He was my great-uncle. His brother, Charlie, is living in Waco, retired by the Espee.—W. F. McCAMMON, JR., Beaumont, Texas.

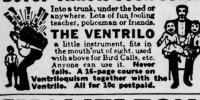

Mainstream / 2 / Sports

The Sports Pulps were a direct outgrowth of the rise in attendance at sports events and the new idolatry of such athletes as Babe Ruth, Bill Tilden, and Jack Dempsey in the early 20's. Street and Smith again led the way in capitalizing on popular trends by publishing *Sport Story Magazine* which presented a wide variety of sports fiction, along with fictionalized narratives of actual events. The field soon expanded to include many competitors, most of which specialized in a single sport.

* * *

"The Yellow Twin," by the still prolific Paul Gallico, appeared in 1928, in *Fight Stories*. Its treatment of courage, honor, and achievement make it a story which could as easily have been set in other surroundings—the West or a war-torn battlefield.

* * *

"From the Bleachers" (1934) is a narrative of an actual event in the career of football star Red Grange. This column by Handley Cross was a regular feature of *Sport Story*, where the author related news and narratives of various sports. It is typical of the columns which provided diversity and flexible filler.

The YELLOW TWIN

By PAUL W. GALLICO

*Two brothers! One who laughed and loved
the thud of wet leather on bare flesh;
the other, who hated it. One was flaming
courage; the other—yellow?*

THERE HAVE been many famous brothers in the boxing game. They have done strange things. Dramatic stories have been told of them, but none so strange or dramatic as the story of the Cassidy boys, Barney and Michael. They were twins. One of them travelled the road to stardom, while the other . . .

The story of the beginning of the Cassidys winds back through years of gruelling, murderous battling for small sums in the fight clubs of the hinterland, unknown, unrecognized. It is traced partially through a bunch of yellowed clippings in the possession of Mother Cassidy, clippings that she values more than the automobile and fine dresses and the comfort she has now.

The first one goes back some eight years. It is from the *Hartford Era*. The Cassidy twins were born in Hartford. When they were ten years old their father, Dennis Cassidy, was killed in the mill where he worked. As the company produced four witnesses who showed that Cassidy died through his own carelessness, disregarding company rules and precautions, there was no compensation. Mother Cassidy did the best she could. They were desperately poor. There were five other children of various ages. As the result of undernourishment, the twins grew up, gangling, skinny and pallid. They were large-mouthed, blue-eyed and freckled, and alike as two peas.

This first one of Mother Cassidy's treasured documents appeared when the twins were seventeen.

Barney Cassidy, a skinny, freckle-faced Irishman, knocked out Mike Galano in the second round of a scheduled four-rounder in the first preliminary at the Sporting Club last night. Barney looked as though a square meal wouldn't do him any harm, but what a sock that kid carries. He is a local boy, and he caught on quick with the fans. They say he has a twin brother who can throw a glove or two himself and who looks so much like Barney they'll have to brand 'em so the fans'll be sure which one is fighting.

When that appeared, the morning after the fight, it was the climax to one of the most exciting nights Mother Cassidy had lived since they brought home what was left of her man to her, but told her she'd better not look at him.

Barney had marched into their shack at ten o'clock that night, with a beautiful welt under his eye, and handed his mother fifteen dollars. Until you've lived like the Cassidys, desperately poor, always hungry, eternally behind, you will never realize what that unlooked-for fifteen dollars meant.

Mother Cassidy read no sermon on the evils of fighting. Instead, she kissed her son, and thanked God that for once seven clamoring stomachs would be stilled.

Michael had eyed his brother worshipfully. "Gee, Barney, fifteen bucks!"

"You could have licked that bird," Barney had said. "Why don't you go down and see Levitsky? Maybe he'll give you a fight."

To which Michael made no reply.

Going back for a moment to that first clipping, it ended with a suggestion, by the boxing writer, that the twins would have to be numbered to tell them apart. Outside the ring, possibly, but inside, never. Their boxing styles were as widely divergent as day and night.

Barney was a wide-open fighter, a happy-go-lucky hitter, who could throw a glove from any angle and who liked to stand toe to toe and trade wallops. His attack was his defense. He learned the trick of bursting suddenly from a shifting figure to a whirlwind of swinging arms. Later on, he also acquired the more important knack of stepping in close and shooting a punch that travelled no more than six inches, but which carried a knockdown.

Michael, on the other hand, came from his corner in a crouch, completely masked behind a pair of gloves, like an ancient warrior looking over or around his shield. He fought carefully, was chary with his leads, preferring to score with counters. He was difficult to hit. Like his brother, he had a punch. But there was also another thing in which he was unlike Barney. There is an indication of what it was in the clippings, in practically the first one that told of the doings of Michael Cassidy.

This excerpt, too, is from the *Hartford Era:*

In the first four-round preliminary, Mike Cassidy blew a decision to Tommy Shevers, after having Tommy on the floor in the first round with the referee counting over him. Tommy got up a nine, brought his right up from the floor with him and popped Mike on the whiskers and Mike was through. He stayed on his feet, but covered up like an old lady going for a walk in the middle of January. Tommy never had a look at him the rest of the fight. You can't tell Mike from his brother Barney, when he's sitting in his corner, but when the bell rings, oh, what a difference!

Michael's first fight was hardly discussed in the Cassidy household. The boy brought home five dollars for his effort when the five dollars was sorely needed.

"Maybe you can meet that Tommy again some time, and show him you're the better man," was all Mother Cassidy said. Michael adored this frail, wan woman with the pale tired blue eyes, and who still retained some of her early beauty. He would have died for her. At the age of seventeen, he was a man of twenty-five. Poverty and privation will do that. The twins had been working in the mills since they were twelve. It broke Mother Cassidy's heart to let them do it, but there were five others who must be fed. So Michael had had no boyhood, nor had Barney.

Mike Cassidy won his next fight in jig time. The *Era* said of it:

Coming out of his corner, Mike ducked under Maguso's lead and caught him flush on the jaw with a right and knocked him stiff. The round had gone less than ten seconds. The Italian was asleep before he started diving for the canvas.

The fans love a hitter, and Mike's first fight was forgotten. Also he contributed to the family exchequer another fifteen dollars. In the meantime, Barney had battered his way to victory twice. His second fight brought him the decision. In his next he knocked out his man in the fourth round.

That year saw an era of semi-prosperity in the Cassidy household. That is, for once there was enough to eat. There was one time that the dynamic Barney brought home fifty dollars. It was that huge sum that practically decided the twins to take up fighting as a profession; that is, devote their entire time to it.

The decision also marked the first time that Mother Cassidy was seized with the illness that later incapacitated her, so that she could no longer contribute to the earnings. The twins gave up their jobs in the mill, and took up their headquarters in the local gym. They were then growing out of the light-weight class.

The *Midvale Reporter* printed the account of their first out-of-town engagement.

The Cassidy twins from Hartford paid a visit to the Arena last night and broke even. Barney pasted Johnny Dugan, the local pride, all over the ring, stopping him in the fifth round of a scheduled six-round semi-final, but Mike took a fine smacking from Young Brodie in another six rounder. Mike had Brodie on the floor twice in the first round and took a dive himself in the second from a belt in the stomach. He set up a cry of foul, but referee Brannick declared the blow fair. Cassidy got up at nine, but stayed in his shell the rest of the night. It took Brodie a round to discover that he wasn't going to be hit any more, and then he gave Mike everything he had, earning the decision. It looks to us as though Mike doesn't like to take it. His brother is a sweet fighter, though.

THERE ARE many clippings covering the next two years. And it was no rosy path the twins were treading. Mother Cassidy can illuminate the cold type.

"There's suffering in here that nigh burnt my heart out," she would say, fingering the treasured notices. "This one from Altoona, the night both Barney and Michael were knocked out. They threw them both out of the club without a cent. Mike was only half-dressed. He hadn't his right senses back yet. Barney got him to the hotel and put him to bed. He used his last dollar to wire me. I borrowed the money and brought them home. Mike was out of his head for three days. I begged them to give up the ring. Barney refused."

She selected a clipping from a Scranton paper.

"Barney beat that boy fairly in Scranton. He could have knocked him out, but held his hand and made the referee stop the fight. Six of 'em beat him up when he left the club after the fight. He couldn't fight for a month."

She came across one that she would pass over hurriedly. "They said Michael quit to him, but he never did. He was struck low. He was in terrible pain. Had I known the pain my boys would have to stand, I would never have let them take to the ring."

A year or so later, Michael got a girl. She was a small, eerie creature, with thin arms and legs. Her name was Mary Loughran. Her father was a foreman in the mill. Her hair was raven black, her eyes sea green, her skin cream-colored. Her mouth was a splash of carmine. She loved Michael. She nursed him and crooned over him when he was hurt, and gloated over him when he was victorious—which he wasn't as often as he should have been. It was strange that she should have taken Michael when there was the dashing Barney—Barney, who battered his careless, fearless, laughing way through numberless ring encounters. But Michael it was she would have. They say it saddened Barney. They were to be married when Michael made enough to support Mary, and still contribute his share to the family. It was Mary who insisted on that. She, too, loved Mother Cassidy.

It was about this time that a New York boxing writer toured the fight clubs of the country in search of championship material and copy. The following is an excerpt from his article:

In Hartford I ran into as sweet a welter-weight as you could wish to lay your eyes on. He is a gangling, pallid, freckle-faced Irishman, who in another year or so will be a natural middleweight. His name is Barney Cassidy, and he fights like his name. He sits in his corner waiting for the bell, with his nostrils distended, and a grin that spreads from ear to ear. That boy just loves to fight. And what a punch! The first time I saw him, he knocked a chap kicking with a swing that suddenly materialized as he was going away from a left hook launched by his opponent.

I met him and talked with him. In the course of conversation, I mentioned short-armed punching. He asked me what that was. I told him, and then showed him how a punch properly delivered had to travel no more than four to five inches to knock a man down.

"Say," he said, "I never thought of that."

He fought again three days later and in the second round stepped in close with a short punch that had his body behind it. It was a crude, unpracticed effort. But it did the trick. It took them five minutes to revive the other fellow. While they were counting him out, he looked over at me and grinned.

Barney has a twin brother, Michael. Mike is no mean ringman himself, except for one thing. Mike is yellow. It is a cruel thing to say, but it is the opinion that has grown up around the clubs where he fights. He gets fights because he has a punch, but a smash or two on the jaw, or in the stomach, is enough to beat him. If he had Barney's fighting heart, he would go far. But he hasn't. I saw him quit to a boy six pounds lighter than he.

The rest of the article dealt with Barney.

The article was the cause of the only scene that ever took place in the Cassidy household.

It took a week or so to reach Hartford, where it was reprinted in its entirety, the idiot who read copy on it neglecting to take out the paragraph referring to Michael.

Barney brought the paper home, opened, to the article and flung it onto the table without saying a word. His usually grinning mouth was set in plain, straight lines.

Michael read the story through. When he finished it, he was quite pale. Neither he nor Barney spoke. At supper that night, even Mother Cassidy was strangely subdued. She appeared to wish to avoid looking at her son Michael. Barney ate gazing squarely at his plate and nowhere else.

Michael misunderstood. In the middle of dinner, he arose suddenly, his face contorted.

"Blast you!" he shouted, "with your looking like that. I hate fighting. I hate it. I've always hated it. If that's being yellow, then I'm yellow. I'm sick every time I go in the ring, I hate it so. I don't want to put another glove on as long as I live. I'm sick of it, sick, sick, SICK!"

He threw the back of his chair into the table so that a glass overturned, running its contents over the floor. Hatless and coatless he ran through the door, out into the street. He went to his Mary.

Shortly after occurred the accident that incapacitated both the twins and once more plunged the family into dangerous poverty. The *Era's* report is brief:

Three were reported killed and seven injured when the Senaca-Wiltonville bus overturned after colliding with a truck between Harrison and Wiltonville. Among the list of the injured appear the names of Barney and Michael Cassidy. The brothers are local boys and have gained some prominence in pugilistic circles. The extent of their injuries has not been ascertained.

A later report in the boxing column gave more details:

The Cassidy twins, favorites at the Sporting Club, are temporarily laid up for repairs, following the crash of the Wiltonville bus on May 19th, in which they were on their way to Wiltonville to fill a date at the Coliseum.

Barney is nursing a broken arm, a fractured wrist and a lacerated scalp. Mike got off with a broken collarbone, a rib or two out of kilter and general cuts and bruises. Both boys will have to hang up their gloves for some time.

A week after that the Cassidys moved away. No one but Mary Loughran knew where they went. She wrote letters and received them. The Cassidy boys dropped out of sight.

IT WAS a year and a half later, to be exact, that a pale, freckled-faced, medium-sized but well set up chap entered the office of the Auditorium in Sidonia, Illinois. In response to the look of inquiry from the swarthy individual seated at a desk, he snapped out:

"I'm Barney Cassidy. I'm looking for a fight. Got anything?"

The swarthy one looked at him disinterestedly. "Yeah? Who's Barney Cassidy, that I should know?"

A lanky man, with a long, solemn nose, got up off the table on which he was seated, and shambled over to the swarthy one. He spoke out of the corner of his mouth.

"If that's the guy he says he is, he's the bird that was stoppin' them all around the Hartford circuit a year or so ago."

The swarthy one showed a spark of interest. "You the Barney Cassidy that was fightin' around by Hartford, yeah?"

"Yup," replied the young man curtly, "I was, until I got scrambled up in an auto wreck."

The lanky one nodded his head. 'Yeah, that's right. I remember somethin' about an auto smash-up."

"You got a brother, ain't you?" asked the swarthy one.

"Yes," assented Barney Cassidy. "Never mind about him."

"Yeah," put in the lanky one, "he's the one they said was yeller—"

"You keep your dirty mouth closed," Cassidy interrupted. "Keep my brother out of this. I'm the one wants to fight. If you've got anything, say so."

"So . . . now . . ." soothed the swarthy one, rising, and placing a hairy paw on Cassidy's arm. "You shouldn't get right away mad. He didn't mean nothing. I want you should shake hands with my partner, Mr. Shinney. I'm Solly Stone—Solitaire Solly. Maybe we could use you in a preliminary if we see you work out. You got a manager?"

Cassidy shook his head.

"No? A manager is good to have. You all right from your injuries?"

"You can tell that when you see me work," said Barney.

Solitaire nodded. "That's so. When we use you, you get ten dollars if you win. Twenty-five for a knockout."

"And if I lose?"

"Nothing."

Cassidy's lip curled. Solitaire noted the look.

"Yeah, but if you win, you get what we said you get, which is more than you do in a lot of places. Solly ain't never gone back on his word. If the customers like you, you get more work. You should be in Levy's gymnasium at four o'clock. Tell him I sent you."

After Cassidy had stepped four rounds at Levy's Gym, Mr. Shinney sidled over to his partner and permitted the following to trickle out of the corner of his mouth:

"That's the guy. I didn't say nothin', but I seen Barney Cassidy fight once. That's Barney all right. Did you see him pop that guy right on the kisser while going backwards? That's Barney's trick. I knew him the minute he come in the office. I thought mebbe he was trying to pass off a stiff arm or somethin' on us, y'know, him gettin' smashed up that way. He's all right. We ought to clean up if he stays around long enough."

Three days later, Solitaire Solly handed Cassidy two ten dollar bills and a five. Although it was only a preliminary of four rounds, the account of the fight drew more than the usual line:

Barney Cassidy, a wild Irishman from Hartford, Conn., made his bow last night at Solitaire Solly's elite palace of pugilism, and after three unimpressive rounds, stood the fans on their ears by knocking out Mickey Toohey in the fourth. Cassidy exhibited a lot of wild swinging and Toohey stepped inside and cut his face to pieces. It was Toohey's fight all the way until the fourth, when the local boy suddenly dropped to the canvas, rolled over and stayed there. Not three men at the ringside saw the blow that did it. We think it was a left hook that moved about four inches. Mickey's seconds drew a big laugh after he revived, when they went over and examined Cassidy's bandages for horseshoes.

And thus began the real rise of Barney Cassidy, and the Cassidy family. But it is interesting to note this item which appeared in an obscure little paper, many miles from Sidonia:

Andy Tucker shaded Mike Cassidy in the first of a series of four rounders at Sportsman's Hall last night.

It indicated the return to the ring of Michael Cassidy.

SOLLY HAD the clipping in his fat fingers when Barney dropped in to see him a week later.

"I see your brother's fightin' again," he said.

Barney nodded briefly.

"Why don't you bring him up?"

Barney looked up angrily.

"You know why!" he snapped.

Solitaire shook his head gravely.

"I ain't never said I believed he was yellow."

Barney suddenly melted, and patted Solly on the back. "You're a good scout, Solly," he said. "Mike's better off where he is."

"Barney, you should have a manager," announced Solitaire earnestly. "I could take you far . . . maybe a championship . . . if . . ."

Barney shook his head. "No. I'll go it alone, Solly."

Strange to say, the *Hartford Era* gives us the next step in the progress of the Cassidy twins. Their boxing writer managed to fill up a hole in his column with the following:

Sam Norstein, who is just back from the west and middle west, reports that Barney Cassidy, once the pride of Hartford, is burning 'em up around Sidonia, under the management of Solitaire Solly, the Sidonia padded glove magnate. Barney is now a full-fledged middleweight and a great favorite with the fans, as he was here.

There is also a tragic note to the report. While selling a

small town about 120 miles from Sidonia, Sam dropped into a little fourth-rate club. There he found Mike Cassidy, Barney's twin brother, stalling through six rounds. Mike, he reports, has no more guts than he ever had. He is just a tramp, while Barney is about due for the big money.

We are not picking these clippings at random, but more with an eye to their importance in this narrative. Thus, right after the above belongs this significant item from the *Sidonia Herald*:

Looks as though Barney Cassidy had a girl. You can't tell us that the petite, black-haired, green-eyed miss who sits back of his corner every time he fights and never takes her eyes off him from the moment he enters the ring until he leaves, isn't interested in him.

And on the payroll of a manufacturing concern in Sidonia, listed as a stenographer, appeared the name of Mary Loughran. All the world loves a winner. It has always been so, it always will be so. Who can blame her?

Barney had gone under Solitaire's management, as indicated in the *Era*. It had come about thus: one afternoon, while Barney was going through his training stunts, Solitaire dropped into Levy's gymnasium and watched him. Finally he spoke to him.

"You ain't right, Barney," he said.

Barney stopped his shadow boxing. "Why, what's the matter with me?"

"You ain't looking right. Maybe you ain't training good. You look tired."

Barney shrugged his shoulders, and turned to the pulleys.

"I was down in Wharton last week," Solly continued.

Barney dropped the pulleys as though they were red hot, and whirled around.

"Yes?" he said tensely.

"Yeah!" continued Solly. "I saw Mike fight."

Barney's eyes widened. "Well . . . ?"

"He ain't doing you no good, Barney," Solly said.

Barney dropped his hands helplessly. "We need the money so, Solly. Ma's nearly always sick now . . ."

"Yeah, I know, Barney. You need a manager. I'm it. Yes?" He looked at Barney gravely. And this time Barney nodded his head in dumb assent.

"Fine," continued Solly. "And Mike . . . I guess Mike don't fight no more. He's bad publicity for Barney Cassidy, the next champ."

Thus the next clipping chronologically is the brief item from the *Staatsburg Post*:

Mike Cassidy, who has been seen several times at the local and neighboring fight clubs, has hung up his gloves and retired from the ring. "I'm cramping my brother's style," was all he said, when asked for a reason. He expects to go into business.

And for a second time, Mike Cassidy dropped out of sight.

IT WAS undeniably due to the experienced Solitaire that Barney got his big chance. "Curtains" Hanford, the world's middleweight titleholder, was barnstorming the middle west, pushing over set-ups for pin money. Curtains, when he was in shape, was a real champion. He got his nickname in that it generally was curtains for his opponents after a couple of rounds. But he didn't like to stay in shape, and there was not much incentive to do so in the clean-up trips through the sticks.

Curtains was matched to meet Kid Lourie, an unknown, in a twelve-round bout in Peoria. A week before the fight, Solitaire visited the Kid, and made him a handsome present of five hundred dollars, spot cash. As a result two days before the fight, the Kid obligingly reported a dislocated shoulder. As the Peoria club had a sell out for the fight, a substitute had to be procured.

At that point, Solitaire kindly offered the services of his Barney. The Peoria club was willing, but Nate Salzman, Curtain's manager, knew a little of Barney's record. He refused to give Solly the match unless he agreed that Barney would take a dive somewhere between the seventh and ninth rounds. In ring parlance, it meant that Barney had three rounds in which to select a blow from Curtains which would look vicious enough to the fans and, on the strength of it, take the count.

And Solly Agreed. Only he neglected to inform Barney of the arrangement. Crooked? Well, maybe. "Don't waste it any time, Barney," Solly instructed him in his corner the night of the fight. "The quicker he's K.O.'ed, the better."

Thus it was that in the second round, one of Barney's windmill swings sent his fist an inch into Curtains' rather fat stomach. The champion doubled up and lowered his guard an instant. The next moment a right chop to the jaw dropped him on his face in the rosin. He never stirred while his own referee counted a ten over him that anywhere else would have amounted to about eighteen seconds. He was revived later in the corner. The title stayed with him, however, as both he and Barney were over the middleweight limit. But the stage was set for Barney.

Exactly forty-eight hours after Mr. Curtains Hanford was stretched on the canvas in Peoria, Solly was in New York putting his name to a contract, binding Barney to fight exclusively for Steve Morley, who was then the greatest promoter of fights in the country. And twenty-four hours after that, the ballyhoo for the great Hanford-Cassidy fight for the middleweight title was under way.

The fight was what is termed a natural. Every sporting writer in New York demanded it, the fans wanted it, and there was a fortune in it for Hanford. And, strange to say, Curtains was not reluctant to enter the ring with Barney. In the first place, the fight would draw him more money than he could earn in three years. In the second, he was sore at being double-crossed. And in the third, he believed that when in condition he could lick Barney. He also realized that until the stigma attached to that knockout was wiped out, his earning powers were considerably impaired. So he signed, after less than the usual amount of dickering and holding off, and the fight was scheduled for American Park, the palatial million dollar ball field of the New York Americans, May 30.

Solitaire moved the entire Cassidy entourage, including Mother Cassidy and the five small Cassidys, to Sea Bright, N.J., to train. There it was I first met and grew to know and like the Cassidys.

STEVE MORLEY was known for the luck he had with weather. The night of the fight was warm and clear. By the time the semi-final bout went on, there were some sixty thousand people in the park. I was the only one with Solitaire Solly and Barney, as Barney dressed for the fight. Barney was horribly nervous. Always pale, he seemed even whiter, that night, his lips bloodless, although he was in first-class condition. His large mouth was set grimly, and he licked his dry lips from time to time. Fifteen minutes before the call, Solitaire spoke to Barney.

"Barney," he said, "I ain't going to tell you you're going out to an easy fight tonight. You ain't. If I told you you was, and you went out there expecting a waltz, and got knocked off, you'd never forgive me. Maybe you feel much worse now, but you'll be better for it when you get out there.

"Barney, you been fightin' small time until now. This is big time. You caught this feller out of shape. He ain't that way now. He's right. He's a tough man. You're goin' to be in a fight tonight if you ever was in one.

"You gotta fight, Barney. You gotta use every trick you ever learned. And you gotta have guts. Hanford's a champion because when he was knocked down five times, he got up and knocked the other fellow out. And he's in there tonight, fightin' for a lot of money. You're fightin' for Mama Cassidy and them kids, and for something else. You know what.

"I ain't gonna give you no advice in your corner. This is your fight. When the bell rings, I can't help you. When you want water thrown on, say so. All I want is you should tell me how you are when you come in after each round. I'll do what's right. If you're a champion, Barney, you're gonna lick this fella. Now go ahead. . . ."

Barney marched out of the dressing room silently, with his lips set. Solitaire followed, and I came behind him. A shadow detached itself from one of the white-washed walls of the corridors, and slipped after us. Solly turned around to me.

"It's Mary Loughran," he whispered out of the corner of his mouth. "Barney don't know it she's here. Fix it so she's with you back by his corner at the ringside. The boy maybe might need her."

I dropped back and the figure drew up alongside. In the semi-darkness I could see only a white face and the glint of eyes. "Better give me your hand," I suggested, "there's a mob."

Without a second's hesitation, a small icy cold hand slipped into mine. Thus, we came out into the park.

There was a thrill to that scene. A giant horseshoe picked out by searchlights all focused on the glaring white patch in the center that constituted the ring and its canopy of brilliant arcs shedding downward their blue-white light. For its lining, the bowl had row upon row of chalky faces that thrust themselves out of the shadowy stands as though the great park was populated by ghosts.

But there was nothing ghostly to the roar that went up as Curtains Hanford climbed into the ring, followed by Salzman and a handler. When I finally fought my way to my seat, back of Barney's corner, and crowded Mary into a few inches of space beside me, the boys were facing the usual battery of cameras. A few minutes later and referee Bill Morton called them to the center for their instructions.

To the fans it looked as though the men were merely listening to Morton's instructions and nodding their heads. As a matter of fact, Curtains Hanford was also addressing words to Barney Cassidy.

"You dirty, double-crossing crook," he said. "You'll never fight again after tonight."

Solitaire, who stood with his arm around Barney's shoulders, could feel him tremble. As they returned to their corners, Barney looked pretty badly off. He appeared to be worried.

"Solly, he knows," I heard him say to Solitaire.

The swarthy manager adjusted Barney's trunks. "He don't know nothing," he said. "That's Curtains' old trick. I should have told you. He's trying to bluff you into a scare. If he talks to you, laugh at him, and try to sock him when his mouth's open. That'll stop him."

The whistle blew. "Beat him Barney," said Solitaire, and climbed out of the ring. Barney rubbed his feet in the rosin a moment. The bell clanged.

CURTAINS CAME out of his corner with a rush. Barney a little listlessly. As a result Barney was still near his corner when they met, and in an instant Curtains had driven him to the ropes and was hammering him with rights and lefts. The mob howled.

"There he goes. Y' got him, Curtains . . ."

"Just a hick; just a hick!"

"Must 'a had lead in his gloves when he socked you out west, Curtains . . ."

Barney ducked a left hook, and ran smack into a right uppercut that sprawled him on the canvas on his hands and knees. Torrents of mad sound rolled over the park as the timer's gong clanged the count. Barney shook his head to clear it, and got up at six, played groggy for a moment, and suddenly released his windmill attack, his gloves thudding off Curtains' head and body like rapid fire. It was a pretty recovery, and the fans rewarded it with shouts of encouragement. Hanford boxed more carefully. The end of the round found them sparring for an opening.

"I'm all right," Barney announced when he sat down. "That was a dumb trick letting him get the jump on me. I stuck my jaw right into his glove on that wallop. If he'd had a real kick in it, you'd be workin' on me still. I'm going to sock him this round."

"Watch him, Barney, he's a slick one," was all Solly said, from his perch outside the ropes. The seconds were industriously rubbing Barney's leg muscles.

When the gong rang for the second round, Barney was out of his corner with both arms flying.

It was evident that Barney's blows were not hurting the champion, because he took what Barney had to give him, while he studied the Irishman carefully. Barney was piling up points with his weird, swinging, unorthodox attack, but I think both men knew that the fight would not go to a decision. Then Curtains coolly stepped inside Barney's flailing arms, and began to hammer at his body. It was exactly what Barney wanted. As Curtains started a right for his stomach, Barney shipped over a terrific left hook that caught Curtains on the side of the jaw and dropped him. The crowd went wild at this turning of the tables.

Curtains took a count of nine, and got up still groggy. Barney closed—too eagerly. The blow he had intended for the knockout just grazed Curtains' jaw and thudded off his shoulder. The champion promptly dove for the canvas and stayed there nine more seconds. When he came up, his head was clear, and Barney's chances had gone glimmering.

"You learned something that time, ain't you?" grunted Solly, as Barney trotted to his corner and sat down, at the end of the round.

Barney nodded his head without speaking.

"Well, it don't hurt you to learn," continued Solitaire, "so long as you watch that feller."

The third round was uneventful. Both men fought warily. They had tasted each other's punch. Each had made an involuntary trip to the canvas. And they respected each other.

It was in the fourth round that Curtains began his clinching. Every time Barney opened up with his swinging attack, he ducked under his arms, and held on. The amount of infighting he did, while close, was negligible. There was no reason for this, as he had completely recovered from the knockdown, as the third round had shown. It was clinch and break, clinch and break. Referee Morton began breaking Curtains from his clinches with a good deal of exasperation. A "boo" or two began to drift upward from the crowd. At the end of the round, the referee went over to Hanford's corner and warned him against continuing his clinching tactics.

Solly was plainly worried when Barney walked to his corner, fresh as a daisy. "It ain't like Curtains to do that," he said. "Keep away from him, Barney."

Again the bell. Barney came shifting out of his corner, wide open as was his style, head shifting, arms waving. Curtains met him in the center, and hooked a left to the chin that snapped Barney's head back. Barney countered on him going away, and Hanford clinched. The referee pried them apart, and Barney rattled three light punches to the champion's face before Curtains again clinched. Angrily Morton sprang at the men to pry Curtains loose. And then it happened.

JUST AS Morton was exerting all his force, Hanford suddenly relaxed and came away, lurching heavily. The result was that the referee lost his balance and went spinning away from the fighters, his back turned. Hanford coiled like a snake about to strike, and then sank his right glove deep into Barney's body, below the line made by his green fighting trunks.

As Barney sank to the canvas, doubled up, and writhing in agony, a veritable tempest of sound broke, hisses, catcalls, boos, cries of "Foul! Foul!" The crowd closest to the ringside attempted to push in, shaking their fists. The police fought them off. And the timer's bell began to clang off the seconds. The referee picked up the count at three. As far as he knew, the blow was fair. He hadn't seen it.

"Four . . . five . . ."

At my side, Solitaire Solly was trying to clamber into the ring, shouting madly, "Foul . . . it was a dirty foul . . . he fouled him . . . four, foul!"

At "five" Barney began his heart-breaking attempt to get up. He lay, eyes turned toward his corner, his face ash gray, his mouth contorted with the fury of pain he was undergoing.

"Six . . . seven . . ."

On his knees, Barney had dragged himself painfully to the ropes. His head was sagging and his eyes were half shut. He grasped the top rope and began the torture of pulling himself erect. The muscles of his arms stood out. His face was wet with perspiration. His nostrils flared wide with the pain.

"Eight . . . NINE . . ."

A scream of pure agony sounded suddenly from the girl at my side. She was on her feet.

"Oh, no! No, no! Michael, Michael my boy . . . don't. It's not worth it. Oh, stop it! Stop it!"

At ten, Barney was on his feet, doubled up, hanging on to the ropes with both hands. Curtains rushed over from the neutral corner to finish it. But Barney had learned a trick. He faced Hanford as he came in, ducked, and slipped to his knees from a brushing blow. He listened to the count of eight on one knee, and got up at nine and clinched. So tightly did he hang on, that by the time Morton pried him off, the bell clanged and the frightful round came to an end.

Barney staggered into Solitaire's arms in his corner. At my side, Mary Loughran was moaning and trying to reach Solly.

"Oh, no, no, no, no, Solly, stop him. They'll kill him, Michael, my boy. . . ."

The referee stepped over to Barney's corner. "Your man's not in shape to continue," he began, when Solly, white and shaking, interrupted him.

"Give him a chance. Give him a chance. You gotta give him a chance. If you'd had your eyes open before, it would be his fight now. Give him one more chance. That boy has suffered more to get this chance than he's suffering now. You watch now. . . ."

He turned to Barney who was sprawled out in his corner, with his handlers working desperately over him.

"Mike!" bawled Solly into the boy's ear. "Mike, you understand, Mike, you *can* go on, Mike. You're not yellow, Mike, you never was! Do you understand what I want, Mike? It's Mike I want, not Barney. Do you understand?"

Barney could not yet speak. But he nodded his head in assent. Solly looked appealingly at the referee. The whistle shrilled and the handlers scrambled out of the ring.

Solly remained in back of Barney, with his arms about him, and now he was crooning into his ear softly.

"Mike, my boy, I wouldn't ask this, but it's for you. If you get through this round, you'll get him. Never mind me or anything else. Go out and fight for Mike now. When you win, you win the biggest fight a man ever won."

THE VIBRATIONS of the bell had not yet died away when Curtains charged out of his corner. Halfway out, he stopped short, his jaw dropping in surprise. The man who came out of the opposite corner was not the man who had faced him in the five previous rounds. Gone was the shifting, open, swinging style. The very contours of the boy's body seemed to have changed, as he shuffled forth, as completely armored in his vulnerable parts as any boxer can be.

His left shoulder suddenly seemed to have elongated and, hunched up, completely covered his chin. The rest of his face was hidden behind the opened glove of his left hand, the elbow coming down forming a protection for the part of the chest and stomach nearest to Curtains. Cassidy's right glove, arm and elbow protected his stomach and wind.

He came out slowly, shuffling sluggishly, partly because it went with the style, and partly because he was still in great pain. His blue eyes blinked and peered from behind the shielding glove.

Then began a curious game of tag. Once over his surprise, Curtains attacked furiously. He rattled blows off Barney's gloves and elbow, which, while they did not hurt him, sent him spinning and bobbing around the ring, his knees bent. The attack was a failure. Cassidy stood swaying and rocking in the center of the ring, while Curtains danced around him and measured him. The referee appeared unconvinced. To his experienced eye, Barney was almost out. He stepped over to the men. And here it was that Barney achieved his greatest triumph. From behind his glove he released a large and deliberate wink at the referee. Then he lashed out with his coiled right arm and caught Curtains flush on the chin, sending him back onto his heels. By the time the champion recovered, Barney had retired into his shell again. He told us afterward that that effort almost cost him the fight then and there. But it did the trick. The referee stepped back.

Mary Loughran saw the wink. I saw it. Solitaire saw it. Solly bubbled over. "What a man! Did you see it, Mary? He's bluffing him . . . he'll win it yet! You got it there a man! Don't you worry no more."

Mary looked at me, and I nodded my head, whereupon she commenced weeping softly.

The bell brought the round to a close, with Cassidy close to his corner. The boy dropped onto the stool and relaxed himself to the attention of his handler.

The next round was a repetition of the last, with the exception that Barney did not strike a blow. His legs were coming back to some extent, and he was more successful rolling and blocking and ducking Curtain's desperate onslaught.

Another round and another, and the fans began to

grow impatient. The fickle crowd that a few moments before had cheered his gameness to the echo, began to grow restless. One or two started to boo. Another section began a steady, "clap, clap, clap."

Curtains began to talk. The referee admonished Barney and warned him to be more aggressive. Barney threw out a few tentative and timid leads. Curtains countered eagerly and rocked Barney's head. So Barney withdrew into his armor once more.

The storm of boos and hisses grew. Individual voices made themselves heard. "Yellow Yellow!" "Go home, you quitter." "Who said you could fight?" A newspaper man at the ringside was excitedly informing those around him: "That ain't Barney Cassidy. It's his brother Mike. He always was yellow. I saw him fight. How the deuce did he get in there?"

The end came suddenly and quietly in the eleventh round. As Barney slouched out of his corner, Hanford danced out to meet him, sneering and talking to him. Barney made a half step that took him in close to the champion, and whipped over three hooks to the jaw. All of them landed. The last one, a left, almost tore the champion's head off. Curtains was out, with his eyes shut even before he started to fall. As the referee counted off the ten seconds, Cassidy started for his corner, with a little grin on his mouth. He teetered gently as he approached it.

"Nine, ten, and out!" said the referee. Barney nodded his head as if in assent, and then collapsed gently into Solly's arms, with Mary Loughran, who had climbed up into his corner, hugging his wet head to her breast.

BARNEY WAS unconscious in his corner. The police made a lane through the surging crowd. Solly and his handlers carried him to his dressing room. Mary Loughran, Mother Cassidy and I followed. Ryan, head of the Boxing Commission, was there. Also the Boxing Commission's doctor. Barney came out of it in ten minutes or so. He started grinning too, as he did so. As Ryan was congratulating him, the door burst open. It was Nate Salzman, Hanford's manager. He was purple in the face. He saw Ryan and exploded.

"Mr. Boxing Commissioner! Mr. Boxing Commissioner! There he is, that crook! That ain't Barney Cassidy. That's his brother Mike. He can't fool me no more. We signed the contract to fight Barney Cassidy for fifteen rounds. It's legal in writing. That ain't Barney we fought. It's a fraud. What are you going to do about it?"

There was a moment of silence. Ryan looked first at the irate Salzman, then at Barney.

"Well," he asked, "what about this?"

The boy's grin faded for a moment. "That's right,"

he said, "I'm Michael Cassidy. There is no Barney. Barney died three years ago. We were in an automobile wreck. It didn't look as though we were hurt much. But Barney's head was hurt inside. He grew sicker and sicker. I knew he was going to die. We moved away from Hartford, where we were living. Barney died from a clot that had formed, a week later. We had no money. Mother was sick. Mary was waiting for me. I hated fighting, and I was a failure at it."

"What's that got to do with us?" interrupted Salzman.

"A lot!" flared up Solitaire Solly, seizing Salzman by the shoulder. "Mike's been fighting under the name Barney Cassidy for two years. He's got a right to use a ring name. It's not our fault you didn't know. You ain't got a kick. You go out."

And Salzman went out.

Solly turned to Michael. "Finish it, Mike," he said.

"I had an idea," continued Michael. "Had it when Barney began to grow worse. That's why we moved away. Barney had made something of a name for himself fighting. I hadn't. I hated fighting. They said I was yellow. I couldn't make money quick, though. I haven't had any learning. The ring was my only chance. I got a job in a packing house. We sorta just made out for a year and a half. I'd boxed with Barney all my life. I knew his style. I knew I'd have a better chance of making money as Barney than as Mike. Barney wasn't yellow, and nobody would know the difference. When I thought I could imitate every move Barney used to make, I went to Solly. He gave me my first fight. I told him I was Barney Cassidy. We had to have money.

"I was afraid some one would ask me about Mike. And I wasn't making much at first. So I used to go a hundred or so miles away, when I could, and fight as Mike. Funny, but when I was fightin' as Barney, I wasn't afraid. It was as if Barney was helping me. Funny thing, I generally got licked when I fought as Mike. Solly discovered what I was doing, and made me stop being Mike. I guess his shouting that name in my ear tonight saved me. It made me come out covered up, the way I used to—"

"Yeah," broke in the beaming Solly, "and if a certain young lady hadn't shouted that name in my ear, I wouldn't have thought of it."

Mary raised her wet face from Michael's chest. "I thought they were killing him," she said. "I couldn't help calling out. He's always been Michael to me, my Michael. . . ."

Solly turned and chased the superfluous spectators out of the room. "To me, he'll be Barney, I hope. Shoo! They want to be alone."

FROM THE BLEACHERS

by HANDLEY CROSS

Big Moments in Sport/Red Grange Strikes
(Illinois vs. Pennsylvania, 1925)

FRANKLIN FIELD, in Philadelphia, on October's last afternoon in 1925. Bright sunshine flooded a white-barred gridiron which a two-day downpour has made a morass of sticky, treacherous mud. Sixty-five thousand excited football fans crowding every inch of the big stands to see "Red" Grange, the Illinois thunderbolt, play his first game in the East.

Even if he is as good as he is said to be, contend the Red-and-Blue rooters, he won't run wild to-day. Old Penn will have a great football team out there this afternoon, even if big Al Kruez, the year's best full back, is nursing a bad leg on the side line. And Red's fast feet will be well anchored in that sticky mud. No, sir, Grange won't run wild to-day!

The big gates down by the Field House swing open. Crash of cymbals! Blare of brass! Boom of the biggest big drum ever seen! A dandy drum major in blue and yellow strutting at their head, the Illinois band swings down the muddy field, turns itself inside out in the way dear to college bands and swings back again. One hundred and fifty undergraduate musicians. The biggest, the gaudiest, the loudest college band ever seen and heard in the East.

But now the crowd's deep roar drowns out even the blare of that monster band. The Illinois squad runs onto the field. "There he is! That's him!" Every eye is on a tall lad who wears a yellow "77" on the back of his blue jersey. Red Grange himself!

Toss up of a coin. Line up of players. Toot of a whistle. Thud of the kick-off. And the battle is on!

For five minutes it is an even battle. Now "Zip" Long, Penn's best punter, boots the ball to the Illinois 45-yard line. An alert Penn end spills the receiver into the mud before he can take a stride.

The Illinois players line up in single file, then swiftly shift into their attacking positions. Grange is the deep back. The center's direct pass goes to him.

He starts like a flash—hits his top speed in two strides. He darts toward the right flank of Penn's line. Just before he hits it, a hole is opened for him—a narrow hole through which he ghosts with a twist of his supple hips.

Now the Pennsylvania secondary-defense men are leaping at him. He dodges to the right, darts to the left. His extended left arm is like an iron bar. Not a tackler gets a hand on him! He's off down the field!

Only the safety man to beat. Red goes past him with a sudden burst of super-speed. There's no one between him and the goal line.

Pennsylvania players pick themselves up out of the mud and give desperate chase. Grange proves that he can outrun any man on the field. He dashes across the goal line with the leaders of the pursuit a good twenty-five yards behind him.

PENNSYLVANIA KICKS off. The ball goes to Grange, standing fifteen yards out from his goal line. He waves his teammates aside. The ball thuds into his arms. He's off again! Whirling, dodging, straight-arming, he speeds over the chalk lines.

Penn tacklers grab him, but they can't hold him. Again he has only the safety man to beat. Approaching him, Red slows down. A Pennsylvania player behind him has been waiting for this chance. He dives desperately, and Grange goes down with a thud and a splash on the Penn 25-yard line. Then the half ends.

The Illinois warriors start the second half with another rush. Before long, Grange makes a first down on the Pennsylvania 38-yard line. Here's a pass! Britton to Grange! Red is downed on the Penn 14-yard line. But now the Red and Blue holds bravely, and Penn takes the ball on downs on her own 1-yard line, and punts to the 37-yard line.

Again the crushing Illinois attack is loosed. Grange and Britton carry the ball to the 26-yard line. Now Britton drops back. A place kick! The ball is snapped. The ball holder takes the pass, kneels, and—passes to Grange! The Red Thunderbolt races to the 13-yard line. On the next play he circles left end for a touchdown.

It's getting along toward the end of the third quarter. Again the Illinois attack surges down the muddy field. With the ball on the Pennsylvania 24-yard line, Britton drops back and takes a long pass from center. He tosses the ball to Kassel, and Kassel hurls it over to Grange, waiting near a side line. Red makes another touchdown.

What's this? Every one in the stadium is standing up, and every one is cheering! Grange is leaving the game!

As he takes off his golden-yellow headguard we see his red hair for the first time. He has finished his day's work. He has scored three of Illinois' four touchdowns, and made the other one possible. He has carried the ball thirty-six times, and gained 363 yards.

There's no more scoring. I'm a little late in getting out of the stands. At the gate, a newsboy sells me an early extra. "Red Grange Beats Pennsylvania!"

Mainstream / 3 / Aviation & War

Probably the one event most responsible for the proliferation of Aviation and War Pulps was Charles Lindbergh's inspiring solo flight from New York to Paris in 1927. The interest in flying created by that event was so great that Aviation became one of the most popular Pulp genres throughout the financially distressed 30's. With the exception of such obscure titles as *Zeppelin Stories,* most of the Aviation Pulps did relatively well.

* * *

The Lone Eagle of course derived its title from one of Lindbergh's best known nicknames (despite the fact that he refused to endorse any commercial product). From one of its 1934 issues comes "The Flaming Arrow," a swashbuckling, World War I story by George Bruce, one of the most graphic and successful writers in this specialized field.

* * *

The Pulps rarely wasted space. Practically every story that did not reach the bottom of the page was followed by some odd scrap such as "Origin of the Lafayette Escadrille Insignia" (*War Birds,* 1934).

* * *

William E. Barrett is best known to today's general public for his moving novel (and later film) *Lilies of the Field.* Those who remember him from the Pulps will recall his many flying stories as well as his often gory detective and mystery stories. "War Planes," (*War Aces* 1930) was one of a series of articles he contributed describing World War I aircraft. Features such as this were very popular, and some magazines also included dictionaries of aviation terminology, plans for building model aircraft, and even "flying lessons."

* * *

The tremendous interest in aviation during the 30's is apparent in the letters which appeared in the readers' column. One of these is "Tarmac Talk," which was conducted by Eddie McCrae in 1936 in *Sky Fighters.* (For the uninitiated, the tarmac is the paved apron in front of an aircraft hangar.) Such columns encouraged interaction with the readers through the formation of "clubs," and membership was usually free. Those who joined were entitled not only to a *bona fide* membership card but often to a "nifty pair of wings" as well.

* * *

Although the World War I flying "ace" was the dominant star in the War Pulps, the glorification of war extended in every conceivable direction as the poem, "Tale of the Transport," by William V. V. Stephens (*Battle Stories,* 1932) would indicate.

The FLAMING

By GEORGE BRUCE

Author of "Courage of the Damned," etc.

Ace Avery

AVERY WIPED his forehead with a wad of grease-soiled waste and pawed ineffectively at the smeared lenses of his goggles. He turned his head from side to side, studying the earth below him. It was a blurred mass of color. He lifted his goggles impatiently and looked for landmarks. He found them, but they did nothing to relieve the tension within his chest. They were German landmarks. He was still within enemy territory, still bait for anything that flew marked with the Black Cross.

His eyes followed a serried line of fresh bullet holes drilled through the right wing of his ship. They began close to the wing tip at the trailing edge, and ran up over the wing, toward the forward fuselage—toward the gas tanks. There was a little shudder within him as he looked at those black dots.

These were not the sharp, clean perforations left by steel-jacketed slugs. They were larger, more ragged. These were the markings of incendiaries.

Ten minutes ago, those holes had not been in that wing. Ten minutes ago a Pfalz had buzzed up ahead of him and, twisting over on a wing, had come screaming down to the attack. A beautiful, new Pfalz, glistening with its black and white paint rubbed to a gloss. Avery

had been almost hypnotized by the sheen of a new propeller spinning in the sunshine, and by the screech of the B. M. W. in the Boche ship.

He had rolled out of a snapping line of white tracers, had whipped into level flight above the wings of the Pfalz, had crashed down upon its tail, pumping lead at it out of both guns. And after an instant he had watched the Pfalz, in all of its bright glory, stagger, wallow around in space and then go into a sagging spin.

One terrific gush of flame and concussion, one immense burst of black smoke. And the Pfalz had become nothing more than a mass of splinters, twisted wire and mashed tubular structure. When the smoke of the explosion lifted, it had no semblance to the graceful, gull-like thing which had soared majestically through the heavens but a moment before. It was ghastly—a charnel pyre.

Kill! The word stalked through Avery's brain. Kill! Smash, crush, destroy! Burn, rend and murder. Kill! Every beautiful thing. Months now, since he had come to the front, that was the one word which haunted him. It lived with him, walked with him, slept with him. Kill! Even in his dreams, he was busy with the

ARROW

*"Ace" Avery Whirls His Crate into
a Maelstrom of Roaring Air Action!*

There was a wave of flame gushing back over the Jerry's head—and then—the war was over for him

business of killing. The faces of the men he had killed, imaginary faces, peered horrifyingly out of the depths of these dreams. He was "Ace" Avery! No identity of his own. Nothing left of the kid who had crossed an ocean from the states to follow the Path of Glory, whose nose was eager to sniff the tang of battle, and whose soul strummed to the thrill of flying. None of that boy left.

Today—only Ace Avery, the flying machine, the perfect machine-gunner, the deadliest man with a Vickers or a Hotchkiss or a Lewis on the front. Ace Avery, the guy who could pick 'em off upside down, on his back, straight up—any old way. Just give him a sight at a Jerry in the ring—and that was the cue for the curtain.

Ace Avery, Killer!

But no one thought about it that way, excepting Avery.

And the funny part about it was that he had such a reputation, they were murdering him. Someone want a tough assignment carried out? Send for Avery. Some squarehead raising hell somewhere along the line? Telephone the field and borrow Avery. And now, when they had given him this rotten Hertreaux assignment, they had the nerve to tell him that no living man could hope to carry it out—but that it had to be done!

AT HERTREAUX, the German engineers had established a plant for the manufacture of a particularly deadly explosive. Avery knew all about that explosive. It had been drilled into his brain by a dozen different intelligence agents. Men had died attempting to penetrate the secrets contained in Hertreaux, but the place's secret had been obtained.

In Hertreaux, the enemy was brewing the most terrible of its war weapons, a combined high explosive and gas. Something so terrible that the German High Command, in possession of the secret of the stuff for two years, had not permitted its manufacture or use. The German High Command had been appalled at the thought of the horror this new agent would unleash.

The new explosive, enough to fill a five pound bomb, would wreck territory over an area of a square mile; would unloose a gas against which no mask possessed by any nation was a defense, and which would kill every living thing within a space of ten seconds. So far, no chemical or other extinguishing agent had been found, able to blot out the flame from this deadly bomb.

But now Germany was fighting with her back to the wall. She must take in hand any weapon that might terrify or destroy her enemies.

So, High Command had reconsidered, and the smoke stacks of Hertreaux were belching black smoke. Night and day, secret manufacture of the new weapon was being pushed to the limit of human and mechanical endurance.

The Intelligence Service had pointed out to Avery that destruction of the Hertreaux plants was vitally necessary. The successful outcome of the war depended upon the destruction of Hertreaux. The lives of millions of combatants and non-combatants depended upon the elimination of the Hertreaux product.

And they had given Avery the job. They had explained that one man had a better chance than a Wing. The Germans were expecting some kind of an attack against their munitions center and they had concentrated around Hertreaux the most complete scheme of defense afforded any defensive point so far in the war.

Murder was in the air over that place. Murder from three squadrons of airplanes assigned to keep enemy flyers out of the sector. Murder from cleverly placed anti-aircraft batteries. Murder from a dozen sources under the canopy of the blue sky. And sixteen men had died flying planes marked with a red, white and blue circle without so much as getting a glimpse of the factories at Hertreaux, before Scott Avery was given the job.

THE STRANGEST thing about the entire assignment was the fact that while the Intelligence officers were talking to him about Hertreaux and Avery was taking on the job, Avery had known that he would die in carrying out the assignment. It was inevitable.

His thinking so was not madness. It was just a knowledge, born out of the queer prescience which becomes a part of every flying man who brushes wings with death a dozen times daily. Avery knew that no one man could defeat the brains and the strength of the German enemy. No man could hope to enter such a contest and escape with his life.

Until this moment, Ace Avery had been lucky. Through the months of his service he had drawn heavily against Time. He was living, breathing, acting upon borrowed time; and in the ten days he had lived through the Hertreaux assignment, his overdrafts on the Bank of Time had grown heavier and heavier.

THERE HAD been the first day, for example. There was an element of surprise connected with his reconnaissance that first day. In spite of magnificent brains and planning abilities, the Germans made mistakes. They had grown to believe that no human would run the gauntlet of death surrounding Hertreaux, no experienced flyer would dare to penetrate eighty kilos behind the enemy lines. That was a defense in itself.

Then, if a red, white and blue marked ship or ships did invite suicide by such an insane flight, they would be immediately subjected to the cross fire of a hundred Archies—and those Archie gunners had the skies above Hertreaux plotted so perfectly that it was not necessary to discover ranges when the guns were fired. Each gun was trained upon a certain point and height, and the gunners merely pumped shells into the breeches without having to worry about targets. The result was a complete barrage from one thousand to twenty thousand feet over the entire Hertreaux area.

So, the pilots and gunners charged with the defense of the factories nodded in satisfaction and considered that they had drawn a very "cushy" billet. They carried out the patrols assigned to them, and they were on the alert, but they didn't believe in their hearts that an enemy would be foolish enough to come.

That first day, Avery had flown very cautiously. Before he crossed the lines, he had taken his Nieuport to its absolute ceiling, laden as it was with two twenty-pound incendiary and demolition bombs. Under bare cruising speed, to silence the motor, Avery had crossed the lines.

There was a mackerel sky in the heights. Below, at ten thousand feet, there were rolling masses of cumulus. Avery knew that far down, even at the bottom of that tremendous void which separated him from the earth, men with delicate "tin ears" were picking up the tiny sound of his motor, recognizing it as a danger signal and trying to locate the source of the sound.

But he also knew that at twenty thousand feet, at

bare cruising speed, the sound would baffle those very clever gentlemen at the "tin ears," and that he could pass over them without danger.

THEN HE knew he must be in the vicinity of Hertreaux, he throttled the motor to a whisper and descended slowly and cautiously in a glide perilously near to a stall. He had his eyes fixed upon the masses of cumulus below him. After a long minute, a grin of satisfaction moved his face. This flight was planned.

He knew the habits of German pilots. They were methodical. They did things by the clock. If he was correct in his reasoning and a seasoned group of pilots was in charge of the Hertreaux defenses, they were due to fly the morning patrol at this hour.

His reasoning was correct. Below him, at eight thousand feet, outlined against the white background of the cumulus, a flight of twelve Fokkers, in echelon, was winging away in a lazy circle toward the southwest.

Avery had held his breath as he hung over them. The sun was behind him. The Fokkers passed under him, flew on, became dots against the horizon. He continued downward in the unhurried glide. He hugged the masking cloud formations and studied the ground below him. After a moment, he made out Hertreaux. It was marked against the sky by a smear of black smoke belching from the high flung stacks of a great factory.

He timed his movements carefully. Three minutes to cover that distance and to go down five thousand feet under throttle. He looked at the belts running up to his guns; looked at the bomb releases attached to the outside of his cockpit. He settled himself in the seat and took a firmer grip on the stick.

PERHAPS THOSE warning voices had given him false information. Perhaps this was going to be a job which on paper was gigantic and impossible, and in fact was nothing more than child's play. Perhaps he was going to have one of those confounding strokes of good fortune which astonish the world. Perhaps he was going to dive down into the middle of those stacks, drop his two deadly bombs into the midst of that piled up mass of horror within the factory—and escape, unscathed, and without firing a shot.

His nerves tautened. He could feel the beat of his heart against his ribs. He pointed the nose of the Nieuport at the stacks, took a sight and went plunging through the clouds. No time for deception or skulking now. This was time for a bold stroke at top speed. This was the time for surprise and velocity.

The Nieuport went ahead with a rush. The wires were screeching. The motor moaned and whined. The tight surfacing of the wings drummed. The slipstream that came back into his face was like a hand clamped over his nostrils and mouth.

The stacks grew nearer and nearer. He saw the first buildings of the factory rising out of the horizon. He kicked a little rudder to aim his flying projectile at the exact center of the group of buildings.

He was intent upon his course.

He never heard the Fokker that dropped in behind him until the whiplash crackling of slugs sounded about his head, and until he saw a tracer flick through the top wing of the Nieuport and explode into tiny bits of phosphorescent smoke. He whirled in his heat with a violence that twisted his neck.

He saw the Fokker. It was close—a hundred and fifty feet behind him. At the first glance the Fokker seemed to be a thing of great eyes, and the eyes were squirting an orange-green venom at his Nieuport. The eyes were the muzzles of twin Spandaus, and the man who handled them was an expert. And he was scoring hits.

The bombs in the Nieuport's rack were contact bombs—delicate things, set to explode at the slightest impact. A slug striking those bombs would result in the Nieuport being blown to atoms. No chance to maneuver, to escape that Fokker with those bombs in the rack.

SO AVERY pulled the releases and sent the twenty pound eggs plunging earthward. There was a fierce sense of frustration within him as he turned them loose. He was being cheated. Hertreaux had been his; life had been his; success had been his—another thirty seconds—and this Fokker had spoiled it all.

He whirled on it with a tigerish ferocity. He was blinded with the desire to destroy this green winged thing behind him. He wanted to trample on it—stomp, tear with his hands, blast it to bits. He pulled up in a straight zoom, giving the Fokker a chance to rake him as he climbed. Five hundred feet up, he twisted over on his back and dived upside down. The Nieuport trembled—but then, it had always trembled under this kind of punishment.

The Fokker slipped sharply to the right. The pilot had his head lifted, studying the Nieuport's maneuver narrowly. He was waiting for the completion of the maneuver. He had watched other ships roll out of a loop and knew the answer to that. How could he know that a dozen times Avery had attacked in his manner—feigning a roll out of a loop, but without ever sliding off his back—and had made his kills shooting in the inverted position?

THE JERRY discovered himself tricked when it was too late. The Nieuport never came out of the inverted dive. The Vickers in the nose of the Nieuport suddenly spurted flame, a short, vicious burst. Every slug in that burst—and they were incendiaries—smacked through the space between the motor and the pilot's cockpit of the Fokker. The fuel tanks of the enemy ship were contained in that space. There was a wave of flame gushing back over the Jerry's head—and then—the war was over for him. His Fokker, burning like a furnace, fell within sight of Hertreaux.

And the Archies on the ground went into action with deadly intent. The sky vomited black puffs and screeching shrapnel. The atmosphere rocked with sharp, nerve-jarring concussion. The Nieuport was tossed about like a cork in a storm at sea.

Above, below, at each side, those blinding red gouts of flame broke out of invisibility and seared Avery's vision. Many times before he had flown through Archie fire—but never anything like this. Half-blinded, half-conscious, he ruddered the Nieuport from side to side, tried to climb, tried to escape the bursts. But he was dealing with the business of aimed firing now.

There was one escape. That was close to the earth. The driving bands of the Archie shells could not be set for less than a thousand feet. Avery stood the Nieuport on its nose and dived madly for the earth. A bit of shrapnel gouged the left upper. The fragile ship spun twice on its axis from a wave of concussion. The controls were ripped out of his hands. He fought to regain control of the Nieuport. The ground leaped up at him.

He brought the ship out with tree branches reaching for him. He flattened it into level flight with the wheels spurning the earth. Dimly he saw machine-guns on the ground spitting flame at him. Once a battalion of troops lifted rifles and there were stabbing streaks of flame—and then then he was over them.

A dozen feet over enemy earth with a red-hot motor, hurdling trees and telegraph wires. Eyes aching with the watch for obstructions. The Fokker flight he had fooled a few minutes before coming in like wolf hounds on the scent of a kill. Spreading out over the sky, straining to head him off, to batter him against the earth flowing under his spreader bar.

MACHINE-GUNS chattering at him—Spandaus, this time. The nervous shock of slugs thudding through the tail section—and the continuance of the mad rush over the earth into the south.

This was a nightmare in the full light of day, this flight through the rocketing maws of hell. Minute after minutes, over those eighty kilos, he waited for the Clerget to blow up, waited for it to grind itself to powder for lack of oil.

Nightmare—the impossible, and he was doing it.

Until at last he had run away from the Fokkers, had leaped across the front, and had dropped on the home field. For minutes after he cut the switch, Avery sat in the cockpit and listened to the Clerget sizzle. It fired for a full minute after the switches were cut. Men gathered around the ship and grinned up at him, men who believed that Ace Avery was a superman who always did the impossible.

When the tremble went out of his legs, he climbed down on the field and grinned with them—though his nerves were jumping and his muscles were twitching.

But he had to grin—he was Ace Avery.

LATER IN the day, an Intelligence Officer came to see him and listened to the story of the flight. There was a queer light in the I. O.'s eyes.

"I don't know," he told Avery. "I'm not a flying man myself, but I don't see how you *could* drop those bombs there, within sight of the objective, knowing how important it was to carry out the job. There you were—by a stroke of good fortune you may never have again—and you didn't go through with it. Somehow, I think that I would have wangled a way to drop those bombs right on the factory."

Avery glanced at the dapper appearance of the officer, at the glossy cordovan riding boots and the impeccable uniform and well-kept hands. He made a might effort to restrain himself from driving his fist down the fellow's throat.

"I'm sorry," he said, instead.

"Well, of course, you're flying the assignment," grumbled the I. O. "But it seemed to me you wasted a golden chance.

"Better luck next time."

"Thanks," grunted Avery. "I'll need it—plenty—"

All that night he was haunted by the Hertreaux factories and the black smudges of shell fire breaking in the skies. From then on it would be tougher—and tougher. They expected him now. They were waiting for him.

And it had been tougher. It had been like battering one's head against a stone wall. Day after day he went out there alone, knowing that a thousand eyes were watching him and a thousand brains were calculating his chances of life and death. When he turned unexpectedly, he found men stopping a conversation with complete abruptness. They were talking about him, discussing him, analyzing him.

And the damned Intelligence Department—those desk polishers who strutted around in the fancy uniforms—thought he was going soft, thought he was going yellow.

He could tell by the way they looked at him. They

were smiling in their sleeves, at the spectacle of Ace Avery—losing the old fire and the old touch. Ace Avery, looking out after his precious hide.

EVEN NOW he wondered where he got the idea. It just had popped into his mind. Maybe, way back in his younger days, he had read it. How the old Indians when they wished to drive an enemy out of a shelter, and couldn't approach the shelter because of deadly defense, used to wrap stuff around the points of arrows, ignite the stuff, and shoot it against the roof, or the dry side of the building.

Flaming arrows—setting fire to the defenses—driving the defenders out into the open to be picked off at will.

Maybe that's where the crazy idea came from.

Maybe it was because they expected things of Avery. Maybe it was because he had to provide the sensational and the dramatic at all costs. He was built up to the point where he could not fail! Had to go on and on—until finally it came—like it had come for Richthofen and Immelmann and the Frog Aces.

Ace Avery! The grim smile played about the corners of his mouth. Ace Avery—the Hero! And he had to go on being the hero—right up to the end of the drama.

BUT THAT was an idea—that packing of the fuselage of the Nieuport with cordite—and that business of stowing a couple of dry cells under his seat with wire running up to a button on the instrument panel. The old Nieuport was heavy under the load—a hundred and fifty pounds of cordite. Enough to blow half of France off the map. Riding behind him—packed into the open space of the after fuselage.

He glanced again at that ragged line of bullet holes through the right wing. If those incendiaries had gone through the camel back, down into that load of explosive! But suppose they had—wasn't that going to happen, anyway?

Hadn't he known it was going to happen from the moment he thought of the idea? There wasn't anything crazy about the impulse. His brain was calm and cool, calmer than it had been in months—and he could think and plan with a razor edge on the planning.

His mechanic—old Bagger—had been appalled when Avery unfolded the idea and when he had insisted on bringing the cordite onto the field in a battered old car. Bagger had flatly refused to do the job. But then, he had always been a softy where Avery was concerned. Bagger had been the perfect mechanic and wet nurse.

But he got the idea right away, about making the Nieuport into a flying torpedo. And between them they had rigged up the ship. Rigged her up to blow hell out of Hertreaux—and hell into Ace Avery.

Even now there was no feeling in him about the business of dying. He felt numb, as though it was going to happen to someone else. Like going to a friend's funeral and trying to work up something that felt like grief.

The old Nieuport flew around with all the lightness and buoyancy gone out of her wings—and Avery stalled for time, saving his gas like a miser, nursing his motor like a mother with a sick baby—waiting— for darkness. He watched the brass ball of the sun sinking toward that unknown place behind the horizon, and tried to understand that this was the last time he would ever see the sun. The last time he would ever float above the earth in the glory of the sunset.

It sounded crazy—why, he'd see a thousand sunsets like this, but his soul was filled with a whispering voice that said over and over: "Last time—look at it—last time—better let it warm you—it'll be cold—in a little while—"

PFALZES WERE the most persistent damned things, like the one coming in on his tail now. Suddenly the whiplashes crackled about Avery's head. He swung the Nieuport over on its side, carried it around in a short circle, with the Pfalz steaming in on his tail.

Last fight maybe—unless he had to fight his way into Hertreaux. Last fight—and growing dark. That Old Man Sun was just a red semi-circle above the horizon. The whole world was bathed in red—like blood. Make the last fight a good one, Ace Avery—have to live up to your medals.

The Nieuport stood up on one wing. Nose up, it began the vertical renversement Avery had dared a couple of times in the past, the damned maneuver that scared guys to death watching it. Just pinning the nose of the crate at the zenith of the sky and holding it steady, while the rudder pulled the ship around in a half arc, and the motor sobbed its heart out under the terrific strain.

One miss, one flop, one flat spot in the air, and it was a question of tumbling nose over tail onto the Nieuport's back. But it was the maneuver of the Ace—and the Pfalz behind him was going to see an Ace put on a show.

Avery even glanced back at the Pfalz as the ship hung upright in space. He saw the head of the Jerry pilot turned upward, the sunlight glinting red upon his goggles, his mouth open in consternation as if he might be watching the antics of a ghost ship.

THE NIEUPORT fell heavily out of the top of the arc. It went into a vertical side-slip, left wing-tip tearing into the atmosphere, the wires shrieking like demons, the wings wrestling with the fuselage. Faster and faster, until it seemed the ship must come apart, and then it was in a headlong plunge—heavy—weighed down by the cordite in the fuselage. And the Pfalz was skidding dangerously to the right, to see what would be the finish to the insane flying.

But the Pfalz never did see the end of the maneuver. Other men in cross-marked ships had waited for the end in the same manner, and had only found the end —for them.

There was a peculiar, wrenching twist at the bottom of the dive, and a shrill shirek of rage from the wires as they changed direction and stress. The Nieuport lunged upward, its guns cutting yellow-green tracks in the gathering darkness. The ghostly whiteness of tracers sped through space, thudded against the Pfalz —and between each tracer were ten incendiaries.

Little sparks broke out upon the surfacing of the Pfalz; little sparks which became tiny flames, like candles seen at a distance. They grew with a hungry rush, becoming liquid fire which engulfed the outline of the enemy ship.

The Nieuport veered away. The Pfalz went diving for the ground. It began vomiting black smoke and sparks. After a minute, it was flaming from nose to tail—fierce rushes of flame which stormed out over the wings.

The red sun was gone. There was a redder sun in the heavens lighting the space between earth and sky with a terrible intensity.

Avery moved this way and that to escape a random Archie burst, unable to keep from watching the Pfalz. It struck the earth—far down—broke into a million sparks. Avery moved his lips. He touched the front of his helmet with his hand. It was a silent gesture of farewell—of salute—almost an automatic gesture, like a devout person who crosses himself in the face of a dreadful sight.

H E TOOK the Nieuport up five thousand feet. No question of the location of Hertreaux. He knew that by instinct. He studied the amount of gas left in the tanks. Just enough.

He pointed the nose of the ship into the gathering darkness.

Ten minutes later, a searchlight from the ground picked him up. It flashed once over his wings, bathed his silver ship in lambent fire, then clung to him with fiery tenacious intent.

He didn't bother to fly away from the light. He knew that once the first light located him, another would inevitably find him. He was almost too high for good Archie practice—and he was going to Hertreaux.

It was in the cards that he was to die at Hertreaux— nothing would happen until he got to the place.

The red flashes of the bursting shells were beautiful against the black velvet of the sky. They broke in a core of white heat, then changed to red. Like fireworks, fifty of them at a time, they put down a curtain of flame before him and above him and on all sides of him.

And when that curtain became a surging, rocking hell of concussion, he knew that Hertreaux was before him, even if he had not been able to see the red flare above the stacks of the factories.

A BLACK SHAPE ripped at him from out of the darkness. Heck—wasn't there anything in the world but Pfalzes? Where had this one come from, bobbing up at him like that out of the dark? He kicked rudder and drove at the Pfalz.

What the devil—they were going the same way— straight down. Might as well have company on the journey. If the Pfalz wanted to dive, it was right up the Nieuport's alley. Twelve thousand feet down was Hertreaux and the objective. For twelve thousand feet, the game of leap frog could go on—

The Pfalz went screaming over the top wing of the Nieuport. There had been a drumming sound from the after fuselage, a succession of tiny shocks throughout the fabric of the Nieuport. Slugs—hammering against longerons, delving through doped linen. Slugs —and a hundred and fifty pounds of cordite under that linen.

The Nieuport dived like a fury. It picked up the Pfalz, a shadowy blur, in the sight. Avery sat there, hounding the Jerry, his thumb on the trigger. Somehow, he didn't feel like hurting that ship in front of him. Then—the pilot decided to out-maneuver the Nieuport.

He pulled up suddenly in a zoom. Avery hadn't wanted to kill that Pfalz—but the fool zoomed right into the path of those deadly little incendiaries.

Smack through the center section of the Pfalz—and the center section was burning—and the fire was showing the face and head of the pilot. He had maneuvered himself out of safety, right into the middle of a blazing furnace. Avery swallowed hard for a moment.

Then suddenly the air about him was alive. Rushing shapes slashed at him. Little trails of fireflies flowed about his Nieuport—a whole flight of the persistent little devils. The Pfalzes flew like wraiths in the night, trying to cut him down.

One thousand feet—and the stacks of Hertreaux were like the flues of hell.

They belched red heat and fury up into the black

skies. The flues of hell—and shed Number Four was right under that line of four stacks in a row.

THE NIEUPORT seemed dissolving. Avery was leaning forward in the seat, driving it faster and faster with the weight of his body. Once he leaned over a black shadow in front of him, and the shadow spouted flame and lead as he went over. He forgot the ships in the air about him, and the frantic play of the searchlight, and the reckless chattering of machine-guns. His eyes were fixed on those four stacks. They grew larger and larger—the flame became hotter and hotter.

His hand moved toward the button on the instrument panel. A jagged, chattering, crackling burst of Spandau slugs ripped above his head, cut the cockpit about him to ribbons, snapped a strut in front of his face—made a hollow, thudding sound from the center of his back.

The Nieuport staggered. A wing ripped from its fittings. The black roof of a shed showed under the spreader bar. There was a large white four on it—in German script.

Avery fell over the tip of the stick—drove it forward with the weight of his body.

The Nieuport crashed through the corrugated roof of the factory.

Avery's thumb jammed down on the button.

There was a rising billow of air which blew the Nieuport back through the galvanized iron roof. A rising billow of air, and then an explosion which seemed to destroy the entire universe with its dull reverberation.

SHOCK SMOTE the world. There was no sound, for there were no eardrums there to hear the sound. There was a mighty avalanche of flame rising higher and higher into the heavens.

And in the flame, the Nieuport disappeared.

Other ships disappeared in that holocaust. The wreckage of the pursuing Pfalzes rained down with the brick and steel and splinters of what had been the Hertreaux hell factories.

*   *   *   *   *

Back on the field a mechanic named Bagger waited—waited for the return of his boss. He sat in a hangar mouth, tears streaming down his face. He waited—because he knew it was his job to wait. He had waited throughout two years for his boss. But this time—the boss was not coming back.

There were the ghostly outlines of gray Nieuports crammed into the hangar behind him. There were other men standing around, digging at the earth with the toes of boots, puffing once or twice on a cigarette and then tossing the cigarette away with an impatient gesture. Pilots and men who had known Ace Avery.

One of them said: "Just what you'd expect of Avery. Just the way he'd pick out to go. Living up to his reputation. Making himself into a blasted flaming arrow and blowing the heck out of that Hertreaux place, and blowing himself into everlasting glory at the same minute."

Bagger lifted his head. "Yes, sir," he said chokingly. "That's almost what he said to me—couple of hours ago—'got to do it—Bagger, my boy,' he said. 'It's expected—when you're an actor, you've got to put on a show—even when they're ringing down the curtain.' Funny like, he said it. Kind of sorry like. Kind of sad like—"

"They'll give him the Congressional posthumously for this," said one of the officers. "They can't miss."

"Yeah," echoed another. "They'll give him the Congressional—he rates it."

ORIGIN OF THE LAFAYETTE ESCADRILLE INSIGNIA

THE FRENCH called it "The Plumed Warrior." The world knew it as the "Whooping Indian"; the insignia of the first and only American volunteer squadron to fly over enemy soil. To the Lafayette Escadrille men it was a symbol of this illustrious squadron, *esprit de corps* and—five bucks.

The feathered Indianhead was inspired by an American five dollar goldpiece.

Captain Georges Thanault,* commanding officer of the Lafayette Escadrille when it was known as the *Escadrille Américaine*, brings this bit of information to light. He is better qualified to speak on this subject than any other one person. He is now a major in the

*Note: Spelled "Thenault" in other war data.

French Air Corps and Air Attaché on duty at the French Embassy, Washington, D.C. His letter has this to say concerning the origin of the motive, the creation of the design, and its adoption:

"Concerning the emblem, I must say that we had some long argument in its choice. The idea of the Indianhead, however, is absolutely mine. I remember some wanted a buffalo, but I stuck to the idea of a fierce Indian visage. I asked for sketches from the mechanics, and one from Lyons, named Suchet, to whom we showed as inspiration a goldpiece from the Treasury representing such a face, drew one which was judged very good and immediately adopted and put on the fuselage."

War Planes

By W. E. BARRETT

The English Handley Page, 1918

THE HANDLEY Page was created in response to the demand for a long-distance bomber capable of making raids far behind the German lines. It was designed primarily to fly at night and the object of its designers was to produce a ship of great lifting and carrying power which would be able to carry sufficient fuel for long flights in addition to destructive quantities of high explosives.

Plans for this ship were drawn as early as December, 1914, but the first Handley Page did not make its appearance until December, 1917. The first model was not successful and was quickly withdrawn to be followed later by the famous 0-400 model which served until the end of the war.

The 0-400 was powered by two Rolls Royce Eagle engines of 375 horse power each and could make an average speed of 90 miles per hour. Its dimensions were heroic. It had a wing span of 100 feet, gap of 11 feet, height of 22 feet and an overall length of 62 feet, 6 inches. No larger ship took the air in its time. The wings were a real feature in that they could be folded back along the fuselage; permitting the ship to be stored in small space.

The crew of each ship consisted of a pilot and two gunners. For armament they carried six fore and aft Lewis guns with 3,000 rounds of ammunition. This was necessary for attack purposes when spotted by German searchlights and for defense purposes against German night flyers. The usual load of destruction, although this varied of course, consisted of sixteen 112-pound bombs and twenty-five 25-pound bombs. The 112 pounders were torpedo shaped and fitted to a rack under the fuselage from which they could be released in succession by means of a lever in the cockpit. The 25 pounders were Cooper bombs, known as grass cutters, and were piled in the cockpit to be tossed over by hand.

The Handley Page 0-400 could operate within a radius of 350 miles and was used with telling effect against the industrial cities of Germany. Among the cities bombed during 1918 were Mainz, Coblenz, Stuttgart, Cologne, and Metz. A bombing squadron was usually composed of ten ships, and 122 Handley Pages were reputed to be in service.

The Handley Page V-1500 came out late in 1918. This carried a crew of seven and was powered by four 350 Rolls Royce engines. The engines were arranged in pairs, one tractor and one pusher on either side. This machine was capable of operating within a radius of 800 miles and there were two of them in France on November 8, 1918, which were charged with the assignment of bombing Berlin. This raid was never accomplished because of the early signing of the armistice.

The ship illustrated is the 0-400. This ship, despite its bulk, was easy to handle and there is one recorded instance of a noted ace standing court-martial for looping the loop in one with several high dignitaries of the British field staff on board.

G REETINGS—buzzards, kiwis, peelots, ack emmas and cloudbusters! You fellows are living in the greatest era of 'em all—the Age of Aviation! Ever since the first man went up in a balloon—and that happened back in the Eighteenth Century, in France—men have predicted that aviation would eventually become the most important factor in national and international life!

Well—it's here now!

The Age of Aviation!

Recent historical events have shown the most cynical observers that the era of the sea has passed and the era of the sky has come.

Airplanes hold the balance of power.

In war, aircraft is supreme; and in peace, travel via the clouds is becoming more popular every day. The new transport liners, many with fine sleeping accommodations, show how we are progressing in this respect.

The Time to Go Ahead

Now is the time to go ahead with all our plans to make America supreme in the air.

England, Italy, Russia, France, Germany—all are awakening to an absorbed interest in aviation—all are working toward increased air forces, leaving no stone unturned and putting no obstacles in the way.

Aviation the World Over

Hop into my crate, fellows, and I'll take you for an aero-tour of the world. Let's review the latest happenings in aviation in many nations!

England—the new *Vega Gull*, accommodating four persons, has made its debut. Powered with a 200 h.p. deHaviland Gypsy-Six, this plane is the most comfortable devised to date. Popularity of the Night Service between London and Paris is growing. G. T. R. Hill, Professor of Engineering in London University, predicts that cruising at a height of 40,000 feet and at a

speed of almost 300 m.p.h. will be a commonplace of airline travel in the near future.

France—Le Bourget is to be improved at a cost of $1,318,000, to make it more modern and practical as an airport. The city of Dieppe is to build another up-to-date airport which will provide a large hangar and passenger depot. Three more seaplanes of the *Lieutenant de Vaissea Paris* type are being built. Test flights of the 350 h.p. Hispano-Suiza powered Breguet-Dorand helicopter show that the craft can attain a speed of at least 62 m.p.h.

Russia—18,000 persons have received emblems for efficiency in the use of parachutes. Gliding is being developed on a large scale.

Now, kiwis, hop off. That's as far as we are going this time, but I'll take you on another tour later on. Let me know how you liked this little jaunt.

Coming Events

Here are things not to miss (if you can get around to them):

The International Aero Exhibition at Stockholm, Sweden, May 16-June 1.

1936 National Air Races at Cleveland, Sept. 3-6.

The 7,060-mile round-trip speed and handicap race between Paris and Saigon, will start from an airport near Paris in October.

Fifteenth International Aeronautical Salon will open at Grand Palais, Paris, in November.

Join AIRMEN OF AMERICA

Maybe you can't be in all those places.

But there's one thing you CAN—and SHOULD— do!

Join the AIRMEN OF AMERICA and you'll be right in the swim with thousands of air-fans the world over! Be one of us. You'll hear from everywhere—if you do your part corresponding with other members.

No dues. No fees. You're welcome to the home tarmac if you share our interest in progress and national air defense. Clip, sign and mail the coupon right away.

Letters! Letters! Letters!

Cloud-busters, your letters are swell! Keep right on sending 'em along! A letter a month from every AIRMAN is what we want.

Here's looking at the home tarmac mail! First off, a note from Robert Frommer, 301 W. 67th St., N.Y.

I think SKY FIGHTERS is swell. I'd like it even better if Ralph Oppenheim wrote some Three Mosquito stories. George Bruce's and Robert Sidney Bowen's stories are perfect. Just keep these authors going and the magazine will zoom right ahead.

I am very interested in aviation and I won't be satisfied until I become a pilot in the United States Army. LEARN TO FLY by Lieut. Jay D. Blaufox and TARMAC TALK are very interesting.

Aubrey Short, Company 5413 at Laurel, Miss., gives us a CCC lad's point of view:

I am going to continue reading SKY FIGHTERS for it is both educational and entertaining.

I am also pleased to know that I have many mail buddies whom I can write to. Will start doing so soon.

This is way down in Mississippi—where the goffers build their nests in the hills in the fall and winter to protect them from the cold winds and frost.

And in a C.C.C. camp here we are preparing the forest for tomorrow. So that airmen can see beauty from the air as they glide along with ease over the landscape of the lonely pine.

Happy landings! I'm on my way for chow.

Mabel Johnstone, who can be reached through Gen-eral Delivery, Chicago, Ill., is the daughter of a Marine stationed in California and asks for mail buddies. She would especially like to hear from people interested in military services. She has taken some lessons in aviation and has been up in an airplane many times. Girls' contingent of the AIRMEN OF AMERICA, deluge her with letters, won't you?

Say, men—the home tarmac has received a special greeting card from the Royal Air Force Association of Canada, wishing us all many happy landings. This important outfit of war fliers all have their hearts in the right place! Three cheers for them!

Tom Shepke, 1401 Stow St., Peoria, Ill., writes:

I became interested in aviation about July, 1933, when the new Peoria Municipal Airport was dedicated. Since then I have saved over 2,000 airplane pictures. I had my first ride on October 19, 1935, in a 1935 Waco Custom Cabin. I thought it was swell and I can't wait until I go up again.

Readers—there sure are bang-up air-thrills in John Scott Douglas' novel, HEROES FROM HELL, which you'll read next month! Also, George Bruce at his best in a novelette, TORTURE, and many other swell yarns in the next issue. See you then.   —Eddie McCrae.

Tale of the Transport

WILLIAM V. V. STEPHENS

Here is a rollicking, stirring bit of verse glorifying those behind-the-lines warriors who fought a real war with the Service of Supply.—EDITOR

THIS IS the tale of the Transport—
The song of the swarming road,
Where we edge along and wedge along
With the moaning, groaning load.
Over the slippery highway,
Over the moorland bleak—
Buddie, your way is my way,
Up where the heavies speak.

We have the eyes of owls,
We drive while the night is thick,
Though the piercing north wind howls,
We'll stick! By God, we'll stick!
We'll hold to the line before us.
We'll cling to the beaten track.
All the hymns of hate in chorus
Never could turn us back.

Oh, it's follow, Buddie, follow!
Hang to the car ahead!
Over the hill and hollow,
Hurry! You'll soon be dead!

Through the deserted village,
By ruins rotten and rank,
With never a chance to pillage,
Where you're crust if you double bank.

Oh, it's onward, ever onward—
Up to the blazing line.
They are waiting, boy, they are waiting—
Up where the star-shells shine!
It is ours to roll and rumble—
To juggle the jag of steel,
Till down like a log we tumble,
Asleep at the quivering wheel.

It isn't a case of nations,
Or color, or caste, or creed;
But the Guns and the Men need rations,
And that is the word we heed.
And as long as the line moves forward,
Or the fires of fury flow,
We'll hold the road with the iron load,
We'll go—by God, we'll go!!

Parallel Forms / 4 / Western & Frontier

The Western Pulps made their first appearance in 1919 with the publication by Street and Smith of *Western Story Magazine.* Like many other types of Pulps, the Westerns presented short stories and novels along with fictionalized accounts of real events, letters-to-the-editor columns and other features. Throughout the years, *Western Story* and its many competitors presented a varied picture of the cowboy's life, ranging from gritty realism to outright fantasy—as fantasy became predominant the American cowboy grew to mythical proportions.

*   *   *

Certainly no one person was more responsible for this metamorphosis than Max Brand. He was fascinated by classical mythology and, in fact, dressed many of its ancient characters in boots, spurs, and ten gallon hats. "The Ghost", one of his earliest short stories, appeared in 1919 in *All-Story Weekly,* and its central character reincarnates the Greek god Pan. (Brand hadn't been out west until after "The Ghost" was published.)

Longing for success as a "serious" writer—a poet—Brand once wrote, "daily I thank God in three languages that I write under a pen name." (He actually wrote under at least 19 pseudonyms, his real name was Frederick Faust.) But despite his negative feelings, he managed to produce a lifetime output of some 30 million words, very little which he would have called "serious."

*   *   *

In contrast to the light tone of "The Ghost", J. E. Grinstead's "Old Pard" (*All Western Magazine,* 1933) has a straightforward quality which suggests a more realistic "Old West." Although there are many violent scenes in the story, Grinstead's descriptions of them are spare, and his portrayal of the cowboy's life appears almost as if it were seen through a dusty haze. Characterization is developed through action, and the ending has all the poetry one associates with the West. It has the kind of plot which could easily be transposed to any of several other settings, the Foreign Legion, for example.

*   *   *

No western anthology would be complete without a story about a cowboy and his horse. "Butler's Nag," by Frank Richardson Pierce, (*Western Story,* 1925) is characteristic of the many Animal Stories regularly featured in the Western Pulps. Pierce's story has a gentle, home-spun humor which is native to the western image.

*   *   *

Western Stories' domain included all new frontiers from Mexico to Alaska. "A Ticket Outside," by Robert Ormond Case, is set in the Yukon and published in 1933 in *Western Story.* Case's story derives its power from his gripping portrayal of the numbing Yukon elements.

*   *   *

Many afficionados of the Western prefer Luke Short's stories to Max Brand's. Certainly he was just as popular word for word, although he was not as prolific. Short's "Tough Enough" (*Argosy,* 1937) demonstrates his ability to create mood and tension within a tight framework of minimum action. Perhaps the most outstanding facet of Short's style is his ability to bring life to his characters through his simple description of minor—but revealing—gestures and dialogue. This visual style was naturally adaptable to film and many of his stories and novels became classic movie Westerns, particularly "Blood on the Moon."

The Ghost

by Max Brand

THE GOLD strike which led the fortune-hunters to Murrayville brought with them the usual proportion of bad men and outlaws. Three months after the rush started a bandit appeared so consummate in skill and so cool in daring that all other offenders against the law disappeared in the shade of his reputation. He was a public dread. His comings were unannounced; his goings left no track. Men lowered their voices when they spoke of him. His knowledge of affairs in the town was so uncanny that people called him the "Ghost."

The stages which bore gold to the railroad one hundred and thirty miles to the south left at the most secret hours of the night, but the Ghost knew. Once he "stuck up" the stage not a mile from town while the guards were still occupied with their flasks of snake-bite. Again, when the stage rolled on at midday, eighty miles south of Murrayville, and the guards nodded in the white-hot sun, the Ghost rose from behind a bush, shot the near-leader, and had the cargo at his mercy in thirty seconds.

He performed these feats with admirable *finesse*. Not a single death lay charged to his account, for he depended upon surprise rather than slaughter. Yet so heavy was the toll he exacted that the miners passed from fury to desperation.

They organized a vigilance committee. They put a price on his head. Posses scoured the region of his hiding-place, Hunter's Cañon, into which he disappeared when hard pressed, and left no more trace than the morning mist which the sun disperses. A hundred men combed the myriad recesses of the cañon in vain. Their efforts merely stimulated the bandit.

While twoscore men rode almost within calling distance, the Ghost appeared in the moonlight before Pat McDonald and Peters and robbed them of eighteen pounds of gold-dust which they carried in their belts. When the vigilance committee got word of this insolent outrage they called a mass-meeting so large that even drunken Geraldine was enrolled.

Never in the history of Murrayville had there been so grave and dry-throated an affair. William Collins, the head of the vigilantes, addressed the assembly. He rehearsed the list of the Ghost's outrages, pointed out that what the community needed was an experienced man-hunter to direct their efforts, and ended by asking Silver Pete to stand up before them. After some urging Pete rose and stood beside Collins, with his hat pushed back from his gray and tousled forelock and both hands tugging at his cartridge-belt.

"Men," went on Collins, placing one hand on the shoulder of the man-killer, "we need a leader who is a born and trained fighter, a man who will attack the Ghost with system and never stop after he takes up the trail. And I say the man we need is Silver Pete!"

Pete's mouth twitched back on one side into the faint semblance of a grin, and he shrugged off the patronizing hand of the speaker. The audience stirred, caught each other with side-glances, and then stared back at Silver Pete. His reputation gave even Murrayville pause, for his reputed killings read like the casualty list of a battle.

"I repeat," said Collins, after the pause, in which he allowed his first statement to shudder its way home, "that Silver Pete is the man for us. I've talked it over with him before this, and he'll take the job, but he needs an inducement. Here's the reward I propose for him or for any other man who succeeds in taking the

Ghost prisoner or in killing him. We'll give him any loot which may be on the person of the bandit. If the Ghost is disposed of in the place where he has cached his plunder, the finder gets it all. It's a high price to pay, but this thing has to be stopped. My own opinion is that the Ghost is a man who does his robbing on the side and lives right here among us. If that's the case, we'll leave it to Silver Pete to find him out, and we'll obey Pete's orders. He's the man for us. He's done work like this before. He has a straight eye, and he's fast with his six-gun. If you want to know Pete's reputation as a fighting man—"

"He'll tell you himself," said a voice, and a laugh followed.

Silver Pete scowled in the direction of the laugh, and his right hand caressed the butt of his gun, but two miners rose from the crowd holding a slender fellow between them.

"It's only Geraldine," said one of them. "There ain't no call to flash your gun, Pete."

"Take the drunken fool away," ordered Collins angrily. "Who let him in here? This is a place for men and not for girl-faced clowns!"

"Misher Collins," said Geraldine, doffing his broad-brimmed hat and speaking with a thick, telltale accent—"Misher Collins, I ask your pardon, shir."

He bowed unsteadily, and his hat brushed the floor.

"I plumb forgot I was in church with Silver Pete for a preacher!" he went on.

The audience turned their heads and chuckled deeply.

"Take him out, will you?" thundered Collins. "Take him out, or I'll come down there and kick him out myself!"

The two men at Geraldine's side turned him about and led him toward the door. Here he struggled away from his guides. "Misher Collins!" he cried in a voice half-whining and half-anger, "if I capture the Ghost do I get the loot?"

A yell of laughter drowned the reply, and Geraldine staggered from the room.

"What do you say, men?" roared Collins, enraged by these repeated interruptions. "Is Silver Pete the man for us?"

There was no shout of approval but a deep muttering of consent.

"I'd hire the devil himself," murmured one man, "if he'd get rid of the Ghost."

"All right," said Collins, and he turned to Pete. "You're in charge here, and it's up to you to tell us what to do. You're the foreman, and we're all in your gang."

The crowd was delighted, for Pete, finding himself deserted before the mass of waiting men, shifted uneasily from one foot to the other and kept changing the angle of the hat upon his mop of gray hair.

"Speech!" yelled a miner. "Give us a speech, Pete!" Silver Pete favored the speaker with a venomous scowl.

"Speech nothin'," he answered. "I ain't here to talk. I ain't no gossipin' bit of calico. I got a hunch my six-gun 'll do my chatterin' for me."

"But what do you want us to do, Pete?" asked Collins. "How are we going to help you?"

"Sit tight and chaw your own tobacco," he said amiably. "I don't want no advice. There's been too many posses around these diggin's. Maybe I'll start and hunt the Ghost by myself. Maybe I won't. If I want help I'll come askin' it."

As a sign that the meeting had terminated he pulled his hat farther down over his eyes, hitched his belt, and stalked through the crowd without looking to either side.

Thereafter Murrayville saw nothing of him for a month, during which the Ghost appeared five times and escaped unscathed. The community pondered and sent out to find Pete, but the search was vain. There were those who held that he must have been shot down in his tracks by the Ghost, and even now decorated some lank hillside. The majority felt that having undertaken his quest alone Pete was ashamed to appear in the town without his victim.

On the subject of the quest Geraldine composed a ballad which he sang to much applause in the eight saloons of the town. It purported to be the narrative of Silver Pete's wanderings in search of the Ghost. In singing it Geraldine borrowed a revolver and belt from one of the bystanders, pushed back his hat and roughed up his hair, and imitated the scowling face of Pete so exactly that his hearers fairly wept with pleasure. He sang his ballad to the tune of "Auld Lang Syne," and the sad narrative concluded with a wailing stanza:

> "I don't expect no bloomin' tears;
>   The only thing I ask
> Is something for a monument
>   In the way of a whisky flask."

Geraldine sang himself into popularity and many drinks with his song, and for the first time the miners began to take him almost seriously. He had appeared shortly after old John Murray struck gold six months before, a slender man of thirty-five, with a sadly drooping mouth and humorous eyes.

He announced himself as Gerald Le Roy Witherstone, and was, of course, immediately christened "Geraldine."

Thereafter he wandered about the town, with no apparent occupation except to sing for his drinks in the saloons. Hitherto he had been accepted as a harmless and amusing man-child, but his ballad gave him at once an Homeric repute, particularly when men remembered that the song was bound to come sooner or later to the ear of Silver Pete.

For the time being Pete was well out of ear-shot. After the meeting, at which he was installed chief man-hunter of the community, he spent most of the evening equipping himself for the chase. Strangely enough, he did not hang a second revolver to his belt nor strap a rifle behind his saddle; neither did he mount a fleet horse. To pursue the elusive Ghost he bought a dull-eyed mule with a pendulous lower lip. On the mule he strapped a heavy pack which consisted chiefly of edibles, and in the middle of the night he led the mule out of Murrayville in such a way as to evade observation. Once clear of the town he headed straight for Hunter's Cañon.

Once inside the mouth of the cañon he began his search. While he worked he might have been taken for a prospector, for there was not a big rock in the whole course of the cañon which he did not examine from all sides. There was not a gully running into Hunter's which he did not examine carefully. He climbed up and down the cliffs on either side as if he suspected that the Ghost might take to wings and fly up the sheer rock to a cave.

The first day he progressed barely a half-mile. The second day he covered even less ground. So his search went on. In the night he built a fire behind a rock and cooked. Through four weeks his labor continued without the vestige of a clue to reward him. Twice during that time he saw posses go thundering through the valley and laughed to himself. They did not even find him, and yet he was making no effort to elude them. What chance would they have of surprising the Ghost?

This thought encouraged him, and he clung to the invisible trail, through the day and through the night, with the vision of the outlaw's loot before him. He ran out of bacon. Even his coffee gave out. For ten days he lived on flour, salt, and water, and then, as if this saintly fast were necessary before the vision, Pete saw the Ghost.

It was after sunset, but the moon was clear when he saw the fantom rider race along the far side of the valley. The turf deadened the sound of the horse's hoofs, and, like another worldly apparition, the Ghost galloped close to the wall of the valley—and disappeared.

Peter rubbed his eyes and looked again. It give him a queer sensation, as if he had awakened suddenly from a vivid dream, for the horse, with its rider, had vanished into thin air between the eyes of Peter and the sheer rock of the valley wall. A little shudder passed through his body, and he cursed softly to restore his courage.

Yet the dream of plunder sent his blood hotly back upon its course. He carefully observed the marks which should guide him to the point on the rock at which the rider disappeared. He hobbled the mule, examined his revolver, and spun the cylinder, and then started down across the cañon.

He had camped upon high ground, and his course led him on a sharp descent to the stream which cut the heart of the valley. Here, for two hundred yards, trees and the declivity of the ground cut off his view, but when he came to the higher ground again he found that he had wandered only a few paces to the left of his original course.

The wall of the valley was now barely fifty yards away, and as nearly as he could reckon the landmarks, the point at which the rider vanished was at or near a shrub which grew close against the rock. For an instant Pete thought that the tree might be a screen placed before the entrance of a cave. Yet the rider had made no pause to set aside the screen. He walked up to it and peered beneath the branches. He even fumbled at the base of the trunk, to make sure that the roots actually entered the earth. After this faint hope disappeared, Pete stepped back and sighed. His reason vowed that it was at this point that the horse turned to air, and Pete's was not a nature which admitted the supernatural.

He turned to the left and walked along the face of the cliff for fifty paces. It was solid rock. A chill like a moving piece of ice went up Pete's back.

He returned to the shrub and passed around it to the right.

At first he thought it merely the black shadow of the shrub. He stepped closer and then crouched with his revolver raised, for before him opened a crevice directly behind the shrub. It was a trifle over six feet high and less than half that in width; a man could walk through that aperture and lead a horse. Pete entered the passage with cautious steps.

Between each step he paused and listened. He put forth a foot and felt the ground carefully with it, for fear of a pebble which might roll beneath his weight, or a twig which might snap. His progress was so painfully slow that he could not even estimate distances in the pitch-dark. The passage grew higher and wider—it turned sharply to the right—a faint light shone.

Pete crouched lower and the grin of expectancy twisted at his lips. At every step, until this moment; he had scarcely dared to breathe, for fear of the bullet which might find him out. Now all the advantage was on his side. Behind him was the dark. Before him was the light which must outline, however faintly, the figure of any one who lurked in wait. With these things in mind he went on more rapidly. The passage widened again and turned to the left. He peered cautiously around the edge of rock and looked into as comfortable a living-room as he had ever seen.

The rock hung raggedly from the top of the cave, but the sides were smooth from the action of running water through long, dead ages. The floor was of level-packed gravel. Silver Pete remained crouched at the sharp angle of the passage until he heard the stamp and snort of a horse. It gave him heart and courage to continue the stealthy progress, inch by inch, foot by foot, pace my pace toward the light, and as he stole forward more and more of the cave developed before him.

A tall and sinewy horse was tethered at one end, and at the opposite side sat a man with his back to Pete, who leveled his revolver and drew a bead on a spot between the shoulder blades. Yet he did not fire, for the thought came to him that if it were an honor to track the Ghost to his abode and kill him, it would be immortal glory to bring back the bandit alive, a concrete testimony to his own prowess.

Once more that catlike progress began until he could see that the Ghost sat on his saddle in front of a level-topped boulder in lieu of a table. The air was filled with the sweet savor of fried bacon and coffee. Pete had crawled to the very edge of the cave when the horse threw up its head and snorted loudly. The Ghost straightened and tilted back his head to listen.

"Up with yer hands!" snarled Silver Pete.

He had his bead drawn and his forefinger tightened around the trigger, but the Ghost did not even turn. His hands raised slowly above his shoulders to the level of his head and remained there.

"Stand up!" said Pete, and rose himself from the ground, against which he had flattened himself. For if the Ghost had decided to try a quick play with his gun the shot in nine cases out of ten would travel breast-high.

"Turn around!" ordered Pete, feeling more and more sure of himself as he studied the slight proportions of the outlaw.

The Ghost turned and showed a face with a sad mouth and humorous eyes.

"By God!" cried Silver Pete, and took a pace back which brought his shoulders against the wall of rock, "Geraldine!"

If the Ghost had had his gun on his hip he could have shot Pete ten times during that moment of astonishment, but his belt and revolver hung on a jutting rock five paces away. He dropped his hands to his hips and smiled at his visitor.

"When they put you on the job, Pete," he said, "I had a hunch I should beat it."

At this inferred compliment the twisted smile transformed one side of Silver Pete's face with sinister pleasure, but there was still wonder in his eyes.

"Damn me, Geraldine," he growled, "I can't believe my eyes!"

Geraldine smiled again.

"Oh, it's me, all right," he nodded. "You got me dead to rights, Pete. What do you think the boys will do with me?"

"And you're—the Ghost?" sighed Silver Pete, pushing back his hat as though to give his thoughts freer play. He had met many a man of grim repute along the "border," but never such nonchalance as he found in the Ghost.

"What'll they do with you?" he repeated, "I dunno. You ain't plugged nobody, Geraldine. I reckon they'll ship you South and let the sheriff handle you. Git away from that gun!"

For Geraldine had stepped back with apparent unconcern until he stood within a yard of his revolver. He obeyed the orders with unshaken good humor, but it seemed to Silver Pete that a yellow light gleamed for an instant in the eyes of the Ghost. It was probably only a reflection from the light of the big torch that burned in a corner of the cave.

"Gun?" grinned Geraldine. "Say, Pete, do you think I'd try and gunplay while *you* have the drop on me?"

He laughed.

"Nope," he went on. "If you was one of those tin-horn gunmen from the town over yonder, I'd lay you ten to one I could drill you and make a getaway, but you ain't one of them, Pete, and, seeing it's you, I ain't going to try no funny stuff. I don't hanker after no early grave, Pete!"

This tribute set a placid glow of satisfaction in Pete's eyes.

"Take it from me, Geraldine," he said, "you're wise. But there ain't no need for you to get scared of me so long as you play the game square and don't try no fancy moves. Now show me where you got the loot stowed and show it quick. If you don't—"

The threat was unfinished, for Geraldine nodded.

"Sure I'll show it to you, Pete," he said. "I know when I got a hand that's worth playing, and I ain't a guy to bet a measly pair of treys against a full house. Take a slant over there behind the rock and you'll find it all."

He indicated a pile of stones of all sizes which lay heaped in a corner. Pete backed toward it with his eye still upon the Ghost. A few kicks scattered the rocks and exposed several small bags. When he stirred these with his foot their weight was eloquent, and the gun-fighter's smile broadened.

"Think of them tin-horns," he said, "that offered all

your pickings to the man that got you dead or alive, Geraldine!"

The Ghost sighed.

"Easy pickings," he agreed. "No more strong-arm work for you, Pete!"

The jaw of Silver Pete set sternly again.

"Lead your hoss over here," he said, "and help me stow this stuff in the saddlebags. And if you make a move to get the hoss between me and you—"

The Ghost grinned in assent, saddled his mount, and led him to Pete. Then in obedience to orders he unbuckled the slicker strapped behind the saddle and converted it into a strong bag which easily held the bags of loot. It made a small but ponderous burden, and he groaned with the effort as he heaved it up behind the saddle and secured it. Pete took the bridle and gestured at the Ghost with the revolver.

"Now git your hands up over your head agin, Geraldine," he said, "and go out down the tunnel about three paces ahead of me."

"Better let me take the torch," suggested the Ghost, "it'll show us the way."

Pete grunted assent, and Geraldine, on his way toward the torch, stopped at the boulder to finish off his coffee. He turned to Pete with the cup poised at his lips.

"Say, Pete," he said genially. "Anything wrong with a cup of coffee and a slice of bacon before we start back?"

"By God, Geraldine," grinned the gun-fighter, "you're a cool bird, but your game is too old!"

Nevertheless his very soul yearned toward the savor of bacon and coffee.

"Game?" repeated the Ghost, who caught the gleam of Pete's eye. "What game? I say let's start up the coffee-pot and the frying-pan. I can turn out flapjacks browner than the ones mother used to make, Pete!"

Pete drew a great breath, for the taste of his flour and water diet of the past few days was sour in his mouth.

"Geraldine," he said at last, "it's a go! But if you try any funny passes I ain't going to wait for explanations. Slide out the chow!"

He rolled a large stone close to the boulder which served as dining-table to the bandit, and sat down to watch the preparations. The Ghost paid little attention to him, but hummed as he worked. Soon a fire snapped and crackled. The coffee can straddled one end of the fire; the frying-pan occupied the other. While the bacon fried he mixed self-rising pancake flour in a tin plate, using water from a tiny stream which trickled down from the rocks at one side of the cave, disappearing again through a fissure in the floor. Next he piled the crisp slices of bacon on a second tin plate and used

the fried-out fat to cook the flapjacks.

"What I can't make out," said Geraldine, without turning to his guest, "is why you'd do this job for those yellow livers over in the town."

Pete moved the tip of his tongue across his lips, for his mouth watered in anticipation.

"Why, you poor nut," he answered compassionately, "I ain't working for them. I'm working for the stuff that's up there behind the saddle."

Geraldine turned on him so suddenly that Pete tightened his grip upon the revolver, but the Ghost merely stared at him.

"Say," he grinned at last, "have you got a hunch they'll really let you walk off with all that loot?"

The face of the gunman darkened.

"I sure think they'll *let* me," he said with a sinister emphasis. "That was the way they talked."

Geraldine sighed in apparent bewilderment, but turned back to his work without further comment. In a few moments he rose with the plates of bacon and flapjacks piled on his left arm and the can of coffee in his right hand. He arranged them on the boulder before Silver Pete, and then sat on his heels on the other side of the big stone. The gun-fighter laid his revolver beside his tin cup and attacked the food with the will of ten. Yet even while he ate the eye which continually lingered on the Ghost noted that the latter stared at him with a curious and almost pitying interest. He came to a pause at last, with a piece of bacon folded in a flapjack.

"Look here," he said, "just what were you aiming at a while ago?"

Geraldine shrugged his shoulders and let his eye wander away as though the subject embarrassed him.

"Damn it!" said Pete with some show of anger, "don't go staring around like a cross-eyed girl. What's biting you?"

"It ain't my business," he said. "As long as I'm done for, I don't care what they do to you."

He stopped and drummed his finger-tips against his chin while he scowled at Pete.

"If it wasn't for you I'd be a free bird," he went on bitterly. "Do you think I'm goin' to weep any of the salt and briny for you, what?"

"Wha'd'ya mean?" Pete blurted. "D'ya mean to say them quitters are going to double-cross me?"

The Ghost answered nothing, but the shrug of his shoulders was eloquent. Pete started up with his gun in his hand.

"By God, Geraldine," he said, "you ain't playin' fair with me! Look what I done for you. Any other man would of plugged you the minute they seen you, but here I am lettin' you walk back safe and sound—treating you as if you was my own brother, almost!"

He hesitated a trifle over this simile. Legend told many things of what Silver Pete had done to his own brother. Nevertheless, Geraldine met his stare with an eye full as serious.

"I'm going to do it," he said in a low voice, as if talking to himself. "Just because you come out here and caught me like a man there ain't no reason I should stand by and see you made a joke of. Pete, I'm going to tell you!"

Pete settled back on his stone with his fingers playing nervously about the handle of his gun.

"Make it short, Geraldine," he said with an ominous softness. "Tell me what the wall-eyed cayuses figure on doin'!"

The Ghost studied him as if he found some difficulty in opening his story in a delicate manner.

"Look here, Pete," he said at last. "There ain't no getting out of it that some of the things you've done read considerable different from Bible stories."

"Well?" snarled Silver Pete.

"Well," said the Ghost, "those two-card Johnnies over to town know something of what you've done, and they figure to double-cross you."

He paused, and in the pause Pete's mouth twitched so that his teeth glinted yellow.

"Anybody could say that," he remarked. "What's your proof?"

"Proof?" echoed the Ghost angrily. "Do you think I'm telling you this for fun? No, Pete," he continued with a hint of sadness in his voice, "it's because I don't want to see those guys do you dirt. You're a real man and they're only imitation-leather. The only way they're tough is their talk."

"Damn them!" commented Pete.

"Well," said Geraldine, settling into the thread of his narrative, "they knew that once you left the town on this job you wouldn't come back until you had the Ghost. Then when you started they got together and figured this way. They said you was just a plain man-killer and that you hadn't any more right to the reward than the man in the moon. So they figured that right after you got back with the Ghost, dead or alive, they'd have the sheriff pay you a little visit and stick you in the coop. They've raked up plenty of charges against you, Peter."

"What?" asked Pete hoarsely.

The Ghost lowered his voice to an insinuating whisper.

"One thing is this. They say that once you went prospecting with a guy called Red Horry. Horace was his right name."

Silver Pete shifted his eyes and his lips fixed in a sculptured grin.

"They say that you went with him and that you was

pals together for months at a time. They say once you were bit by a rattler and Red Horry stuck by you and saved you and hunted water for you and cared for you like a baby. They say you got well and went on prospecting together and finally he struck a mine. It looked rich. Then one day you come back to Truckee and say that Red Horry got caught in a landslide and was killed and you took the mine. And they say that two years later they found a skeleton, and through the skull, right between the eyes, was a little round hole, powerful like a hole made by a .45. They say—"

"They lie!" yelled Silver Pete, rising. "And you lie like the rest of them. I tell you it was—it was—"

"Huh!" said Geraldine, shrugging away the thought with apparent scorn. "Of course they lie. Nobody could look at you and think you'd plug a pal—not for nothing."

Pete dropped back to his stone.

"Go on," he said. "What else do they say?"

"I don't remember it all," said the Ghost, puckering his brows with the effort of recollection, "but they got it all planned out when you come back with the loot they'll take it and split it up between them—one-third to Collins, because he made the plan first.

"They even made up a song about you," went on Geraldine, "and the song makes a joke out of you all the way through, and it winds up like this—you're supposed to be talking, see?

"I don't expect no bloomin' tears;
    The only thing I ask
Is something for a monument
    In the way of a whisky flask."

"Who made up the song, Geraldine?" asked Pete.

"I dunno," answered the Ghost. "I reckon Collins had a hand in it."

"Collins," repeated the gun-fighter. "It sounds like him. I'll get him first!"

"And it was Collins," went on the Ghost, leaning a little forward across the boulder, while he lowered his voice for secrecy. "It was Collins who got them to send out three men to watch you from a distance. They was to trail you and see that if you ever got to the Ghost you didn't make off with the loot without showing up in town. Ever see anybody trailing you, Pete?"

The gun-fighter flashed a glance over his shoulder toward the dark and gaping opening of the passage from the cave. Then he turned back to the Ghost.

"I never thought of it," he whispered. "I didn't know they was such skunks. But, by God, they won't ever see the money! I'll take it and line out for new hunting grounds."

"And me?" asked the Ghost anxiously.

"You?" said Silver Pete, and the whisper made the words trebly sinister. "I can't leave you free to track me up, can I? I'll just tie you up and leave you here."

"To starve?" asked the Ghost with horror.

"You chose your own house," said Pete, "an' now I reckon it's good enough for you to live in it."

"But what'll you do if they're following you up?" suggested the Ghost. "What'll you do if they've tracked you here and the sheriff with them? What if they get you for Red Horry?"

The horse had wandered a few paces away. Now its hoof struck a loose pebble which turned with a crunching sound like a footfall.

"My God!" yelled the Ghost, springing up and pointing toward the entrance passage, "they've got you, Pete!"

The gun-fighter whirled to his feet, his weapon poised and his back to the Ghost. Geraldine drew back his arm and lunged forward across the boulder. His fist thudded behind Silver Pete's ear. The revolver exploded and the bullet clicked against a rock, while Pete collapsed upon his face, with his arms spread out crosswise. The Ghost tied his wrists behind his back with a small piece of rope. Silver Pete groaned and stirred, but before his brain cleared his ankles were bound fast and drawn up to his wrists, so that he lay trussed and helpless. The Ghost turned him upon one side and then, strangely enough, set about clearing up the tinware from the boulder. This he piled back in its niche after he had rinsed it at the runlet of water. A string of oaths announced the awakening of Silver Pete. Geraldine went to him and leaned over his body.

Pete writhed and cursed, but Geraldine kneeled down and brushed the sand out of the gun-fighter's hair and face. Then he wiped the blood from a small cut on his chin where his face struck a rock when he fell.

"I have to leave you now, Pete," he said, rising from this work of mercy. "You've been good company, Pete, but a little of you goes a long way."

He turned and caught his horse by the bridle.

"For God's sake!" groaned Silver Pete, and Geraldine turned. "Don't leave me here to die by inches. I done some black things, Geraldine, but never nothing as black as this. Take my own gun and pull a bead on me and we'll call everything even."

The Ghost smiled on him.

"Think it over, Pete," he said. "I reckon you got enough to keep your mind busy. So-long!"

He led his horse slowly down the passage, and the shouts and pleadings of Silver Pete died out behind him. At the mouth of the passage his greatest shout rang no louder than the hum of a bee.

Grimly silent was the conclave in Billy Hillier's saloon. That evening, while the sunset was still red in the west, the Ghost had stopped the stage scarcely a mile from Murrayville, shot the sawed-off shotgun out of the very hands of the only guard who dared to raise a weapon, and had taken a valuable packet of the "dust." They sent out a posse at once, which rode straight for Hunter's Cañon, and arrived there just in time to see the fantom horseman disappear in the mouth of the ravine. They had matched speed with that rider before, and they gave up the vain pursuit. That night they convened in Hillier's, ostensibly to talk over new plans for apprehending the outlaw, but they soon discovered that nothing new could be said. Even Collins was silent, twisting his glass of whisky between his fingers and scowling at his neighbors along the bar.

It was small wonder, therefore, if not a man smiled when a singing voice reached them from a horseman who cantered down the street:

> "I don't expect no bloomin' tears;
>   The only thing I ask
> Is something for a monument
>   In the way of a whisky flask."

The sound of the gallop died out before the saloon, the door opened, and Geraldine staggered into the room, carrying a small but apparently ponderous burden in his arms. He lifted it to the bar which creaked under the weight.

"Step up and liquor!" cried Geraldine in a ringing voice. "I got the Ghost!"

A growl answered him. It was a topic over which they were not prepared to laugh.

"Get out and tell that to your hoss, son," said one miner. "We got other things to think about than your damfoolery."

"Damfoolery?" echoed Geraldine. "Step up and look at the loot! Dust, boys, real dust!"

He untied the mouth of a small buckskin bag and shoved it under the nose of the man who had spoken to him. The latter jumped back with a yell and regarded Geraldine with fascinated eyes.

"By God, boys," he said, "it *is* dust!"

Geraldine fought off the crowd with both hands.

"All mine!" he cried. "Mine, boys! You voted the loot to the man who caught the Ghost!"

"And where's the Ghost?" asked several men together.

"Geraldine," said Collins, pushing through the crowd, "if this is another joke we'll hang you for it!"

"It's too heavy for a joke," grinned Geraldine. "I'll put the loot in your hands, Collins, and when I show you the Ghost I'll ask for it again."

Collins caught his shoulder in a strong grasp.

"Honest to God?" he asked. "Have you got him?"

"I have," said Geraldine, "and I'll give him to you on one ground."

"Out with it," said Collins.

"Well," said Geraldine, "when you see him you'll recognize him. He's been one of us!"

"I knew it," growled Collins; "some dirty dog that lived with us and knifed us in the back all the time."

"But, remember," said Geraldine, "he never shot to kill, and that's why you sha'n't string him up. Is it a bargain?"

"It's a bargain," said Collins, "we'll turn him over to the sheriff. Are you with me, boys?"

They yelled their agreement, and in thirty seconds every man who had a horse was galloping after Collins and Geraldine. At the shrub beside the wall of the valley Geraldine drew rein, and they followed him in an awed and breathless body into the passage.

"I went out scouting on my own hook," explained Geraldine, as he went before them, "and I saw the Ghost ride down the cañon and disappear in here. I followed him."

"Followed up this passage all alone?" queried Collins.

"I did," said Geraldine.

"And what did you do to him?"

"You'll see in a minute. There was only one shot fired, and it came from his gun."

They turned the sharp angle and entered the lighted end of the passage. In another moment they crowded into the cave and stood staring at the tightly bound figure of Silver Pete. His eyes burned furiously into the face of Geraldine. The men swarmed about his prostrate body.

"Untie his feet, boys," said Collins, "and we'll take him back. Silver Pete, you can thank your lucky stars that Geraldine made us promise to turn you over to the law."

"How did you do it?" he continued, turning to Geraldine.

"I'm not very handy with a gun," said the Ghost, "so I tackled him with my fists. Look at that cut on his jaw. That's where I hit him!"

A little murmur of wonder passed around the group. One of them cut the rope which bound Pete's ankles together, and two more dragged him to his feet.

"Stand up like a man, Pete," said Collins, "and thank Geraldine for not cutting out your rotten heart!"

But Silver Pete, never moving his eyes from the face of the Ghost, broke into a long and full-throated laugh.

"Watch him, boys!" called Collins sharply. "He's going looney! Here, Jim, grab on that side and I'll take him here. Now start down the tunnel."

Yet, as they went forward, the rumbling laugh of the gun-fighter broke out again and again.

"I got to leave you here," said the Ghost, when they came out from the mouth of the passage. "My way runs east, and I got a date at Tuxee for to-night. I'll just trouble you for that there slicker with the dust in it, Collins."

Without a word the vigilance men unstrapped the heavy packet which he had tied behind his saddle. He fastened it behind Geraldine's saddle and then caught him by the hand.

"Geraldine," he said, "you're a queer cuss! We haven't made you out yet, but we're going to take a long look at you when you come back to Murrayville to-morrow."

"When I come back," said Geraldine, "you can look at me as long as you wish."

His eyes changed, and he laid a hand on Collins's shoulder.

"Take it from me," he said softly, "you've given me your word that the boys won't do Pete dirt. Remember, he never plugged any of you. He's got his hands tied now, Collins, and if any of the boys try fancy stunts with him—maybe I'll be making a quick trip back from Tuxee. Savvy?"

His eyes held Collins for the briefest moment, and then he swung into his saddle and rode east with the farewell yells of the posse ringing after him. By the time they were in their saddles Geraldine had topped a hill several hundred yards away and his figure was black against the moon. A wind from the east blew back his song to them faintly:

> "I don't expect no bloomin' tears;
>   The only thing I ask
> Is something for a monument
>   In the way of a whisky flask."

"Look at him, boys," said Collins, turning in his saddle. "If it wasn't for what's happened to-night, I'd lay ten to one that that was the Ghost on the wing for his hiding-place!"

OLD PARD

By

J. E. GRINSTEAD

*Few men knew where Old Pard came from, and fewer cared
to ask. It was enough for him to be known as a "top hand" . . .
then came the day when he had to talk and all men called
him a Prince.*

THEY CALLED him Old Pard, because he had been with the Y Bar outfit for ten years and had never had a partner. He rarely spoke, unless he was spoken to, and then as few words as he could get along with. He spoke a queer jargon. A mixture of cow-country and something else. That is, he would be talking plain cow talk, and all of a sudden he would use words, and say things that— Well, that stuck out from his language, like one silver conch on a pair of old, mildewed, worn out chaps. Then Old Pard would look ashamed, and talk plain cow talk for a long time afterwards. He was like a man who forgets, and busts out in a foreign tongue that the rest of the company don't understand.

A bunch of the Y Bar boys had ridden into Wellman. It was just an old frontier cowtown. Big store, saloon and dance hall, hotel, livery stable, saddle-shop and a few houses. Plenty more like it.

The boys left their horses at the hitch rack, and all trailed into the Shorthorn Saloon, to take on a little fuel for the grade up to the dance hall, and maybe to play poker or monte for a while. Old Pard was with the boys. He would go along that way occasionally. Once in a great while he would take more than one drink. When he did, he was likely to take several. Then he would talk easy and smooth. He would clip his words off in a queer way, and they would sound like raindrops falling in a little pool. No cow talk at all.

There was a young fellow who had been with the outfit about a month, and he didn't have a partner, either. Not that he didn't want one, but because he was so green, and clumsy with his rope and things that nobody wanted to tie up with him. His name was Monty Clark.

When the gang lined up at the bar, it so happened that Monty was at the back end. He took his place, with one hoof on the rail. Never was a fellow that tried harder to be a natural cowhand than Monty Clark. He looked like a boy, and wasn't much more than one. Something was always surprising him, and he was always showing it in his pretty brown eyes. Old Pard, tall, straight and stiff with queer, squinty blue eyes, his mustache cropped short, was right next to Monty.

The boys took one round of drinks. Next time, Old Pard turned his glass down. It wasn't his night to take more than one drink. The boys knew that when he turned his glass down, it was down for the night. They didn't argue with him. He would just turn it upside down on the bar, and say to the barkeep:

"Just leave it there, Chub, and take out one for me when you make change. I don't want to hurt the house, but the liquor is better off in your bottles than it would be in my system."

The boys took a few more drinks, and by that time some of them were missing the rail when they tried to put their feet on it. You know how that is. One of these was Monty. Liquor always went to his hands and his feet, instead of his head, but he would drink it, because he wanted to be a natural cowhand.

Now, there was a ranch in that country that ran the Hour Glass brand. The Y Bar boys called it the Saddle Blanket outfit, to one another, because the Hour Glass covered a Y Bar so good. Old Bill Givens, of the Hour Glass, and his hands, knew they were called that behind their backs, and they didn't like it. Bill had a pretty big outfit, and also a pretty tough one. You know the kind. Everybody in the country suspected them, but nothing had been proved on them, so they worked cattle with the rest.

Bill Givens and half a dozen of his hands had been playing some poker in the back, and got dry, so they came to the bar for a drink and stopped at the back end. Monty had heard the other Y Bar boys call them the Saddle Blanket outfit, so he thought it was all right.

"Hi, boys," says he. "Come up and take a drink with us, all you Saddle Blanket fellers."

Monty didn't know he had said anything wrong, as he edged toward Old Pard, to make room. Old Pard squinted his blue eyes, like he expected something to bust in his face, and turned facing the Hour Glass men.

"I'll cover you with a saddle blanket, damn you," snarled Bill Givens. Then he gave Monty an open-handed slap on the side of his face that rocked his head on his shoulders.

Bill Givens had slapped a tiger, and didn't know it. No one else knew it, then. They just thought Monty had let his mouth go off, and would have to take his medicine, and that was all there was to it.

Monty's hands were so limber that it looked like he never would get his gun. Bill Givens had turned facing the bar, and yelled for his drink. Old Pard just backed away from Monty a little, his eyes still squinted. Seemed like he was still expecting something to bust and fly in his face, and it did.

"Jerk yo' gun off, and get ready," says Monty, soft and easy like. "I'm goin' to whip hell out of you with my fists."

Bill Givens turned his head to see what the noise was about, and almost punched his eyes out of the muzzle of Monty's gun. Bill was a giant of a fellow. If he'd had his way about it, he would just have pulled off his gun and spanked Monty. As it was, instead of a fight, it turned out to be a battle. A couple of Hour Glass punchers set their guns to smoking, to distract attention so Bill could get his head away from where it was. They shot into the floor, at first, and then they didn't. Old Pard stepped to the side of Monty, and his eyes were squinted until he looked like he was blind.

Bill Givens threw up his hand and knocked Monty's gun aside, just as Monty pulled trigger, meaning to shoot Bill's head off. Being slapped in the face was an insult to Monty, and Bill didn't know it. Monty's bullet went through a picture of Dan Patch, on the wall back of the bar. Old Pard's gun was out and smoking, and a lot more followed his bad example. In about a second there was more smoke and lead, and less light; more cripples and less dead men, in the Shorthorn, than that old joint ever saw at one time, and it had seen plenty.

T HEN THE smoke finally settled, and somebody made a light, there was not an Hour Glass man in the place, but there was a well defined trail of blood leading to the back door, where they had gone out.

"That's damn funny," said Old Pard. "Looks like they'd stop long enough to help clean up, and pay their part of the damage."

Then Old Pard turned around and looked at Monty The boy was leaning against the bar. His face was white. He had his gun in his left hand, and his gun and his brown eyes were both fixed on that back door.

"What's the matter, Monty?" asked Old Pard.

"Got me in the right arm," said Monty, through his set teeth.

"Let's have a look." Old Pard rolls back the sleeve and looks where a forty-five bullet had crawled through Monty's arm, right close to the elbow joint, just missing the bone.

Pard grabbed a bottle of raw alcohol and poured the wound full of it. Then he bandaged it with a clean bar cloth that Chub gave him. Monty just leaned against the bar, his face white, his teeth clenched, and hand shaking a little, but he didn't even grunt. Nerve? He had a plenty of it.

Nobody had been killed. Some of the other boys had some little burns and scratches that they doctored. Then all hands put another helping of healing balm on the inside, because the party seemed to be over, and there was nothing to do but go home. Any way, the fiddlers were gone.

Tell Bates, the owner of the Y Bar, was one hard-boiled old he-cattle baron, but he was square and white as they make 'em, and wiser than a prairie-dog-hole full of owls. Bates was playing poker with some of his men, in the bunkhouse, when the boys got home. Tully Grimes, the cleanest, gamest cowhand that ever forked a horse, and Old Man Tell's right bower, told the old man what had happened.

"That's damn funny," said Bates, just like Old Pard had said it. There was not anything funny about it, especially to Monty Clark. Bates squinted at his poker hand about a minute, without seeing it, then went on: "When fellers is that quick on trigger, they are nervous about something. You boys have been calling them the Saddle Blanket outfit for a year, and hurrahing about how easy the Hour Glass would cover the Y Bar, and I didn't pay you no mind. Thought you just wanted to ride somebody, like natural. But, now, damfi—" He pushed back his chair and got up. "Better turn in, boys. Reck'n we'll ride that Hour Glass range some in the morning."

Next morning the boys all saddled up by daylight. Old Pard roped out Monty's horse, and saddled it for him. Monty had his right arm in a sling.

"Shore hate it that you can't go, Monty," said Old Man Tell, as Monty stood waiting for the word to mount.

"I'm going," said Monty.

"Hell, no!" roared Bates. "You'll take cold in that arm and lose it, or else you'll open the wound and bleed to death."

"I'm going," repeated Monty.

"All right, you damn fool," snapped Bates. "Go if you insist on it, but don't say I'm to blame for anything that happens."

With that, the old Man threw in his spurs and led out. Monty makes two or three tries, before he gets to his saddle. Then him and Old Pard rides away from the Y Bar together; partners. If anybody saw one of them after that he saw them both, as long as Old Pard lived. The queer old puncher had seen something in Monty that night while the fight was on, that he just had to have in a partner. Monty had it, and he just tied to Monty without any talk.

WELL, THE Y Bar outfit just rode on to the Hour Glass range, without sending up any signals, or anything else. It was all open range, and anybody had a right to ride it where he pleased. It was in the afternoon. Bates and his men had seen nothing out of the ordinary. Then the Old Man saw a steer with an Hour Glass brand that didn't look just right.

"Throw that steer," he commanded.

In about a pair of seconds that steer was on the ground, hog-tied and breathing hard. Tell Bates looked at the brand, and a wrinkle came between his eyes.

"Turn him loose," he growled. "Now, you boys listen to me. That's a burnt Y Bar. A drunken Indian could tell that. The brand ain't been burnt two hours. Reck'n he gets away, and starts to drift back to the home range. I been suspecting that Hour Glass outfit, same as everybody else, but I didn't think they was in the wholesale business. Come on."

Well, they crossed a ridge, and looked right down into a low valley in the edge of the foothills, and there it was. Bill Givens, with about forty hands, was branding cattle in that valley. That would have been all right, if Old Man Tell had not seen that burned Y Bar steer. Bates had not only caught them with the goods, but had caught them producing more.

"Come on, boys," snapped Bates. "I'm going in there."

Tully Grimes was riding with Old Man Bates, as the outfit stormed down the slope. Bates thought the thieves would drop their running-irons and leave, when they saw him, but they didn't. If anybody tells you that a thief won't fight when he's cornered, he never saw a cattle rustler. There was a real fight. They fought all over that little valley. A dozen rustlers were down, but Bates had lost six of his twenty men, and was getting decidedly the worst of it, but he was not quitting just yet.

The Y Bar outfit had driven a flying wedge, with Old Man Tell and Tully Grimes for a point, right through the middle of the Saddle Blanket boys. The result was that instead of one main battle, there was a flock of little fights going on, all over the valley. Part of the Saddle Blanket boys gave back in front of Bates, Tully Grimes and a few others. Bill Givens was with that detachment, and Bill couldn't afford to give up. There was a real fight going on over there.

In that manner, Old Pard and Monty got shunted off to the west side of the valley, away from the others. Half a dozen rustlers decided the Y Bar had too many men, and set in to cut the outfit down by at least two.

They were not having a whole lot of luck. Monty Clark was doing some of the meanest left-handed shooting, for a right-handed man, that had ever been done in that country, while Old Pard was a regular he-tiger, with claws a foot long. Five of the six rustlers got off their horses, accidentally, and the other one was weaving in his saddle, when a fresh bunch came tearing across the valley.

Meantime, Old Man Bates had seen that he had picked up something that was too hot to handle, and was drawing his men off. It was almost sunset. Bates waved his hat at Old Pard and Monty, as he and what men he had left tore south, out of the valley. Bates had not seen the fresh helping of rustlers that were making for Monty and Old Pard so he and his men rode on over the ridge, thinking that Monty and Old Pard were coming right on behind them.

A hundred yards west of where Monty and Old Pard had made their stand, and ruined a lot of otherwise good rustlers, there was a little ridge of malpais rock. Old Pard knew all the rocks in that country by their first names. They gained them, just as the sun went down, but they were both afoot. The rustlers had killed both their horses. On top of the little ridge they turned facing the enemy, not so much because they were brave, but because the Saddle Blanket riders were right on them, and something had to be done. Plenty was done, all right. The first thing that happened, the two foremost rustlers went from their saddles. The next thing, Monty Clark threw up his hands, fell, and rolled down the other side of the little ridge.

Then, the last wink of the setting sun fell on something that was unusual, even for that land of violence. It was the tall, gaunt form of Old Pard, giving back slowly across the top of that tiny ridge, his gun spouting methodically, and doing terrible damage. He had backed to the slope, when the band of rustlers charged and poured in a storm of lead. Old Pard's knees buckled, he fell, and rolled on down the hill. Even then, the rustlers didn't care to see what was on the other side of the ridge, but turned and tore away to join Givens and the others.

The rest of the badly beaten Y Bar outfit stormed on south. Given rallied his men, and rode for the Hour Glass, which was only two miles away, to the north of the battleground. Old Tell Bates was not quitting. Not a bit of it. He knew he could get help at the Cross T, for they had suspected Givens, too.

A LITTLE while after midnight, the combined outfits fell on the Hour Glass, and that cow outfit was only a memory. There was simply no room in that part of the country for wholesale rustlers, and these fellows had been caught with the goods.

At daylight next morning, Bates and his Y Bar boys were riding the little valley, looking for their dead.

"Well," said Old Man Bates, at last, "we have found everybody but Monty and Old Pard. They're dead, or the fighting fools are still shooting, if they ain't out of cartridges. Anybody got an idea where we'll find em?"

"I have," said Tully Grimes. "They were over at the north side of the valley when you waved at 'em, but they were busy, and I guess they didn't follow us."

"Looks like they didn't," growled Bates. "Queer pair. First time I ever knowed Old Pard to take a partner in a fight. He generally plays a lone hand, and plays it to win. Take some of the boys, Tully, and see if you can locate 'em."

When Tully and the other boys crossed the little ridge, they saw Old Pard and Monty. They were sitting on the ground, back to back, and their heads slumped forward. They were both bareheaded, and both pale, but Old Pard's face was that cold blue gray that no one could mistake.

Poor Old Pard was cold in death, and already stiff. Monty was not dead, but he was clean out. They examined him, and found that wads of cloth had been placed in a terrible wound in his right breast, and then bandaged with Old Pard's shirt.

They took them up and carried them, along with the other dead, back to the Y Bar. A doctor looked at Monty, who lay limp in his bunk, and shook his head.

"That boy's spirit don't want to go anywhere. If it did, the door's wide open. He hasn't got a chance in the world. Hole in his lung that you could drive a wagon through sideways. Still, I'll do what I can. Make him easy, anyway."

Well, the doctor was mistaken, as doctors sometimes are, the same as other people. Monty refused to die. For a week, he lay babbling in delirium. Old Man Bates was in the bunkhouse one day when Monty had one of his wild talking spells on him, and they had to hold him in the bed. When he was finally quieted, Bates said:

"Huh. Monty must of read that in a book. He couldn't talk like that to save his life, if he was sane. Sounded like Old Pard, when he's drunk."

Then one evening about dusk, when there was nobody about the bunkhouse but Tully Grimes, Monty opened his big brown eyes; bigger now than ever.

"Hello, Tully," he croaked. "Where's—where's Old Pard?"

"He's— You better not try to talk now, partner. You're pretty weak, and all, and——"

"Oh, that's all right, Tully. I recollect, now. Was there—was there something in my pocket when you boys found me?"

"Shore was, old timer. I put it away for you. Better go to sleep now, if you can."

Monty turned over and went to sleep. He began to mend at once, but it was months before he could ride again. The next spring—no, it must have been two years after that, for Monty was pretty weak for a year. Anyway, it was the spring that grass was good, water plentiful, and rustlers thick as green-head flies in all that part of the cow country. Monty's right arm was always stiff, from that gunshot wound, but he never did suit trying to be a natural cowhand, and before the end he was one. For some reason, Tully Grimes and Monty became partners, after Monty got able to ride. Maybe it was because Tully's partner was killed in that same mess.

Monty never mentioned Old Pard but once, after he got able to go about a little. That was when Tully gave him the things he had found in Monty's pocket, over there by the malpais ridge. Among them was a curious gold watch that Old Pard had always carried. Tully had pried open the back one day, and saw the picture of a beautiful woman's face in it. He had closed it reverently. When Grimes gave Monty the things, Monty said:

"Where did you all bury Old Pard?"

"Out there in that sorty Boot Hill we got, under them big mesquites."

"Will you show me the grave?"

"Shore will, partner." They went to the graveyard, a little way from the ranch house. "There they are. Seven in the lot. Four in one row, and three in the other. Old Pard is the last one to the right, in the row of three. We left a place for you by the side of him, because you was the only partner he ever had, and we thought you was goin' then."

"Sure that's right?" asked Monty.

"Shore am."

"Thank you, Tully. I'll find a flat rock, and mark it. I might—somebody might—" Monty broke off, and the incident was closed, except that Monty found a big flat rock, and laboriously made the inscription with an old horseshoe rasp, "Old Pard." Then he planted it firmly at the head of the grave.

AS I was saying, that spring grass was good, water plentiful, and the market right, but thieves and rustlers worked the stock something awful. There had been a lot of fierce northers the winter before, and the Y Bar cattle tried to drift clean into Mexico. So, when the grass gets good, one of the Y Bar wagons and a little bunch of men were working the Wolf Creek country, fifty miles south of headquarters. One morning when they went to saddle up, four of the best horses in the remuda were gone.

Of course that wouldn't do. Tully Grimes was rodding the little outfit, and Monty Clark was riding with him, like always. They left the camp and the remuda with the cook and the wrangler, and all hands set out to find the lost horses, and maybe a rustler or two. The country was rough and rocky, for it was in close to some foothills and some bad roughs. The trail was hard to find, and in a little while the men were scattered, and out of sight of each other, riding in pairs.

Tully and Monty finally struck the trail, about five miles from camp, and heading straight for some deep canyons. They took the trail, and followed on for another five miles. They were riding two of the best and fastest horses in the outfit. Then in a broad, flat-bottomed draw they came upon two old sore-backed crow-baits, the sweat still dried on their backs, that the rustlers had discarded when they got good horses. That meant that there were only two of the rustlers. No real cowhand asked for anything more than an even break, so Grimes and Monty pushed on up the draw.

They came at last to a considerable thicket in the bottom of the draw. At the lower end of the thicket the tracks were quite fresh. One man had gone on each side of the thicket, for some reason, and each had a led horse. That was why they had made such poor time. Tully Grimes rode up on a little hill, and took a look. He could see far beyond the thicket. There was no one in sight.

"Monty," he said, "them fellers are in that thicket, and we got to get 'em out. We—no we ain't. Look!" Two men had bolted from the upper end of the thicket, but neither of them had a led horse. "They saw us, and have left the led horses in the thicket. We've got to catch 'em inside a mile, or they'll make it, to the canyons, where the devil couldn't catch 'em with a pitchfork. Come on. We can catch 'em."

The thieves had seen them. There could be no stalking the game now. It was just a plain horse race, for a mile, slightly up hill, and the thieves almost a quarter mile in the lead. It looked like a slim chance, but there was nothing to do but take it, or lose two good horses.

On they tore. The better horses and better horsemanship of the cowboys was steadily closing the gap between them. One of the men was a tall fellow, and the other short. They had yet more than a hundred yards to go before they reached the mouth of the canyon, when Tully fired, and the bullet whined low over their heads. They ducked, and lost speed. They heard the pounding hoofs behind them, now. Almost, they had reached one of nature's sanctuaries for wild beasts and wilder men, but not quite. They saw they

could never make it, for more bullets were whining about them. They separated, one going to the right and the other to the left. They probably figured that the two cowboys would stay together, giving at least one of them a chance to get away.

That was a bad guess. Of all the cowboys in the west, none were better satisfied with an even break than these two. The big man turned to the left, and Monty being on that side took after him, while Tully gave chase to the squatty one. Tully Grimes not only was not afraid, but few men had a chance with him in a gunfight. He knew that rustler was scared. If he were not, he would not be running.

The rustler was not idle. Bullets were whining about Tully Grimes, but he was holding his fire, and riding for good pistol range. A duel followed. Both their horses were plunging about, and even Tully Grimes missed, but he put his last bullet where it belonged, and the thief pitched from his saddle dead. Tully's horse had stopped dead still. Tully had been burnt a little across one arm, but when he looked across the draw to where Monty fought the other man, he forgot all about it. Telling about it afterward, Tully said:

"I slammed in my spurs, to go to Monty, but the horse didn't move. When I had him half gutted with the rowels, I found out that the rustler's last bullet had broke his foreleg. I jumped off, and tried to make it to Monty on foot, but all I could do was see the fight. There was a little gully that would make some protection. The big thief had been trying to get to that when Monty headed him off. Did Monty try to get into the gully? Not any. He's taken' it in the open, like a real hand. I was wishing he'd duck into the holler, while both of 'em were reloading, but all they did was reload, and start it all over. Aw, hell, fellers. I hope you don't never see anything like what I seen then."

Tully stopped and rolled a smoke. He burnt the cigarette up, before he went on.

"Before I could take a step, I seen it happen. They both comes up to the scratch, but that old stiff elbow of Monty's made him a little slow. They fired almost together, but not quite. The big rustler went from his saddle plum sudden and natural. Monty just leans over his saddle horn, and then slides to the ground, like a fellow with a bad bellyache."

TULLY WOULD always stop there, and smoke a while. If he was not prodded, he wouldn't tell the rest of it. What really happened was this: Tully ran on across the draw. When he got there, the thief was dead, and he saw that it was Bill Givens! Monty lay on the ground. His face was pale, and his eyes were squinted, like those of Old Pard.

"Get you deep, Monty?" asked Grimes, as he stooped over the boy on the ground.

"Yep," said Monty, "but I reck'n maybe he won't slap my face again."

"I'll get you on your horse, and take you to camp," said Tully. "It's about ten mile, but we can make it."

"No. Couldn't make it, partner," said Monty, a grim smile coming to his white face. "He—he got me right through the bread-basket. It won't be long, but I got something to do."

"What is it, Monty?"

"You—you remember Old Pard, don't you?"

"Of course I do. What about Old Pard?"

"Well, that night behind the malpais ridge, when the Saddle Blanket outfit left him and me for dead, I found out something. When he had plugged up the hole in me, and rolled me a smoke, Old Pard propped us up back-to-back so we wouldn't fall over. Then he talked. I never heard no talk like that before. I can't tell you what he said, because I can't speak that language, and any way I wouldn't have time, but —Tully, he was doctor, preacher, father, mother and friends, all rolled into one, as we sat looking up at the stars. He——"

Monty broke off and struggled with his pain, in silence, for a moment. Then he fumbled in an inside pocket, brought out a little leather pouch, and said:

"Take this, partner. Maybe you can deliver it some time. You can try, any way, and that's all I could do."

"What is it?" asked Monty.

"Old Pard's watch, and a little locket. When he had talked a while, that night out there under the stars, he hands me these, and says, plumb quiet, just like he's cashing in and quitting a poker game: 'Monty, I'll be going pretty quick. I'm taking cold in my heart, right now. Most of the sands of my life are already in my boots. Take this.'

"Then he gives me the watch and the locket. I still remember how cold his hand was as it touched mine. 'Monty,' he says, 'maybe you won't understand, but I'm an English Lord, in my own right. When I'm gone, write to the address I'll give you, in England,

and when you are sure, send these. I didn't do anything wrong, to bring me to this country. I just came away, because—there was a woman. She—she might care to know, now. When you write to them, tell them I died with my face to the enemy, like a gentleman. No, not that—like a real cowhand—it's the same thing, d'ya know.'

"He had to rest a little while, just like I'm doing now." Monty stopped and rested a moment. "Old Pard didn't say anything for a little bit, and then he sorta whispers, 'Monty, here's the address.' We had no paper and pencil. 'Try to remember it.' Then he told me, but you know these English names don't spell like an Englishman says them. When I got well, I wrote, but the letters all came back. Maybe you can do better.

"Just keep the things until you get it all straight, then send them, like Old Pard said. That picture in the back of the watch is a Lady Somebody, and Old Pard was a lord, a prince, a King, or anything else that is big and good. I'd like to do that much for Old Pard. He—he saved my life. Hadn't been for him, I'd of went that night, and wouldn't had no chance to square it with Bill Givens."

"All right, partner," said Tully Grimes, gently. "I'll do my dangdest. Tell me the address."

Monty's eyes had closed, sleepily. He opened them and stared at Tully in a doubtful manner, then said:

"Shore, the address. I was about to forget. It is—" There was just a little gasp. That was all.

Tully Grimes made camp a little while after nightfall. He had brought in Monty's body, and five horses. The crippled one he shot. They had to bury Monty, out there on the head of Wolf Creek. It was too far to the place that they had kept for him, by the side of Old Pard.

The big fat rock may still be lying under the big mesquites at the old Y Bar. In the Old Country, he may have been a prince, and may have worn diamonds; out here in the cow country he was a natural cowhand, and wore chaps and a gun. As he said, it is all the same thing, if a man is right. No one knows what his name was. The cow country called him— Old Pard.

Butler's Nag

by Frank Richardson Pierce

Author of "The Split," etc.

I T WAS a raw day, the tail end of winter. The wind coming down from the mountains carried an edge that cut through heavy woolens with ease; people hurried about their business and grumbled. Several weeks before, the buds had appeared, and it had looked like an early spring. Then winter had given a laugh, nipped the buds with frost, and gladdened the hearts of fuel dealers.

The wind ruffled the horse's coat, and he set his stiff legs and trembled. The edge of the wind bit deep, almost chilling his old heart. Once his black coat had been like velvet; once he had faced the blizzard with contempt, and led a band of wild horses over an empire. Men had called him Blackie and coveted him. Now——

He shook violently at times, regained control of his muscles with an effort, then continued to nibble at the tufts of grass that defied the cold. The green blades, scant as they were, held a promise of spring, and instinctively Blackie sensed that spring held a promise even for an old horse with thin blood. He would no longer lead a band of wild horses, but he was entitled to the reward of age—food, comfort, and reflection, with a little work, perhaps.

There had been a time when thousands had cheered him to the echo; when, though men held his prisoner, no man was his master. They held him with ropes, saddled him, put men on his back, then freed him. His wild blood had leaped in resentment in those days; he had shaken himself with fury, hurled the man from his back, and stamped the saddle into the dust with his hoofs.

Then "Glue" Butler had appeared. Butler had not earned such a nickname without reason. He could stick to any horse like glue. The first two days Blackie tossed Glue with ease, and over Glue's face came an expression of deep admiration and a trace of affection. The third day it had been a battle royal, and Blackie had won just when he believed himself beaten.

The fourth day Glue Butler rode him straight up without pulling leather. Roars of approval came from thousands of throats. It was a tribute to a great broncho buster and a great horse. Blackie sensed firmness in Butler's attitude, yet kindness. Though he fought it at first, his affection went out toward the man. They became rare partners. Butler trained Blackie to come in reponse to a peculiar little whistle. Sometimes when Butler overslept on the range, for he was not as young as some of the other cowmen, Blackie would roll him over with his nose until he awakened. Those had been great days.

Then one day Butler had launched himself from Blackie's back. His hands had clutched at a steer's long horns, gripped, and the steer and Butler had gone down together. Blackie had swerved and galloped on; some one caught him; the stands became hushed, and they carried a limp form away on a stretcher.

Perhaps Blackie reflected on all this as he trembled in the cold. Like mankind, he had been carried to the crest, heard the cheers of the crowd, then been forgotten, hardly a memory except where old men gathered and talked of another day. At times, Blackie certainly must have recalled Glue Butler. What had become of Glue? Old, discarded, no longer wanted, left to shift for himself by a world that had once cheered. Blackie was hungry, so he continued nibbling at the scant grass. It took steady nibbling all day long to gather even a partial meal.

And then some one who had noticed Blackie, day after day, had paused long enough in her busy life to do something. She telephoned the police department. "He's old, I don't know how old and pitifully thin. Sometimes when he is tired he lies down on the wet ground and that stiffens his joints so that he has a difficult time in getting up again."

"Who owns him!"

"No one wants him. He was turned loose several weeks ago when he could no longer work. The people have moved. Something should be done!"

"All right," came a cheerful voice. "We'll take care of it!"

Later a member of the department who knew horses looked Blackie over. "You poor devil!" he muttered. "Somebody should have shot you weeks ago. H'm! Well, there's only one thing to do, and I hate like sin to do it. You are useless; your day is done. It's a tough world, for something tells me you were a great nag in your day."

Blackie did not understand, but he sensed friendship in the hand that slapped him so gently. He looked back curiously. Maybe this man would lead him away to a warm barn and food. Blackie's sides were caked with mud; he had not been curried in years.

Then the man drove away in a small car. Stray horses were rare indeed in this day and age. He looked into certain ordinances, and then he telephoned Blackie's location.

The following day two men drove up in a truck. It was built particularly to transport animals with a minimum of effort.

"Here's the old crow bait," said one roughly. "Looks like he had some good points in his day."

"Still has," replied the other man with an attempt at humor. "You can hang your hat on some of them!" He tossed his hat onto the old horse and proved it. The men laughed, then with some difficulty loaded Blackie into the truck. "This nag and old man Butler would make a great team—they were both good in their day." He laughed loudly—the thoughtless laugh of the young.

"Queer about Butler. Every time we bring some old horse down to the plant, he hangs around and shakes his head. He's a little off upstairs, I guess; a horse is a horse." He started the truck. "Butler once asked me if a horse ever saved my life. He's a little off; harmless enough, though. We've never missed anything."

An hour later the truck had passed nearly across the city and stopped before an evil-smelling establishment. Here ended the trail of many living things. While the Chicago stock yards might utilize everything but the squeal, it was the boast of the "refining" plant that it used everything but the stiffness in an old horse's joints.

Blackie's once glossy coat would make good leather; his bones gelatine, glue. By a strange trick of fate it was Glue who had tamed him; now glue would claim him. He had known the wild, had heard the cheers of those who admired him. He had felt the bite of the lash as he labored, and the deeper bite of the cold in age. Now Blackie took new hope, for ahead was a shelter and some hay. He walked stiffly from the truck.

They would not need him for a day or so. Until then he would be fed.

From his little ranch on top of the hill Glue Butler looked down at the scene below. He liked to call his little place a ranch. It reminded him of the old days. Really it was a small clearing in the timber. When the city ceased its northward growth and turned south, the ranch would vanish and bungalows would spring up by the score. Taxes made a deep hole in his returns, for he was really ranching on residential land, but with good garden crops and rigid economy, he managed to hold his own.

Each morning he looked below and tried to imagine that he was on a bench, and the flat ground at his feet was a grassy cañon floor on which contented cattle grazed. When one is old and has seen much, when the eyesight is dim, it is not difficult to paint beautiful scenes over squalid reality. And this morning a horse stood in the south pasture beyond the ranch houses.

"B'gosh!" he muttered aloud. "I went cold all over at sight of that old horse down there; something about the way he ambled, reminded me of Blackie." He rubbed his hand over his eyes. "Blackie, ah yes; good old Blackie. The night of the stampede he saved my life. Another time——"

Glue Butler was lost in a past so vivid as to seem real. The bad lands, canteen empty, and Blackie plodding steadily with his nearly unconscious rider lurching in the saddle; the swollen tongue, cracked lips, the laugh of death, then water. Blackie found it; it was in his old stamping grounds.

Glue Butler straightened up in sudden bewilderment. "Golly," he breathed. There was a trace of disappointment in his tone "Golly, I thought I was young again, with Blackie. I musta been asleep. That horse down there in the corral sure reminded me of Blackie the way he walked. I wonder——" He shook his head in sad denial. "No, fate wouldn't give old Blackie any such break as that. Fate is hard at times, but not that hard; still——" He recalled a number of harsh decrees fate had issued. Then he made his way down the steep trail to the corral.

The horse was eating again. He heard men talking about him. Some thoughtless person had turned him loose to die, and because he was game, he had not died. The refinery people now had him without cost. It was tough.

"Tough!" Butler muttered. "And he does look like Blackie. For Blackie's sake I ought to do something, but I can't. I couldn't buy him, and I could hardly afford to feed him until spring. I guess I'd better go."

Butler turned away, but something turned him back again. He stood in doubt. Then he felt that nameless chill akin to excitement sweep through his body as it had done the moment he noticed the horse. He puckered his lips and gave a peculiar whistle.

The horse seemed to shake age from its tottering limbs. The head came up with something of the old pride, the eyes rolled around roguishly.

"B'gosh!" the man cried, then whistled again.

The horse stumbled toward him in a pathetic attempt to gallop. The man compressed his lips real tight, and two tears came from his faded eyes. "It *is* Blackie!" he cried.

Glue Butler climbed stiffly over the corral and placed his arms about the horse's neck.

Then after a long time Glue Butler left the corral and climbed stiffly up the hill. He estimated various costs necessary to clearing a bit of the timber away and make pasture land. Slowly he shook his head.

"I can't do it!" he muttered. "And when they found I wanted Blackie, they asked fifty dollars for him; trying to cash in on sentiment—it ain't right!"

It was night with just a bit of cold wind coming from the mountains. Down below the refinery a watchman was making his rounds. Butler looked down and listened. The wind was just right to carry a whistle. Just supposing a man on a bench wanted his horse in the cañon to come to him? He took a deep breath, thrust his fingers into his mouth, and whistled.

Below he heard the thud of hurrying hoofs, then silence. Again he whistled, and waited. Something crashed, and it sounded very much as if a heavy body had forced its way through a fence. The hoof beats became louder and louder.

The watchman was hurrying toward the corral, lighting his way with an electric flash light. Presently he found the place where the horse had broken through. There were no human footprints in the wet ground, just hoofprints. He scratched his head.

"Never knew a half-starved horse to leave a manger full of hay before. I can't figure it. Well, morning will tell what happened."

On the bench above him a gnarled hand reached into the darkness and felt a familiar nose. He rubbed it. "Blackie," Butler whispered. "You old pirate, I knew you'd come. Have a doughnut, Blackie; you used to like 'em fine!"

The horse accepted the doughnut with apparent relish, then followed Butler to the shack that was to serve as a stable, temporarily.

"Now tie in to that grain and we'll get some meat on your bones. Here's a blanket I've fixed up until you are stronger."

Even after he had done everything possible to make the horse comfortable, Glue Butler lingered and relived the old days. Somewhat abruptly he remembered there would be a tomorrow and consequences to face. He would fight. It was the least he could do for old Blackie, who had saved his life twice. With a final slap of affection, Butler left Blackie to warmth and slumber.

Voices aroused Butler early the following morning. The refinery superintendent, watchman, and a policeman were there.

"Horse stealing!" announced the police officer briefly.

The superintendent nodded. "An old cowman like you should have known better than to steal a horse. In the old days they'd string you up."

"Yep! And I didn't steal any horse. That horse out in the barn is old Blackie. He was stolen from me while I was in the hospital years ago. I got the papers to prove title to him. He came to me last night, and I took him in same as I would take in any old pardner."

"Tell all that to the judge," said the policeman, "and come along."

The superintendent turned to the watchman. "Take the old nag back where he belongs. Tell the boys to start things going!"

Glue Butler froze in his tracks. He knew what that order meant. He leveled an indignant finger at the superintendent. "Get this!" he snarled. "I've got mighty little to live for, and you've got a lot. If you kill old Blackie for glue, so help me, I'll drill you if it's the last act of my life! I mean that!"

The other laughed easily. "You heard that, officer? Threatens to murder me." He turned to the watchman. "Get the horse," he repeated. "And be quick about it!"

At the foot of the steep trail the patrol wagon was waiting. Butler was hustled in and driven away. He caught a final glimpse of the watchman coming down the trail. Blackie followed, bracing his stiff legs, sometimes sliding, again walking slowly, as if sensing his fate.

"B'gosh!" Butler panted. "I'll drill him!"

Then his thoughts became bitter. What chance had a poor old man like himself fighting a wealthy corporation? None! It took money in this man's country to get justice. He had no chance. When it was all over, he would take the law into his own hands—the old law of the West—the justice not written on books.

They booked him at police headquarters, and that afternoon he faced Judge Sloane for a preliminary hearing. Stealing a horse was good for a term in State's prison. The judge was known as a "mean cuss!" Ask any offender in the reformatory or prison whether Judge Sloane ever gave a man leniency. Besides that, the judge had just received his annual tax statement, and he was in a very bad mood. Who wouldn't be? He gave one man a short shrift; "threw the book" at a second, and then the clerk called:

"Butler! Charged with horse stealing, your honor!"

"Horse thief, eh? Well, what have you to say for yourself, Butler. You are bow-legged, I observe; ridden horses a lot. You should know better!"

The refinery superintendent was called. He was an old friend, the judge called him Sam. Butler heard it, and saw the look of understanding that the superintendent flashed at the judge. Butler felt that he had not a chance.

The judge listened attentively.

"And," the witness concluded, "he threatened to kill me if we killed the horse!"

The judge remembered his tax statement just then. "Threatened to kill you?" he roared. "How about it, Butler!"

"Yes, I guess I did say something like that. I did discover my old nag down there in the corral, and I did try to buy it. This cuss asked me fifty dollars; tried to cash in on my love for an old friend. I'd just paid my last year's taxes, and that left me flat broke."

"Taxes, eh? I know all about taxes. Go ahead, Butler, you didn't buy this horse because you'd paid your taxes, and because they wanted fifty dollars for him. So you stole him? Is that it?"

A prisoner squirmed. "The old boy is yowling for raw meat to-day; he'll throw the book at that old guy and bang him over the head with the gavel for good luck," he whispered.

"I didn't steal him," said Butler. "He came to me in the night, and I took him in. I never went near the corral!"

"The watchman tells me he heard a peculiar whistle, and the old horse responded instantly," exclaimed the superintendent hurriedly.

The judge frowned. "Were you whistling last night, Butler?" he demanded.

"Some, just two or three notes!"

"Butler, you are constructively guilty of inducing that horse to leave Sam's stable. In my eyes that is guilt. Do you think Blackie or any horse is worth the trouble you've gotten yourself into!"

"Yes, sir!" answered Butler promptly.

"Sam, let's see your title to this horse," demanded Sloane.

"You understand, your honor, that the horse was a stray animal, and the police department——"

"Was there an auction sale as provided by ordinance ——"

"No, because we are the only firm hereabouts engaged in such work. An auction is a useless expense!"

The judge frowned at Butler, the prisoners, and finally at Sam. He was thinking of the tax statement. It was little short of robbery, official robbery it was, and beyond the reach of any judge.

"Sam, confound your skin, I'm ashamed of you. Taxing a man's love for an old horse, and taxing without the color of title. Sam, get out of my sight. If that horse isn't in Butler's possession by ten o'clock to-night, I shall regard you in the light of a thief."

Glue Butler jumped to his feet. "Thanks, your honor, for——"

"Sit down, you horse thief!" shouted Sloane. "Now, Sam——"

"I gave orders for the horse to be killed, your honor, and in case this has been done, I'll appreciate it if you'll fix a price that shall be paid to Butler in view of your unusual ruling."

"Sam, if they've killed that horse, I'd hate to be in your shoes. Butler looks to me like he'd been a wild cat in his day, and still had a yowl or two left in his system. There's the telephone."

The superintendent's hands were shaking as he dialed the plant number. "He did?" he exclaimed in surprise. "He has? No, there is nothing to be done now!"

Glue Butler looked stunned. Yes, there was justice in the courts for a man without funds, but it had been thwarted at the eleventh hour. He wished he had brought his gun. Failing in that, he still had his hands. Perhaps before court police could pull him off, he might get his revenge.

The superintendent was speaking. "Blackie got away; kicked one of my men and broke three ribs. Knocked down the fence, and went up the trail to Butler's place."

Sam mopped his brow. A sigh escaped him as he saw Glue Butler relax slightly, then quickly reach for his hat.

"Next case!" growled the court.

A TICKET OUTSIDE

By ROBERT ORMOND CASE

Author of "Twenty Pokes Of Gold," etc.

WITH THE upriver wind howling at his back, "Wild Pete" Judson mushed alone on the Dawson-Whitehorse Trail. The temperature was already far below zero. Chill tides of air, sweeping up the mighty Yukon Basin, bore on their breath a hint of impending and vaster deeps of cold. High crags moaned beneath the flaming stars and ghostly banners of wind-driven snow wavered and streamed from hummock and ridge.

It was the kind of night in which experienced mushers did not put forth on the trail for any reason short of life and death. They preferred, rather, to crouch beside red-bellied heaters with fuel stacked high near by, while stout walls shook. Stay close to heat that was life, so the wisdom of the North whispered. And let 'er blow!

Wild Pete knew all this, having spent thirty-four winters on the Yukon. He had his reasons for braving the terrors that drummed and trumpeted through the arctic night. Those reasons were sufficient, according to his lights. He hugged them close as he stumbled behind the sled in the swirling gloom. He chuckled over them, like a miser counting gold. The hate that was in him, the accumulated spleen of thirty years, roared through his veins in defiance of the thundering forces of cold and dark.

He whipped his dogs on, though the starved and scarecrow animals were already weaving over the trail from exhaustion. No musher could have driven dogs against such a wind. Few could have driven them with it, at these temperatures. He was killing the team, he knew; but what of it? He would have no further use for them after he got to Whitehorse. He couldn't give them away. They were worthless, broken in body and spirit, half-blind and crippled. The Mounties wouldn't let him turn them loose to starve. If the team would take him a few miles farther—until he had passed Joe Platt on the trail—he would abandon them and go on to Whitehorse on foot. Folks would have plenty to say about a musher who would leave dogs in that condition on the trail. Whatever they said wouldn't scorch his, Pete's, ears. He'd be on his way Outside. Let them talk! To blazes with them all!

He laughed aloud as he swung around the bend and came into view of the Hootalinqua stage station. It was perfect. He had planned it all to a nicety, and it was developing as planned. He would have time to stop five minutes, maybe more, at the stage station. He would tell old "Porcupine" Smith, stage tender, all about it. Porcupine, in turn, would tell the rest of the boys downriver. There would be no misunderstanding as to why, and under what exact circumstances, Wild Pete Judson was heading Outside!

He pulled up on the trail just outside the glowing,

ice-spangled window. He could see old Porcupine vaguely, crouching beside the roaring heater. Only the single room was lighted; the rest of the building, with its various log lean-tos, bulked darkly in the gloom to right and left. The instant he halted, the dogs fell immediately to the snow. They peered at him through frost-rimmed eyes, without hope. When he made no move to unharness them, they curled up in shuddering balls, heads resting on paws, their plumed tails protecting muzzles and eyes from the speeding surface snow.

Wild Pete threw his whip upon the sled and stamped to the threshold. Before his fumbling hand found the latch, the door was flung open. He was seized upon, dragged inside, and the door slammed shut. Swift as the maneuver had been, a blast of wind swirled across the room. The heater roared. The oil lamp flickered.

"Phooey!" said Porcupine Smith, the station tender, peering at him through faded eyes and dusting his hands with a significant gesture, "I thought you was Joe Platt. He's due any minute now. You got dogs out there, Judson? Why don't you turn 'em loose?"

"Ain't staying but a minute," returned Wild Pete.

H E WRIGGLED out of his parka and cast it and his mittens upon the floor. He had been a booming man, huge and arrogant, when he had come down the Yukon with gold-mad thousands, Klondike-bound. Now, though his frame was shrunken and his features seared and twisted by bitter decades, he thought of himself as booming and swashbuckling still. He peered knowingly at Porcupine as he strode to the heater and extended gnarled hands into its sphere of warmth.

The old station tender said nothing. He knew that Wild Pete was fairly bursting to answer questions, and he stubbornly refused to ask them. He threw more fuel into the heater. A can of hot toddy was simmering on the hearth. He pushed it farther back. He had prepared it for Joe Platt, to warm Joe's insides when he pulled in with the stage from upriver; but Joe had not yet arrived.

"Cold, ain't it?" said Wild Pete. "Listen to 'er blow!"

"I been listening to 'er," returned Porcupine, "and thinking about Joe. He'll be chilled to the marrow by the time he rolls in. Facing the wind all the while! But I got some hot toddy fixed for him. That'll warm him up."

"Hot toddy, eh?" said Wild Pete, licking his lips.

"For Joe," repeated Porcupine.

Wild Pete grunted, shrugging his shoulders. He looked hard at Porcupine and grinned, displaying huge, broken fangs.

"Yeah," he said, nodding. "Joe'll be cold, plenty cold.

Driving a horse stage like that ain't like mushing behind dogs. You got to set and take it. Hell of a job he's got, eh?"

Porcupine said nothing. He drew forth his pipe and filled it, studying Wild Pete with placid eyes. The latter rubbed his hands together, cocking his head as the wind whistled and screamed about the eaves.

"Well," he said loudly, turning away. "I guess I'll shove off before my dogs get too stiff to travel. I'm leaving this blasted country, old son. Let the wolves have it. You and the rest of the optimists and half-wits can rot here. Particularly Joe Platt. You know why I'm pushing through to-night? I'll tell you why." His voice was muffled and growling as he wriggled into his parka. "Because I want to pass Joe Platt on the trail."

"Sure," Porcupine nodded, pretending to understand. "You used to be pardners with Joe. Now you're going Outside. He's staying on. You'll never meet up again. So you crave to tell him good-by." He nodded, puffing on his pipe. "That's fine, Pete."

"Bah!" said Pete, his sullen features swelling with rage. "You couldn't have missed it further if you'd put your alleged mind to it. You don't get the picture a-tall." He delved in the pocket of his parka, drew forth a moosehide poke and waved it aloft. "See that? It's dust. Eighty ounces! It's my ticket Outside. It's a stake for them soft an' easy years. Down yonder where the sun's shining and the birds are singing and the wind don't blow. It's the Promised Land Joe's always dreamed about. He'll never make it. He's driving his blasted stage, chained to his penny-ante job in this God-forsaken wilderness. I pass him on the trail, heading up-river. *And laugh!* Got it now?"

"Hm-m-m," said Porcupine. "Sounds like you've been nourishing some sort of a grudge." He eyed the poke narrowly. "Judson, where'd you get that dust?"

"Dragged it from the pot," Pete boasted. "A little here and a little there. Salted it away. Good ol' Joe didn't miss it. He was always so pop-eyed and trusting like that. It's a laugh I've been saving for thirty years. Feel sorry for me all the while, will he? Tell the world there's real dirt under all my oneriness? There was, at that. Eighty ounces is what it totals."

He returned the poke to his pocket with a flourish. He stooped and picked up his mittens.

Y OU MEAN to say," continued Porcupine, with a species of awe, "that you had that stake when Joe paid your fine down to Dawson? You had it when he took this stage job to keep the both of you from starving this winter? You had it five years ago when he dragged you from the mush ice and nursed you through that spell of pneumonia? You had it when he was freighting to Birch Creek and grubstaked you on the Little Cultus stampede?"

"I started the ol' retirement fund on the Little Cultus." Pete grinned. "That claim was supposed to be a blank, you savvy. Joe figures it was to this day."

"Well, Judson," said Porcupine, knocking the ashes from his pipe, "I thought I'd met up with some snakes in my time. You're the lowest reptile that ever crawled and crept. Any average two-by-four crook can knife his fellow man. You're worse than that. You've consistently and deliberately gouged the only lad in the North who held faith in you to the end. Yes, by gravy, and then you make a brag about it!"

"Go on," urged Pete, with relish. He drew on his mittens, grinning still. "That's music, ol' son."

"Hm-m-m," said Porcupine. "Are you *that* low? Can't be reached, is that it? What'd you tell me all this for, Judson?"

"I'll tell you what for," said Pete. He spoke with sudden, savage emphasis. "So you'd tell Joe, when he rolls in. In case I didn't have time to give him the whole picture when I pass him. He'd figure it was too cold to leave his horses stand long. So you and Joe could talk it over, shaking your heads and nodding in unison. So all the other old-timers down the river would know about it, and whisper and cuss and tell the world they never heard of such oneriness. Blast the whole lot of you! You've been down on me from the first, more than thirty years ago. I was a crook and that's all there was to it!"

"And you *were* a crook," Porcupine insisted. "Look at the record. You've been robbing Joe blind from the first."

"And from the first," said Pete, "Ol' sanctimonious Joe's been pointing out the error of my ways. 'You got the wrong slant on things, Pete,' he'd tell me. You're headin' for Hades in a handbasket. You got to do right by your fellow man,' he says. 'You got to shoot square. Otherwise you'll get tripped up at the show-down. It's one of them natural laws.' " He slapped the pocket that held the gold. "That's O. K. by me, you understand, Porcupine. Let Joe have the credit. Let him be one of those square guys. Me, I got the dust."

For a space Porcupine stared at him beneath lowered brows. Then he removed the pipe from his lips and pointed with it toward the door.

"This station's too small for you, Judson. The Yukon likewise. Doggone it, man! You an' Joe are both coming into the home stretch. You're old, broken down. There ain't but a few springs left for you both to see. What kind of dreams you going to have out yonder, amongst the flowers and sunshine, thinking of Joe?"

"Whenever I think of him," said Pete, "I'll laugh, a regular guffaw. Between the two of us, who was the sap, after all? Who held 'em in the show-down?"

"Phooey!" said Porcupine. "If Joe wasn't so easygoing I wouldn't give much for your chances when you pass him on the trail. Leave the door open a mite when you go out, Judson. This place needs airing."

IT WAS hard to start the dogs. In a matter of minutes they had become cold-blooded, their exhaustion chaining them to the snow. But Pete had mastered the Eskimo trick of laying his lash on a dime at ten paces. He flicked the right ear of his lead dog and grinned as the animal leaped up in agony. It was the leader's sore ear. In a reverse motion, bringing the lash back, he raked the flank of his wheeler, at a point where scars of ancient battle had left the hair short. He knew the vulnerable points of each of the dogs, and his mittened right hand rose and fell with an expert motion.

Because death on the trail was preferable to being cut to ribbons as they lay, the team staggered up one by one. Pete broke out the sled. A blast of wind pressing on them from the rear, icy as interstellar space, helped the outfit to get under way. With gathering momentum they drifted on into the dark like black and ghostly shadows fleeing before the storm.

The Dawson-Whitehorse Trail was broad and smooth where the wind paralleled its course. Where the icy tides rolled obliquely across it, the man-made trough had narrowed. Surface snow, hard as fine sand and infinitely more cold, flowed eternally with the current. On the Hootalinqua grade, where the trail rose over a mountain spur, following the edge of the cliff, a huge drift sloped down almost sheer for two hundred feet to the frozen bosom of the river.

His dogs were toiling midway up this grade when Pete heard the sound of approaching bells. The stage was coming. He swung the team over to the river side but did not take to the snow. He halted them there, flung down his whip and pushed back the hood of his parka.

Since the Klondike, when horses had replaced dogs on the Dawson-Whitehorse run, an unwritten law of the North had evolved. Horsedrawn traffic, on a narrow trail, must swing into the deep snow and leave the right of way to the dogs. Thus as the bells rang forth nearer and clearer at the top of the grade, and the horses dipped down, coming at a fast trot, Pete stood his ground. He could see Joe's swaddled figure, muffled to the ears in robes. He knew that his own outfit was equally visible to Joe.

Pete laid hold on his poke with a mittened hand and dragged it forth, grinning. Joe would not stop long. Two minutes, perhaps three. It would be long enough to comprise a perfect moment, a scene, a setting, that would stay with him, Pete, down through the fat, sun-lit years. Every detail of it would be etched upon his memory—the scream of the wind above them; the flaming stars and the cold; Joe peering at him in bewilderment, his shoulders hunched. Man, what a picture!

As the horses bore down upon him, Pete's jovial mood turned to surprise, then to disbelief, and finally —all but too late—to searing rage. For it was plain that Joe, recognizing him all too well, was attempting to run him down.

"Pull over!" Pete bellowed. "Pull over, blast you!"

The dogs leaped desperately from underfoot. The horses, without slackening speed, crowded together in passing. Heavy runners sheared into the rickety sled, overturned it, crushed it. Only by a furious lunge that sent him wallowing over the crest and on the face of the mighty drift, was Pete himself able to avoid being trampled and ground underfoot.

Holding himself with outspread arms and legs from sliding down into the depths, Pete peered up through the berserk rage that had given him his name in the North. He glimpsed Joe's face. Joe was grinning. He held his horses to undiminished speed. The music of the bells faded down the grade, dwindled and were finally lost on the flat below.

PETE LOOKED about him slowly. The dogs had broken loose from the sled. Rolling and tumbling in a snarl of harness, they had completed the long descent to the frozen bosom of the river. One had clawed free from its moosehide bonds. It let off across the ice; the others followed, harnessed still. They ran at a spraddling, ungainly lope, quartering across the wind. Something in the quality of their undeviating flight—suggesting bondage, death, and an unloved master left far behind—told Pete that he was looking his last upon them. They would chew loose from their harness. They would hole in until the storm blew over. If they lived, they would scatter into the wilds. Having known Wild Pete Judson, the paths of man would see them no more.

The loss of his dogs, the wrecking of his sled, the scattering of his equipment, these were minor matters. *He had lost his gold!* Somewhere in his frenzied leap to safety, he had loosened his grip upon the poke. It was gone.

He was all but submerged in the loose face of the drift. Only his shoulders, arms, and head projected above its surface. He inched himself upward slowly, thrusting deep with hands and feet, and holding what he had gained. Wind-driven pellets bit into his face like myriad tiny fangs. He groped blindly as he mounted, burrowing like a mole, searching for his

gold; but he knew even before he had achieved the crest that the search was in vain. His every effort, impacted through the fluffy mass that was itself poised on the brink of crumbling, was sending the heavy poke deeper into the abyss.

It was gone! The gold would stay in the drift until the spring thaw, and the thaw would carry it into the river.

Though he faced this fact and knew it was final, he searched for minutes longer, mouthing imprecations, his voice rising in a hoarse, sobbing note. He crawled along the trail, prowled like a jackal among the ruins of his sled. All hope died, presently. Only his rage was left. He rose up, snarling, and at a stumbling run, charged down the grade into the teeth of the wind.

Joe had arrived at the station, long since. The horses had already been put away. The stage stood deserted in the snow, whitened and still. Wild Pete leaped past it, clawed the latch upward and burst through the door. He slammed it shut behind him and stood leaning against it, arms outspread.

"Where's Joe?"

Porcupine, standing alone beside the stove, made no reply. A bleakness in his face mellowed a little as he heard Pete's blasphemous story.

"Lost your dust, eh, Judson? Joe crowded you off the trail, wrecked your sled and cut your unfortunate dogs loose?" He clucked sympathetically. "Well, well! Come along. Joe's out back."

He led the way to the woodshed, lamp in hand. The frost in the walls glittered and twinkled all about them. The feeble light flickered. Joe was seated on a chopping-block, his back to a tier of wood. His mittened hands were outstretched, as though they still grasped reins.

"The horses followed the trail and fetched him in," Porcupine explained. "I've said all the while he was too old for the winter run. Too cold! Froze where he sat. Well, why not? He couldn't hope to see but a few more springs. He didn't suffer. He ain't cold now."

Pete studied Joe's face. It was rigid, as though cast in stone. He knew it had been thus long before they had passed on the trail. Strangely enough, here was engraved no memory of cold, loneliness, weariness, or defeat. Joe's smile, rather, was that of one who has fallen asleep on a sunlit bench, in a region where flowers bloom and birds sing always, and storms never blow.

"He beat you Outside, after all," said Porcupine. "Pushed you off the trail and made you lose your dust, eh? Well, well, Judson! On second thought, just you step inside. We'll kill that hot toddy I had fixed for Joe. We'll drink him luck across the River. *And we'll all laugh together!*"

Tough Enough

By LUKE SHORT
Author of "King Colt," etc.

WHEN KATE saw him ride in from the north, a tall, big-boned man with caution in his manner, she thought he was one of Drury Warms' riders, and she almost looked away. But when he stopped in front of Warms' Emporium, turned in his saddle and looked sharply at the station and its stockpens, then at this single street of a half dozen buildings paralleling the tracks that was the town of Warms, she knew he was looking for something: not the hotel where she stood behind the wide windows, not the saloon which he could have seen as easily, and not for a man—most of all, not for a man. She knew that because she was sure now he was a stranger, and when he went on down the dusty road out of sight to McGrew's feed stable, she set down the pitcher of water for the window geraniums and watched.

Over where the four cars were waiting against the stock pens, she saw Wilsey Boone leave his conversation with the telegrapher, mount his horse and ride the hundred yards across the baked, sage-stripped frontage to the saloon. He was watching the stranger, his head turned down street.

A rider came out of Warms' Emporium, looked down toward McGrew's, then hurried across the street. He passed Kate at the window and went in the saloon.

"Like a rock thrown in a quiet pool," Kate thought, as she went back to the kitchen for some more water.

When she returned with the pitcher full, Drury Warms had come in from the saloon and was seated in the lobby with Wilsey Boone, and he said to her curtly, "He didn't stop here, did he?"

"No."

Drury sat quietly, the cigar poised unlit in his frail fingers, as he looked past Wilsey at the street. It was formula, Kate thought, remembering the last man who had ridden into town this way. That was three months ago, and he was still here, this George Dufreese, tending bar next door, one of Drury Warms' men. Of course, George was weak, or it never would have happened. His horse had disappeared the night of his arrival, and, since a man must have either a horse or a train to take him across these endless sage and alkali flats, he had stayed. And he had been greeted the same way the new man had been—scrutinized from the same chair Drury Warms now sat in.

"He picked a bad time," Wilsey Boone said, and shifted his burly body restlessly in his chair, watching Warms and the street with those quiet, hard, black eyes.

Drury said nothing. He lighted his cigar now and settled back in his chair, watching, utterly patient, utterly confident.

"You don't suppose he's a marshal?" Wilsey said.

"Where would he come from?" Drury said impatiently, without looking at him.

"That's right."

Two riders came in from the north and turned and went past the window toward the saloon, and Wilsey said, "There's the boys," and got no answer from Drury.

Then Drury said, "Here *he* comes."

Kate picked up her pitcher and started toward the kitchen with it, and Drury said without looking at her, "You stay here."

KATE OBEDIENTLY turned and came back to the desk, her face blank, a little tight, but resigned. The only thing betraying her nervousness or her distaste was a small gesture of brushing back her hair. It lay smooth and sleek and corn-colored against her temples and fell to a low knot at the base of her neck where it met the collar of her basque.

She heard the door open and looked up from the geraniums in the window and said pleasantly, "Good evening," wanting to make up for Drury's stare.

"Evening," the man said. He was a little taller than she thought he would be, but dusty, more saddle stiff than he looked at first. There was little flesh on his skull, so that his cheekbones seemed high and sharp, but not high enough to hide the hard insolent stare he gave Drury and Wilsey while he still contrived to touch his hat. He tramped in with the heavy walk of a tired man and dropped his warbag and canteen at his feet. He leaned on the counter, while Kate pulled out the register.

"A hot ride," he said.

"Yes, in any direction," Kate answered, smiling a little.

When he had signed his name she said, "I'll show you your room," but he held out his hand for the key and said, "I'll find it."

"It's the third on your right then, upstairs."

Again he looked at Drury, this time a little longer, and then ignoring Wilsey, he walked up the stairs, his boots loud and deliberate on the treads and in the hall above.

"Well?" Wilsey said.

Drury rose and went through the side door into the saloon, Wilsey trailing him, looking up the stairs with those hard speculative eyes.

"Frank Sessions," Kate said reading in the register. No town given—as if he weren't even going to bother to bluff, as if he didn't believe this scattering of buildings fronting a railroad that ran straight across these endless miles of sagebrush flats had the power to hurt him.

She went back to the kitchen to help Mrs. Sais with supper, but she found herself unaccountably restless, expectant. But when she heard the cattle coming, she dropped her work and went back into the lobby.

She found him looking out the big front window, his big hands rammed in his hip pockets. Out in the dusk, where minutes before the air had been so clear that she had been able to see the distinct bulk of the Seven Sleepers eighty miles to the south, there was a fog of stirred dust; and she could make out the jogging backs of a thick stream of cattle wedging its bawling way past the hotel and toward the stockpens. Five riders harried them, their cries sharp in the still air.

And then she saw Drury, who had been watching Sessions from the door into the saloon. Quickly, Kate walked past Drury up to the desk and began fumbling beneath it, her head down. Drury's step as he walked past her up to Sessions was firm, slow.

Kate rose. Drury was standing behind and a little to one side of Sessions, who had not seen him.

"Nice cattle," Drury said, removing the cigar from his mouth.

SESSIONS TURNED slowly, indolently, and regarded Drury a moment, his profile sharp and hard to Kate.

"They were. They've been pushed hard," Sessions said, without criticism, almost without interest.

"That's the railroad's fault," Drury said. "You drive when they can spare the train—not before, not after."

"I don't see it here," Sessions said.

Drury's bland face settled into hardness and then suddenly he laughed noiselessly. "You wait a few minutes. It'll be in before the cattle are loaded."

Sessions waited a silent moment then wheeled and went over to a chair. Drury went back into the saloon, and when he was gone, Kate felt Sessions' hard inquisitive look bearing on her.

He said suddenly, "I reckon I rode in here at the wrong time."

"Yes," Kate said, almost inaudibly, then added, even more softly, "If you can, you'd better go."

Sessions only scowled, but did not move. Under his gaze, Kate picked up some paper and headed back for the kitchen, feeling her face hot as she went.

She heard his steps behind her and then his voice, "Miss . . ."—He was right there in front of her when she turned, his hard face curious, down-looking, intent —"Somebody makes big tracks around here. Is he the one?"

He was referring to Drury, of course, and she said, "Mr. Warms? Yes. It's his town."

He looked sharply at the saloon door and then back at her and grinned faintly. And then he left, Kate watching him as he tramped his heavy way into the saloon. She was still watching when Wilsey came in the front door on the heel of Sessions' exit, and walked past her, pausing with one foot on the stair. He jerked his head toward the saloon. "Did he leave his key?"

"No."

Wilsey went silently up the stairs, his square, bent back almost a banner of his vindictiveness.

In the saloon, Drury saw Sessions enter and go to the bar. The four other men playing poker with Drury under the newly-lit kerosene lamp, watched Drury.

who said quietly, "Let's make this stud," while he shuffled the deck without looking.

The far-off wail of a train whistle sounded before the hole card was dealt, and Drury shuttled his gaze over to the two men at the far end of the bar. In answer to their look, he nodded imperceptibly. Then he called, "George."

The bartender lounged off the back bar and came over to him. He was a middle-aged man in shirtsleeves, colorless, his saddle of sandy red hair dividing his bald skull. Only his eyes, reserved, untroubled, would have given a man a key to his character.

"Go get supper, George," Drury said. George turned away and Drury said distinctly, "Tell your customer to step over, please."

In a moment, Sessions walked over.

Drury said with graciousness, "I didn't want to close bar on your pleasure, but my help must eat." He indicated the bottles on the green felt at his elbow. "Join us, if you care to."

Sessions waited for the introductions which would be Warms' quiet way of forcing him to give a name, but Drury only waited, too, silent, as Sessions regarded the players with a kind of arrogant thoughtfulness, and then reached for a chair.

"I'll even buy in the game," Sessions said quietly, "if it's open."

The train clanged in just as the first hand was dealt. George untied his apron and put it under the shelf when a man entered the room and came over to the bar.

IT WAS Berry, the telegrapher, and he wanted a drink. While he waited, he ripped off his alpaca cuffs, watching Drury's game, then took his own bottle and walked over to the table. As George went out, he saw Berry sit down and heard him call for a hand.

Outside, George leaned against the door a moment, listening, knowing that the time had finally come and welcoming it, but with an enormous excitement. He was a plain-looking man at best, his collarless shirt soiled at the neck, his hands white and soft and contrasting strangely with his thin and hair-fuzzed arms. Automatically, he reached for a cigar in his shirt pocket and then started back down the corridor to the dining room, the cigar forgotten.

Kate spoke to him as he passed through the dining room and he went into the kitchen and out the back door. At the pump, he made a quick racket, but did not wash. Turning away, he sought the shadow of the hotel and walked down it to the street. It was empty, dark, and he walked across it toward the station.

Out in the stockpens, by the light of several lanterns, the cattle were being loaded, the rough shouts of the riders, the bawling concert of cattle and the clanking breath of the engine giving him cover enough for what he wanted.

He went quickly in the shabby waiting room and turned to the agent's wicket. The door was unlocked. Inside, a kerosene lamp was burning low in its bracket. Crossing the room, he glanced quickly at the telegraph key and then leaned over and blew out the light. Darkness fell like a blanket and he waited a moment, motionless, listening.

The key was silent. Seating himself in front of it, he reached out and by feel and hearing he started its swift rat-a-plan—C.H., C.H., C.H., over and over in growing excitement. It was the agent's call in Jungo, a county seat, a hundred and forty miles to the west. Insistently, monotonously, he called, then ceased, ready for acknowledgment, and when it did not come he called again. The hard sharp patter of his key became more insistent. He shifted faintly in his chair as he stopped again, and then suddenly, as hard and almost as sharp as a gun report, his call was answered. He smiled a little. Out there in dry, wind-bitten Jungo, the agent was waiting.

Hard, expertly, George stuttered out his message, picking his own story out by ear in that thick darkness. When he was finished, he signalled *repeat*, and went through it again. Then, without waiting for acknowledgment, he stood up and walked to the lamp. It was cool now. He placed it on the floor, under the desk, struck a match, lit it, placed it in its bracket and let himself out of the office.

Out in the night, he listened again for a moment, then walked swiftly back to the hotel, entering, as he had left, through the kitchen. Once there, he seemed to know what he was about. Ignoring the cook, he poured himself a cup of coffee, took a cake from several dozen lying on a floured board, and then leaned against the cupboard, eating it, watching the cook, his eyes veiled, his face impassive.

"Supper's on," the cook said presently.

"Not hungry," George replied, setting his coffee down and grimacing. He put a soft hand to his stomach. "Too many cigars, not enough air."

"*Es verdad*," the cook said idly.

In the dining room, the stranger was eating alone. Kate was over by the sideboard, counting out the silver.

"Your supper's ready, George," she said, as George passed her.

"Not hungry," he said, "I ate a little in the kitchen."

Kate looked up swiftly at him, about to speak her amazement, when George, who had stopped, smiled faintly, watching her. "I said, I ate in the kitchen. Don't you remember?"

She did not answer, and George turned and walked

out into the lobby, his face settling into slackness and stupidity again. One of Drury's riders was sitting in the deep leather chair where he could see the entrance to the dining room.

"How's things, George?" the rider said.

"*Poco-poco.* But I'm off my feed, Ed," George answered, and turned wearily into the saloon.

THE GAME was still going on; Berry still had a hand in the game. George put on his apron and drew out a toothpick and leaned against the back bar, picking his teeth, staring at space with that peculiar air of brooding which is the exclusive property of bartenders. After one of the McGrew kids came in with a bucket and he drew beer for her, George drew the *Stockman's Gazette* from beneath the bar, spread it on the sleek mahogany and read it—or pretended to. But he listened.

He heard Drury Warms and Wilsey Boone and Berry, the telegrapher, go in to eat. He saw Sessions come in, and Sessions asked him if he had any Oregon papers and George gave him some. Sessions sat down at a vacant table and read. Drury and Wilsey and Berry came back, and after that, the man who had been watching Sessions from the street disappeared.

Still George listened. When he heard a rider out on the walk, he looked up. The rider entered, slapping dust from his Stetson and went over to Drury and said, "All up, Drury."

Wilsey Boone and the telegrapher got up then and went out with the rider. In another ten minutes, George heard the train pull out and he breathed deeply. Turning, he poured himself a glass of whiskey and found Sessions watching him, those bleached eyes probing, curious.

George patted his stomach and grinned sourly. "You don't see many of us behind the bar drink, do you?"

Sessions said, "No."

"My stomach." George said wryly. He reached in his shirt pocket and brought out a cigar and held it up, saying. "Too many of these. They don't let me feed right," after which he lighted up and went back to the *Gazette.*

He was glad when six cowhands, Wilsey Boone among them, tramped in and demanded drinks. He was working hard. A little of the tension had eased off now, but George wasn't deceived. Through it all, he managed to avoid watching the door, so that he didn't appear to see Berry bolt through the door and walk straight over to Warms.

"Can I see you a minute, Drury?" Berry said in a hard swift voice that stopped the game dead.

Drury got up and walked into the lobby after Berry. "What is it?" he asked, as soon as the door was closed

behind him. Then, before Berry could answer, Drury said, "Kate, get out of here."

Kate picked up her knitting and went back into the dining room. "Now what is it?" asked Drury.

"Somebody's been on that key," Berry said. He told it all with a kind of bitter, frightened violence. "I heard my call and answered. It was Jungo, asking for a repeat. I says 'what repeat?' and Holden—he's agent at Jungo—says am I crazy. I said 'send it back.'" He drew a paper from his shirt pocket and handed it to Drury and Drury unfolded it, reading Berry's scrawled message:

Four carloads of stolen cattle leave Warms on No. 4 tonight. Cut out and hold and get in touch with Tuscarorah and Weybolt, Oregon County sheriffs. Refer my authority to U. S. Marshal, W. C. Preston, Reno., and come make arrests.

"Stop the train," Drury said.

"Hell, I can't. It's clear all the way to Jungo."

Drury looked at the paper, his face white with fury. "You mean you can't do a thing—can't wire it's a joke, can't stop the train, can't get it around Jungo."

"That's it, they've wired Preston and got an answer," Berry said desperately. "It's Sheriff Jelke in Jungo wantin' to verify those counties."

"Then Holden has got it to Jelke," Drury said more quietly.

"To Jelke and Preston."

Drury rammed the paper in his pocket and took out a cigar and looked at it absently, almost with surprise at seeing it in his hand.

"They'll be swarmin' over here day after tomorrow, with a railroad investigator, too," Berry said hoarsely.

"Yes."

"Ain't you—what do you aim to do?"

"What time did that message go out from here?" Drury asked mildly.

"I don't know. I didn't—"

"Go and find out then."

Berry hesitated a second, then started. At the door he said, "What will I tell Holden?"

"Details later," Drury said.

DRURY STOOD in that same spot until Berry came back and said, "It went out at seven three."

Drury wheeled and went back into the dining room. Kate was reading at one of the tables and looked up at him as he entered.

"Get Mrs. Sais," he ordered.

"She's gone to bed, I think."

"Get her."

Kate went out. When she returned with the cook, Drury had not moved. He had a fresh unlit cigar in his mouth, and he said, "Sit down, both of you."

When they were seated he said to Kate, "You were in here when that stranger—Sessions—ate supper?"

"Yes."

"All the time?"

"Yes."

"He didn't leave, then."

Kate said with a faint stirring of anger. "You ought to know. You had a man watching him, so he wouldn't go near the pen."

Drury did not smile; he simply ignored this. "Who all have you served tonight?"

"You and Sessions and Wilsey and McGrew and ourselves," Kate said. "That's all."

"Not George?" Drury said quickly. "He didn't eat?"

Kate hesitated a moment. "He ate in the kitchen, I think."

Drury shuttled his hot gaze to Mrs. Sais, "Did he?"

"Si."

"Speak English!"

"Yes."

"Was he there all the time?" Drury asked.

Mrs. Sais' face started to go blank, the presage of that feigned stupidity which has been the sanctuary of her people, but one look at Drury Warms' face changed her mind. She said sullenly. "I don't know."

"Think," Drury said mildly. "Think hard—awful hard."

Mrs. Sais said hurriedly, "No. She's go out."

"Where?"

"The pump."

"For how long?"

"Quien sabe?" she said sullenly, and when Drury started to walk over to her, she slid out of her chair and stood behind it. "Veree long," she said quickly shrinking back.

Drury looked now at Kate. "I used to expect those lies from your mother. So you've started too?"

He wheeled and walked out and said to Berry, waiting in the lobby, "Get Wilsey."

When Boone came out, Drury said quietly, "George is the marshal, not Sessions. He tipped our hand to the sheriff in Jungo. Your name's on the waybill, isn't it?"

Wilsey nodded.

"Then you'll have to hide out for a stretch." He held out his hand. "Give me a gun."

Wilsey flipped out a gun and Drury took it, hefting it, then brushed back his coat tails and rammed it in his hip pocket and said, "Maybe you better come along too."

GEORGE KNEW what was up when Drury approached the bar, but not by Drury's face, which was as bland and inscrutable and prideful as ever. It showed in the face of Wilsey Boone, although George had not realized Boone's eyes could be more baleful than they always were. Something had gone wrong. Ten feet down the bar and under it was the shotgun—too far. George thought mildly behind his relaxed, impassive face, "Now isn't that hell? Isn't that hell?"—no more, only that, as he looked up at Drury and said, "Yessir, Mr. Warms. What'll it be, the same?"

Drury did not answer him immediately. He was looking at the array of bottles on the back bar. Then his gaze shuttled to George and he smiled thinly and said, "I've got a cold, George. Have you any rock and rye?"

"Rock and rye," George echoed and turned promptly. In the bar mirror he saw Drury's hand leave the counter, his arm bend. He laughed between his teeth even as he gripped the bottle and turned and threw it in Drury's face. Before it struck, a shot hammered out hard and flat and queerly explosive and Wilsey Boone drove into the counter, his gun clattering to the floor. George only caught a glimpse of Sessions standing by the table, gun leveled, as he dived down for the shotgun. He came up with it cocked to see Drury Warms standing away from the bar, one arm across his mouth. The other weaving arm held out a gun which he fired, then. George just laid the shotgun on the bar and pulled the trigger and watched Drury knocked over backwards; and then it occurred to him that he had every man at the corner poker table covered—every man in this room, with the exception of Sessions.

George said quietly, "Do the right thing, boys. I've still got a load here and it's not birdshot. If you'll look down there on the floor you'll see what it can do to a man."

They were standing now and their hands came up. Berry came running in now from the lobby, and he was well within the room before he caught sight of George.

"Walk over and take their guns, Berry," George invited. "Just put them on the table. When you're through, you'd better go—all of you. There's a deputy U. S. Marshal in town tonight, and if you can beat his wire to those lower Oregon counties, you're luckier than I think you are."

Afterwards, when they were gone George pulled out a cigar and leaned over the bar and looked down at Wilsey and then at Drury—and then at Sessions.

"Why did you do that?" he asked curiously. "I thought I looked like a bartender. And if it hadn't been for you I would of looked like a pretty dead bartender."

"Instinct," Sessions replied. "I didn't even like to see a man who looks like a bartender shot in the back. I don't play that way."

There was a knock on the lobby door and George picked up his shotgun and said, "Come in. And come with your hands empty."

Kate stood in the doorway. Drury Warms was out of her line of sight, and almost casually, Sessions yanked the green felt from his table and spread it over Warms, so that it hid him.

George said, "I don't know who this'll make the happiest, Miss Kate—you or me. Warms is dead."

When Kate looked over at Sessions she noticed the gun in his hand. He did too. He rammed it back in its holster and George said, "After I light this cigar, I'm going to work. Maybe you better step back and wait for us, Miss."

She left, George took off his apron and came out and knelt by Wilsey Boone, saying, "Since you ain't allowed to take scalps anymore, this ain't so much fun."

He emptied Wilsey's pockets, and when he came to a letter, he picked it up and read the name, "Frank Sessions," aloud. He read the letter inside, taking a long time to do it.

Then for a time he sat staring at the letter, thinking.

He did not see Sessions move his chair away. He heard him clear his throat, and George said quickly, "Don't that beat hell? Wilsey Boone was Frank Sessions. I remember his description come through back when I was working with Preston four months ago."

He gave Sessions plenty of time and then looked up at him. "He's wanted for an old murder, this Sessions was," George went on, and he studied Sessions thoughtfully.

Sessions said nothing, his eyes less hard, more curious.

George said, "The way I remember it, it was a killing in one of them Arizona feuds when Sessions was a lad of sixteen."

"That's a long time to remember a killing," Sessions said quietly. "Seems people ought to forget sometime."

"Uh-huh. Seems like one of the other outfits come into a little sudden money and got a bench warrant out for all the Sessions. They tell me warrants can be bought in some places in Arizona if a man puts up a little bounty money to boot."

Sessions said nothing. George took the letter and laid it on the bar and looked down at Wilsey. "Well," he said gravely, looking at Sessions. "You killed Sessions. You feel like taking reward money? There's two thousand, if I remember right. And you're the one that brought him down."

"Give it away," Frank Sessions said in a level voice.

When Drury and Boone lay side by side on the floor, George locked the door and blew the light and the two of them went into the lobby of the hotel.

Kate sat quite still, watching them, when George said, "If you'll come back with me, Miss Kate, I'll give you some help."

They left Frank there. He stood in the middle of the lobby, bewildered. That letter—it had been in his warbag. And it was found on Boone who probably stole it. And this marshal believed it—or did he? Frank Sessions could not decide.

"I've got to get out of here," Frank thought. He went upstairs. When he came down with his canteen and warbag, George and Kate were waiting for him.

"I'll walk down to McGrew's with you both," she said.

The town was really deserted now—not a horse at the long hitchrack, the only light in town at McGrew's shack, behind the stable. McGrew was gone, the stable deserted.

When they got to the corral behind it, there was one horse standing by the down poles which the other horses had been stampeded through. It was Frank's horse. George looked at it and said, "Did you ever hear that a U. S. Deputy Marshal can commandeer a mount as well as help?"

Frank stirred a little and looked down at Kate, who was watching him. "I hadn't," he said.

"Sure." George said softly. "I'm a coward. I've got to take your horse." He looked at Kate and said, "If I wasn't such a coward, I'd stay here and see you through this, Miss Kate. If they come back, there'll be trouble you know."

"There's nothing left. It's all over," Kate said.

George saddled up and then shoved some bills into Frank's hand and mounted. "I've got to run before they stop to figure out just how big that bluff was."

"Goodbye," Kate said. "You know I can't thank you."

George reached in his pocket and pulled out a folded piece of paper. "I almost forgot to give you that," he said to Kate.

He shook her hand, and then shook Frank's.

"You know," he said quietly, "if a man ever tried it, he'd find this was pretty good range." He wheeled his horse and rode off west, soon losing himself in the shadows of the stockpens.

They watched him go, and then Kate took the paper he had left her and ripped it in half and dropped it and started to go.

"Wait," Frank said. He knelt and picked up the paper and unfolded it and pieced it together in the dim light of the lantern which hung in the archway. It was the page of hotel register containing his name. Below it was scrawled, "Don't burn your bridge before you cross it."

Frank looked up. "He knew. I was wondering."

"Yes," Kate said. "He knew. He knew a great many things."

"But why?" Frank asked softly. "Why did he do it?"

Kate smiled faintly. "I know what he said to me."

"What?"

"He said, 'You kick a man around long enough and he's going to get tough. He's tough enough right now.' "

Frank pondered this a moment, the paper still in his hand. Then he looked down at it again and read, " 'Don't burn your bridge before you cross it.' What does that mean?"

Kate looked at him a long moment, her face serene, calm. "You don't know?"

"No."

"My stepfather, Drury Warms, owned this town—all of it. He owned a ranch too. They're mine now. Frank Sessions is dead, buried, acknowledged so by the testimony of a Deputy United States Marshal." She paused, "Don't you see, Frank? This is the one place you can live, where your past is buried and no one will be curious?" When he said nothing, she went on, "He seemed to know about you. He told me that you were foreman on a New Mexico spread for seven years until you got word of this warrant. It's unfair. He knew it. So do I. So do you. He was trying to make it square."

"But the bridge. What did he mean?" Frank asked quietly.

"This is your bridge—this, here. Cross it to safety. Burn it, go away, and—and you'll get tough, Frank. Don't you see?"

"I see," Frank said softly. He fell in beside her as they started up the deserted street. Presently, he felt her hand through his arm, and the tightness that had gathered in him seemed to dissolve.

"Do you want the job—as my foreman?"

Frank put a very large hand on her small one and said quietly:

"I'm plumb out of matches, Kate. I couldn't burn anything—not a bridge, anyway."

Where our reading and writing waddies get together with **POWDER RIVER BILL**

CLIMB DOWN, hombres an' hombresses, an' rest for a mite. Because soon as we shake out the kinks we gotta fork leather again an' hunt for three missin' hombres. Yes siree. This *Stampede* posse has plumb important work to do *muy pronto!*

The first of these lost jaspers is Leonard Olson o' Everett, Washington—the second is William LaMarr of Parkersburg, W. Va.—and the third hairpin is none other than our own Dishpan Charlie!

Whoa! Hold 'er tight, waddies. Yup, Dishpan has plumb disappeared. I'll tell you all 'bout him later. But first comes Leonard Olson as his big brother is sure anxious to find him. Here's what his brother says:

Western Trails, 1931

2725 Nassau St.,
Everett, Wash.

Dear Bill:

I have a brother that I am very anxious to see. His name is Leonard Olson. He is eighteen years of age, blond and about 5 feet 10 inches tall.

Haven't seen him for a number of years, but would like to locate him, and be responsible for his welfare. I got his description from the people where he last stayed. I'm sure he reads your WESTERN TRAILS so it would help a lot. Thanks very much,

Yours,

LOUIS OLSON.

We sure will take a look-see, Louis, an' do all we can to corral that lost kid brother of yours. An' you let us know how you make out on your private hunt. For if he doesn't show up at seein' this, we o' the *Stampede* will keep right on lookin' for him. Yuh betcha!

Now hombres an' hombresses, curly-haired Miss Mabel here is kind enough to say a few words on behalf o' William La Marr's mother who is worried 'bout him.

Step right up, Miss Mabel.

725 Market St.,
Parkersburg, W. Va.

Howdy Bill:

The WESTERN TRAILS is the best magazine that I ever read.

Here's my description—I have grey eyes, brown curly hair, five feet six inches tall. Tip the scales at 113 pounds, fair complexion.

I do hope that this letter will bring me just lots of letters from the far west. For I certainly do love to write letters.

Oh come on, boys and girls both, and write to this lonesome factory lass.

Bill, won't you please tell William La Marr to write to his mother. She is very much worried about him. She lives at the same place.

Most sincerely,
MABEL CAMPBELL.

Sure thing, Miss Mabel, we'd be plumb glad to scout around for this La Marr maverick. If he takes a look-see in at the W. T. spread our buckaroos will sure talk with him an' tell him 'bout his mother. Well, so you want some Pen Pards? The quickest way to get 'em is to amble over to the Pen Pards' bunkhouse across the way an' sign up.

Well, hombres an' hombresses, I'll tell you all I know o' the disappearance o' Dishpan Charlie. It was night before last that I was sittin' in the bunkhouse mendin' the strap on my saddle. The rest of the boys had gone into Cowtown Junction. I'd have gone, too—but Glenn Vernam an' Joe Archibald got together an' cleaned me purty. All of a sudden I hears Dishpan a-singin' out on the corral bar. Hombres, it sure was singin'. Ole Dishpan was puttin' his whole heart into the song.

Then Dishpan became quiet—
The next mornin' he was gone—lock, stock an' barrel!

We have to find ole Dishpan, folks, an' I want you-all to pitch in. Everyone o' you what has an idea what happened to that singin' chuck-wrassler write it down an' send it to me. We'll go over 'em all an' ride where the trail leads. . . .

S'long, pards, see yuh on Dishpan Charlie's trail.

Parallel Forms / 5 / Detective & Mystery

The late, mystery writer Raymond Chandler once presumed that someone "would determine just how and when and by what steps the popular mystery story shed its refined good manners and went native." Furthermore he maintained, "it takes a very open mind indeed to look beyond the unnecessarily gaudy covers, trashy titles and barely acceptable advertisements of the pulps to . . . recognize the authentic power of a kind of writing that, even at its most mannered and artificial, made most of the fiction of the time taste like a cup of lukewarm consomme at a spinsterish tearoom."

In his examination of this "power" Chandler speculated that its source was not plot or character, but "the smell of fear which these stories managed to generate. Their characters lived in a world gone wrong, a world in which, long before the atom bomb, civilization had created the machinery for its own destruction, and was learning to use it with all the moronic delight of a gangster trying out his first machine gun."

Implicitly this "smell of fear" was a response to and a reflection of the anxiety following World War I. It was not merely characters in stories who "lived in a world gone wrong," but everyone who had served in the trenches, or read of the horrors of warfare, or turned on the radio to hear of the latest Prohibition gang-land slaying.

*   *   *

Until the early 20's, the Detective and Mystery Pulps contained stories which were, by nature, narrative puzzles. Plot and character were only important insofar as they led the reader to the denouement. "Hard-boiled" characters were being written about by authors such as Carroll John Daly in *Black Mask Magazine,* but for the most part the solution of the puzzle was still the key to detective fiction as it had been since Edgar Allan Poe. This changed when Joseph T. Shaw became editor of *Black Mask* in the mid-20's. Shaw had returned to the States after five years abroad, during and following World War I. The attitude he brought to *Black Mask* would seem to reflect much of the expatriate's cynicism about life in these United States. Whatever his reasons, he meditated about shifting the emphasis of story values to those of character and the problems inherent in human behavior. Feeling that "the creation of a new pattern was a writer's rather than an editor's job," Shaw studied the authors who were already writing for *Black Mask.* He was most impressed with the work of Dashiell Hammett because "he told his stories with a new kind of compulsion and authenticity." Hammett had unknowingly shared Shaw's feelings for some time and was enthusiastic about his ideas. With Hammett in the vanguard, *Black Mask* became the model for many magazines which imitated its "hard-boiled" school of writers.

As Shaw noted, in the new pattern the main theme was character conflict; the crime or its threat was incidental. Raymond Chandler, who was perhaps the most fluent of the brittle *Black Mask* stylists, went on to describe the "hard-boiled" story's emotional basis: "it does not believe that murder will out and justice will be done—unless some very determined individual makes it his business to see that justice is done. The stories were about the men who made that happen." Describing the technical basis for the *Black Mask* type of story he said that "scene outranked the plot, in the sense that a good plot was one which made good scenes. The ideal mystery was one you would read if the end was missing."

The first four stories in this section show the evolution of the "hard-boiled dick," starting with a traditional expository puzzle story, and continuing with a trilogy of "hard-boiled" stories, each progressively broader in style. The last of these three, a "Dan Turner" story from the 40's, is so intensely colored that it becomes a parody of itself.

*   *   *

"Mr. Alias, Burglar," by Rodrigues Ottolengui appeared in 1916, in one of the first issues of the first of the specialized Detective Pulps, Street and Smith's *Detective Story Magazine*. A pastiche of the typical Sherlock Holmes mystery, it commits the cardinal sin of unravelling a stream of essential clues in the denouement instead of planting them for the reader to discover during the plot development. Nevertheless, it is great fun, and if you listen to the dialogue closely, perhaps you will hear the voices of Basil Rathbone as "Holmes" and Lionel Atwill as the arch-criminal, "Professor Moriarity."

*   *   *

"One Hour" was one of Dashiell Hammett's first "Continental Op" stories, appearing in 1924 in *Black Mask*. The "Op," a nameless investigator for Hammett's fictional Continental Detective Agency, grew out of his previous experience as a Pinkerton operative after World War I. "One Hour" incorporates many of the elements of Hammett's early stories: direct style, minimum of unessential detail, and maximum of action. Hammett keeps himself outside of the story, and lets his characters demonstrate everything. What makes this short-short story exceptional is the fact that all of the action takes place within the framework of one hour's time. The pace is fast, and to paraphrase what an admirer said of him, he shows how to attain the shortest distance between two points.

*   *   *

T. T. Flynn's "The Deadly Orchid" (*Detective Fiction Weekly*, 1933) sacrifices some of Hammett's terseness for a more free-swinging style. The dialogue is racier and reminiscent of the competitive wise-cracking of the memorable detective team, Mr. and Mrs. North. The story makes good use of locale as well as an unusual plot device involving bicycles, demonstrating the kind of color which was responsible for much of the popularity of the "hard-boiled dicks." Typical of the form at its peak, description of violence is kept to a minimum—the reader must fill in the details—and the story comes to a quick, neat close. "The Deadly Orchid" has such enjoyable scenes that the plot and its outcome become relatively unimportant—fulfilling the Chandler ideal.

*   *   *

"Death's Passport" by Robert Leslie Bellem completes the "hard-boiled" trilogy. It appeared in 1940 in *Spicy Detective*, an under-the-counter offshoot of this typically non-erotic, socially conscious genre. Bellem achieved a modicum of fame for his use of racy dialogue and characterization. In fact, his language was so colorful that the plot frequently disappears from sight and the characters parody themselves. Bellem's stories furnished S. J. Perelman with material for one of his funniest essays, "Somewhere a Roscoe . . ." The outer limits of Bellem's sexual inventiveness are further explored in "Labyrinth of Monsters" in the section dealing with sex.

*   *   *

Many writers who later achieved literary prominence, weathered the Depression on money provided by the Pulps—notably MacKinlay Kantor, whose novel *Andersonville* won the 1956 Pulitzer Prize. His introspective and atmospheric mystery story, "The Torture Pool," was published in 1932 in *Detective Fiction Weekly*.

*   *   *

Best known for his tales of fantasy and science-fiction, Ray Bradbury—Master of the Macabre—wrote for many of the Detective and mystery Pulps as well. "Wake for the Living" which first appeared in 1947 in *Dime Mystery Magazine*, is an unusual little "tongue-in-cheek" piece.

Mr. Alias, Burglar
by Rodrigues Ottolengui

A PERSON to see you, sir," announced Mr. Mitchel's man, Williams, entering the library and presenting a card.

"A person, Williams?" queried Mr. Mitchel, taking the card. He looked at his valet, and wondered why he should have spoken thus.

"Hope I'm not presuming, sir. He's a stranger, sir, and then his card—that's why I——"

"I see," said Mr. Mitchel, looking at the bit of pasteboard intently. "You may show him up. There will be entertainment for me to-day, after all."

The card was, indeed, an oddity. It was of the finest material and beautifully engraved. It bore the name, "Mr. Alias," under which was written in pencil, "Burglar."

Mr. Alias proved to be in appearance a gentleman. He was attired in clothing evidently made by a good tailor—fashionable without being extreme in style. Mr. Mitchel judged him to be between thirty-five and forty years of age; and noted that his keenly intelligent face was what men would call attractive, while women might use a more complimentary term.

"Mr. Alias, I believe," said Mr. Mitchel, rising, but not advancing to meet him.

"Yes. Have I the pleasure of addressing Mr. Mitchel?"

"Mitchel is my name. May I ask your business?"

"Burglary. You have my card."

"Your business with me, I mean?"

"I understand, but I need not modify my previous answer."

"Your business with me, you say, is burglary? Do you mean that you have come to rob my house?"

"I do not think I will say yes to that question. It would be too incriminating, and besides, such a reply would be lacking in finesse. Still, I do not mind admitting that when I go it would not surprise me if I should take some of your property with me."

"It would surprise me, however," said Mr. Mitchel tartly.

"That brings us to the object of my call," said Mr. Alias. "You have not asked me to be seated, but as our conversation may be long, I will put myself at ease. You will pardon my removing my overcoat? You keep your rooms quite warm."

He proceeded to take off his coat, which, with his soft hat, he placed on a table. Then he selected a comfortable chair and seated himself with the air of an old acquaintance. Mr. Mitchel admired the man's cool audacity.

"Of course," continued Mr. Alias, "I recognize that my card and my actions must arouse considerable curiosity in your mind, and I am afraid you have thus far formed rather a poor opinion of me. I do not blame you, for the fact is, I am not proud of my manner of introducing myself to you. It has been a little too theatrical, not in the best of taste. No, I hold that an offense against good form is almost a crime."

"While burglary, I presume, is one of the fine arts," interposed Mr. Mitchel sarcastically.

"That is according to the point of view. My calling, as I myself practice it, is, I flatter myself, almost an art. Burglary, though, hardly fits it. It is a bad word, a vulgar word, if you please, and somewhat inapplicable."

"Thievery perhaps might be better."

"Yes, perhaps so." Mr. Alias spoke musingly as though he were seeking the word that would most accurately express his thought. "It has a broader significance, and so applies to more conditions. Burglary, on the other hand, is connected in the mind with housebreaking. Now, I do not think I ever—no, I am quite sure I never have broken into a house. It is a boast of mine that when compelled to make forcible entrance I do not damage the building in any way, leaving marks for stupid policemen to quarrel over and for the press to chatter about as clews. That sort of thing is very inartistic. Ordinarily I prefer to gain entrance by use of my brains, rather than of my hands."

"As you have entered here, for example?"

"Quite so. I see you are beginning to comprehend, but I am not surprised, as from all that I have heard of you, I was quite prepared to do battle with a keen intellect."

"Then you have heard something of me?"

"Yes, indeed, or I should not be here. And I must admit that, considering my profession, pardon my calling it so, what I heard of you made me most anxious to meet you."

"May I ask what it is in particular that you have heard?"

"I am told that you rather despise men of my calling, that you belittle the skill of the average burglar. That I am not prepared to dispute with you, but then there are a few of us above the average. I have also heard that you think very little of detectives, claiming that their success depends largely upon the blunders of the criminals whom they detect. Have I been correctly informed?"

"I certainly have expressed such views."

"Then I understand that though deprecating the detective work of other men, you have done a little in that line yourself. In fact, that you have not as yet failed to solve any little affair to which you have deigned to bend your energies?"

"It is true I have not met with failure."

"I am very glad to find that I have been accurately informed; otherwise, all the fun of this adventure would be lost. Now to come to the point, for which you have waited with most commendable patience. I have called because I, too, have never met with failure."

"You mean that in the practice of thievery, you have never been detected?"

"That is the situation exactly. I have had a somewhat remarkable career, and though I have appropriated—I like that word better than any that you might suggest—though I have appropriated much of other people's property, I have never been detected, nay, never even suspected. Thus you with your record and I with mine were inevitably bound to meet, and, to use an astronomical term, as the conjunction promised to be interesting, I thought it well to hasten the moment."

"But, why? The mere fact that you are a thief, even though the most skillful of your class, is of no interest to me. Where is the problem?"

"You shall have it. But first, one more question. Unless I am mistaken, judging you now by myself, and placing myself, as it were, in your position, I should imagine that you would feel capable of thwarting a criminal, of preventing a crime; of detecting him as it were before he might accomplish his purpose. Am I right?"

"No. You are wrong," said Mr. Mitchel coldly, but watching his man keenly while apparently gazing out of the window. "You have mistaken my character entirely. I am not a policeman."

"But I thought you have maintained that such work is not done by policemen?"

"True. It is not, but it ought to be. Certainly it is not the work of a gentleman."

"Then why, pray, did you work on that suicide case?"

"What suicide case?" said Mr. Mitchel, turning on the man and speaking quickly.

"Why, the one where you prevented the woman from killing herself."

"Oh, that case," said Mr. Mitchel, apparently lapsing into a condition of apathetic attention. "That was merely a little experiment, by way of amusement."

"Still, you have made such broad claims, it seems to me," urged Mr. Alias, "that my little problem might afford you sufficient amusement to make it attractive to you."

"Well, what is your problem?"

"I have told you that I have never been detected in any of my—what shall I call them?—adventures. I sent you a card on which I had written a secret known only to a trusted few. My main object in coming here was to announce that I intend to undertake a burglary within a week and to suggest that you try to prevent it."

"That must depend upon two conditions. In the first place, I would not care to bother with the affair during the next seven days, as I have more important matters to engage my attention."

"Let us say, then, that the 'adventure' must occur between the eighth and fifteenth day from to-day. You see, I am very accommodating."

"Very. Now, as to what you mean by prevent? Make the word detect, and I will pit my skill against yours."

"But if you can detect, why should you not prevent?"

"I may prefer to permit you to carry out your scheme, and I may not. I must be free to act as I will. But if I detect, I do, in effect, prevent."

"This time I do not follow you."

"I mean that if you enter some house and possess yourself of certain property, your success is nullified if, on the following day, I can meet you with such proof as would convict you of the crime and make your imprisonment certain."

"I see your meaning, and will allow you so much latitude. To make this affair more diverting, might I suggest a little supper at a specified date after the 'adventure,' the expense to be assumed by the loser in this contest of brains?"

"That will be quite agreeable to me," said Mr. Mitchel. "Where shall the supper be served?"

"I suppose," said Mr. Alias, looking around him, "it would be too much trouble for us to eat here, in this room."

"No," replied Mr. Mitchel, laughing heartily. "We will have supper in this room by all means." Then he laughed again, but as though the cause of his merriment were some inward thought. Then he continued: "If you do not mind, I will make a little memorandum of our wager, for that is what it comes to."

"By all means; a proper precaution."

Mr. Mitchel seated himself at his desk and began to write. Evidently the pen did not suit him, for he wrenched it from the holder and threw it into the wastebasket, ignoring the good old saw that warns one not to throw away dirty water before procuring clean. He seemed to have considerable trouble in finding another pen. He rummaged among his papers and pulled out drawer after drawer in his search. From one of these a small parcel fell to the floor, where the soft tissue paper became unwound and revealed a magnificent diamond necklace. That Mr. Mitchel should have such a treasure is not surprising when we remember his hobby for collecting rare jewels. That he should be so careless as to expose the brilliants to a stranger apparently betokened that his search for the pen had for the moment cost him his self-control. It could have been only for a moment, however, for Mr. Mitchel snatched the parcel from the floor so quickly that it was questionable whether Mr. Alias had seen the necklace at all, especially as this gentleman had gone to the table to take a handkerchief from his overcoat pocket. Mr. Mitchell suddenly grasped a box of pens that had all the while been right before him, exclaiming under his breath:

"Had it been a snake, it must have bitten me!"

Then he wrote out rapidly the substance of the wager and handed the paper to his visitor.

"Is that your idea of what we undertake?" asked Mr. Mitchel.

"It seems quite accurate," said the other, after reading it.

"Then we will both sign it," said Mr. Mitchel; which they did.

"Why do you not sign your true name?" said Mr. Mitchel, rubbing his hand over the blotter.

"Oh! Then you do not think that my name is Alias?"

"I am hardly so stupid as that," said Mr. Mitchel, smiling. "It is only your *alias*."

"You are right. You are shrewder even than I had supposed. It is an *alias*, but I flatter myself rather an artistic touch. You see, your common burglar starts out with his own name. In some way, he earns a nickname from his companions, such as 'The Dude.' At first he is John Jones *alias* 'The Dude.' After he has dodged the police of several cities, he is caught, and his name in print is a succession of *aliases* all more or less stupid, especially as the true name heads the list. With me it is different. I adopted the name 'Alias,' as my stage name, partly to prevent the word being used in connection with myself, printed as it generally is in italics. More especially, however, I chose a new name because I fancy that my good old mother and father would not approve of my method of living."

"So your parents are still alive?"

"Alive and highly respected in a small town where they live quite happily and innocently on the proceeds of my roguery."

"I should think that with your keen sense of the fitness of things, that is, of some things, you would hesitate to send the old folks your ill-gotten gains."

"Money is money. I send mine to my people with as little compunction as you show when you buy fine raiment for your wife with Wall Street profits. It is all a matter of custom. Well, I think we understand each other. I'll be here promptly at seven on the night appointed." While talking, he was getting into his overcoat. Taking up a silk hat from the table and placing it on his head, he turned to Mr. Mitchel and said:

"I must thank you for your very courteous treatment of a stranger. Good morning!"

He was passing out when Mr. Mitchel detained him by touching him on the arm and saying:

"I will thank you to replace my silk hat where you found it. Your own, a soft one, is in your overcoat pocket, where you put it while I was looking for a pen, and when you were pretending to be getting a handkerchief."

"With pleasure. I return your property. You score first. Good morning."

Mr. Mitchel wrote a note to Mr. Barnes, asking the detective to call as soon as convenient, which he did on the following day.

"What can I do for you?" asked the detective, when he had been ushered into Mr. Mitchel's presence.

"Do you know a man who calls himself Mr. Alias?" asked Mr. Mitchel.

"Why, certainly," said Mr. Barnes.

"Is he a burglar?"

"He may be, though he has never been caught at it. But a crook is liable to turn his hand to anything to make a dishonest dollar. That is a maxim with detectives."

"And this fellow is known as a crook to the police?"

"He is a confidence man, the most expert in New York."

"Has he ever been caught and punished?"

"Yes. He has been in prison twice in this State, and I believe elsewhere also. But, of course, he would deny it. Has he tried any of his schemes on you?"

"You know that I am interested in problems involving the prevention of crime," said Mr. Mitchel, not giving a direct reply. "Well, I have information from which I am led to believe that this man will attempt burglary within the next two weeks. Can you have him watched for me?"

"Certainly. Night and day if you desire it."

"Do so. Put a good man on his trail, and let me have a report daily. That is all. I need not detain you longer to-day."

During the next two weeks the reports from Mr. Barnes' office reached Mr. Mitchel regularly. The first one that enlisted his active interest did not come in until only two days remained of the time during which Mr. Alias had undertaken to effect his crime. This report read as follows:

Alias to-day again met the servant girl who lives with the Randolphs, and from her we discovered that she has been bribed to admit him into the house between ten and eleven to-morrow night, while the family will be at the opera. If you wish, there will be no difficulty in arranging to have you admitted to the house, together with my man, prior to that hour. BARNES.

On the evening appointed for the supper at Mr. Mitchel's house, Mr. Alias arrived promptly, attired in a perfectly fitting dress suit of recent cut. Williams, who admitted him, apologized for Mr. Mitchel, who had been unexpectedly called out, but who would return within a quarter of an hour. A few minutes later Mr. Barnes arrived, having received an invitation from Mr. Mitchel. The note of invitation, however, had contained no intimation as to whom Mr. Barnes would meet. Less than ten minutes later, Mr. Mitchel came in and repeated the excuses which had been made for him by his man. He then formally introduced the two men and ordered supper to be served.

The repast was delightful. The viands were of the best and deliciously cooked, while the wines were plentifully supplied and of excellent quality. The three men chatted pleasantly, nothing whatever being said either by Mr. Mitchel or by Mr. Alias of the occasion of the meeting until the coffee and cigars were reached.

"I trust the meal has been to your liking, Mr. Alias," said Mr. Mitchel.

"It could not have been better had I ordered it myself," said that gentleman.

"Of course," pursued Mr. Mitchel, "under the circumstances, it was needful to keep account of the cost. Consequently, though the service has been with my own things, the eatables and the wines have been supplied by a caterer. Williams," said Mr. Mitchel, turning to his man, "you may present the bill to Mr. Alias."

Mr. Alias took the paper, looked it over carefully, and coolly replied:

"Very reasonable, considering the quality of everything." Then he tossed the bill to Mr. Mitchel, adding: "You pay it, I presume."

"I think not," said Mr. Mitchel, calmly lighting a fresh cigar and slipping down into a more comfortable position in his chair.

"Why not?"

"I think I ought to explain what we are talking about," said Mr. Mitchel, turning to Mr. Barnes. "This supper was the stake of a little wager between Mr. Alias and myself, the loser to pay the bill. Perhaps the story would interest you?"

"I am all attention," said Mr. Barnes.

"The affair is a little out of the ordinary," began Mr. Mitchel. "Mr. Alias called upon me two weeks ago and announced that he intended to commit a burglary. He offered to wager that I could not prevent him. I changed the word 'prevent' to 'detect,' and took the wager. I also asked for two weeks instead of one, as he had first suggested. I win the wager because I can explain every detail of the robbery which occurred last night, when Mr. Alias came into this room and abstracted a diamond necklace from my desk. Moreover, he has the property in his pocket now and I will thank him to restore it."

The detective and the crook looked first at Mr. Mitchel and then at one another in a quizzical manner. Mr. Alias was the first to regain his self-possession.

"This is but an assertion on your party and does not constitute legal proof," said he. "Proof sufficient for conviction, I think we agreed upon."

"You shall have all the proof you want," said Mr. Mitchel. "And, by the way, Mr. Barnes," he continued, turning toward the detective, "I have won your wagers for you also, have I not?"

"My wagers?" said Mr. Barnes, apparently mystified.

"Innocent, eh!" laughed Mr. Mitchel. "Well, you two are not so clever as you thought yourselves. Fooling with Mr. Mitchel is just a little like touching a moving buzz saw to see if it is sharp. Pardon the conceit. Now, I presume you two want the details."

Neither answered, and Mr. Mitchel continued:

"When Mr. Alias called here his mode of introducing himself was so unique, and his manner after I had admitted him was so good, that for a short time I was greatly puzzled and almost dared to hope that at last I had met with a crook who really had some brains. But while better than the average, a claim which he made for himself, I soon found that he was not above making slips, slips that were fatal."

"What slips?" asked Mr. Alias.

"You knew altogether too much about me," said Mr. Mitchel. Some things you may have heard from various sources, and therefore told me nothing. When you approached certain exclusive knowledge, even you seemed to realize that you were treading on dangerous ground. You wished to get to the point that I am interested in preventing crime, and you thought yourself clever to say that placing yourself in my position you would suppose that I would feel capable of preventing a crime. I doubted at once that you had arrived at that idea by purely deductive process of reasoning, but it was necessary for me to know positively. I therefore set a trap for you. You expected me to admit that I would take an interest in such matters, and I astonished you by flatly denying your proposition. You lost your head at once, and a moment later argued the point with me and asked why I had undertaken to prevent a case of suicide. That was sufficient. I had the whole scheme plainly before my mind instantly, and could afford to appear to drop back into my former attitude. You see, no one but Mr. Barnes knew about that suicide affair, and my management of it. Consequently I knew that he had sent you here."

"Why should I do that?" asked Mr. Barnes, with assumed innocence.

"Making a little test of my boasted skill, I suppose," said Mr. Mitchell, "and following the lead I gave you in the Remington affair. But there was another reason. Mr. Alias here had made a wager with you first, that he could conduct a robbery without detection by me; and secondly, that he could, unknown to me, steal something from this room. How I know this will appear later. He tried to win at least one bet from you when he deliberately attempted to walk off with my silk hat. But that was a poor compliment to me after he had warned me at the beginning of his visit, by saying that he would not be surprised if when he left the house he should take something with him. How did I detect him in that? To explain I must touch on another feature. After the true reason of his call had been stated there was no way for me to know where his intended robbery would occur. I received a hint of what was in his mind, however, when he audaciously suggested that the supper should be served in this room. That made me laugh. I laughed because by that speech, Mr. Alias, you placed the game entirely in my own hands. You were so sure of your own cleverness that you thought to add to your triumph by making me pay for a supper served in the very room where the robbery should have occurred. I took the reins at once, and from that moment really conducted the whole affair."

"You are not lacking in conceit yourself, are you?" sneered Mr. Alias.

"No, only mine is founded on fact and yours only on imagination. I suggested putting the agreement in writing as a means of going to my desk. I threw away my pen and searched for another for two reasons. I thus gave you a chance to steal something or to prepare to steal something, while all your movements were easily observed by me in a mirror which you had overlooked in your haste to accept the seeming opportunity. Thus I saw you put your soft hat in your overcoat pocket and also try on my hat. The rest was easy.

"Next, I purposely dropped the diamond necklace on the floor because when you came here on your errand I wished that you should steal that in preference to anything else. The temptation was too great for you."

"How do you know?"

"You will recall that I asked for an additional week? During that time I arranged my apparatus for automatic detection of my smart burglar, Mr. Alias. Be assured everything was ready for you on your arrival, including my absence?"

"Your absence?"

"Suspecting that Mr. Barnes had sent you here, I asked him to assist me by having you watched. How he must have chuckled to himself when writing out his fictitious reports to me daily. I do not suppose, Mr. Barnes, you even suspected that I had another detective from another agency watch this man, or you would not have told me all about his movements in this city when he was really out of town for five days."

"You beat me there," said Mr. Barnes.

"Of course, Mr. Barnes was, in a measure, your confederate. He was willing to lose his wager with you to defeat me, while his winning from you would, in a measure, soothe his feelings in case of failure. In due time, I was told by Mr. Barnes of your intention to rob Mr. Randolph's house, and I had the chance to enter the house with the connivance of the maidservant. I waited there until I felt assured that you had finished your job here. Meanwhile, what had occurred here? You called and asked for me. My man told you I had gone out, but would soon be back, and he brought you into this room. On retiring, he closed the door behind him, and everything seemed to be in your hands. You lost no time, but went over to my desk. You chuckled and even muttered aloud, 'This is too easy,' when you found the desk unlocked. You found the package containing the diamonds, and, reaching out, you took hold of it. The parcel seemed caught in some way, and you were obliged to pull a little hard to get it. Just then a slight buzzing noise overhead caused you to look up. Almost instantly there was a smothered explosion, a brilliant flash of light, and then complete darkness. You barely had time to thrust the parcel in your pocket when my man opened the door and looked in on you, saying:

"'Don't be alarmed, the fuse had blown out. Step this way and I'll light the gas in another room; there is none in this room.'

"You replied that you would not wait any longer, but asked him to tell me that you would be on hand promptly to-night."

"You seem well informed," said Mr. Alias.

"Very well informed. From the time that you entered the room every sound that you made was registered by a graphophone, the usual trifling noise of which I had effectually stilled by blowing powdered graphite into the works. The machine was started by Williams when he left the room the first time. When you went over to my desk and took hold of the parcel, as soon as you pulled on it you started the buzzing noise which was electrically produced. This noise made you look up and face a camera which was pointing toward you, properly focused. When you stepped on the rug in front of the desk, you, of course, had no idea that under it was a sheet of zinc resting over a bulb connecting with the shutter of the camera. When you stepped on it the shutter opened. When you stepped off after the explosion the shutter closed. The buzzing sound which caused you to look up was likewise a signal to Williams, who instantly touched a button, thus setting off a magnesium flash lamp by electricity, while with the other hand he then shut off the lights in this room, and hurried in to give you an explanation which you might accept, and which, apparently, did satisfy you. I hand you a very good print from the negative for which you unconsciously posed last night. You will see that the likeness is startlingly good, and you will also observe that the necklace is in your hand. If you desire, I will now start up the graphophone and permit you to hear yourself say: 'This is too easy.'"

"I'll take your word for it, I guess," said Mr. Alias, looking at the photograph.

"There is another little matter. May I look at the bottom of your shoes? Thank you. All has happened as I supposed. I noted when you called that you wore handsome patent-leather shoes, so I presumed there would be no reason why you should wear others to-night, or on the occasion of your burglarious visit. It is evidently your habit. Assuming, then, that you would come here with the same shoes worn last night, and as a precaution against the possibility that my electrical mechanisms might not work, I obtained a few thumb tacks from which I removed the points, and soldered to them instead points taken from small fish hooks. When you stepped on the rug you picked up, so to speak, two or three of these tacks, two to be exact. Since then, noticing something unusual in walking, you have torn off the heads of the tacks, but the fishhook ends resisted and are still in your soles."

"How did you know," said Mr. Barnes, "that he has the diamonds with him, and how is it that you risked his taking such valuables when he might have made off with the booty without coming here to-night?"

"I purposely arranged to be out when you two called to-night. But my phonograph was at home. During supper, Williams has received the message from the instrument, which he adroitly wrote out and smuggled to me with one of my plates. From this I learned the conversation that occurred between you two, while awaiting me, in which the bets between you are mentioned; the last words are in your voice, Mr. Barnes:

"'Put the things in your pocket. Quick! Here he comes!'"

"As to risking my valuables, the risk was slight, as they are but a duplicate set in paste of my wife's real stones."

One Hour

by DASHIELL HAMMETT

(Author of "The Tenth Clew")

*Like all of Mr. Hammett's detective stories, this tale
starts with a very ordinary police case, and just as you
think you have it all figured out, it takes several
unexpected turns and ends up with a bang.*

THIS IS Mr. Chrostwaite," Vance Richmond said.

Chrostwaite, wedged between the arms of one of the attorney's large chairs, grunted what was perhaps meant for an acknowledgment of the introduction. I grunted back at him, and found myself a chair.

He was a big balloon of a man—this Chrostwaite—in a green plaid suit that didn't make him look any smaller than he was. His tie was a gaudy thing, mostly of yellow, with a big diamond set in the center of it, and there were more stones on his pudgy hands. Spongy fat blurred his features, making it impossible for his round purplish face to even hold any other expression that the discontented hoggishness that was habitual to it. He reeked of gin.

"Mr. Chrostwaite is the Pacific Coast agent for the Mutual Fire Extinguisher Manufacturing Company," Vance Richmond began, as soon as I had got myself seated. "His office is on Kearny Street, near California. Yesterday, at about two-forty-five in the afternoon, he went to his office, leaving his machine—a Hudson touring car—standing in front, with the engine running. Then minutes later, he came out. The car was gone."

I looked at Chrostwaite. He was looking at his fat knees, showing not the least interest in what his attorney was saying. I looked quickly back at Vance Richmond; his clean grey face and lean figure were downright beautiful beside his bloated client.

"A man named Newhouse," the lawyer was saying, "who was the proprietor of a printing establishment on California Street, just around the corner from Mr.

Chrostwaite's office, was run down and killed by Mr. Chrostwaite's car at the corner of Clay and Kearny Streets, five minutes after Mr. Chrostwaite had left the car to go into his office. The police found the car shortly afterward, only a block away from the scene of the accident—on Montgomery near Clay.

"The thing is fairly obvious. Some one stole the car immediately after Mr. Chrostwaite left it; and in driving rapidly away, ran down Newhouse; and then, in fright, abandoned the car. But here is Mr. Chrostwaite's position; three nights ago, while driving perhaps a little recklessly out—"

"Drunk," Chrostwaite said, not looking up from his plaid knees; and though his voice was hoarse, husky—it was the hoarseness of a whiskey burnt throat—there was no emotion in his voice.

"While driving perhaps a little recklessly out Van Ness Avenue," Vance Richmond went on, ignoring the interruption, "Mr. Chrostwaite knocked a pedestrian down. The man wasn't badly hurt, and he is being compensated very generously for his injuries. But we are to appear in court next Monday to face a charge of reckless driving, and I am afraid that this accident of yesterday, in which the printer was killed, may hurt us.

"No one thinks that Mr. Chrostwaite was in his car when it killed the printer—we have a world of evidence that he wasn't. But I am afraid that the printer's death may be made a weapon against us when we appear on the Van Ness Avenue charge. Being an attorney, I know just how much capital the prosecuting attorney —if he so chooses—can make out of the really insignificant fact that the same car that knocked down the man on Van Ness Avenue killed another man yesterday. And, being an attorney, I know how likely the prosecuting attorney is to so choose. And he can handle it in such a way that we will be given little or no opportunity to tell our side.

"The worst that can happen, of course, is that, instead of the usual fine, Mr. Chrostwaite will be sent to the city jail for thirty or sixty days. That is bad enough, however, and that is what we wish to—"

Chrostwaite spoke again, still regarding his knees.

"Damned nuisance!" he said.

"That is what we wish to avoid," the attorney continued. "We are willing to pay a stiff fine, and expect to, for the accident on Van Ness Avenue was clearly Mr. Chrostwaite's fault. But we—"

"Drunk as a lord!" Chrostwaite said.

"But we don't want to have this other accident, with which we had nothing to do, given a false weight in connection with the slighter accident. What we want, then, is to find the man or men who stole the car and ran down John Newhouse. If they are apprehended before we go to court, we won't be in danger of suffering for their act. Think you can find them before Monday?"

"I'll try," I promised; "though it isn't—"

The human balloon interrupted me by heaving himself to his feet, fumbling with his fat jeweled fingers for his watch.

"Three o'clock," he said. "Got a game of golf for three-thirty." He picked up his hat and gloves from the desk. "Find 'em, will you? Damned nuisance going to jail!"

And he waddled out.

CHAPTER II

FROM THE attorney's office, I went down to the Hall of Justice, and, after hunting around a few minutes, found a policeman who had arrived at the corner of Clay and Kearny Streets a few seconds after Newhouse has been knocked down.

"I was just leaving the Hall when I seen a bus scoot around the corner at Clay Street," this patrolman—a big sandy-haired man named Coffee—told me. "Then I seen people gathering around, so I went up there and found this John Newhouse stretched out. He was already dead. Half a dozen people had seen him hit, and one of 'em had got the license number of the car that done it. We found the car standing empty just around the corner on Montgomery Street, pointing north. There was two fellows in the car when it hit Newhouse, but nobody saw what they looked like. Nobody was in it when we found it."

"In what direction was Newhouse walking?"

"North along Kearny Street, and he was about three-quarters across Clay when he was knocked. The car was coming north on Kearny, too, and turned east on Clay. It mightn't have been all the fault of the fellows in the car—according to them that seen the accident. Newhouse was walking across the street looking at a piece of paper in his hand. I found a piece of foreign money—paper money—in his hand, and I guess that's what he was looking at. The lieutenant tells me it was Dutch money—a hundred-florin note, he says."

"Found out anything about the men in the car?"

"Nothing! We lined up everybody we could find in the neighborhood of California and Kearny Streets—where the car was stolen from—and around Clay and Montgomery Streets—where it was left at. But nobody remembered seeing the fellows getting in it or getting out of it. The man that owns the car wasn't driving it— it was stole all right, I guess. At first I thought maybe there was something shady about the accident. This John Newhouse had a two- or three-day-old black eye on him. But we run that out and found that he had a attack of heart trouble or something a couple days ago, and fell, fetching his eye up against a chair. He'd been home sick for three days—just left his house half an hour or so before the accident."

"Where'd he live?"

"On Sacramento Street—way out. I got his address here somewhere."

He turned over the pages of a grimy memoranda book, and I got the dead man's house number, and the names and addresses of the witnesses to the accident that Coffee had questioned.

That exhausted the policeman's information, so I left him.

CHAPTER III

MY NEXT play was to canvass the vicinity of where the car had been stolen and where it had been deserted, and then interview the witnesses. The fact that the police had fruitlessly gone over this ground made it unlikely that I would find anything of value; but I couldn't skip these things on that account. Ninety-nine per cent of detective work is a patient collecting of details—and your details must be got as nearly first-hand as possible, regardless of who else has worked the territory before you.

Before starting on this angle, however, I decided to run around to the dead man's printing establishment—only three blocks from the Hall of Justice—and see if any of his employees had heard anything that might help me.

Newhouse's establishment occupied the ground floor of a small building on California, between Kearny and Montgomery. A small office was partitioned off in front, with a connecting doorway leading to the press-room in the rear.

The only occupant of the small office, when I came in from the street, was a short, stocky, worried-looking blond man of forty or thereabouts, who sat at the desk in his shirt-sleeves, checking off figures in a ledger, against others on a batch of papers before him.

I introduced myself, telling him that I was a Continental Detective Agency operative, interested in Newhouse's death. He told me his name was Ben Soules, and that he was Newhouse's foreman. We shook hands, and then he waved me to a chair across the desk; pushed back the papers and book upon which he had been working, and scratched his head disgustedly with the pencil in his hand.

"This is awful!" he said. "What with one thing and another, we're heels over head in work, and I got to fool with these books that I don't know anything at all about, and—"

He broke off to pick up the telephone, which had jingled.

"Yes . . . This is Soules . . . We're working on them now . . . I'll give 'em to you by Monday noon at the least. . . . I know we promised them for yesterday, but . . . I know! I know! But the boss's death set us back. Explain that to Mr. Chrostwaite. And . . . And I'll promise you that we'll give them to you Monday morning, sure!"

Soules slapped the receiver irritably on its hook and looked at me.

"You'd think that since it was his own car that killed the boss, he'd have decency enough not to squawk over the delay!"

"Chrostwaite?"

"Yes—that was one of his clerks. We're printing some leaflets for him—promised to have 'em ready yesterday—but between the boss's death and having a couple new hands to break in, we're behind with everything. I've been here eight years, and this is the first time we ever fell down on an order—and every damned customer is yelling his head off. If we were like most printers they'd be used to waiting; but we've been too good to them. But this Chrostwaite! You'd think he'd have some decency, seeing that his car killed the boss!"

I nodded sympathetically, slid a cigar across the desk, and waited until it was burning in Soules' mouth before I asked:

"You said something about having a couple new hands to break in. How come?"

"Yes. Mr. Newhouse fired two of our printers last week—Fincher and Keys. He found that they belonged to the I. W. W., so he gave them their time."

"Any trouble with them or anything against them except that they were Wobblies?"

"No—they were pretty good workers."

"Any trouble with them after he fired them?" I asked.

"No real trouble, though they were pretty hot. They made red speeches all over the place before they left."

"Remember what day that was?"

"Wednesday of last week, I think. Yes, Wednesday, because I hired two new men on Thursday."

"How many men do you work?"

"Three, besides myself."

"Was Mr. Newhouse sick very often?"

"Not sick enough to stay away very often, though every now and then his heart would go back on him, and he'd have to stay in bed for a week or ten days. He wasn't what you could call real well at any time. He never did anything but the office work—I run the shop."

"When was he taken sick this last time?"

"Mrs. Newhouse called up Tuesday morning and said he had had another spell, and wouldn't be down for a few days. He came in yesterday—which was Thursday—for about ten minutes in the afternoon, and said he would be back on the job this morning. He was killed just after he left."

"How did he look—very sick?"

"Not so bad. He never looked well, of course, but I couldn't see much difference from usual yesterday. This last spell hadn't been as bad as most, I reckon—he was usually laid up for a week or more."

"Did he say where he was going when he left? The reason I ask is that, living out on Sacramento Street, he would naturally have taken a car at that street if he been going home, whereas he was run down on Clay Street."

"He said he was going up to Portsmouth Square to sit in the sun for half an hour or so. He had been cooped up indoors for two or three days, he said, and he wanted some sunshine before he went back home."

"He had a piece of foreign money in his hand when he was hit. Know anything about it?"

"Yes. He got it here. One of our customers—a man named Van Pelt—came in to pay for some work we had done yesterday afternoon while the boss was here. When Van Pelt pulled out his wallet to pay his bill, this piece of Holland money—I don't know what you call it—was among the bills. I think he said it was worth something like thirty-eight dollars. Anyway, the boss took it, giving Van Pelt his change. The boss said he wanted to show the Holland money to his boys—and he could have it changed back into American money later."

"Who is this Van Pelt?"

"He's a Hollander—is planning to open a tobacco importing business here in a month or two. I don't know much about him outside of that."

"Where's his home, or office?"

"His office is on Bush Street, near Sansome."

"Did he know that Newhouse had been sick?"

"I don't think so. The boss didn't look much different from usual."

"What's this Van Pelt's full name?"

"Hendrik Van Pelt."

"What does he look like?"

Before Soules could answer, three evenly spaced buzzes sounded above the rattle and whirring of the presses in the back of the shop.

I slid the muzzle of my gun—I had been holding it in my lap for five minutes—far enough over the edge of the desk for Ben Soules to see it.

"Put both of your hands on top of the desk," I said.

He put them there.

The press-room door was directly behind him, so that, facing him across the desk, I could look over his

shoulder at it. His stocky body served to screen my gun from the view of whoever came through the door, in response to Soules' signal.

I didn't have long to wait.

Three men—black with ink—came to the door, and through it into the little office. They strolled in careless and casual, laughing and joking to one another.

But one of them licked his lips as he stepped through the door. Another's eyes showed white circles all around the irises. The third was the best actor—but he held his shoulders a trifle too stiffly to fit his otherwise careless carriage.

"Stop right there!" I barked at them when the last one was inside the office—and I brought my gun up where they could see it.

They stopped as if they had all been mounted on the same pair of legs.

I kicked my chair back, and stood up.

I didn't like my position at all. The office was entirely too small for me. I had a gun, true enough, and whatever weapons may have been distributed among these other men were out of sight. But these four men were too close to me; and a gun isn't a thing of miracles. It's a mechanical contraption that is capable of just so much and no more.

If these men decided to jump me, I could down just one of them before the other three were upon me. I knew it, and they knew it.

"Put your hands up," I ordered, "and turn around!"

None of them moved to obey. One of the inked men grinned wickedly; Soules shook his head slowly; the other two stood and looked at me.

I was more or less stumped. You can't shoot a man just because he refuses to obey an order—even if he is a criminal. If they had turned around for me, I could have lined them up against the wall, and, being behind them, have held them safe while I used the telephone.

But that hadn't worked.

My next thought was to back across the office to the street door, keeping them covered, and then either stand in the door and yell for help, or take them into the street, where I could handle them. But I put that thought away as quickly as it came to me.

These four men were going to jump me—there was no doubt of that. All that was needed was a spark of any sort to explode them into action. They were standing stiff-legged and tense, waiting for some move on my part. If I took a step backward—the battle would be on.

We were close enough for any of the four to have reached out and touched me. One of them I could shoot before I was smothered—one out of four. That meant that each of them had only once chance out of four of being the victim—low enough odds for any but the most cowardly of men.

I grinned what was supposed to be a confident grin—because I was up against it hard—and reached for the telephone: I had to do something! Then I cursed myself! I had merely changed the signal for the onslaught. It would come now when I picked up the receiver.

But I couldn't back down again—that, too, would be a signal—I had to go through with it.

The perspiration trickled across my temples from under my hat as I drew the phone closer with my left hand.

The street door opened! An exclamation of surprise came from behind me.

I spoke rapidly, without taking my eyes from the four men in front of me.

"Quick! The phone! The police!"

With the arrival of this unknown person—one of Newhouse's customers, probably—I figured I had the edge again. Even if he took no active part beyond calling the police in, the enemy would have to split to take care of him—and that would give me a chance to pot at least two of them before I was knocked over. Two out of four—each of them had an even chance of being dropped—which *is* enough to give even a nervy man cause for thinking a bit before he jumps.

"Hurry!" I urged the newcomer.

"Yes! Yes!" he said—and in the blurred sound of the "s" there was evidence of foreign birth.

Keyed up as I was, I didn't need any more warning that that.

I threw myself sidewise—a blind tumbling away from the spot where I stood. But I wasn't quite quick enough.

The blow that came from behind didn't hit me fairly, but I got enough of it to fold up my legs as if the knees were hinged with paper—and I slammed into a heap on the floor. . . .

Something dark crashed toward me. I caught it with both hands. It may have been a foot kicking at my face. I wrung it as a washerwoman wrings a towel.

Down my spine ran jar after jar. Perhaps somebody was beating me over the head. I don't know. My head wasn't alive. The blow that had knocked me down had numbed me all over. My eyes were no good. Shadows swam to and fro in front of them—that was all. I struck, gouged, tore at the shadows. Sometimes I found nothing. Sometimes I found things that felt like parts of bodies. Then I would hammer at them, tear at them. My gun was gone.

My hearing was no better than my sight—or not so good. There wasn't a sound in the world. I moved in a silence that was more complete than any silence I had ever known. I was a ghost fighting ghosts.

I found presently that my feet were under me again, though some squirming thing was on my back, and kept me from standing upright. A hot, damp thing like a hand was across my face.

I put my teeth into it. I snapped my head back as far as it would go. Maybe it smashed into the face it was meant for. I don't know. Anyhow the squirming thing was no longer on my back.

Dimly I realized that I was being buffeted about by blows that I was too numb to feel. Ceaselessly, with head and shoulders and elbows and fists and knees and feet, I struck at the shadows that were around me. . . .

Suddenly I could see again—not clearly—but the shadows were taking on colors; and my ears came back a little, so that grunts and growls and curses and the impact of blows sounded in them. My straining gaze rested upon a brass cuspidor six inches or so in front of my eyes. I knew then that I was down on the floor again.

As I twisted about to hurl a foot into a soft body above me, something that was like a burn, but wasn't a burn, ran down one leg—a knife. The sting of it brought consciousness back into me with a rush.

I grabbed the brass cuspidor and used it to club a way to my feet—to club a clear space in front of me. Men were hurling themselves upon me. I swung the cuspidor high and flung it over their heads through the frosted glass door into California Street.

Then we fought some more.

But you can't throw a brass cuspidor through a glass door into California Street between Montgomery and Kearny without attracting attention—it's too near the heart of daytime San Francisco. So presently—when I was on the floor again with six or eight hundred pounds of flesh hammering my face into the boards—we were pulled apart, and I was dug out of the bottom of the pile by a squad of policemen.

Big sandy-haired Coffee was one of them, but it took a lot of arguing to convince him that I was the Continental operative who had talked to him a little while before.

"Man! Man!" he said, when I finally convinced him. "Them lads sure—God! have worked you over! You got a face like a wet geranium!"

I didn't laugh. It wasn't funny.

I looked out of the one eye, which was working just now, at the five men lined up across the office—Soules, the three inky printers, and the man with the blurred "s," who had started the slaughter by tapping me on the back of the head.

He was a rather tall man of thirty or so, with a round ruddy face that wore a few bruises now. He had been, apparently, rather well-dressed in expensive black clothing, but he was torn and ragged now. I knew who he was without asking—Hendrik Van Pelt.

"Well, man, what's the answer?" Coffee was asking me.

By holding one side of my jaw firmly with one hand I found that I could talk without too much pain.

"This is the crowd that ran down Newhouse," I said, "and it wasn't an accident. I wouldn't mind having a few more of the details myself, but I was jumped before I got around to all of them. Newhouse had a hundred-florin note in his hand when he was run down, and he was walking in the direction of police headquarters—was only half a block away from the Hall of Justice.

"Soules tells me that Newhouse said he was going up to Portsmouth Square to sit in the sun. But Soules didn't seem to know that Newhouse was wearing a black eye—the one you told me you had investigated. If Soules didn't see the shiner, then it's a good bet that Soules didn't see Newhouse's face that day!

"Newhouse was walking from his printing shop toward police headquarters with a piece of foreign paper money in his hand—remember that!

"He had frequent spells of sickness, which, according to friend Soules, always before kept him at home for a week or ten days at a time. This time he was laid up for only two and a half days.

"Soules tells me that the shop is three days behind with its orders, and he says that's the first time in eight years they've ever been behind. He blames Newhouse's death—which only happened yesterday. Apparently, Newhouse's previous sick spells never delayed things—why should this last spell?

"Two printers were fired last week, and two new ones hired the very next day—pretty quick work. The car with which Newhouse was run down was taken from just around the corner, and was deserted within quick walking distance of the shop. It was left facing north, which is pretty good evidence that its occupants went south after they got out. Ordinary car thieves wouldn't have circled back in the direction from which they came.

"Here's my guess: This Van Pelt is a Dutchman, and he had some plates for phoney hundred-florin notes. He hunted around until he found a printer who would go in with him. He found Soules, the foreman of a shop whose proprietor was now and then at home for a week or more at a time with a bad heart. One of the printers under Soules was willing to go in with them. Maybe the other two turned the offer down. Maybe Soules didn't ask them at all. Anyhow, they were discharged, and two friends of Soules were given their places.

"Our friends then got everything ready, and waited for Newhouse's heart to flop again. It did—Monday night. As soon as his wife called up next morning and said he was sick, these birds started running off their counterfeits. That's why they fell behind with their regular work. But this spell of Newhouse's was lighter than usual. He was up and moving around within two days, and yesterday afternoon he came down here for a few minutes.

"He must have walked in while all of our friends were extremely busy in some far corner. He must have spotted some of the phoney money, immediately sized up the situation, grabbed one bill to show the police, and started out for police headquarters—no doubt thinking he had not been seen by our friends here.

"They must have got a glimpse of him as he was leaving, however. Two of them followed him out. They couldn't, afoot, safely knock him over within a block or two of the Hall of Justice. But, turning the corner, they found Chrostwaite's car standing there with idling engine. That solved their getaway problem. They got in the car and went on after Newhouse. I suppose the original plan was to shoot him—but he crossed Clay Street with his eyes fastened upon the phoney money in his hand. That gave them a golden chance. They piled the car into him. It was sure death, they knew—his bum heart would finish the job if the actual collision didn't kill him. Then they deserted the car and came back here.

"There are a lot of loose ends to be gathered in—but this pipe-dream I've just told you fits in with all the facts we know—and I'll bet a month's salary I'm not far off anywhere. There ought be a three-day crop of Dutch notes cached somewhere! You people—"

I suppose I'd have gone on talking forever—in the giddy, head-swimming intoxication of utter exhaustion that filled me—if the big sandy-haired patrolman hadn't shut me off by putting a big hand across my mouth.

"Be quiet, man," he said, lifting me out the chair, and spreading me flat on my back on the desk. "I'll have an ambulance here in a second for you."

The office was swirling around in front of my one open eye—the yellow ceiling swung down toward me, rose again, disappeared, came back in odd shapes. I turned my head to one side to avoid it, and my glance rested upon the white dial of a spinning clock.

Presently the dial came to rest, and I read it—four o'clock.

I remembered that Chrostwaite had broken up our conference in Vance Richmond's office at three, and I had started to work.

"One full hour!" I tried to tell Coffee before I went to sleep.

THE POLICE wound up the job while I was lying on my back in bed. In Van Pelt's office on Bush Street they found a great bale of hundred-florin notes. Van Pelt, they learned, had considerable reputation in Europe as a high-class counterfeiter. One of the printers came through, stating that Van Pelt and Soules were the two who followed Newhouse out of the shop, and killed him.

Detectograms—A Puzzle Feature

By Lawrence Treat

2. Murder Hunch

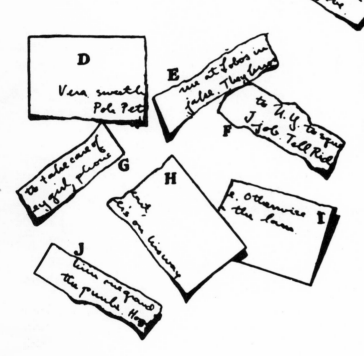

Magruder walked in without knocking. Vera was about to empty a trash basket into the incinerator, but Magruder prevented her. While he asked her rather vague questions, he stared at the contents of the trash basket.

If you were Magruder and saw these torn bits of paper at the bottom of the basket, what could you learn and what would you do about it?

1. In how many longitudinal strips had the letter been torn? □ 1 □ 2 □ 3 4 ☒ Because every strip has at least one straight edge.
2. Was the letter signed? □ Yes □ No
3. Is the entire letter apparently here? □ Yes □ No
4. Do you think it was from Healy? □ Yes □ No
5. Do you think the writer knows anything about the Jameson kidnaping? □ Yes □ No
6. Who was on his way (strip H)? □ Pal Healy □ Rider □ Pole Peter □ Chi □ Lobo □ jake
7. Where was he going? □ To N.Y. □ To Chi □ To Lobo's
8. For what purpose? □ To phone □ To tell Rider □ To squeal □ To take care of someone □ To take it on the lam
9. For what purpose is one grand (strip J) to be used? □ To get to N.Y. □ To take care of Vera □ To get hold of Pole Peter □ To take care of "me" □ To take care of the punk
10. Who is the punk? □ Vera □ Pal Healy □ Rider □ Lobo □ Pole Peter □ Chi □ Honey □ jake
11. Does the writer reveal his whereabouts? □ No □ Yes, where he is staying □ Yes, how he may be reached
12. Would it be advisable to arrest Vera at once? □ Yes □ No
13. Name the two people whose immediate arrests are the most important, for questioning or otherwise. □ Vera □ Honey □ jake □ Pal Healy □ Pole Peter □ Chi □ Rider □ Lobo
14. Write the complete letter.

DIRECTIONS

Read the statement. Study the documents. Answer the questions by checking the box next to the correct answer. The first question has been done and explained to show you the type of reason you should have in mind, although you need not write it out.

DON'T GUESS. There is a definite, logical clue to every answer.

STATEMENT

Detective Magruder, on a hunch that Pal Healy was the man wanted for kidnaping and murdering young Jameson, paid a visit to Vera Rawlins, Pal Healy's girl, in New York.

Ace High Detective, 1936

The Deadly Orchid

By T. T. FLYNN

Detective Harris Sighed Dreamily as Gloria Whitney Pressed Her Delicate Body Close to Him—But He Had Been Warned She Was as Dangerous as a Cobra.

"They're gone! Every stone and setting; while you played the fool and I played bridge."

THOMPSON, EASTERN manager of the Blaine Agency, said to me in the hotel room in Jacksonville, "Do dames fall for towheads like you, Mike?"

"Dames fall for anyone with a good line," I said, and waited. Six years' sleuthing with the Blaine agency had taught me that a fellow never knew what was coming next.

"You'll need a good line," Thompson grinned, fishing an old cigar stub out of his vest pocket. "There's a dame in Palm Beach who's responsible for the deaths of two men that we know of. And she's about ready to put a third scalp in her belt. I want you to meet her."

"Says you," I told him. "Figuring me for the third corpse, I suppose?"

"You never can tell." Thompson scraped a match under the edge of his chair and sucked on the cigar, rolling an eye at me as sober as a deacon.

"Who is this female execution squad—and where do I come in?" I asked him.

"She was baptized Gloria Whitney and has a string of aliases. Her nickname is the Orchid. Her specialty is blackmail. When she hooks a man he may as well pay up, take it on the front page, or write his own ticket. They fished one of her boy friends out of the

river below New Orleans, and found another in his Park Avenue apartment with a bullet through his head. Not a bit of proof to connect the Orchid with either, of course. But there's no law against guessing."

"They should call her Aconite, the poison flower," I wisecracked. "And what do I do with this hothouse assassin?"

Thompson rolled the cigar to the corner of his mouth and grinned at me. "I'm counting on that well known sex appeal of yours I've been hearing about from Trixie Meehan."

I damned Trixie Meehan for spreading those yarns. She panned me every chance she got.

Thompson grinned again, and then became serious.

"The Orchid is one of the smoothest crooks in the country, Mike. She makes big money and makes it easy. As near as we can find out, she's got a partner or so who don't show often. She's been in Palm Beach for a month, and made a killing—all but the collecting."

"Or the suicide," I suggested.

"Exactly!" Thompson snapped. "I talked to the poor devil this morning. It won't take much to make him reach for a gun. He's Waldo Maxwell of the State Truth."

"Not *the* Waldo Maxwell?"

"None other," Thompson assured me. "No fool like an old widower, and he took it hook, line and sinker, and put it on paper. He won't stand a chance in court. And it will cost him a cool quarter of a million to buy back the evidence."

"Holy catfish!" I gasped. "What a haul! Why doesn't he take the publicity and save the dough?"

"Be yourself!" Thompson said. "He'd be the laughing stock of the country. Men who formerly trusted his judgment would think him doddering and senile. No telling what it would do to his financial strength. Not to speak of winding up a distinguished career as the country's prize clown. He'll pay if we can't settle it some other way."

Thompson was right. Waldo Maxwell had been a national figure for forty years. His bank was a Gibraltar of finance; he was the ultimate in conservative respectability. He'd be finished, out, if the scandal sheets got a thing like this.

"Maxwell retained the Blaine Agency," Thompson continued. "The sky is the limit on expense. And we're giving it to you. The Orchid is at the Palm Beach Palo Verde, registered as Miss Gloria Dean and maid. We don't know anything about the maid. It's a cinch she's crooked too. Got any ideas?"

"Plenty," I said, thinking fast. "First, make good on that expense account. And I'll want a good looking woman with brains. Got one this side of New York?"

"Trixie Meehan is due here in the morning from Chicago. She'll work with you."

I groaned, knowing Trixie.

Next morning I bought luggage, evening clothes, dress shirts, shoes, hats, all the clutter an oil millionaire from west Texas would be likely to have.

Trixie Meehan blew in, had a conference with Thompson before he left town, did some whirlwind shopping herself. We made the train together with enough luggage to do a theatrical troupe.

AN HOUR before dinner that evening we rolled into Palm Beach in two taxis, one packed with luggage. The Palo Verde was four stories high, with sprawling wings, acres of velvet lawns and a golf course; shrubbery, flower beds, palms, and the blue surf of the open Atlantic creaming in on the white sand beach before it. We wheeled up a wide shell driveway and stopped before a long marquee. Four uniformed bellboys ran out to meet us.

Trixie kicked me on the ankle.

"Out, ape!" she hissed under her breath. "Husbands always help the little woman tenderly."

"There you go!" I snarled. "Trying to start something right off the bat!"

"Yes, darling," cooed Trixie for the driver's benefit as I helped her out to the sidewalk.

Trixie Meehan was a little frail slip of a thing with forget-me-not eyes, a knock 'em dead face, and a clinging vine manner that covered concentrated hell. She had a razor tongue, muscles like steel springs, a brain that made me dizzy at times, and absolutely no fear. And here she was cuddling close and cooing up into my face while the taxi driver eyed me like a sap.

I paid him and left the baggage for the bellhops.

"Lay off that googoo talk when you don't have to use it," I growled as we went into the lobby. "You get my goat."

Trixie grabbed my arm and snuggled close. "You big strong he-man!" she sighed.

I couldn't shove here there in the lobby, so I took it out on the clerk. "A suite. Two bedrooms. Best you have. Ocean exposure, on the third floor, if possible."

"A *quiet* suite, dear," Trixie trilled.

"A *quiet* suite!" I snapped to the clerk.

"I think we have one that will be entirely satisfactory," he beamed at me. "And I can give it to you for only eighty dollars a day, since that is late in the season."

"Eighty a what?" I gagged.

"Eighty dollars a day," the clerk repeated firmly, and managed to chill me with one eye while he eyed our mountainous luggage, just coming in, with the other.

Trixie pinched my arm, and smiled brightly. "Eighty dollars a day is quite satisfactory, darling," she cooed. "Can't you remember that we have oil wells now?"

The clerk caught it. His face cleared instantly. He handed me a registry card and a fountain pen. I registered Mr. and Mrs. Blaine, San Antonio, Texas.

We looked like wealthy young globe trotters, for our old luggage was plastered with labels from everywhere. Undercover work for the Blaine Agency means travel. When the bellhops got their toll and left us alone in the suite, I went to the connecting door of the bedrooms and moved the key to my side.

"Verboten," I grunted at Trixie. "None of your blasted tricks now. I want some peace on this case."

Trixie threw her hat on the bed and made a face at me. "Be yourself, ape. Nobody's pursuing you. What has your massive brain planned for this evening?"

"The Orchid and her maid have three rooms at the end of the hall," I snapped. "I meet her, I make her, and then we take her."

"Just as easy as that," Trixie marveled. "Well, here's hoping. But don't forget we're married, darling, and I get some of this Palm Beach whoopee."

"Nix," I grinned. "That's for me and the Orchid.

You're the neglected wife who mopes in her room."

"You'll have whiskers to your ankles when I do that," Trixie said through her teeth.

THE IDLE rich! The wisecracker who said that never had more than a week's pay on hand in his life. Golf, tennis, swimming, riding, dancing—and bridge thrown in whenever Trixie could scare up a game. Three days of that to put us in the public eye and get our lines out.

The unlimited expense account made it possible; oil millionaires from Texas, hicks, from the sticks, lathery with money. Trixie shopped at those exclusive little Fifth Avenue branch shops. They came to the hotel collect, and we had war the first night.

"Whose little gold digger are you?" I yelped. "Look at these bills I settled today! I knew you were a tough case, but I didn't know you had mucilage fingers. Any dumbwit you drag to the altar will be going for a cleaning instead of a honeymoon. Sixty-seven berries for a hat, and I could wear it for a felt thumb protector!"

"So!" said Trixie with a glitter in her eye. "You were snooping in my packages like a second story mug, Michael Harris?"

"When I pay sixty-seven crackers for a cardboard box and four yards of tissue paper and ribbon, I want to see what I'm stung with!" I gave her.

And Trixie moved in close for battle.

"Listen to me, you sack of wind! Nobody ever dragged you to the altar and they never will. Pull those popeyes in and get this straight! I'll send the beach up here collect if I feel like it, and you'll pay and thank me. Whose bank account is getting nicked? Not yours! Hand you a five dollar bill and you'd start jawing J. P. Morgan. Gold digger, am I, for providing a little atmosphere? Next time I hear a—"

I slammed the door on the rest. That acid tongue of Trixie's could lift the skin off a cigar store Indian.

We buried the subject of clothes. After all it wasn't my money. I took a flier or so in the market those three days. And the tips I ladled out everywhere disturbed my sleep nights. But they were good advertising. By the second day every flunkey in sight was bowing and scraping when I appeared. Funny how oil millions can spread. We were the gossip of the hotel. Some turned up their noses, and some fell over themselves to glad-hand us.

The Orchid did neither.

I spotted her the first evening in the dining room, and the waiter cinched it. "That is Miss Dean, sir."

"Pretty girl to be dining alone."

"Miss Dean seldom has anyone at her table, sir. She is, if I may be so free, a retiring woman." And the waiter rolled an expectant eye at Trixie.

"Perhaps, dear," says Trixie sweetly, "you would like to leave me and join her?"

And the waiter went off satisfied.

The Orchid had everything Thompson had outlined. I didn't try to guess her age. She was like an orchid, slender, graceful, dainty, fragile. She was a natural blonde—Trixie admitted that reluctantly—with a shell pink complexion and ripe red lips. Her eyelashes were long and dreamy, her makeup a bit of art, her expression tender and demure.

One look at her there in dainty solitude and I was willing to swear Thompson was a liar and Waldo Maxwell a lecherous old reprobate. A second look and I was hardboiled again. I've seen enough crooks to have an extra sense about them. Her eyes wandered over and caught my grin. She took me in from hair to second button on my dinner coat, and then went on eating without a change of expression. But my neck hairs stiffened. She was like a beautiful leopard, lazily lapping cream. Claws were sheathed behind that fragile daintiness.

Trixie was on tap as usual. "All right, cave man, go into your act," she said under her breath.

"Rats to you," I said. "This is going to take technique."

The waiter returned and Trixie cooed: "Yes, dear." And we had honeymoon the rest of the dinner.

I didn't make a move for three days. But now and then when the Orchid was on the horizon I caught her studying me. The wild and woolly west, with a wagon load of money, and extra luggage in the wife, had come to Palm Beach. I spent as little time with Trixie as possible. I ogled the women when the Orchid was around. I flashed the bankroll and made a fool of myself. Anyone with half an eye could see I was ripe picking for a smart dame.

But it was Palmer, a natty customers' man for Trenholme and Edwards' branch brokerage office, who gave me my break. A little about oil wells and flyers in the market made him my man. He was a good looking young chap, a little too soft and polite; but he knew his Palm Beach, and the Orchid by sight when I pointed her out on the hotel veranda.

"Corker, isn't she?" Palmer sighed. "Haven't met her, but I hope to. See her all the time at Corey's. Say, that's a place you might like. Been there yet?"

"A big gambling joint, isn't it?"

"Yes."

"I'll be glad to take you and Mrs. Blaine there any time."

"Tonight," I said. "Mrs. Blaine will be busy. We'll go alone."

I'D HEARD about Corey's place; to gambling what Palm Beach was to society. With its clientele a Broadway gambler would have retired in six months. Strict cards of admission were required, and your name almost had to be in the social register to get one. Formal evening dress, of course, and once inside the old lavishly furnished frame building, set back in a tangle of trees and tropical growth, the sky was the limit. Private rooms upstairs for really high play. The drinks and food were on the house. The service was in keeping with the crowd who went there.

Palmer got a card some way. Things like that were his business. I went with a fat billfold, a boiled shirt, tails and everything—and tried to forget that in a few weeks I might be impersonating a longshoreman around the East river docks.

It was a joy to lose the first three hundred, of someone else's money. We shifted from game to game for an hour and a half. Cool, perfumed air, beautiful women —some of them—men whose names made the newspapers, the hum and chatter of conversation, the quiet voices of the house men, now and then a black dressed automation moving about with a tray. But no Orchid.

And then she came in, wrapped in a black coat with a roll of white around the collar. Stunning? I skipped a breath. "Palmer," I said, "I'm going to need the rest of the evening to myself. Would you mind ordering a Rolls outside in case I need it?"

And I went to the roulette table where the Orchid had drifted. For a few minutes I watched her lose five dollar chips, and then I slipped into an empty place at her side and slapped down five hundred. I lost and raised to a thousand. And won, and won the next time, and the next. By that time I had the Orchid and everyone else at the table with me.

A fifty dollar bill was slipped into my palm, and I met a cool smile. "Will you play it?" the Orchid asked. "I think you are lucky tonight."

We won together.

Since it wasn't my money I didn't get the cold chills as I pushed my luck. I played the Blaine oil wells in public that night, and had the customers hanging on the edge of the table and standing three deep behind us. No, I didn't break the bank. They tell me no one ever does that at Corey's. But I put on a good show, won six thousand when the plays were evened up, and broke the ice with the Orchid.

I stuffed the winnings in my pocket and grinned at the Orchid. "I always quit while I'm cool, ma'am. Would a little drive along the ocean front cap your luck?"

"It might," the Orchid agreed as she folded her cut. "Shall we try it?"

The motor of that big Rolls purred and so did the Orchid. Her technique would have made Delilah quit. "You were so calm over those big stakes," she sighed.

"Shucks, ma'am, back in Texas, our stud games would make that piker play tonight."

"Your're from Texas?"

"West Texas," I gave her breezily. "Out in the oil country."

"How fascinating! Have you an oil well?"

"A dozen," I grinned. "An' two more spudding-in this week on proved ground. I always told Susan that when I passed my first million I was coming to Palm Beach. And here I am. But I never thought I'd be riding around with a beautiful woman like you."

"You flatter me," said the Orchid absently. "Your wife—does she like it? I've noticed her. She's a beautiful little thing."

"Susan's pretty enough," I agreed without enthusiasm. "But she says she'd rather be back home where she can be a big frog in a little puddle instead of a little frog in a big puddle like she is here."

The Orchid laughed softly.

"Perhaps she is right at that. A woman has to be used to this life before she can get the most out of it. I owe you more thanks than I can repay for making it possible for me to stay here a little longer."

"I don't understand," I mumbled and waited for her line.

"The money you won for me," she explained. "That was almost my last fifty dollars I gave you."

"I thought you were—"

"—rich?" She laughed shortly. What an actress! "One thinks that about everyone here. A little insurance money can create quite an effect. But when it's gone—" She broke off on a quaver.

I put a hand over hers. "I understand."

"I thought you would," the Orchid murmured. "Now forget about me and tell me about Texas."

So I spun her a few yarns about how I started as a poor kid in the oil fields and finally got in the money. When I spoke about oil field life she looked out the window, and when I mentioned big money she was all ears again.

"I want you to meet Susan," I said finally.

"No, I don't think I'd better," the Orchid said sadly. "Wives don't seem to like me. They get jealous. We'll keep this to ourselves."

"Perhaps we'd better," I agreed—and wondered what her game was.

Trixie saw the powder on my coat lapel when I came in the sitting room, and said acidly, "Necking?"

"With the Orchid. I wanted her to meet my dear little wife, Susan, but she begged off. Wives don't usually like her."

"*Susan?*" Trixie had fire in her eye. "I could skin you for that, Mike Harris! Why not Abigail to that hussy?"

"Why not? Susan Abigail it is."

I got the door locked just in time.

THOMPSON LONG distanced from Washington in the morning.

"She's putting the screws on Maxwell," he crabbed over the wire. "Wants her dough quick, or else. The old man's frantic. He thought he'd have a couple of weeks yet anyway. Haven't you done anything?"

"It looks like I've done too much," I decided. "She wants Maxwell cleaned up before she cleans me."

"Well, get some action!" Thompson yelled. "If this thing goes sour on you, you're washed up with the Blaine Agency. It's that important."

"Button your lip," I advised. "They can hear you across the hall here. Tell Maxwell to put another padlock on his checkbook. No dame's going to toss a quarter of a million away by getting rash. He's safe enough as long as he stalls."

Thompson's groan traveled clear down from Washington. "I hope for your sake that's right," he warned.

And so did I. The Blaine Agency had a little trick of loading all the responsibility on the ones who drew a case, and then if they didn't come through, heads began to fall. It worked nine times out of ten. But Waldo Maxwell's quarter of a million and the Orchid were a big bite.

She was a wise one, dangerous as dynamite.

Trixie heard me out.

"You can't stall any longer, loud mouth," she decided. "Necking parties may be your forte, but you'll have to cut them short. I've been watching that hussy. She never speaks to anyone who might be in the racket with her. And a dime to a promise that those letters are not in her hotel room here. She wouldn't dare keep them so close."

"She has a maid."

"I've seen the maid!" Trixie snapped.

And so had I. A beauty, and a crook, if I knew my way around. "We've got to pull a fast one," I decided.

"He thinks," Trixie marveled. "Well, produce before we both get fired."

"I'm going swimming," I told her.

I met the Orchid on the beach where she had said the night before she'd be. She wore black beach pajamas trimmed with white, and against her creamy skin they were enough to stop the breath and scuttle good resolutions. She gave me a smile to go with them. "Where is your wife?"

"Reading. No sunburn wanted."

"You poor neglected boy. It must be lonesome at times."

I held my breath until my face got red and stuttered, "N-not when I'm with you." And we got along famously.

All the time I was wondering where she kept those letters of Maxwell's. Trixie was right. Not in her room. That would be the first place private dicks would look. And despite the fact that Trixie had seen no one with her, Thompson's hint that she did not work alone kept pricking at my mind.

So I admired the big diamond ring on her finger and told her about the jewels I had bought the little woman since the oil wells came in. Three hundred grand worth, diamonds, pearls, emeralds and what not.

The Orchid swallowed the hook. "What a fortunate woman your wife is," she sighed. "I haven't seen her wearing any."

I grinned. "She's afraid to. Jewel thieves. So she keeps them in the bottom of her trunk."

The Orchid lay there on the sand like a lazy cat. Her pink finger nails dug in gently when I said that. I saw her leg muscles stiffen slightly. But she didn't bat an eye.

"How dangerous," she warned abruptly. "She should keep them in a safety deposit box."

"Susan doesn't think so," I yawned. "She likes to take them out and play with them. She's like a kid. Always wanted a diamond ring—and then got a lapful. And she's convinced no one would ever think of looking in the false bottom she had built into her trunk."

"I suppose she's right," the Orchid nodded lazily. "But just the same if they were mine I wouldn't take chances."

"Not you," I thought. Aloud I said: "Let's forget 'em. If she is robbed, I'll buy her some more. And how about taking a ride with me this evening? The wife is going to be downstairs playing bridge until late. I may have to leave tomorrow. Got a wire from my partner."

She looked at me through her lashes smiling, mysterious, inscrutable. "Do you really want to?" she murmured.

"Try me," I dared.

"At eight," she said.

And I wondered whether I was being a fool after all. She looked soft and inviting as honey—and I knew she was dangerous as a cobra.

WALDO MAXWELL said harshly, "You are a fool!"

"I know I am," I agreed. "We all act the fool now and then."

He winced, said something savagely under his breath and prowled back and forth. I had run him down in one of those fantastic villas that huddled up little narrow drives just off the beach. Simplicity by the hundred thousand dollars' worth. Handkerchief sized lawns, tile roofs, and luxury inside that would dim the Arabian nights.

It was indiscreet, I knew. I shouldn't have gone near him. But I needed action quick, and he was the only one who could give it to me. And there he prowled around the room like an enraged old bear, his dewlaps shaking, his white hair mussed where he had shoved his fingers through it, a scowl deepening the wrinkles over his rimless eyeglasses.

Waldo Maxwell might have been able to tame a multimillionaire board of directors, but he had never tried Michael Harris of the Blaine Agency before. "Do I get it?" I demanded.

"It is an insane request!" he blurted violently.

"I know. I've thought it all over. If something isn't done quick, you're going to be splashed on the front pages, or out a quarter of a million," I reminded. "You haven't a thing on that dame. She's got you by your reputation and you can't even yip. Unless I'm wrong about the contents of those letters."

"No—no! I was out of my mind when I wrote them. Don't mention them! Are you certain you can control this insane—this plan of yours?"

I would have felt sorry for him, if I hadn't remembered he could sign his name to a check for five million, and still have plenty left in the sock. "What would you give to have her come begging for mercy?" I asked.

Waldo Maxwell showed his teeth in a smile, gentle as a wolf's. "It would be some consolation for the humiliation I have been put to," he confessed.

"Then come through with what I need."

He glanced at a platinum cased watch and made up his mind abruptly. "They will be delivered to your hotel some time before six," he promised.

"Can I count on that?"

"Young man, you heard me. Some time before six."

So I left, satisfied.

And he came through.

I opened the sealed brown paper package and poured the contents on the sitting room table. Trixie took one look and squealed: "Mike, where did you get these?"

"Kris Kringle," I grinned. "Now do you believe in fairies?"

"I've never seen such good looking imitations."

"I'll bet you never have," I agreed. "Not a phony among them. Every stone and setting is the real McCoy."

And I didn't blame Trixie for going pale and sick when she looked at me. That mess of diamond rings, bracelets, necklaces and whatnots needed a lot of explaining. Trixie picked up a pearl necklace and ran it through her fingers. "Tell me, Mike," she commanded.

"Waldo Maxwell," I admitted. "It was like pulling eye teeth, but I got him to buy the lot on consignment. If they're returned, he gets his money back. If not—he'll probably have a heart seizure."

Trixie put her little hands on her little hips and looked me up and down with her lips pressed tightly together. "Have you gone insane, Mike Harris?"

"That has a familiar ring," I recalled. "Maxwell wanted to know the same thing."

"I think you have! What are you going to do with all this jewelry? Why, it—it must be worth a fortune."

"It is," I agreed. "And we're going to put it all in that little false bottom in your trunk, and you're going downstairs this evening and play bridge, and I'm sneaking off for an automobile ride with the Orchid."

"Exactly."

"And leave all this up here?"

Trixie bristled. "Now I know you're out of your mind! We'll do nothing of the sort! You can waste another evening making sheep's eyes at that cat if you care to, but I'm staying in and sit on this jewelry, to take it down to the hotel safe."

"Jealous?"

Trixie tossed her head. "Of you, big mouth?"

"We'll do as I say."

"If we do," Trixie snapped, "something tells me we are in for grief. I think that massive brain of yours is cracking under the strain."

"Don't think," I advised. "It's dangerous."

IF I had stopped to think I would have gone shaky myself. For I knew what Waldo Maxwell and Trixie did not—that lot of jewelry was in greater danger than if I had tossed it on the lobby floor and walked off. It might have been returned from there. And I didn't dare use phonies. A slick crook would have spotted them the first look. So I shut my eyes and walked into the manager's office and asked for four young bellhops who could ride bicycles, keep their mouths shut and stay honest for a twenty dollar bill.

He looked at me as if I were addled. "Of course, Mr. Blaine—I mean to say, we strive to furnish every service, but—"

"Then service me," I cut him off. "I'm serious and in a hurry."

Grant the Palm Beach Palo Verde service. They delivered. I chased the manager out of his office, talked turkey to those bellhops, and hung a hundred dollar prize to sweeten their twenties. All four of them could outthink the average guest they roomed. In five minutes I drilled them letter perfect, and they scattered with expense money.

The Orchid sighed dreamily. "Isn't the surf lovely?"

"Great," I agreed, and held her hand tight while I looked over to the beach.

Sure enough, there was a surf frothing in through the moonlight. Pretty, too, if a fellow had time to look at it. I didn't. My mind was on Trixie back there in the hotel playing bridge. And on my five bellhops, and the Orchid beside me on the front seat of the big rented sedan. No chauffeur this time. I didn't want to be bothered in case quick action was needed.

But for the time being we had no action as we loafed south in the moonlight with the open sea on the left. Some night. Some scenery. Some girl. I forgot the times I had called myself a fool for throwing in with the Blaine Agency. Nights when the rain ran down my neck, and guns barked out of the blackness. Days when nerves were worn to a frazzle matching wits with the smartest crooks in the country. A dog's life, until I met the moon and the sea, and the Orchid went limp inside my arms as we loafed along through the miles. She was concentrating forgetfulness in a gorgeous shell.

Only I didn't forget. When I wrap my arm around a snake I watch it. I tested her out. "We'd better be getting back, beautiful."

"Not yet," she sighed, and came over another inch. "It's so lovely out here tonight. I could drive until morning."

"You won't sister," I thought—and gave her three miles more before I turned and stepped on the gas.

"You are driving too fast," the Orchid protested.

I patted her knee. "I'm a fast chap."

"You're a fresh one," she said, and tried to steer me over to Lake Worth and down through West Palm Beach, stalling for time.

"Little girls shouldn't be out so late," I stalled back. "I have a headache, and I'm going to turn in. I'll stay over another day and we'll take this up tomorrow night."

"But I will not be free tomorrow night."

"My loss," I mourned, and rolled her back to the hotel far faster than she had gone away from it.

The Orchid said good night without much graciousness and went in the front entrance. When I parked the car one of the four bellhops popped out of the night. His eyes were wide with suppressed excitement.

"Your room was entered. Mr. Blaine!" he said breathlessly. "A thin man with a black mustache. About twenty minutes ago."

"Any trouble? Where are the others?"

"They haven't come back yet. I've been waiting here for you."

"Be back in a few minutes," I told him, and hurried inside, lifted Trixie from her bridge game and took her up to the suite.

"Powder on your coat again," Trixie sniffed while I unlocked the door. "I'm getting sick of a half baked Romeo underfoot all the time."

"It's my charm," I grinned.

"It's your oil wells!" Trixie snapped as she marched into the room.

She beat me to the trunk while I was closing the door. And a moment later pulled her hand out of the hidden compartment in the bottom and whirled on me.

"They're gone! Every stone and setting; while you played the fool and I play bridge like you ordered! Oh, why did Thompson ever put an idiot like you on this?" She stamped her foot, grabbed my arm and shook it. "Say something! Don't stand there grinning like an idiot! They're gone, I tell you!"

"That's great," I said heartily. And Trixie almost swooned.

While she was getting her breath back I came out of my room sliding a clip into my automatic. "Hat and coat," I directed. "We're going out."

"Where?"

"Ask me something I know. It's a great night."

AND TRIXIE almost swooned again. But she was ready in sixty seconds, slipping a small edition of my automatic in her purse. Tucked away somewhere, too, was a fountain pen gas gun. Trixie never went without it.

A second bellhop was waiting when we got outside, his bicycle tipped on the grass. "What luck?" I asked him, and held my breath for the answer. It might mean the end of Waldo Maxwell's diamonds and pearls. If it did, it was my finish.

"Over in West Palm Beach," he said quickly. "Two of the boys are watching."

"Get in the back," I ordered. "We'll talk as we drive."

"Who are they?" Trixie demanded as we all tumbled in.

"Bellhops."

"It doesn't make sense."

"Nothing does." And as I drove, the boys in the back seat talked fast. One of them had been in an empty room where he could watch the door of our suite; another outside covering the windows; and the other two had been downstairs near a telephone.

There had been no second story work. A well dressed man had walked down the hall, fitted a key into the door of our suite, stepped inside, remained a few minutes, and stepped out again, natural and easy. He had walked out of the hotel into a waiting car—and three bellhops had jumped on waiting bicycles and followed. Simple as that.

"And you didn't tell them to call the house detective?" Trixie asked thinly.

"Think of the publicity, my dear."

"I think you are a reckless idiot!" Trixie flared.

"You've called me that before," I reminded. "He who steals and runs away will surely pay some other day."

"Mad!" Trixie muttered despairingly. "Stark, raving mad!"

Cross west on the brightly lighted bridge over Lake Worth and you come into another world. The coast highway runs through West Palm Beach, and now and then a tourist stops off and settles. Apartment buildings, cottages, cozy houses—it was like getting home from phantasy land. We found the other two bellhops beside their bikes at a corner in the residential section.

Their dope was short and sweet. The car they had followed had turned into a driveway in the middle of the block, and was still in there.

"Stay here with the car," I said to Trixie.

And she said: "Never again. You need someone with sense to watch you."

"Meaning a woman," I said sarcastically. "Nevertheless, you stay here. This isn't a tea party."

So she stayed, and two of the bellhops walked down one side of the street and the other guided me to the one story stucco cottage where Waldo Maxwell's jewels had flitted. One side room was lighted. The window shades were down.

I sent the kid across the street and walked to the back of the house. A big car was standing in the driveway, heading toward the street.

No one was worried inside—and why should they be, after strolling out of the Palo Verde so easily? A radio was playing jazz. The screen door on the back porch was unlocked, and so was the kitchen door. I pulled my automatic as I stepped inside.

A swinging door opened out of the kitchen, a hall beyond that, and to the left was an archway into a dining room. A voice said: "God, Harry, this bracelet ought to be worth five grand anyway. The emerald is good for two, and most of the diamonds will bulge a carat and a half."

And a second voice, "Shall we split this necklace and peddle the pearls separate?"

"I wouldn't," I advised as I stepped in. "That's a sucker trick."

There were two of them, sleek, good looking young fellows. One knocked over a chair as he jumped back and reached under his coat. When he saw my gun he stood still.

Waldo Maxwell's bait was spread over the table. They hadn't been able to keep their hands off it. Harry had a little black mustache that jerked as he got out: "What are you doing here?"

"Don't be so formal," I said. "This is a pinch."

And Harry gasped, "It's a frame! He talks like a dick!"

"You mind reader," I said. "He is a dick. Turn around while I collect your rods, suckers."

Harry took a chance, dodged and grabbed for his gun. I shot him through the shoulder. The next instant the light went out as his sidekick reached the wall switch. They both cut loose as I dropped to the floor behind the table. Four shots that were almost one—and a door slammed. . . .

I was alone with my ears ringing and the radio blaring away in the next room.

That was what slowed me up! My ears and the radio. I couldn't hear their movements, had to go slow for fear they were waiting for me. The motor in the driveway suddenly spun. Gears whined as it rushed toward the street.

And just as I opened the front door there was a terrific crash at the street. They had run into another car in front of the driveway as they turned sharp to avoid it.

I ran out.

Two groping, stumbling figures reeled on the sidewalk, fighting at their eyes. I backed away quick from the thin drifting vapor they were trying to escape.

It was my rented car they had run into. Trixie joined me, and said coolly: "I drove up when I heard the shots, and blocked them. I let them have the gas through the open window of their car."

"Good girl!" I yelled. "Tell those bellhops to collar 'em until the cops get here!" And I ran back into the house while the neighbors poured out into the street.

I reached the street again just as the police car slid up. We settled the rest in the station house. It took the jewels on the dining room table, the testimony of the bellhops, our credentials and a telephone call to Waldo Maxwell to clear Trixie and me enough so we could leave for the evening.

And at that we were told it was damn queer business, and there was going to be a lot of explaining before the matter was settled.

"There will be," I promised.

Trixie was wild as a taxi took us back to the Palo Verde.

"See what you've done with that idiotic jewelry!" she stormed. "A man shot, two cars wrecked, serious charges plastered everywhere—with all the publicity it will bring—and Maxwell is as bad off as ever!"

"We'll ask the Orchid about that," I said.

TRIXIE WAS still breathing hard when I knocked on the Orchid's door. The maid, almost as good looking as the Orchid, answered it. She took one look at Trixie and informed us that Miss Dean had retired.

"Too bad," I regretted. "Get her up." And I pushed on in.

The Orchid met us in a frothy negligee that was enough to stop the breath. "What does this mean?" Her voice was knife-edged.

"Harry and his sidekick are in the West Palm Beach police station," I told her. "They were caught with the jewelry. It belonged to Waldo Maxwell."

I saw the maid, standing in the doorway, turn pale and press a hand against her throat. But the Orchid's eyes began to blaze past her long lashes.

"So you tricked me!" she said through her teeth.

"Gloria," I sighed, "it broke my heart to do it. But you've been loose long enough."

"Waldo Màxwell is behind this!"

"Sad—but so."

I've seen a furious tigress behind the bars. But never have I been so close to one. The Orchid's face turned marble white. Her eyes narrowed to points.

"Maxwell won't get away with this!" she blazed. "I'll spread his name over every paper in the country! Tell him he'd better run here and settle it quick! If those men aren't out by tomorrow, I'll call the reporters in and give them the story of their lives!"

"Can you back it up?"

"Certainly! I have letters!"

"You had," I corrected. "What do you think I planted that jewelry for? I wanted to uncover your boy friends who were probably holding Maxwell's letters. I found them in the bottom of a suitcase in their house. You might call Maxwell from the police station tonight and ask him for a little mercy. He's got an answer all ready."

She spat at me like a cat.

Trixie said later that gave her hope for me.

Narrative Cross-Word Puzzle

A GOOD JOKE ON A PICKPOCKET
By Richard Hoadley Tingley

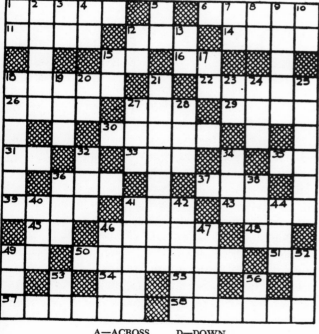

A—ACROSS   D—DOWN

The train was (A 43), and the platform of the Interborough (D 18) station at 168th Street and St. Nicholas Avenue was (A 1) with activity and crowded with men and women (D 34) anxious to be on their way downtown.

"(A 51) my!" complained one of the young (D 9) to her chum. "(A 48) is me, (D 12) a wreck! That brute nearly stove in my ribs, the horrid man!"

"We'll have to wear (A 46) corsets soon if this sort of (A 30) keeps up," moaned her friend (D 1), with a rattle and a rumble, the train pulled in (A 49) the station.

"(A 29)!" whispers Sergeant (D 53) Jenkins to his colleague, Patrolman (D 13) Lardner, as he drops his nickel into the (D 46) at the turnstile and (A 58) the platform to (D 24) with the ever-increasing mob. "Watch that miserable looking (D 32) over there with the gray (A 50) suit. He's (A 12) Castro, a sneak thief. Used to be a (D 36) driver. Now don't (D 41). He knows me and is looking this way. I'll bet he's up to some monkey business (A 54) other with that nob (D 20) front of him."

"(A 55)?" responded the cop. "Who's the swell? Know him (D 44)?"

"Sure I know him," answered Jenkins with an (D 49) of superiority. "He's Mr. (D 47) Garcia of the Amalgamated Cigar Company, (D 28) of the big (A 22) in the social register, and a (A 18) substantial man; probably has a (D 19) of money on him. (A 31) can't afford to (A 6) here on the sidelines when there's trouble brewing. Let's (A 35) a little nearer and (D 7) in on the fun if there is any. (D 4) is our duty to (A 16) all we can to protect such men."

"(D 5) Sergeant," replied the cop. "The place for (A 45) is where things are doing, and (D 23) how I would like to be in (D 17) a good scrimmage! I consider I (A 15) a match for any of (D 10), and, besides, (D 8) like a good yarn to (A 57) to the boys at Headquarters, and (D 27) reporters who are always looking around for a (D 2)."

The gray-suited man was seen (D 3) slip his hand into the pocket of his victim, but (A 33) he could draw it (D 40) a bystander jarred (D 52) arm, and with that the row began!

(A 27) much the smaller man, Garcia (A 41) up a stiff fight, while, with (D 42) interest, the crowd watched the tussle. The crook appeared to be having the (D 15 Prefix) vantage until, with a rush, the two officers of the (D 38) took a hand. And when they got through with Castro (D 56) must have felt like a piece of (A 14) cheese.

"Thank you for (A 39) help, boys," graciously said Mr. Garcia as he got (A 26) his feet and picked up his hat. "I (D 25) as hard as I could, but it might have gone (A 37) with me, and that thug might have got off (A 11) free if you hadn't been here on the job. (A 36) the joke of it all is that I have only (D 21) cents in my clothes!"

A**T FIRST I** thought I must have sponged up too much Vat 69 at Abe Pilwyn's pre-wedding party before staggering home that midnight. At least I'd never gandered any spooks when I was sober. But I was certainly seeing one now.

I stepped back from my threshold and bleated: "Okay. I'll sign the pledge. I'll never touch another drop if you promise you won't turn into a pink elephant."

The guy's smile was cadaverous. "I'm not dead, Dan," he said from down near his shoelaces. And he barged into my stash, went to the cellarette, helped himself to a jorum of skee.

Then I realized he was genuine. For one thing, ghosts don't imbibe giggle-juice. Moreover, this bird had been a crony of mine in the old days; knew where I stored my Scotch. And he hadn't forgotten. "Len Kensington!" I whispered.

He downed his dollop. "Yes."

I irrigated my jitters with a nip of the same medicine. It's a hell of a shock to meet a bozo you've considered fish-food the past six months. By rights, Kensington should have been a skeleton festooning Davy Jones' locker instead of pacing my carpet like an underfed lion in a cage.

I could still see him taking off from Glendale Airport on the flight that erased him from this mundane slate. He'd been a star since silent days; one of the few to retain popularity after talkies came in. Eventually, though, his vogue had faded and he found himself unwanted by any of the major studios.

That was when Pildex Productions, an independent outfit run by Abe Pilwyn and financed from a distance by an investment broker named Sam Dexter, decided to gamble on him. Casting him as a speed-demon flyer in a quickie aviation opus, they laid plans for the juiciest publicity coup that ever came out of Poverty Row.

I**N PRIVATE** life Kensington held an amateur pilot's license. So Pildex Productions bought a Lockheed monoplane; announced that their star would attempt a non-stop record flight to Honolulu and back. The story hit the headlines simultaneously with Kensington's takeoff and the quickie's release. It was swell timing; drew customers into the theaters the way a dead horse draws flies.

I'd been present when Len lifted his ship into the swallowing night. I'd watched Lanya, his curvesome brunette wife, blow teary kisses after him as if she never expected to see him again. I'd tabbed Abe Pilwyn, the producer, soothing her by putting his arm around her dainty waist. And that was the end of it.

The end of Len Kensington; but not of his aviation

The man was dead and his widow was about to take a new husband. And then the dead man had to turn up at Dan Turner's apartment to upset everything!

DEATH'S

pic. Four days later the newspapers blatted: *"Flyer Missing At Sea" "Star Lost On Pacific Hop!"* It shoved the war news off the front pages—and it shoved audiences into movie houses from hell to Halifax. Everybody wanted a hinge at the hero who'd disappeared while on a genuine flight paralleling the one in his last cinema opus. Morbid curiosity, maybe; but it coined bales of lettuce for Pildex Productions.

It was still reaping copious shekels in the neighborhood dives six months later when Kensington had long since been given up for croaked. Only he wasn't croaked. He was alive, prowling my carpet and swigging my whiskey.

I said: "What the hell happened, Len? Did a boat pick you up? When did you get back?"

"I never left," he muttered grimly.

That didn't make sense. I said: "You must have a screw loose. I saw you take off that night!"

He flushed. "Yes. But you didn't see me land on the coast this side of San Diego an hour later and give my ship to another pilot."

"I'll feed you a mouthful of your own teeth," he grated.

By
ROBERT
LESLIE
BELLEM

PASSPORT

"You mean—?"

"I was yellow," he said. "I was scared to go through with it. So I secretly arranged for a substitute flyer to take my place—a guy whose name I never even knew because he wouldn't tell me. He was down on his luck, glad for a chance to pick up five thousand bucks while I got the glory."

I began to get it. "This anonymous slob was to make the hop, bring the plane back to your hidden spot and turn it over to you?" I asked. "Then you'd have flown into Los Angeles, pretending you'd been at the controls to Honolulu and back?"

Kensington jerked me a nod. "I gave that poor devil his passport to death, Turner. He didn't make the grade. I can't understand why, because the plane was okay. I went over it myself—"

A hunch nipped me. I said: "Did you have any enemies who might have wanted to bump you? Somebody who might have sabotaged the ship, thinking you were really going to fly it?"

"Impossible!" he shook his head. "Whatever hap-

pened was an accident. But that doesn't change things. The guy was lost and I'm responsible. I'll pay as long as I live. God knows I've already paid plenty. Six months of hell; of keeping under cover; hiding because my pride wouldn't let me show myself. . . ."

"You haven't told anybody the score?"

"Nobody but you, now. Not even the girl who took me in and gave me a bed because she got a yen for me. . . ."

I could understand that. If he revealed his identity he would have been forced to admit his cowardice; compelled to confess he'd sent another pilot in his stead. That would have branded him for life—and no dyed-in-the-wool actor, accustomed to feeding his ego on years of public adulation, could take that kind of rap. It was easy to see why Kensington had preferred to let the world consider him defunct.

"Then why the hell come to me now?" I asked him.

"I'm tired, Dan. Tired of taking charity from this poor little jane who's been looking after me. I'm hungry, not for food but for my wife. You're a friend of mine; a smart private dick. I—I thought you might help me regain what I've lost. . . ."

A sudden brainstorm slugged me. I yelped: "Suffering tripes, I've got to move fast!" And I grabbed my hat, lunged at the door.

"Wh-where are you going?"

"Stay here and don't ask questions!" I said. "I'll be back soon—I hope." Then I hurled myself out of the flat. I had less than thirty minutes in which to stop Len Kensington's wife from committing Arizona bigamy with Abe Pilwyn. It was their elopement shindig I'd attended that evening, just before coming home to find Kensington himself haunting my portal.

A SLENDER blonde wren was passing along the corridor as I arrowed out. I smacked into her before I could drag anchor. The impact knocked her upside down. I stumbled over her kicking stems, landed on top of her. She unleashed a gasping moan as my weight flattened her resilient curves.

For an instant I was all tangled up in slim legs and bare thighs and fluttering skirt. The sensation was pleasant enough but I didn't have time to enjoy it. I scrambled upright, pulled her with me, steadied her. When I got a swivel at her startled puss, I recognized her. She was an extra chick around the studios; I'd been on a few parties with her in the old days. "Vonnie Vale!" I said.

She pushed the mussed golden hair out of her glims, tugged at her girdle, twisted her brassiere back into position beneath the bodice of her frock and gasped: "Hello, D-Dan. You're so impetuous! You ought to carry a Klaxon."

If I'd had more time I might have volunteered to help adjust that brassiere; its plump contents intrigued me. But there were other matters more immediately pressing right then. I said: "Sorry, babe. I'll get in touch with you some rainy evening and make amends. Just now I'm in a hell of a yank." Then I blew her a kiss, hurled my heft downstairs to the basement garage and aimed my jalopy toward Glendale Airport.

A BLUE-PAINTED private monoplane was just trundling off the tarmac as I gained the field in a shower of sparks. An attendant with a badge tried to halt me at the gate and I dished him up a helping of knuckles, sent him skidding on his pistol pockets. I catapulted across the runway, waving my arms and yelling fit to split my adenoids.

The blue plane's motor coughed, died; its wheels locked to a stop. I wrenched the door open and said: "Pardon my rough exterior, folks, but the wedding is off."

In the cabin's rear twin-seat, Abe Pilwyn sat with a fat arm around Lanya Kensington's waist. Up front, Sam Dexter—the money guy behind Pildex Productions—twisted away from his controls; glued the focus on me. "Turner!" he said. "What on earth—"

I poked a thumb at his partner and Lanya. "They can't get hitched in Yuma tonight. Or any other night. Her husband's still alive."

Lanya's dark lamps widened; her tempting kisser made a startled crimson zero. I could see the sudden surge of her gorgeous whatchacallems under her fawn

Before I could drag anchor, I'd smacked into her.

jersey frock; they swelled until I thought the material was going to split open—which would have been jake with me. She had a figure that was damned pleasant medicine for the orbs. "Len alive?" she gasped. "Oh-h-h, thank God! Thank God!" It sounded sincere enough.

A wheezing oath of frustration erupted from Pilwyn's pudgy throat. "You're crazy!" he choked. "Kensington's dead! We collected his insurance; I'm marrying Lanya. You can't tell me—"

"But I *am* telling you," I said. And I spilled the story as Len had given it to me.

Pilwyn yeeped: "He can't have Lanya! She's mine!"

"No, Abe," the brunette twist spoke for herself. "Len's the one I love. I was marrying you because I thought he was d-dead . . . and because you'd been good to me. But everything's changed now." She popped out of the plane in a flurry of fawn jersey skirt and a twinkling of silk-smooth legs; grabbed at me. "Where is Len? Take me to him. Please!"

I drew a thrill from her nearness; envied Kensington the kisses he'd garner when the reunion took place. Lanya was a choice morsel in any man's book. "He's at my tepee," I said. "But we've got to dope up a scheme to bring him back to the public without making a heel of him."

SAM DEXTER turned his ship over to a ground crew and we all went to the depot's waiting room. Abe Pilwyn growled: "Who the hell wants him back?"

I said: "You will when I show you how to make a stack of geetus from the publicity." Then I set fire to a gasper, went into details.

We could fake a note in a bottle, I pointed out, and have somebody pretend to find it. The note would ostensibly give Kensington's position on some south sea island. Pildex Productions could then outfit a rescue yacht, go through the motions of saving their lost star from his Robinson Crusoe jam.

Of course he'd be on the yacht all the time; but the newspapers would go wild when he was brought back to Hollywood. That aviation pic could be reissued; a new quickie made with Len in the leading role. It was a natural.

Sam Dexter thought so, too. So I said: "You go attend to the note in the bottle. Abe can see about chartering a boat. Lanya will go home and I'll bring Len to her so she can hide him out. Okay?"

They chorused okay and lammed. I felt like a boy scout as I went toward my rambling wreck. I'd fixed it for Kensington to resume his career, get his wife back. And I'd probably earned a fat fee for myself in the bargain; Pildex Productions would certainly cut me in for a slice of the cabbage they stood to make.

That was an important item; I'm trying to save up a retirement fund before some sharp disciple whittles my name on a bullet.

The future looked so damned rosy I didn't even get sore when that airport gate-guard tried to put the arm on me as I left the field. He was boiling because I'd bopped him; wanted to take me down to the gow on an assault charge. It cost me an argument and a ten-spot to poultice his bruised dignity; but what the hell? I had time to spare and dough in sight.

Presently he subsided, turned me loose. I climbed into my heap and drove home. I opened the door of my stash and called: "It's all set, Len—*Good God!*"

Len Kensington would never need to be rescued from a desert island. He was sprawled on my floor with three .38 slugs in his guts. The slugs had rendered him deader than the 1918 Armistice.

THE APARTMENT was infested with plainclothes cops captained by my friend Dave Donaldson of the homicide squad. Dave piped me entering and yowled: "I've been waiting for you to turn up, dammit! Maybe you can explain what goes on here!"

My elly-bay was doing nip-ups and I had to fight to keep from jettisoning my pancakes. "He's dead!" I whispered.

"You must be psychic," Donaldson sneered.

I said: "Who chilled him?"

"That's what I crave to know!" Dave roared at me. "Your next-door neighbors heard three blasts and saw a blonde frill powering down the stairs. They put in a quick beef to headquarters and this is what I found. You got anything to spill, Sherlock? Such as who this lug was, and what he was doing in your dump, and who had the curse on him?"

I shook my noggin. It took a couple minutes for Dave's information to seep into my soggy grey matter. Then a hunch sneaked up my leg. I said: "A blonde wren, hunh?" and pivoted to the door; slammed myself out of the apartment.

Donaldson tried to block me but he was too slow on his dogs. I pelted down to the basement, climbed into my bucket and souped the kidneys out of it; bored a hole through the night with my radiator ornament. Pretty soon I parked in front of a bungalow on a side street near Rampart; raced toward the porch.

The cottage was where Vonnie Vale hung out. I kept remembering how I'd smacked into her in the corridor of my apartment stash a while back; how startled she had seemed. Maybe she hadn't merely been passing by; maybe she'd been eavesdropping on my conversation with Len Kensington. . . .

. . . Len had mentioned a jane who'd taken him in, given him a bed. Which might possibly add up to

"It's not so!" she whimpered. "I didn't shoot him."

Vonnie Vale being the she-male in question. If my guess made a bull's-eye, hell was about to pop. I don't like corpses strewn around my living room; especially when they leak lots of juice. It costs coin to have your rugs cleaned.

RINGING THE bell, I schemed up a campaign. In itself Vonnie Vale's presence outside my door a little earlier wasn't conclusive proof of her connection with the Kensington kill; wouldn't warrant an actual accusation. Even if the neighbors fingered her as the chick who had lammed out of the building after those shots were fired, she could still defy the police to pin anything on her chemise.

But if she *had* been in on the croaking, I knew a way to find it out. All I had to do was watch her reactions. . . .

I jingled again. This time she opened up. "Why— why, hello, Hawkshaw!" she said in a voice that quavered around the fringes.

I moved in; fastened the appreciative focus on her. She was embellished in a nightgown three shades thinner than watered whiskey and a lot more potent. Through the gossamer material I could tab her various tempting thems and those—including a pair of tapered white gams, a set of lyric hips, and a duet of curves that made my fingers tingle up to the elbows. Some damsels are built that way: just looking at them makes you pine for your vanished youth.

"Hi, kiddo," I said. "Did I disturb your slumbers?"

"W-well, I *was* asleep." Which was a lie and I knew it. She still had her makeup on, and I know she would never go to bed without cold-creaming her piquant puss. She added: "What brings you here at such an hour, Dan?"

I perched on the divan, pulled her alongside me. "I just wanted to apologize for ramming into you tonight," I said.

Her rouge became more noticeable as her cheeks whitened. "Oh, th-that's all right. I'd forgotten all about it."

I said: "Have you forgotten all about this?" and slipped an arm around her; hunted for her lips with my kisser.

She didn't try to fight me off. She gave me what I wanted—but her heart wasn't in it. The kiss was mechanical. She was just going through the motions.

I poured on more coal; pressed her backward and started to examine the quality of the nightie she was wearing. "Nice piece of goods, babe," I remarked. My hand touched more than silk as I said it.

"I—I'm glad you like it, Dan." Her voice was tight, edgy. Then she made a weak effort to push me up. "Let's n-not wrestle tonight, do you mind?"

"It's been a long time," I reminded her. I danced my fingers over her shoulders and down her smooth bare arms. "Can I help it if I'm human?"

She struggled for a phony smile. "All right, handsome. I guess we're b-both human. . . ." She let me take her lips again; cuddled close to me when I began hunting a spot to pat with my palm.

It was nice to snuggle her that way. She was soft, feminine; her hair smelled good. For a minute I almost forgot my original purpose in starting the joust. If she hadn't been so damned passive, I might have got my arteries steamed up.

But there wasn't much fun to it when she merely relaxed on the cushions and let me do all the leading. Competition is the life of trade—and this was like taking candy away from a baby. So I pulled her shoulder straps back into place and said: "Maybe I've lost my technic."

"Oh-h-h, no. . . ." She didn't mean a word of it.

I said: "Or maybe you've got a boyfriend you like better."

"N-not any more . . . I mean—"

"You mean you haven't got a boyfriend because you croaked him!" I snarled. And I stood up, jerked her to her feet. "I was testing you—and you reacted just the way I expected. I knew damned well you wouldn't be in any mood to pitch woo with a murder on your conscience!"

The rouge-spots were ugly splotches against her colorless cheeks. "My God—you don't th-think I k-killed him? No, Dan! I didn't! Oh, please—you've got to believe me—"

I said: "So you admit knowing he's dead. Which means you're the jane I'm looking for. You're the one who gave Len Kensington a home. You loved him. Tonight you followed him to my wikiup; heard him asking me to help him get back to his wife."

"Y-yes, but—"

"Sooner than give him up to another woman, you creamed him. Deny it and I'll feed you a meal of your own teeth!" I commenced shaking her until her thing-umbobs jiggled like mounds of aspic in an earthquake—

SHE CLAWED at my map; broke free. "It's not so!" she whimpered. "I didn't shoot him! I admit I went into your apartment after you left—"

"Why?"

"To talk Len into coming back to me. We argued a long time. Then somebody knocked. Len thought it was you. He thought you were bringing his wife in to see him—"

"And?"

"He didn't want her to catch him with another woman. So he pushed me into the bedroom, shut me in there. Then I heard him opening the front door of the flat . . . and there were three shots . . . someone fell . . . someone also ran away. . . ."

The story rang true. I said: "What happened then?"

"I came out of the bedroom," she said tonelessly. "Len was on the floor, d-dead. I got panicky. I was afraid I'd be suspected. I raced out of the building and came home. . . ."

"You didn't see anybody who might have done the triggering?"

"N-no. . . ." She came close to me, clung to me like a terrified child. "Please believe me, Dan! I—I'll do anything to prove I'm telling the truth!" And she jammed her pouting figure against my shirt-front; offered me the bribery of her lips, her body.

It wasn't necessary. I had a hunch she was leveling. I said: "Okay, sweet. If what you say is true you needn't worry about a murder rap; somebody else pulled the kill and you'll be in the clear if you come clean with the bulls."

"I've got to go the p-police?"

"It's best," I told her gently. "You want Len's murderer nabbed, don't you?"

"Y-yes."

"So maybe your evidence will help," I said. "Get your threads on an' let's go."

She went into the boudoir, and started to dress. Don't blame me if there was a mirror placed where

I could tab each little movement; after all, I'm as curious as the next slob.

WHEN SHE was frocked and shod we piled into my chariot; I headed for home. Just as I expected, Dave Donaldson was still on deck when we ankled in—although Kensington's corpse had been taken away in the meat wagon. Dave rasped: "So you came back. I thought you would, so I waited. Who's this number?"

"The blonde the neighbors saw lamming," I said. "Go ahead, Vonnie; spill your story to the nice apoplectic detective before he blows a fuse."

She faltered out her side of the mess; then I added what I knew. When I got through spouting, Donaldson growled: "So the dead guy was Len Kensington, hunh? That's all I need to know. It hands me the killer, by Gahd!"

"How come it does?" I asked him.

He said: "Kensington left a message before he kicked the bucket; wrote it on your rug with his own blood."

Vonnie Vale moaned quietly; sagged against me. She'd been through hell that night; she was still going through it. I supported her and kept listening to Donaldson.

"I discovered the message after you rushed off," he told me. "But up until now I couldn't savvy the connection." And he pointed to a wavery brown scrawl on the floor.

I leaned forward; stared. The gooey finger-marks spelled out a lower case "p-i-l—" ending in a squiggly round hieroglyphic that trailed off to nothing.

"You see?" Donaldson crowed. "He tried to tell us it was Abe Pilwyn who drilled him."

I said: "Yeah?"

"Yeah! P-I-L spells the start of the name, doesn't it?"

"Could be," I said.

He snapped: "The whole thing's plain as hell. Pilwyn wanted Kensington's wife. He couldn't stand the thought of losing her to a guy that was supposed to be dead. So he decided to make her a widow—a real widow this time. That was his motive—"

Before I could interrupt him, my phone-bell jangled. I unforked the receiver and said: "Dan Turner talking. Make it brief. I'm busy."

"Dan—this is Lanya Kensington. Come quick—bring Len with you—Abe and Mr. Dexter are fighting here—Abe's threatening to k-kill him—"

I yowled: "The hell you yodel!" and hung up, whirled around. I grabbed Vonnie Vale, gestured at Donaldson. "Let's go thumb a killer!"

We whooshed down to the street. I jammed Vonnie into the tonneau of Dave's official police chariot,

wedged myself beside her while Dave took the wheel. He said: "You better be taking me to Abe Pilwyn, by Gahd!"

"I am. Goose this thing." And I gave him Lanya Kensington's address.

I'LL SAY one thing for Dave Donaldson: when he scents a pinch in the offing he can drive like a maniac. He blooped that sedan up to seventy from a standing start; kicked the everlasting tripes out of it. The yellow-haired Vale cutie shivered against me like a cat coughing lamb-chops; she must have thought she was headed for the pearly gates. Her even little teeth chattered like pennies in a Salvation Army tambourine.

I snuggled her, told her not to worry. But I didn't sound very convincing. Especially when we zipped around a corner on two wheels and a miracle. Vonnie and I resembled two hunks of popcorn rattling around in a hopper and I didn't like it a damned bit. I could-not even hold onto her where the holding was nicest because she kept bouncing so much I wasn't able to pick my spots.

It was a hell of a wild ride; but pretty soon we were at the end of the line. Dave slammed to a halt in front of Lanya Kensington's modest shebang, scuttled from under his wheel and said: "Now what?"

I stuck a match in my mouth, tried to light it with a gasper. When my nerves quit screaming I ordered Vonnie Vale to stay in the car; then I dragged Donaldson toward the house.

Len Kensington's cuddly brunette widow was on the porch to greet us. She looked pale, jittery. "Wh-where's Len? You promised to bring him—"

I ducked the issue. "Take us to Pilwyn and Dexter."

She led us inside, pointed to a closed library door. From within the room I could hear Abe Pilwyn snarling: "You're going to do as I say, Sam."

"And toss away a fortune?" That was Dexter's worried voice. "Don't be foolish. Put away that gun."

"Like hell! When Kensington shows up, we're going to hand him a fistful of cash, send him on his way. He can be bought. He's *got* to be bought! I won't let him have Lanya, understand? I'll croak him first. And you too if you—"

I yanked on the knob, bounced over the threshold, whipped out the .32 automatic I always carry in a shoulder holster. On the far side of the library Abe Pilwyn was aiming a roscoe at his partner. I shouted: "Hold it, Abe. Save him for the gas-chamber!" Then I said: "Dexter, you're under arrest for murdering Len Kensington."

The finance man of Pildex Productions gave me a wild-eyed glare; edged toward the French window behind him. "I don't know what the hell you're talking about!"

I said: "You shot Kensington because you didn't want to disgorge the insurance fortune you collected when he was declared legally dead—a policy you took out on him before the Honolulu hop. You made the profit because you own Pildex Productions; Abe Pilwyn is just a front man."

"That's not murder proof."

"Kensington left his own proof. He wrote your name in blood before he signed off."

Donaldson said: "Cripes, Dan, it was Pilwyn's name—"

I shook my head. "It all goes back to an insurance swindle pulled by Dexter. He wanted to collect on Kensington's policy without actually killing the guy."

"How could I do that?" Dexter sneered.

I said: "By arranging for Kensington to vanish and having him declared croaked. But he refused to stay vanished, so this time you were forced to bump him.

"You were one of the only four possible suspects who knew he was in my apartment. The other three were Vonnie Vale, Lanya Kensington, and Abe Pilwyn. Want me to tell you how I eliminated them?"

"Help yourself."

I SAID: "It was simple logic. Before he died, Kensington wrote 'pil' without capitals, and another letter that looked like a zero. The only way you can make a word of that is by adding a 't'—and then you get 'pilot.'"

"What pilot?"

I said: "Obviously the anonymous one who had doubled for him on the Honolulu hop. In other words, a man he didn't know by name. Which cleared Vonnie and Lanya. Of the four persons who knew Kensington was at my stash, only you and Abe Pilwyn were left.

"But Abe wasn't a flyer. And he'd been at the airport when Kensington started that Honolulu jaunt. So you, Dexter, were the guy with the roscoe.

"As financial backer of Pildex Productions you'd always stayed away from the studio; Kensington had never met you. Therefore he didn't suspect your identity when you told him you were an out-of-luck aviator. He turned his plane over to you and went into hiding. That was the crux of your scheme. You sank the plane in the ocean, got back to shore and allowed the world to believe Len Kensington had been lost at sea.

"You figured he wouldn't dare show himself after that. You were safe in having him declared defunct so you could collect the insurance. But he fooled you. He turned up. So you had to bump him. He still didn't know you, even as you were shooting him. He merely realized you were his substitute pilot—and that's the word he tried to write. Satisfied?"

Dexter grinned in my teeth. "Sure. I'm satisfied you can't prove a word of it, even if it were true."

Somehow I'd been anticipating that. So I said: "You're wrong, rat. An eye-witness saw you do your triggering. She was in my bedroom at the time and she's outside in a police car now, ready to put the finger on you."

That got him. "You dirty son!" he yelled; and he hurled himself backward through the French window in a shower of glass.

I launched my bulk across the room. Dave Donaldson made his move at the same instant. We collided. I said: "Damn you for a clumsy ox!" and landed on my hands and knees. By the time I got going again, Dexter was a blur in the distant shadows. I saw him making for Donaldson's sedan; saw the glitter of a cannon in his duke—

The cannon yammered: *Kachow! Chow!* and vomited twin flame-streaks at Vonnie Vale in the car's tonneau. But even as I saw it, more gun-thunder roared from behind my shoulder. That was Donaldson's service .38 doing its stuff. Up ahead, Sam Dexter screamed and pitched forward on his smeller.

By the time I reached him he was as dead as a Hitler promise. Vonnie Vale was whimpering inside the car, bleeding from a bullet-nick in her arm.

I grabbed her, snagged a strip from her dress, bandaged the scratch. That ruined the frock; left a lot of loveliness on display. She moaned: "Oh-h-h, Dan . . . I th-think I'm going to faint! Please . . . take care of me. . . ."

So I took her home and cared for her.

The Torture Pool

By MacKINLAY KANTOR

*They Were Only Chinquapin Seeds,
but They Sprouted the Clew
That Was Deeply Rooted
in an Old and Gruesome Mystery.*

ALONG ABOUT this time of year, Willard Mott was apt to become meditative. Day after day, as the bright sunlight lay like warm yellow paint across the wide valley, he would sit in his tiny, cluttered shop, his high boots hoisted across the counter, his old chair tipped so that he could gaze through the open door.

Sitting thus, his pipe warm in his hand, he would settle his straight gray gaze on Gar Island. For hours at a time he would sit thinking many perplexed thoughts.

Mostly, these thoughts concerned a murder.

"Now it's five years," Willard Mott reflected. "Six summers gone, and I ain't done anything about it."

It was easy to tell himself that he had done all that a mortal could do. He had been at old Sheriff Sickles' side, from the moment the news reached Deerskin. Together they had scouted around the scene of the crime; together they had poked in the marsh, fingered the body of the victim, as if hoping to quicken it into telling them the name of the man who had done this thing. Together, a posse stringing behind them, they had carried torches on that slippery, midnight trail when the bloodhounds went yelping along the margin of Gar Slough.

But all that was five years ago, and in those five years Willard Mott had done precious little about the business on Gar Island. You could understand his eagerness to avenge, understand the balked hatred which rose in his breast, when you knew that the murdered man was Willard Mott's brother.

"Lily Louis" Mott, people called him. A bent, gangling hermit, fifteen years older than his brother Willard, he lived in a tiny hut on the forested ridge which crept above the narrow island like the backbone of a boar. To the apothecary shops, to the old-fashioned housewives of Deerskin, came the dried and bunched herbs that Lily Louis collected in shady coves among the twisting wilderness of channels.

Few men know the Winneshiek country. But Lily Louis Mott knew as much of it as any man. He had poled his flat-bottomed boat through the grassy, sluggish channels ever since most of the inhabitants of Deerskin could remember. As boys, he and Sheriff Sickles had fished together up and down the river. As a young man, Louis had taught his little brother Willard the eerie secrets of more than one hidden fastness where the warblers whistled unafraid. But a lifetime spent amid those grasses had not served to warn Louis Mott of the death which would come to him in the mist of early morning.

Rich. That was what people whispered. They argued that a man couldn't sell as much ginseng and flagroot, as many mushrooms and water-cresses and herbs as old Lily Louis sold, and not get rich. The tiny, narrow handcart which he carried with him in his boat was a familiar sight for twenty-five miles up and down the river. It was a touch of color, of pastoral greenness, to see the stoop-shouldered, brown-faced man trudging along the street as he pushed before him the laden hand-cart. And always he decorated it with chinquapins and white lilies; always his battered cow-bell tinkled out its message. "Medicine," Lily Louis would call. "Good tonic for what ails you. Nature's own remedies . . . Also ginseng, flagroot candy, and flower seeds . . . Medicine . . ."

AND SO, in the fifty-eighth year of his life, Louis Mott was murdered. Who did it, no one could more than guess. But the people who had whispered those supposititious tales about his secreted wealth seemed justified. The body of Lily Louis was found in the muck of Gar Slough, hidden by the umbrella leaves of the big yellow chinquapins which he had loved. A hundred yards away stood his little cabin, open and to all appearances undisturbed. But on the grassy ridge behind the hut was all the evidence of motive which anyone could need. A hole had been scooped out, on that low hill; a deep hole—dirt and clods flung heedlessly aside. And battered open beside the excavation was a small iron box. It was empty, but a silver dollar lay in the dirt nearby.

Lily Louis had lost his buried treasure and lost his life at the same time. A fisherman, drawn to the scene by the queer activities of birds, had discovered the body. Sheriff Sickles, estimating roughly, had placed the time of death at sunrise on August 23. The doctor said that Louis had been dead about thirty hours, and people had seen him in his boat on the evening of August 22.

"Five years." Willard Mott fumbled for a match, and struck it, and held it above the bowl of his chewed, black pipe. "And I ain't yet got track of the fellow who done it."

When the murder was discovered, Mott and the sheriff had made a thorough check-up of the town's inhabitants. To the best of their discovery, only three men from Deerskin had been abroad at an early hour on August 23. These were two old fishermen named Kennedy, and a young drug clerk named Dwight Heyward.

Each of the three men, it developed, had been fishing separately, in boats somewhere near Gar Island. But no one of them could offer a single clew. They had heard nothing, seen nothing. The gray mist of morning was cool and thick and all-enveloping.

Willard Mott shook his head over the Kennedy brothers.

"Good enough fellows, in their way," he told his friend Sickles. "Louis and I know them all our lives. If they had wanted to kill Louis, they had plenty of opportunities to do it before this. Naturally I want to keep tab on them. But I don't think they done this."

The drug clerk offered more possibilities for justifiable suspicion. He had been in town only a few months; no one knew much about him. His story seemed frank and entirely above-board, however. There was none of the furtiveness common to men of the criminal class, and when Mott made a special trip to LaCross and looked up the boy's record, he found it satisfactory. No clew came up to point in Heyward's direction.

Accordingly, they concentrated on the villages up and down the river. But weeks of searching led to nothing. No drifters but gave perfect alibis. No riverman blossomed out with sudden wealth.

Bloodhounds, taken hurriedly to the island that first night, had bayed and yapped heedlessly along the shore. An optimistic sleuth might judge that when a bloodhound trots repeatedly back and forth on an indefinite trail which leads nowhere, the criminal has done the same thing. Bloodhound men don't reason that way.

And so, five years afterward, things stood as they had stood at the beginning. Lily Louis was dead—slammed on the head with a pick-axe. They found the pick-axe in the muck near his body, but people of the Winneshiek don't go in for finger-printing. And within a few hours that pick-axe had been handled so much, anyway, that it would have yielded only a composite record of the chief citizens of Deerskin.

ONE OF the Kennedy brothers was dead, but the other was still fishing—just as poor and just as ordinary as ever. Dwight Heyward had left the drug store and gone into summer real estate, and made some money. Now he was an energetic, lively young business man instead of a drug clerk. He owned a colony of summer bungalows down at Reese's Point. He advertised in big middle-western papers. He drove a glistening roadster. There was money in land along the Mississippi, if you went after it in the right way.

That was the one thing which stuck, now, in Willard Mott's craw. He couldn't swallow that; it kept coming up and choking him, month after month. Where did Dwight Heyward ever get his first money to embark on this venture?

An aunt of his died in Madison, some people said. Others thought that he had saved the money, clerking at the store, and had started out in a very small way. One lot at a time . . . clever manipulating . . . and then more lots. He owned an interest in the ferry, too.

But it seemed to Will Mott that Heyward had made his money too rapidly, at the beginning.

"Can't quite get it down," he told himself, and the intelligence was harder and harder to digest the more he thought about it. Dwight Heyward was out on that river the morning when Lily Louis Mott was brained with the pick-axe. And now Dwight Heyward, the rising young summer-real-estate-colonist, had a lot of money.

"If I had anything to go on," thought Will Mott. "One single thing . . . I've tried, and I can't find nothing that points in his direction. Well. So be it . . ."

And on this afternoon, this sixth of August, this fifth year since Louis was killed, he shrugged his shoulders and leaned back again in his old chair. And then, suddenly, he tipped forward and stood up, and slid the chair against the wall. A man was coming along the plank walk which led to Will Mott's shop.

Mott went to the door to meet him.

The newcomer gazed in mild astonishment around the interior of the shop, where fishing tackle, mounted deers' heads, varnished pickerel, garden tools and cartridges were crowded on the little shelves or clustered on the walls.

He was a tourist, in baggy knickers and straw hat; Mott had seen men like him a thousand times, which was well, because he made his living from men like that.

"They told me I could get a guide here," began the tourist.

"Sure can. Or a fishing license, or artificial bait, or tobacco and sody water, or about anything else."

"I've just got a few hours to spend here. But Deerskin is a kind of historic spot, and I'd like to look around. What do you charge?"

The arrangement was concluded satisfactorily; Will Mott closed and locked the front door of his establishment, setting in position a much-thumbed cardboard placard on which he had drawn with blue crayon a representation of a clock. *Back at* read the sign, and the wooden hands were set at four o'clock. He made more money guiding tourists, by the hour or day or week, than he could ever make in the business of retailing cartridges, trout line and chewing tobacco.

"What do you want to see?" he inquired, when he was seated in his patron's touring car.

"The works. Take me around to all points of interest near by. Especially the old Indian battleground."

MOTT AGREED

"We can go out there first, then stop at Horsethief Cave and Lovers' Leap on the way back. You'll want to see the Colored Rocks, too—a fairyland of natural beauty," he added, lapsing for a moment into his prepared monologue. Young Rev. Witler had written it for him, years before, and the tourists were invariably impressed.

They drove east from the long, shambling main street, and crept up Snake Hill. At the summit, turning from a wide panorama of green miles which spread before him, the tourist pointed toward a rustic shack before which a flag fluttered and garden flowers bloomed. " 'The Relic House,' " he read from the sign above the log gateway. "What's that?"

"Just a real estate place," replied Will Mott. "That's Dwight Heyward's headquarters. He sells cottages and stuff."

"Are there really relics, inside?"

"Sure. Scads of them. But you wanted—"

The tourist stopped his car decisively before the gateway.

"I want to go in there. Indian stuff—that's what interests me."

"All right," grunted Mott. He was mildly disgusted whenever a transient voiced such approval of Heyward's gaudy shack, with its white-painted antlers and fake totem-pole in the yard. Sucker bait—all that stuff was. But as long as he got paid, it made no difference.

He led the way up the graveled path and thrust his head inside. "Dwight."

No answer.

"Guess he ain't here. But we can look around, anyway."

They entered the room; Heyward's office was at one end, behind a railing, but most of the chamber was given over to a miscellaneous museum. Stuffed animals, stone axes, pressed flowers, bottles of colored sand packed in gaudy designs—there was little here to entice an expert in any line, zoölogical or archaeological. But the tourist emitted occasional grunts of pleasure as he leisurely moved from exhibit to exhibit.

"This here," explained Mott, "is an old .69 musket. Buck-and-ball, they called 'em. They used that kind, some, in the Civil War . . . These are arrowheads; Sioux manufacture, I guess . . . That's a stuffed mink— pretty poor fur, too. And this—" He paused abruptly as Heyward entered the room from the back door.

He was a slick, black-haired young man with white hands on which yellow-bellied rings caught the light. His clothes were the affected, extreme sports togs of a country man suddenly become clothes-conscious.

"Good afternoon, Mr. Mott," Heyward breezed. "Grand day, isn't it? Grand—"

"Hello, Dwight," muttered Mott. "I was taking this gentleman around to look at a few sights. But he wanted to stop in here and see your stuff—"

"Indian things," volunteered the stranger. "I'm great on that stuff. Any of these for sale?"

Heyward's small eyes traveled swiftly over the tourist. His clothes . . . shoes . . . this man had money. Heyward didn't make a rule of selling relics; once in a while he let someone have a few arrow-heads for fifty cents apiece; but when opportunity knocked, Dwight Heyward was not one to keep opportunity waiting.

"To tell the truth," he purred, "I'm not in the habit of selling my curios. No, indeed. Buying—well, that's more the thing I do. Ha, ha. But—of course—"

The tourist brightened.

"If you've got something really good, I'd like to see it. Real old stuff is what I like. Mound builders' relics, and—"

THE REAL estate owner rubbed his hands. "Of course—you wouldn't be interested in trash. Let's see . . . in fact—" He was sparring for time. Here was a man, obviously possessed of an open purse, and Dwight Heyward didn't have anything worth offering. No tourist, no matter how daft over relics he might be, would pay a round sum for a splintered spearhead or a stone pipe of ordinary appearance. He wondered whether it might not be wise to attempt the sale of a lot in Komfort Kove Kamp Kolony.

If only he had something to pass off . . . something—

"—and old pottery and junk like that. I don't know

much about it, but all that stuff is pretty interesting. We got some dandy prehistoric vases in Taos, New Mexico. And—"

Rebuilding that scene, months later, Will Mott tried to trace the train of thought which must have been started in Dwight Heyward's brain. Vases, he thought, was the word which did it. Vases . . . flowers . . . lilies —or seeds. Flowers . . . Often, he wondered about it. Maybe his own presence there had brought up the wraith of Lily Louis.

At any rate, it was only a moment before Heyward was at his desk, rummaging in a bottom drawer.

"I've got something here—something extremely unusual." His tone implied that he might have a nail from the True Cross, or a finger of John the Baptist.

"Come here, if you don't mind. These—"

The tourist joined Heyward at the desk, and Mott followed him, more out of boredom than any interest in the proceedings.

Dwight Heyward displayed a cigar box, half full of small brown spheres that looked like clay marbles. "These," said Heyward, "are seeds. They were dug out of an ancient Indian grave, up the river a ways. The jar crumbled to pieces but— Here they are. Nobody could guess how old."

"Seeds, eh?" The tourist bent over the box. "Must be fifty or a hundred of them. What kind of seeds?"

Heyward rolled up his eyes.

"I haven't an idea. Maybe some plant—some ancient plant that—"

"Pshaw," interrupted Willard Mott. "Those are chinquapin seeds."

"Chinquapin?"

"Lotus seeds. Yellow water-lily, some folks call 'em. But that ain't the right name. Lotus, or chinquapin. That's what they are."

Heyward nodded. "They must be. I remember, now. People have them around here, sometimes. They sell them, don't they?"

"Used to." Mott thought guiltily of the box of lotus seeds hidden under a counter in his little shop. "It's against the law, since all those river islands was made into a government nature preserve. But folks still do sell them, I guess, once in awhile. The tourists come through here and see those big beds of pretty yellow flowers, and they go crazy over them. Want to take some seeds home . . . The Indians used to eat the seeds," he added meditatively. "But I never heard tell of finding the seeds in Indian graves."

Heyward shrugged.

"You've heard of it, now. A fellow came in here one day; he had driven a plow through an old mound, and he found these in there with a lot of other relics. Maybe they're thousands of years old. Who knows?"

The stranger stared with fascination at the mass of hard, brown balls.

"Want to sell them?"

"Well, I don't know. I thought you'd like to see them. Of course, I might sell a few—"

"Sell me half of them," the man offered. "What are they worth?"

Heyward squinted.

"Let's see. I paid—guess I paid a pretty stiff price for them and—"

Will Mott thought:

"And maybe not. You're a slick business man, Dwight Heyward." But he said nothing.

The tourist drew out a roll of bills.

"I'll give you fifty dollars for half of them."

HEYWARD PROTESTED, but not too volubly. He didn't like to sell the seeds, after all. They were unusual—some day a museum might pay a large sum and— He protested, but not too long. At length he allowed himself to be cajoled to the point where he counted out thirty of the round pellets and received fifty dollars in exchange.

Mott watched the proceedings in disgust. But he was thinking, hard. Lotus seeds in Indian graves. He had never heard of that—

"Can't remember the name of that fellow who sold you them things, can you?" he asked of Heyward before departing.

Heyward became wrapped in thought.

"Let's see. Was it Al Metzger? No, I guess not. Maybe Charley Underwood, or— No, I can't remember. Some old farmer up the river somewhere. He had some spear-heads and bones, too. I've got those around somewhere," he concluded, vaguely.

"Just wondered," said Mott. "Thought maybe it was Barney Lickstein. You can't trust him."

"It wasn't Barney Lickstein," replied Heyward. "These are straight stuff. I would never have sold them to this gentleman if there was the least doubt about their genuineness. You know that, Mott."

"Of course, of course," the guide agreed. "Sure you wouldn't, Heyward." But in his mind he remarked, "Can't remember the name. Hm."

He watched the tourist stow the little box of seeds carefully in the side pocket of his touring car. Heyward had placed them in an empty cracker box; not tied up, or anything. Hm.

They drove, then, to the old Indian battleground, and to a cave, and the inevitable Lovers' Leap, and the inevitable tree where a horse-thief was once hanged. Will Mott heard himself speaking his monologue, telling tales of early river days, of fur traders. But it seemed as if someone else was doing the talking.

Back at the shop, he received two dollars and the visitor's thanks. "Interesting country," the man said, heartily. He mopped his shiny, red face. "I've heard a lot about Deerskin, and always meant to stop off when I was driving near here. And those seeds." He slapped the side pocket. "You don't come across something like that every day."

From the bottom of his heart, Mott pitied this gullible pilgrim. "No, you sure don't . . . Say." He looked around with a show of caution. "Like a drink?"

The tourist nodded. "How much?" he whispered.

"Nothing. This is just my personal treat. But my wife lives up there—" he pointed to a small white cottage on a ledge of the hill a hundred yards above the shop— "and I don't want her to see me going down cellar with you. She'll know blame well what we were up to. So you go around to the back of the shop and open the cellar door. Go right down the steps and leave the door open, so's you can see. There's a demijohn on a shelf, and a glass right beside it. Help yourself and drink hearty."

As the delighted stranger scurried out of sight, Will Mott slid his brown hand into the side pocket of the car and brought out the little cracker box. In one quick gesture he had poured the seeds into his own trouser pocket. Then, moving speedily but without nervous alarm, he crossed to the front door of the shop, turned the key, and admitted himself. He could hear his patron moving about in the cellar, humming, making noises. That helped.

From beneath the counter, Mott produced a box of forbidden lotus seeds. He counted swiftly . . . twenty-eight, twenty-nine . . . In another moment he had closed the little cracker box on thirty chinquapin seeds, but chinquapin seeds dug from beneath his own counter rather than from any Indian grave.

THEN THE tourist made his heavy and florid way up the cellar steps, around the shop and along the little shale path, he found Will Mott standing with one lazy foot on the running board, gazing speculatively out upon the drowsy street and riverside.

"Good stuff?"

"Swell. What was it?"

"A kind of brandy. Make it myself. Got the recipe years ago from my brother, Louis Mott. He used to live over there." Will pointed toward Gar Island. "But he's dead now . . . Well, mister. Better come up here for a fishing trip before cold weather. I'll give you one of my cards."

He presented the man with one of the printed oblongs which displayed his tanned face above the uncomfortable whiteness of a collar. The picture was taken fifteen years before. *W. P. Mott. Sporting Goods,*

Souvenirs and Novelties. Private parties guided reasonable. Deerskin, Wis.

He received the man's thanks, and as he watched him drive away toward the ferry, his hand caressed the bumpy wad of lotus seeds in his pocket.

Ten minutes later, he strolled into Sheriff Sickles' office in the tobacco-smelling, cobwebby building at the other end of town, where the business of official Mesquakie County was not exactly rushing.

Sickles stared sleepily from under his stained hat-brim.

" 'Lo, Will." He took his feet off the desk.

Mott sat down on the desk, and went about the serious business of filling his pipe.

"Sickles, do you know much about chinquapins?"

"Chinquapins?" The sheriff yawned. "Lotus? Naw, not much . . . Your brother Louis was the fellow for chinquapins. Flowers and such. Louis knowed all that stuff."

"He sure did." Will puffed dreamily at his pipe. "Loved 'em."

"Sure did. Great fellow, Lily Louis."

"Ever have any new ideas about who killed him?"

"Naw. I've finally come to the notion that it was a drifter. Some tramp or maybe an Indian, sneaking down the river."

Mott grunted.

"Maybe so. Never felt any more suspicions about Kennedy, did you?"

"Naw. Nor young Heyward."

"Heyward's got a lot of money."

"Yep. But he's a slick one. He made that all."

Mott agreed.

"Maybe so. Bloodhounds didn't show us a thing, way I remember it."

Sickles switched the cud of tobacco to his other cheek.

"Just ran up and down the slough. Maybe they had a trail. If so, the fellow who did the killing came in a boat. Came in a boat, got out, went over to the ridge. Maybe got in a tussle with Louis, and then killed him. Took his body over to the edge of the slough, dropped it into the mud, slung the axe in there, and got back into the boat and rowed away."

"The Kennedy boys and Heyward was in boats, that morning."

"Say." Sickles chuckled with weak amusement. "You're a great one. Come in here, five years after the killing, and try to get worked up over the Kennedys and Heyward. You ought to remember that we give them up, long ago. Didn't we?"

"Yes. Yes. But I was just thinking a while—"

"What about?"

"Chinquapin seeds. The Indians used to eat 'em."

"They did, I guess."

"Ever hear of Indians burying them in their graves? I mean the real old Indians that made these animal mounds—effigy mounds, the summer folks call them. Ever hear of chinquapin seeds being dug out of mounds?"

"Never did. Did you?"

"I've heard tell of it," said Mott, as he sauntered toward the door. "But—we'll see."

Sickles stared after him as Mott went down the hall. Several times he started to replace his feet on the desk, but each time he would catch himself as a new thought, vague and ill-defined, crept into his brain.

"Chinquapins . . . Wonder what's eating him." He sighed. Lily Louis was a blame good fellow. Everybody liked him . . . Five years dead.

THE LAST smile of summer still held sway in the Winneshiek. The birds were going south in long V's of smoke against the pale blue sky, the cottonwood leaves were fluttering down like gold coins, but the air of daylight was still warm. Cold mists came at night, and colder hours when there was no mist, but bare-armed men still went trolling in the quiet backwaters.

Will Mott, standing on the threshold of The Relic House, was proposing no trolling journey, however. He knew that Dwight Heyward was too busy and important a personage in the community to spend much time at fishing, any more.

"It's a real Indian mound, all right," he told Heyward. "I dug into it a little way and found some old clay and fire ash. Likely there's plenty of relics inside."

Heyward nodded, cannily. That experience of selling lotus seeds to the red-faced tourist had convinced him that there was more than the value of publicity in such curios.

"Where'd you say it was?"

"Right along Gar Slough, up that little channel that runs east from the big island. It used to connect with Four Mile Bayou, but the connection is pretty well dried up, now. I just happened to stumble on it, crossing the marsh."

Again Heyward nodded. There would be no spoof about this. Will Mott knew those tortuous channels, and there were plenty of remote spots where few hunters or fishermen ever wandered.

"Could you take me over there this afternoon? I'll pay you well if it turns out to be anything."

"I guess this afternoon would be good." Mott's mild gaze scanned the driftless blue overhead. "I got a party to guide, tomorrow and Thursday, so maybe we better make it this afternoon."

They went across in the soggy, unpainted old scow which Mott's outboard motor drove methodically beyond the wider current.

"Better than a row-boat or canoe," he explained to Heyward. "Have to walk quite a ways when we get there, but it'll take less time than paddling through the shallows."

At the narrow head of navigation in Gar Slough, they beached the boat and struck out into the tangled labyrinths. For ten minutes they followed a narrow, well-trodden path, but at length Mott headed into tall grass.

"How about snakes?" inquired Heyward a trifle nervously. "I'm not afraid of mud—these are old clothes—but I haven't got high boots on."

"Noticed that you didn't. But don't worry. It's a little marshy, but I haven't seen no rattlers. I'll go ahead."

For another ten minutes they floundered in the tangling grasses. In this short time they had progressed far into the swamp—perhaps not more than a mile from the main channel, but probably two miles from the nearest human being, and as much cut off from civilization as if they had been in darkest Africa.

Heyward grunted and puffed behind the lean guide, slapping away the insects, and muttering that they'd have to be good relics to be worth all this.

"Won't be long now," Mott cheered him. "See those willows right ahead? They're on the higher ground where the mound is."

Beyond the border of elderly, water-soaked willow trunks stretched a lake of arrow-head and lotus thickets, still green under the early autumn sky.

"Right here." Mott pointed to an indefinite, grassy tunnel under the dark shadow of willows. "This is the longer way around, but you better take it. I've got high boots, so I'll go the quick way." He turned abruptly, and moved into the weedy brake, disappearing from the young realtor's gaze.

HEYWARD LOOKED unhappily at the grassy trail. It seemed damp, but safe enough. He grunted, swore, and skipped rapidly ahead. His first leap landed him on a knoll of seeming security, but as his weight centered on the surface there was an ominous crackling; Heyward plunged above his knees into a churning quagmire.

He cursed, volubly, and tried to climb out. But as he lifted his weight from one leg, the other slid down into unplumbed depths.

"Mott!" cried Heyward. His frantic hands clawed at the nearer tufts of grass, but they were evanescent things which came loosely away in his grasp.

"Mott!" he bellowed wildly.

The bushes parted, and Mott's gray eyes looked at him in surprise.

"You damn fool!" screamed Heyward. "Help me out of this! You said the path was solid and safe. You—" Something seemed to be gripping his legs in soft, formless tentacles.

Mott grunted: "By God. That's right. Seems like I—"

"Quicksand!" screeched the victim. "Can't you see? I'm going down. Look, it's almost up to my waist. Do something!"

Moving with hateful tardiness, the guide circled cautiously toward the landward side of the marsh, fumbled in the weeds, and brought forth a coil of rope. He tossed one end of the rope to Heyward. "Take it under your arms. That's right . . . Tie a good knot. That's it . . ."

Then, quite surprisingly, he had drawn the rope taut against a stout limb of the willow, taken a hitch about the limb, and knotted the coil loosely around a broken stub jutting from the trunk. He squatted on his heels, pipe gripped in his mouth, gazing at the man who struggled, half-submerged, before his eyes.

Heyward rolled a glassy stare in his direction.

"Pull!" he wailed. "Pull me out! That rope—" Globules of sweat stood out on his muddy forehead.

"Plenty of time for that," drawled Mott. "Figure we'll have a little talk first. You can't go much lower—not much."

Heyward's face turned livid with the surge of his exertions and a horrid realization which clutched at his heart. "That rope. It— Mott, you—" His tongue found itself amid horrible epithets. "What kind of a joke is this, anyway? You sent me into this pool, damn you. You had that rope hidden in the weeds. You—"

The tanned face nodded.

"Guessed right, Dwight. Only this ain't a joke. This is the third degree."

"Third degree? Third degree! What do you mean? God!" He bellowed "Help, help—somebody— He's torturing me—"

"That's a good word for it," agreed Will Mott. "Torture. Yes. I see stories about police and things in the movies, and they treat folks rough and make as if to kill them, and call it third degree. But this is more like real torture. And you can yell till hell won't hold it, and that's all the good it will do you. This is a lonesome country, out here in these sloughs."

Heyward's little eyes glowed, hateful and alive above his muddy face. "What do you want of me?" he snarled.

"Just a little torture," said Mott soothingly. "I read about this kind of thing, once't, in a magazine. Long time ago, in the Dark Ages, they found that this was a good way to make folks confess things. Works, usually."

The young man struggled for a moment in ugly silence. There was no sound other than his grunting

and straining at the rope. But the marsh drew him tighter at each twist of his body. "I—don't know what you—mean," he gasped.

"Just tell me about how you killed Lily Louis, that's all."

"Damn you," snarled the anguished Heyward. "It's a lie. I didn't—"

FOR REPLY, Mott rose calmly to his feet and unfastened the knot of rope. Burning quickly against the willow trunk, the brown strand jerked downward. Dwight Heyward sank a little deeper into the greasy slime.

"Mott," he gargled. "For God's sake—"

"Dwight, I'd just as soon kill you as kill a rat. It'll be easy, too—easiest thing I ever did. All I got to do is untie this rope, and down you go, rope and all. Nobody would ever get you out of there. When I was a boy, I've seen deer go into these places—cattle, too. And more than one man is down underneath that mud, probably. It'll be easy." He knotted the rope about the tree trunk once more.

Only Heyward's head and shoulders and gaunt, twisting arms protruded above the whistling muck.

"I know you killed my brother, Dwight. All I got to do is unhitch that rope and . . . Think it over. I'll give you one minute and down you go another notch." Calmly, Mott drew out his watch and scrutinized the dial.

"Thirty seconds gone," he said.

Heyward's face was green, a corpse face with eyes like coals.

"Forty-five seconds . . ." Mott arose; his free hand reached for the rope.

"I'll tell you," gasped Heyward. "I—I killed him."

"Ain't no news to me. I want to know all about it. How come, and why, and what happened? Don't think I'd go to the bother of torturing anybody to find out something I already know, do you?"

Heyward was silent. The other man's fingers touched the strand of hemp.

"I'll tell the whole business," gabbled Heyward.

Mott nodded. Unfastening the rope, he braced himself and swung his tough body against the rude pulley with a terrific lunge. Heyward grunted, but he was drawn up a few inches above the morass. Again his torturer fastened the knot.

"Well?" he inquired.

"I was fishing," groaned the young man. "Lost my bait can overboard. Thought I'd—go ashore on the Island and get some bait. Stopped at Louis' cabin to get a shovel. I came out of the mist, and there he was —digging on that little hill behind there. When he saw me, he let out a yell. I—"

He was silent, trembling, palsied.

"Shall I let her slide?" asked Mott quietly.

HEYWARD SNARLED, "No. For God's sake, I—
All right. He ordered me out of there. But— I had
heard stories about him having—money. I wanted to
take a look and— You won't believe it, but it was self-
defense. We got to fighting and—the pick-axe—"

"Self-defense," grunted Will Mott. "Sure. You killed
him in self-defense, and then took his money and beat
it. Robbery was the motive, I guess."

"Oh, hell," cried Dwight Heyward. "How could I
help it? He was dead and— Well, I thought I might as
well see what was in the hole. I finished digging. I
guess maybe he was taking that box out to get something out of it, or— I broke open the box. There were
some little sacks. I put them in my pockets. Then I
lugged him over to the slough and left him."

"What'd you do with the sacks?"

"I put them all in my undershirt, tied up with a
rock. Let them down on a strand of fish-line fastened
to an old drift. Came back later and—got them—"

"How about the chinquapin seeds, Dwight?"

Heyward's weary head lolled to one side.

"I didn't know what they were. I was afraid to throw
them away. Afraid somebody would find them, or
they'd grow or— I kept them in that cigar box in my
desk. For years. Forgot about them until that day last
summer. Thought I'd—cash in on them. Just a lot of—
old seeds."

"Yes," muttered Will Mott. "He set a great store by
them seeds, Louis did. Probably those was 'specially
choice ones that he had saved. You know, he was
always growing lotuses—moving them to new sloughs,
and things like that. Just some of his favorite seeds, I
guess. No wonder he kept them in the box. How about
the money?"

"There wasn't a lot. About two thousand—some bills,
and a little silver and gold."

"And you took it easy, didn't you? Sort of brought
the money out by degrees. It helped you get started,
I reckon."

Heyward nodded clammily.

Will Mott struggled with the rope, bending his stout
arms to bring about the necessary leverage. Occasionally he paused to rest, but always Dwight Heyward
was a little further out of the slime. At last Mott drew
him free, and dragged the man, a ghastly thing of
greasy blackness, up to the safety of solid ground.

Heyward rested, breathing heavily, his eyes still
darting about with hunted shrewdness. His body was
sore and bruised, but— On the way back. There might
be a chance. He didn't have a gun, but probably Mott
didn't have one either.

"Well," said Will. "Guess I got your confession."

Heyward nodded. "Looks that way." He grinned
inwardly; swell chance Mott would have of ever
proving—

"No witnesses, though," added Mott. "At least none
in sight."

Heyward shot a swift glance behind him. The weeds
swayed. Old Sheriff Sickles stepped out, looking very
grim, a small board in his hand.

"That board," Mott pointed out, "will do for a writing desk. You can write that confession out, Dwight,
as soon as you get rested up and washed off. We don't
stir from here until it's done. And it'll be all signed, of
course, and witnessed by me and the sheriff of Mesquakie County. I guess Sickles has got the main facts
noted down, but we want them complete and in your
own handwriting."

Heyward sobbed aloud.

"And then," drawled Mott, "we'll all go down the
river to Tomahawk Landing and put you in jail. Once't
we had a bad accident in Deerskin, when a murderer
was left overnight in jail there. We don't want it to
happen again. And don't get the idea that Sickles had
anything to do with this. He didn't know what I was
up to. It ain't reasonable to expect a sheriff to help
torture anybody.

"I thought it all out myself. Can't see any harm in
doing a little torturing, especially when you're certain
you got the right party."

Sickles eyed the huddled Heyward, and then gazed
sternly at Will Mott. "That's the only thing I can't
understand. How you was so certain—"

"Chinquapin seeds," said Will, "that Dwight claimed
was dug up in a mound twenty thousand years old. I
had never heard of that, so I took the ones that the
fellow bought off Dwight, and substituted a few of my
own. Nature's wonderful, Sickles. Chinquapin seeds
grow under the muddy water, but nature will let them
stay out of water seven years and still be fertile. That's
to take care of the droughts we get up here, sometimes."

He emptied out his pipe.

"Louis taught me that, years ago. But only seven
years is all the longer the stay fertile. They got to have
water that soon. I planted them, and I tended them
careful, and they started to grow. So I knew they
couldn't be dug out of no Indian mound. And Dwight
had to have some good reason, near as I could see, for
telling such a long lie about a few chinquapin seeds."

WAKE FOR THE LIVING

*"If you must know," snarled old Charles,
"I'm building my own coffin . . ."*

By RAY BRADBURY

*"That's a strange coffin you're building," Richard Braling said. "It's
almost big enough for two . . ."*

THERE WAS any amount of banging and hammering for a number of days along with deliveries of metal parts and oddments which Mr. Charles Braling took into his little workshop with feverish anxiety. He was a dying man, a badly dying man, and he seemed to be in a great hurry, between racking coughs and spitting, to piece together one last invention.

"What are you doing?" inquired his younger brother, Richard Braling. He had listened with increasing difficulty and much curiosity to that banging and rattling about, and now he stuck his head through the workroom door.

"Go far, far away and let me alone," said Charles Braling, who was seventy, trembly and wet-lipped most of the time. He trembled nails into place and trembled a hammer down with a weak blow upon a large timber and then stuck a small metal ribbon down into an intricate machine, and, all in all, was having a carnival of labor.

Richard looked on, bitter-eyed, for a long moment. There was a hatred between them. It had gone on for

some years and now was neither better nor worse for the fact that Charlie was dying. Richard was delighted to know of the impending death, if he thought of it at all. But this busy fervor of his brother's stimulated him.

"Pray tell," he asked, not moving from the door.

"If you must know," snarled old Charles, fitting in an odd thingumabob on the box before him, "I'll be dead in another week and I'm—I'm building my own coffin!"

"A coffin, my dear Charlie; that doesn't *look* like a coffin. A coffin isn't that complex. Come on now, what *are* you up to?"

"I tell you it is a coffin! An odd coffin, yes, but, nevertheless—" the old man moved his fingers around within the large box—"nevertheless a coffin!"

"But it would be easier to buy one."

"Not one like this! You couldn't buy one like this any place, ever. Oh, it will be a really fine coffin, all right."

"You're obviously lying." Richard moved forward. "Why, that coffin is a good twelve feet long. Six feet longer than normal size!"

"Oh, yes?" The old man laughed quietly.

"And that transparent top; who ever heard of a coffin lid you can see through? What good is a transparent lid to a corpse?"

"Oh, just never you mind at all," sang the old man heartily. "La!" And he went humming and hammering about the shop.

"This coffin is terribly thick," shouted the young brother over the din. "Why, it must be five feet thick; how utterly unnecessary!"

"I only wish I might live to patent this amazing coffin," said old Charlie. "It would be a God-send to all the poor peoples of the world. Think how it would eliminate the expense of most funerals. Oh, but, of course, you don't know how it would do that, do you? How silly of me. Well, I shan't tell you. If this coffin could be mass-produced—expensive at first, naturally—but then when you finally got them made in vast quantities, ah, but the money people would save."

"To hell with it!" And the younger brother stormed out of the shop.

IT HAD been an unpleasant life. Young Richard had always been such a bounder he had never had two coins to clink together at one time; all of his money had come from old brother Charlie, who had the indecency to remind him of it at all times. Richard spent many hours with his hobbies; he dearly loved piling up bottles with French wine labels, in the garden. "I like the way they *glint*," he often said, sitting and sipping and sipping and sitting. He was the man in the county who could hold the longest gray ash on a fifty-cent cigar for the longest recorded time. And he knew how to hold his hands so his diamonds jangled in the light. But he had not bought the wine, the diamonds, the cigars—no! They were all gifts. He was never allowed to buy anything himself. It was always brought to him and given to him. He had to ask for everything, even writing paper. He considered himself quite a martyr to have put up with taking things from that rickety old brother for so long a time. Everything Charlie ever laid his hand to turned to money; everything Richard ever tried in the way of a leisurely career had failed.

And now, here was this old mole of a Charlie whacking out a new invention which would probably bring Charlie additional specie long after his bones were slotted in the earth!

Well, two weeks passed.

One morning the old brother toddled upstairs and stole the insides from the electric phonograph. Another morning he raided the gardener's greenhouse. Still another time he received a delivery from a medical company. It was all young Richard could do to sit and hold his long gray cigar ash steady while these murmuring excursions took place.

"I'm finished!" cried old Charlie on the fourteenth morning, and dropped dead.

Richard finished out his cigar and, without showing his inner excitement, he laid down his cigar with its fine long whitish ash, two inches long, a real record, and arose.

He walked to the window and watched the sunlight playfully glittering among the fat beetle-like champagne bottles in the garden.

He looked toward the top of the stairs where dear old brother Charlie lay peacefully sprawled against the banister. Then he walked to the phone and perfunctorily dialed a number.

"Hello, Green Lawn Mortuary? This is the Braling residence. Will you send around a wicker, please? Yes. For brother Charlie. Yes. Thank you. Thank you."

As the mortuary people were taking brother Charles out in their wicker, they received instructions. "Ordinary casket," said young Richard. "No funeral service. Put him in a pine coffin. He would have preferred it that way—simple. Good-bye."

"Now!" said Richard, rubbing his hands together. "We shall see about this 'coffin' built by dear Charlie. I do not suppose he will realize he is not being buried in his 'special' box. Ah."

He entered the downstairs shop.

The coffin sat before some wide-flung French windows, the lid shut, complete and neat, all put together like the fine innards of a Swiss watch. It was vast, and it rested upon a long long table with rollers beneath for easy maneuvering.

The coffin interior, as he peered through the glass lid, was six feet long. There must be a good three feet of false body at both head and foot of the coffin, then. Three feet at each end which, covered by secret panels that he must find some way of opening, might very well reveal—exactly what?

Money, of course. It would be just like Charlie to suck his riches into his grave with himself, leaving Richard with not a cent to buy a bottle with. The old tightwad!

He raised the glass lid and felt about, but found no hidden buttons. There was a small sign studiously inked on white paper, thumb-tacked to the side of the satin-lined box. It said:

THE BRALING ECONOMY CASKET. Simple to operate. Can be used again and again by morticians and families with an eye to the future.

Richard snorted thinly. Who did Charlie think he was fooling?

There was more writing:

DIRECTIONS: SIMPLY PLACE BODY IN COFFIN.

What a fool thing to say. Put body in coffin! Naturally! How else would one go about it? He peered intently and finished out the directions:

SIMPLY PLACE BODY IN COFFIN—AND MUSIC WILL START.

"*It can't be!*" Richard gaped at the sign. "Don't tell me all this work has been for a—" He went to the open door of the shop, walked out upon the tiled terrace and called to the gardener in his greenhouse. "Rogers!" The gardener stuck his head out. "What time is it?" asked Richard.

"Twelve o'clock, sir," replied Rogers.

"Well, at twelve-fifteen, you come up here and check to see if everything is all right, Rogers." "Yes, sir," said the gardener. Richard turned and walked back into the shop. "We'll find out—" he said, quietly.

There would be no harm in lying in the box, testing it. He noticed small ventilating holes in the sides. Even if the lid were closed down there'd be air. And Rogers would be up in a moment or two. Simply place body in coffin—and music will start. Really, how naive of old Charlie. Richard hoisted himself up.

H E WAS like a man getting into a bathtub. He felt naked and watched over. He put one shiny shoe into the coffin, and crooked his knee and eased himself up and made some little remark to nobody in particular; then he put in his other knee and foot and crouched there, as if undecided about the temperature of the bath-water. Edging himself about, chuckling softly, he lay down, pretending to himself; "for it was fun pretending" that he was dead, that people were dropping tears on him, that candles were fuming and illuminating and that the world was stopped in midstride because of his passing. He put on a long pale expression, shut his eyes, holding back the laughter in himself behind pressed, quivering lips. He folded his hands and decided they felt waxen and cold.

Whirr! Spung! Something whispered inside the box-wall. *Spung!*

The lid slammed down on him!

From outside, if one had just come into the room, one would have imagined a wild man was kicking, pounding, blathering and shrieking inside a closet! There was a sound of a body dancing and cavorting. There was a thudding of flesh and fists. There was a squeaking and a kind of wind from a frightened man's lungs. There was a rustling like paper and a shrilling as of many pipes simultaneously played. Then there was a real fine scream. Then—silence.

Richard Braling lay in the coffin and relaxed. He let loose all his muscles. He began to chuckle. The smell of the box was not unpleasant. Through the little perforations he drew more than enough air to live comfortably on. He need only push gently up with his hands, with none of this kicking and screaming, and the lid would open. One must be calm. He flexed his arms.

The lid was locked.

Well, still there was no danger. Rogers would be up in a minute or two. There was nothing to fear.

The music began to play.

It seemed to come from somewhere inside the head of the coffin. It was fine music. Organ music, very slow and melancholy, typical of Gothic arches and long black tapers. It smelled of earth and whispers. It echoed high between stone walls. It was so sad that one almost cried listening to it. It was music of potted plants and crimson and blue-stained glass windows. It was late sun at twilight and a cold wind blowing. It was a dawn with only fog and a far away fog-horn moaning.

"Charlie, Charlie, Charlie, you old fool, you! So this is your odd coffin!" Tears of laughter welled into Richard's eyes. "Nothing more than a coffin which plays its own dirge. Oh, my sainted grandma!"

He lay and listened critically, for it was beautiful music and there was nothing he could do until Rogers came up and let him out. His eyes roved aimlessly; his fingers tapped soft little rhythms on the satin cushions. He crossed his legs, idly. Through the glass lid he saw sunlight shooting through the French windows, dust particles dancing on it. It was a lovely blue day with wisps of clouds overhead.

The sermon began.

The organ music quieted and a gentle voice said:

"We are gathered together, those who loved and those who knew the deceased, to give him our homage and our due—"

"Charlie, bless you, that's *your* voice!" Richard was delighted. A mechanical, transcribed funeral, by God! Organ music and lecture, on records! And Charlie giving his own oration for himself!

The soft voice said, "We who knew and loved him are grieved at the passing of—"

"What was *that*?" Richard raised himself, startled. He didn't quite believe what he had heard. He repeated it to himself just the way he had heard it:

"We who knew and loved him are grieved at the passing of Richard Braling."

That's what the voice had said.

"Richard Braling," said the man in the coffin. "Why, *I'm* Richard Braling."

A slip of the tongue, naturally. Merely a slip. Charlie had meant to say, *Charles* Braling. Certainly. Yes. Of course. Yes. Certainly. Yes. Naturally. Yes.

"Richard was a fine man," said the voice, talking on. "We shall see no finer in our time."

"My name, *again*!"

Richard began to move about uneasily in the coffin.

Why didn't Rogers come?

It was hardly a mistake, using that name twice. Richard Braling. Richard Braling. We are gathered here. We shall miss . . . We are grieved. No finer man. No finer in our time. We are gathered here. The deceased. Richard Braling. *Richard* Braling.

Whirrrr! Spunng!

Flowers! Six dozen bright blue, red, yellow, sun-brilliant flowers leaped up from behind the coffin on concealed springs!

The sweet odor of fresh-cut flowers filled the coffin. The flowers swayed gently before his amazed vision, tapping silently on the glass lid. Others sprang up, and up, until the coffin was banked with petals and color and sweet odors. Gardenias and dahlias and petunias and daffodils, trembling and shining.

"Rogers!"

The sermon continued.

". . . Richard Braling, in his life, was a connoisseur of great and good things. . . ."

The music sighed, rose and fell, distantly.

". . . Richard Braling savored of life as one savors of a rare wine, holding it upon the lips. . . ."

A SMALL panel in the side of the box flipped open. A swift bright metal arm snatched out. A needle stabbed Richard in the thorax, not very deeply. He screamed. The needle shot him full of a colored liquid before he could seize it. Then it popped back into a receptacle and the panel snapped shut.

"Rogers!"

A growing numbness. Suddenly he could not move his fingers or his arms or turn his head. His legs were cold and limp.

"Richard Braling loved beautiful things. Music. Flowers," said the voice.

"Rogers!"

This time he did not scream it. He could only think it. His tongue was motionless in his anaesthetized mouth.

Another panel opened. Metal forceps issued forth on steel arms. His left wrist was pierced by a huge sucking needle.

His blood was being drained from his body.

He heard a little pump working somewhere.

". . . Richard Braling will be missed among us. . . ."

The organ sobbed and murmured.

The flowers looked down upon him, nodding their bright-petalled heads. Six candles, black and slender, rose up out of hidden receptacles and stood behind the flowers, flickering and glowing.

Another pump started to work. While his blood drained out one side of his body, his right wrist was punctured, held, a needle shoved into it, and the second pump began to force formaldehyde into him.

Pump, pause, *pump*, pause, *pump*, pause, *pump*, pause.

The coffin moved.

A small motor popped and chugged. The room drifted by on either side of him. Little wheels revolved. No pallbearers were necessary. The flowers swayed as the casket moved gently out upon the terrace under a blue clear sky.

Pump, pause. *Pump*, pause.

"Richard Braling will be missed by all his. . . ."

Sweet soft music.

Pump, pause.

"Ah, sweet mystery of life, at last . . ." Singing.

"Braling, the gourmet . . ."

"Ah, I know at last the secret of it all. . . ."

Staring, staring, his eyes egg-blind, at the little card out of the corners of his eyes: THE BRALING ECONOMY CASKET.

Directions: Simply place body in coffin—and music will start.

A tree swung by overhead. The coffin rolled gently through the garden, behind some bushes, carrying the voice and the music with it.

"Now it is the time when we must consign this part of this man to the earth. . . ."

Little shining spades leaped out of the sides of the casket.

They began to dig.

He saw the spades toss up dirt. The coffin settled. Bumped, settled, dug, bumped, and settled, dug, bumped and settled again.

Pump, pause, *pump*, pause, *pump*, pause, *pump*, pause.

"Ashes to ashes, dust to dust. . . ."

The flowers glistened and waved. The box was deep. The music played.

The last thing Richard Braling saw was the spading arms of the Braling Economy Casket reaching up and pulling the hole in after it.

"Richard Braling, Richard Braling, Richard Braling, Richard Braling, Richard Braling. . . ."

The record was stuck.

Nobody minded. Nobody was listening.

Exploiting the Girls / 6 / Innocence

In 1912 women were campaigning vigorously for equal rights with men and Pulp publisher W. M. Clayton probed a virgin market with the first tentative serving of quasi-erotica, *Snappy Stories*. The primly attired girls who adorned its covers might deceive the innocent; but the public whose prurient interest *Snappy Stories* intended to exploit was tipped off by the subtitle: "A Magazine of Entertaining Fiction." The key word was, of course, "Entertaining," and it was to send a trend for other code-words such as "zippy," "peppy," and "saucy." The field was entered in 1915 by another magazine of note, *The Parisienne*. Although it did not use catchwords on its cover as a come-on, *The Parisienne* did wreath its title page in cigarette smoke, titillatingly produced by a pair of crossed cigarettes. (At the time, cigarette smoking by women in public was a sign of emancipation and "fastness," as drinking was to become a few years later.)

To avoid incurring the displeasure of the authorities these Pulps devoted a large proportion of the contents to romantic fiction, poetry, and anecdotes, often by writers of some prominence, and generally glorifying the virtues and qualities of Woman. Most of the suggestive material now seems quaint, though it was written in what was considered to be a sophisticated style at the time. The themes usually concerned women who were exposed to the temptations of emotional excess: single girls who found themselves involved with the "wrong kind" of men, such as underworld figures; wives flirting with men other than their husbands; and women faced with a choice between adventure and marriage. The threat underlying the latter situation ran the gamut—from "missing one's chance" to developing a callousness undesirable in a wife. Complications developed only through excesses of emotional involvement; sleeping together was not even so much as implied in these early magazines.

Most story endings fell into one of three types: the woman triumphed over temptation; she succumbed to the lure of her feelings and was either dishonored or lost out on "the better things in life"; or she was forgiven for her flirtation by the fiance or husband she had scorned.

These early Pulps split into two groups in the early 20's. The "respectable" material, following Hollywood's lead, became the basis for a new Pulp, *Love Story*, published by Street and Smith. It was characterized by deeply emotional and romantically idealized fiction completely devoid of sexual connotations. *Love Story* became a best-seller and model for dozens of other magazines and flourished as a Pulp until the 50's.

The more suggestive material fostered a bolder group of Pulps with titles such as *Zest, Pep,* and *Droll Stories*. Their covers boasted "Lively Stories Sizzling with Speed-Spice-Sparkle," hinting that the sexual intentions of the heroes and heroines would be described and that sleeping together would be implied. This was accomplished by leaving the prospective lovers in seclusion and closing the paragraph with three dots.

Many of the stories were written under pen-names and the magazines themselves were sold "under the counter." Since the ads in these Pulps were aimed at women as well as men, it would indicate that they successfully attracted both audiences.

*   *   *

"Hot Rompers", by Russ West, appeared in 1931 in *Parisienne Life*, an under-the-counter Pulp. Passing for pornography in its day, "Hot Rompers" is suggestive enough to form a link between the early Pulps such as *Snappy Stories* and their really salacious successors such as *Spicy Detective* and *Spicy Mystery,* which first appeared in 1934.

* * *

The rest of the material in this section is the type of camouflage which was published by the early above-the-counter Pulps in their effort to maintain a respectable appearance.

* * *

The poem, "Enter the Vampire", (Saucy Stories, 1917) was written by the prolific author, anthologist and teacher, Clement Wood, who was also a bitter and volatile critic of racial and social injustice.

* * *

"Seeing New York by Kiddie Car" is a sketch written by noted author Philip Wylie. It was published in *Zest* in 1926 when Wylie was 23 years old and working on the staff of *The New Yorker.*

* * *

John Held, Jr. achieved fame as a cover-artist for the old *Life* during the 20's and 30's. His series of sketches entitled "Kitty the Kisser" (*Snappy Stories,* 1924) foreshadows the style of his more famous later work.

* * *

"A Plea for the Old Music", by Richard Le Gallienne, a popular poet of the period, appeared in 1919 in *Snappy Stories.* It is one of many poems by him which that magazine published.

* * *

Harry Irving Shumway was another frequent contributor to these Pulps. His poem, "A Place for Everything", also appeared in *Snappy Stories* in 1919.

* * *

Almost every story was followed by a page-filling poem, a vignette, or "one-liners" like Carrington North's "Wisdom" (*Saucy Stories,* 1920).

* * *

Hot Rompers

By RUSS WEST

"Hamlin was entertaining a brace of cuties—"

MFERDINAND DE BRISSAC had it in his head to shoot an American. The reason was plain: Bert Hamlin, the American, had been making headway with Ferdinand's carefree and capricious wife, Jenni. What is meant by headway? Well, he'd taken a pair of Jennie's panties—Ferdinand suspected he'd taken them right off the warm flesh they'd originally clothed—and shown them around to his friends as a boast and a souvenir. One of these "friends," having some regard for Ferdinand, had reported this. Certainly it wasn't very gentlemanly of Hamlin to have acted thus.

Ferdinand, a wine merchant, had been forced to make a tour of the Meuse Valley, recently, to inspect the grape industry. On his return he'd found a pair of Bert Hamlin's shoes—the name was stamped on the insole—in Jenni's closet. He'd been shocked beyond belief to discern, hanging on the same hook with Jenni's ripped nightie, a pair of Hamlin's monogrammed pajamas. Is it any wonder that he should want to shoot the American?

The enraged husband was slumped at a table in the Club du Nord with a loaded lead-dealing instrument in his pocket. Just a few yards away, Hamlin, drunkenly unconscious of Ferdinand's designs on his irresponsible life, was entertaining a brace of cuties. They were the typical *femmes de joie* and daughters of sin. One wore a skirt slit so severely up the side that Ferdinand could see not only the limits of her misty stockings but spacious inches of woman-flesh where her white thigh looped out softly and became something more personal. Her breasts, all but bared by the dazzling, daring economy of her brilliant-sewn bodice, were like perfectly shaped, tender and carefully bleached gourds studded with coral. Her red damask lips moved in ardent phrases, probably flattery; her passion-fueled eyes gleamed soft, melting, beseeching into Bert Hamlin's as he stroked her knee with insinuating privilege.

The other girl had stretched herself across Hamlin's lap. Her rhinestone heels were on the table. The satin of her gown tautened about her flagrant form with the smugness of nudity itself. The entire length of her legs

was on view. Hamlin quite openly was fingering the curves that would have made this cocotte's breasts ideal material for any artist's canvas.

It infuriated Ferdinand, for the scene made him think of the hours this gutter dog from the States must have spent with Jenni. In fact the more he looked at the passionate abandon and insinuating posture of the girl on Hamlin's lap the more she seemed to resemble Jenni in the throes of ecstasy. Ferdinand had to turn his face away many times to keep from shooting Bert Hamlin right there in cold blood. He had to be cautious, that was certain. He wanted to be alone with the American—at least more alone than he was now—to address a few remarks to him before he should extinguish his life. And, of course, he earnestly wished to escape once he'd given his wife's lover what the *cochon* deserved.

Hence this show of patience.

Suddenly the place seemed electrified, however. A spotlight had torn through the bluish, smoke-filled atmosphere and pinned its revealing circle on a nude figure advancing from a doorway beside the orchestra rostrum. Anisia, the dancer! A small, silver leaf was her entire drapery. That and the pearls that held it in place composed a complete costume for the daring dance in which Anisia was now tumbling her hips. Waveringly, lambently, her bosom shook. Sinuously

she moved her hips in time to the music. Now she crouched like a crab, now she sprang high, madly in the air. And in whatever posture eyes beheld her, her glorious, mordant whiteness was intimately on display; her glaring nudity a spectacle of plump contours and smooth, rounded girlishness.

Even Ferdinand sat up straight to watch. This dancer had the most exciting body he'd beheld in months. And of course the man he'd come to murder was all but standing on his chair, in order to miss no whirling detail or sensuous gesture of Anisia's roving thighs.

"I must send a note back to that girl," Ferdinand was thinking. "An hour or two with Anisia would certainly be delightful." But his errand in coming there intruded itself.

"No," Ferdinand concluded to himself, "I must first deal with this love burglar of an American. Until I have had satisfaction of him I have no time for women nor spirit to enjoy myself."

Anisia was finishing her dance in a clamorous throbbing and heaving of her body, a mad orgy of frenzied sinfulness that threatened to dislodge the small, jeweled trifle she was wearing as a "costume." It fell to the floor. The lights went out. Anisia must have fled in the darkness for they went on again instantly and Anisia wasn't there.

Ferdinand, somehow, was first on to the dance floor to retrieve the tiny silver leaf with its now dangling strands of pearls. The entire gathering was laughing at the rush almost every man in the place had made. For whoever picked up this badge of Anisia's delectable depravity had the privilege of returning it to her—in private.

Almost absently Ferdinand stuck the intimate trinket in his pocket. The patrons whom he had defeated in the rush to pick it up returned to their tables variously smiling and disgruntled. Ferdinand, however, felt no sense of triumph or jubilation. He'd simply jumped up and grasped the loin decoration instinctively after seeing it fall to the floor.

And now he was worried because Bert Hamlin, his proposed victim, had apparently got away from him and taken one of the impassioned cocottes with him. The other was still sitting where she'd been left, alone and apparently looking about for quarry.

Ferdinand went directly to her.

"What has become of *M'sieur* Hamlin, your escort of a moment ago, *M'mselle*?" he asked in French.

The snappy *fille* gave a flirtatious flutter of her eyelids.

"I think he has taken my companion upstairs, *M'sieur*. Shall we follow?" As she spoke she had been drawing her skirt back along her immaculate, garter-striped thigh in the age-old gesture of the inveterate flirt.

"*I'll* follow, you stay here," Ferdinand cautioned.

Upstairs was one of the many Paris hotels in which you hire rooms not by the day or week but by the *hour*. It was going to be a trial finding Bert Hamlin's "withdrawing room" with many rooms occupied and nobody required to register. But if he hurried he might catch up to Hamlin and his flame in the corridor, before they had time to enter any of the rooms. In that frame of mind Ferdinand hastened through the halls upstairs.

It was while he was prowling down one of the corridors, intent on listening at keyholes until he should hear a voice resembling Bert Hamlin's, that he had a most peculiar accident. A girl suddenly opened a door and emerged into the corridor in nothing but the least important part of her undies. She was staggering and laughing alcoholically. The wisp of unimportant drape added a touch of mystery, but absolutely no disguise to the lively pink contours of her pinkly pert person.

She threw her arms about Ferdinand, laughing crazily, and began to writhe and tremble in his embrace. Ferdinand's stick was knocked off his arm and clattered against a door on his left. He disengaged himself from the maudlin, half-mad creature who had thrown herself at him and she staggered off down the corridor. Ferdinand bent to pick up his stick. At the same time the door against which it had rattled opened. Also, as

he bent over, the silver leaf, he had picked up on the dance floor downstairs, fell out of his pocket.

"Did you knock?"

Ferdinand straightened to behold Anisia, trimly pink, alive and almost nude in a chiffon dressing sac. Her rich black hair was caught in a twisted silver bandeau. Luxuriant dark fringe framed her purple eyes. Her lips seemed to be pursed and holding kisses on their soft surface. And once again he looked at the live color, the natural, vibrant pink contours showing through her chiffon wrap.

"Oh, you brought my fig leaf," Anisia seemed to take the matter for granted. "Come in quickly."

Almost before Ferdinand knew it he was alone with Anisia in her suite.

"You're an American!" he said in some amazement.

Anisia sat down on a low divan, crossing her legs with an all-revealing sweep.

"Yes, would you like to hear my story?"

Ferdinand thought of declining, offering as his excuse the fact that he had come there to kill a man. But he didn't want to shock Anisia. He simply nodded dumbly.

"Come here and sit down beside me," Anisia invited. And almost immediately she was a throbbing, panting, wanting bundle of mobile femininity in his arms. Ferdinand couldn't have explained quite how it happened. He'd sat down beside her, felt the pull of her lips on his emotions, and the next thing they were wildly enmeshed in the passions that neither could deny.

Marvelously yielding, yet poignantly firm, Anisia's figure seemed to give of its warmth and its ardor. Caressing her gave Ferdinand the impression of touching delight with his bare hands. They writhed in a hurricane of undisciplined liberty.

But Ferdinand's troublesome mission kept him from completely enjoying himself. And at last he straightened with the words.

"Anisia, you must excuse me. I'm afraid that should I not do right now what I came here to do, I shall not care to be bothered later."

"But who's stopping you, dear one?" It's barely possible that Anisia misinterpreted Ferdinand's statement! "I seem to have forgotten to give you my biography. Know what they used to call me at school, back in the U. S. A.? 'Little Hot Rompers'—I went for the boys in such generous style. So you see this is no ordinary playmate you've picked yourself."

Ferdinand was quite well aware of that by this time, so he sank back in indolent compliance. Anisia was threshing about, acting restless. But Ferdinand soon soothed her with kisses, with caresses.

There is an end to all things, however, even the most delightful. At a later hour, therefore, Ferdinand was bidding the adorable Anisia adieu. Their lips met in deep, frantic embrace. Their forms merged in splendid fervor. Somewhat weakly, shakenly, Ferdinand turned and opened the door into the corridor. At the same instant he stiffened. He was face to face with Bert Hamlin, who leered at him in amiable, drunken lack of recognition!

Ferdinand's hand flew to his hip. He rushed the pistol out of his pocket and aimed it smack at Hamlin's head. A woman's scream cracked the silence. Ferdinand's arm was battered down, the automatic belched aimlessly, and fingers seized Ferdinand's ear with a relentless grip which he recognized at once as Jenni's expert grip.

"At last you come out, eh, *mon gros renard!* I saw you come in here and have waited in the corridor for hours, not knowing which of these rooms you occupied. But you come home with me now and I keep my eye on you from this time on!" Petite, modish Jenni was pouring over him a very cataract of information and abuse.

"Oh, I shay," Bert Hamlin exclaimed, staggering after the pair quite unharmed. "I shay, Jenni, aren't you gonna speak to me?"

"To you? You were just an interlude, *mon ami.* I have forgotten I ever knew you. Now, I must worry about my husband!"

Ferdinand stopped wincing from the pull on his ear long enough to crease his Gallic face in a smile.

"You won't have to worry about me, Jenni, if I don't have to worry about you and this American. And *merci beaucoup* for knocking that weapon out of my hand.

I'd much rather go home with you than go to jail."

Enter the Vampire
CLEMENT WOOD

THE Vampire once was not a bit respectable;
   They called her quite exotic and outré;
And tho' the taste was bloody, they thought her thirst
      too ruddy;
   Meals should be made in some more usual way.
So ducking vampires all declared delectable—
   Or burning them—it didn't matter which;
A maid who drank corpuscles was seized by brawny
      muscles
   And treated like an ordinary witch.

The style in maidens then was Lydia Languishy;
   The fragile dame must simply drizzle weeps.
She must be apt at fainting, and water-color painting;
   She seemed to be the favorite for keeps.
She passed—and, tired of poses weak and anguishy,
   Sweet brainless Beauty now was all the rage;
And Pickford and her sisters were the chosen of the
      Misters—
   Until the Vampire seized upon the stage.

And now she writhes and wriggles thru' the photoplay,
   And gloats upon her victim's very gore;
She violently vexes each admirer she annexes;
   She vamps—need we elaborate it more?
Yet since she's got to thrill us the *in toto* play,
   She has to keep it up five weary reels.
Tho' we may say, in passing, just to soften the
      harassing,
   She has to vamp, to earn her daily meals.

Saucy Stories, 1917

Seeing New York By Kiddie Car

By Philip G. Wylie

DOWN TOWN

MRS. RICHARD FILBERT, of Sioux Rapids, Iowa, looked eagerly down one of the many side streets that ball up traffic in and about Times Square, New York City. It was the ninth of September—no, it was the tenth, because Sarah came down with rheumatism on the ninth, and that was a Thursday.

"There," she said, "are the Kiddie Cars." And, sure enough, there they were; for, whatever else the worthy vice president of the Ladies' Aid was, she was not a liar.

The small man at her side to whom she had spoken was her husband, and it was more her fault than any one else's that he always looked as though he had just swallowed the stump of a cigar. As a matter of fact, she never allowed him to smoke, so the possibility of swallowing even one cigar-butt was plainly all too remote.

They hurried up to the Kiddie Cars, passing Ed's Ready Lunch en route. "We're off!" cried Mrs. Filbert as one and all the sightseers grasped the steering mechanisms of the stanch little vehicles and commenced to paddle toward a policeman who weighed about one hundred and ninety-five pounds. Filbert nodded in agreement, at the same time jamming the wheel hard over to avoid hitting Pony de Beer, of New Orleans, who was crossing the street at the time. Up ahead a man with a megaphone had already started to point out the many interesting sights which their gray-brown-tickets entitled them to see. The heart of the great city closed about them, and far away indeed the Filberts felt from bee-helmets and Shetland ponies.

"You are now on Broadway," the man was shouting, although nobody understood him, "the Great White Way, home of the sucker and the Flea Circus, and the best advertising medium for chewing gum in the United States. On your right is the Paramount Building. Mr. Paramount may be seen entering the front door. . . . Ah, Mr. Paramount!"

The guide, or lecturer, waved a friendly greeting toward the gentleman he had pointed out. The guide was named Jasper after his father. From now on we will call him Jasper. Hey, Jasper—like that.

"I'll bet he's rich," Mrs. Filbert said in an awed tone, referring to Mr. Paramount.

Jasper overheard the exclamation and fixed a monocle in his eye. For a long time he stared at Mrs. Filbert. Then he said, "Mercy!" and after that she breathed more easily. Jasper resumed his hollering:

"If you get tired pushing with one foot, change to the other. Please keep in line, Mr—?"

"Pevis."

"Mr. Pevis. We are now approaching City Hall, where the laws of New York are made and broken. New York has the cleverest Mayor in the world. For instance, he couldn't keep away from cabarets, so he made a law closing them at two o'clock. Next year, if he isn't too busy eating lunches, he is going to make another law requiring all people to procure hunting licenses before entering shooting galleries."

Mrs. Filbert sighed ecstatically. "There's the City Hall, Ed," she said to a total stranger.

"Pardon, madam, that is a bank," Jasper interrupted her. "Over there is the City Hall," and he pointed to a little hutch that resembled a fairly large county jail, although uglier and smaller. "And there is the Woolworth Building—they tried to make it as high as Eiffel tower, but there weren't enough nickels and dimes in the country. It falls over every once in a while, and the tourists miss it for a day or two, but nowadays it only takes four or five hours to build a thing like that, and nothing is really expected to be permanent."

"Well, well!" Mr. Filbert said, "That's the first airedale I've seen in New York." And right he was, except that there was a little collie in the dog. Years afterward he used to say, "Sure I saw the Woolworth Building. There was an airedale in front of it. I'll never forget it—only the dog wasn't as big." And every one in Sioux Rapids would slap their thighs and go on whittling.

Jasper's voice pierced the hushed silence of Lower Broadway. "There goes the Mayor himself. He's the one carrying the coal scuttle." The Mayor waved his hat, and the little procession stopped while news reels of the event were being made. Then the Mayor made a speech of welcome and the Fire Department Band played "Annie Laurie," and one and all, including the reporters, voted him a good fellow, without a single dissenting voice.

"Write down the things we've seen," Mrs. Filbert said, and Mr. F. wrote, "Times Building, Flea Circus, lame man, Degan's Drug Store, Mayor, airedale, Woolworth Building, Mr. Paramount, City Hall, postmen (7), Brooklyn Bridge."

"Why did you put in Brooklyn Bridge?" she asked.

"I thought I caught a glimpse of it," he said sheepishly.

They passed the Tombs, where they noticed that the cracksmen and the embezzlers were giving a little cake sale for the benefit of the Park Avenue débutantes. Then they came to the Bowery. "Everything is quiet here now," Jasper yelled, "because the crooks gave up trying to make as much noise as they do in Chicago. There was a murder here last night, though." Mrs. Filbert shivered happily and speeded up to get a little closer to her husband. "A desperado named Wiggins brutally dispatched a cat known as 'Dora' with a hob-nail boot."

"Did you hear that?" she said.

Filbert, wise in the wickedness of the world as he was, made no reply.

"The tale of the Bowery is an old and romantic one," Jasper went on, in spite of the fact that he was a little hoarse. "John L. Sullivan used to stalk proudly down this street, hitching up his trousers, and making frightful faces at the street urchins. I'll never forget the face he made at me one day. I keep it locked away in a trunk in my mother's attic in Jersey City. Every St. Swithin's day I unwrap it from its sheath of cabbage leaves. What memories it conjures up!"

The sightseers looked at their guide with awakened interest.

From the Bowery they went to Chinatown, which was even dirtier. There they learned that the real Chinaman who lived almost in Chinatown except for Farragut Avenue coming between had been arrested for carrying a concealed slingshot, and so, while the wheel on the car being run by the lady from Duluth was being repaired, they put a wreath on his front porch. Mrs. F. wanted to leave a note with the wreath, but her husband wouldn't let her. "It might start a Tong War," he said darkly.

"Ridiculous!" she answered, not knowing what he meant, but assuming anything he said would be, anyway.

"And now we'll go on to the Aquarium at the Battery," Jasper announced. "The Aquarium is at one end

Kitty the Kisser   By John Held, Jr.

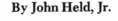
She was kissed on the dance floor

She was kissed in the park

She was kissed on the beach

Snappy Stories, 1924

of Manhattan Island, and the Zoo is at the other. That is so people won't get the animals confused with the fish. We'll have to rush—it closes at five o'clock, because the fish get tired looking at the public."

With busy legs they hurried on, Jasper leading the way over hill and dale. Mr. Filbert stood for a long time looking at the shad. Then he sat down in front of the turtles and cried a little, until his wife came up with a very angry attendant.

"What's the trouble now?" Filbert inquired.

"I just asked him if we could get a shore dinner here," Mrs. F. said. "And he arrested me."

There was an embarrassed silence, and then Filbert shook hands with the attendant.

"All aboard for home," Jasper called.

"I'm not going home," Mrs. Filbert replied stubbornly.

"Why?"

"Because of the walrus. He's just like my brother John who lives in the Philippine Islands and has a daughter three months old."

"Nonsense!" her husband said. "Come along, and I'll buy you a nice new telephone-booth."

"There!" Jasper shouted in a relieved tone. And presently outside the Aquarium, the wheels began to turn beneath the kiddie cars, and the reunited party swept merrily past the Cunard Building, the blinds of which were symmetrically drawn half way down.

Needless to say, the voyagers slept soundly that night, dreaming of Chinatown and the Battery and perhaps of the Great Pyramids of Egypt. Who knows?

A Plea for the Old Music

By RICHARD LE GALLIENNE

PLAY me some old gavotte
  Or minuet—
To-day I would forget,
And live in *the Forgot*:
I want to hear the dead folk dancing,
I want to see the dead eyes glancing,
I want dead ladies and dead lords,
The wigs, the furbelows, the swords.
I weary of the sansculotte,
The unkempt northern hordes
That pour their muddy streams
Across our dreams,
Fouling the sacred fire
With bestial desire,
Knowing no law
Only to glut the sensual appetite,
Or cram the brutish maw.

Yea, master of the magic strings,
Bring back the fair old-fashioned things,
The gallant bows, the curtseys sweeping,
Of that brave world that's gone a-sleeping,
Where love was none the less a passion
Because fine manners were the fashion.

Play me some old gavotte.
I weary of the carmagnole,
I weary of the sansculotte,
With his Pan-Slavic "soul"—
Bring back pavane and rigadoon,
And Watteau—the rising moon.

Snappy Stories, 1919

Kitty had been kissed 'most every way there was

She was kissed on the golf links

But after she was married, it was swell to be kissed with her shoes off!

A Place For Everything

By HARRY IRVING SHUMWAY

KISSES—
I have had many.
One was like the pretty
Peck of a robin;
Another seemed like
Honey from a lovely flower;
And one I remember was
A summer zephyr, cool, sweet, delicious;
But the one that
Knocked me dead
Was a bit of lightning
From Nora's lips
When the glims went bad
In a subway train.

Snappy Stories, 1919

Wisdom

By CARRINGTON NORTH

SHE moved slowly and spoke seldom, and men thought her mysterious and soulful and restful. They laid their hearts at her feet and worshiped her as a super-woman.

She took their gifts and smiled, for she knew that she limped slightly when she hurried, and that when she talked she disclosed an abysmal ignorance of the English language.

THE woman with a rake for a husband has the comforting knowledge that no matter what she does, his record will be blacker than hers.

Exploiting the Girls / 7 / Straight Out Sex

In April, 1934, openly erotic material finally burst on the under-the-counter scene in the form of a violent, new magazine with the relatively innocent title, *Spicy Detective Stories*. On its cover, cowering in the foreground, was a tender but terrified blonde, clad only in the flimsiest of undergarments, one limp stocking dangling around her ankle. At her feet were a few fragments of her dress. The rest of it was clutched in the ape-like fist of the object of her terror—a man behind her, ready to spring. He was small and compact. A black-vest half covered his shoulder-holster. A white shirt made him look even swarthier than he was. His black hair was wild, his teeth were bared in a suggestive leer. His face was bloody where it had been raked by the girl's finger-nails. There was no mistaking his intention. The title of the cover-story was next to the girl's knee, "The Love Nest Murder" by Jon Le Baron. There was no mistaking Culture Publications' intention, either.

Spicy Detective was the first in a line which quickly expanded to include *Spicy Adventure, Spicy Mystery,* and *Spicy Western.* The degree and type of eroticism varied according to the editorial policy of each of the four, but certain factors remained uniform. The heroes and heroines were always unmarried; and either could instigate a sexual encounter. If the girl did, it was because she was menaced by some threat of harm which evoked her sexual desire for the hero. If the hero did, it was because her appearance, and his protective feelings, made him, in Robert Bellem's immortal words, "as human as the next gazabo." Villains generally had rape on their minds, but in the case of *Spicy Mystery*, sadism was a frequent motive.

These Pulps were eagerly searched for "hot parts" by their readers, since the heroes were permitted to expose (and even indulge) their sexual desires for the first time. Girls were no longer described merely in terms of height, weight, and coloring. They were dished up in terms of quality of flesh (creamy expanses) and the material which covered it (diaphanous, barely able to conceal its straining contents). Men were allowed, at last, to explore anything except the pelvic area and descriptions were vivid. But at the ultimate moment the shades—as in earlier Pulps—were pulled down on the action . . .

Recognizing that the *Spicy* titles were satisfying only one portion of society's needs, Popular Publications introduced a new sub-genre, its intent cloaked under the guise of mystery and horror. These Pulps had titles such as *Horror Stories, Terror Tales,* and *Dime Mystery.* Their exquisitely executed and artistically imaginative covers portrayed every conceivable form of torture and perversity which could be inflicted anywhere on the female (and sometimes the male) anatomy (excepting the pelvis, of course). That hero and heroine were usually married suggests editorial sensitivity to a latent psycho-sexual drama of the Depression—an era with an unusually emasculating effect on the breadwinner. Villains were generally crazed friends, bent only on inflicting the most violent forms of torture on the heroines; straight sex was never their intent. Descriptions were vivid.

* * *

"The Purple Heart of Erlik" appeared in 1936 in *Spicy Adventure,* under the pen-name, Sam Walser. A completely unknown story by a writer who developed a large following among supernatural fans, it is reprinted here for the first time in hard cover. The author was Robert E. Howard, who achieved prominence in that field through his "sword and sorcery" stories, particularly those involving his character "Conan the Barbarian." Most of Howard's most popular work appeared in *Weird Tales* during the 30's, but he also wrote for the Western and Adventure Pulps as well. This story presents a sharp contrast to his more familiar work, of which a sample, "The Valley of the Worm", appears in the supernatural section.

*　　*　　*

Another contrast in style is illustrated by "Labyrinth of Monsters" (*Spicy Mystery,* 1937), by Robert Leslie Bellem, whose Dan Turner story "Death's Passport" appears in the detective section. Comparison between the two Bellem stories reveals a similarity of structure and character, and a dissimilarity of language. Many of the devices remain the same: in particular, Bellem was the master of the "cheap feel." In the jail-cell scene at the end of "Labyrinth of Monsters" he achieved the ultimate in his craft by pulling off the sneakiest and most thorough "quickie" in literary history.

*　　*　　*

"The Dinner Cooked in Hell" appeared in 1940 in *Startling Mystery Magazine,* one of the Popular Publications Pulps. It was written by Mindret Lord who employed some pretty gruesome devices. Although the Spicy group's writers often approached the level of gore achieved in this story, they generated a level of enthusiasm which was reflected in their writing. Those who wrote for the really sadistic Pulps on the other hand appear either to have sluffed over their writing or belabored it. The result was that many of their stories appear forced and self-conscious.

By SAM WALSER (ROBERT E. HOWARD)

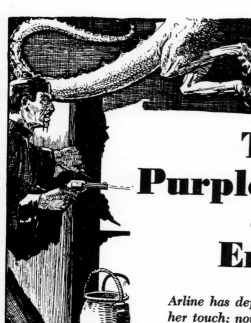

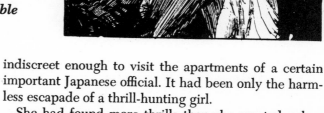

She laughed and, with a choking cry, Woon Yuen turned the gun, fired at her.

The Purple Heart of Erlik

Arline has defamed the ruby by her touch; now the ruby and its Chinese high priest plan terrible vengeance.

"**Y**OU'LL DO what I tell you—or else!" Duke Tremayne smiled cruelly as he delivered his ultimatum. Across the table from him Arline Ellis clenched her white hands in helpless rage. Duke Tremayne, world adventurer, was tall, slim, darkly mustached, handsome in a ruthless way; and many women looked on him with favor. But Arline hated him, with as good reason as she feared him.

But she ventured a flare of rebellion.

"I won't do it! It's too risky!"

"Not half as risky as defying me!" he reminded her. "I've got you by the seat of your pretty pants, my dear. How would you like to have me tell the police why you left Canton in such a hurry? Or tell them *my* version of that night in Baron Takayami's apartment—"

"Hush!" she begged. She was trembling as she glanced fearfully about the little curtained alcove in which they sat. It was well off the main floor of the Bordeaux Cabaret; even the music from the native orchestra came only faintly to their ears. They were alone, but the words he had just spoken were dynamite, not even safe for empty walls to hear.

"You know I didn't kill him—"

"So you say. But who'd believe you if I swore I *saw* you do it?"

She bent her head in defeat. This was the price she must pay for an hour of folly. In Canton she had been

Spicy Adventure, 1936

indiscreet enough to visit the apartments of a certain important Japanese official. It had been only the harmless escapade of a thrill-hunting girl.

She had found more thrills than she wanted, when the official had been murdered, almost before her eyes, by his servant, who she was sure was a Russian spy. The murderer had fled, and so had she, but not before she had been seen leaving the house by Duke Tremayne, a friend of the slain official. He had kept silent. But the murderer had taken important documents with him in his flight, and there was hell to pay in diplomatic circles.

It had been an international episode, that almost set the big guns of war roaring in the East. The murder and theft remained an unsolved mystery to the world at large, a wound that still rankled in the capitals of the Orient.

ARLINE HAD fled the city in a panic, realizing she could never prove her innocence, if connected with the affair. Tremayne had followed her to Shanghai and laid his cards on the table. If she did not comply with his wishes, he'd go to the police and swear he saw her murder the Jap. And she knew his testimony would send her to a firing squad, for various governments were eager for a scape-goat with which to conciliate the wrathful Nipponese.

Terrified, Arline submitted to the blackmail. And now Tremayne had told her the price of his silence. It was not what she had expected, though, from the look in his eyes as he devoured her trim figure from blonde hair to French heels, she felt it would come to that eventually. But here in the Bordeaux, a shady rendezvous in the shadowy borderland between the European and the native quarters, he had set her a task that made her flesh crawl.

He had commanded her to steal the famous Heart of Erlik, the purple ruby belonging to Woon Yuen, a Chinese merchant of powerful and sinister connections.

"So many men have tried," she argued. "How can I hope to succeed? I'll be found floating in the Yangtze with my throat cut, just as they were."

"You'll succeed," he retorted. "They tried force or craft; we'll use a woman's strategy. I've learned where he keeps it—had a spy working in his employ and he learned that much. He keeps it in a wall safe that looks like a dragon's head, in the inner chamber of his antique shop, where he keeps his rarest goods, and where he never admits anybody but wealthy women collectors. He entertains them there alone, which makes it easy."

"But how am I going to steal it, with him in there with me?"

"Easy!" he snapped. "He always serves his guests tea. You watch your chance and drop this knock-out pill in his tea."

He pressed a tiny, faintly odorous sphere into her hand.

"He'll go out like a candle. Then you open the safe, take the ruby and skip. It's like taking candy from a baby. One reason I picked you for this job, you have a natural gift for unraveling Chinese puzzles. The safe doesn't have a dial. You press the dragon's teeth. In what combination, I don't know. That's for you to find out."

"But how am I going to get into the inner chamber?" she demanded.

"That's the cream of the scheme," he assured her. "Did you ever hear of Lady Elizabeth Willoughby? Well, every antique dealer in the Orient knows her by sight or reputation. She's never been to Shanghai, though, and I don't believe Woon Yuen ever saw her. That'll make it easy to fool him. She's a young English woman with exotic ideas and she spends her time wandering around the world collecting rare Oriental art treasures. She's worth millions, and she's a free spender.

"Well, you look enough like her in a general way to fit in with any description Woon Yuen's likely to have heard. You're about the same height, same color of hair and eyes, same kind of figure—" his eyes lit with admiration as they dwelt on the trim curves of bosom and hips. "And you can act, too. You can put on an English accent that would fool the Prince of Wales, and act the high-born lady to a queen's taste.

"I've seen Lady Elizabeth's cards, and before I left Canton I had one made, to match. You see I had this in mind, even then." He passed her a curious slip of paper—thin jade, carved with scrawling Chinese characters.

"Her name, of course, in Chinese. She spends a small fortune on cards like that, alone. Now go back to your apartment and change into the duds I had sent up there—scarlet silk dress, jade-green hat, slippers with ivory heels, and a jade brooch. That's the way Lady Elizabeth always dresses. Eccentric? You said it! Go to Woon Yuen's shop and tell him you want to see the ivory Bon. He keeps it in the inner chamber. When you get in there, do your stuff, but be careful! They say Woon Yuen worships that ruby, and burns incense to it. But you'll pull the wool over his eyes, all right. Be careful he doesn't fall for you! Couldn't blame him if he did."

Against his thickly muscled arms, her struggles were vain.

H E WAS leaning toward her, and his hand was on her knee. She flinched at the feel of his questing fingers. She loathed his caresses, but she dared not repulse him. He was arrogantly possessive, and she did not doubt that when—and if—she returned with the coveted gem, he would demand the ultimate surrender. And she knew she would not dare refuse him. Tears of helpless misery welled to her eyes, but he ignored them. Grudgingly he withdrew his hand and rose.

"Go out by the back way. When you get the ruby, meet me at room Number 7, in the Alley of Rats—you know the place. Shanghai will be too hot for you, and we'll have to get you out of town in a hurry. And remember, sweetheart," his voice grew hard as his predatory eyes, and his arm about her waist was more a threat than a caress, "if you double-cross me, or if you flop on this job, I'll see you stood before a Jap firing squad if it's the last thing I do. I won't accept any excuses, either. Get me?"

His fingers brushed her chin, trailed over the soft white curve of her throat, to her shoulder; and as he voiced his threat, he dug them in like talons, emphasizing his command with a brutality that made Arline bite her lip to keep from crying out with pain.

"Yes, I get you."

"All right. Get going." He spanked her lightly and pushed her toward a door opposite the curtained entrance beyond which the music blared.

The door opened into a long narrow alley that eventually reached the street. As Arline went down this alley, seething with rebellion and dismay for the task ahead of her, a man stepped from a doorway and stopped her. She eyed him suspiciously, though concealing a secret throb of admiration for a fine masculine figure.

H E WAS big, broad-shouldered, heavy-fisted, with smoldering blue eyes and a mop of unruly black hair under a side-tilted seaman's cap. And he was Wild Bill Clanton, sailor, gun-runner, blackbirder, pearl-poacher, and fighting man de luxe.

"Will you get out of my way?" she demanded.

"Wait a minute, Kid!" He barred her way with a heavy arm, and his eyes blazed as they ran over the smooth bland curves of her blond loveliness. "Why do you always give me the shoulder? I've made it a point to run into you in a dozen ports, and you always act like I had the plague."

"You have, as far as I'm concerned," she retorted.

"You seem to think Duke Tremayne's healthy," he growled resentfully.

She flinched at the name of her master, but answered spiritedly: "What I see in Duke Tremayne's none of your business. Now let me pass!"

But instead he caught her arm in a grip that hurt.

"Damn your saucy little soul!" he ripped out, anger fighting with fierce desire in his eyes. "If I didn't want you so bad, I'd smack your ears back! What the hell! I'm as good a man as Duke Tremayne. I'm tired of your superior airs. I came to Shanghai just because I heard you were here. Now are you going to be nice, or do I have to get rough?"

"You wouldn't dare!" she exclaimed. "I'll scream—"

A big hand clapped over her mouth put a stop to that.

"Nobody interferes with anything that goes on in alleys behind dumps like the Bordeaux," he growled, imprisoning her arms and lifting her off her feet, kicking and struggling. "Any woman caught here's fair prey."

He kicked open the door through which he had reached the alley, and carried Arline into a dim hallway. Traversing this with his writhing captive, he shoved open a door that opened on it. Arline, crushed against his broad breast, felt the tumultuous pounding of his heart, and experienced a momentary thrill of vanity that she should rouse such stormy emotion in Wild Bill Clanton, whose exploits with the women of a hundred ports were as widely celebrated as his myriad bloody battles with men.

He entered a bare, cobwebby room, and set her on her feet, placing his back against the door.

"Let me out of here, you beast!" She kicked his shins vigorously.

He ignored her attack.

"Why don't you be nice?" he begged. "I don't want to be rough with you. Honest, kid, I'd be good to you —better than Tremayne probably is—"

For answer she bent her blonde head and bit his wrist viciously, even though discretion warned her it was probably the worst thing she could do.

"You little devil!" he swore, grabbing her. "That settles it!"

Scornful of her resistance he crushed her writhing figure against his chest, and kissed her red lips, her furious eyes, her flaming cheeks and white throat, until she lay panting and breathless, unable to repel the possessive arms that drew her closer and closer.

She squirmed and moaned with mingled emotions as he sank his head, eagerly as a thirsty man bending to drink, and pressed his burning lips to the tender hollow of her throat. One hand wandered lower, to her waist, locked her against him despite her struggles.

In a sort of daze she found herself on the dingy cot, with her skirt bunched about her hips. The gleam of her own white flesh, so generously exposed, brought her to her senses, out of the maze of surrender into

Not even Wild Bill could stand up under a clout like that.

which his strength was forcing her. Her agile mind worked swiftly. As she sank back, suddenly she shrieked convulsively.

"My back! Something's stabbed me! A knife in the mattress—"

"What the hell?" He snatched her up instantly and whirled her about, but she had her hands pressed over the small of her back, and was writhing and moaning in well-simulated pain.

"I'm sorry, kid—" he began tearing the mattress to pieces, trying to find what had hurt her, and as he turned his back, she snatched a heavy pitcher from the wash-stand and smashed it over his head.

Not even Wild Bill Clanton could stand up under a clout like that. He went down like a pole-axed ox—or bull, rather—and she darted through the door and down the hall. Behind her she heard a furious roar that lent wings to her small high heels. She sprang into the alley and ran up it, not stopping to arrange her garments.

As she emerged into the street, a backward glance showed her Clanton reeling out into the alley, streaming blood, a raging and formidable figure. But she was on a semi-respectable street, with people strolling past and Sikh policemen within call. He wouldn't dare

come out of the alley after her. She walked sedately away, arranging her dress as she went. A few loungers had seen her run from the alley, but they merely smiled in quiet amusement and made no comment. It was no novelty in that quarter to see a girl run from a back alley with her breasts exposed and her skirt pulled awry.

But a few deft touches smoothed out her appearance, and a moment later, looking cool, unruffled and demure as though she had just stepped out of a beauty shop, she was headed for her apartment, where waited the garments she must don for her dangerous masquerade.

AN HOUR later she entered the famous antique shop of Woon Yuen, which rose in the midst of a squalid native quarter like a cluster of jewels in a litter of garbage. Outside it was unpretentious, but inside, even in the main chamber with its display intended to catch the fancy of tourists and casual collectors, the shop was a colorful riot of rich artistry.

A treasure trove in jade, gold, and ivory was openly exhibited, apparently unguarded. But the inhabitants of the quarter were not fooled by appearances. Not one would dare to try to rob Woon Yuen. Arline fought down a chill of fear.

A cat-footed Chinese bowed before her, hands concealed in his wide silken sleeves. She eyed him with the languid indifference of an aristocrat, and said, with an accent any Briton would have sworn she was born with: "Tell Woon Yuen that Lady Elizabeth Willoughby wishes to see the ivory Bon." The slant eyes of the impassive Chinese widened just a trifle at the name. With an even lower bow, he took the fragment of jade with the Chinese characters, and kowtowed her into an ebony chair with dragon-claw feet, before he disappeared through the folds of a great dark velvet tapestry which curtained the back of the shop.

She sat there, glancing indifferently about her, according to her role. Lady Elizabeth would not be expected to show any interest in the trifles displayed for the general public. She believed she was being spied on through some peephole. Woon Yuen was a mysterious figure, suspected of strange activities, but so far untouchable, either by his many enemies or by the authorities. When he came, it was so silently that he was standing before her before she was aware of his entrance. She glanced at him, masking her curiosity with the bored air of an English noblewoman.

Woon Yuen was a big man, for a Chinese, squattily built, yet above medium height. His square, lemon-tinted face was adorned with a thin wisp of drooping mustachios, and his bull-like shoulders seemed ready to split the seams of the embroidered black silk robe he wore. He had come to Shanghai from the North, and there was more Mongol than Chinese in him, as emphasized by his massive forearms, impressive even beneath his wide sleeves. He bowed, politely but not obsequiously. He seemed impressed, but not awed by the presence of the noted collector in his shop.

"Lady Elizabeth Willoughby does my humble establishment much honor," said he, in perfect English, sweeping his eyes over her without any attempt to conceal his avid interest in her ripe curves. There was a natural arrogance about him, an assurance of power. He had dealt with wealthy white women before, and strange tales were whispered of his dealings with some of them. The air of mystery and power about him made him seem a romantic figure to some European women.

"The Bon is in the inner chamber," he said. "There, too, are my real treasures. These," he gestured contemptuously about him, "are only a show for tourists. If milady would honor me—"

She rose and moved across the room, with the assured bearing of a woman of quality, certain of deference at all time. He drew back a satin curtain on which gilt dragons writhed, and following her through, drew it together behind them. They went along a narrow corridor, where the walls were hung with black velvet and the floor was carpeted with thick Bokhara rugs in which her feet sank deep.

A soft golden glow emanated from bronze lanterns, suspended from the gilt-inlaid ceiling. She felt her pulse quicken. She was on her way to the famous, yet mysterious, inner chamber of Woon Yuen, inaccessible to all but wealthy and beautiful women, and in which, rumor whispered, Woon Yuen had struck strange bargains. He did not always sell his antiques for money, and there were feminine collectors who would barter their virtue for a coveted relic.

WOON YUEN opened a bronze door, worked in gold and ebon inlay, and Arline entered a broad chamber, over a silvery plate of glass set in the threshold. She saw Woon Yuen glance down as she walked over it, and knew he was getting an eyeful. That mirror placed where a woman must walk over it to enter the chamber was a typical Chinese trick to allow the master of the establishment to get a more intimate glimpse of the charms of his fair customers, as reflected in the mirror. She didn't care, but was merely amused at his ingenuity. Even Woon Yuen would hardly dare to make a pass at Lady Elizabeth Willoughby.

He closed the door and bowed her to an ornate mahogany chair.

"Please excuse me for a moment, milady. I will return instantly."

He went out by another door, and she looked about her at a display whose richness might have shamed a shah's treasure-house. Here indeed were the real treasures of Woon Yuen—what looked like the plunder of a thousand sultans' palaces and heathen temples. Idols in jade, gold, and ivory grinned at her, and a less sophisticated woman would have blushed at some of the figures, depicting Oriental gods and goddesses in amorous poses of an astonishing variety. She could imagine the effect these things would have on some of his feminine visitors.

Even her eyes dilated a trifle at the sight of the smirking, pot-bellied monstrosity that was the ivory Bon, looted from God only knew what nameless monastery high in the forbidden Himalayas. Then every nerve tingled as she saw a gold-worked dragon head jutting from the wall beyond the figure. Quickly she turned her gaze back to the god, just as her host returned on silent, velvet-shod feet.

He smiled to see her staring at the idol and the female figure in its arms.

"That is only one of the conceptions of the god—the Tibetan. It is worth, to any collector—but let us delay business talk until after tea. If you will honor me—"

With his guest seated at a small ebon table, the Mongol struck a bronze gong, and tea was served by a slim, silent-footed Chinese girl, clad only in a filmy jacket which came a little below her budding hips, and which concealed none of her smooth-skinned, lemon-tinted charms.

This display, Arline knew, was in accord with the peculiar Chinese belief that a woman is put in a properly receptive mood for amorous advances by the sight of another woman's exposed charms. She wondered, if, after all, Woon Yuen had designs—but he showed no signs of it.

The slave girl bowed herself humbly out with a last salaam that displayed her full breasts beneath the low-necked jacket, and Arline's nerves tightened. Now was the time. She interrupted Woon Yuen's polite trivialities.

"That little jade figure, over there on the ivory shelf," she said, pointing. "Isn't that a piece of Jum Shan's work?"

"I will get it!"

AS HE rose and stepped to the shelf, she dropped the knock-out pellet into his tea-cup. It dissolved instantly, without discoloring the liquid. She was idly sipping her own tea when the Mongol returned and placed the tiny figure of a jade warrior before her.

"Genuine Jum Shan," said he. "It dates from the tenth century!" He lifted his cup and emptied it at a draught, while she watched him with a tenseness which she could not wholly conceal. He sat the cup down empty, frowning slightly and twitching his lips at the taste.

"I would like to call your attention, milady—" he leaned forward, reaching toward the jade figure—then slumped down across the table, out cold. In an instant she was across the room, and her white, tapering fingers were at work on the teeth of the carved dragon's head. There was an instinct in those fingers, a super-sensitiveness such as skilled cracksmen sometimes have.

In a few moments the jaws gaped suddenly, revealing a velvet-lined nest in the midst of which, like an egg of some fabled bird of paradise, burned and smoldered a great, smooth, round jewel.

She caught her breath as awedly she cupped it in her hands. It was a ruby, of such deep crimson that it looked darkly purple, the hue of old wine, and the blood that flows near the heart. It looked like the materialization of a purple nightmare. She could believe now the wild tales she had heard—that Woon Yuen worshiped it as a god, sucking madness from its sinister depths, that he performed terrible sacrifices to it—

"Lovely, is it not?"

The low voice cracked the tense stillness like the heart-stopping blast of an explosion. She whirled, gasping, then stood transfixed. Woon Yuen stood before her, smiling dangerously, his eyes slits of black fire. A frantic glance sped to the tea-table. There still sprawled a limp, bulky figure, identical to Woon Yuen in every detail.

"What—?" she gasped weakly.

"My shadow," he smiled. "I must be cautious. Long ago I hit upon the expedient of having a servant made up to resemble me, to fool my enemies. When I left the chamber a little while ago, he took my place, and I watched through the peep-hole. I supposed you were after the Heart.

"How did you guess?" She sensed the uselessness of denial.

"Why not? Has not every thief in China tried to steal it?" He spoke softly, but his eyes shone reddishly, and the veins swelled on his neck. "As soon as I learned you were not what you pretended, I knew you had come to steal something. Why not the ruby? I set my trap and let you walk into it. But I must congratulate you on your cleverness. Not one in a thousand could have discovered the way to open the dragon's jaws."

"How did you know I wasn't Lady Elizabeth?" she whispered, dry-lipped; the great ruby seemed to burn her palms.

"I knew it when you walked across the mirror and I saw your lower extremities reflected there. I have never seen Lady Elizabeth, but all dealers in jade know her peculiarities by reputation. One of them is such a passion for jade that she always wears jade-green step-ins. Yours are lavender."

"What are you going to do?" she panted, as he moved toward her.

A light akin to madness burned in his eyes.

"You have defamed the Heart by your touch! It must drink of all who touch it save me, its high priest! If a man, his blood! If a woman—"

NO NEED for him to complete his abominable decree. The ruby fell to the thick carpet, rolled along it like a revolving, demoniac eyeball. She sprang back, shrieking, as Woon Yuen, no longer placid, but with his convulsed face a beast's mask, caught her by the wrist. Against his thickly muscled arms her struggles were vain. As in a nightmare, she felt herself lifted and carried kicking and scratching, through heavily brocaded drapes into a curtained alcove. Her eyes swept the room helplessly; she saw the ivory Bon leering at her as through a mist. It seemed to mock her.

The alcove was walled with mirrors. Only Chinese cruelty could have devised such an arrangement, where, whichever way she twisted her head she was confronted by the spectacle of her own humiliation, reflected from every angle. She was at once actor and spectator in a beastly drama. She could not escape the shameful sight of her own writhings and the eager brutish hands of Woon Yuen remorselessly subduing her hopeless, desperate struggles.

As she felt the greedy yellow fingers on her cringing flesh, she saw in the mirrors, her quivering white breasts, her dress torn—dishevelled, the scarlet skirt in startling contrast to the white thighs, with only a wisp of silk protecting them as they frantically flexed, twisted and writhed—then with a sucking gasp of breath between his grinding teeth, Woon Yuen tore the filmy underthings to rags on her body. . . .

At the tea-table the senseless Chinese still sprawled, deaf to the frantic, agonized shrieks that rang again and again through the inner chamber of Woon Yuen.

AN HOUR later a door opened into a narrow alley in the rear of Woon Yuen's antique shop, and Arline was thrust roughly out, her breasts almost bare, her dress ripped to shreds. She fell sprawling from the force of the shove, and the door was slammed, with a brutal laugh. Dazedly she rose, shook down the remains of her skirt, drew her dress together, and tottered down the alley, sobbing hysterically.

Inside the room from which she had just been ejected, Woon Yuen turned to a lean, saturnine individual, whose pigtail was wound tightly about his head, and from whose wide silk girdle jutted the handle of a light hatchet.

"Yao Chin, take Yun Kang and follow her. There is always some man behind the scenes, when a woman steals. I let her go because I wished her to lead us to that man, send Yun Kang back to me. On no account kill him yourself. I, and only I, must feed the Heart with their vile blood—hers and his."

The hatchetman bowed and left the room, his face showing nothing of his secret belief that Woon Yuen was crazy, not because he believed the Heart drank human blood, but because he, a rich merchant, insisted on doing murder which others of his class always left to hired slayers.

In the mouth of a little twisting alley that ran out upon a rotting abandoned wharf, Arline paused. Her face was haggard and desperate. She had reached the end of her trail. She had failed, and Tremayne would not accept any excuse. Ahead of her she saw only the black muzzles of a firing squad to which he would deliver her—but first there would be torture, inhuman torture, to wring from her secrets her captors would think she possessed. The world at large never knows the full story of the treatment of suspected spies.

With a low moan she covered her eyes with her arm and stumbled blindly toward the edge of the wharf— then a strong arm caught her waist and she looked up into the startled face of Wild Bill Clanton.

"What the hell are you fixin' to do?"

"Let go!" she whimpered. "It's my life! I can end it if I want to!"

"Not with me around," he grunted, picking her up and carrying her back away from the wharf-lip. He sat down on a pile and took her on his lap, like a child. "Good thing I found you," he grunted. "I had a hell of a time tracin' you after you slugged me and ran up that alley, but I finally saw you duckin' down this one. You pick the damndest places to stroll in. Now you tell me what the trouble is. A classy dame like you don't need to go jumpin' off of docks."

He seemed to hold no grudge for that clout with the pitcher. There was possessiveness in the clasp of his arms about her supple body, but she found a comforting solidity in the breast muscles against which her flaxen head rested. There was a promise of security in his masculine strength. Suddenly she no longer resented his persistent pursuit of her. She needed his strength— needed a man who would fight for her.

In a few words she told him everything—the hold Tremayne had on her, the task he had set for her, and what had happened in Woon Yuen's inner room.

He swore at the narrative.

"I'll get that yellow-belly for that! But first we'll go to the Alley of Rats. Try to stall Tremayne along to give you another chance. In the meantime I'll work on a Eurasian wench I know who could tell me plenty about him—and she will, too, or I'll skin her alive. He's been mixed up in plenty of crooked rackets. If we get somethin' hot on him, we can shut his mouth, all right. And we'll get somethin', you can bet."

When they entered the Alley of Rats, in a half-abandoned warehouse district in the native quarter, they did not see two furtive figures slinking after them, nor hear the taller whisper: "Yun Kang, go back and tell our master she had led us to a man! I will watch the alley till he comes."

Clanton and Arline turned into a dingy doorway, and went down a corridor that seemed wholly deserted. Groping along it, in the dusk, she found the room she sought and led Clanton into it. She lit a candle stub stuck on a shelf, and turned to Clanton: "He'll be here soon."

"I'll wait in the next room," he said, reluctantly taking his arm from about her waist. "If he gets rough, I'll come in."

Alone in the candle-lighted room she tried to compose herself; her heart was beating a wild tattoo, loud in the stillness. Somewhere rats scampered noisily. Time dragged insufferably. Then quick, light steps sounded in the hall, and Duke Tremayne burst through the door, his eyes blazing with greed. They turned red as he read defeat in her eyes; his face contorted.

"Damn you!" His fingers were like talons as he gripped her shoulders. "You failed!"

"I couldn't help it!" she pleaded. "He knew I was a fake. Please don't hurt me, Duke. I'll try again—"

"Try again? You little fool! Do you think that Chinese devil will give you another chance?" Tremayne's suavity was gone; he was like a madman. "You failed, after all my planning! All right! I'll have a little profit out of you! Take off that dress—" Already in shreds, the garment ripped easily in his grasp, baring a white breast which quivered under his gaze.

The inner door swung open. Tremayne wheeled, drawing a pistol, but before he could fire, Clanton's fist crashed against his jaw and stretched him senseless. Clanton bent and picked up the gun, then whirled as the hall door opened behind him. He stiffened as a tranquil voice spoke: "Do not move, my friend!"

He looked into the muzzle of a gun in Woon Yuen's hand.

"So you are the man?" muttered the Mongol. "Good! The Heart drinks—"

HE COULD fire before Clanton could lift the pistol he held. But behind the American Arline laughed suddenly, unexpectedly.

"It worked, Bill!" she exclaimed. "Our man will get

the ruby while we hold Woon Yuen here! The fool! He hasn't yet guessed that we tricked him to draw him away from his shop after I'd found where he hid the gem."

Woon Yuen's face went ashen. With a choking cry he fired, not at Clanton but at the girl. But his hand was shaking like a leaf. He missed, and like an echo of his shot came the crack of Clanton's pistol. Woon Yuen dropped, drilled through the head.

"Good work, kid!" Clanton cried exultantly. "He fell for it—hard!"

"But they'll hang us for this!" whimpered the girl. "Listen! Someone's running up the hall! They've heard the shots!"

Stooping swiftly Clanton folded Duke Tremayne's fingers about the butt of the smoking pistol, and then kicked the man heavily in the shins. Tremayne grunted and showed signs of returning consciousness. Clanton drew Arline into the other room and they watched through the crack of the door.

The hall door opened and Yao Chin came in like a panther, hatchet in hand. His eyes blazed at the sight of Woon Yuen on the floor, Tremayne staggering to his feet, a pistol in his hand. With one stride the hatchet-man reached the reeling blackmailer. There was a flash of steel, an ugly butcher-shop *crunch*, and Tremayne slumped, his skull split. Yao Chin tossed the reeking hatchet to the floor beside his victim and turned away.

"Out of here, quick!" muttered Clanton, shaking Arline who seemed threatened with hysteria. "Up the alley—in the other direction."

She regained her poise in their groping flight up the darkened alley, as Clanton muttered: "We're in the clear now. Tremayne can't talk, with his head split, and that hatchetman'll tell his pals Tremayne shot their boss."

"We'd better get out of town!" They had emerged into a narrow, lamp-lit street.

"Why? We're safe from suspicion now." A little tingle of pleasure ran through her as Clanton turned into a doorway and spoke to a grinning old Chinaman who bowed them into a small neat room, with curtained windows and a couch.

As the door closed behind the old Chinese, Clanton caught her hungrily to him, finding her red lips, now unresisting. Her arms went about his thick neck as he lifted her bodily from the floor. Willingly she yielded, responded to his eager caresses.

She had only exchanged masters, it was true, but this was different. There was a delicious sense of comfort and security in a strong man who could fight for her and protect her. There was pleasure in the dominance of his strong hands. With a blissful sigh she settled herself luxuriously in his powerful arms.

By
ROBERT
LESLIE
BELLEM

Never in the wildest nightmare of hell-spawned horrow could Travis imagine such creatures as menaced the girl who invaded his bungalow that night.

With all his strength he heaved the pitcher at the little monster's head.

Labyrinth of MONSTERS

WITH THE coming of midnight, a thick, glutinous fog had billowed in from the sea. Now the impenetrable grey pall settled silently over the little coast resort of Ghost Cove, blotting out the rows of summer cottages which clustered at the edge of the bay's whispering waters.

Wet mists collected on tree-limbs and cottage eaves; and droplets of moisture fell slowly, monotonously, like the *drip-drip-drip* of blood flowing from a hundred raw wounds. In the far distance, toward the frowning cliffs which imprisoned the cove, a loon shrilled eerily. Nearer, there came a faint shuffling sound in the sand, as of laggard footsteps dragging.

Within the bedroom of his rented duplex bungalow, Travis Brant stirred uneasily on his hard cot. He snapped on his flashlight, looked at the clock alongside his bed. Twenty minutes past midnight, the hands showed. Through an open window, curling tentacles of fog drifted into the room, like the ectoplasmic arms of a seeking, groping blind monster.

Brant arose to close the window. And as he thrust his feet into carpet-slippers, he stiffened. *What in God's name was that?*

It came again, a weird, wailing cry that stabbed through the night's ghostly mist. Ululant with terror, laden with dread, it seemed to come from the other half of the duplex bungalow. Soul-chilling, spine-curdling, the scream rang out still a third time.

With a curse, Travis Brant hurled his two hundred pounds of brawny body toward his front door; smashed out into the engulfing fog. A gust of salt-tanged breeze brushed his cheek like the touch of ghost-fingers; and the fog-mists eddied and parted for a brief moment.

Brant stared downward at the floor of the small porch on which he stood. And then he drew a great, gulping breath; and icy talons of nameless dread clutched deep into his heart. The porch was wet and glistening with spilled, crimson blood!

Even as Travis Brant's eyes widened, he heard again that weird and horrifying scream. This time there was no mistaking its source. The sound came from the other half of Brant's duplex.

Snatching up a dressing-gown Brant lunged toward the door from which that wailing cry had gibbered into the night. He saw that the portal was open; saw a faint light within. He hurled himself inside the place.

And as he crossed the threshold he plummeted into a soft and yielding form, a warm, trembling body that suddenly clung to him in sheer, crystalline terror.

"What the hell!" Travis Brant gritted; and then he swung the beam of his flashlight full upon the form that had clutched at him. He drew a sharp breath of amazement and stupefied admiration.

It was a girl, a young, brown-haired girl of breath-taking beauty. She was clad in shimmering, diaphanous pajamas, and there was a splotch of blood on her bare, lovely shoulder. Her brown eyes were wide, staring, filled with the slithering seeds of fear-madness. Her crimson, kissable lips were parted, contorted.

Through the gauzy thinness of the pajamas, Travis Brant could see the girl's heaving, panting breasts, twin ripe half-melons of cream-white flesh that strained at the pajama jacket like swelling mounds of enchantment. Her hips were lush, feminine, rounded; and her entire body was filled with a terror-trembling that was not pleasant to behold.

Even as Travis Brant stared at her, the brown-haired girl flung herself upon him once more. Her arms went about his neck, and her fragrant, feminine body blended and merged with his own, as if she sought to fuse herself upon him and to hide herself in his protecting masculinity.

SOMETHING OF the girl's icy terror seemed to leap from her veins and enter Travis Brant's blood like a frigid rip-tide. And then, from somewhere in the house behind her, Brant heard a slithering, susurrant whisper of sound, as though a scuttling *thing* were moving across the floor.

"Oh, God!" the brown-haired girl gulped spasmodically, as a paroxysm of fear throbbed through her. "Take me away—before it grabs me and . . . tears out my throat . . . *the way it tore out that other girl's throat!*"

"Good Lord!" Travis Brant grated. "What are you talking about?" His arms enfolded the brown-haired girl. He shook her, trying to restore sanity to her staring eyes. "Who are you? What's it all about?" he rasped.

"I—my name's Anne Barnard. I live here in this half of the duplex. I j-just moved in this afternoon. . . ."

"Yes. Go on!"

"A while ago, I—I was asleep. Something awakened me. Foosteps outside. . . . Then my front door opened. Somebody staggered into my bedroom. It was a girl, a Chinese girl. She was naked . . . and bleeding from a raw wound in her throat."

"That accounts for the blood I saw here on the porch!" Travis Brant clipped out.

"Yes! I—I switched on my lights, stared at the Chinese girl. There . . . there was *something* . . . clinging to her breast. At first I thought it was an infant. And then—and then I saw . . ." Anne Barnard's voice quivering and gurgled into a low-pitched moan of sheer horror.

"Go on! You saw what?" Travis Brant whispered.

"The—the *thing* at the Chinese girl's breast was not an infant. It was . . . something else. Something foul—horrible—impossible! Its talons were fastened in her b-breasts; its fangs were at her throat. It was *drinking her blood!*"

"God!" Travis Brant rasped. "What was it? What was the thing?"

"I—I don't know!" the brown-haired Anne Barnard wailed shrilly. "It was horribly hairy . . . all over! It was tiny, and white . . . and its face was dripping with the Chinese girl's blood! It had no legs—*and four long arms!*"

Travis Brant stared at the girl. Was she mad? Was she suffering from the delusions of insanity? Then he noticed her blood-stained shoulder. He touched it. "This—?" he whispered.

"I—I tried to tear the *thing* loose from the naked Chinese girl. It snarled at me, clutched me with one of its four hands. Its claws scratched my flesh! I screamed and ran out of the house. Then I bumped into you!" Abruptly, Anne Barnard went limp; collapsed utterly.

TRAVIS BRANT caught her as she slumped. Caught her, lifted her, carried her into his own half of the duplex. He laid her on his own bed; stared down at her for a single instant. His eyes took in the swelling glories of her firm breasts through her thin pajama-coat; swept over the lilting contours of her torso, her hips, her thighs. Then he whirled and dashed back out into the fog.

He reached the open front door of the adjoining half of his duplex cottage, the half occupied by Anne Barnard. He plunged inside. And as he passed the portal, it seemed as though slimy tentacles of oozing dread reached into his soul with questing, cold gelatinous fingers. For a single instant he hesitated, and salt sweat dribbled from his forehead into his eyes, his mouth. Then he squared his shoulders; forced himself forward.

He reached Anne Barnard's bedroom. His eyes went wide, and he felt the blood draining from his strained features. "My God!" he cried wildly, savagely. "My God!"

Thick nausea nibbled at his churning belly. He felt sickening revulsion sweeping over him like a black tidal wave. His eyes were riveted as though hypnotically magnetized, upon a sprawled, outstretched form on the floor at his feet. . . .

The dead body of a naked woman, a girl. A dark-haired Asiatic girl, slant-eyed, lovely, young and yet thick with maturity. Her heavy, swelling breasts were bruised and lacerated; her almond eyes were wide, glazing, sightless. Her throat was a ripped and bleeding wound—a great, gory gash from which the crimson had spewed in a thick freshet, running down over her breasts, her rounded ivory body.

And then, from the shadows of a far corner, Travis Brant heard a sudden, mewling, threadlike wail—a tiny cry of utter, demoniac, nameless evil. It was as

The iron spike split through the bone as if it had been tissue paper; pierced the brain.

though a damned soul had spoken from the slimy slopes of hell itself!

Travis Brant's gaze went toward that sound. And then he felt his knees going weak, and a chill terror gripping his intestines. Something was moving toward him, moving crablike across the floor, horribly, obscenely.

NEVER IN the wildest nightmares of hell-ridden, fiend-spawned horror could such a creature be envisioned. Its tiny white-ivory body was covered with fine, thin black hair through which the flesh showed with scaly luster. It had no legs; but from its shoulders grew four long, flaccid arms, many-jointed and snake-like.

All four arms ended in clawing, long-nailed caricatures of human hands. The creature's face was a God-less obscenity. It had no eyes, no ears; and where its nose should have been, there were two distended, bloody holes. Its mouth was a slavering red slash that ran from cheek to cheek, and from the curled-back lips, sharp jagged fangs protruded redly. And yet, despite the unutterable, fantastic hideousness of that fact, there was some faint quality of humanness about it—as though the thing were a blasphemous travesty of a human infant, fashioned by a sadistic Satan in the foulest reaches of hell.

It was moving toward Travis Brant, pulling itself blindly with its four groping, tentacle-like arms. And as it moved, there issued from its mouth a series of those thin, thread-like mewling cries, blood-hungry and horrible.

Suddenly it reached the Chinese girl's body. Like a flash, it battened itself upon the corpse's breasts, cling-ing with all four clawing hands, the sharp nails digging demoniacally into dead, pliant flesh. . . . Its fanged slash of a mouth fastened on the girl's gory, torn throat. Then, while Travis Brant watched in nauseated fascination, it began to suck the dead woman's clotting, congealing blood.

Abruptly, the thralls of Travis Brant's icy paralysis were broken. With a wild oath, he leaped forward, picked up a heavy pitcher from the wash-stand, hurled it with all his strength full at the tiny monster's blood-battening head. The pitcher smashed into crimson-dripping shards against that evil little skull.

There came the sound like the splitting of a ripe cocoanut, and the miniature hell-beast sprawled lifelessly backward, kicking and squirming spasmodically in the throes of its death-agony. Its brains made a spewing grey ooze on the rug . . . then, slowly, it stiffened and grew still.

Sobbing in his constricted throat, Travis Brant turned and raced out of the room, out of the house, into the spectral-damp fog outside. He plunged into his own half of the duplex cottage, hurtled into his bedroom.

T HE BROWN-HAIRED Anne Barnard was sitting up in the bed. Her hand was pressed over her left breast, as if to still the wild, insane thrumming of her heart. "You—you saw the *thing?*" she whispered.

"Yes!" Travis Brant muttered thickly. "I saw it! And we've got to get the police—right away!"

Abruptly the girl sprang from the cot. She threw herself at Brant; clung to him hotly, thrillingly, frantically. "You—you can't leave me here!" she panted.

"Then come along!" he grated grimly. His arm encircled her lithe waist; and as if magnetized, his hand drew upward toward the swelling base of her breast. His fingers pressed into that firm, rounded mound. Together, they raced from the cottage, into the fog-bound night.

Ahead of them, two blobs of yellow light suddenly loomed through the glutinous grey mist. An automobile's headlights! Travis Brant sprang toward the machine—and as he drew near it, he gulped a great, gasping breath of sheer relief. It was the official police car of Ghost Cove—and Patrolman Dennis Mahony was at the wheel!

M AHONY WAS a big, raw-boned Irishman, an intrepid, steady-eyed man with whom Travis Brant had got fairly well acquainted during the past few weeks. They'd fished together in the Cove, two or three times; had played a little poker in the town's tiny jail-building. Now Travis Brant sprang on the policeman's running-board.

"Mahony—for the love of God, man!" he rasped. "Come with me quick! There's been a murder!"

The officer's eyes narrowed. "Murder, ye say?" he barked. He leaped from his machine. "Where? Where's the body?"

Travis Brant clutched Mahony's arm, dragged him back toward the duplex cottage. Anne Barnard followed fearfully. Mahony's service .38 was in his steady fist as they entered the front doorway of Anne Barnard's portion of the duplex.

Into the dimly-lighted bedroom they swept. "Look!" Travis Brant whispered. He pointed to the corpse of the mutilated Chinese girl. And then he went white.

The carcass of that blood-drinking little monster— the bestial and tiny thing of evil which Brant had slain with the water-pitcher—was gone! The bloody little dead thing had vanished, utterly and completely!

"Who was this dame? What killed her?" Mahony, the policeman, muttered thickly.

"I don't know who she was!" Travis Brant rapped out. "But I know what killed her. It was a small, foul, beast-like monster that ripped out her throat. I saw it —I killed it—and now it's disappeared!"

Mahony stared at Brant, as though he entertained doubts as to the man's sanity. And then Anne Barnard choked out a frightened, gasping whisper. "When— when the Chinese girl came into my bedroom, she gurgled something about Dr. Zenarro having killed her."

"Dr. Zenarro, is it?" Patrolman Dennis Mahony grunted. "I know the buzzard! He lives in that big, spooky house by the cliffs. They do say he deals with banshees and omadhauns! We'll go and question that laddy-buck right now!"

As he spoke, the officer picked up the Chinese girl's blood-stained cadaver, slung it over his shoulder.

And as he carried his gruesome burden toward the front door, he looked at Anne Barnard. "I'll be wanting you to come along, miss," he said grimly. "I'll be wanting you to tell about this dame's accusation, right to Dr. Zenarro's ugly mug!"

The brown-haired girl shrank backward. "You—you want me to go to that gloomy house of Dr. Zenarro? I —I'm afraid!"

Then Travis Brant slipped a hard arm about Anne Barnard's warm, thrillingly-feminine waist. "It's all right!" he whispered. "I'm going along with you!"

S HE CAST him a frightful, grateful glance; and there was something in the passionate depths of her lovely eyes that filled Brant with leaping tingles of desire, of anticipation.

Out in the swirling, thickening fog, Dennis Mahony stuffed the corpse of the Asiatic girl in the back of his sedan. Then he slid under his steering-wheel; and Anne Barnard and Travis Brant got in beside him. The machine moved slowly, ominously through the wraith-tentacles of fog.

Ten minutes later they drew up before a vast, rambling black house set midway up the high and frowning cliffs overlooking Ghost Cove. The place was a somber, spectral structure of slimy grey stone, wet and viscid in the dripping night.

Brant and Anne Barnard followed the bulky figure of Patrolman Mahony as he stepped up to the porch of the house. And as the officer raised his huge fist and knocked thunderously on the heavy oaken door, Travis Brant felt a cold premonition creeping through his veins, like the oozing of some primordial fear.

He held Anne Barnard closer to him; and the warmth-fragrance of her tender body was like a bulwark to which he fastened his sanity and his courage.

A long moment they waited, in that fog-shrouded night of unreality and nightmare-horror. And then footsteps resounded hollowly within the house of Dr. Zenarro, like the echoing dim treads of doom. The heavy door swung open. Travis Brant tensed.

The man who had opened the door was a huge, ungainly, shuffling creature clad in butler's livery. But there was something bestial and obscene about the fellow—a weird, chilling aura of utter evil. The man's long arms hung almost beyond his knees, and his head was sunk low between his broad, sloping shoulders. Hairy, his hands were, and his face was a thing of stark malignance.

Fang-like teeth jutted from between slavering, drooling lips; the eyes were oddly narrow, eerily gleaming with some demoniac and hell-born inward glow.

Patrolman Dennis Mahony spoke sharply. "I want to see your master, Dr. Zenarro. Take me to him."

"Yes," the liveried servant growled deep in his barrel-chest. "I am Gorill, and I will take you to him. You will come inside." There was something in the servant's voice that prickled the short red hairs at the nape of Travis Brant's neck. A sudden desire flamed in Brant's brain—a seething impulse to leap forward and smash his hammer-like fists into the butler's leering, evil features.

But he restrained himself. He followed Patrolman Mahony into the dark, dank house; and Anne Barnard clung to his arm, trembling strangely. The butler led them into a tiny ante-room, lighted a small electric lamp. "You will wait here!" he snarled.

Dennis Mahony shook his head grimly, "No. I'll follow you. You'll take me to Dr. Zennaro. My friends here, will wait in this room for me."

Silently the servant nodded; but there was a sardonic, saturnine flare in his yellow-gleaming eyes.

He led the police-officer out of the little ante-room; closed the door. And now Travis Brant was alone with Anne Barnard.

She turned to Brant, crept toward him. "I—I'm afraid in this place!" she whispered falteringly. "There's something evil, horrible, about it . . . like the odor of a tomb!"

Brant drew her toward him. "It's all right!" he told her gently. "I'll take care of you." Then, on impulse, he tilted her tremulous chin, lowered his mouth to her parted lips.

She returned his kiss, ardently, warmly, thrillingly. Brant felt the fluttering tip of her moist little tongue, and lancing shivers of desire coursed through him. His hand crept to the front of her pajama-jacket, unfastened it, explored tentatively within the silken-gauzy garment. She pressed her body closer to his.

AND then, suddenly, Brant heard a faint, hissing sound. "*What's that?*" he gasped. He disengaged Anne's arms from about his neck; turned swiftly, seeking the source of that susurrant sound. At the same instant, he felt an abrupt choking sensation in his throat, and the blood began to pound strangely in his ears his temples.

He looked at Anne Barnard. She had gone corpse-pale; was swaying toward him. Her breath was coming in sobbing gasps. "I—I can't breathe!" she whimpered. "Something's choking me!"

And it was choking, strangling, Travis Brant at the same time. An acrid, reeking agony was throttling the breath in his lungs, his throat. He whirled, hurled himself at the ante-room's closed door.

"God in Heaven!" he rasped. "It's locked! *We're prisoners!*"

And then he realized that the room was air-tight, hermetically-sealed, and that through some secret vent, an anaesthetizing gas was being introduced into the chamber! A gas that was robbing him of his senses, his consciousness.

Again he smashed against the locked door. It repulsed him. He felt himself swaying, toppling, falling. Anne Barnard had already slumped to the floor. Now he joined her, and the roaring in his ears became a hellish horror of sound which ended in nothingness.

When he opened his eyes, he was in a moisture-dripping subterranean passageway, dank and humid and filled with a smothering necrotic odor, the odor of decayed bodies, of long-dead, putrescent flesh. Someone was shaking him savagely, trying to arouse him.

He looked up—and stared into the fiend-gleaming eyes of a tall, broad-shouldered man clad entirely in black—clad in hell-black tights, black mask, black skull-cap. Through slits in the mask, the man's eyes glowed redly, Satanically.

"Come, come, my snooping friend!" the black-clad man growled evilly. "Get up! You are going on a nice journey through my labyrinth of caves!"

Dim electric lights glowed in the earthen walls of the underground passage, and seeping wetness stained the jutting rocks. From somewhere far along the tunnel, Travis Brant heard a series of mewling wails, foul and demoniac. Where had he heard such weird, eerie sounds before? And then he remembered. That tiny, furry creature which had battened on the Asiatic girl's life-blood—it had emitted exactly the same wailing cries!

Brant staggered to his feet; saw a snub-nosed automatic in the steady hand of the black-clad, demoniac man who was his captor. From the man's black mask came a rasping, guttural, snarling laugh. "I will let you sample the hospitality of Dr. Zenarro!" he chuckled softly, ominously.

"You—you are Zenarro?"

"Aye. I'm Zenarro, my friend. As you will learn to your sorrow!" The black-clad, mysterious one prodded Brant with the automatic. "Get going!"

AS TRAVIS Brant stumbled forward, he beheld a cringing, fettered feminine figure before him. "Anne! Anne! Barnard!" he choked.

The brown-haired girl turned frightened, pleading eyes toward him. Her pajamas had been ripped from her lovely body, until only a thin gauzy shred remained about her middle. Her figure was hauntingly beautiful, a symphony in white girl-flesh. Her tapered legs melted fluidly into the columns of her creamy thighs; her lithe waist swelled upward toward the prominences of her alluring young breasts. There was horror in the tremulous twist of her red lips, and in the slithering fear that dwelt in her eyes. "Travis!" she whimpered.

"Move on!" the black-clad, demon-like Dr. Zenarro rasped. "There is no time to be wasted!"

For an instant, Travis Brant contemplated the thought of flinging himself at Zenarro; facing that automatic, chancing death, gambling against impossible odds. It was as if Zenarro had read his thoughts, for the man's finger squeezed on the trigger. The weapon belched flame, vomited a bullet past Travis Brant's head. "The next one will not miss, my friend!" the doctor whispered silkily.

Brant's shoulders sagged. Dully, he realized that he stood no chance in combat with Zenarro, as long as the man held that automatic. He must wait until Zenarro was off-guard.

Now they were shambling along that subterranean passageway. They rounded a bend. Far below, Travis Brant heard the whispering murmur of the surf, and knew that this cave must be in the cliffs behind Zenarro's house above Ghost Cove. Propped in an angle of earthen corridor, Brant suddenly perceived a slumped figure—recognized it.

It was the body of Patrolman Dennis Mahony, clad in his olive-drab uniform, trussed, helpless, motionless, white-faced!

Brant's heart sank. No use looking for help from Mahony, now! Stiffly the officer lay there in that underground niche, as though deep in unconsciousness.

And then, abruptly, Dr. Zenarro prodded his two prisoners into a great cavernlike chamber, lighted with weird bluish effulgence from two semi-concealed, ghost-sputtering Cooper-Hewitt lamps. But it was not the evil blue glow that brought a choking sob of horror to Travis Brant's dry throat. It was something else.

His eyes widened. What hellish nightmare was this? The place was lined with barred cages, and with medieval-looking instruments of torture. There was a rack, and there were branding-irons, and sharp-spiked torture-tables.

BUT THE cages! God above! Travis Brant felt his stomach churning to a black froth of despair. In each of the iron-barred apertures there was a half-naked woman! There were white women, and negresses, and Japs and Chinese and Filipinos. And each creature held infantile forms—monster-nightmares of unutterable foulness!"

One girl's arms cradled a malignant, two-headed creature— at tiny *thing* with one body and two heads, so that each of its twin mouths nuzzled at the woman's two white breasts. The dull gleam of stark insanity was in the mother's lack-luster eyes, and she rocked the evil little monstrous infant with solicitous maternal affection.

In another cage, a black woman gibbered and crooned over a hairy, miniature shape that had five legs and no arms, no eyes, almost no head. In still another, a brown-skinned Malay girl tended the wants of a hell-spawned *thing* whose arms grew out of its thighs, and whose mouth was located foully in the center of its forehead.

The black-clad Zenarro chuckled fiendishly. "Quite a collection, eh, my friend?" he whispered. "And they all belong to me! Soon I will sell these freak-monsters to European circuses, for much money! And then I will raise a new herd to replace them."

"You beast out of hell!" Travis Brant rasped unsteadily. "You—you father of monsters!"

"But no!" Zenarro corrected softly. "I am not the father. I am merely what, in show parlance, you might call the *entrepreneur*. I raise these creatures for profit. But the father is my huge and shambling servant, the man Gorill, who admitted you to my house."

"You—you mean—?"

"I will explain, since you seem interested. You may recall the case of a fellow named. Modescu, a Rumanian miner in the Pennsylvania coal fields. The newspapers gave it much publicity at the time. This Modescu's wife gave birth to a monster infant—a nightmare horror, abominably deformed. Modescu went mad; killed his wife and the newborn child. He was incarcerated in an asylum—but later he escaped. Well, my friend, that same Modescu is none other than my servant, whom I have re-named Gorill—after the gorilla, you understand."

TRAVIS BRANT stared at the black-masked, black-clad Dr. Zenarro. Understanding was beginning to dawn in Brant's reeling brain, and his marrow crawled as though filled with maggots of madness.

Zenarro went on calmly. "This servant of mine has an unfortunate glandular affliction which causes all his offspring to be monsters. I rescued him from his pursuers and brought him here. And now he serves me well. I make much money from his . . . er, glandular peculiarity. I bring women here, force them to mate with Gorill. They bear monster-children, whom I sell to European circuses. A very profitable enterprise.

"Unfortunately, there is occasionally born a monster more savage than the rest—one which perhaps demands living blood instead of mother's milk. Such was the case of that Chinese girl who escaped from here tonight."

"God!" Brant gasped thickly. "That—that crab-like *thing* was her own child?"

"Yes. And it killed her, clung to her as she escaped. She could not free herself of it. It tore out her throat. I am sorry you killed that little monstrosity, my friend. I could have got a good price for it. However, I will breed another to replace it. In fact, this girl who came here with you tonight shall be mother to a new monster!"

Anne Barnard suddenly went white. She raised her fettered hands to her mouth; tried to run, to dart out of this chamber of foul horror. But Zenarro tripped her, and she went sprawling. At the same instant, Travis Brant lunged at the black-clad fiend.

But Zenarro was even swifter. He raised the muzzle of his automatic, smashed it down on Brant's unprotected skull. Blinding facets of light crashed across Brant's eyes, and he sagged into semi-stupor, with a constellation of agony stabbing at his brain.

Dimly he perceived the huge, ungainly, ape-like form of the liveried butler coming forward, lifting him,

The masked man brought down the whip-lash again and again. Welts appeared on the girl's flesh.

carrying him to a wall of the chamber. He felt iron rings being clamped about his wrists; the rings attached to a clanking chain; the chain drawn through a huge spike jutting from the wall. He sagged limply against his iron bonds.

THROUGH BLURRED eyes, he saw Zenarro bend forward, lift Anne Barnard to her feet. The black-clad doctor pawed at her quivering breasts. Then Zenarro's guttural voice drifted to Travis Brant's pain-dulled ears. The doctor was addressing Anne Barnard—

"You will be Gorill's mate, my dear. He will be the father of your child. Will you go to his arms willingly?"

"Never!" the girl wailed. "I'll die first!"

"No! But you will suffer much . . . until you either go mad, or accept Gorill's caresses!" Swiftly, savagely, Zenarro thrust the almost-nude brown-haired girl against a wooden cruciform frame; strapped her wrists to the cross-member, spread-eagled her ankles, tied them tight to the lower part of the framework. Pinioned, pilloried, she was held there by her bonds. Her eyes were wide with horror.

Zenarro picked up a long whip-lash. "Now!" he grated. He raised the quirt, brought it singing; stinging down across Anne Barnard's cringing body. Great, red welts appeared on her white flesh, like living ser-

*She clung to him in sheer,
crystalline terror.*

pents under her milky skin. Again and again Zenarro
lashed at her, savagely, horribly.

And then the girl sagged. Her head lolled, and her
eyes closed in the merciful oblivion of unconsciousness.

Zenarro spat disgustedly through a slit in his mask.
"Pfah! She has fainted!" He turned to his hulking servant. "I am going back to the house, Gorill. Watch the
girl—and when she regains her senses, signal me. You
understand?"

The shambling, ape-like man nodded. Then Zenarro
turned and left the cavern.

In the far corner, Travis Brant's numbed, pain-dulled
senses were gradually clearing. His mind was beginning to function once more. He saw the gorilla-like
servant approaching Anne Barnard's bound, unconscious form. The man was untying, untrussing Anne's
limp arms and ankles. "I will carry you to the mating-
chamber!" Gorill was muttering. "I will revive you
with my kisses; and then we will make love . . . much
love! We do not need Dr. Zenarro to watch!"

And then the ape-like brute lifted Anne, cradled her
in his huge arms, carried her out of the cavern!

STRENGTH SEEPED back into Travis Brant's
sinews. Cold horror was on him, and a dread chill,
a savage red rage. Anne Barnard—sweet, innocent—at
the mercy of that foul beast-man! It was too much for
sanity to contemplate. Brant gathered his muscles,

gained his feet, plunged against the chains that held
him.

Again, again, again, he plummeted forward. And
then, suddenly, he went sprawling. The iron spike had
pulled out from the wall!

He was free!

Like a flash, he gathered up the long length of chain.
His wrists were still bound together by those iron
bracelet-rings; but he was otherwise untrammeled! He
bounded out of the cavern. He must find Patrolman
Dennis Mahony; and together, the two of them would
rescue Anne Barnard—

Brant was in the subterranean passageway now. He
came to the niche where Mahony lay stiffly, lifelessly.
He bent down over the policeman.

"God!" he rasped in his throat as his fingers recoiled

from those cold, waxen features. Brant straightened, whirled, hurled himself back along the passageway. He passed the cavern of cages, the cave of monsters and mad, insane, mindless, unwilling mothers . . . Then at last, he reached another, smaller chamber in the earth.

Within that chamber, the ape-like servant was forcing Anne Barnard toward a cot. The girl had recovered consciousness, and she was fighting with all her vain, useless strength. Gorill was bending her backward. . . .

With a mighty, snarling oath, Travis Brant leaped into that foul place. In his iron-bound hands he grasped the spike which he had pulled from the wall. He raised it high—brought it plunging down into the liveried servant's skull. The iron spike split through bone as though it had been tissue-paper; pierced Gorill's brain. The servant slumped lifelessly to the earthen floor, limp, dead.

Travis Brant sprang at Anne Barnard, swept her into his arms. And at that instant, a harsh voice floated through the labyrinth of caverns. Dr. Zenarro's voice. "Gorill—where are you? What have you done with that girl? Gorill—Gorill!"

The voice was coming closer now. Travis Brant's face was white, grim, set. "Listen, Anne darling!" he whispered. "This is our only chance of overcoming that mad doctor. Are you willing?" And he whispered something into the girl's ear.

She clung to him, pressed her body close to his own. "Y-yes!" she answered faintly.

And then Travis Brant sprang at the liveried, dead servant; stripped the corpse of its butler's garb. He drew the trousers on over his own pajamas; and since he could not don the coat because his wrists were fettered by the iron chains, he merely placed the livery over his shoulders like a cape. Then, in the semi-darkness, he pressed Anne Barnard back toward the cot . . .

She moaned with fright, with pain. Brant's mouth was pressed upon her lips, and his chained hands touched her breasts, fondled those swelling mounds of enticement. Darting thrills ran through his veins at the intimate contact with her body . . .

And then Brant stiffened. Footsteps had stopped directly outside the chamber. He heard Zenarro's chuckling, evil voice. "So you decided to mate with her before I got back, eh, Gorill?" the man rasped.

ZENARRO entered the little cave; came close to the cot. And as he leaned forward, unsuspecting, Travis Brant hurled himself upright, gathered his muscles, sprang—full at the black-masked doctor's throat.

Cat-like, Zenarro leaped backward. His eyes widened

behind his mask as he perceived that the man in livery was not his servant, but was his supposed prisoner, Travis Brant, the man he intended to kill. Zenarro's hand whipped up. It held the automatic. He fingered the trigger spasmodically.

Flame roared from the gun's muzzle, and Travis Brant felt a scalding slug tear into his shoulder. But no bullet could stop Brant's mighty leap. He smashed himself full at his enemy, raised his blood-stained iron spike, drove it home in Zenarro's heart.

Zenarro collapsed, coughing bloody, crimson-frothed spew from behind his mask. He twisted, writhed—and suddenly became very still, with the stillness of sudden death.

Travis Brant lurched toward the prone body. "You know who this man was?" he whispered harshly to Anne Barnard.

"N-no. Who?"

"A man nobody would ever have suspected. I myself would never have guessed, except that I tried to arouse that unconscious figure of our friend Patrolman Dennis Mahony, out in the passageway. And when I tried to arouse him, I discovered—*that it was a wax figure! A dummy placed there to fool anyone who might stumble upon it!*"

"You mean—?"

"I mean that Dennis Mahony was a policeman part of the time; and the rest of the time he was Dr. Zenarro!" Travis Brant gritted. He whipped away the mask from the dead man's features, and disclosed the face of Mahony, the Irish cop! "That accounts for the disappearance of the little monster that killed the Chinese girl!" Brant breathed harshly. "He was right there on the scene all the time, probably looking for his escaped victim. While I was in my bedroom with you, he was in your half of the duplex, making away with the corpse of the monster. He had time to get back to his sedan before you and I ran out into the fog and came upon him!"

Anne Barnard crept close to Brant. "W-what is to be done now? she whispered.

"We'll get out of here, notify the authorities. Those poor caged, insane women will be sent to some asylum. Their monster-children will be mercifully destroyed. And meanwhile, you and I—"

"Y-yes, Travis Brant? What about you and me?"

Brant caught her with his iron-gyved hands. "We'll find a minister who'll marry us!" he answered softly, gently.

She smiled at him; pressed herself thrillingly against him. And then, together, they wended their way upward out of the cavern-labyrinth of horror. And when at last they reached the open, they saw that the fog had dispersed, and the stars were very bright.

The Dinner Cooked in Hell

By MINDRET LORD

*That grisly meal was prepared in the
kitchen of hell and served by the beautiful,
evil daughter of the devil. And afterward,
for entertainment, I had to watch my wife
and friends twist to the tortures contrived
by this Princess of Pain and her
ungodly followers . . .*

TO ME, it seems so much more horrible because
it happened right in my own house in the middle of New York City. It would have been
ghastly enough, God knows, no matter where it happened—but in my own house!

That afternoon my wife had been to a matinee, and
she called for me at my office so that we could drive
home together. As we got into the car, I noticed that
the sky was dark over the river. One of those sudden
and dramatic summer storms was sweeping in from
New Jersey.

My wife said, "Oh dear! I hope there's not going to
be any thunder!"

I laughed at her. "What's the matter, Dora? I never
knew you to be afraid, before."

"It's our maid, Martha, I'm worried about. She's
told me several times that she's terrified of thunder.
She says when the Thunder God speaks, it means
death."

"That's nonsense," I said. "And if you ask me, I
think we ought to get rid of her. She's cracked. And if
it does thunder tonight, she can lock herself in a closet
and we'll go out to dinner."

"We can't," Dora told me. "Michael and Mary Royce
are dining with us—"

Thunder growled in the sky and a few drops of rain
began to fall on the traffic-crowded streets. It was
sultry and threatening, but it was still not raining hard
when we parked the car and entered the doorway of
the three-floor house where we lived.

In answer to our ring, the door opened, but it was
not the familiar Martha who opened it. Instead, it was
a girl whom neither of us had ever seen before. She
was dark and rather handsome in a bold, Italian way,
and the figure that filled the maid's uniform was much
too voluptuously curving to suit the costume.

Dora said, "What does this mean? Where is Martha?
Who are you?"

The girl smiled apologetically. "Martha was suddenly taken sick and she asked me if I would help out,
tonight. I hope you don't mind, madam?"

Dora hesitated. "Well—we're having guests, so there
doesn't seem much we can do about it. Do you know
how to cook and serve?"

"Oh yes, madam."

"And what did you say your name was?"

"Lucia, madam."

"Very well, Lucia. I'm going up to dress now. We'll
dine at a quarter to seven."

Dora went upstairs. I went to the bar to mix myself
a drink, and asked Lucia to bring me some ice. In a
moment she returned with it and asked, "May I help
you, sir?"

"No," I said. "I'll put it in, myself."

"Yes, sir."

I dropped a couple of cubes into the whiskey and
soda and then looked up. She was still standing there.

"What's the matter?" I asked.

Her black eyes were shining and her deep red lips
were soft and moist.

"It's the thunder, sir," she said.

"Oh lord! Are you afraid of it, too?"

"Oh no, sir! I love it! It—it—" I don't know what she was going to say, but apparently she thought better of it and merely repeated. "I love it!" But there was something about the way she said those words that made me shudder. It was as if she were speaking of a passionate sweetheart.

At that instant, lightning flashed through the window drapes, and in the few seconds that elapsed before the following thunder, I looked at Lucia. I could see that some strange and intense excitement was causing her breast to swell against the black silk of her uniform. Her eyes sought mine in an ecstatic stare. Then came the deep roll of thunder. Lucia sighed heavily and without another word, turned and left me gazing after her. For some reason my hand was shaking when I raised my glass to my lips.

I WENT up to see Dora and found her combing her long, flaxen hair. She made some comment about what bad luck it was to have a new maid on a night when company was expected and then she asked, "By the way—you didn't happen to hear what's the matter with Martha, or where she is?"

"No—but I don't suppose it's anything serious. Anyhow, she wouldn't have been any good in this storm."

"Well," said Dora. "I'd rather have Martha even though she was scared to death—than that one downstairs."

I showered and dressed and got downstairs just as Mike and Mary Royce arrived. They're a good-looking young couple, about our age. Lucia had let them in and I noticed Mike's eyes following her as she left the room.

Mary said, "I see you've got a new maid." I explained about it and then Dora joined us. For a few minutes we sat around, talking about nothing important. Then Lucia came in with a tray and four glasses.

Dora looked at it and laughed. "A tomato juice cocktail! I didn't even know there was any in the house. Oh well, it's good for us."

We each took a glass and drank it politely, but at the time, I remember thinking, "If that's tomato juice, I'm the Queen of the May." I didn't know what it was —it was so cold and so highly seasoned—but after I had swallowed it, I knew I didn't want any more.

At dinner, I think that all of us were nervous and jumpy. It was partly the storm that now crashed directly over Manhattan, and partly the dinner, itself. I don't know how to explain about that meal—the food was good and it was well served, but nobody seemed very hungry. Lucia had carved the roast in the kitchen, and as Dora helped herself, she asked, "What is this, Lucia? I ordered roast beef for tonight."

The girl shrugged her shoulders and smiled as if to say, "I cooked what was there."

"The butcher must have made a mistake." Dora cut a piece and tasted it. "Pork," she said. And to Mary, "I hope you like pork?"

"Of course," said Mary. "We both do. And this is perfectly done. Your new girl's a treasure."

"It is good, isn't it?" Dora agreed—somewhat curiously, I thought.

The meat was good—very white and very fine-textured. But I noticed that nobody ate much.

When Lucia removed our plates, before bringing on the dessert, she must have left the kitchen door open, for I heard a voice speaking in a cautious undertone— so low that the words could not be distinguished.

Dora heard it, too, and asked, "Who is out in the kitchen, Lucia?"

"Just someone who is waiting to take me home, madam. Would you prefer that he waited outside?"

"No," said Dora slowly. "No—it's all right."

It occurred to me that there must be more than one person waiting out there—unless he was talking to himself. However, I said nothing about it.

MEANWHILE, Mike Royce's behavior had done nothing to make the dinner more pleasant. He seemed to be in a kind of stupid daze. When he was spoken to, he scarcely heard. If the remark were repeated, he mumbled some inadequate reply. Dora and I felt embarrassed for Mary and tried to keep up a sprightly conversation, but it was far from easy— particularly when Lucia entered the room. Then, Mike's eyes would follow her every movement, even though he pretended to be looking at his plate.

Dessert was ice cream with a thick, dark wine sauce that tasted more like—like what that tomato juice cocktail had tasted—than like wine. Not that it was actually bad. It was just different from anything any of us had tasted before. We ate a few bites and then went into the living room where Lucia was to serve coffee.

Instead of passing over, the storm was increasing in intensity, so it was no great surprise when the lights suddenly flickered out.

I said, "They'll probably come back on in a second."

While we waited in the dark, the flash of lightning behind the drapes was almost continuous and the peals of thunder seemed to overlap, so that there was a constant, uninterrupted roar. I lit a cigarette. Before I blew out the match, I noticed that Mike Royce was no longer in the room. I didn't mention it, of course, and the girls seemed unaware of his absence.

Finally, Dora said to me, "George—there are some

candles in a box in the basement. Don't you think you'd better go down and get them?"

I groped my way through the dining room to the kitchen, half expecting to find Mike there, with Lucia. But I was wrong. There was nobody in the kitchen at all—as I could see by the ghostly glow of the gas stove's pilot light. I thought that Lucia had probably decided to go home with whomever had been waiting for her, without bothering to finish her job.

I struck a match and went down the flight of wooden stairs to the basement. At the bottom, the match went out, but I knew my way well enough, and the lightning was frequent enough, so that I could move without danger of cracking my head against the low beams. The box I was looking for was on an old carpenter's bench, against the farther wall. I crossed the basement, felt the side of the bench against my thigh and put out my hand to where the box ought to have been. My hand met something that froze me with horror—incredible, unbelieving horror! It *couldn't* be!— and yet, that first grisly touch—when my hand rested on cold flesh and wet, sticky blood—told me the truth, whether my brain would admit it or not. Before I could draw my hand away, the lightning flashed and I had a momentary glimpse of the mutilated thing that once had been a woman.

Nausea gripped me. It was as if some terrible, live thing had suddenly jumped in my stomach. I wanted to strike a light—but more than anything in the world, I wanted to get away from there. I turned and ran three steps before the top of my head seemed to explode. I don't even remember falling. . . .

I AWOKE TO the din of thunder, the clamor of the storm—to a blinding, splitting headache—and to the sound of men's voices near me.

"I think he's coming to," one said. "Will the ropes hold?"

"Sure. They're strong."

"Shall we carry him?"

"No—make him walk."

"I don't see why we don't finish him off right here."

"Lucia would be sore if we did. Besides, it'll be half the fun to watch him when we go to work on his wife—"

At that, I opened my eyes and saw two nightmarish figures bending over me. Even in the feeble light of the flickering candle that one of them held, I could see that these men were mad. Degeneracy was written upon their lantern-jawed faces and in their piggish, cunning eyes. And I, with my arms roped behind me, was completely helpless to defend either my wife or myself.

I opened my mouth to speak, but I never got the words out. One of them kicked me hard in the ribs, and the other yanked me to my feet. Then, between them, they dragged me up the stairs and through the kitchen. As we passed the stove, something caught in the pocket of my coat and ripped it down. It was the handle that turns on the gas in the oven. I didn't know whether it had opened the valve, or not.

There was nobody on the first floor of the house and the men who held me did not stop as we went through. Instead they took me up the stairs and into the big bedroom that was Dora's and mine. They threw the door wide and shoved me in.

A fire had been started in a coal brazier, and the red flames lit the scene of terror. Hanging from the heavy, rustic ceiling beam, was the stripped body of Mary Royce. Hanging beside her, naked to the waist, was Dora, my wife! Michael was suspended a short distance away. Behind him, Lucia held a glowing poker within inches of his bare back. In her left hand was a vicious, snake-like whip.

As I stumbled into the room, Lucia whirled and faced me, her eyes blazing with raging madness. "Good!" she said. "I was afraid you had gotten away—"

"Damn you!" I shouted. "What—"

"Shut up! One word out of you—and both you and your wife will get worse than this!"

"But what do you want?" I begged. "I'll give you anything—"

"I want your lives," she said, matter-of-factly. "I am the Thunder God's bride—and I want your lives for him—tonight!"

As if in confirmation of her crazy statement, a clap of thunder literally shook the house. When it died away, Lucia pointed to a chair and said, "Sit there! And remember—one word—one sound—one movement. . . ."

She didn't need to finish the threat. What could I do but obey?

Mike Royce hung perfectly still—staring vacantly at the tortured, writhing body of his wife. Now that my eyes were more accustomed to the light, I could see that his back was scorched and burnt to such an extent, that he had gone insane from the pain.

While one of my lunatic guards remained near me, the other took the cooling poker from Lucia's hand and exchanged it for another which he withdrew from the fire. But Lucia waved it aside and lifted her whip. The slow, inhuman punishment began again. Mary's slender body was soon torn and bleeding in a hundred places as the merciless lash bit deeply into her tender flesh again, and again. . . .

The room was reverberating with sound—the thunder, Mary's screams, the mad laughter of the men—

yet through it all, I heard Dora's voice raised in a shriek of agony . . . and at that moment, I knew the terrible misery of helplessness.

IF I had been roped into my chair so that I could not possibly move, it might have been easier for me to bear. But to be able to get to her side and yet not be able to fight for her—

Lucia yelled, "What are you doing, you fool? I told you to leave her alone until I was ready for her!"

The idiot answered like a petulant child. "I just burnt her a little bit. Why can't I have some fun, sometimes?"

"Oh well," said Lucia. "All right. But I warn you—don't kill her!"

Almost instantly, Dora cried out again—cried my name, begging me to help her. My arms were slippery with blood, but still the ropes would not give.

I was so concentrated upon my struggle to free my arms that I scarcely saw the ghastly tableau before me, and I have no clear idea of how long it lasted. Finally, however, Lucia halted.

"She's dead," she said, tonelessly, and raised her whip to strike Dora.

At this instant, there was a sudden gust of hot wind that blasted through the bedroom door, followed by a sound that was something like a gigantic sigh. The floor heaved, the windows blew out and the ceiling crashed down. I knew what had happened—when my coat caught on the stove, it had opened one of the burners and the gas had collected in the kitchen until the pilot light had exploded it.

Unthinkingly, the three men raced out of the room and down the stairs. The heavy beams had fallen on Mary's dead body, and they had also caught Michael and Lucia. He was dead, with a point of the splintered wood through his skull. Lucia was alive, though crushed and unable to move.

I backed up to the brazier, pulled one of the irons from the embers and managed to burn through the ropes around my arms. Then, it was the work of a moment to release the chains that bound Dora. I took her in my arms, climbed through one of the shattered windows and set her on the wide ledge, outside.

Lucia was still alive when the firemen took Dora and me down their ladder, but when they asked me if there was anyone else to be saved before the house burned to ashes, I lied about it. I told them that everybody else in the house was dead. Anyway, she couldn't have lasted long—not nearly long enough to suffer for the ghastly carnage she had caused. . . .

*　　*　　*

Several days later, we found out what happened. Martha, our maid, had once been confined in a private asylum for the insane from which she had been discharged as cured just before she came to us. Lucia and the three men had been patients in the same asylum—and when they broke out, they came directly to their old friend, Martha. They were violent, to begin with, but the thunderstorm aroused them to even greater violence.

As for Martha, herself—my wife will never know what happened to her downstairs, in the cellar. I will bear that nauseating memory alone.

Extension of the Finite / 8 / Supernatural

Few publications of any kind can claim greater artistic integrity, commitment to an audience and persistence in the face of almost overwhelming obstacles than *Weird Tales*. First published in 1923 by Clark Henneberger, who, somewhat incongruously, was also the proprietor of *College Humor, The Magazine of Fun,* and some underground semi-pornographic magazines, *Weird Tales,* in 30 years of publication, never made money. In fact, its various publishers often sacrificed their other magazines in order to maintain its financial stability and lofty editorial philosophy. Other publishers attempted fantasy titles but fared even worse, probably because they lacked the commitment of the publishers of *Weird Tales*.

From the start Henneberger had problems and little more than a year after the first issue had to sell *Weird Tales*. Editor Edward Baird was replaced by Farnsworth Wright, who had been a first reader and author for *Weird Tales* as well as a critic for trade magazines in the music field. Wright injected new editorial vitality. But in 1938, when *Weird Tales* was sold again, he was replaced by Dorothy McIlwraith, former editor of *Short Stories,* who edited *Weird Tales* until the last issue in 1954.

The horror story permits us to act out our fears under "safe" circumstances. Its timeless appeal to children, for example, is the product of a constant testing of the environment in an unconscious attempt to define the identity. The imagination is extended as far as one wishes, fulfilling the need to express courage which does not always rally when needed in real life.

Horror stories make demands of the reader. Clearly, they require a more active participation than heroic fiction. Even science-fiction is not so demanding: there the imagination employs the intellect as its tool in relating to the unknown, whereas in the supernatural tale, the imagination triggers the emotions.

* * *

The formidable talent of Pulitzer Prize winner Thomas Lanier "Tennessee" Williams matured at an early age; he was only 16 when he earned $35 for his first story, "The Vengeance of Nitocris" (*Weird Tales,* 1928). Although the story suffers somewhat from the excesses of youthful zeal, Williams has said that it is "a prelude to the violence that is considered my trademark." It is presented here for the first time in book form —the first professional work ever published by one of our greatest playwrights.

* * *

H. P. Lovecraft has become recognized as *the* American writer of horror fiction, second only to Edgar Allan Poe. A coterie "name" with *Weird Tales* readers for many years, he died prematurely in the late 1930's. He is currently being "discovered" in France, and one of his best known works, "The Dunwich Horror," was recently produced here as a film. For the uninitiated, his poetry, not his prose, is presented along with that of some of his contemporaries.

* * *

Writing in the best tradition of Edgar Rice Burroughs, Robert E. Howard achieved popularity which rivalled that of Lovecraft among *Weird Tales* readers. He was best known for his "sword and sorcery" stories, especially those of his character "Conan". Set in the prehistoric Ice Age, these stories of barbarian adventure appeared mainly in *Weird Tales* in the 20's and 30's and are currently experiencing revived popularity in paperback. (Howard spent most of his life in Texas, never living far from his mother. Despondent over her impending death, he committed suicide in 1936 at the age of 30.)

"The Valley of the Worm" (*Weird Tales*, 1934) is reprinted for the first time in hardcover, and is similar to the "Conan" series lacking the latter's sexual scenes, but characteristically fast-moving and powerful in its elements of primitive thought, action, and emotion. ("The Purple Heart of Erlik" in the chapter dealing with sex, is an undiscovered work and the only identified example of an unknown facet of Howard's talent.)

*　　*　　*

Mary Elizabeth Counselman has been widely anthologized and much of her work appeared in such magazines as *The Saturday Evening Post, Collier's,* and *Ladies Home Journal.* Her skillfully constructed "The Green Window" was published in *Weird Tales* in 1949. Few popular magazines other than the low-paying *Weird Tales* offered such a showcase for writing so clearly done for the pure enjoyment of the artist.

*　　*　　*

Malcolm Jameson started writing after leaving the Navy because of ill health. He sold his first story at the age of 38, and although his career as a writer lasted only seven years before he died, he had demonstrated unusual promise and ability in science-fiction. The Train for Flushing" (*Weird Tales*, 1940) is one of his few supernatural fantasies.

*　　*　　*

The protegé of San Francisco poet George Sterling, Clark Ashton Smith first achieved recognition in 1912 at the age of 19 when his book of fantasy verse, *The Startreader* was an extraordinary success. Although he was completely self-educated, Smith acquired one of the largest vocabularies of any American writer, and became extremely popular with the readers of *Weird Tales* when he turned to fiction after 1929. A life-long recluse, he died in 1961. His story "The Seed From the Sepulcher" appeared in 1933 in *Weird Tales.* It demonstrates his unusual imagination, although it does not employ his predominant theme of ancient sorcerery.

*　　*　　*

Editor Farnsworth Wright was astonished by the brilliant technique and originality apparent in the first drawings submitted in 1935 by unknown artist Virgil Finlay. But he had doubts about his ability to reproduce Finlay's exquisitely detailed line and stipple work on rough, pulp paper. One drawing was successfully tested and Finlay immediately became the leading artist for *Weird Tales.* Others such as Hannes Bok and Boris Dolgov continued in the Finlay tradition, but no one surpassed him in illustrating the realm of the imagination. The drawing reproduced here illustrates a few of Longfellow's poetic lines—typical of many full-page works, which were inspired by such literary giants as Dante and Shakespeare.

*　　*　　*

This section, then, is dedicated to the purists who sustained *Weird Tales* throughout its precarious years. For the reader's protection, it is suggested that Page Cooper's poem, "Incantation" (*Weird Tales*, 1950), page 172, be read aloud before proceeding.

The Vengeance of Nitocris

By THOMAS LANIER "TENNESSEE" WILLIAMS

HUSHED WERE the streets of many-peopled Thebes. Those few who passed through them moved with the shadowy fleetness of bats near dawn, and bent their faces from the sky as if fearful of seeing what in their fancies might be hovering there. Weird, high-noted incantations of a wailing sound were audible through the barred doors. On corners groups of naked and bleeding priests cast themselves repeatedly and with loud cries upon the rough stones of the walks. Even dogs and cats and oxen seemed impressed by some strange menace and foreboding and cowered and slunk dejectedly. All Thebes was in dread. And indeed there was cause for their dread and for their wails of lamentation. A terrible sacrilege had been committed. In all the annals of Egypt none more monstrous was recorded.

Five days had the altar fires of the god of gods, Osiris, been left unburning. Even for one moment to allow darkness upon the altars of the god was considered by the priests to be a great offense against him. Whole years of dearth and famine had been known to result from such an offense. But now the altar fires had been deliberately extinguished, and left extinguished for five days. It was an unspeakable sacrilege.

Hourly there was expectancy of some great calamity to befall. Perhaps within the approaching night a mighty earthquake would shake the city to the ground, or a fire from heaven would sweep upon them, or some monster from the desert, where wild and terrible monsters were said to dwell, would rush upon them and Osiris himself would rise up, as he had done before, and swallow all Egypt in his wrath. Surely some such dread catastrophe would befall them ere the week had passed. Unless—unless the sacrilege were avenged.

But how might it be avenged? That was the question high lords and priests debated. Pharaoh alone had committed the sacrilege. It was he, angered because the bridge, which he had spent five years in constructing so that one day he might cross the Nile in his chariot as he had once boasted that he would do, had been swept away by the rising waters. Raging with anger, he had flogged the priests from the temple. He had barred the temple doors and with his own breath had blown out the sacred candles. He had defiled the hallowed altars with the carcasses of beasts. Even, it was said in low, shocked whispers, in a mock ceremony of worship he had burned the carrion of a hyena, most abhorrent of all beasts of Osiris, upon the holy altar of gold which even the most high of priests forbore to lay naked hands upon!

Surely, even though he be Pharaoh, ruler of all

Egypt and holder of the golden eagle, he could not be permitted to commit such violent sacrileges without punishment from man. The god Osiris was waiting for them to inflict that punishment, and if they failed to do it, upon them would come a scourge from heaven.

Standing before the awed assembly of nobles, the high Kha Semblor made a gesture with his hands. A cry broke from those who watched. Sentence had been delivered. Death had been pronounced as doom for the pharaoh. The heavy, barred doors were shoved open. The crowd came out, and within an hour a well-organized mob passed through the streets of Thebes, directed for the palace of the pharaoh. Mob justice was to be done.

Within the resplendent portals of the palace the pharaoh, ruler of all Egypt, watched with tightened brow the orderly but menacing approach of the mob. He divined their intent. But was he not their pharaoh? He could contend with gods, so why should he fear mere dogs of men?

A woman clung to this stiffened arm. She was tall and as majestically handsome as he. A garb of linen, as brilliantly golden as the sun, entwined her body closely and bands of jet were around her throat and forehead. She was the fair and well-loved Nitocris, sister of the pharaoh.

"Brother, brother!" she cried, "light the fires! Pacify the dogs! They come to kill you."

Only more stern grew the look of the pharaoh. He thrust aside his pleading sister, and beckoned to the attendants.

"Open the doors!"

Startled, trembling, the men obeyed.

The haughty lord of Egypt drew his sword from its sheath. He slashed the air with a stroke that would have severed stone. Out on the steep steps leading between tall, colored pillars to the doors of the palace he stopped. The people saw him. A howl rose from their lips.

"Light the fires!"

The figure of the pharaoh stood inflexible as rock. Superbly tall and muscular, his bare arms and limbs glittering like burnished copper in the light of the brilliant sun, his body erect and tense in his attitude of defiance, he looked indeed a mortal fit almost to challenge gods.

The mob, led by the black-robed priests and nobles who had arrived at the foot of the steps, now fell back before the stunning, magnificent defiance of their giant ruler. They felt like demons who had assailed the heavens and had been abashed and shamed by the mere sight of that which they had assailed. A hush fell over them. Their upraised arms faltered and sank down. A moment more and they would have fallen to their knees.

What happened then seemed nothing less than a miracle. In his triumph and exultation, the pharaoh had been careless of the crumbling edges of the steps. Centuries old, there were sections of these steps which were falling apart. Upon such a section had the gold-sandaled foot of the pharaoh descended, and it was not strong enough to sustain his great weight. With a scuttling sound it broke loose. A gasp came from the mob—the pharaoh was about to fall. He was palpitating, wavering in the air, fighting to retain his balance. He looked as if he were grappling with some monstrous, invisible snake, coiled about his gleaming body. A hoarse cry burst from his lips; his sword fell; and then his body thudded down the steps in a series of somersaults, and landed at the foot, sprawled out before the gasping mob. For a moment there was breathless silence. And then came the shout of a priest.

"A sign from the god!"

That vibrant cry seemed to restore the mob to all of its wolflike rage. They surged forward. The struggling body of the pharaoh was lifted up and torn to pieces by their clawing hands and weapons. Thus was the god Osiris avenged.

A week later another large assembly of persons confronted the brilliant-pillared palace. This time they were there to acknowledge a ruler, not to slay one. The week before they had rended the pharaoh and now they were proclaiming his sister empress. Priests had declared that it was the will of the gods that she should succeed her brother. She was famously beautiful, pious, and wise. The people were not reluctant to accept her.

When she was borne down the steps of the palace in her rich litter, after the elaborate ceremony of the coronation had been concluded, she responded to the cheers of the multitude with a smile which could not have appeared more amicable and gracious. None might know from that smile upon her beautiful carmined lips that within her heart she was thinking, "These are the people who slew my brother. Ah, god Issus, grant me power to avenge his death upon them!"

Not long after the beauteous Nitocris mounted the golden throne of Egypt, rumors were whispered of some vast, mysterious enterprise being conducted in secret. A large number of slaves were observed each dawn to embark upon barges and to be carried down the river to some unknown point, where they labored through the day, returning after dark. The slaves were Ethiopians, neither able to speak nor to understand the Egyptian language, and therefore no information could be gotten from them by the curious as to the object of their mysterious daily excursions. The general opinion, though, was that the pious queen was having a great temple constructed to the gods and that when it was finished, enormous public banquets would be held within it before its dedication. She meant it to be a surprise gift to the priests who were ever desirous of some new place of worship and were dissatisfied with their old altars, which they said were defiled.

Throughout the winter the slaves repeated daily their excursions. Traffic of all kinds plying down the river was restricted for several miles to within forty yards of one shore. Any craft seen to disregard that restriction was set upon by a galley of armed men and pursued back into bounds. All that could be learned was that a prodigious temple or hall of some sort was in construction.

It was late in the spring when the excursions of the workmen were finally discontinued. Restrictions upon river traffic were withdrawn. The men who went eagerly to investigate the mysterious construction returned with tales of a magnificent new temple, surrounded by rich, green, tropical verdure, situated near the bank of the river. It was a temple to the god Osiris. It had been built by the queen probably that she might partly atone for the sacrilege of her brother and deliver him from some of the torture which he undoubtedly suffered. It was to be dedicated within the month by a great banquet. All the nobles and the high priests of Osiris, of which there were a tremendous number, were to be invited.

Never had the delighted priests been more extravagant in their praises of Queen Nitocris. When she passed through the streets in her open litter, bedazzling eyes by the glitter of her golden ornaments, the cries of the people were almost frantic in their exaltation of her.

True to the predictions of the gossipers, before the month had passed the banquet had been formally announced and to all the nobility and the priests of Osiris had been issued invitations to attend.

The day of the dedication, which was to be followed by the night of banqueting, was a gala holiday. At noon the guests of the empress formed a colorful assembly upon the bank of the river. Gayly draped barges floated at their moorings until preparations should be completed for the transportation of the guests to the temple. All anticipated a holiday of great merriment, and the lustful epicureans were warmed by visualizations of the delightful banquet of copious meats, fruits, luscious delicacies and other less innocent indulgences.

When the queen arrived, clamorous shouts rang deafeningly in her ears. She responded with charming smiles and gracious bows. The most discerning observer could not have detected anything but the greatest cordiality and kindliness reflected in her bearing toward those around her. No action, no fleeting expression upon her lovely face could have caused anyone to suspect anything except entire amicability in her feelings or her intentions. The rats, as they followed the Pied Piper of Hamlin through the streets, entranced by the notes of his magical pipe, could not have been less apprehensive of any great danger impending than were the guests of the empress as they followed her in gayly draped barges, singing and laughing down the sun-glowing waters of the Nile.

The most vivid descriptions of those who had already seen the temple did not prepare the others for the spectacle of beauty and grandeur which it presented. Gasps of delight came from the priests. What a place in which to conduct their ceremonies! They began to feel that the sacrilege of the dead pharaoh was not, after all, to be so greatly regretted, since it was responsible for the building of this glorious new temple.

The columns were massive and painted with the greatest artistry. The temple itself was proportionately large. The center of it was unroofed. Above the entrance were carved the various symbols of the god Osiris, with splendid workmanship. The building was immensely big, and against the background of green foliage it presented a picture of almost breath-taking beauty. Ethiopian attendants stood on each side of the doorway, their shining black bodies ornamented with bands of brilliant gold. On the interior the guests were inspired to even greater wonderment. The walls were hung with magnificent painted tapestries. The altars were more beautifully and elaborately carved than any seen before. Aromatic powders were burning upon them and sending up veils of scented smoke. The sacramental vessels were of the most exquisite and costly metals. Golden coffer and urns were piled high with perfect fruits of all kinds.

Ah, yes—a splendid place for the making of sacrifices, gloated the staring priests.

As, yes indeed, agreed the Queen Nitocris, smiling with her closed eyes, it was a splendid place for sacrifices—especially the human sacrifice that had been planned. But all who observed that guileful smile interpreted it as gratification over the pleasure which her creation in honor of their god had brought to the priests of Osiris. Not the slightest shadow of portent was upon the hearts of the joyous guests.

The ceremony of dedication occupied the whole of the afternoon. And when it drew to its impressive conclusion, the large assembly, their nostrils quivering from the savory odor of the roasting meats, were fully ready and impatient for the banquet that awaited them. They gazed about them observing that the

whole building composed an unpartitioned amphitheater and wondering where might be the room of
the banquet. However, when the concluding proces-
sional chant had been completed, the queen summoned
a number of burly slaves, and by several iron rings
attached to its outer edges they lifted up a large slab
of the flooring, disclosing to the astonished guests the
fact that the scene of the banquet was to be an immense subterranean vault.

Such vaults were decidedly uncommon among the
Egyptians. The idea of feasting in one was novel and
appealing. Thrilled exclamations came from the eager,
excited crowd and they pressed forward to gaze into
the depths, now brightly illuminated. They saw a room
beneath them almost as vast in size as the amphitheater
in which they were standing. It was filled with banquet
tables upon which were set the most delectable foods
and rich, sparkling wines in an abundance that would
satiate the banqueters of Bacchus. Luxurious, thick
rugs covered the floors. Among the tables passed
nymphlike maidens, and at one end of the room
harpists and singers stood, making sublime music.

The air was cool with the dampness of under-earth,
and it was made delightfully fragrant by the perfumes
of burning spices and the savory odors of the feast.
If it had been heaven itself which the crowd of the
queen's guests now gazed down upon they would
not have considered the vision disappointing. Perhaps
even if they had known the hideous menace that
lurked in those gay-draped walls beneath them, they
would still have found the allurement of the banquet
scene difficult to resist.

Decorum and reserve were almost completely forgotten in the swiftness of the guests' descent. The
stairs were not wide enough to afford room for all
those who rushed upon them, and some tumbled over,
landing unhurt upon the thick carpets. The priests
themselves forgot their customary dignity and aloof-
ness when they looked upon the beauty of the maiden
attendants.

Immediately all of the guests gathered around the
banquet tables, and the next hour was occupied in
gluttonous feasting. Wine was unlimited and so was
the thirst of the guests. Goblets were refilled as quickly
as they were empty by the capacious mouths of the
drinkers. The singing and the laughter, the dancing
and the wild frolicking grew less and less restrained
until the banquet became a delirious orgy.

The Queen alone, seated upon a cushioned dais from
which she might overlook the whole room, remained
aloof from the general hilarity. Her thick black brows
twitched; her luminous black eyes shone strangely
between their narrow painted lids. There was something peculiarly feline in the curl of her rich red lips.

Now and again her eyes sought the section of wall
to her left, where hung gorgeous braided tapestries
from the East. But it seemed not the tapestries that
she looked upon. Color would mount upon her brow
and her slender fingers would dig still tighter into the
cushions she reclined upon.

In her mind the Queen Nitocris was seeing a ghastly
picture. It was the picture of a room of orgy and feasting suddenly converted into a room of terror and
horror; human beings one moment drunken and lustful, the next screaming in the seizure of sudden and
awful death. If any of those present had been empowered to see also that picture of dire horror, they would
have clambered wildly to make their escape. But none
was so empowered.

With increasing wildness the banquet continued into
the middle of the night. Some of the banqueters, dis-
gustingly gluttonous still gorged themselves at the
greasy tables. Others lay in drunken stupor, or lolled
amorously with the slave-girls. But most of them,
formed in a great, irregular circle, skipped about the
room in a barbaric, joy-mad dance, dragging and
tripping each other in uncouth merriment and making
the hall ring with their ceaseless shouts, laughter and
hoarse song.

When the hour had approached near to midnight,
the Queen, who had sat like one entranced, arose from
the cushioned dais. One last intent survey she gave to
the crowded room of banquet. It was a scene which
she wished to imprint permanent upon her mind.
Much pleasure might she derive in the future by recall-
ing that picture, and then imagining what came afterward—stark, searing terror rushing in upon barbarious
joy!

She stepped down from the dais and walked swiftly
to the steps. Her departure made no impression upon
the revelers. When she arrived at the top of the stairs
she looked down and observed that no one had
marked her exit.

Around the walls of the temple dim-lit and fantastic-
looking at night, with the cool wind from the river
sweeping through and bending the flames of the tallest
candelabra, stalwart guardsmen were standing at their
posts, and when the gold-cloaked figure of the Queen
arose from the aperture, they advanced toward her
hurriedly. With a motion, she directed them to place
the slab of rock in its tight-fitting socket. With a swift
noiseless hoist and lowering, they obeyed the command. The Queen bent down. There was no change
in the boisterous sounds from below. Nothing was yet
suspected.

Drawing the soft and shimmering folds of her cloak
about her with fingers that trembled with eagerness,
excitement and the intense emotion which she felt, the

Queen passed swiftly across the stone floor of the temple toward the open front through which the night wind swept, blowing her cloak in sheenful waves about her tall and graceful figure. The slaves followed after in silent file, well aware of the monstrous deed about to be executed and without reluctance to play their parts.

Down the steps of the palace into the moon-white night passed the weird procession. Their way led them down an obviously secreted path through thick ranks of murmuring palms which in their low voices seemed to be whispering shocked remonstrances against what was about to be done. But in her stern purpose the Queen was not susceptible to any discussion from god or man. Vengeance, strongest of passions, made her obdurate as stone.

Out upon a rough and apparently new-constructed stone pier the thin path led. Beneath, the cold, dark waters of the Nile surged silently by. Here the party came to a halt. Upon this stone pier would the object of their awful midnight errand be accomplished.

With a low-spoken word, the Queen commanded her followers to hold back. With her own hand she would perform the act of vengeance.

In the foreground of the pier a number of fantastic, wand-like levers extended upward. Toward these the Queen advanced, slowly and stiffly as an executioner mounts the steps of the scaffold. When she had come beside them, she grasped one upthrust bar, fiercely, as if it had been the throat of a hated antagonist. Then she lifted her face with a quick intake of breath toward the moon-lightened sky. This was to her a moment of supreme ecstasy. Grasped in her hand was an instrument which could release awful death upon those against whom she wished vengeance. Their lives were as securely in her grasp as was this bar of iron.

Slowly, lusting upon every triumph-filled second of this time of ecstasy, she turned her face down again to the formidable bar in her hand. Deliberately she drew it back to its limit. This was the lever that opened the wall in the banquet vault. It gave entrance to death. Only the other bar now intervened between the banqueters, probably still reveling undisturbed, and the dreadful fate which she had prepared for them. Upon this bar now her jeweled fingers clutched. Savagely this time she pulled it; then with the litheness of a tiger she sprang to the edge of the pier. She leaned over it and stared down into the inky rush of the river. A new sound she heard above the steady flow. It was the sound of waters suddenly diverted into a new channel—an eager, plunging sound. Down to the hall of revelry they were rushing—these savage waters—bringing terror and sudden death.

A cry of triumph, wild and terrible enough to make even the hearts of the brutish slaves turn cold, now broke from the lips of the Queen. The pharaoh was avenged.

And even he must have considered his avenging adequate had he been able to witness it.

After the retiring of the Queen, the banquet had gone on without interruption of gayety. None noticed her absence. None noticed the silent replacing of the stone in its socket. No premonition of disaster was felt. The musicians, having been informed beforehand of the intended event of the evening, had made their withdrawal before the queen. The slaves, whose lives were of little value to the queen, were as ignorant of what was to happen as were the guests themselves.

Not until the wall opened up with a loud and startling crunch did even those most inclined toward suspicion feel the slightest uneasiness. Then it was that a few noticed the slab to have been replaced, shutting them in. This discovery, communicated throughout the hall in a moment, seemed to instill a sudden fear in the hearts of all. Laughter did not cease, but the ring of dancers were distracted from their wild jubilee. They all turned toward the mysteriously opened wall and gazed into its black depths.

A hush fell over them. And then became audible the mounting sound of rushing water. A shriek rose from the throat of a woman. And then terror took possession of all within the room. Panic like the burst of flames flared into their hearts. Of one accord, they rushed upon the stair. And it, being purposely made frail, collapsed before the foremost of the wildly screaming mob had reached its summit. Turbulently they piled over the tables, filling the room with a hideous clamor. But rising above their screams was the shrill roar of the rushing water, and no sound could be more provoking of dread and terror. Somewhere in its circuitous route from the pier to the chamber of its reception it must have met with temporary blockade; for it was several minutes after the sound of it was first detected that the first spray of that death-bringing water leapt into the faces of the doomed occupants of the room.

With the ferocity of a lion springing into the arena of a Roman amphitheater to devour the gladiators set there for its delectation, the black water plunged in. Furiously it surged over the floor of the room, sweeping tables before it and sending its victims, now face to face with their harrowing doom, into a hysteria of terror. In a moment that icy, black water had risen to their knees, although the room was vast. Some fell instantly dead from the shock, or were trampled upon by the desperate rushing of the mob. Tables were clambered upon. Lamps and candles were extinguished. Brilliant light rapidly faded to twilight, and a ghastly dimness fell over the room as only the suspended lanterns remained lit. And what a scene of chaotic and hideous horror might a spectator have beheld! The gorgeous trumpetry of banquet invaded by howling waters of death! Gayly dressed merry-makers caught suddenly in the grip of terror! Gasps and screams of the dying amid tumult and thickening dark!

What more horrible vengeance could Queen Nitocris have conceived than this banquet of death? Not Diablo himself could be capable of anything more fiendishly artistic. Here in the temple of Osiris those nobles and priests who had slain the pharaoh in expiation of his sacrilege against Osiris had now met their deaths. And it was in the waters of the Nile, material symbol of the god Osiris, that they had died. It was magnificent in its irony!

I would be content to end this story here if it were but a story. However, it is not merely a story, as you will have discerned before now if you have been a student of the history of Egypt. Queen Nitocris is not a fictitious personage. In the annals of ancient Egypt she is no inconspicuous figure. Principally responsible for her prominence is her monstrous revenge upon the slayers of her brother, the narration of which I have just concluded. Glad would I be to end this story here; for surely anything following must be in the nature of an anticlimax. However, being not a mere story-teller here, but having upon me also the responsibility of a historian, I feel obligated to continue the account to the point where it was left off by Herodotus, the great Greek historian. And, therefore, I add this postscript, anticlimax though it be.

The morning of the day after the massacre in the temple, the guests of the Queen not having made their return, the citizens of Thebes began to glower with dark suspicions. Rumor came to them through divers channels that something of a most extraordinary and calamitous nature had occurred at the scene of the banquet during the night. Some had it that the temple had collapsed upon the revelers and all had been killed. However, this theory was speedily dispelled when a voyager from down the river reported having passed the temple in a perfectly firm condition but declared that he had seen no signs of life about the place—only the brightly canopied boats, drifting at their moorings.

Uneasiness steadily increased throughout the day. Sage persons recalled the great devotion of the Queen toward her dead brother, and noted that the guests at the banquet of last night had been composed almost entirely of those who had participated in his slaying.

When in the evening the Queen arrived in the city, pale, silent, and obviously nervous, threatening crowds blocked the path of her chariot, demanding roughly an explanation of the disappearance of her guests. Haughtily she ignored them and lashed forward the horses of her chariot, pushing aside the tight mass of people. Well she knew, however, that her life would be doomed as soon as they confirmed their suspicions. She resolved to meet her inevitable death in a way that befitted one of her rank, not at the filthy hands of a mob.

Therefore, upon her entrance into the palace she ordered her slaves to fill instantly her boudoir with hot and smoking ashes. When this has been done, she went to the room, entered it, closed the door and locked it securely, and then flung herself down upon a couch in the center of the room. In a short time the scorching heat and the suffocating thick fumes of the smoke overpowered her. Only her beautiful dead body remained for the hands of the mob.

Incantation

By PAGE COOPER

LORD of the unseen,
 Of ghosts that howl through musty corners of the mind
 And stir the hideous sightless fears that grope to find
A strangling clutch on this poor terror-palsied hand,
Oh keep them blind.

 Lord of the unspoken,
  Of viper words that suck the poisoned wounds of red
  And festered old betrayals; e'er my lips have fed
  Their venom to a heart as yet unstabbed, unbled,
  Oh strike them dead.

Weird Tales, 1950

The Valley of the Worm

By ROBERT E. HOWARD

*A stirring tale of a hideous
monster from the elder world,
that came in conflict with the
yellow-haired sons of Aryan.*

*"He fell through the air
full upon the monster's back."*

I WILL tell you of Niord and the Worm. You have
heard the tale before in many guises wherein the
hero was named Tyr, or Perseus, or Siegfried, or
Beowulf, or Saint George. But it was Niord who met
the loathly demoniac thing that crawled hideously up
from hell, and from which meeting sprang the cycle
of hero-tales that revolves down the ages until the very
substance of the truth is lost and passes into the limbo
of all forgotten legends. I know whereof I speak, for
I was Niord.

As I lie here awaiting death, which creeps slowly
upon me like a blind slug, my dreams are filled with
glittering visions and the pageantry of glory. It is not
of the drab, disease-racked life of James Allison I
dream, but all the gleaming figures of the mighty
pageantry that have passed before, and shall come
after; for I have faintly glimpsed, not merely the
shapes that come after, as a man in a long parade
glimpses, far ahead, the line of figures that precede him
winding over a distant hill, etched shadow-like against
the sky. I am one and all the pageantry of shapes and
guises and masks which have been, are, and shall be
the visible manifestations of that illusive, intangible,
but vitally existent spirit now promenading under the
brief and temporary name of James Allison.

Each man on earth, each woman, is part and all of
a similar caravan of shapes and beings. But they can
not remember—their minds can not bridge the brief,
awful gulfs of blackness which lie between those unstable shapes, and which the spirit, soul or ego, in
spanning, shakes off its fleshy masks. I remember. Why
I can remember is the strangest tale of all; but as I lie
here with death's black wings slowly unfolding over

me, all the dim folds of my previous lives are shaken
out before my eyes, and I see myself in many forms
and guises—braggart, swaggering, fearful, loving, foolish, all that men have been or will be.

I have been Man in many lands and many conditions; yet—and here is another strange thing—my line
of reincarnation runs straight down one unerring
channel. I have never been any but a man of that
restless race men once called Nordheimr and later
Aryans, and today name by many names and designa-
tions. Their history is my history, from the first mewling wail of a hairless white ape cub in the wastes of
the arctic, to the death-cry of the last degenerate
product of ultimate civilization, in some dim and
unguessed future age.

My name has been Hialmar, Tyr, Bragi, Bran, Horsa,
Eric, and John. I strode red-handed through the deserted streets of Rome behind the yellow-maned
Brennus; I wandered through the violated plantations
with Alaric and his Goths when the flame of burning
villas lit the land like day and an empire was gasping
its last under our sandalled feet; I waded sword in
hand through the foaming surf from Hengist's galley
to lay the foundations of England in blood and pillage; when Leif the Lucky sighted the broad white
beaches of an unguessed world, I stood beside him
in the bows of the dragon-ship, my golden beard blowing in the wind; and when Godfrey of Bouillon led
his Crusaders over the walls of Jerusalem, I was among
them in steel cap and brigandine.

But it is of none of these things I would speak. I
would take you back with me into an age beside which
that of Brennus and Rome is as yesterday. I would take

you back through, not merely centuries and millenniums, but epochs and dim ages unguessed by the wildest philosopher. Oh far, far and far will you fare into the nighted Past before you win beyond the boundaries of my race, blue-eyed, yellow-haired, wanderers, slayers, lovers, mighty in rapine and wayfaring.

It is the adventure of Niord Worm's-bane of which I would speak—the rootstem of a whole cycle of hero-tales which has not yet reached its end, the grisly underlying reality that lurks behind time-distorted myths of dragons, fiends and monsters.

Yet it is not alone with the mouth of Niord that I will speak. I am James Allison no less than I was Niord, and as I unfold the tale, I will interpret some of his thoughts and dreams and deeds from the mouth of the modern I, so that the saga of Niord shall not be a meaningless chaos to you. His blood is your blood, who are sons of Aryan; but wide misty gulfs of eons lie horrifically between, and the deeds and dreams of Niord seem as alien to your deeds and dreams as the primordial and lion-haunted forest seems alien to the white-walled city street.

IT WAS a strange world in which Niord lived and loved and fought, so long ago that even my eon-spanning memory can not recognize landmarks. Since then the surface of the earth has changed, not once but a score of times; continents have risen and sunk, seas have changed their beds and rivers their courses, glaciers have waxed and waned, and the very stars and constellations have altered and shifted.

It was so long ago that the cradle-land of my race was still in Nordheim. But the epic drifts of my people had already begun, and blue-eyed, yellow-maned tribes flowed eastward and southward and westward, on century-long treks that carried them around the world and left their bones and their traces in strange lands and wild waste places. On one of these drifts I grew from infancy to manhood. My knowledge of that northern homeland was dim memories, like half-remembered dreams, of blinding white snow plains and ice fields, of great fires roaring in the circle of hide tents, of yellow manes flying in great winds, and a sun setting in a lurid wallow of crimson clouds, blazing on trampled snow where still dark forms lay in pools that were redder than the sunset.

That last memory stands out clearer than the others. It was the field of Jotunheim, I was told in later years, whereon had just been fought that terrible battle which was the Armageddon of the Æsir-folk, the subject of a cycle of hero-songs for long ages, and which still lives today in dim dreams of Ragnarok and Goetterdaemmerung. I looked on that battle as a mewling infant; so I must have lived about—but I will not

name the age, for I would be called a madman, and historians and geologists alike would rise to refute me.

But my memories of Nordheim were few and dim, paled by memories of that long, long trek upon which I had spent my life. We had not kept to a straight course, but our trend had been for ever southward. Sometimes we had bided for a while in fertile upland valleys or rich river-traversed plains, but always we took up the trail again, and not always because of drouth or famine. Often we left countries teeming with game and wild grain to push into wastelands. On our trail we moved endlessly, driven only by our restless whim, yet blindly following a cosmic law, the workings of which we never guessed, any more than the wild geese guess in their flights around the world. So at last we came into the Country of the Worm.

I will take up the tale at the time when we came into jungle-clad hills reeking with rot and teeming with spawning life, where the tom-toms of a savage people pulsed incessantly through the hot breathless night. These people came forth to dispute our way— short, strongly built men, black-haired, painted, ferocious, but indisputably white men. We knew their breed of old. They were Picts, and of all alien races the fiercest. We had met their kind before in thick forests, and in upland valleys beside mountain lakes. But many moons had passed since those meetings.

I believe this particular tribe represented the easternmost drift of the race. They were the most primitive and ferocious of any I ever met. Already they were exhibiting hints of characteristics I have noted among black savages in jungle countries, though they had dwelt in these environs only a few generations. The abysmal jungle was engulfing them, was obliterating their pristine characteristics and shaping them in its own horrific mold. They were drifting into head-hunting, and cannibalism was but a step which I believe they must have taken before they became extinct. These things are natural adjuncts to the jungle; the Picts did not learn them from the black people, for then there were no blacks among those hills. In later years they came up from the south, and the Picts first enslaved and then were absorbed by them. But with that my saga of Niord is not concerned.

We came into that brutish hill country, with its squalling abysms of savagery and black primitiveness. We were a whole tribe marching on foot, old men, wolfish with their long beards and gaunt limbs, giant warriors in their prime, naked children running along the line of march, women with tousled yellow locks carrying babies which never cried—unless it were to scream from pure rage. I do not remember our numbers, except that there were some five hundred fighting-men—and by fighting-men I mean all males, from the child just strong enough to lift a bow, to the oldest of the old men. In that madly ferocious age all were fighters. Our women fought, when brought to bay, like tigresses, and I have seen a babe, not yet old enough to stammer articulate words, twist its head and sink its tiny teeth in the foot that stamped out its life.

Oh, we were fighters! Let me speak of Niord. I am proud of him, the more when I consider the paltry crippled body of James Allison, the unstable mask I now wear. Niord was tall, with great shoulders, lean hips and mighty limbs. His muscles were long and swelling, denoting endurance and speed as well as strength. He could run all day without tiring, and he possessed a co-ordination that made his movements a blur of blinding speed. If I told you his full strength, you would brand me a liar. But there is no man on earth today strong enough to bend the bow Niord handled with ease. The longest arrow-flight on record is that of a Turkish archer who sent a shaft 482 yards. There was not a stripling in my tribe who could not have bettered that flight.

AS WE entered the jungle country we heard the tom-toms booming across the mysterious valleys that slumbered between the brutish hills, and in a broad, open plateau we met our enemies. I do not believe these Picts knew us, even by legends, or they had never rushed so openly to the onset, though they outnumbered us. But there was no attempt at ambush. They swarmed out of the trees, dancing and singing their war-songs, yelling their barbarous threats. Our heads should hang in their idol-hut and our yellow-haired women should bear their sons. Ho! ho! ho! By Ymir, it was Niord who laughed then, not James Allison. Just so we of the Æsir laughed to hear their threats—deep thunderous laughter from broad and mighty chests. Our trail was laid in blood and embers through many lands. We were the slayers and ravishers, striding sword in hand across the world, and that these folk threatened us woke our rugged humor.

We went to meet them, naked but for our wolfhides, swinging our bronze swords, and our singing was like rolling thunder in the hills. They sent their arrows among us, and we gave back their fire. They could not match us in archery. Our arrows hissed in blinding clouds among them, dropping them like autumn leaves, until they howled and frothed like mad dogs and changed to hand-grips. And we, mad with the fighting joy, dropped our bows and ran to meet them, as a lover runs to his love.

By Ymir, it was a battle to madden and make drunken with the slaughter and the fury. The Picts were as ferocious as we, but ours was the superior physique, the keener wit, the more highly developed fighting-brain. We won because we were a superior race, but it was no easy victory. Corpses littered the blood-soaked earth; but at last they broke, and we cut them down as they ran, to the very edge of the trees. I tell of that fight in a few bald words. I can not paint the madness, the reek of sweat and blood, the panting, muscle-straining effort, the splintering of bones under mighty blows, the rending and hewing of quivering sentient flesh; above all the merciless abysmal savagery of the whole affair, in which there was neither rule nor order, each man fighting as he would or could. If I might do so, you would recoil in horror; even the modern I, cognizant of my close kinship with those times, stand aghast as I review that butchery. Mercy was yet unborn, save as some individual's whim, and rules of warfare were as yet undreamed of. It was an age in which each tribe and each human fought tooth and fang from birth to death, and neither gave nor expected mercy.

So we cut down the fleeing Picts, and our women came out on the field to brain the wounded enemies with stones, or cut their throats with copper knives. We did not torture. We were no more cruel than life demanded. The rule of life was ruthlessness, but there is more wanton cruelty today than ever we dreamed of. It was not wanton bloodthirstiness that made us butcher wounded and captive foes. It was because we knew our chances of survival increased with each enemy slain.

Yet there was occasionally a touch of individual mercy, and so it was in this fight. I had been occupied with a duel with an especially valiant enemy. His tousled thatch of black hair scarcely came above my chin, but he was a solid knot of steel-spring muscles, than which lightning scarcely moved faster. He had an iron sword and a hide-covered buckler. I had a knotty-headed bludgeon. That fight was one that glutted even my battle-lusting soul. I was bleeding from a score of flesh wounds before one of my terrible, lashing strokes smashed his shield like cardboard, and an instant later my bludgeon glanced from his unprotected head. Ymir! Even now I stop to laugh and marvel at the hardness of that Pict's skull. Men of that age were assuredly built on a rugged plan! That blow should have spattered his brains like water. It did lay his scalp open horribly, dashing him senseless to the earth, where I let him lie, supposing him to be dead, as I joined in the slaughter of the fleeing warriors.

When I returned reeking with sweat and blood, my club horridly clotted with blood and brains, I noticed that my antagonist was regaining consciousness, and that a naked tousle-headed girl was preparing to give him the finishing touch with a stone she could scarcely lift. A vagrant whim caused me to check the blow. I had enjoyed the fight, and I admired the adamantine quality of his skull.

WE MADE camp a short distance away, burned our dead on a great pyre, and after looting the corpses of the enemy, we dragged them across the plateau and cast them down in a valley to make a feast for the hyenas, jackals and vultures which were already gathering. We kept close watch that night, but we were not attacked, though far away through the jungle we could make out the red gleam of fires, and could faintly hear, when the wind veered, the throb of tom-toms and demoniac screams and yells—keenings for the slain or mere animal squallings of fury.

Nor did they attack us in the days that followed. We bandaged our captive's wounds and quickly learned his primitive tongue, which, however, was so different from ours that I can not conceive of the two languages having ever had a common source.

His name was Grom, and he was a great hunter and fighter, he boasted. He talked freely and held no grudge, grinning broadly and showing tusk-like teeth, his beady eyes glittering from under the tangled black mane that fell over his low forehead. His limbs were almost ape-like in their thickness.

He was vastly interested in his captors, though he could never understand why he had been spared; to the end it remained an inexplicable mystery to him. The Picts obeyed the law of survival even more rigidly than did the Æsir. They were the more practical, as shown by their more settled habits. They never roamed as far or as blindly as we. Yet in every line we were the superior race.

Grom, impressed by our intelligence and fighting qualities, volunteered to go into the hills and make peace for us with his people. It was immaterial to us, but we let him go. Slavery had not yet been dreamed of.

So Grom went back to his people, and we forgot about him, except that I went a trifle more cautiously about my hunting, expecting him to be lying in wait to put an arrow through my back. Then one day we heard a rattle of tom-toms, and Grom appeared at the edge of the jungle, his face split in his gorilla-grin, with the painted, skin-clad, feather-bedecked chiefs of the clans. Our ferocity had awed them, and our sparing of Grom further impressed them. They could not understand leniency; evidently we valued them too cheaply to bother about killing one when he was in our power.

So peace was made with much pow-wow, and sworn to with many strange oaths and rituals—we swore only by Ymir, and an Æsir never broke that vow. But they swore by the elements, by the idol which sat in the fetish-hut where fires burned for ever and a withered crone slapped a leather-covered drum all night long, and by another being too terrible to be named.

Then we all sat around the fires and gnawed meat-bones, and drank a fiery concoction they brewed from wild grain, and the wonder is that the feast did not end in a general massacre; for that liquor had devils in it and made maggots writhe in our brains. But no harm came of our vast drunkenness, and thereafter we dwelt at peace with our barbarous neighbors. They taught us many things, and learned many more from us. But they taught us iron-workings, into which they had been forced by the lack of copper in those hills, and we quickly excelled them.

We went freely among their villages—mud-walled clusters of huts in hilltop clearings, overshadowed by giant trees—and we allowed them to come at will among our camps—straggling lines of hide tents on the plateau where the battle had been fought. Our young men cared not for their squat beady-eyed women, and our rangy clean-limbed girls with their tousled yellow heads were not drawn to the hairy-breasted savages. Familiarity over a period of years would have reduced the repulsion on either side, until the two races would have flowed together to form one hybrid people, but long before that time the Æsir rose and departed, vanishing into the mysterious hazes of the haunted south. But before that exodus there came to pass the horror of the Worm.

I HUNTED with Grom and he led me into brooding, uninhabited valleys and up into silence-haunted hills where no men had set foot before us. But there was one valley, off in the mazes of the southwest, into which he would not go. Stumps of shattered columns, relics of a forgotten civilization, stood among the trees on the valley floor. Grom showed them to me, as we stood on the cliffs that flanked the mysterious vale, but he would not go down into it, and he dissuaded me when I would have gone alone. He would not speak plainly of the danger that lurked there, but it was greater than that of serpent or tiger, or the trumpeting elephants which occasionally wandered up in devastating droves from the south.

Of all beasts, Grom told me in the gutturals of his tongue, the Picts feared only Satha, the great snake, and they shunned the jungle where he lived. But there was another thing they feared, and it was connected in some manner with the Valley of Broken Stones, as the Picts called the crumbling pillars. Long ago, when his ancestors had first come into the country, they had dared that grim vale, and a whole clan of them had perished, suddenly, horribly, and unexplainably. At least Grom did not explain. The horror had come up out of the earth, somehow, and it was not good to talk of it, since it was believed that It might be summoned by speaking of It—whatever It was.

But Grom was ready to hunt with me anywhere else; for he was the greatest hunter among the Picts, and many and fearful were our adventures. Once I killed, with the iron sword I had forged with my own hands, that most terrible of all beasts—old saber-tooth, which men today call a tiger because he was more like a tiger than anything else. In reality he was almost as much like a bear in build, save for his unmistakably feline head. Saber-tooth was massive-limbed, with a low-hung, great, heavy body, and he vanished from the earth because he was too terrible a fighter, even for that grim age. As his muscles and ferocity grew, his brain dwindled until at last even the instinct of self-preservation vanished. Nature, who maintains her balance in such things, destroyed him because, had his super-fighting powers been allied with an intelligent brain, he would have destroyed all other forms of life on earth. He was a freak on the road of evolution—organic development gone mad and run to fangs and talons, to slaughter and destruction.

I killed saber-tooth in a battle that would make a saga in itself, and for months afterward I lay semi-delirious with ghastly wounds that made the toughest warriors shake their heads. The Picts said that never before had a man killed a saber-tooth single-handed. Yet I recovered, to the wonder of all.

While I lay at the doors of death there was a secession from the tribe. It was a peaceful secession, such as continually occurred and contributed greatly to the peopling of the world by yellow-haired tribes. Forty-five of the young men took themselves mates simultaneously and wandered off to found a clan of their own. There was no revolt; it was a racial custom which bore fruit in all the later ages, when tribes sprung from the same roots met, after centuries of separation, and cut one another's throats with joyous abandon. The tendency of the Aryan and the pre-Aryan was always toward disunity, clans splitting off the main stem, and scattering.

So these young men, led by one Bragi, my brother-in-arms, took their girls and venturing to the southwest, took up their abode in the Valley of Broken Stones. The Picts expostulated, hinting vaguely of a monstrous doom that haunted the vale, but the Æsir laughed. We had left our own demons and weirds in the icy wastes of the far blue north, and the devils of other races did not much impress us.

When my full strength was returned, and the grisly wounds were only scars, I girt on my weapons and strode over the plateau to visit Bragi's clan. Grom did not accompany me. He had not been in the Æsir camp for several days. But I knew the way. I remembered well the valley, from the cliffs of which I had looked down and seen the lake at the upper end, the trees thickening into forest at the lower extremity. The sides of the valley were high sheer cliffs, and a steep broad ridge at either end cut it off from the surrounding country. It was toward the lower or southwestern end that the valley-floor was dotted thickly with ruined columns, some towering high among the trees, some fallen into heaps of lichen-clad stones. What race reared them none knew. But Grom had hinted fearsomely of a hairy, apish monstrosity dancing loathsomely under the moon to a demoniac piping that induced horror and madness.

I CROSSED the plateau whereon our camp was pitched, descended the slope, traversed a shallow vegetation-choked valley, climbed another slope, and plunged into the hills. A half-day's leisurely travel brought me to the ridge on the other side of which lay the valley of the pillars. For many miles I had seen no sign of human life. The settlements of the Picts all lay many miles to the east. I topped the ridge and looked down into the dreaming valley with its still blue lake, its brooding cliffs and its broken columns jutting among the trees. I looked for smoke. I saw none, but I saw vultures wheeling in the sky over a cluster of tents on the lake shore.

I came down the ridge warily and approached the silent camp. In it I halted, frozen with horror. I was not easily moved. I had seen death in many forms, and had fled from or taken part in red massacres that spilled blood like water and heaped the earth with corpses. But here I was confronted with an organic devastation that staggered and appalled me. Of Bragi's embryonic clan, not one remained alive, and not one corpse was whole. Some of the hide tents still stood erect. Others were mashed down and flattened out, as if crushed by some monstrous weight, so that at first I wondered if a drove of elephants had stampeded across the camp. But no elephants ever wrought such destruction as I saw strewn on the bloody ground. The camp was a shambles, littered with bits of flesh and fragments of bodies—hands, feet, heads, pieces of human debris. Weapons lay about, some of them stained with a greenish slime like that which spurts from a crushed caterpillar.

No human foe could have committed this ghastly atrocity. I looked at the lake, wondering if nameless amphibian monsters had crawled from the calm waters whose deep blue told of unfathomed depths. Then I saw a print left by the destroyer. It was a track such as a titanic worm might leave, yards broad, winding back down the valley. The grass lay flat where it ran, and bushes and small trees had been crushed down into the earth, all horribly smeared with blood and greenish slime.

With berserk fury in my soul I drew my sword and started to follow it, when a call attracted me. I wheeled, to see a stocky form approaching me from the ridge. It was Grom the Pict, and when I think of the courage it must have taken for him to have over-come all the instincts planted in him by traditional teachings and personal experience, I realize the full depths of his friendship for me.

Squatting on the lake shore, spear in his hands, his black eyes ever roving fearfully down the brooding tree-waving reaches of the valley, Grom told me of the horror that had come upon Bragi's clan under the moon. But first he told me of it, as his sires had told the tale to him.

Long ago the Picts had drifted down from the north-west on a long, long trek, finally reaching these jungle-covered hills, where, because they were weary, and because the game and fruit were plentiful and there were no hostile tribes, they halted and built their mud-walled villages.

Some of them, a whole clan of that numerous tribe, took up their abode in the Valley of the Broken Stones. They found the columns and a great ruined temple back in the trees, and in that temple there was no shrine or altar, but the mouth of a shaft that vanished deep into the black earth, and in which there were no steps such as a human being would make and use. They built their village in the valley, and in the night, under the moon, horror came upon them and left only broken walls and bits of slime-smeared flesh.

In those days the Picts feared nothing. The warriors of the other clans gathered and sang their war-songs and danced their war-dances, and followed a broad track of blood and slime to the shaft-mouth in the temple. They howled defiance and hurled down boulders which were never heard to strike bottom. Then began a thin demoniac piping, and up from the well pranced a hideous anthropomorphic figure danc-ing to the weird strains of a pipe it held in its mon-strous hands. The horror of its aspect froze the fierce Picts with amazement, and close behind it a vast white bulk heaved up from the subterranean darkness. Out of the shaft came a slavering mad nightmare which arrows pierced but could not check, which swords carved but could not slay. It fell slobbering upon the warriors, crushing them to crimson pulp, tearing them to bits as an octopus might tear small fishes, sucking their blood from their mangled limbs and devouring them even as they screamed and struggled. The sur-

vivors fled, pursued to the very ridge, up which, apparently, the monster could not propel its quaking mountainous bulk.

After that they did not dare the silent valley. But the dead came to their shamans and old men in dreams and told them strange and terrible secrets. They spoke of an ancient, ancient race of semi-human beings which once inhabited that valley and reared those columns for their own weird inexplicable purposes. The white monster in the pits was their god, summoned up from the nighted abysses of mid-earth uncounted fathoms below the black mold, by sorcery unknown to the sons of men. The hairy anthropomorphic being was its servant, created to serve the god, a formless elemental spirit drawn up from below and cased in flesh, organic but beyond the understanding of humanity. The Old Ones had long vanished into the limbo from whence they crawled in the black dawn of the universe, but their bestial god and his inhuman slave lived on. Yet both were organic after a fashion, and could be wounded, though no human weapon had been found potent enough to slay them.

Bragi and his clan had dwelt for weeks in the valley before the horror struck. Only the night before, Grom, hunting above the cliffs, and by that token daring greatly, had been paralyzed by a high-pitched demon piping, and then by a mad clamor of human scream-ing. Stretched face down in the dirt, hiding his head in a tangle of grass, he had not dared to move, even when the shrieks died away in the slobbering, repul-sive sounds of a hideous feast. When dawn broke he had crept shuddering to the cliffs to look down into the valley, and the sight of the devastation, even when seen from afar, had driven him in yammering flight far into the hills. But it had occurred to him, finally, that he should warn the rest of the tribe, and return-ing, on his way to the camp on the plateau, he had seen me entering the valley.

So SPOKE Grom, while I sat and brooded darkly, my chin on my mighty fist. I can not frame in modern words the clan-feeling that in those days was a living vital part of every man and woman. In a world where talon and fang were lifted on every hand, and the hands of all men raised against an individual, ex-cept those of his own clan, tribal instinct was more than the phrase it is today. It was as much a part of a man as was his heart or his right hand. This was neces-sary, for only thus banded together in unbreakable groups could mankind have survived in the terrible environments of the primitive world. So now the per-sonal grief I felt for Bragi and the clean-limbed young men and laughing white-skinned girls was drowned in a deeper sea of grief and fury that was cosmic in its depth and intensity. I sat grimly, while the Pict squatted anxiously beside me, his gaze roving from me to the menacing deeps of the valley where the accursed columns loomed like broken teeth of cackling hags among the waving leafy reaches.

I, Niord, was not one to use my brain over-much. I lived in a physical world, and there were the old men of the tribe to do my thinking. But I was one of a race destined to become dominant mentally as well as physically, and I was no mere muscular animal. So as I sat there, there came dimly and then clearly a thought to me that brought a short fierce laugh from my lips.

Rising, I bade Grom aid me, and we built a pyre on the lake shore of dried wood, the ridge-poles of the tents, and the broken shafts of spears. Then we collected the grisly fragments that had been parts of Bragi's band, and we laid them on the pile, and struck flint and steel to it.

The thick sad smoke crawled serpent-like into the sky, and turning to Grom, I made him guide me to the jungle where lurked that scaly horror, Satha, the great serpent. Grom gaped at me; not the greatest hunters among the Picts sought out the mighty crawling one. But my will was like a wind that swept him along my course, and at last he led the way. We left the valley by the upper end, crossing the ridge, skirting the tall cliffs, and plunged into the fastnesses of the south, which was peopled only by the grim denizens of the jungle. Deep into the jungle we went, until we came to a low-lying expanse, dank and dark beneath the great creeper-festooned trees, where our feet sank deep into the spongy silt, carpeted by rotting vegetation, and slimy moisture oozed up beneath their pressure. This, Grom told me, was the realm haunted by Satha, the great serpent.

Let me speak of Satha. There is nothing like him on earth today, nor has there been for countless ages. Like the meat-eating dinosaur, like old saber-tooth, he was too terrible to exist. Even then he was a survival of a grimmer age when life and its forms were cruder and more hideous. There were not many of his kind then, though they may have existed in great numbers in the reeking ooze of the vast jungle-tangled swamps still farther south. He was larger than any python of modern ages, and his fangs dripped with poison a thousand times more deadly than that of a king cobra.

He was never worshipped by the pure-blood Picts, though the blacks that came later deified him, and that adoration persisted in the hybrid race that sprang from the negroes and their white conquerors. But to other peoples he was the nadir of evil horror, and tales of him became twisted into demonology; so in later ages

Satha became the veritable devil of the white races, and the Stygians first worshipped, and then, when they became Egyptians, abhorred him under the name of Set, the Old Serpent, while to the Semites he became Leviathan and Satan. He was terrible enough to be a god, for he was a crawling death. I had seen a bull elephant fall dead in his tracks from Satha's bite. I had seen him, had glimpsed him writhing his horrific way through the dense jungle, had seen him take his prey, but I had never hunted him. He was too grim, even for the slayer of old saber-tooth.

But now I hunted him, plunging farther and farther into the hot, breathless reek of his jungle, even when friendship for me could not drive Grom farther. He urged me to paint my body and sing my death-song before I advanced farther, but I pushed on unheeding.

In a natural runway that wound between the shouldering trees, I set a trap. I found a large tree, soft and spongy of fiber, but thick-boled and heavy, and I hacked through its base close to the ground with my great sword, directing its fall so that when it toppled, its top crashed into the branches of a smaller tree, leaving it leaning across the runway, one end resting on the earth, the other caught in the small tree. Then I cut away the branches on the under side, and cutting a slim tough sapling I trimmed it and stuck it upright like a prop-pole under the leaning tree. Then, cutting away the tree which supported it, I left the great trunk poised precariously on the prop-pole, to which I fastened a long vine, as thick as my wrist.

Then I went alone through that primordial twilight jungle until an overpowering fetid odor assailed my nostrils, and from the rank vegetation in front of me, Satha reared up his hideous head, swaying lethally from side to side, while his forked tongue jetted in and out, and his great yellow terrible eyes burned icily on me with all the evil wisdom of the black elder world that was when man was not. I backed away, feeling no fear, only an icy sensation along my spine, and Satha came sinuously after me, his shining eighty-foot barrel rippling over the rotting vegetation in mesmeric silence. His wedge-shaped head was bigger than the head of the hugest stallion, his trunk was thicker than a man's body, and his scales shimmered with a thousand changing scintillations. I was to Satha as a mouse is to a king cobra, but I was fanged as no mouse ever was. Quick as I was, I knew I could not avoid the lightning stroke of that great triangular head; so I dared not let him come too close. Subtly I fled down the runway, and behind me the rush of the great supple body was like the sweep of wind through the grass.

He was not far behind me when I raced beneath the dead-fall, and as the great shining length glided under the trap, I gripped the vine with both hands and jerked desperately. With a crash the great trunk fell across Satha's scaly back, some six feet back of his wedge-shaped head.

I had hoped to break his spine but I do not think it did, for the great body coiled and knotted, the mighty tail lashed and thrashed, mowing down the bushes as if with a giant flail. At the instant of the fall, the huge head had whipped about and struck the tree with a terrific impact, the mighty fangs shearing through bark and wood like simitars. Now, as if aware he fought an inanimate foe, Satha turned on me, standing out of his reach. The scaly neck writhed and arched, the mighty jaws gaped, disclosing fangs a foot in length, from which dripped venom that might have burned through solid stone.

I believe, what of his stupendous strength, that Satha would have writhed from under the trunk, but for a broken branch that had been driven deep into his side, holding him like a barb. The sound of his hissing filled the jungle and his eyes glared at me with such concentrated evil that I shook despite myself. Oh, he knew it was I who had trapped him! Now I came as close as I dared, and with a sudden powerful cast of my spear, transfixed his neck just below the gaping jaws, nailing him to the tree-trunk. Then I dared greatly, for he was far from dead, and I knew he would in an instant tear the spear from the wood and be free to strike. But in that instant I ran in, and swinging my sword with all my great power, I hewed off his terrible head.

THE HEAVINGS and contortions of Satha's prisoned form in life were naught to the convulsions of his headless length in death. I retreated, dragging the gigantic head after me with a crooked pole, and at a safe distance from the lashing, flying tail, I set to work. I worked with naked death then, and no man ever toiled more gingerly than did I. For I cut out the poison sacs at the base of the great fangs, and in the terrible venom I soaked the heads of eleven arrows, being careful that only the bronze points were in the liquid, which else had corroded away the wood of the tough shafts. While I was doing this, Grom, driven by comradeship and curiosity, came stealing nervously through the jungle, and his mouth gaped as he looked on the head of Satha.

For hours I steeped the arrowheads in the poison, until they were caked with a horrible green scum, and showed tiny flecks of corrosion where the venom had eaten into the solid bronze. I wrapped them carefully in broad, thick, rubber-like leaves, and then, though night had fallen and the hunting beasts were roaring on every hand, I went back through the jungled hills, Grom with me, until at dawn we came again to the high cliffs that loomed above the Valley of Broken Stones.

At the mouth of the valley I broke my spear, and I took all the unpoisoned shafts from my quiver, and snapped them. I painted my face and limbs as the Æsir painted themselves only when they went forth to certain doom, and I sang my death-song to the sun as it rose over the cliffs, my yellow mane blowing in the morning wind.

Then I went down into the valley, bow in hand.

Grom could not drive himself to follow me. He lay on his belly in the dust and howled like a dying dog.

I passed the lake and the silent camp where the pyre-ashes still smoldered, and came under the thickening trees beyond. About me the columns loomed, mere shapeless heads from the ravages of staggering eons. The trees grew more dense, and under their vast leafy branches the very light was dusky and evil. As in twilight shadow I saw the ruined temple, cyclopean walls staggering up from masses of decaying masonry and fallen blocks of stone. About six hundred yards in front of it a great column reared up in an open glade, eighty or ninety feet in height. It was so worn and pitted by weather and time that any child of my tribe could have climbed it, and I marked it and changed my plan.

I came to the ruins and saw huge crumbling walls upholding a domed roof from which many stones had fallen, so that it seemed like the lichen-grown ribs of some mythical monster's skeleton arching above me. Titanic columns flanked the open doorway through which ten elephants could have stalked abreast. Once there might have been inscriptions and hieroglyphics on the pillars and walls, but they were long worn away. Around the great room, on the inner side, ran columns in better state of preservation. On each of these columns was a flat pedestal, and some dim instinctive memory vaguely resurrected a shadowy scene wherein black drums roared madly, and on these pedestals monstrous beings squatted loathsomely in inexplicable rituals rooted in the black dawn of the universe.

There was no altar—only the mouth of a great well-like shaft in the stone floor, with strange obscene carvings all about the rim. I tore great pieces of stone from the rotting floor and cast them down the shaft which slanted down into utter darkness. I heard them bound along the side, but I did not hear them strike bottom. I cast down stone after stone, each with a searing curse, and at last I heard a sound that was not the dwindling rumble of the falling stones. Up from the well floated a weird demon-piping that was a symphony of madness. Far down in the darkness I glimpsed the faint fearful glimmering of a vast white bulk.

I retreated slowly as the piping grew louder, falling back through the broad doorway. I heard a scratching, scrambling noise, and up from the shaft and out of the doorway between the colossal columns came a prancing incredible figure. It went erect like a man, but it was covered with fur, that was shaggiest where its face should have been. If it had ears, nose and a mouth I did not discover them. Only a pair of staring red eyes leered from the furry mask. Its misshapen hands held a strange set of pipes, on which it blew weirdly as it pranced toward me with many a grotesque caper and leap.

Behind it I heard a repulsive obscene noise as of a quaking unstable mass heaving up out of a well. Then I nocked an arrow, drew the cord and sent the shaft singing through the furry breast of the dancing monstrosity. It went down as though struck by a thunderbolt, but to my horror the piping continued, though the pipes had fallen from the malformed hands. Then I turned and ran fleetly to the column, up which I swarmed before I looked back. When I reached the pinnacle I looked, and because of the shock and surprize of what I saw, I almost fell from my dizzy perch.

Out of the temple the monstrous dweller in the darkness had come, and I, who had expected a horror yet cast in some terrestrial mold, looked on the spawn of nightmare. From what subterranean hell it crawled in the long ago I know not, nor what black age it represented. But it was not a beast, as humanity knows beasts. I call it a worm for lack of a better term. There is no earthly language which has a name for it. I can only say that it looked somewhat more like a worm than it did an octopus, a serpent or a dinosaur.

It was white and pulpy, and drew its quaking bulk along the ground, worm-fashion. But it had wide flat tentacles, and fleshy feelers, and other adjuncts the use of which I am unable to explain. And it had a long proboscis which it curled and uncurled like an elephant's trunk. Its forty eyes, set in a horrific circle, were composed of thousands of facets of as many scintillant colors which changed and altered in never-ending transmutation. But through all interplay of hue and glint, they retained their evil intelligence—intelligence there was behind those flickering facets, not human nor yet bestial, but a night-born demoniac intelligence such as men in dreams vaguely sense throbbing titanically in the black gulfs outside our material universe. In size the monster was mountainous; its bulk would have dwarfed a mastodon.

But even as I shook with the cosmic horror of the thing, I drew a feathered shaft to my ear and arched it singing on its way. Grass and bushes were crushed flat as the monster came toward me like a moving mountain and shaft after shaft I sent with terrific force and deadly precision. I could not miss so huge a target. The arrows sank to the feathers or clear out of sight in the unstable bulk, each bearing enough poison to have stricken dead a bull elephant. Yet on it came, swiftly, appallingly, apparently heedless of both the shafts and the venom in which they were steeped. And all the time the hideous music played a maddening accompaniment, whining thinly from the pipes that lay untouched on the ground.

My confidence faded; even the poison of Satha was futile against this uncanny being. I drove my last shaft almost straight downward into the quaking white mountain, so close was the monster under my perch. Then suddenly its color altered. A wave of ghastly blue surged over it, and the vast bulk heaved in earthquake-like convulsions. With a terrible plunge it struck the lower part of the column, which crashed to falling shards of stone. But even with the impact, I leaped far out and fell through the empty air full upon the monster's back.

The spongy skin yielded and gave beneath my feet, and I drove my sword hilt-deep, dragging it through the pulpy flesh, ripping a horrible yard-long wound, from which oozed a green slime. Then a flip of a cable-like-tentacle flicked me from the titan's back and spun me three hundred feet through the air to crash among a cluster of giant trees.

The impact must have splintered half the bones in my frame, for when I sought to grasp my sword again and crawl anew to the combat, I could not move hand or foot, could only writhe helplessly with my broken back. But I could see the monster and I knew that I had won, even in defeat. The mountainous bulk was heaving and billowing, the tentacles were lashing madly, the antennae writhing and knotting, and the nauseous whiteness had changed to a pale and grisly green. It turned ponderously and lurched back toward the temple, rolling like a crippled ship in a heavy swell. Trees crashed and splintered as it lumbered against them.

I wept with pure fury because I could not catch up my sword and rush in to die glutting my berserk madness in mighty strokes. But the worm-god was death-stricken and needed not my futile sword. The demon pipes on the ground kept up their infernal tune, and it was like the fiend's death-dirge. Then as the monster veered and floundered, I saw it catch up the corpse of its hairy slave. For an instant the apish form dangled in midair, gripped round by the trunk-like proboscis, then was dashed against the temple wall with a force that reduced the hairy body to a mere shapeless pulp. At that the pipes screamed out horribly, and fell silent for ever.

The titan staggered on the brink of the shaft; then

another change came over it—a frightful transfiguration the nature of which I can not yet describe. Even now when I try to think of it clearly, I am only chaotically conscious of a blasphemous, unnatural transmutation of form and substance, shocking and indescribable. Then the strangely altered bulk tumbled into the shaft to roll down into the ultimate darkness from whence it came, and I knew that it was dead. And as it vanished into the well, with a rending, grinding groan the ruined walls quivered from dome to base. They bent inward and buckled with deafening reverberation, the columns splintered, and with a cataclysmic crash the dome itself came thundering down. For an instant the air seemed veiled with flying debris and stone-dust, through which the tree-tops lashed madly as in a storm or an earthquake convulsion. Then all was clear again and I stared, shaking the blood from my eyes. Where the temple had stood there lay only a colossal pile of shattered masonry and broken stones, and every column in the valley had fallen, to lie in crumbling shards.

IN THE silence that followed I heard Grom wailing a dirge over me. I bade him lay my sword in my hand, and he did so, and bent close to hear what I had to say, for I was passing swiftly.

"Let my tribe remember," I said, speaking slowly. "Let the tale be told from village to village, from camp to camp, from tribe to tribe, so that men may know that not man nor beast nor devil may prey in safety on the golden-haired people of Asgard. Let them build me a cairn where I lie and lay me therein with my bow and sword at hand, to guard this valley for ever; so if the ghost of the god I slew comes up from below, my ghost will ever be ready to give it battle."

And while Grom howled and beat his hairy breast, death came to me in the Valley of the Worm.

In Mayan Splendor

By FRANK BELKNAP LONG, JR.

IN dim dreams and shadowed memories
   Of fabled cities I have dwelt apace;
    And from strange springs and guardian trees
Have slaked my thirst, and scornful of the face
Of harsh reality have stooped to trace
Dark figures on the sands of alien keys:
In Mayan splendor I have spanned the seas
And clothed myself in legendary grace.

In Copan I have dwelt where serpent stones
And skies of dusky violet merge to form
A glimmering gate of wonder whereto bones
Of warrior dead are gathered in a storm
Of whirling clouds and crimson flames that roar
Beneath the sky-vault where great condors soar.

The Green Window

BY MARY ELIZABETH COUNSELMAN

What was there about the window?
Look long enough and you shall know!
Heading by Vincent Napoli

IT IS one of those old Colonial structures, with great fluted columns in front and a kitchen detached from the house by a long hall-porch. There are half a dozen just like it in Stuartsboro—but if you are driving through here, if you will ask any of our leisurely-moving inhabitants, they will gladly direct you to "the house with the green window." Anyone, that is, except myself. I would not go near the place for any reason whatsoever. I'll never go back there. *Never.*

There is nothing to see. The beautiful old grounds have grown up now in mustard and Jimson seed. The large plaster fountain on the lawn runs no more; it is full of stagnant rain water, probably, at this season, and choked with last autumn's leaves that drifted down from the giant whiteoaks standing like sentinels before the house. Furthermore, the windows have been boarded up—even that queer opaque one to the left of the fan-lighted door. Especially that one . . . There are ten-penny nails in the heavy planks that cover it from sight. Otherwise, Aunt Millicent insists, passing tourists would swarm in with claw hammers and rip them off, to take a peek at those panes. The American tourist is a predatory animal; he would break pieces off the Venus de Milo to take home a souvenir to the folks. Several times the "window lights," as panes are called locally, have been broken

Weird Tales, 1949

out by the curious, by would-be detectives of the supernatural who yearn to give that weird green glass a laboratory test.

I wish I could see their faces when they smugly take it out of pocket or handbag, back home again, with a tale to tell the neighbors. For, whatever it is that causes the glass in that one particular window of the old Dickerson home to cloud over, it disappears about half an hour after the panes are removed from the windowframe. I don't know why. Jeb and Mark and I, as children, have scraped them with razor blades, peered at them under our toy microscopes, and smeared all sorts of acids on them. But the green scum—that is what it looks like; a foul gray-ish-green scum on the surface of a pool—seems to be *inside* the glass, under surface. I could not tell you how many times the opaque discolored panes have been replaced by ordinary glass, only to cloud over again by sunset of the next day.

BUT THAT is not its attraction. The "green window" is supposed to be a prophetic window, an opening into the future; or, more accurately, a mirror for tomorrow. The story is: when Great-great Grandpa Dickerson was thrown from his horse and lay dying in that room, over a century ago, he called for an old slave on the Place, a wizened old negress purported to be a *mamaloi*. The plantation was heavily in debt, and it seems the old boy was worried about the welfare of his wife and two small sons. Lying there on the brocaded couch, with his spine broken from the fall, he had begged the old voodoo woman to look into the future for him, to help his widow make necessary plans.

She had done so, the story goes, using that window as a sort of "psychic screen." All the Evil Ones that crowd about someone who is dying, she had summoned to that spot—it was their fetid breath, she explained, that clouded the glass panes. But there was only one trick of dark magic in her power: to make a mirror of that opaque window, in which could be seen the dim reflection of the room where her master lay dying. A reflection of the room, yes—not as it looked at the moment, but as it *would* look, at some unnamed future date, when the *next* person in the house should die. The mental picture of that mumbling old black crone, of the sobbing wife cuddling her two terrified children before that slowly darkening window, has always been vivid to me.

All my life, of course, I have heard family tales about its prophecies. But the old Place itself has become a white elephant, tax-ridden and run-down. Mother married a Virginian and moved away, but she would never sell her equity in the property to Mark's father or to Jeb's mother, my uncle and aunt. Jeb's mother married a local lawyer and moved across town, but Mark and his father lived on at the old Homeplace, selling off some of the land when the old man had his stroke. It was, I may add, somewhat of a disappointment that this actual death occurred in a hospital. I think half the people in Stuartsboro had planned to "drop in" at the moment of his demise, for a peek into that prophetic window. No death had occurred in the house for seventy-two years—a fact I believe people resentfully accused our family of arranging, just for spite.

As a matter of fact, none of my generation believed in the hoodoo. We grinned about it fondly, the way others smile at myths about Santa Claus or the Easter Bunny. Mark, Jeb, and I—children of the Depression and the Second World War—were not inclined to believe in anything we couldn't see and touch. Jeb took over his father's meagre law practice in Stuartsboro, and managed to support himself and his widowed mother. Mark sold off more and more land, then went into the Air Corps. He came back with a charming little bride, a redhead with a bright gamin-face and a Brooklyn accent you could cut with a knife.

They were such a gay fun-loving young couple that I began visiting them, or Jeb, every summer after my teaching job closed in June. Mark was small, arrogant, with the lazy good looks of a Spanish don. Jeb was tall, lanky, good-humored, and wore glasses that ruined whatever good looks he might have inherited from Aunt Millicent. As a girl, I often toyed with the idea of marrying one or the other of them, if they had not been my first cousins. Occasionally we would pretend among ourselves that they were my brothers.

But after Sherry came, with her light laugh and boundless energy, I had to take a backseat as their "best girl." Mark worshipped his little redhead; he became restless and bored unless they were in the same room.

It was apparent, too, that Jeb was in love with her, in that quiet awkward way of his. I felt sorry for him, because it was just as easy to see that Sherry's attention was all for her husband.

The plantation had dwindled now to only the grounds around the house, hardly an acre. Small houses had sprung up like mushrooms all about it, making it look like a dignified old dowager drawing her skirts haughtily away from a flock of tenement children. Mark started a real estate office, failed at it; built a movie drive-in outside of town and had to sell it at a loss; found two more jobs, and lost them. Then the family—especially Jeb Randolph and I—became distressed because of his drinking. He drank all the time now, lounging around the house in an old dressing-gown with a highball tinkling in his hand.

We all worked at getting him back on his feet. Jeb and I dropped in several times a day to pull him out of one of his moody spells. And Sherry was never more cheerful and loving. I often noticed the stiff pained look on Jeb's face when she sat down in Mark's lap, throwing her arms around him and kissing him with the childlike abandon that was her greatest charm. She invented things to amuse him around the house— small tasks to take his mind off his failures; little games to coax him out of his despondency.

ONE afternoon when we dropped by, she had been cleaning out the attic, and had come across an old letter wedged into a skylight. It was brown with age, streaky with rain, and almost illegible. But Sherry had made out the fine cramped old-fashioned handwriting, and was perched on Mark's chair arm, reading it aloud to him excitedly.

"Liz, Jeb—it's about the green window!" she called as we entered. "Some relative of yours, way back there . . . It's signed 'Lucy.' There's a blot on it, See? It's unfinished; she must have been writing to somebody, and spilled ink on her letter. Then the skylight rattled, and she or the servants stuffed the page in to wedge it . . ."

"Detective," Mark laughed, jerking a thumb at her. "She's got it all figured out . . . Jeb," he chuckled, "the 'Lucy' was Aunt Lucy Dickerson, Grandfather's maiden sister. She never did have all her buttons, I remember Dad used to say. And this letter proves it!"

"Something about the window?" I asked, amused at Sherry's excitement, "What'd the old gal say? Read it!"

"Well, it starts off in the middle of a sentence," Sherry said importantly. "Must have been the second page of her letter, or some such. She's thanking somebody for the funeral flowers they sent, as I make it out. '. . . beautiful wreath,' it starts out. 'There were so many lovely flowers, and poor dear Ellen looked so natural, lying there in the casket . . .'"

Mark, Jeb, and I yelped with laughter in chorus.

"That's Aunt Lucy, all right!" Jeb nodded. "She was always going on about somebody's funeral. Liked to cry, so she went to 'em all! What else does it say?"

Sherry made a face at us. "All right! Laugh! I'll skip a few sentences, where she tells what the pastor said about . . . Allen? No, it's Ellen . . ."

"That was Grandma," Mark told her. "Died of cancer, poor old gal . . . Say" he burst out, suddenly interested. "She *was* the last person to die here in the house, wasn't she? Aunt Lucy nursed her for years. Old maid. She lived for the family; never had any life of her own."

Jeb and I nodded. Sherry was poring over the stained letter-fragment again, trying to make out the words in faded ink.

". . . *my dear, what I saw in the window! You'd never believe . . .*" she read. "*Never believe . . .* something-something; it's blotted out. "*. . . 'twas an Oriental,*" she made out another phrase or two. "*Sitting there in Father's chair with a turban on his head—if indeed 'twas a man, dear Martha—and . . .*"

We laughed again uproariously.

"Good old Aunt Lucy!" Mark hooted. "Wasn't that about the time of the Yellow Peril talk? When everybody thought the Chinese were going to take over the country? And the gals sneaked around, reading Indian love-lyrics?"

Jeb grinned, nodding. "Guess Aunt Lucy took it

from there, planting a rajah in our parlor! She had so little romance in her life . . ."

SHERRY GAVE him a sharp look I could not translate. Aunt Lucy isn't the only one," she muttered cryptically. "Don't you even want to hear the rest of it? All about a thief breaking in to steal the rajah's treasure, and the Oriental shoots him—she saw it all in the mirror, the letter says. There's a cap pulled down over the burglar's face. When the Oriental sees who he's shot, he falls sobbing on the body of the young boy. Maybe his brother, she says, or his son . . ."

"Good grief! How corny!" Jeb held his nose expressively. "Mother told me Aunt Lucy used to read dime novels all the time—and I can well believe it! Kept 'em hidden between the leaves of a *Godey's Ladies' Book* . . ."

Sherry gave us one glance of disgust. She flung the wadded letter into the fireplace, then whirled on us, directing most of her temper at Mark.

"All right, of course it's silly! But we could *pretend*, couldn't we? You three are so . . . stuffy about everything! Mark half drunk all the time, and we never go anywhere any more! I never have any new clothes or . . . or . . ." Tears welled into her pretty brown eyes. "Or anything but family pride!"

Mark went white, averting his eyes from our faces. I could not think of a word to say, but Jeb, with admirable tact, leaped into the breach.

"Sure," he said gently. "We're getting to be a bunch of stick-in-the-muds. That's why Liz and I ran by this morning, to persuade you two to go to the Lindsay's dance at the country club. We . . ."

"Not going," Mark snapped. "Sally Lindsay yapping in my ear, and Jay handing out those dishwater cocktails like they were champagne . . . !"

Sherry looked at him, temper sparkling in her eyes. She compressed her lips, fighting for self-control, then burst the dam:

"Maybe *you're* not going. But *I* am! Jeb will take me, and Liz can go with that drip of a Joe Kimball who keeps trying to marry her off. She's too smart, though! Marriage is . . . a bog hole! Ours is, anyhow! . . . Come on Liz," she whirled and swept out of the room to run upstairs. "I'll take some clothes, and dress at Jeb's with you. Mark can sit here and *drown* in his cheap rye. I'll spend the night at Aunt Millicent's!"

She came running down again with a lavender tulle dress, slip, and gold sandals, and stalked out to the car with no further word to Mark. Jeb and I mumbled something to our cousin; but he was already gulping down several slugs of whiskey in white-lipped anger, and did not reply. We followed Sherry out to the car, and drove away, not blaming her, only wishing Mark would find his way again and return to his old self.

On the way to Aunt Millicent's, Sherry became contrite, but covered it by chattering about the letter she had found in the attic.

"Oriental potentate!" she laughed. "With a turban on his head, and a flowered robe! She really dreamed that one up, didn't she! It's not so fantastic, though. The window didn't predict the date, by any chance? Say, December 7th, 1941 . . .?"

We fell in with her mood and began to kid each other about the Japanese Invasion of Stuartsboro that might have actually come off in 1941, but hadn't quite made it. At noon I discreetly called Mark on the phone, but he sounded very drunk when he answered. Sighing, I hung up, and went ahead with our plans for the dance.

What I had forgotten to tell Sherry was, it was a masquerade ball. She was disappointed, for she had a lovely little Pierrette costume at home. She would not go back after it, however, so I promised to get her some kind of costume, if I had to lend her my own "Colonial belle" outfit—inherited from Grandmother, complete with powdered wig and hoopskirt.

Meanwhile, Mark was sulking in the big cool parlor, with a mystery novel held upside-down in his hand and a half-empty decanter beside him on the floor. He was in pajamas and dressing robe, as usual, with a two-day growth of beard on his puffy face. He also had a splitting headache, and had tied a rubber icebag on his head. I could picture him when I phoned —a tragi-comic figure, sulking there in the semi-gloom.

He sat there, pretending to read, until the sun sank below the Blue Ridge foothills. Then, still muttering things he wished he had thought to say, he fell into an alcoholic doze . . .

ABOUT MIDNIGHT, he awakened with a start. His head was pounding. The dim light from a lamp in the hall illuminated the high-ceiled room palely. Mark heard a faint scraping noise to his right. Somebody was prying at the window that faced on the garden, trying to open it, trying to get in.

Dizzily, his heart pounding, Mark slid out of his chair and made his way over to a cabinet where his father had kept a collection of pistols and knives. His fumbling hand found one weapon, a blunt automatic. Mark could not remember whether it was loaded or not; but, he thought, it might scare the prowler. He waited, motionless in the half-dark, eyes glued to that window across the room. Beside it, locked as always, the green window—the prophetic green window— —gleamed back at him like a shadowy mirror.

The window raised slowly. A figure in slouchy pants and a patched white shirt climbed up stealthily, shin-ning up the trellis outside. A tweed cap was pulled far down over the intruder's eyes. A knife held between the teeth, a knife that had been used to pry open the window, gave the lower part of the face an evil distorted look.

Mark took careful aim, and pulled the trigger. No one was more startled than he was at the deafening explosion that rocked the room, filling it with the acrid stench of cordite.

The intruder screamed—a high-pitched cry of anguish and pain—then toppled forward over a chair, knocking it to the floor. Mark quickly switched on the light, aiming at the marauder again. But a gasping cry stopped him.

"Mark! Don't shoot—it's me! I left my latchkey! Thought you were in bed."

Then Mark cried out, throwing himself to his knees beside the still figure lying face up on the rug. It was Sherry—in an old pair of Jeb's pants, a shirt of mine, and someone's borrowed cap: the "Bowery thug" costume she wore to the masquerade dance. Moaning, Mark gathered her up in his arms. He rocked back and forth, crooning to her as her blood flowed out over his dressing gown.

And the green window began to glow with a weird radiance, mirroring the room as it had many times before, according to my parents and grandparents. A picture began to take shape in its shadowy frame, like a dim movie. My cousin Mark raised his head, holding his dead wife in his arms and watching the pattern of the future unfold in those green panes.

The day before the funeral, Jeb left Stuartsboro abruptly. Even Aunt Millicent could not explain his sudden departure, following a decision to join a law firm in New York. I was there, standing beside Mark as a loving sister might uphold a bereaved brother. He seemed stunned and vague. Now and again I caught him staring at me all during the service. There was a deep bewilderment in his piercing gaze, a look of horror that transcended even what I expected him to feel. Was it only his great sense of loss?

"Mark dear," I whispered. "Get hold of yourself. I'm still around."

After the interment of pretty shallow little Sherry, we were riding back from the cemetery. At my words, Mark broke his sober silence abruptly.

"Liz," he said quietly, "I have a hunch she was running away with Jeb, that night after the dance. He must have been waiting for her. She just came back for her clothes, probably—though I let Jeb believe it was to make up with me . . . She wasn't. You see, I know. I lost Sherry, not by death," he said heavily, "but a long time ago, to Jeb. Didn't you suspect?"

I stared at him, amazed. "Sherry? I knew he was in

love with *her*, but . . . Whatever gave you the idea that she . . .? Why, Sherry adored you!"

"No." Mark's smile twisted. "She didn't," he said heavily. "She told me over a year ago that she'd married me for a meal-ticket, one of those war marriages. If Jeb would have taken her, she'd have left me long ago . . . but I played on his sympathy, let myself go to seed, just to keep her. Out of loyalty to me, he held out against her . . . until the night of the dance, is my bet. He blames himself for the whole mess, but of course I should have given her up to him long ago. Well . . ." He straightened his shoulders with an effort. "That's all over now. Think I'll go back into the Army. And, Liz . . ." He hesitated queerly. "It might be well for you to sell the old place. We must never go back there, the three of us. I told Jeb if we did, there'd be tragedy. That I saw *murder* in the green window that night . . ."

MY EYES widened. "Mark!" I took his hand in both of mine; he stared oddly at our entwined fingers. "You told him *that*? No wonder he left so suddenly! He must have thought you meant you were going to kill him, or he you! . . . Oh, Mark!" I sighed. "The three of us grew up together. We've been so close, I couldn't bear this town without you both. Look here!" I laughed. "Are you forcing me to marry Joe Kimball and move to Idaho with him? No sir! I won't do it! I'll stay here with Aunt Millicent and grow into a lonely old maid like Aunt Lucy, without you and Jeb around . . . Mark, I'm ashamed to confess I've rather resented Sherry barging in and taking both my . . . my best beaux! So now, please, I'd like to have you back! With a little teamwork, we could make the old Place into a tourist hotel. Call it "The Three Cousins' . . ."

Mark did not respond to my attempt at levity.

His dark eyes were still searching my face with that bewildered expression. He shook his head slowly, and patted my hand.

"No . . . we've got to board it up. Don't . . . don't ever open it, Liz . . . How little people really know about each other!" he muttered. "I about Jeb, or he about me, or both of us about . . . Only the green window really *knows* . . ." He passed a shaky hand over his forehead. "I wonder. If I'd been forewarned by that letter, could I have prevented the accident to Sherry? Do you think . . .? Liz, if we never go near the old home again, the three of us together, how can it happen, the thing I saw . . .?"

I shivered at the peculiar look of dread on my cousin's face. The car had rolled to a halt in front of the old Dickerson home, built by our great-great-grandfather nearly two centuries ago. The murky green window stared out at us like a blind eye, seeing not the present but the future—the incredible future, like that strange trick of fate which had caused Mark to shoot his adored wife and Jeb to leave his hometown forever.

"Mark," I demanded, "what did you see in the window, the night poor Sherry . . .? Mark, she's gone now, and you and Jeb must forgive each other! We three have to stick together, as we did when we were children. Blood is thicker than water, Mark, and . . ."

My cousin looked at me, and all at once he began to laugh harshly.

"Blood?" he said queerly. "That's what I saw, Liz! Blood all over the room, that shadow-room inside the window, our parlor as it will look . . . I don't know when. Next month. Next year. I don't know. Jeb and I were lying there on the floor, hacked to pieces. And someone was standing over us with . . . with an ax. Still . . . still *chopping* . . . That's what I saw.

I shuddered and hid my face against his shoulder. "Oh, Mark! How awful! But it couldn't ever happen, of course," I laughed nervously. "Jeb has gone, and you'll be gone next week . . . D—did you see who it was? I mean, the face? Did it look like anyone we know?"

"Yes," my cousin held my hand tightly for a moment, then answered quietly. "Yes, I saw the face. Liz . . . it was *you*."

"Not all the devils in Hell nor all the angels in Heaven shall stop me!"

Train for Flushing

By MALCOLM JAMESON

An odd and fascinating story that runs backward instead of forward—a curious tale of the Flying Dutchman.

THEY OUGHT never to have hired that man. Even the most stupid of personnel managers should have seen at a glance that he was mad. Perhaps it is too much to expect such efficiency these days—in *my* time a thing like this could not have happened. They would have known the fellow was under a curse! It only shows what the world has come to. But I can tell you that if we ever get off this crazy runaway car, I intend to turn the Interboro wrong-side out. They needn't think because I am an old man and retired that I am a nobody they can push around. My son Henry, the lawyer one, will build a fire under them—he knows people in this town.

"And I am not the only victim of the maniac. There is a pleasant, elderly woman here in the car with me. She was much frightened at first, but she had recognized me for a solid man, and now she stays close to me all the time. She is a Mrs. Herrick, and a quite nice woman. It was her idea that I write this down—it will help us refresh our memories when we come to testify.

"Just at the moment, we are speeding atrociously *downtown* along the Seventh Avenue line of the subway—but we are on the *uptown* express track! The first few times we tore through those other trains it was terrible—I thought we were sure to be killed—and even if we were not, I have to think of my heart. Dr. Steinback told me only last week how careful I should be. Mrs. Herrick has been very brave about it, but it is a scandalous thing to subject anyone to, above all such a kindly little person.

"The madman who seems to be directing us (if charging wildly up and down these tracks implies *direction*), is now looking out the front door, staring horribly at the gloom rushing at us. He is a big man and heavy-set, very weathered and tough-looking. I am nearing eighty and slight.

"There is nothing I can do but wait for the final crash; for crash we must, sooner or later, unless some Interboro official has brains enough to shut off the current to stop us. If *he* escapes the crash, the police will know him by his heavy red beard and tattooing on the backs of his hands. The beard is square-cut and there cannot be another one like it in all New York.

"But I notice I have failed to put down how this insane ride began. My granddaughter, Mrs. Charles L. Terneck, wanted me to see the World's Fair, and was to come in from Great Neck and meet me at the subway station. I will say that she insisted someone come with me, but I can take care of myself—I always have —even if my eyes and ears are not what they used to be.

THE train was crowded, but somebody gave me a seat in a corner. Just before we reached the stop, the woman next to me, this Mrs. Herrick, had asked if I knew how to get to Whitestone from Flushing. It was while I was telling her what I knew about the busses, that the train stopped and let everybody off the car but us. I was somewhat irritated at missing the station, but knew that all I had to do was stay on the car, go to Flushing and return. It was then that the maniac guard came in and behaved so queerly.

"This car was the last one in the train, and the guard had been standing where he belongs, on the platform. But he came into the car, walking with a curious rolling walk (but I do not mean to imply he was drunk, for I do not think so) and his manner was what you might call masterful, almost overbearing. He stopped at the middle door and looked very intensely out to the north, at the sound.

"'*That* is not the Scheldt!' he called out, angrily, with a thick, foreign accent, and then he said 'Bah!' loudly, in a tone of disgusted disillusionment.

"He seemed of a sudden to fly into a great fury. The train was just making its stop at the end of the line, in Flushing. He rushed to the forward platform and somehow broke the coupling. At the same moment, the car began running backward along the track by which we had come. There was no chance for us to get off, even if we had been young and active. The doors were not opened, it happened so quickly.

"Then he came into the car, muttering to himself. His eye caught the sign of painted tin they put in the windows to show the destination of the trains. He snatched the plate lettered 'Flushing' and tore it to bits with his rough hands, as if it had been cardboard, throwing the pieces down and stamping on them.

"'That is not Flushing. Not *my* Flushing—not *Vlissingen!* But I will find it. I will go there, and not all the devils in Hell nor all the angels in Heaven shall stop me!'

"He glowered at us, beating his breast with his clenched fists, as if angry and resentful at us for having deceived him in some manner. It was then that Mrs. Herrick stooped over and took my hand. We had gotten up close to the door to step out at the World's Fair station, but the car did not stop. It continued its wild career straight on, at dizzy speed.

"'*Rugwaartsch!*' he shouted, or something equally unintelligible. '*Back* I must go, like always, but yet will find my Vlissingen!'

"Then followed the horror of pitching headlong into those trains! The first one we saw coming, Mrs. Herrick screamed. I put my arm around her and braced myself as best I could with my cane. But there was no crash, just a blinding succession of lights and colors, in quick winks. We seemed to go straight through that train, from end to end, at lightning speed, but there was not even a jar. I do not understand that, for I saw it coming, clearly. Since, there have been many others. I have lost count now, we meet so many, and swing from one track to another so giddily at the end of runs.

"But we have learned, Mrs. Herrick and I, not to dread the collisions—or say, passage—so much. We are more afraid of what the bearded ruffian who dominates this car will do next—surely we cannot go on this way much longer, it has already been many, many hours. I cannot comprehend why the stupid people who run the Interboro do not do something to stop us, so that the police could subdue this maniac and I can have Henry take me to the District Attorney."

SO READ the first few pages of the notebook turned over to me by the Missing Persons Bureau. Neither Mrs. Herrick, nor Mr. Dennison, whose handwriting it is, has been found yet, nor the guard he mentions. In contradiction, the Interboro insists no guard employed by them is unaccounted for, and further, that they never had had a man of the above description on their payrolls.

On the other hand, they have as yet produced no satisfactory explanation of how the car broke loose from the train at Flushing.

I agree with the police that this notebook contains matter that may have some bearing on the disappearances of these two unfortunate citizens; yet here in the Psychiatric Clinic we are by no means agreed as to the interpretation of this provocative and baffling diary.

The portion I have just quoted was written with a fountain pen in a crabbed, tremulous hand, quite exactly corresponding to the latest examples of old Mr. Dennison's writing. Then we find a score or more of pages torn out, and a resumption of the record in indelible pencil. The handwriting here is considerably stronger and more assured, yet unmistakably that of the same person. Farther on, there are other places where pages have been torn from the book, and evidence that the journal was but intermittently kept. I quote now all that is legible of the remainder of it.

JUDGING by the alternations of the cold and hot seasons, we have now been on this weird and pointless journey for more than ten years. Oddly enough, we do not suffer physically, although the interminable rushing up and down these caverns under the streets becomes boring. The ordinary wants of the body are strangely absent, or dulled. We sense heat and cold, for example, but do not find their extremes particularly uncomfortable, while food has become an item of far distant memory. I imagine, though, we must sleep a good deal.

"The guard has very little to do with us, ignoring us most of the time as if we did not exist. He spends his days sitting brooding at the far end of the car, staring at the floor, mumbling in his wild, red beard. On other days he will get up and peer fixedly ahead, as if seeking something. Again, he will pace the aisle in obvious anguish, flinging his outlandish curses over his shoulder as he goes. 'Verdoemd' and 'verwenscht' are the commonest ones—we have learned to recognize them—and he tears his hair in frenzy whenever he pronounces them. His name, he says, is Van Der Dechen,

and we find it politic to call him 'Captain.'

"I have destroyed what I wrote during the early years (all but the account of the very first day); it seems rather querulous and hysterical now. I was not in good health then, I think, but I have improved noticeably here, and that without medical care. Much of my stiffness, due to a recent arthritis, has left me, and I seem to hear better.

"Mrs. Herrick and I have long since become accustomed to our forced companionship, and we have learned much about each other. At first, we both worried a good deal over our families' concern about our absence. But when this odd and purposeless kidnapping occurred, we were already so nearly to the end of life (being of about the same age) that we finally concluded our children and grand-children must have been prepared for our going soon, in any event. It left us only with the problem of enduring the tedium of the interminable rolling through the tubes of the Interboro.

"In the pages I have deleted, I made much of the annoyance we experienced during the early weeks due to flickering through oncoming trains. That soon came to be so commonplace, occurring as it did every few minutes, that it became as unnoticeable as our breathing. As we lost the fear of imminent disaster, our riding became more and more burdensome through the deadly monotony of the tunnels.

"Mrs. Herrick and I diverted ourselves by talking (and to think in my earlier entries in this journal I complained of her garrulousness!) or by trying to guess at what was going on in the city above us by watching the crowds on the station platforms. That is a difficult game, because we are running so swiftly, and there are frequent intervening trains. A thing that has caused us much speculation and discussion is the changing type of advertising on the bill-posters. Nowadays they are featuring the old favorites—many of the newer toothpastes and medicines seem to have been withdrawn. Did they fail, or has a wave of conservative reaction overwhelmed the country?

"Another marvel in the weird life we lead is the juvenescence of our home, the runaway car we are confined to. In spite of its unremitting use, always at top speed, it has become steadily brighter, more new-looking. Today it has the appearance of having been recently delivered from the builders' shops.

I LEARNED half a century ago that having nothing to do, and all the time in the world to do it in, is the surest way to get nothing done. In looking in this book, I find it has been ten years since I made an entry! It is a fair indication of the idle, routine life in this wandering car. The very invariableness of our existence has discouraged keeping notes. But recent developments are beginning to force me to face a situation that has been growing ever more obvious. The cumulative evidence is by now almost overwhelming that this state of ours has a meaning—has an explanation. Yet I dread to think the thing through—to call its name! Because there will be two ways to interpret it. Either it *is* as I am driven to conclude, or else I . . .

"I must talk it over frankly with Nellie Herrick. She is remarkably poised and level-headed, and understanding. She and I have matured a delightful friendship.

"What disturbs me more than anything is the trend in advertising. They are selling products again that were popular so long ago that I had actually forgotten them. And the appeals are made in the idiom of years ago. Lately it has been hard to see the posters, the station platforms are so full. In the crowds are many uniforms, soldiers and sailors. We infer from that there is another war—but the awful question is, 'What war?'

"Those are some of the things we can observe in the world over there. In our own little fleeting world, things have developed even more inexplicably. My health and appearance, notably. My hair is no longer white! It is turning dark again in the back, and on top. And the same is true of Nellie's. There are other similar changes for the better. I see much more clearly and my hearing is practically perfect.

"The culmination of these disturbing signals of retrogression has come with the newest posters. It is their appearance that forces me to face the facts. Behind the crowds we glimpse new appeals, many and insistent—'BUY VICTORY LOAN BONDS!' From the number of them to be seen, one would think we were back in the happy days of 1919, when the soldiers were coming home from the World War.

MY TALK with Nellie has been most comforting and reassuring. It is hardly likely that we should both be insane and have identical symptoms. The inescapable conclusion that I dreaded to put into words is *so*—it must be so. In some unaccountable manner, we are *unliving* life! Time is going backward! '*Rugwaartsch*,' the mad Dutchman said that first day when he turned back from Flushing; 'we will go backward'—to *his* Flushing, the one he knew. Who knows what Flushing he knew? It must be the Flushing of another age, or else why should the deranged wizard (if it is he who has thus reversed time) choose a path through time itself? Helpless, we can only wait and see how far he will take us.

"We are not wholly satisfied with our new theory. Everything does not go backward; otherwise how could it be possible for me to write these lines? I think we are like flies crawling up the walls of an elevator cab while it is in full descent. Their own proper movements, relative to their environment, are upward, but all the while they are being carried relentlessly downward. It is a sobering thought. Yet we are both relieved that we should have been able to speak it. Nellie admits that she has been troubled for some time, hesitating to voice the thought. She called my attention to the subtle way in which our clothing has been changing, an almost imperceptible de-evolution in style.

WE ARE now on the lookout for ways in which to date ourselves in this headlong plunging into the past. Shortly after writing the above, we were favored with one opportunity not to be mistaken. It was the night of the Armistice. What a night in the subway! Then followed, in inverse order, the various issues of the Liberty Bonds. Over forty years ago—counting time both ways, forward, then again backward—*I* was up there, a dollar-a-year man, selling them on the streets. Now we suffer a new anguish, imprisoned down here in this racing subway car. The evidence all around us brings a nostalgia that is almost intolerable. None of us knows how perfect his memory is until it is thus prompted. But we cannot go up there, we can only guess at what is going on above us.

"The realization of what is really happening to us has caused us to be less antagonistic to our conductor. His sullen brooding makes us wonder whether he is not a fellow victim, rather than our abductor, he seems so unaware of us usually. At other times, we regard him as the principal in this drama of the gods and are bewildered at the curious twist of Fate that has entangled us with the destiny of the unhappy Van Der Dechen, for unhappy he certainly is. Our anger at his arrogant behavior has long since died away. We can see that some secret sorrow gnaws continually at his heart.

"'There is *een vloek* over me,' he said gravely, one day, halting unexpectedly before us in the midst of one of his agitated pacings of the aisle. He seemed to be trying to explain—apologize for, if you will—our situation. 'Accursed I am, damned!' He drew a great breath, looking at us appealingly. Then his black mood came back on him with a rush, and he strode away growling mighty Dutch oaths. 'But I will best them—God Himself shall not prevent me—not if it takes all eternity!'

OUR ORBIT is growing more restricted. It is a long time now since we went to Brooklyn, and only the other day we swerved suddenly at Times Square and cut through to Grand Central. Considering this circumstance, the type of car we are in now, and our costumes, we must be in 1905 or thereabouts. That is a year I remember with great vividness. It was the year I first came to New York. I keep speculating on what will become of us. In another year we will have plummeted the full history of the subway. What then? Will that be the end?

"Nellie is the soul of patience. It is a piece of great fortune, a blessing, that since we were doomed to this wild ride, we happened in it together. Our friendship has ripened into a warm affection that lightens the gloom of this tedious wandering.

IT MUST have been last night that we emerged from the caves of Manhattan. Thirty-four years of darkness is ended. We are now out in the country, going west. Our vehicle is not the same, it is an old-fashioned day coach, and ahead is a small locomotive. We cannot see engineer or fireman, but Van Der Dechen frequently ventures across the swaying, open platform and mounts the tender, where he stands firmly with wide-spread legs, scanning the country ahead through an old brass long-glass. His uniform is more nautical than railroadish—it took the sunlight to show that to us. There was always the hint of salt air about him. We should have known who he was from his insistence on being addressed as Captain.

"The outside world *is* moving backward! When we look closely at the wagons and buggies in the muddy trails alongside the right of way fence, we can see that the horses or mules are walking or running backward. But we pass them so quickly, as a rule, that their real motion is inconspicuous. We are too grateful for the sunshine and the trees after so many years of gloom, to quibble about this topsy-turvy condition.

FIVE YEARS in the open has taught us much about Nature in reverse. There is not so much difference as one would suppose. It took us a long time to notice that the sun rose in the west and sank in the east. Summer follows winter, as it always has. It was our first spring, or rather, the season that we have come to regard as spring, that we were really disconcerted. The trees were bare, the skies cloudy, and the weather cool. We could not know, at first sight, whether we had emerged into spring or fall.

"The ground was wet, and gradually white patches of snow were forming. Soon, the snow covered everything. The sky darkened and the snow began to flurry, drifting and swirling upward, out of sight. Later we saw the ground covered with dead leaves, so we thought it must be fall. Then a few of the trees were seen to have leaves, then all. Soon the forests were in the full glory of red and brown autumn leaves, but in a

few weeks those colors turned gradually through oranges and yellows to dark greens, and we were in full summer. Our 'fall,' which succeeded the summer, was almost normal, except toward the end, when the leaves brightened into paler greens, dwindled little by little to mere buds and then disappeared within the trees.

"The passage of a troop train, its windows crowded with campaign-hatted heads and waving arms tells us another war has begun (or more properly, ended). The soldiers are returning from Cuba. *Our* wars, in this backward way by which we approach and end in anxiety! More nostalgia—I finished that war as a major. I keep looking eagerly at the throngs on the platforms of the railroad stations as we sweep by them, hoping to sight a familiar face among the yellow-legged cavalry. More than eighty years ago it was, as I reckon it, forty years of it spent on the road to senility and another forty back to the prime of life.

"Somewhere among those blue-uniformed veterans am I, in my original phase, I cannot know just where, because my memory is vague as to the dates. I have caught myself entertaining the idea of stopping this giddy flight into the past, of getting out and finding my way to my former home. Only, if I could, I would be creating tremendous problems—there would have to be some sort of mutual accommodation between my *alter ego* and me. It looks impossible, and there are no precedents to guide us.

"Then, all my affairs have become complicated by the existence of Nell. She and I have had many talks about this strange state of affairs, but they are rarely conclusive. I think I must have over-estimated her judgment a little in the beginning. But it really doesn't matter. She has developed into a stunning woman and her quick, ready sympathy makes up for her lack in that direction. I glory particularly in her hair, which she lets down some days. It is thick and long and beautifully wavy, as hair should be. We often sit on the back platform and she allows it to blow free in the breeze, all the time laughing at me because I adore it so.

"Captain Van Der Dechen notices us not at all, unless in scorn. His mind, his whole being, is centered on getting back to Flushing—*his* Flushing, that he calls Vlissingen—wherever that may be in time or space. Well, it appears that he is taking us back, too, but it is backward in time for us. As for him, time seems meaningless. He is unchangeable. Not a single hair of that piratical beard has altered since that far-future day of long ago when he broke our car away from the Interboro train in Queens. Perhaps he suffers from the same sort of unpleasant immortality the mythical Wandering Jew is said to be afflicted with—otherwise why should he complain so bitterly of the curse he says is upon him?

"Nowadays he talks to himself much of the time, mainly about his ship. It is that which he hopes to find since the Flushing beyond New York proved not to be the one he strove for. He says he left it cruising along a rocky coast. He has either forgotten where he left it or it is no longer there, for we have gone to all the coastal points touched by the railroads. Each failure brings fresh storms of rage and blasphemy; not even perpetual frustration seems to abate the man's determination or capacity for fury.

THAT DUTCHMAN has switched trains on us again! This one hasn't even Pintsch gas, nothing but coal oil. It is smoky and it stinks. The engine is a woodburner with a balloon stack. The sparks are very bad and we cough a lot.

"I went last night when the Dutchman wasn't looking and took a look into the cab of the engine. There is no crew and I found the throttle closed. A few years back that would have struck me as odd, but now I have to accept it. I did mean to stop the train so I could take Nell off, but there is no way to stop it. It just goes along, I don't know how.

"On the way back I met the Dutchman, shouting and swearing the way he does, on the forward platform. I tried to throw him off the train. I am as big and strong as he is and I don't see why I should put up with his overbearing ways. But when I went to grab him, my hands closed right through. The man is not real! It is strange I never noticed that before. Maybe that is why there is no way to stop the train, and why nobody ever seems to notice us. Maybe the train is not real, either. I must look tomorrow and see whether it casts a shadow. Perhaps even *we* are not . . .

"But Nell is real. I *know* that.

THE OTHER night we passed a depot platform where there was a political rally—a torchlight parade. They were carrying banners. 'Garfield for President.' If we are ever to get off this train, we must do it soon.

"Nell says no, it would be embarrassing. I try to talk seriously to her about us, but she just laughs and kisses me and says let well enough alone. I wouldn't mind starting life over again, even if these towns do look pretty rough. But Nell says that she was brought up on a Kansas farm by a step-mother and she would rather go on to the end and vanish, if need be, than go back to it.

"That thing about the end troubles me a lot, and I wish she wouldn't keep mentioning it. It was only lately that I thought about it much, and it worries me more than death ever did in the old days. *We know when it will be!* 1860 for me—on the third day of August. The last ten years will be terrible—getting smaller, weaker, more helpless all the time, and winding up as a messy, squally baby. Why, that means I have only about ten more years that are fit to live; when I was this young before, I had a lifetime ahead. It's not right! And now *she* has made a silly little vow—'Until birth do us part!'—and made me say it with her!

IT IS too crowded in here, and it jolts awfully. Nell and I are cooped up in the front seats and the Captain stays in the back part—the quarterdeck, he calls it. Sometimes he opens the door and climbs up into the driver's seat. There is no driver, but we have a four-horse team and they gallop all the time, day and night. The Captain says we must use a stagecoach, because he has tried all the railroad tracks and none of them is right. He wants to get back to the sea he came from and to his ship. He is not afraid that it has been stolen, for he says most men are afraid of it—it is a haunted ship, it appears, and brings bad luck.

"We passed two men on horses this morning. One was going our way and met the other coming. The other fellow stopped him and I heard him holler, 'They killed Custer and all his men!' and the man that was going the same way we were said, 'The bloodthirsty heathens! I'm a-going to jine!'

NELLIE CRIES a lot. She's afraid of Indians. I'm not afraid of Indians. I would like to see one.

"I wish it was a boy with me, instead of this little girl. Then we could do something. All she wants to do is play with that fool dolly. We could make some bows and arrows and shoot at the buffaloes, but she says that is wicked.

"I tried to get the Captain to talk to me, but he won't. He just laughed and laughed, and said,

"'*Een tijd kiezan voor—op schip!*'

"That made me mad, talking crazy talk like that, and I told him so.

"'Time!' he bellows, laughing like everything. ' 'Twill all be right in time!' And he looks hard at me, showing his big teeth in his beard. 'Four—five—six hundred years—more—it is nothing. I have all eternity! But one more on my ship, I will get there. I have sworn it! You come with me and I will show you the sea—the great Indian Sea behind the Cape of Good Hope. Then some day, if those accursed head winds abate, I will take you home with me to Flushing. That I will, though the Devil himself, or all the——' And then he went off to cursing and swearing the way he always does in his crazy Dutchman's talk.

NELLIE IS mean to me. She is too bossy. She says she will not play unless I write in the book. She says I am supposed to write something in the book every day. There is not anything to put in the book. Same old stagecoach. Same old Captain. Same old everything. I do not like the Captain. He is crazy. In the night-time he points at the stars shining through the roof of the coach and laughs and laughs. Then he gets mad, and swears and curses something awful. When I get big again, I am going to kill him— I wish we could get away—I am afraid—it would be nice if we could find mamma——"

THIS TERMINATES the legible part of the notebook. All of the writing purporting to have been done in the stagecoach is shaky, and the letters are much larger than earlier in the script. The rest of the contents is infantile scribblings, or grotesque childish drawings. Some of them show feathered Indians drawing bows and shooting arrows. The very last one seems to represent a straight up and down cliff with wiggly lines at the bottom to suggest waves, and off a little way is a crude drawing of a galleon or other antique ship.

This notebook, together with Mr. Dennison's hat and cane and Mrs. Herrick's handbag, were found in the derailed car that broke away from the Flushing train and plunged off the track into the Meadows. The police are still maintaining a perfunctory hunt for the two missing persons, but I think the fact they brought this journal to us clearly indicates they consider the search hopeless. Personally, I really do not see of what help these notes can be. I fear that by now Mr. Dennison and Mrs. Herrick are quite inaccessible.

Speak, speak, thou fearful guest,
Who, with thy hollow chest,
All in rude armor dressed,
Comest to daunt me!

—Longfellow: *The Skeleton in Armor*

Weird Tales, 1938

The Seed From the Sepulcher

By CLARK ASHTON SMITH

*A horror-tale of the Venezuelan jungle, and a diabolical plant
that lived on human life.*

YES, I found the place," said Falmer. "It's a queer sort of place, pretty much as the legends describe it." He spat quickly into the fire, as if the act of speech had been physically distasteful, and half averting his face from the scrutiny of Thone, stared with morose and somber eyes into the jungle-matted Venezuelan darkness.

Thone, still weak and dizzy from the fever that had incapacitated him for continuing their journey to its end, was curiously puzzled. Falmer, he thought, had undergone an inexplicable change during the three days of his absence: a change that was too elusive in some of its phases to be fully defined or delimited.

Other phases, however, were all too obvious. Falmer, even during extreme hardship or illness, had heretofore been unquenchably loquacious and cheerful. Now he seemed sullen and uncommunicative, as if preoccupied with far-off things of disagreeable import. His bluff face had grown hollow—even pointed—and his eyes had narrowed to secretive slits. Falmer was troubled by these changes, though he tried to dismiss his impressions as mere distempered fancies due to the influence of ebbing fever.

"But can't you tell me what the place was like?" he persisted.

"There isn't much to tell," said Falmer, in a queer, grumbling tone. "Just a few crumbling walls and falling pillars."

"But didn't you find the burial-pit of the Indian legend, where the gold was supposed to be?"

"I found it . . . but there was no treasure." Falmer's voice had taken on a forbidding surliness; and Thone decided to refrain from further questioning.

"I guess," he commented lightly, "that we had better stick to orchid-hunting. Treasure-trove doesn't seem to be in our line. By the way, did you see any unusual flowers or plants during the trip?"

"Hell, no," Falmer snapped. His face had gone suddenly ashen in the firelight, and his eyes had assumed a set glare that might have meant either fear or anger.

"Shut up, can't you? I don't want to talk. I've had a headache all day—some damned Venezuelan fever coming on, I suppose. We'd better head for the Orinoco tomorrow. I've had all I want of this trip."

James Falmer and Roderick Thone, professional orchid-hunters, with two Indian guides, had been following an obscure tributary of the upper Orinoco. The country was rich in rare flowers; and, beyond its floral wealth, they had been drawn by vague but persistent rumors among the local tribes concerning the existence of a ruined city somewhere on this tributary; a city that contained a burial-pit in which vast treasures of gold, silver and jewels had been interred together with the dead of some nameless people. The two men had thought it worth while to investigate these rumors. Thone had fallen sick while they were still a full day's journey from the site of the ruins, and Falmer had gone on in a canoe with one of the Indians, leaving the other to attend Thone. He had returned at nightfall of the third day following his departure.

Thone decided after a while, as he lay staring at his companion, that the latter's taciturnity and moroseness were perhaps due to disappointment over his failure to find the treasure. It must be that, together with some tropical infection working in the man's blood. However, he admitted doubtfully to himself, it was not like Falmer to be disappointed or downcast under such circumstances.

Falmer did not speak again, but sat glaring before him as if he saw something invisible to others beyond the labyrinth of fire-touched boughs and lianas in which the whispering, stealthy darkness crouched. Somehow, there was a shadowy fear in his aspect. Thone continued to watch him, and saw that the Indians, impassive and cryptic, were also watching him, as if with some obscure expectancy. The riddle was too much for Thone, and he gave it up after a while, lapsing into restless, fever-turbulent slumber from which he awakened at intervals, to see the set face of Falmer, dimmer and more distorted each time with the slowly dying fire and the invading shadows.

THONE FELT stronger in the morning: his brain was clear, his pulse tranquil once more; and he saw with mounting concern the indisposition of Falmer, who seemed to rouse and exert himself with great difficulty, speaking hardly a word and moving with singular stiffness and sluggishness. He appeared to have forgotten his announced project of returning toward the Orinoco, and Thone took entire charge of the preparations for departure. His companion's condition puzzled him more and more: apparently there was no fever, and the symptoms were wholly ambiguous. However, on general principles, he administered a stiff dose of quinine to Falmer before they started.

The paling saffron of sultry dawn sifted upon them through the jungle-tops as they loaded their belongings into the dugouts and pushed off down the slow current. Thone sat near the bow of one of the boats, with Falmer in the rear, and a large bundle of orchid roots and part of their equipment filling the middle. The two Indians occupied the other boat, together with the rest of their supplies.

It was a monotonous journey. The river wound like a sluggish olive snake between dark, interminable walls of forest from which the goblin faces of orchids leered. There were no sounds other than the splash of paddles, the furious chattering of monkeys, and petulant cries of fiery-colored birds. The sun rose above the jungle and poured down a tide of torrid brilliance.

Thone rowed steadily, looking back over his shoulder at whiles to address Falmer with some casual remark or friendly question. The latter, with dazed eyes and features queerly pale and pinched in the sunlight, sat dully erect and made no effort to use his paddle. He offered no reply to the queries of Thone, but shook his head at intervals with a sort of shuddering motion that was plainly involuntary. After awhile he began to moan thickly, as if in pain or delirium.

They went on in this manner for hours. The heat grew more oppressive between the stifling walls of jungle. Thone became aware of a shriller cadence in the moans of his companion. Looking back, he saw that Falmer had removed his sun-helmet, seemingly oblivious of the murderous heat, and was clawing at the crown of his head with frantic fingers. Convulsions shook his entire body, and the dugout began to rock dangerously as he tossed to and fro in a paroxysm of manifest agony. His voice mounted to a high, unhuman shrieking.

Thone made a quick decision. There was a break in the lining palisade of somber forest, and he headed the boat for shore immediately. The Indians followed, whispering between themselves and eyeing the sick man with glances of apprehensive awe and terror that puzzled Thone tremendously. He felt that there was some devilish mystery about the whole affair; and he could not imagine what was wrong with Falmer. All the known manifestations of malignant tropical diseases rose before him like a rout of hideous fantasms; but, among them, he could not recognize the thing that had assailed his companion.

Having gotten Falmer ashore on a semicircle of liana-latticed beach without the aid of the guides, who seemed unwilling to approach the sick man, Thone administered a heavy hypodermic injection of morphine from his medicine-chest. This appeared to ease Falmer's suffering, and the convulsions ceased. Thone, taking advantage of their remission, proceeded to examine the crown of Falmer's head.

He was startled to find amid the thick, dishevelled hair a hard and pointed lump which resembled the tip of a beginning horn, rising under the still unbroken skin. As if endowed with erectile and resistless life, it seemed to grow beneath his fingers.

At the same time, abruptly and mysteriously, Falmer opened his eyes and appeared to regain full consciousness. For a few minutes he was more his normal self than at any time since his return from the ruins. He began to talk, as if anxious to relieve his mind of some oppressing burden. His voice was peculiarly thick and toneless, but Thone was able to follow his mutterings and piece them together.

"The pit! the pit!" said Falmer—"the infernal thing that was in the pit, in the deep sepulcher! . . . I wouldn't go back there for the treasure of a dozen El Dorados. . . . I didn't tell you much about those ruins, Thone. Somehow it was hard—impossibly hard—to talk. . . .

I GUESS the Indian knew there was something wrong with the ruins. He led me to the place . . . but he wouldn't tell me anything about it; and he waited by the riverside while I searched for the treasure.

"Great gray walls there were, older than the jungle —old as death and time. They must have been quarried and reared by people from some forgotten continent, or some lost planet. They loomed and leaned at mad, unnatural angles, threatening to crush the trees about them. And there were columns, too: thick, swollen columns of unholy form, whose abominable carvings the jungle had not wholly screened from view.

"There was no trouble finding that accursed burial-pit. The pavement above had broken through quite recently, I think. A big tree had pried with its boa-like roots between the flagstones that were buried beneath centuries of mold. One of the flags had been tilted back on the pavement, and another had fallen through into the pit. There was a large hole, whose bottom I could see dimly in the forest-strangled light. Something glimmered palely at the bottom; but I could not be sure what it was.

"I had taken along a coil of rope, as you remember. I tied one end of it to a main root of the tree, dropped the other through the opening, and went down like a monkey. When I got to the bottom I could see little at first in the gloom, except the whitish glimmering all around me, at my feet. Something that was unspeakably brittle and friable crunched beneath me when I began to move. I turned on my flashlight, and saw that the place was fairly littered with bones. Human skeletons lay tumbled everywhere. They must have been very old, for they broke into powder at a touch.

"It was the burial-chamber of the legend. Looking about with the flashlight, I found the steps that led to the blocked-up entrance. But if any treasure had been buried with the bodies, it must have been removed long ago. I groped around amid the bones and dust, feeling pretty much like a ghoul, but couldn't find anything of value, not even a bracelet or a finger-ring on any of the skeletons.

"It wasn't till I thought of climbing out that I noticed the real horror. In one of the corners—the corner nearest to the opening in the roof—I looked up and saw it in the webby shadows. Ten feet above my head it hung, and I had almost touched it, unknowing, when I descended the rope.

"It looked like a sort of white lattice-work at first. Then I saw that the lattice was partly formed of human bones—a complete skeleton, very tall and stalwart, like that of a warrior. A pale, withered thing grew out of the skull, like a set of fantastic antlers ending in myriads of long and stringy tendrils that had spread themselves on the wall, climbing upward till they reached the roof. They must have lifted the skeleton, or body, along with them as they climbed.

"I examined the thing with my flashlight. It must have been a plant of some sort, and apparently it had started to grow in the cranium. Some of the branches had issued from the cloven crown, others through the eye-holes, the mouth and the nose-hole, to flare upward. And the roots of the blasphemous thing had gone downward, trellising themselves on every bone. The very toes and fingers were ringed with them, and they drooped in writhing coils. Worst of all, the ones that had issued from the toe-ends *were rooted in a second skull*, which dangled just below, with fragments of the broken-off root-system. There was a litter of fallen bones on the floor in the corner. . . .

"The sight made me feel a little weak, somehow, and more than a little nauseated—that abhorrent, inexplicable mingling of the human and the plant. I started to climb the rope, in a feverish hurry to get out, but the thing fascinated me in its abominable fashion, and

I couldn't help pausing to study it a little more when I had climbed half-way. I leaned toward it too far, I guess, and the rope began to sway, bringing my face lightly against the leprous, antler-shaped boughs above the skull.

"Something broke—possibly a sort of pod on one of the branches. I found my head enveloped in a cloud of pearl-gray powder, very light, fine and scentless. The stuff settled on my hair, it got into my nose and eyes, nearly choking and blinding me. I shook it off as well as I could. Then I climbed on and pulled myself through the opening. . . ."

As if the effort of coherent narration had been too heavy a strain, Falmer lapsed into disconnected mumblings. The mysterious malady, whatever it was, returned upon him, and his delirious ramblings were mixed with groans of torture. But at moments he regained a flash of coherence.

"My head! my head!" he muttered. "There must be something in my brain, something that grows and spreads. I tell you, I can feel it there. I haven't felt right at any time since I left the burial-pit. . . . My mind has been queer ever since. . . . It must have been the spores of the ancient devil-plant. The spores have taken root . . . the thing is splitting my skull, going down into my brain—a plant that springs out of a human cranium, as if from a flower-pot!"

The dreadful convulsions began once more, and Falmer writhed uncontrollably in his companion's arms, shrieking with agony. Thone, sick at heart, and shocked by his sufferings, abandoned all effort to restrain him and took up the hypodermic. With much difficulty, he managed to inject a triple dose, and Falmer grew quiet by degrees, and lay with open, glassy eyes, breathing stertorously. Thone, for the first time, perceived an odd protrusion of his eyeballs, which seemed about to start from their sockets, making it impossible for the lids to close, and lending the drawn features an expression of mad horror. It was as if something were pushing Falmer's eyes from his head.

Thone, trembling with sudden weakness and terror, felt that he was involved in some unnatural web of nightmare. He could not, dared not, believe the story Falmer had told him, and its implications. Assuring himself that his companion had imagined it all, had been ill throughout with the incubation of some strange fever, he stooped over and found that the horn-shaped lump on Falmer's head had now broken through the skin.

With a sense of unreality, he stared at the object that his prying fingers had revealed amid the matted hair. It was unmistakably a plant-bud of some sort, with involuted folds of pale green and bloody pink that seemed about to expand. The thing issued from above the central suture of the skull.

A nausea swept upon Thone, and he recoiled from the lolling head and its baleful outgrowth, averting his gaze. His fever was returning; there was a woeful debility in all his limbs; and he heard the muttering voice of delirium through the quinine-induced ringing in his ears. His eyes blurred with a deathly and miasmal mist.

HE FOUGHT to subdue his illness and impotence. He must not give way to it wholly; he must go on with Falmer and the Indians and reach the nearest trading-station, many days away on the Orinoco, where Falmer could receive medical aid.

As if through sheer volition, his eyes cleared, and he felt a resurgence of strength. He looked around for the guides, and saw, with a start of uncomprehending surprize, that they had vanished. Peering further, he observed that one of the boats—the dugout used by the Indians—had also disappeared. It was plain that he and Falmer had been deserted. Perhaps the Indians had known what was wrong with the sick man, and had been afraid. At any rate, they were gone, and they had taken much of the camp equipment and most of the provisions with them.

Thone turned once more to the supine body of Falmer, conquering his repugnance with effort. Resolutely, he drew out his clasp-knife, and stooping over the stricken man, he excised the protruding bud, cutting as close to the scalp as he could safety. The thing was unnaturally tough and rubbery; it exuded a thin, sanious fluid; and he shuddered when he saw its internal structure, full of nerve-like filaments, with a core that suggested cartilage. He flung it aside quickly on the river sand. Then, lifting Falmer in his arms, he lurched and staggered toward the remaining boat. He fell more than once, and lay half swooning across the inert body. Alternately carrying and dragging his burden, he reached the boat at last. With the remnant of his failing strength, he contrived to prop Falmer in the stern against the pile of equipment.

His fever was mounting apace. After much delay, with tedious, half-delirious exertions, he pushed off from the shore and got the boat into midstream. He paddled with nerveless strokes, till the fever mastered him wholly and the oar slipped from oblivious fingers. . . .

He awoke in the yellow glare of dawn, with his brain and his senses comparatively clear. His illness had left a great languor, but his first thought was of Falmer. He twisted about, nearly falling overboard in his debility, and sat facing his companion.

Falmer still reclined, half sitting, half lying, against the pile of blankets and other impedimenta. His knees were drawn up, his hands clasping them as if in tetanic rigor. His features had grown as stark and ghastly as those of a dead man, and his whole aspect was one of mortal rigidity. It was not this, however, that caused Thone to gasp with unbelieving horror.

During the interim of Thone's delirium and his lapse into slumber, the monstrous plant-bud, merely stimulated, it would seem, by the act of excision, had grown again with preternatural rapidity from Falmer's head. A loathsome pale-green stem was mounting thickly, and had started to branch like antlers after attaining a height of six or seven inches.

More dreadful than this, if possible, similar growths had issued from the eyes, and their stems, climbing vertically across the forehead, had entirely displaced the eyeballs. Already they were branching like the thing that mounted from the crown. The antlers were all tipped with pale vermilion. They appeared to quiver with repulsive animation, nodding rhythmically in the warm, windless air. . . . From the mouth, another stem protruded, curling upward like a long and whitish tongue. It had not yet begun to bifurcate.

Thone closed his eyes to shut away the shocking vision. Behind his lids, in a yellow dazzle of light, he still saw the cadaverous features, the climbing stems that quivered against the dawn like ghastly hydras of tomb-etiolated green. They seemed to be waving toward him, growing and lengthening as they waved. He opened his eyes again, and fancied, with a start of new terror, that the antlers were actually taller than they had been a few moments previous.

After that, he sat watching them in a sort of baleful hypnosis. The illusion of the plant's visible growth and freer movement—if it was illusion—increased upon him. Falmer, however, did not stir, and his parchment face appeared to shrivel and fall in, as if the roots of the growth were draining his blood, were devouring his very flesh in their insatiable and ghoulish hunger.

THONE WRENCHED his eyes away and stared at the river-shore. The stream had widened and the current had grown more sluggish. He sought to recognize their location, looking vainly for some familiar landmark in the monotonous dull-green cliffs of jungle that lined the margin. He felt hopelessly lost and alienated. He seemed to be drifting on an unknown tide of madness and nightmare, companioned by something that was more frightful than corruption itself.

His mind began to wander with an odd inconsequence, coming back always, in a sort of closed circle, to the thing that was devouring Falmer. With a flash of scientific curiosity, he found himself wondering to what genus it belonged. It was neither fungus nor pitcher-plant, nor anything that he had ever encountered or heard of in his explorations. It must have come, as Falmer had suggested, from an alien world: it was nothing that the Earth could conceivably have nourished.

He felt, with a comforting assurance, that Falmer was dead. That, at least, was a mercy. But, even as he shaped the thought, he heard a low, guttural moaning, and peering at Falmer in horrible startlement, saw that his limbs and body were twitching slightly. The twitching increased, and took on a rhythmic regularity, though at no time did it resemble the agonized and violent convulsions of the previous day. It was plainly automatic, like a sort of galvanism; and Thone saw that it was timed with the languorous and loathsome swaying of the plant. The effect on the watcher was insidiously mesmeric and somnolent; and once he caught himself beating the detestable rhythm with his foot.

He tried to pull himself together, groping desperately for something to which his sanity could cling. Ineluctably, his illness returned: fever, nausea, and revulsion worse than the loathliness of death. But, before he yielded to it utterly, he drew his loaded revolver from the holster and fired six times into Falmer's quivering body. He knew that he had not missed, but, after the final bullet, Falmer still twitched in unison with the evil swaying of the plant, and Thone, sliding into delirium, heard still the ceaseless, automatic moaning.

THERE WAS no time in the world of seething unreality and shoreless oblivion through which he drifted. When he came to himself again, he could not know if hours or weeks had elapsed. But he knew at once that the boat was no longer moving; and lifting himself dizzily, he saw that it had floated into shallow water and mud and was nosing the beach of a tiny, jungle-tufted isle in mid-river. The putrid odor of slime was about him like a stagnant pool; and he heard a strident humming of insects.

It was either late morning or early afternoon, for the sun was high in the still heavens. Lianas were drooping above him from the island trees like uncoiled serpents, and epiphytic orchids, marked with ophidian mottlings, leaned toward him grotesquely from lowering boughs. Immense butterflies went past on sumptuously spotted wings.

He sat up, feeling very giddy and light-headed, and faced again the horror that companioned him. The thing had grown incredibly: the three-antlered stems, mounting above Falmer's head, had become gigantic and had put out masses of ropy feelers that tossed uneasily in the air, as if searching for support—or new provender. In the topmost antlers, a prodigious blossom had opened—a sort of fleshy disk, broad as a man's face and white as leprosy.

Falmer's features had shrunken till the outlines of every bone were visible as if beneath tightened paper. He was a mere death's-head in a mask of human skin; and beneath his clothing, the body was little more than a skeleton. He was quite still now, except for the communicated quivering of the stems. The atrocious plant had sucked him dry, had eaten his vitals and his flesh.

Thone wanted to hurl himself forward in a mad impulse to grapple with the growth. But a strange paralysis held him back. The plant was like a living and sentient thing—a thing that watched him, that dominated him with its unclean but superior will. And the huge blossom, as he stared, took on the dim, unnatural semblance of a face. It was somehow like the face of Falmer, but the lineaments were twisted all awry, and were mingled with those of something wholly devilish and non-human. Thone could not move —and he could not take his eyes from the blasphemous abnormality.

By some miracle, his fever had left him; and it did not return. Instead, there came an eternity of frozen fright and madness, in which he sat facing the mesmeric plant. It towered before him from the dry, dead shell that had been Falmer, its swollen, glutted stems and branches swaying gently, and the huge flower leering perpetually upon him with its impious travesty of a human face. He thought that he heard a low singing sound, ineffably, demoniacally sweet, but whether it emanated from the plant or was a mere hallucination of his overwrought senses, he could not know.

The sluggish hours went by, and a gruelling sun poured down its beams like molten lead from some titanic vessel of torture. His head swam with weakness and the fetor-laden heat, but he could not relax the rigor of his posture. There was no change in the nodding monstrosity, which seemed to have attained its full growth above the head of its victim. But after a long interim Thone's eyes were drawn to the shrunken hands of Falmer, which still clasped the drawn-up knees in a spasmodic clutch. From the ends of the fingers, tiny white rootlets had broken and were writhing slowly in the air—groping, it seemed, for a new source of nourishment. Then, from the neck and chin, other tips were breaking, and over the whole body the clothing stirred in a curious manner, as if with the crawling and lifting of hidden lizards.

At the same time the singing grew louder, sweeter, more imperious, and the swaying of the great plant assumed an indescribably seductive tempo. It was like the allurement of voluptuous sirens, the deadly languor of dancing cobras. Thone felt an irresistible compulsion: a summons was being laid upon him, and his drugged mind and body must obey it. The very fingers of Falmer, twisting viperishly, seemed beckoning to him. Suddenly he was on his hands and knees in the bottom of the boat.

Inch by inch, with terror and fascination contending in his brain, he crept forward, dragging himself over the disregarded bundle of orchid-plants—inch by inch, foot by foot, till his head was against the withered hands of Falmer, from which hung and floated the questing roots.

Some cataleptic spell had made him helpless. He felt the rootlets as they moved like delving fingers through his hair and over his face and neck, and started to strike in with agonizing, needle-sharp tips. He could not stir, he could not even close his lids. In a frozen stare, he saw the gold and carmine flash of a hovering butterfly as the roots began to pierce his pupils.

Deeper and deeper went the greedy roots, while new filaments grew out to enmesh him like a witch's net. . . . For a while, it seemed that the dead and the living writhed together in leashed convulsions. . . . At last Falmer hung supine amid the lethal, ever-growing web. Bloated and colossal, the plant lived on; and in its upper branches, through the still, stifling afternoon, a second flower began to unfold.

Continuity

By H. P. LOVECRAFT

THERE is in certain ancient things a trace
Of some dim essence—more than form or
    weight;
A tenuous aether, indeterminate,
Yet linked with all the laws of time and space.
A faint, veiled sign of continuities
That outward eyes can never quite descry,
Of locked dimensions harboring years gone by,
And out of reach except for hidden keys.

It moves me most when slanting sunbeams glow
On old farm buildings set against a hill,
And paint-with life the shapes which linger still
From centuries less a dream than this we know.
In that strange light I feel I am not far
From the fixt mass whose sides the ages are.

Weird Tales, 1947

The Gardens of Yin
By H. P. LOVECRAFT

Beyond the wall, whose ancient masonry
Reached almost to the sky in moss-thick towers,
There would be terraced gardens rich with flowers,
And flutter of bird and butterfly and bee.
There would be walks, and bridges arching over
Warm lotus-pools reflecting temple eaves,
And cherry trees with delicate boughs and leaves
Against a pink sky where the herons hover.

All would be there, for had not old dreams flung
Open the gate to that stone-lanterned maze
Where drowsy streams spin out their winding ways,
Trailed by green vines from bending branches hung?
I hurried, but when the wall rose, grim and great,
I found there was no longer any gate.

Weird Tales, 1939

Extension of the Finite / 9 / Science Fiction

In April 1926, publisher Hugo Gernsback inaugurated a new Pulp, *Amazing Stories*. It bore the startling description, "The Magazine of Scientification." Gernsback (his firm was appropriately titled Experimenter Publishing Company) had been publishing non-fiction science and radio magazines which occasionally included in their contents some science-fiction material. But with *Amazing Stories* he created the first Science-Fiction Pulp.

Three months later, in a editorial entitled "Fiction versus Facts," he clarified *Amazing's* editorial policy, in response to certain readers who had questioned the believability of some of its stories. He wrote: "We reject stories often on the ground that, in our opinion, the plot or action is not in keeping with science as we know it today. For instance, when we see a plot wherein the hero is turned into a tree, later on into a stone, and then again back to himself, we do not consider this science, but, rather, a fairy tale, and such stories have no place in *Amazing Stories*." Quoting one science-fiction author, he went on to say: "beauty lies only in the things that are mysterious . . . scientifiction goes out into the remote vistas of the universe, where there is still mystery and so still beauty." With these aims in mind Gernsback set the standard for what was to become one of the most popular Pulp categories.

Amazing Stories rapidly reached a circulation of 100,000, an unusually high figure for a Pulp selling for the extravagant sum of 25 cents. But stories in the tradition of Jules Verne and H. G. Wells, while faithful to "scientifiction," were not imaginative enough to maintain *Amazing's* circulation after its competitor, *Astounding Stories*, made an editorial breakthrough in 1934.

Astounding Stories had entered the science-fiction field in 1930. Unlike *Amazing* it emphasized action fantasy (closely related to the Burroughs tradition) rather than scientific plausibility. Unable to gain ground from *Amazing*, it was on the verge of collapse by 1933. However, later that year F. Orlin Tremaine assumed editorship, and pumped new vitality into *Astounding's* life-stream. His formula was simple: get the best science-fiction fantasy material—that which strains the frontiers of the imagination. Within 12 months *Astounding* became number one.

Tremaine's policies continued until 1938, when John Campbell replaced him. Campbell was probably the greatest science-fiction editor of all time. His policies were more profound than Tremaine's; he required material of greater depth, which speculated on the implications of future scientific discoveries for humans—emotionally, philosophically, and sociologically. Campbell's impact on science-fiction was so powerful that there has been no significant divergence in the field in more than 30 years.

Today an abundance of highly sophisticated science-fiction is being published, and many of the better-known stories are available in current anthologies or as reprints. This section has therefore been limited to two generous selections from the middle 30's employing themes which have all but vanished from the literary scene.

* * *

"Wanderer of Infinity" (*Astounding Stories*, 1933), is by Harl Vincent, a Gernsback discovery who in the 30's became one of the more popular science-fiction writers. It has highly moral overtones not usually employed—and similar to those of many classic horror stories—based on themes of "meddling" with processes which trespass on the realm of

God. The religious symbolism of its leading character, the anti-heroic "alien", is obvious.

The villains of "Wanderer of Infinity" are "BEMs", a coterie term for Bug-Eyed-Monsters. Just prior to and concurrently with World War II, a new group of Pulps flourished: *Planet Stories, Startling Stories, Thrilling Wonder Stories,* and *Marvel Science Stories.* Their action-fantasy stories employed BEMs as villains, resulting in a surge in circulation which dropped off after the war. That stories of this nature achieved a wide audience during that period denotes their vicarious, satisfying, and addictive appeal as a release from anxiety.

*　　*　　*

"Parasite Planet" by Stanley G. Weinbaum is significant in two respects: it presents the rare theme of exploration of an alien world; and it was written by a man whose total output, although lasting little more than one year, inspired a whole new direction of science-fiction writing.

All of Weinberg's 31 stories were published in a 15-month period during 1934 and 1935. A Louisville chemist with a promising career as a writer, he died at the age of 33 of throat cancer. However, his name was permanently established in science-fiction by his introduction of vivid new elements, including believable love-interests, realistic dialogue, and endowment of alien beings with believable yet distinctively alien personalities. Until then aliens had been represented either as humanoids with human personalities or as monsters with animal ones. Weinberg's aliens were given thought processes and emotional characteristics which were neither human nor animal but, more logically, matched the creatures' physical structure, and even incorporated environmental factors. The lushly descriptive, "Parasite Planet" presents a terrifying journey through an alien environment. It was published in 1935 in *Astounding Stories.*

Wanderer of Infinity

By HARL VINCENT

LENVILLE! BERT Redmond had never heard of the place until he received Joan's letter. But here it was, a tiny straggling village cuddled amongst the Ramapo hills of lower New York State, only a few miles from Tuxedo. There was a prim, white-painted church, a general store with the inevitable gasoline pump at the curb, and a dozen or so of weatherbeaten frame houses. That was all. It was a typical, dusty crossroads hamlet of the vintage of thirty years before, utterly isolated and apart from the rushing life of the broad concrete highway so short a distance away.

Bert stopped his ancient and battered flivver at the corner where a group of overalled loungers was gathered. Its asthmatic motor died with a despairing cough as he cut the ignition.

"Anyone tell me where to find the Carmody place?" he sang out.

No one answered, and for a moment there was no movement amongst his listeners. Then one of the loungers, an old man with a stubble of gray beard, drew near and regarded him through thick spectacles.

"You ain't aimin' to go up there alone, be you?" the old fellow asked in a thin cackled voice.

"Certainly. Why?" Bert caught a peculiar gleam in the watery old eyes that were enlarged so enormously by the thick lenses. It was fear of the supernatural that lurked there, stark terror, almost.

"Don't you go up to the Carmody place, young feller. There's queer doin's in the big house, is why. Blue lights at night, an' noises inside—an'—an' cracklin' like thunder overhead—"

"Aw shet up, Gramp!" Another of the idlers, a youngster with chubby features, and downy of lip and chin, sauntered over from the group, interrupting the old man's discourse. "Don't listen to him," he said to Bert. "He's cracked a mite—been seein' things. The big house is up yonder on the hill. See, with the red chimbley showin' through the trees. They's a windin' road down here a piece."

Bert followed the pointing finger with suddenly anxious gaze. It was not an inviting spot, that tangle of second-growth timber and underbrush that hid the big house on the lonely hillside; it might conceal almost anything. And Joan Parker was there!

The one called Gramp was screeching invectives at the grinning bystanders. "You passel o' young idjits!" he stormed. "I seen it, I tell you. An'—an' heard things, too. The devil hisself is up there—an' his imps. We'd oughtn't to let this feller go. . . ."

Bert waited to hear no more. Unreasoning fear came to him that something was very much amiss up there at the big house, and he started the flivver with a thunderous barrage of its exhaust.

The words of Joan's note were vivid in his mind: "Come to me, Bert, at the Carmody place in Lenville. Believe me, I need you." Only that, but it had been sufficient to bring young Redmond across three states to this measly town that wasn't even on the road maps.

Bert yanked the bouncing car into the winding road that led up the hill, and thought grimly of the quarrel with Joan two years before. He had told her then, arrogantly, that she'd need him some day. But now that his words had proved true the fact brought him no consolation nor the slightest elation. Joan was there in this lonely spot, and she did need him. That was enough.

He ran nervous fingers through his already tousled mop of sandy hair—a habit he had when disturbed— and nearly wrecked the car on a gray boulder that encroached on one of the two ruts which, together, had been termed a road.

Stupid, that quarrel of theirs. And how stubborn both had been! Joan had insisted on going to the big city to follow the career her brother had chosen for her. Chemistry, biology, laboratory work! Bert sniffed, even now. But he had been equally stubborn in his insistence that she marry him instead and settle down on the middle-Western fruit farm.

With a sudden twist, the road turned in at the entrance of a sadly neglected estate. The grounds of the place were overrun with rank growths and the driveway was covered with weeds. The tumble-down gables of a decrepit frame house pepped out through the trees. It was a rambling old building that once had been a mansion—the "big house" of the natives. A musty air of decay was upon it, and crazily askew window shutters proclaimed deep-shrouded mystery within.

Bert drew up at the rickety porch and stopped the flivver with its usual shuddering jerk.

AS IF his coming had been watched for through the stained glass of its windows, the door was flung violently open. A white-clad figure darted across the porch, but not before Bert had untangled the lean six feet of him from under the flivver's wheel and bounded up the steps.

"Joan!"

"Bert I—I'm sorry."

"Me too." Swallowing hard, Bert Redmond held her close.

"But I won't go back to Indiana!" The girl raised her chin and the old defiance was in her tearful gaze.

Bert stared. Joan was white and wan, a mere shadow of her old self. And she was trembling, hysterical.

"That's all right," he whispered. "But tell me now, what is it? What's wrong?"

With sudden vigor she was drawing him into the house. "It's Tom," she quavered. "I can't do a thing with him; can't get him to leave here. And something terrible is about to happen, I know. I thought perhaps you could help, even if—"

"Tom Parker here?" Bert was surprised that the fastidious older brother should leave his comfortable city quarters and lose himself in this God-forsaken place. "Sure, I'll help, dear—if I can."

"You can; oh, I'm sure you can," the girl went on tremulously. A spot of color flared in either cheek. "It's his experiments. He came over from New York about a year ago and rented this old house. The city laboratory wasn't secluded enough. And I've helped him until now in everything. But I'm frightened; he's playing with dangerous forces. He doesn't understand —won't understand. But I saw. . . ."

And then Joan Parker slumped into a high-backed chair that stood in the ancient paneled hall. Soft waves of her chestnut hair framed the pinched, terrified face, and wide eyes looked up at Bert with the same horror he had seen in those of the old fellow in the village. A surge of the old tenderness welled up in him and he wanted to take her in his arms.

"Wait," she said, swiftly rising. "I'll let you judge for yourself. Here—go into the laboratory and talk with Tom."

She pushed him forward and through a door that closed softly behind him. He was in a large room that was cluttered with the most bewildering array of electrical mechanisms he had ever seen. Joan had remained outside.

TOM PARKER, his hair grayer and forehead higher than when Bert has seen him last, rose from where he was stooping over a work bench. He advanced, smiling, and his black eyes were alight with genuine pleasure. Bert had anticipated a less cordial welcome.

"Albert Redmond!" exclaimed the older man. "This is a surprise. Glad to see you, boy, glad to see you."

He meant it, Tom did, and Bert wrung the extended hand heartily. Yet he dared not tell of Joan's note. The two men had always been the very best of friends— except in the matter of Joan's future.

"You haven't changed much," Bert ventured.

Tom Parker laughed. "Not about Joan, if that is what you mean. She likes the work and will go far in it. Why, Bert—"

"Sa-ay, wait a minute." Bert Redmond's mien was solemn. "I saw her outside, Tom, and was shocked. She isn't herself—doesn't look at all well. Haven't you noticed, man?"

The older man sobered and a puzzled frown creased his brow. "I have noticed, yes. But it's nonsense, Bert, I swear it is. She has been having dreams—worrying a lot, it seems. Guess I'll have to send her to the doctor?"

"Dreams? Worry?" Bert thought of the old man called Gramp.

"Yes. I'll tell you all about it—what we're working on here—and show you. It's no wonder she gets that way, I guess. I've been a bit loony with the marvel of it myself at times. Come here."

Tom led him to an intricate apparatus which bore some resemblance to a television radio. There were countless vacuum tubes and their controls, tiny motors belted to slotted disks that would spin when power was applied, and a double eyepiece.

"Before I let you look," Tom was saying, I'll give you an idea of it, to prepare you. This is a mechanism I've developed for a study of the less-understood dimensions. The results have more than justified my expectations—they're astounding. Bert, we can actually see into these realms that were hitherto unexplored. We can examine at close range the life of these other planes. Think of it!"

"Life—planes—dimensions?" said Bert blankly. "Remember, I know very little about this science of yours."

HAVEN'T YOU read the newspaper accounts of Einstein's researches and of others who have delved into the theory of relativity?"

"Sa-ay! I read them, but they don't tell me a thing. It's over my head a mile."

"Well, listen: this universe of ours—space and all it contains—is a thing of five dimensions, a continuum we have never begun to contemplate in its true complexity and immensity. There are three of its dimensions with which we are familiar. Our normal senses perceive and understand them—length, breadth and thickness. The fourth dimension, time, or, more properly, the time-space interval, we have only recently understood.

And this fifth dimension, Bert, is something no man on earth has delved into—excepting myself."

"You don't say." Bert was properly impressed; the old gleam of the enthusiastic scientist was in Tom's keen eyes.

"Surest thing. I have called this fifth dimension the interval of oscillation, though the term is not precisely correct. It has to do with the arrangement, the speed and direction of movement, and the polarity of protonic and electronic energy charges of which matter is comprised. It upsets some of our old and accepted natural laws—one in particular. Bert, two objects *can* occupy the same space at the same time, though only one is perceptible to our earthbound senses. Their differently constituted atoms exist in the same location without interference—merely vibrating in different planes. There are many such planes in this fifth dimension of space, all around us, some actually inhabited. Each plane has a different atomic structure of matter, its own oscillation interval of the energy that is matter, and a set of natural laws peculiar to itself. I can't begin to tell you; in fact, I've explored only a fraction. But here—look."

He attacked it in vain with his fists

TOM'S INSTRUMENT set up a soft purring at his touch of a lever, and eery blue light flickered from behind the double eyepiece, casting grotesque shadows on walls and ceiling, and paling to insignificance the light of day that filtered through the long-unwashed windows.

Bert squinted through the hooded twin lenses. At first he was dazzled and confused by the rapidly whirling light-images, but these quickly resolved into geometric figures, an inconceivable number of them, extending off into limitless space in a huge arc, revolving and tumbling like the colored particles in an old-fashioned kaleidoscope. Cubes, pyramids and cones of variegated hues. Swift-rushing spheres and long slim cylinders of brilliant blue-white; gleaming disks of polished jet, spinning. . . .

Abruptly the view stabilized, and clear-cut stationary objects sprang into being. An unbroken vista of seamed chalky cliffs beside an inky sea whose waters rose and fell rhythmically yet did not break against the towering palisade. Waveless, glass-smooth, these waters. A huge blood-red sun hanging low in a leaden though cloudless sky, reflecting scintillating flecks of gold and purple brilliance from the ocean's black surface.

At first there was no sign of life to be seen. Then a mound was rising up from the sea near the cliff, a huge tortoiselike shape that stretched forth several flat members which adhered to the vertical white wall as if held by suction disks. Ponderously the thing turned over and headed up from the inky depths, spewing out from its concave under side an army of furry brown bipeds. Creatures with bloated torsos in which head and body merged so closely as to be indistinguishable one from the other, balanced precariously on two spindly legs, and with long thin arms like tentacles, waving and coiling. Spiderlike beings ran out over the smooth dark surface of the sea as if it were solid ground.

JUPITER!" BERT looked up from the eyepiece, blinking into the triumphant grinning face of Tom Parker. "You mean to tell me these creatures are real?" he demanded. "Living here, all around us, in another plane where we can't see them without this machine of yours?"

"Surest thing. And this is but one of many such planes."

"They can't get through, to our plane?"

"Lord no, man, how could they?"

A sharp crackling peal of thunder rang out overhead and Tom Parker went suddenly white. Outside, the sky was cloudless.

"And that—what's that?" Bert remembered the warning of the old man of the village, and Joan's obvious fear.

"It—it's only a physical manifestation of the forces I use in obtaining visual connection, one of the things that worries Joan. Yet I can't find any cause for alarm. . . ."

The scientist's voice droned on endlessly, technically. But Bert knew there was something Tom did not understand, something he was trying desperately to explain to himself.

Thunder rumbled once more, and Bert returned his eyes to the instrument. Directly before him in the field of vision a group of the spider men advanced over the pitchy sea with a curiously constructed cage of woven transparent material which they set down at a point so close by that it seemed he could touch it if he stretched out his hand. The illusion of physical nearness was perfect. The evil eyes of the creatures were fastened upon him; tentacle arms uncoiled and reached forth as if to break down the barrier that separated them.

And then a scream penetrated his consciousness, wrenching him back to consideration of his immediate surroundings. The laboratory door burst open and Joan, pale and disheveled, dashed into the room.

TOM SHOUTED, running forward to intercept her, and Bert saw what he had not seen before, a ten-foot circle of blue-white metal set in the floor and illuminated by a shaft of light from a reflector on the ceiling above Tom's machine.

"Joan—the force area!" Tom was yelling. "Keep away!"

Tom had reached the distraught girl and was struggling with her over on the far side of the disk.

There came a throbbing of the very air surrounding them, and Bert saw Tom and Joan on the other side of the force area, their white faces indistinct and wavering as if blurred by heat waves rising between. The rumblings and cracklings overhead increased in intensity until the old house swayed and creaked with the concussions. Hazy forms materialized on the lighted disk—the cage of the transparent, woven basket—dark spidery forms within. The creatures from that other plane!

"Joan! Tom!" Bert's voice was soundless as he tried to shout and his muscles were paralyzed when he attempted to hurl himself across to them. The blue-white light had spread and formed a huge bubble of white brilliance, a transparent elastic solid that flung him back when he attacked it in vain with his fists.

Within his confines he saw Joan and her brother scuffling with the spider men, tearing at the tentacle arms that encircled them and drew them relentlessly into the basketweave cage. There was a tremendous thump and the warping of the very universe about them all. Bert Redmond, his body racked by insupportable tortures, was hurled into the black abyss of infinity. . . .

HIS WAS not death, nor was it a dream from which he would awaken. After that moment of mental agony and ghastly physical pain, after a dizzying rush through inky nothingness, Bert knew suddenly that he was very much alive. If he had lost consciousness at all, it had been for no great length of time. And yet there was this sense of strangeness in his surroundings, a feeling that he had been transported over some nameless gulf of space. He had dropped to his knees, but with the swift return of normal faculties he jumped to his feet.

A tall stranger confronted him, a half-nude giant with bronzed skin and of solemn visage. The stalwart build of him and the smooth contours of cheek and jaw proclaimed him a man not yet past middle age, but his uncropped hair was white as the driven snow.

They stood in a spherical chamber of silvery metal, Bert and this giant, and the gentle vibration of delicately balanced machinery made itself felt in the structure. Of Joan and Tom there was no sign.

"Where am I?" Bert demanded. "And where are my friends? Why am I with you, without them?"

Compassion was in the tall stranger's gaze—and something more. The pain of a great sorrow filled the brown eyes that looked down at Bert, and resignation to a fate that was shrouded in ineffable mystery.

"Trust me," he said in a mellow slurring voice. "Where you are, you shall soon learn. You are safe. And your friends will be located."

"*Will* be located! Don't you *know* where they are? Bert laid hands on the big man's wrists and shook him impatiently. The stranger was too calm and unmoved in the face of this tremendous thing which had come to pass.

"I know where they have been taken, yes. But there is no need of haste out here in infra-dimensional space, for time stands still. We will find it a simple matter to reach the plane of their captors, the Berdeks, within a few seconds after your friends arrive there. My plane segregator—this sphere—will accomplish this in due season."

STRANGELY, BERT believed him. This talk of dimensions and planes and of the halting of time was incomprehensible, but somehow there was communicated to his own restless nature something of the placid serenity of the white-haired stranger. He regarded the man more closely, saw there was an alien look about him that marked him as different and apart from the men of Earth. His sole garment was a wide breech clout of silvery stuff that glinted with changing colors—hues foreign to nature on Earth. His was a superhuman perfection of muscular development, and there was an indescribable mingling of gentleness and sternness in his demeanor. With a start, Bert noted that his fingers were webbed, as were his toes.

"Sa-ay," Bert exclaimed, "who are you, anyway?"

The stranger permitted himself the merest ghost of a smile. "You may call me Wanderer," he said. "I am the Wanderer of Infinity."

"Infinity! You are not of my world?"

"But no."

"You speak my language."

"It is one of many with which I am familiar."

"I—I don't understand." Bert Redmond was like a man in a trance, completely under the spell of his amazing host's personality.

"It is given to few men to understand." The Wanderer fell silent, his arms folded across his broad chest. And his great shoulders bowed as under the weight of centuries of mankind's cares. "Yet I would have you understand, O Man-Called-Bert, for the tale is a strange one and is heavy upon me."

It was uncanny that this Wanderer should address him by name. Bert thrilled to a new sense of awe.

"But," he objected, "my friends are in the hands of the spider men. You said we'd go to them. Good Lord, man, I've got to do it!"

"You forget that time means nothing here. We will go to them in precise synchronism with the proper time as existent in that plane."

THE WANDERER'S intense gaze held Bert speechless, hypnotized. A swift dimming of the sphere's diffused illumination came immediately, and darkness swept down like a blanket, thick and stifling. This was no ordinary darkness, but utter absence of light—the total obscurity of Erebus. And the hidden motors throbbed with sudden new vigor.

"Behold!" At the Wanderer's exclamation the enclosing sphere became transparent and they were in the midst of a dizzying maelstrom of flashing color. Brilliant geometric shapes, there were, whirling off into the vastness of space, as Bert had seen them in Tom Parker's instrument. A gigantic arc of rushing light-forms spanning the black gulf of an unknown cosmos. And in the foreground directly under the sphere was a blue-white disk, horizontally fixed—a substantial and familiar object, with hazy surroundings likewise familiar.

"Isn't that the metal platform in my friend's laboratory?" asked Bert, marveling.

"It is indeed." The mellow voice of the Wanderer was grave, and he laid a hand on Bert's arm. "And for so long as it exists it constitutes a serious menace to your civilization. It is a gateway to your world, a means of contact with your plane of existence for those many vicious hordes that dwell in other planes

of the fifth dimension. Without it the Bardeks had not been able to enter and effect the kidnapping of your friends. Oh, I tried so hard to warn them—Parker and the girl—but could not do it in time."

A measure of understanding came to Bert Redmond. This was the thing Joan had feared and which Tom Parker had neglected to consider. The forces which enabled the scientist to see into the mysterious planes of this uncharted realm were likewise capable of providing physical contact between the planes, or actual travel from one to the other. Tom had not learned how to use the forces in this manner, but the Bardeks had.

WE TRAVEL now along a different set of co-ordinates, those of space-time," said the Wanderer. "We go into the past, through eons of time as it is counted in your world."

"Into the past," Bert repeated. He stared foolishly at his host, whose eyes glittered strangely in the flickering light.

"Yes, we go to my home—to what *was* my home."

"To your home? Why?" Bert shrank before the awful contorted face of the Wanderer. A spasm of ferocity had crossed it on his last words. Some fearful secret must be gnawing at the big man's vitals.

"Again you must trust me. To understand, it is necessary that you see."

The gentle whir of machinery rose to a piercing shriek as the Wanderer manipulated the tiny levers of a control board that was set in the smooth transparent wall. And the rushing light-forms outside became a blur at first, then a solid stream of cold liquid fire into which they plunged at breakneck speed.

There was no perceptible motion of the sphere, however. It was the only object that seemed substantial and fixed in an intangible and madly gyrating universe. Its curved wall, though transparent, was solid, comforting to the touch.

Standing by his instrument board, the Wanderer was engrossed in a tabulation of mathematical data he was apparently using in setting the many control knobs before him. Plotting their course through infinity! His placid serenity of countenance had returned, but there was a new eagerness in his intense gaze and his strong fingers trembled while he manipulated the tiny levers and dials.

OUTSIDE THE apparently motionless sphere, a never-ending riot of color surged swiftly and silently by, now swirling violently in great sweeping arcs of blinding magnificence, now changing character and driving down from dizzying heights as a dim-lit column of gray that might have been a blast of steam from some huge inverted geyser of the cosmos.

Always there were the intermittent black bands that flashed swiftly across the brightness, momentarily darkening the sphere and then passing on into the limbo of this strange realm between planes.

Abruptly then, like the turning of a page in some gigantic book, the swift-moving phantasmagoria swung back into the blackness of the infinite and was gone. Before them stretched a landscape of rolling hills and fertile valleys. Overhead, the skies were a deep blue, almost violet, and twin suns shone down on the scene. The sphere drifted along a few hundred feet from the surface.

"Urtraria!" the Wanderer breathed reverently. His white head was bowed and his great hands clutched the small rail of the control board.

In a daze of conflicting emotions, Bert watched as this land of peace and plenty slipped past beneath them. This, he knew, had been the home of Wanderer. In what past age or at how great a distance it was from his own world, he could only imagine. But that the big man who called himself Wanderer loved this country there was not the slightest doubt. It was a fetish with him, a past he was in duty bound to revisit time and again, and to mourn over.

Smooth broad lakes, there were, and glistening streams that ran their winding courses through well-kept and productive farmlands. And scattered communities with orderly streets and spacious parks. Roads, stretching endless ribbons of wide metallic surface across the countryside. Long two-wheeled vehicles skimming over the roads with speed so great the eye could scarcely follow them. Flapping-winged ships of the air, flying high and low in all directions. A great city of magnificent dome-topped buildings looming up suddenly at the horizon.

The sphere proceeded swiftly toward the city. Once a great air liner, flapping huge gossamerlike wings, drove directly toward them. Bert cried out in alarm and ducked instinctively, but the ship passed *through* them and on its way. It was as if they did not exist in this spherical vehicle of the dimensions.

W E ARE here only as onlookers," the Wanderer explained sadly, "and can have no material existence here. We can not enter this plane, for there is no gateway. Would that there were."

Now they were over the city and the sphere came to rest above a spacious flat roof where there were luxurious gardens and pools, and a small glass-domed observatory. A woman was seated by one of the pools, a beautiful woman with long golden hair that fell in soft profusion over her ivory shoulders and bosom. Two children, handsome stalwart boys of probably ten and twelve, romped with a domestic animal which resembled a foxhound of Earth but had glossy short-haired fur and flippers like those of a seal. Suddenly these three took to the water and splashed with much vigor and joyful shouting.

The Wanderer gripped Bert's arm with painful force. "My home!" he groaned. "Understand, Earthling? This was my home, these my wife and children —destroyed through my folly. Destroyed, I say, in ancient days. And by my accursed hand—when the metal monsters came."

There was madness in the Wanderer's glassy stare, the madness of a tortured soul within. Bert began to fear him.

"We should leave," he said. "Why torment yourself with such memories? My friends. . . ."

"Have patience, Earthling. Don't you understand that I sinned and am therefore condemned to this torment? Can't you see that I *must* unburden my soul of its ages-old load, that I must revisit the scene of my crime, that others must see and know? It is part of my punishment, and you, perforce, must bear witness. Moreover, it is to help your friends and your world that I bring you here. Behold!"

A MAN was coming out of the observatory, a tall man with bronzed skin and raven locks. It was the Wanderer himself, the Wanderer of the past, as he had been in the days of his youth and happiness.

The woman by the pool had risen from her seat and was advancing eagerly toward her mate. Bert saw that the man hardly glanced in her direction, so intent was he upon an object over which he stood. The object was a shimmering bowl some eight or ten feet across, which was mounted on a tripod near the observatory, and over whose metallic surface a queer bluish light was playing.

It was a wordless pantomime, the ensuing scene, and Bert watched in amazement. This woman of another race, another age, another plane, was pleading with her man. Sobbing soundlessly, wretchedly. And the man was unheeding, impatient with her demonstrations. He shoved her aside as she attempted to interfere with his manipulations of some elaborate contrivance at the side of the bowl.

And then there was a sudden roaring vibration, a flash of light leaping from the bowl, and the materialization of a spherical vessel that swallowed up the man and vanished in the shaft of light like a moth in the flame of a candle.

At Bert's side, the Wanderer was a grim and silent figure, misty and unreal when compared with those material, emotion-torn beings of the rooftop. The woman, swooning, had wilted over the rim of the bowl, and the two boys with their strange amphibious pet splashed out from the pool and came running to her, wide-eyed and dripping.

The Wanderer touched a lever and again there was the sensation as of a great page turned across the vastness of the universe. All was hazy and indistinct outside the sphere that held them, with a rushing blur of dimly gray light-forms. Beneath them remained only the bright outline of the bowl, an object distinct and real and fixed in space.

"It was thus I left my loved ones," the Wanderer said hollowly. "In fanatical devotion to my science, but in blind disregard of those things which really mattered. Observe, O Man-Called-Bert, that the bowl is still existent in infra-dimensional space—the gateway I left open to Urtraria. So it remained while I, fool that I was, explored those planes of the fifth dimension that were all around us though we saw and felt them not. Only I had seen, even as your friend Tom has seen. And like him, I heeded not the menace of the things I had witnessed. We go now to the plane of the metal monsters. Behold!"

THE SPHERE shuddered to the increased power of its hidden motors and another huge page seemed to turn slowly over, lurching sickeningly as it came to rest in the new and material plane of existence. Here, Bert understood now, the structure of matter was entirely different. Atoms were comprised of protons and electrons whirling at different velocities and in different orbits—possibly some of the electrons in reverse direction to those of the atomic structure of matter in Urtraria. And these coexisted with those others in the same relative position in time and in space. Ages before, the thing had happened, and he was seeing it now.

They were in the midst of a forest of conical spires whose sides were of dark glittering stuff that reminded Bert of the crystals of carborundum before pulverizing for commercial use. A myriad of deep colors were reflected from the sharply pointed piles in the light of a great cold moon that hung low in the heavens above them.

In the half light down there between the circular bases of the cones, weird creatures were moving. Like great earthworms they moved, sluggishly and with writhing contortions of their many-jointed bodies. Long cylindrical things with glistening gray hide like armor plate and with fearsome heads that reared upward occasionally to reveal the single flaming eye and massive iron jaws each contained. There were riveted joints and levers, wheels and gears that moved as the creatures moved; darting lights that flashed forth from trunnion-mounted cases like the searchlights of a battleship of Earth; great swiveled arms

with grappling hooks attached. They were mechanical contrivances—the metal monsters of which the Wanderer had spoken. Whether their brains were comprised of active living cells or whether they were cold, calculating machines of metallic parts, Bert was never to know.

"See, the gateway," the Wanderer was saying. "They are investigating. It is the beginning of the end of Urtraria—all as is occurred in the dim and distant past."

He gripped Bert's arm, pointing a trembling finger, and his face was a terrible thing to see in the eery light of their sphere.

A SHARPLY OUTLINED circle of blue-white appeared down there in the midst of the squirming monsters. The sphere drifted lower and Bert was able to see that a complicated machine was being trundled out from an arched doorway in the base of one of the conical dwellings. It was moved to the edge of the light circle which was the bowl on that rooftop of Urtraria. The same bowl! A force area like that used by Tom Parker, an area existent in many planes of the fifth dimension simultaneously, an area where the various components of wave motion merged and became as one. The gateway between planes!

The machine of the metal monsters was provided with a huge lens and a reflector, and these were trained on the bowl. Wheels and levers of the machine moved swiftly. There came an orange light from within that was focused upon lens and reflector to strike down and mingle with the cold light of the bowl. A startling transformation ensued, for the entire area within view was encompassed with a milky diffused brightness in which two worlds seemed to intermingle and fuse. There were the rooftops of the city in Urtraria and its magnificent domes, a transparent yet substantial reality superimposed upon the gloomy city of cones of the metal monsters.

"Jupiter!" Bert breathed. "They're going through!"

"They are, Earthling. More accurately, they did—thousands of them; millions." Even as the Wanderer spoke, the metal monsters were wriggling through between the two planes, their enormous bodies moving with menacing deliberation.

On the rooftops back in Urtraria could be seen the frantic fleeing forms of humanlike beings—the Wanderer's people.

There was a sharp click from the control panel and the scene was blotted out by the familiar maze of geometric shapes, the whirling, dancing light-forms that rushed madly past over the vast arch which spanned infinity.

"WHERE WERE you at the time?" asked Bert. Awed by what he had seen and with pity in his heart for the man who had unwittingly let loose the horde of metal monsters on his own loved ones and his own land, he stared at the Wanderer.

The big man was standing with face averted, hands clutching the rail of the control panel desperately. "I?" he whispered. "I was roaming the planes, exploring, experimenting, immersed in the pursuits that went with my insatiable thirst for scientific data and the broadening of my knowledge of this complex universe of ours. Forgetting my responsibilities. Unknowing, unsuspecting."

"You returned—to your home?"

"Too late I returned. You shall see; we return now by the same route I then followed."

"No!" Bert shouted, suddenly panicky at thought of what might be happening to Joan and Tom in the land of the Bardeks. "No Wanderer—tell me, but don't show me. I can imagine. Seeing those loathsome big worms of iron and steel, I can well visualize what they did. Come now, have a heart, man; take me to my friends before. . . ."

"Ah-h!" The Wanderer looked up and a benign look came to take the place of the pain and horror which had contorted his features. "It is well, O Man-Called-Bert. I shall do as you request, for I now see that my mission has been well accomplished. We go to your friends, and fear you not that we shall arrive too late."

"Your—your mission?" Bert calmed immediately under the spell of the Wanderer's new mood.

"My mission throughout eternity, Earthling—can't you sense it? Forever and ever I shall roam infra-dimensional space, watching and waiting for evidence that a similar catastrophe might be visited on another land where warm-blooded thinking humans of similar mold to my own may be living out their short lives of happiness or near-happiness. Never again shall so great a calamity come to mankind anywhere if it be within the Wanderer's power to prevent it. And that is why I snatched you up from your friend's laboratory. That is why I have shown to you the—"

"Me, why me?" Bert exclaimed.

"Attend, O Earthling, and you shall hear."

The mysterious intangibilities of the cosmos whirled by unheeded by either as the Wanderer's tale unfolded.

"WHEN I returned," he said, the gateway was closed forever. I could not reenter my own plane of existence. The metal monsters had taken possession; they had found a better and richer land than their own, and when they had completed their migration they destroyed the generator of my force area. They had shut me out; but I could visit Urtraria—as an outsider, as a wraith—and I saw what they had done. I saw the desolation and the blackness of my once fair land. I saw that—that none of my own kind remained. All, all were gone.

"For a time my reason deserted me and I roamed infra-dimensional space a madman, self-condemned to the outer realms where there is no real material existence, no human companionship, no love, no comfort. When reason returned, I set myself to the task of visiting other planes where beings of my own kind might be found and I soon learned that it was impossible to do this in the body. To these people I was a ghostly visitant, if they sensed my presence at all, for my roamings between planes had altered the characteristics of atomic structure of my being. I could no longer adapt myself to material existence in these planes of the fifth dimension. The orbits of electrons in the atoms comprising my substance had become fixed in a new and outcast oscillation interval. I had remained away too long. I *was* an outcast, a wanderer—the Wanderer of Infinity."

There was silence in the sphere for a space, save only for the gentle whirring of the motors. Then the Wanderer continued:

"Nevertheless, I roamed these planes as a nonexistent visitor in so far as their peoples were concerned. I learned their languages and came to think of them as my own, and I found that many of their scientific workers were experimenting along lines similar to those which had brought disaster to Urtraria. I swore a mighty oath to spend my lifetime in warning them, in warding off a repetition of so terrible a mistake as I had made. On several occasions I have succeeded.

"And then I found that my lifetime was to be for all eternity. In the outer realms time stands still, as I have told you, and in the plane of existence which was now mine—an extra-material plane—I had no prospect of aging or of death. My vow, therefore, is for so long as our universe may endure instead of for merely a lifetime. For this I am duly thankful, for I shall miss nothing until the end of time.

"I VISITED planes where other monsters, as clever and as vicious as the metal ones who devastated Urtraria, were bending every effort of their sciences toward obtaining actual contact with other planes of the fifth dimension. And I learned that such contact was utterly impossible of attainment without a gateway in the realm to which they wished to pass—a gateway such as I had provided for the metal monsters and such as that which your friend Tom Parker has provided for the Bardeks, or spider men, as you term them.

"In intra-dimensional space I saw the glow of Tom

Parker's force area and I made my way to your world quickly. But Tom could not get my warning: he was too stubbornly engrossed in the work he was engaged in. The girl Joan was slightly more susceptible, and I believe she was beginning to sense my telepathic messages when she sent for you. Still and all, I had begun to give up hope when you came on the scene. I took you away just as the spider men succeeded in capturing your friends, and now my hope has revived. I feel sure that my warning shall not have been in vain."

"But," objected Bert, "you've warned *me*, not the scientist of my world who is able to prevent the thing—"

"Yes, *you*," the Wanderer broke in. "It is better so. This Tom Parker is a zealot even as was I—a man of science thinking only of his own discoveries. I am not sure he would discontinue his experiments even were he to receive my warning in all its horrible details. But you, O Man-Called-Bert, through your love of his sister and by your influence over him, will be able to do what I can not do myself: bring about the destruction of this apparatus of his; impress upon him the grave necessity of discontinuing his investigations. You can do it, and you alone, now that you fully understand."

"Sa-ay! You're putting it up to me entirely?"

"Nearly so, and there is no alternative. I believe I have not misjudged you; you will not fail, of that I am certain. For the sake of your own kind, for the love of Joan Parker—you will not fail. And for me— for this small measure of atonement it is permitted that I make or help to make possible—"

"No, I'll not fail. Take me to them, quick." Bert grinned understandingly as the Wanderer straightened his broad shoulders and extended his hand.

There was no lack of substantiality in the mighty grip of those closing fingers.

AGAIN THE sphere's invisible motors increased speed, and again the dizzying kaleidoscope of color swept past them more furiously.

"We will now overtake them—your friends," said the Wanderer, "in the very act of passing between planes."

"Overtake them. . . ." Bert mumbled. "I don't get it at all, this time traveling. It's over my head a mile."

"It isn't time travel really," explained the Wanderer. "We are merely closing up the time-space interval, moving to the precise spot in the universe where your friend's laboratory existed at the moment of contact between planes with your world and that of the Bardeks. We shall reach there a few seconds after the actual capture."

"No chance of missing?" Bert watched the Wanderer as he consulted his mathematical data and made new adjustments of the controls.

"Not the slightest; it is calculated to a nicety. We could, if we wished, stop just short of the exact time and would see the reoccurrence of their capture. But only as unseen observers—you can not enter the plane as a material being during your own actual past, for your entity would then be duplicated. Of course, I can not enter in any case. But, moving on to the instant *after* the event, as we shall do, you may enter either plane as a material being or move between the two planes at will by means of the gateway provided by Tom Parker's force area. Do you not now understand the manner in which you will be enabled to carry out the required procedure?"

"H-hm!" Bert wasn't sure at all. "But this moving through time," he asked helplessly, "and the change from one plane of oscillation to another—they're all mixed up—what have they to do with each other?"

"All five dimensions of our universe are definitely interrelated and dependent one upon the other for the existence of matter in any form whatsoever. You see —but here we are."

THE MOTORS slowed down and a titanic page seemed to turn over in the cosmos with a vanishing blaze of magnificence. Directly beneath them glowed the disk of blue-white light that was Tom's force area. The sphere swooped down within its influence and came to rest.

"Make haste," the Wanderer said. "I shall be here in the gateway though you see me not. Bring them here, speedily."

On the one side Bert saw familiar objects in Tom's laboratory, on the other side the white cliff and the pitchy sea of the Bardek realm. And the cage of basket-weave between, with his friends inside struggling with the spider men. It was the instant after the capture.

"Joan! Tom!" Bert shouted.

A side of the sphere had opened and he plunged through and into the Bardek plane—to the inky surface of the sea, fully expecting to sink in its forbidding depths. But the stuff was an elastic solid, springy under his feet and bearing him up as would an air-inflated cushion. He threw himself upon the cage and tore it with his fingers.

The whimpering screams of the spider men were in his ears, and he saw from the corner of his eye that other of the tortoiselike mounds were rising up out of the viscid black depths, dozens of them, and that hundreds of the Bardeks were closing in on him from all directions. Weapons were in their hands, and a huge engine of warfare like a caterpillar tractor was skimming over the sea from the cliff wall with a great grinding and clanking of its mechanisms.

But the cage was pulling apart in his clutches as if made of reeds. With Joan in one encircling arm he was battling the spider men, driving swift short-arm jabs into their soft bloated bodies with devastating effect. And Tom, recovering from the first surprise of his capture, was doing a good job himself, his flailing arms scattering the Bardeks like ninepins. The Wanderer and his sphere, both doomed to material existence only in infra-dimensional space, had vanished from sight.

A bedlam rose up from the reinforcing hordes as they came in to enter the force area. But Bert sensed the guiding touch of the Wanderer's unseen hand, heard his placid voice urging him, and, in a single wild leap was inside the sphere with the girl.

With Joan safely in the Wanderer's care, he rushed out again for Tom. Then followed a nightmare of battling those twining tentacles and the puffy crowding bodies of the spider men. Wrestling tactics and swinging fists were all that the two Earthlings had to rely upon, but, between them, they managed to fight off a half score of the Bardeks and work their way back into the glowing force area.

"It's no use," Tom gasped. "We can't get back."

"Sure we can. We've a friend—here—in the force area."

Tom Parker staggered: his strength was giving out. "No, no, Bert," he moaned. "I can't. You go on. Leave me here."

"Not on your life!" Bert swung him up bodily into the sphere as he contacted with the invisible metal of its hull. Kicking off the nearest of the spider men, he clambered in after the scientist.

THE TABLEAU then presented in the sphere's interior was to remain forever imprinted on Bert's memory, though it was only a momentary flash in his consciousness at the time: the Wanderer, calm and erect at the control panel, his benign countenance alight with satisfaction; Tom Parker, pulling himself to his feet, clutching at the big man's free arm, his mouth opened in astonishment; Joan, seated at the Wanderer's feet with awed and reverent eyes upturned.

There is no passing directly between the planes. One must have the force area as a gateway, and, besides, a medium such as the cage of the Bardeks, the orange light of the metal monsters, or the sphere of the Wanderer. Bert knew this instinctively as the sphere darkened and the flashing light-forms leaped across the blackness.

The motors screamed in rising crescendo as their speed increased. Then, abruptly, the sound broke off into deathly silence as the limit of audibility was passed. Against the brilliant background of swift color changes and geometric light-shapes that so quickly merged into the familiar blur, Bert saw his companions as dim wraithlike forms. He moved toward Joan, groping.

Then came the tremendous thump, the swinging of a colossal page across the void, the warping of the very universe about them, the physical torture and the swift rush through Stygian inkiness. . . .

"Farewell." A single word, whispered like a benediction in the Wanderer's mellow voice, was in Bert's consciousness. He knew that their benefactor had slipped away into the mysterious regions of intra-dimensional space.

RAISING HIMSELF slowly and dazedly from where he had been flung, he saw they were in Tom's laboratory. Joan lay over there white and still, a pitiful crumpled heap. Panicky, Bert crossed to her. His trembling fingers found her pulse; a sobbing breath of relief escaped his lips. She had merely swooned.

Tom Parker, exhausted from his efforts in that other plane and with the very foundations of his being wrenched by the passage through the fifth dimension, was unable to rise. Only semiconscious, his eyes were glazed with pain, and incoherent moaning sounds came from his white lips when he attempted to speak.

Bert's mind was clearing rapidly. That diabolical machine of Tom's was still operating, the drone of its motors being the only sound in the laboratory as the inventor closed his mouth grimly and made a desperate effort to raise his head. But Bert had seen shapes materializing on the lighted disk that was the gateway between planes and he rushed to the controls of the instrument. That starting lever must be shifted without delay.

"Don't!" Tom Parker had found his voice; his frantic warning was a hoarse whistling gasp. He had struggled to his knees. "It will kill you, Bert. Those things in the force area—partly through—the reaction will destroy the machine and all of us if you turn it off. Don't, I say!"

"What then?" Bert fell back appalled. Hazily, the steel prow of a war machine was forming itself on the metal disk; caterpillar treads moved like ghostly shadows beneath. It was the vanguard of the Bardek hordes!

"Can't do it that way!" Tom had gotten to his feet and was stumbling toward the force area. "Only one way—during the change of oscillation periods. Must mingle other atoms with those before they stabilize in our plane. Must localize annihilating force. Must—"

What was the fool doing? He'd be in the force area in another moment. Bert thrust forward to intercept him; saw that Joan had regained consciousness and was sitting erect, swaying weakly. Her eyes widened with horror as they took in the scene and she screamed once despairingly and was on her feet, tottering.

"Back!" Tom Parker yelled, wheeling. "Save yourselves."

BERT LUNGED toward him but was too late. Tom had already burst into the force area and cast himself upon the semitransparent tank of the spider men. A blast of searing heat radiated from the disk and the motors of Tom's machine groaned as they slowed down under a tremendous overload.

Joan cried out in awful despair and moved to follow, but her knees gave way beneath her. Moaning and shuddering, she slumped into Bert's arms, and he drew her back from the awful heat of the force area.

Then horrified, they watched as Tom Parker melted into the misty shape of the Bardek war machine. Swiftly his body merged with the half-substance of the tank and became an integral part of the mass. For a horrible instant Tom, too, was transparent—a ghost shape writhing in a ghostly throbbing mechanism of another world. His own atomic structure mingled with that of the alien thing and yet, for a moment, he retained his Earthly form. His lean face was peaceful in death, satisfied, like the Wanderer's when they had last seen him.

A terrific thunderclap rent the air and a column of flame roared up from the force area. Tom's apparatus glowed to instant white heat, then melted down into sizzling liquid metal and glass. The laboratory was in sudden twilight gloom, save for the tongue of fire that licked up from the force area to the paneled ceiling. On the metal disk, now glowing redly, was no visible thing. The gateway was closed forever.

WHAT MORE fearful calamity might have befallen had the machine been switched off instead, Bert was never to know. Nor did he know how he reached his parked flivver with Joan a limp sobbing bundle in his arms. He only knew that Tom Parker's sacrifice had saved them, had undoubtedly prevented a horrible invasion of Earth; and that the efforts of the Wanderer had not been in vain.

The old house was burning furiously when he climbed in under the wheel of his car. He held Joan very close and watched that blazing funeral pyre in wordless sorrow as the bereaved girl dropped her head to his shoulder.

A group of men came up the winding road, a straggling group, running—the loungers from the village. In the forefront was the beardless youth who had directed Bert, and, bringing up the rear, limping and scurrying, was the old man they had called Gramp. He was puffing prodigiously when the others gathered around the car, demanding information.

And the old fellow with the thick spectacles talked them all down.

"What'd I tell you?" he screeched. "Didn't I say they was queer doin's up here? Didn't I say the devil was here with his imps—an' the thunder? You're a passel o' idjits like I said—"

The roar of Bert's starting motor drowned out the rest, but the old fellow was still gesticulating and dancing about when they clattered off down the winding road to Lenville.

AN HOUR later Joan had fallen asleep, exhausted. Night had fallen and, as mile after mile of smooth concrete unrolled beneath the flivver's wheels, Bert gave himself over to thoughts he had not dared to entertain in nearly two years. They'd be happy, he and Joan, and there'd be no further argument. If she still objected to living on the fruit farm, that could be managed easily. They'd live in Indianapolis and he'd buy a new car, a good one, to run back and forth. If, when her grief for Tom had lessened, she wanted to go on with laboratory work and such—well, that was easy, too. Only there would be no fooling around with this dimensional stuff—she'd had enough of that, he knew.

He drew her close with his free arm and his thoughts shifted far out in infra-dimension space to dwell upon the man of the past who had called himself the Wanderer of Infinity. He who would go on and on until the end of time, until the end of all things, watching over the many worlds and planes. Warning peoples of human-like mold and emotions wherever they might dwell. Helping them. Atoning throughout infinity. Suffering.

Parasite Planet

By STANLEY G. WEINBAUM

Two humans beat their way through the peculiar—and perilous—Venusian jungle. A masterpiece of fantasy.
Illustrated by Elliot Dold

He shifted the girl to his left arm, then fired into the leaping horrors above.

LUCKILY FOR "Ham" Hammond it was mid-winter when the mud-spout came. Mid-winter, that is, in the Venusian sense, which is nothing at all like the conception of the season generally entertained on Earth, except possibly, by dwellers in the hotter regions of the Amazon basin, or the Congo.

They, perhaps, might form a vague mental picture of winter on Venus by visualizing their hottest summer days, multiplying the heat, discomfort and unpleasant denizens of the jungle by ten or twelve.

On Venus, as is now well known, the seasons occur alternately in opposite hemispheres, as on the Earth, but with a very important difference. Here, when North America and Europe swelter in summer, it is winter in Australia and Cape Colony and Argentina. It is the northern and southern hemispheres which alternate their seasons.

But on Venus, very strangely, it is the eastern and western hemispheres, because the seasons of Venus depend, not on inclination to the plane of the ecliptic, but on libration. Venus does not rotate, but keeps the same face always toward the Sun, just as the Moon does toward the earth. One face is forever daylight, and the other forever night, and only along the twilight zone, a strip five hundred miles wide, is human habitation possible, a thin ring of territory circling the planet.

Toward the sunlit side it verges into the blasting heat of a desert where only a few Venusian creatures live, and on the night edge the strip ends abruptly in the colossal ice barrier produced by the condensation of the upper winds that sweep endlessly from the rising air of the hot hemisphere to cool and sink and rush back again from the cold one.

The chilling of warm air always produces rain, and at the edge of the darkness the rain freezes to form these great ramparts. What lies beyond, what fantastic forms of life may live in the starless darkness of the frozen face, or whether that region is as dead as the airless Moon—those are mysteries.

But the slow libration, a ponderous wabbling of the planet from side to side, does produce the effect of seasons. On the lands of the twilight zone, first in one hemisphere and then the other, the cloud-hidden Sun seems to rise gradually for fifteen days, then sink for the same period. It never ascends far, and only near the ice barrier does it seem to touch the horizon; for the libration is only seven degrees, but it is sufficient to produce noticeable fifteen-day seasons.

But such seasons! In the winter the temperature drops sometimes to a humid but bearable ninety, but, two weeks later, a hundred and forty is a cool day near the torrid edge of the zone. And always, winter and summer, the intermittent rains drip sullenly down to be absorbed by the spongy soil and given back again as sticky, unpleasant, unhealthy steam.

And that, the vast amount of moisture on Venus, was the greatest surprise of the first human visitors; the clouds had been seen, of course, but the spectroscope denied the presence of water, naturally, since it was analyzing light reflected from the upper cloud surfaces, fifty miles above the planet's face.

That abundance of water has strange consequences. There are no seas or oceans on Venus, if we except the probability of vast, silent, and eternally frozen oceans on the sunless side. On the hot hemisphere evaporation is too rapid, and the rivers that flow out of the ice mountains simply diminish and finally vanish, dried up.

A further consequence is the curiously unstable nature of the land of the twilight zone. Enormous subterranean rivers course invisibly through it, some boiling, some cold as the ice from which they flow. These are the cause of the mud eruptions that make human habitation in the Hotlands such a gamble; a perfectly solid and apparently safe area of soil may be changed suddenly into a boiling sea of mud in which buildings sink and vanish, together, frequently, with their occupants.

There is no way of predicting these catastrophes; only on the rare outcroppings of bed rock is a structure safe, and so all permanent human settlements cluster about the mountains.

SAM HAMMOND was a trader. He was one of those adventurous individuals who always appear on the frontiers and fringes of habitable regions. Most of these fall into two classes; they are either reckless daredevils pursuing danger, or outcasts, criminal or otherwise, pursuing either solitude or forgetfulness.

Ham Hammond was neither. He was pursuing no such abstractions, but the good, solid lure of wealth. He was, in fact, trading with the natives for the sporepods of the Venusian plant *xixtchil*, from which terrestrial chemists would extract trihydroxyl-tertiary-tolunitrile-beta-anthraquinone, the xixtline or triple-T-B-A that was so effective in rejuvenation treatments.

Ham was young and sometimes wondered why rich old men—and women—would pay such tremendous prices for a few more years of virility, especially as the treatments didn't actually increase the span of life, but just produced a sort of temporary and synthetic youth.

Gray hair darkened, wrinkles filled out, bald heads grew fuzzy, and then, in a few years, the rejuvenated person was just as dead as he would have been, anyway. But as long as triple-T-B-A commanded a price about equal to its weight in radium, why, Ham was willing to take the gamble to obtain it.

He had never really expected the mudspout. Of course it was an ever-present danger, but when, staring idly through the window of his shack over the writhing and steaming Venusian plain, he had seen the sudden boiling pools erupting all around, it had come as a shocking surprise.

For a moment he was paralyzed; then he sprang into immediate and frantic action. He pulled on his enveloping suit of rubberlike transkin; he strapped the great bowls of mudshoes to his feet; he tied the precious bag of spore-pods to his shoulders, packed some food, and then burst into the open.

The ground was still semisolid, but even as he watched, the black soil boiled out around the metal walls of the shack, the cube tilted a trifle, and then sank deliberately from sight, and the mud sucked and gurgled as it closed gently above the spot.

Ham caught himself. One couldn't stand still in the midst of a mudspout, even with the bowllike mudshoes as support. Once let the viscous stuff flow over the rim and the luckless victim was trapped; he couldn't raise his foot against the suction, and first slowly, then more quickly, he'd follow the shack.

So Ham started off over the boiling swamp, walking with the peculiar sliding motion he had learned by much practice, never raising the mudshoes above the surface, but sliding them along, careful that no mud topped the curving rim.

It was a tiresome motion, but absolutely necessary. He slid along as if on snowshoes, bearing west because that was the direction of the dark side, and if he had to walk to safety, he might as well do it in coolness. The area of swamp was unusually large; he covered at least a mile before he attained a slight rise in the ground, and the mudshoes clumped on solid, or nearly solid, soil.

He was bathed in perspiration; and his transkin suit was hot as a boiler room, but one grows accustomed to that on Venus. He'd have given half his supply of xixtchil pods for the opportunity to open the mask of the suit, to draw a breath of even the steamy and humid Venusian air, but that was impossible; impossible, at least, if he had any inclination to continue living.

One breath of unfiltered air anywhere near the warm edge of the twilight zone was quick and very painful death; Ham would have drawn in uncounted millions of the spores of those fierce Venusian molds, and they'd have sprouted in furry and nauseating masses in his nostrils, his mouth, his lungs, and eventually in his ears and eyes.

Breathing them wasn't even a necessary requirement; once he'd come upon a trader's body with the molds springing from his flesh. The poor fellow had somehow torn a rip in his transkin suit, and that was enough.

The situation made eating and drinking in the open a problem on Venus; one had to wait until a rain had precipitated the spores, when it was safe for half an hour or so. Even then the water must have been recently boiled and the food just removed from its can; otherwise, as had happened to Ham more than once, the food was apt to turn abruptly into a fuzzy mass of molds that grew about as fast as the minute hand moved on a clock. A disgusting sight! A disgusting planet!

T HAT LAST reflection was induced by Ham's view of the quagmire that had engulfed his shack. The heavier vegetation had gone with it, but already avid and greedy life was emerging, wriggling mud grass and the bulbous fungi called "walking balls." And all around a million little slimy creatures slithered across the mud, eating each other rapaciously, being torn to bits, and each fragment re-forming to a complete creature.

A thousand different species, but all the same in one respect; each of them was all appetite. In common with most Venusian beings, they had a multiplicity of both legs and mouths; in fact some of them were little more than blobs of skin split into dozens of hungry mouths, and crawling on a hundred spidery legs.

All life on Venus is more or less parasitic. Even the plants that draw their nourishment directly from soil and air have also the ability to absorb and digest—and, often enough, to trap—animal food. So fierce is the competition on that humid strip of land between the fire and the ice that one who has never seen it must fail even to imagine it.

The animal kingdom wars incessantly on itself and the plant world; the vegetable kingdom retaliates, and frequently outdoes the other in the production of monstrous predatory horrors that one would even hesitate to call plant life. A terrible world!

In the few moments that Ham had paused to look back, ropy creepers had already entangled his legs; transkin was impervious, of course, but he had to cut the things away with his knife, and the black, nauseating juices that flowed out of them smeared on his suit and began instantly to grow furry as the molds sprouted. He shuddered.

"Hell of a place!" Ham growled, stooping to remove his mudshoes, which he slung carefully over his back.

He slogged away through the writhing vegetation, automatically dodging the awkward thrusts of the Jack Ketch trees as they cast their nooses hopefully toward his arms and head.

Now and again he passed one that dangled some trapped creature, usually unrecognizable because the molds had enveloped it in a fuzzy shroud, while the tree itself was placidly absorbing victim and molds alike.

"Horrible place!" Ham muttered, kicked a writhing mass of nameless little vermin from his path.

He mused; his shack had been situated rather nearer the hot edge of the twilight zone; it was a trifle over two hundred and fifty miles to the shadow line, though of course that varied with the libration. But one couldn't approach the line too closely, anyway, because of the fierce, almost inconceivable, storms that raged where the hot upper winds encountered the icy blasts of the night side, giving rise to the birth throes of the ice barrier.

So a hundred and fifty miles due west would be sufficient to bring coolness, to enter a region too temperate for the molds, where he could walk in comparative comfort. And then, not more than fifty miles north, lay the American settlement Erotia, named, obviously, after that troublesome mythical son of Venus, Cupid.

Intervening, of course, were the ranges of the Mountains of Eternity, not those mighty twenty-mile-high peaks whose summits are occasionally glimpsed by Earthly telescopes, and that forever sunder British Venus from the American possessions, but, even at the point he planned to cross, very respectable mountains indeed. He was on the British side now; not that any one cared. Traders came and went as they pleased.

Well, that meant about two hundred miles. No reason why he couldn't make it; he was armed with both automatic and flame-pistol, and water was no problem, if carefully boiled. Under pressure of necessity, one could even eat Venusian life—but it required hunger and thorough cooking and a sturdy stomach.

It wasn't the taste so much as the appearance, or so he'd been told. He grimaced; beyond doubt he'd be driven to find out for himself, since his canned food couldn't possibly last out the trip. Nothing to worry about, Ham kept telling himself. In fact, plenty to be glad about; the xixtchil pods in his pack represented as much wealth as he could have accumulated by ten years of toil back on Earth.

No danger—and yet, men had vanished on Venus, dozens of them. The molds had claimed them, or some fierce unearthly monster, or perhaps one of the many unknown living horrors, both plant and animal.

Ham trudged along, keeping always to the clearings about the Jack Ketch trees, since these vegetable omnivores kept other life beyond the reach of their greedy nooses. Elsewhere progress was impossible, for the Venusian jungle presented such a terrific tangle of writhing and struggling forms that one could move only by cutting the way, step by step, with infinite labor.

Even then there was the danger of Heaven only knew what fanged and venomous creatures whose teeth might pierce the protective membrane of·transskin, and a crack in that meant death. Even the unpleasant Jack Ketch trees were preferable company, he reflected, as he slapped their questing lariats aside.

Six hours after Ham had started his involuntary journey, it rained. He seized the opportunity, found a place where a recent mudspout had cleared the heavier vegetation away, and prepared to eat. First, however, he scooped up some scummy water, filtered it through the screen attached for that purpose to his canteen, and set about sterilizing it.

Fire was difficult to manage, since dry fuel is rare indeed in the Hotlands of Venus, but Ham tossed a thermide tablet into the liquid, and the chemicals boiled the water instantly, escaping themselves as gases. If the water retained a slight ammoniacal taste —well, that was the least of his discomforts, he mused, as he covered it and set it by to cool.

He uncapped a can of beans, watched a moment to see that no stray molds had remained in the air to infect the food, then opened the visor of his suit and swallowed hastily. Thereafter he drank the blood-warm water and poured carefully what remained into the water pouch within his transkin, where he could suck it through a tube to his mouth without the deadly exposure to the molds.

Ten minutes after he had completed the meal, while he rested and longed for the impossible luxury of a cigarette, the fuzzy coat sprang suddenly to life on the remnants of food in the can.

II.

AN HOUR later, weary and thoroughly soaked in perspiration, Ham found a Friendly tree, so named by the explorer Burlingame because it is one of the few organisms on Venus sluggish enough to permit one to rest in its branches. So Ham climbed it, found the most comfortable position available, and slept as best he could.

It was five hours by his wrist watch before he awoke, and the tendrils and little sucking cups of the Friendly tree were fastened all over his transkin. He tore them away very carefully, climbed down, and trudged westward.

It was after the second rain that he met the dough-

pot, as the creature is called in British and American Venus. In the French strip, it's the *pot à colle*, the "paste pot"; in the Dutch—well, the Dutch are not prudish, and they call the horror just what they think it warrants.

Actually, the doughpot is a nauseous creature. It's a mass of white, dough-like protoplasm, ranging in size from a single cell to perhaps twenty tons of mushy filth. It has no fixed form; in fact, it's merely a mass of de Proust cells—in effect, a disembodied, crawling, hungry cancer.

It has no organization and no intelligence, nor even any instinct save hunger. It moves in whatever direction food touches its surfaces; when it touches two edible substances, it quietly divides, with the larger portion invariably attacking the greater supply.

It's invulnerable to bullets; nothing less than the terrific blast of a flame-pistol will kill it, and then only if the blast destroys every individual cell. It travels over the ground absorbing everything, leaving bare black soil where the ubiquitous molds spring up at once—a noisome, nightmarish creature.

Ham sprang aside as the doughpot erupted suddenly from the jungle to his right. It couldn't absorb the transkin, of course, but to be caught in that pasty mess meant quick suffocation. He glared at it disgustedly and was sorely tempted to blast it with his flame-pistol as it slithered past at running speed. He would have, too, but the experienced Venusian frontiersman is very careful with the flame-pistol.

It has to be charged with a diamond, a cheap black one, of course, but still an item to consider. The crystal, when fired, gives up all its energy in one terrific blast that roars out like a lightning stroke for a hundred yards, incinerating everything in its path.

The thing rolled by with a sucking and gulping sound. Behind it opened the passage it had cleared; creepers, snake vines, Jack Ketch trees—everything had been swept away down to the humid earth itself, where already the molds were springing up on the slime of the doughpot's trail.

The alley led nearly in the direction Ham wanted to travel; he seized the opportunity and strode briskly along, with a wary eye, nevertheless, on the ominous walls of jungle. In ten hours or so the opening would be filled once more with unpleasant life, but for the present it offered a much quicker progress than dodging from one clearing to the next.

It was five miles up the trail, which was already beginning to sprout inconveniently, that he met the native galloping along on his four short legs, his pincerlike hands shearing a path for him. Ham stopped for a palaver.

"*Murra*," he said.

The language of the natives of the equatorial regions

of the Hotlands is a queer one. It has, perhaps, two hundred words, but when a trader has learned those two hundred, his knowledge of the tongue is but little greater than the man who knows none at all.

The words are generalized, and each sound has anywhere from a dozen to a hundred meanings. *Murra,* for instance, is a word of greeting; it may mean something much like "hello," or "good morning." It also may convey a challenge—"on guard!" It means besides, "Let's be friends," and also, strangely, "Let's fight this out."

It has, morever, certain noun senses; it means peace, it means war, it means courage, and, again, fear. A subtle language; it is only recently that studies of inflection have begun to reveal its nature to human philologists. Yet, after all, perhaps English, with its "to," "too," and "two," its "one," "won," "wan," "wen," "win," "when," and a dozen other similarities, might seem just as strange to Venusian ears, untrained in vowel distinctions.

Moreover, humans can't read the expressions of the broad, flat, three-eyed Venusian faces, which in the nature of things must convey a world of information among the natives themselves.

But this one accepted the intended sense. "*Murra,*" he responded, pausing. "*Usk?*" That was, among other things, "Who are you?" or "Where did you come from?" or "Where are you bound?"

Ham chose the latter sense. He pointed off into the dim west, then raised his hand in an arc to indicate the mountains. "Erotia," he said. That had but one meaning, at least.

The native considered this in silence. At last he grunted and volunteered some information. He swept his cutting claw in a gesture west along the trail. "*Curky,*" he said, and then, "*Murra.*" The last was farewell; Ham pressed against the wriggling jungle wall to permit him to pass.

Curky meant, together with twenty other senses, trader. It was the word usually applied to humans, and Ham felt a pleasant anticipation in the prospect of human company. It had been six months since he had heard a human voice other than that on the tiny radio now sunk with his shack.

T RUE ENOUGH, five miles along the doughpot's trail Ham emerged suddenly in an area where there had been a recent mudspout. The vegetation was only waist-high, and across the quarter-mile clearing he saw a structure, a trading hut. But far more pretentious than his own iron-walled cubicle; this one boasted three rooms, an unheard-of luxury in the Hotlands, where every ounce had to be laboriously transported by rocket from one of the settlements. That was

expensive, almost prohibitive. Traders took a real gamble, and Ham knew he was lucky to have come out so profitably.

He strode over the still spongy ground. The windows were shaded against the eternal daylight, and the door—the door was locked. This was a violation of the frontier code. One always left doors unlocked; it might mean the salvation of some strayed trader, and not even the most dishonorable would steal from a hut left open for his safety.

Nor would the natives; no creature is as honest as a Venusian native, who never lies and never steals, though he might, after due warning, kill a trader for his trade goods. But only after a fair warning.

Ham stood puzzled. At last he kicked and tramped a clear space before the door, sat down against it, and fell to snapping away the numerous and loathsome little creatures that swarmed over his transkin. He waited.

It wasn't half an hour before he saw the trader plowing through the clearing—a short, slim fellow; the transkin shaded his face, but Ham could make out large, shadowed eyes. He stood up.

"Hello!" he said jovially. "Thought I'd drop in for a visit. My name's Hamilton Hammond—you guess the nickname!"

The newcomer stopped short, then spoke in a curiously soft and husky voice, with a decidedly English accent. "My guess would be 'Boiled Pork,' I fancy." The tones were cold, unfriendly. "Suppose you step aside and let me in. Good day!"

Ham felt anger and amazement. "The devil!" he snapped. "You're a hospitable sort, aren't you?"

"No. Not at all." The other paused at the door. "You're an American. What are you doing on British soil? Have you a passport?"

"Since when do you need a passport in the Hotlands?"

"Trading, aren't you?" the slim man said sharply. "In other words, poaching. You've no rights here. Get on."

Ham's jaw set stubbornly behind his mask. "Rights or none," he said, "I'm entitled to the consideration of the frontier code. I want a breath of air and a chance to wipe my face, and also a chance to eat. If you open that door I'm coming in after you."

An automatic flashed into view. "Do, and you'll feed the molds."

Ham, like all Venusian traders, was of necessity bold, resourceful, and what is called in the States "hard-boiled." He didn't flinch, but said in apparent yielding:

"All right; but listen, all I want is a chance to eat."

"Wait for a rain," said the other coolly and half turned to unlock the door.

As his eyes shifted, Ham kicked at the revolver; it

went spinning against the wall and dropped into the weeds. His opponent snatched for the flame-pistol that still dangled on his hip; Ham caught his wrist in a mighty clutch.

Instantly the other ceased to struggle, while Ham felt a momentary surprise at the skinny feel of the wrist through its transkin covering.

"Look here!" he growled. "I want a chance to eat, and I'm going to get it. Unlock that door!"

He had both wrists now; the fellow seemed curiously delicate. After a moment he nodded, and Ham released one hand. The door opened, and he followed the other in.

AGAIN, UNHEARD-OF magnificence. Solid chairs, a sturdy table, even books, carefully preserved, no doubt, by lycopodium against the ravenous molds that sometimes entered Hotland shacks in spite of screen filters and automatic spray. An automatic spray was going now to destroy any spores that might have entered with the opening door.

Ham sat down, keeping an eye on the other, whose flame-pistol he had permitted to remain in its holster. He was confident of his ability to outdraw the slim individual, and, besides, who'd risk firing a flame-pistol indoors? It would simply blow out one wall of the building.

So he set about opening his mask, removing food from his pack, wiping his steaming face, while his companion—or opponent—looked on silently. Ham watched the canned meat for a moment; no molds appeared, and he ate.

"Why the devil," he rasped, "don't you open your visor?" At the other's silence, he continued: "Afraid I'll see your face, eh? Well, I'm not interested; I'm no cop."

No reply.

He tried again. "What's your name?"

The cool voice sounded: "Burlingame. Pat Burlingame."

Ham laughed. "Patrick Burlingame is dead, my friend. I knew him." No answer. "And if you don't want to tell your name, at least you needn't insult the memory of a brave man and a great explorer."

"Thank you." The voice was sardonic. "He was my father."

"Another lie. He had no son. He had only a——" Ham paused abruptly; a feeling of consternation swept over him. "Open your visor!" he yelled.

He saw the lips of the other, dim through the transkin, twitch into a sarcastic smile.

"Why not?" said the soft voice, and the mask dropped.

Ham gulped; behind the covering were the delicately modeled features of a girl, with cool gray eyes in a face lovely despite the glistening perspiration on cheeks and forehead.

The man gulped again. After all, he was a gentleman despite his profession as one of the fierce, adventurous traders of Venus. He was university-educated—an engineer—and only the lure of quick wealth had brought him to the Hotlands.

"I—I'm sorry," he stammered.

"You brave American poachers!" she sneered. "Are all of you so valiant as to force yourselves on women?"

"But—how could I know? What are you doing in a place like this?"

"There's no reason for me to answer your questions, but"—she gestured toward the room beyond—"I'm classifying Hotland flora and fauna. I'm Patricia Burlingame, biologist."

He perceived now the jar-enclosed specimens of a laboratory in the next chamber. "But a girl alone in the Hotlands! It's—it's reckless!"

"I didn't expect to meet any American poachers," she retorted.

He flushed. "You needn't worry about me. I'm going." He raised his hands to his visor.

Instantly Patricia snatched an automatic from the table drawer. "You're going, indeed, Mr. Hamilton Hammond," she said coolly. "But you're leaving your xixtchil with me. It's crown property; you've stolen it from British territory, and I'm confiscating it."

He stared. "Look here!" he blazed suddenly. "I've risked all I have for that xixtchil. If I lose it I'm ruined—busted. I'm not giving it up!"

"But you are."

He dropped his mask and sat down. "Miss Burlingame," he said, "I don't think you've nerve enough to shoot me, but that's what you'll have to do to get it. Otherwise I'll sit here until you drop of exhaustion."

Her gray eyes bored silently into his blue ones. The gun held steadily on his heart, but spat no bullet. It was a deadlock.

At last the girl said, "You win, poacher." She slapped the gun into her empty holster. "Get out, then."

"Gladly!" he snapped.

He rose, fingered his visor, then dropped it again at a sudden startled scream from the girl. He whirled, suspecting a trick, but she was staring out of the window with wide, apprehensive eyes.

HAM SAW the writhing of vegetation and then a vast whitish mass. A doughpot—a monstrous one, bearing steadily toward their shelter. He heard the gentle *clunk* of impact, and then the window was blotted out by the pasty mess, as the creature, not quite large enough to engulf the building, split into two masses that flowed around and merged on the other side.

Another cry from Patricia. "Your mask, fool!" she rasped. "Close it!"

"Mask? Why?" Nevertheless, he obeyed automatically.

"Why? That's why! The digestive acids—look!"

She pointed at the walls; indeed, thousands of tiny pinholes of light were appearing. The digestive acids of the monstrosity, powerful enough to attack whatever food chance brought, had corroded the metal; it was porous; the shack was ruined. He gasped as fuzzy molds shot instantly from the remains of his meal, and a red-and-green fur sprouted from the wood of chairs and table.

The two faced each other.

Ham chuckled. "Well," he said, "you're homeless, too. Mine went down in a mudspout."

"Yours would!" Patricia retorted acidly. "You Yankees couldn't think of finding shallow soil, I suppose. Bed rock is just six feet below here, and *my* place is on pilons."

"Well, you're a cool devil! Anyway, your place might as well be sunk. What are you going to do?"

"Do? Don't concern yourself. I'm quite able to manage."

"How?"

"It's no affair of yours, but I have a rocket call each month."

"You must be a millionaire, then," he commented.

"The Royal Society," she said coldly, "is financing this expedition. The rocket is due——"

She paused; Ham thought she paled a little behind her mask.

"Due when?"

"Why—it just came two days ago. I'd forgotten."

"I see. And you think you'll just stick around for a month waiting for it. Is that it?"

Patricia stared at him defiantly.

"Do you know," he resumed, "what you'd be in a month? It's ten days to summer and look at your shack." He gestured at the walls, where brown and rusty patches were forming; at his motion a piece the size of a saucer tumbled in with a crackle. "In two days this thing will be a caved-in ruin. What'll you do during fifteen days of summer? What'll you do without shelter when the temperature reaches a hundred and fifty—a hundred and sixty? I'll tell you—you'll die."

She said nothing.

"You'll be a fuzzy mass of molds before the rocket returns," Ham said. "And then a pile of clean bones that will go down with the first mudspout."

"Be still!" she blazed.

"Silence won't help. Now I'll tell you what you can do. You can take your pack and your mudshoes and walk along with me. We may make the Cool Country before summer—if you can walk as well as you talk."

"Go with a Yankee poacher? I fancy not!"

"And then," he continued imperturbably, "we can cross comfortably to Erotia, a good American town."

Patricia reached for her emergency pack, slung it over her shoulders. She retrieved a thick bundle of notes, written in aniline ink on transkin, brushed off a few vagrant molds, and slipped it into the pack. She picked up a pair of diminutive mudshoes and turned deliberately to the door.

"So you're coming?" he chuckled.

"I'm going," she retorted coldly, "to the good British town of Venoble. Alone!"

"Venoble!" he gasped. "That's two hundred miles south! And across the Greater Eternities, too!"

III.

PATRICIA WALKED silently out of the door and turned west toward the Cool Country. Ham hesitated a moment, then followed. He couldn't permit the girl to attempt that journey alone; since she ignored his presence, he simply trailed a few steps behind her, plodding grimly and angrily along.

For three hours or more they trudged through the endless daylight, dodging the thrusts of the Jack Ketch trees, but mostly following the still fairly open trail of the first doughpot.

Ham was amazed at the agile and lithe grace of the girl, who slipped along the way with the sure skill of a native. Then a memory came to him; she *was* a native, in a sense. He recalled now that Patrick Burlingame's daughter was the first human child born on Venus, in the colony of Venoble, founded by her father.

Ham remembered the newspaper articles when she had been sent to Earth to be educated, a child of eight; he had been thirteen then. He was twenty-seven now, which made Patricia Burlingame twenty-two.

Not a word passed between them until at last the girl swung about in exasperation.

"Go away" she blazed.

Ham halted. "I'm not bothering you."

"But I don't want a bodyguard. I'm a better Hotlander than you!"

He didn't argue the point. He kept silent, and after a moment she flashed:

"I hate you, Yankee! Lord, how I hate you!" She turned and trudged on.

An hour later the mudspout caught them. Without warning, watery muck boiled up around their feet, and the vegetation swayed wildly. Hastily, they strapped on their mudshoes, while the heavier plants sank with sullen gurgles around them. Again Ham marveled at the girl's skill; Patricia slipped away across the unstable surface with a speed he could not match, and he shuffled far behind.

Suddenly he saw her stop. That was dangerous in a mudspout; only an emergency could explain it. He hurried; a hundred feet away he perceived the reason. A strap had broken on her right shoe, and she stood helpless, balancing on her left foot, while the remaining bowl was sinking slowly. Even now black mud slopped over the edge.

She eyed him as he approached. He shuffled to her side; as she saw his intention, she spoke.

"You can't," she said.

Ham bent cautiously, slipping his arms about her knees and shoulders. Her mudshoes was already embedded, but he heaved mightily, driving the rims of his own dangerously close to the surface. With a great sucking gulp, she came free and lay very still in his arms, so as not to unbalance him as he slid again into careful motion over the treacherous surface. She was not heavy, but it was a hairbreadth chance, and the mud slipped and gurgled at the very edge of his shoe-bowls. Even though Venus has slightly less surface gravitation than Earth, a week or so gets one accustomed to it, and the twenty per cent advantage in weight seems to disappear.

A hundred yards brought firm footing. He sat her down and unstrapped her mudshoes.

"Thank you," she said coolly. "That was brave."

"You're welcome," he returned dryly. "I suppose this will end any idea of your traveling alone. Without both mudshoes, the next spout will be the last for you. Do we walk together now?"

Her voice chilled. "I can make a substitute shoe from tree skin."

"Not even a native could walk on tree skin."

"Then," she said, "I'll simply wait a day or two for the mud to dry and dig up my lost one."

He laughed and gestured at the acres of mud. "Dig where?" he countered. "You'll be here till summer if you try that."

She yielded. "You win again, Yankee. But only to the Cool Country; then you'll go north and I south."

THEY TRUDGED on. Patricia was as tireless as Ham himself and was vastly more adept in Hotland lore. Though they spoke but little, he never ceased to wonder at the skill she had in picking the quickest route, and she seemed to sense the thrusts of the Jack Ketch trees without looking. But it was when they halted at last, after a rain had given opportunity for a hasty meal, that he had real cause to thank her.

"Sleep?" he suggested, and as she nodded: "There's a Friendly tree."

He moved toward it, the girl behind.

Suddenly she seized his arm. "It's a Pharisee!" she cried, jerking him back.

None too soon! The false Friendly tree had lashed down with a terrible stroke that missed his face by inches. It was no Friendly tree at all, but an imitator, luring prey within reach by its apparent harmlessness, then striking with knife-sharp spikes.

Ham gasped. "What is it? I never saw one of those before."

"A Pharisee! It just looks like a Friendly tree."

She took out her automatic and sent a bullet into the black, pulsing trunk. A dark stream gushed, and the ubiquitous molds sprang into life about the hole. The tree was doomed.

"Thanks," said Ham awkwardly. "I guess you saved my life."

"We're quits now." She gazed levelly at him. "Understand? We're even."

Later they found a true Friendly tree and slept. Awakening, they trudged on again, and slept again, and so on for three nightless days. No more mudspouts burst about them, but all the other horrors of the Hotlands were well in evidence. Doughpots crossed their path, snake vines hissed and struck, the Jack Ketch trees flung sinister nooses, and a million little crawling things writhed underfoot or dropped upon their suits.

Once they encountered a uniped, that queer, kangaroolike creature that leaps, crashing through the jungle on a single mighty leg, and trusts to its ten-foot beak to spear its prey.

When Ham missed his first shot, the girl brought it down in mid-leap to thresh into the avid clutches of the Jack Ketch trees and the merciless molds.

On another occasion, Patricia had both feet caught in a Jack Ketch noose that lay for some unknown cause on the ground. As she stepped within it, the tree jerked her suddenly, to dangle head down a dozen feet in the air, and she hung helplessly until Ham managed to cut her free. Beyond doubt, either would have died alone on any of several occasions; together they pulled through.

Yet neither relaxed the cool, unfriendly attitude that had become habitual. Ham never addressed the girl unless necessary, and she in the rare instances when they spoke, called him always by no other name than Yankee poacher. In spite of this, the man found himself sometimes remembering the piquant loveliness of her features, her brown hair and level gray eyes, as he had glimpsed them in the brief moments when rain made it safe to open their visors.

At last one day a wind stirred out of the west, bringing with it a breath of coolness that was like the air of heaven to them. It was the underwind, the wind that blew from the frozen half of the planet, that breathed cold from beyond the ice barrier. When Ham experimentally shaved the skin from a writhing weed, the molds sprang out more slowly and with encouraging sparseness; they were approaching the Cool Country.

They found a Friendly tree with lightened hearts; another day's trek might bring them to the uplands where one could walk unhooded, in safety from the molds, since these could not sprout in a temperature much below eighty.

Ham woke first. For a while he gazed silently across at the girl, smiling at the way the branches of the tree had encircled her like affectionate arms. They were merely hungry, of course, but it looked like tenderness. His smile turned a little sad as he realized that the Cool Country meant parting, unless he could discourage that insane determination of hers to cross the Greater Eternities.

He sighed, and reached for his pack slung on a branch between them, and suddenly a bellow of rage and astonishment broke from him.

His xixtchil pods! The transkin pouch was slit; they were gone.

Patricia woke startled at his cry. Then, behind her mask, he sensed an ironic, mocking smile.

"My xixtchil!" he roared. "Where is it?"

She pointed down. There among the lesser growths was a little mound of molds.

"There," she said coolly. "Down there, poacher."

"You——" He choked with rage.

"Yes. I slit the pouch while you slept. You'll smuggle no stolen wealth from British territory."

Ham was white, speechless. "You damned devil!" he bellowed at last. "That's every cent I had!"

"But stolen," she reminded him pleasantly, swinging her dainty feet.

Rage actually made him tremble. He glared at her; the light struck through the translucent transkin, outlining her body and slim rounded legs in shadow. "I ought to kill you!" he muttered tensely.

His hand twitched, and the girl laughed softly. With a groan of desperation, he slung his pack over his shoulders and dropped to the ground.

"I hope—I hope you die in the mountains," he said grimly, and stalked away toward the west.

A hundred yards distant he heard her voice.

"Yankee! Wait a moment!"

He neither paused nor glanced back, but strode on.

HALF AN hour later, glancing back from the crest of a rise, Ham perceived that she was following him. He turned and hurried on. The way was upward now, and his strength began to outweigh her speed and skill.

When next he glimpsed her, she was a plodding speck far behind, moving, he imagined, with a weary doggedness. He frowned back at her; it had occurred to him that a mudspout would find her completely helpless, lacking the vitally important mudshoes.

Then he realized that they were beyond the region of mudspouts, here in the foothills of the Mountains of Eternity, and anyway, he decided grimly, he didn't care.

For a while Ham paralleled a river, doubtless an unnamed tributary of the Phlegethon. So far there had been no necessity to cross watercourses, since naturally all streams on Venus flow from the ice barrier across the twilight zone to the hot side, and therefore, had coincided with their own direction.

But now, once he attained the tablelands and turned north, he would encounter rivers. They had to be crossed either on logs or, if opportunity offered and the stream was narrow, through the branches of Friendly trees. To set foot in the water was death; fierce fanged creatures haunted the streams.

He had one near catastrophe at the rim of the table-land. It was while he edged through a Jack Ketch clearing; suddenly there was a heave of white corruption, and tree and jungle wall disappeared in the mass of a gigantic doughpot.

He was cornered between the monster and an impenetrable tangle of vegetation, so he did the only thing left to do. He snatched his flame-pistol and sent a terrific, roaring blast into the horror, a blast that incinerated tons of pasty filth and left a few small fragments crawling and feeding on the debris.

The blast also, as it usually does, shattered the barrel of the weapon. He sighed as he set about the forty-minute job of replacing it—no true Hotlander ever delays that—for the blast had cost fifteen good American dollars, ten for the cheap diamond that had exploded, and five for the barrel. Nothing at all when he had had his xixtchil, but a real item now. He sighed again as he discovered that the remaining barrel was his last; he had been forced to economize on everything when he set out.

Ham came at last to the table-land. The fierce and predatory vegetation of the Hotlands grew scarce; he began to encounter true plants, with no power of movement, and the underwind blew cool in his face.

He was in a sort of high valley; to his right were the gray peaks of the Lesser Eternities, beyond which lay Erotia, and to his left, like a mighty, glittering rampart, lay the vast slopes of the Greater Range, whose peaks were lost in the clouds fifteen miles above.

He looked at the opening of the rugged Madman's Pass where it separated two colossal peaks; the pass itself was twenty-five thousand feet in height, but the mountains out-topped it by fifty thousand more. One man had crossed that jagged crack on foot—Patrick Burlingame—and that was the way his daughter meant to follow.

Ahead, visible as a curtain of shadow, lay the night edge of the twilight zone, and Ham could see the incessant lightnings that flashed forever in this region of endless storms. It was here that the ice barrier crossed the ranges of the Mountains of Eternity, and the cold underwind, thrust up by the mighty range, met the warm upper winds in a struggle that was one continuous storm, such a storm as only Venus could provide. The river Phlegethon had its source somewhere back in there.

Ham surveyed the wildly magnificent panorama. Tomorrow, or rather, after resting, he would turn north. Patricia would turn south, and, beyond doubt, would die somewhere on Madman's Pass. For a moment he had a queerly painful sensation, then he frowned bitterly.

Let her die, if she was fool enough to attempt the pass alone just because she was too proud to take a rocket from an American settlement. She deserved it. He didn't care; he was still assuring himself of that as he prepared to sleep, not in a Friendly tree, but in one of the far more friendly specimens of true vegetation and in the luxury of an open visor.

The sound of his name awakened him. He gazed across the table-land to see Patricia just topping the divide, and he felt a moment's wonder at how she managed to trail him, a difficult feat indeed in a country where the living vegetation writhes instantly back across one's path. Then he recalled the blast of his flame-pistol; the flash and sound would carry for miles, and she must have heard or seen it.

Ham saw her glancing anxiously around.

"Ham!" she shouted again—not Yankee or poacher, but "Ham!"

He kept a sullen silence; again she called. He could see her bronzed and piquant features now; she had dropped her transkin hood. She called again; with a despondent little shrug, she turned south along the divide, and he watched her go in grim silence. When the forest hid her from view, he descended and turned slowly north.

Very slowly; his steps lagged; it was as if he tugged against some invisible elastic bond. He kept seeing her anxious face and hearing in memory the despondent call. She was going to her death, he believed, and, after all, despite what she had done to him, he didn't want that. She was too full of life, too confident, too young, and above all, too lovely to die.

True, she was an arrogant, vicious, self-centered devil, cool as crystal, and as unfriendly, but—she had gray eyes and brown hair, and she was courageous. And at last, with a groan of exasperation, he halted his lagging steps, turned, and rushed with almost eager speed into the south.

TRAILING the girl was easy here for one trained in the Hotlands. The vegetation was slow to mend itself, here in the Cool Country, and now again he found imprints of her feet, or broken twigs to mark her path. He found the place where she had crossed the river through tree branches, and he found a place where she had paused to eat.

But he saw that she was gaining on him; her skill and speed outmatched his, and the trail grew steadily older. At last he stopped to rest; the table-land was beginning to curve upward toward the vast Mountains of Eternity, and on rising ground he knew he could overtake her. So he slept for a while in the luxurious comfort of no transkin at all, just the shorts and shirt that one wore beneath. That was safe here; the eternal underwind, blowing always toward the Hotlands, kept drifting mold spores away, and any brought in on the fur of animals died quickly at the first cool breeze. Nor would the true plants of the Cool Country attack his flesh.

He slept five hours. The next "day" of traveling brought another change in the country. The life of the foothills was sparse compared to the table-lands; the vegetation was no longer a jungle, but a forest, an unearthly forest, true, of treelike growths whose boles rose five hundred feet and then spread, not into foliage, but flowery appendages. Only an occasional Jack Ketch tree reminded him of the Hotlands.

Farther on, the forest diminished. Great rock outcroppings appeared, and vast red cliffs with no growths of any kind. Now and then he encountered swarms of the planet's only aerial creatures, the gray, mothlike dusters, large as hawks, but so fragile that a blow shattered them. They darted about, alighting at times to seize small squirming things, and tinkling in their curiously bell-like voices. And apparently almost above him, though really thirty miles distant, loomed the Mountains of Eternity, their peaks lost in the clouds that swirled fifteen miles overhead.

Here again it grew difficult to trail, since Patricia scrambled often over bare rock. But little by little the signs grew fresher; once again his greater strength began to tell. And then he glimpsed her, at the base of a colossal escarpment split by a narrow, tree-filled canyon.

She was peering first at the mighty precipice, then at the cleft, obviously wondering whether it offered a means of scaling the barrier, or whether it was necessary to circle the obstacle. Like himself, she had discarded her transkin and wore the usual shirt and shorts of the Cool Country, which, after all, is not very cool by terrestrial standards. She looked, he thought, like some lovely forest nymph of the ancient slopes of Pelion.

He hurried as she moved into the canyon. "Pat!" he shouted; it was the first time he had spoken her given name. A hundred feet within the passage he overtook her.

"You!" she gasped. She looked tired; she had been hurrying for hours, but a light of eagerness flashed in her eyes. "I thought you had—I tried to find you."

Ham's face held no responsive light. "Listen here, Pat Burlingame," he said coldly. "You don't deserve any consideration, but I can't see you walking into death. You're a stubborn devil but you're a woman. I'm taking you to Erotia."

The eagerness vanished. "Indeed, poacher? My father crossed here. I can, too."

"Your father crossed in midsummer, didn't he? And midsummer's to-day. You can't make Madman's Pass in less than five days, a hundred and twenty hours, and by then it will nearly winter, and this longitude will be close to the storm line. You're a fool."

She flushed. "The pass is high enough to be in the upper winds. It will be warm."

"Warm! Yes—warm with lightning." He paused; the faint rumble of thunder rolled through the canyon. "Listen to that. In five days that will be right over us." He gestured up at the utterly barren slopes. "Not even Venusian life can get a foothold up there—or do you think you've got brass enough to be a lightning rod? Maybe you're right."

Anger flamed. "Rather the lightning than you!" Patricia snapped, and then as suddenly softened. "I tried to call you back," she said irrelevantly.

"To laugh at me," he retorted bitterly.

"No. To tell you I was sorry, and that——"

"I don't want your apology."

"But I wanted to tell you that——"

"Never mind," he said curtly. "I'm not interested in your repentance. The harm's done." He frowned coldly down on her.

Patricia said meekly: "But I——"

A crashing and gurgling interrupted her, and she screamed as a gigantic doughpot burst into view, a colossus that filled the canyon from wall to wall to a six-foot height as it surged toward them. The horrors were rarer in the Cool Country, but larger, since the abundance of food in the Hotlands kept subdividing them. But this one was a giant, a behemoth, tons and tons of nauseous, ill-smelling corruption heaving up the narrow way. They were cut off.

Ham snatched his flame-pistol, but the girl seized his arm.

"No, no!" she cried. "Too close! It will spatter!"

PATRICIA WAS right. Unprotected by transkin, the touch of a fragment of that monstrosity was deadly, and, beyond that, the blast of a flame-pistol would shower bits of it upon them. He grasped her wrist and they fled up the canyon, striving for vantage way enough to risk a shot. And a dozen feet behind

surged the doughpot, traveling blindly in the only direction it could—the way of food.

They gained. Then, abruptly, the canyon, which had been angling southwest, turned sharply south. The light of the eternally eastward Sun was hidden; they were in a pit of perpetual shadow, and the ground was bare and lifeless rock. And as it reached that point, the doughpot halted; lacking any organization, any will, it could not move when no food gave it direction. It was such a monster as only the life-swarming climate of Venus could harbor; it lived only by endless eating.

The two paused in the shadow.

"Now what?" muttered Ham.

A fair shot at the mass was impossible because of the angle; a blast would destroy only the portion it could reach.

Patricia leaped upward, catching a snaky shrub on the wall, so placed that it received a faint ray of light. She tossed it against the pulsing mass; the whole doughpot lunged forward a foot or two.

"Lure it in," she suggested.

They tried. It was impossible; vegetation was too sparse.

"What will happen to the thing?" asked Ham.

"I saw one stranded on the desert edge of the Hotlands," replied the girl. "It quivered around for a long time, and then the cells attacked each other. It ate itself." She shuddered. "It was—horrible!"

"How long?"

"Oh, forty to fifty hours."

"I won't wait that long," growled Ham. He fumbled in his pack, pulling out his transkin.

"What will you do?"

"Put this on and try to blast that mass out of here at close range." He fingered his flame-pistol. "This is my last barrel," he said gloomily, then more hopefully: "But we have yours."

"The chamber of mine cracked last time I used it, ten or twelve hours ago. But I have plenty of barrels."

"Good enough!" said Ham.

He crept cautiously toward the horrible, pulsating wall of white. He thrust his arm so as to cover the greatest angle, pulled the trigger, and the roar and blazing fire of the blast bellowed echoing through the canyon. Bits of the monster spattered around him, and the thickness of the remainder, lessened by the incineration of tons of filth, was now only three feet.

"The barrel held!" he called triumphantly. It saved much time in recharging.

Five minutes later the weapon crashed again. When the mass of the monstrosity stopped heaving, only a foot and a half of depth remained, but the barrel had been blown to atoms.

"We'll have to use yours," he said.

Patricia produced one, he took it, and then stared at

it in dismay, The barrels of her Enfield-made weapon were far too small for his American pistol stock!

He groaned. "Of all the idiots!" he burst out.

"Idiots!" she flared. "Because you Yankees use trench mortars for your barrels?"

"I meant myself. I should have guessed this." He shrugged. "Well, we have our choice now of waiting here for the doughpot to eat himself, or trying to find some other way out of this trap. And my hunch is that this canyon's blind."

It was probable, Patricia admitted. The narrow cleft was the product of some vast, ancient upheaval that had split the mountain in halves. Since it was not the result of water erosion, it was likely enough that the cleft ended abruptly in an unscalable precipice, but it was possible, too, that somewhere those sheer walls might be surmountable.

"We've time to waste, anyway," she concluded. "We might as well try it. Besides——" She wrinkled her dainty nose distastefully at the doughpot's odor.

STILL IN his transkin, Ham followed her through the shadowy half dusk. The passage narrowed, then veered west again, but now so high and sheer were the walls that the Sun, slightly south of east, cast no light into it. It was a place of shades like the region of the storm line that divides the twilight zone from the dark hemisphere, not true night, nor yet honest day, but a dim middle state.

Ahead of him Patricia's bronzed limbs showed pale instead of tan, and when she spoke her voice went echoing queerly between the opposing cliffs. A weird place, this chasm, a dusky, unpleasant place.

"I don't like this," said Ham. "The pass is cutting closer and closer to the dark. Do you realize no one knows what's in the dark parts of the Mountains of Eternity?"

Patricia laughed; the sound was ghostly. "What danger could there be? Anyway, we still have our automatics."

"There's no way up here," Ham grumbled. "Let's turn back."

Patricia faced him. "Frightened, Yankee?" Her voice dropped. "The natives say these mountains are haunted," she went on mockingly. "My father told me he saw queer things in Madman's Pass. Do you know that if there is life on the night side, here is the one place it would impinge on the twilight zone? Here in the Mountains of Eternity?"

She was taunting him; she laughed again. And suddenly her laughter was repeated in a hideous cacophony that hooted out from the sides of the cliffs above them in a horrid medley.

She paled; it was Patricia who was frightened now.

They stared apprehensively up at the rock walls where strange shadows flickered and shifted.

"What—what was it?" she whispered. And then: "Ham! Did you see that?"

Ham had seen it. A wild shape had flung itself across the strip of sky, leaping from cliff to cliff far above them. And again came a peal of hooting that sounded like laughter, while shadowy forms moved, flylike, on the sheer walls.

"Let's go back!" she gasped. "Quickly!"

As she turned, a small black object fell and broke with a sullen pop before them. Ham stared at it. A pod, a spore-sac, of some unknown variety. A lazy, dusky cloud drifted over it, and suddenly both of them were choking violently. Ham felt his head spinning in dizziness, and Patricia reeled against him.

"It's narcotic!" she gasped. "Back!"

But a dozen more plopped around them. The dusty spores whirled in dark eddies, and breathing was a torment. They were being drugged and suffocated at the same time.

Ham had a sudden inspiration. "Mask!" he choked, and pulled his transkin over his face.

The filter that kept out the molds of the Hotlands cleaned the air of these spores as well; his head cleared. But the girl's covering was somewhere in her pack; she was fumbling for it. Abruptly she sat down, swaying.

"My pack," she murmured. "Take it out with you. Your—your——" She broke into a fit of coughing.

He dragged her under a shallow overhang and ripped her transkin from the pack. "Put it on!" he snapped.

A score of pods were popping.

A figure flitted silently far up on the wall of rock. Ham watched its progress, then aimed his automatic and fired. There was a shrill, rasping scream, answered by a chorus of dissonant ululations, and something as large as a man whirled down to crash not ten feet from him.

The thing was hideous. Ham stared appalled at a creature not unlike a native, three-eyed, two-handed, four-legged, but the hands, though two-fingered like the Hotlanders', were not pincer-like, but white and clawed.

And the face! Not the broad, expressionless face of the others, but a slanting, malevolent, dusky visage with each eye double the size of the natives'. It wasn't dead; it glared hatred and seized a stone, flinging it at him with weak viciousness. Then it died.

Ham didn't know what it was, of course. Actually it was a *triops noctivivans*—the "three-eyed dweller in the dark," the strange, semi-intelligent being that is as yet the only known creature of the night side, and a member of that fierce remnant still occasionally found in the sunless parts of the Mountains of Eternity. It is perhaps the most vicious creature in the known planets, absolutely unapproachable, and delighting in slaughter.

At the crash of the shot, the shower of pods had ceased, and a chorus of laughing hoots ensued. Ham seized the respite to pull the girl's transkin over her face; she had collapsed with it only half on.

Then a sharp crack sounded, and a stone rebounded to strike his arm. Others pattered around him, whining past, swift as bullets. Black figures flickered in great leaps against the sky, and their fierce laughter sounded mockingly. He fired at one in mid-air; the cry of pain rasped again, but the creature did not fall.

Stones pelted him. They were all small ones, pebble-sized, but they were flung so fiercely that they hummed in passage, and they tore his flesh through his transkin. He turned Patricia on her face, but she moaned faintly as a missile struck her back. He shielded her with his own body.

THE POSITION was intolerable. He must risk a dash back, even though the doughpot blocked the opening. Perhaps, he thought, armored in transkin he could wade through the creature. He knew that was an insane idea; the gluey mass would roll him into itself to suffocate—but it had to be faced. He gathered the girl in his arms and rushed suddenly down the canyon.

Hoots and shrieks and a chorus of mocking laughter echoed around him. Stones struck him everywhere. One glanced from his head, sending him stumbling and staggering against the cliff. But he ran doggedly on; he knew now what drove him. It was the girl he carried; he *had* to save Patricia Burlingame.

Ham reached the bend. Far up on the west wall glowed cloudy sunlight, and his weird pursuers flung themselves to the dark side. They couldn't stand daylight, and that gave him some assistance; by creeping very close to the eastern wall he was partially shielded.

Ahead was the other bend, blocked by the dough-pot. As he neared it, he turned suddenly sick. Three of the creatures were grouped against the mass of white, eating—actually eating!—the corruption. They whirled, hooting, as he came, he shot two of them, and as the third leaped for the wall, he dropped that one as well, and it fell with a dull gulping sound into the doughpot.

Again he sickened; the doughpot drew away from it, leaving the thing lying in a hollow like the hole of a giant doughnut. Not even that monstrosity would eat these creatures.*

But the thing's leap had drawn Ham's attention to a twelve-inch ledge. It might be—yes, it was possible that he could traverse that rugged trail and so circle the doughpot. Nearly hopeless, no doubt, to attempt it under the volley of stones, but he must. There was no alternative.

He shifted the girl to free his right arm. He slipped a second clip in his automatic and then fired at random into the flitting shadows above. For a moment the hail of pebbles ceased, and with a convulsive, painful struggle, Ham dragged himself and Patricia to the ledge.

Stones cracked about him once more. Step by step he edged along the way, poised just over the doomed doughpot. Death below and death above! And little by little he rounded the bend; above him both walls glowed in sunlight, and they were safe.

At least, *he* was safe. The girl might be already dead, he thought frantically, as he slipped and slid through the slime of the doughpot's passage. Out on the daylit slope he tore the mask from her face and gazed on white, marble-cold features.

IT WAS not death, however, but only drugged torpor. An hour later she was conscious, though weak and very badly frightened. Yet almost her first question was for her pack.

"It's here," Ham said. "What's so precious about that pack? Your notes?"

"My notes? Oh, no!" A faint flush covered her features. "It's—I kept trying to tell you—it's your xixtchil."

"What?"

"Yes. I—of course I didn't throw it to the molds. It's yours by rights, Ham. Lots of British traders go into the American Hotlands. I just slit the pouch and hid it here in my pack. The molds on the ground were only some twigs I threw there to—to make it look real."

"But—but—why?"

The flush deepened. "I wanted to punish you," Patricia whispered, "for being so—so cold and distant."

"I?" Ham was amazed. "It was you!"

"Perhaps it was, at first. You forced your way into my house, you know. But—after you carried me across the mudspout, Ham—it was different."

Ham gulped. Suddenly he pulled her into his arms. "I'm not going to quarrel about whose fault it was," he said. "But we'll settle one thing immediately. We're going to Erotia, and that's where we'll be married, in a good American church if they've put one up yet, or by a good American justice if they haven't. There's no more talk of Madman's Pass and crossing the Mountains of Eternity. Is that clear?"

She glanced at the vast, looming peaks and shuddered. "Quite clear!" she replied meekly.

*Note: It was not known then that while the night-side life of Venus can eat and digest that of the day side, the reverse is not true. No day-side creature can absorb the dark life because of the presence of various metabolic alcohols, all poisonous.

Extension of the Finite / 10 / Paper Tigers — The Hero Pulps

Like mighty avengers they rose out of the gloom of the Depression to battle the forces of crime and injustice. One by one they advanced in the name of humanity, until their legion numbered 50 strong, to strike terror into the souls of evildoers and courage into the faint hearts of small boys. They were the Pulp Heroes, fearlessly and selflessly devoted to ridding the country of its growing plague of crime.

Each was unique. Each had his special arsenal of super-powers, his distinctive clan of specially talented comrades in arms. If you were black, yellow, red, or white, too skinny, too tall, too short, or too fat, were plagued with pimples or overbite, hated school, were scared of girls or terrified of bullies, somewhere within the pulpy pages of the Hero Pulps there was an idol (or at least an assistant) through whom you could assert that part of you which you secretly knew was invincible.

Before their arrival crime had been fought with the standard equipment: guts and guns. But in the early 30's police didn't seem to be making much progress with that equipment—not against the ruthlessly efficient gangs like those of Dillinger and Ma Barker. Then, quite by accident, a new kind of hero was born. Street and Smith was doing a radio series based on stories from *Detective Story Magazine*. Writer Harry Charlot suggested an announcer to be called "The Shadow." Dave Chrisman and Bill Sweets of the program's advertising agency expanded the role to that of narrator—an eerie disembodied all-knowing voice. It was so successful as a concept that Street and Smith, in order to protect the idea, created the first Hero Pulp, The Shadow. Suddenly the forces of evil panicked and mothers and teachers trembled as small boys donned black capes and slouch hats and affected strange laughter from behind locked doors:

> Weird mirth that, as it faded, rang with a note that symbolized triumph over crime:
> The laugh of The Shadow!

That laugh was to become an immortal symbol to countless followers, perhaps the most famous trait of any American hero in history. But who was The Shadow? Where had he come from? For the neophyte crime-fighter a short resume was included in every issue:

THE SHADOW KNOWS

In crime capitals the world over, criminals gather in secret and smugly plan attacks on the populace at large. Hell's Kitchen in New York—Limehouse in London—under the shadows of the Sacre Coeur in Paris—along the Tiber in Rome—in the back streets of Berlin—beside the Bund in Shanghai—in San Francisco's Chinatown—in cities the globe over, crooks mumble their plans of murder, arson, theft—every crime known to man!

But hidden in a sanctum in New York, a being in black ponders beneath a blue light and slyly chuckles to himself as he peruses reports of his agents. For The Shadow knows! Before crime plans have been put into being, word has come from his agents in far-flung corners of the world—and The Shadow has laid plans to thwart the hordes of evil!

Earphones on the wall lead to Burbank, contact man—and through him go the Master of Darkness' instructions to his aids. Instructions to Harry Vincent to report on the scene of incipient crime, to lay the groundwork for The Shadow's approach; to Hawkeye and Cliff Marsland, in their underworld guise, the paths they are to follow; to Clyde Burke, reporter for the Classic, the necessary information to be gained through newspaper channels; to Moe Shrevnitz, taxi driver of the first rank, word of transporting the Master Fighter to his field of battle; to Rutledge Mann, hiding behind the "front" of an investment broker, the word to be ready with his invaluable aid; to Jericho, giant African, the stand-by message to aid, if necessary, with his terrible strength.

Agents obey orders—and then from the sanctum glides a being in black—to reach the scene of crime and strike swiftly with blazing automatics. The Shadow against minions of the underworld! One gun against many! But when the triumph laugh peals out under a midnight sky, there has been but one ending: The Shadow has vanquished his foes, and crime for the time being has been stilled.

To two persons only is The Shadow's true identity known—that of Kent Allard, internationally famous aviator—and those persons are Xinca Indians, servants picked up by Allard during a stay among their tribe in Central America. A guise often used by The Shadow is that of Lamont Cranston, world-renowned big-game hunter and traveler, when Cranston is away on his travels. This is by the leave of the real Cranston, a man of deep understanding.

"Crime must go!'—thus The Shadow's slogan.

There was beef behind that slogan, too. For the "Master of Darkness" had a special philosophy which emerged to the dismay of those foolish enough to cross him:

The Shadow's aim was certain. The attacking gunmen were clear targets for his unerring marksmanship. For cowardly murders. The Shadow had no quarter. Snarling, bestial fiends fell with dying curses on their evil lips.

No quarter! Bullies fell snarling in small imaginations, everywhere!
The Shadow's entrance was always dramatic:

It was a night of madness, this, indoors and out. Through the thick, ugly fog came basso blares of river whistles, singularly like tones of doom. Amid the thick swirl, Griff and his expert crew had spread out to patrol the district, with the fog as perfect cover.

Strangest of all was the ghostly shape that glided through the neighboring streets like the stalking figure of death itself. It seemed a human shape plucked from night's own blackness, visible only where it stirred the mist, disappearing in the grimy background beyond the swirls of fog.

The Shadow was seeking an arch-foe whom he had never seen nor heard of, but whose existence was a matter beyond all doubt: Professor MacAbre, the brain of Voodoo crime!

Wherever evil dwelt, The Shadow would find it. Nothing escaped those eyes:

They were eyes that burned from darkness; the eyes of a shrouded, unseen observer, black-cloaked and hatted, . . .
The watcher was The Shadow.

But of all his characteristics it was his laugh by which he was known and respected, feared and hated:

Silent, ominous, The Shadow stood. From unseen lips came a low sound of shuddering, whispered mirth. It was the laugh of The Shadow—that weird, knowing mockery that characterized this strange, unknown master of the night.

It conjured forgotten memories:

His laugh took a recollective note.

It uplifted the spirit:

The Shadows sibilant laugh carried an encouraging note.

It communicated whole paragraphs:

It was Harry who caught the strange note in The Shadow's laugh: a tone telling that his chief would prefer to drive back into the pursuing swarm and snatch Li Husang from their midst, as final proof that Ying Ko was superior in power.

Regardless of the supply of oxygen, its stamina could be counted on:

It promised to be a long undertaking for The Shadow, but breathless. Rising to fierce crescendo, the mockery flung its challenge in no doubtful terms.
It was the laugh of The Shadow!

It had a good beat and could be downright musical:

Tuned almost to The Shadow's laugh came the chime of a distant clock striking eleven. Those reverberations seemed to stimulate the whispered mirth that Fred heard.

But first and last, it was the finest weapon of psychological warfare ever evoked:

He wanted the taunt to be heard by Professor Durand, creator of the mechanical contraption. Fierce, strident, the tone filled the courtyard like a challenge to all-comers.
It brought results, that mirth.

It reduced all who heard it to jelly:

His sudden appearance at their flank, the taunt of his mighty laugh close to their ears, was sufficient to send them scurrying.

Even in large numbers:

It seemed that nothing could stop the fury of the on-rushing mob. Then, like a cry from another world, came a mighty challenge that stopped the fanatics in their tracks.
It was a laugh, so weird and sinister that no human listener could ignore its defiance.
The laugh of The Shadow!

Above all—The Shadow had style!

Amid those deadly gun coughs, The Shadow laughed. His tone came strident through the thickness, inviting enemies to do their utmost. Maybe they took it as a bluff, for with one accord they charged, shouting to each other to "get The Shadow."

Shots from thrusting guns stabbed at a common target, looming blackness that could only represent The Shadow since there was no one else about. Instead of collapsing, that shape loomed higher and grew huge, as though magnified by the fog. The Shadow seemed to be gaining a gigantic stature, his taunting laugh rising with him.

The burst of guns was drowning the metallic clang of bullets, otherwise Griff's marksmen might have realized what their target was before they reached it. Coming together at the focal spot, they saw the thing they had mistaken for The Shadow take its rightful shape. The bulking monstrosity was the steep, covered stairway leading up to the elevated line!

It was one of those stairways with several turns, which accounted for its massive appearance. It was made of metal; steps, rails and all, a zigzag pill-box towering up into the foggy night. Already well up the steps, The Shadow was laughing down at the foemen from whose very midst he had escaped.

Griff snarled the order for attack and with a mad surge, six gunmen stormed the stairs, blasting shots upward at every turn. Either The Shadow was out of shots or saving them, for his laugh was the only response.

This was an express station, where the central track mounted to a superstructure above the local platform. Down the line, approaching lights were twinkling upward through the mist, announcing that an express was taking the rise toward the double platform of the superstructure.

Reaching the edge of the platform at full speed, The Shadow launched himself in the air. His was the action of a broad jumper, perfectly performed. A capable jumper can cover twenty feet and the width of the track pit was considerably under that distance. But few athletes would have taken the chance in circumstances such as these.

The Shadow's leap carried him right across the path of the onrushing train, the gleaming headlight growing as if to swallow him. His flight through air seemed painfully slow as the metal juggernaut roared toward him, but his timing was perfect. The Shadow struck the far platform and reeled onward, half a second ahead of the mighty mass that threatened to smash him.

Above the groan of the halting train, a weird laugh floated back from the stairs beyond the opposite platform. The Shadow hadn't waited to witness the frustration of his pursuers; having let the train cut them off, he was on his way elsewhere, taking advantage of the time that would elapse before Griff's tribe could follow.

Only they didn't. They wanted flight, knowing that The Shadow was somewhere at large in the dank fog, probably prepared to chop them down at leisure, if they crossed his deadly path. They weren't even going back to get their truck.

They were lucky, those scattering gunners who had dared The Shadow. He was letting them go their way —for The Shadow had another person to consider: Margo Lane.

Turning in the misty gloom, The Shadow gave a brief departing laugh as he started back along the avenue to cover the few blocks to the abandoned lair of Professor MacAbre.

That kind of action appeared in 325 novel-length stories "from the private annals of The Shadow, as told to Maxwell Grant." Who was this Grant? Was he a mere stenographer, secretly taking dictation from a mysteriously shrouded figure under a blue light in an abandoned warehouse, somewhere in the swirling mists of the night? It was thrilling to think so. But it wasn't the case.

Maxwell Grant was, at various times, the alias of five different writers. The most prolific was Walter Gibson, who wrote 285 of the novels, including the first 15 years' worth. Figuring about 60,000 words for each bi-weekly novel, that comes to better than 17 million words just for his work on The Shadow. But Gibson put it in his own words and his figures are most striking:

. . . to meet The Shadow's schedule I had to hit 5,000 words or more per day. I geared for that pace and found that instead of being worn out by 5,000 words I was just reaching my peak. I made 10,000 words my goal and found I could reach it. Some stories I wrote in four days each, starting early Mon- day morning and finishing late Thursday night. On these occasions I averaged 15,000 words a day, or nearly 60 typewritten pages, a pace of four to five pages an hour for 12 to 15 hours. By living, thinking, even dreaming the story in one continued process, ideas came faster and faster. Sometimes the typewriter keys would fly so fast that I wondered if my fingers could keep up with them. And at the finish of the story I often had to take a few days off as my finger-tips were too sore to begin work on the next book.

But in spite of the pace, Gibson reminisced affectionately, "I remember mostly the fun and excitement of those hectic years."

Gibson wasn't the only writer to maintain that kind of energy. Lester Dent (who, incidentally, contributed one Shadow episode) was essentially responsible for another great Street and Smith Pulp Hero who, although he piled up fewer installments, achieved longer lasting popularity. Was it because of his inspiring use of science in his battles against crime? Was it because he offered hope to the weak through his methods of self-development? Or again, could it have been something in the flicker of those "flake-gold eyes" or even the fact that he was "inscrutable" (as most shy boys were)? Whatever it was, the "Man of Bronze," Doc Savage, became the Hero *par excellence,* and dozens of his exploits are being resurrected in paperback today.

Getting your problem to Doc Savage wasn't easy. He operated out of a fortress at the top of a skyscraper and was surrounded by an amazing clan of crime-busters. In the true Pulp Hero tradition, a resumé came with each novel:

RENNY. One of Doc's most valued assistants, an engineer of world-wide reputation and, as it happens, a whale of a guy in any kind of a fight. He tops six feet in height, and he's 200 pounds in perfect shape.

MONK. Also a great rough-and-tumble fighter. But more—he's a renowned chemist. He doesn't look it, though. He's a hairy, homely man—which doesn't keep him from thinking he's a wow with the ladies. His nickname fits him better than his real name—nothing less than Andrew Blodgett Mayfair, if you please.

HAM. A lawyer—and part of the cream of his profession. Brigadier General Theodore Marley Brooks—which is how is mail is addressed—looks the part,

too. He's one of the half dozen best dressed men in the country. And can he fight! His favorite weapon for special occasions is a useful sword-cane, tipped with a drug which puts his opponents into a quick and harmless slumber.

LONG TOM. Major Thomas J. Roberts, an electrical wizard, sturdy of mind, frail of physique.

JOHNNY. An authority on geology and archaeology. Those are big words, but they're nothing to the many-syllabled tongue-twisters that William Harper Littlejohn—Johnny to you—uses in intimate conversation. He's gaunt and unhealthy-looking—a fact which has led many a thug to get the very erroneous idea that he's a pushover in a fight.

Entrance to Doc's command post was tricky, as girl animal trainer Lion Ellison found out in one episode:

She'd read about this particular building, so she'd been prepared to be awed. But not prepared quite sufficiently. It was exactly what they'd said it was. Stupendous. Eighty-six stories it towered, not counting the dirigible mooring mast that some dreamer architect had added to the top, and which had proved about as useful as a pair of tonsils.

She walked into the place and was awed by its modernistic magnitude. The size, if nothing else, made the lobby breath-taking. There was a phalanx of elevators.

Lion went to a uniformed elevator starter, asked, "Doc Savage's office?"

"Private lift in the rear," the starter said.

Lion moved toward the back of the lobby.

The elevator, she discovered, was an automatic one. There was no operator. There were merely two buttons, one labeled "Up," the other "Down." And a small plaque over the "Up" button said, "Clark Savage, Jr.," with modest letters. Lion shrugged and gave the button a poke.

The door shut silently and the cage raised upward so swiftly that Lion had to swallow and pump at her ears with her palms to equalize the pressure. Then the cage stopped. The door, however, did not open.

Lion jumped when a voice addressed her from overhead.

"If you will remove that knife from your purse," the voice said, "you will be admitted."

Lion glanced upward, saw where the voice came from—there was a small loud-speaker, hitherto unnoticed, in the cage roof. But just how the unseen speaker had known there was a knife in her handbag was a dumfounding mystery.

"Who are you?" Lion asked uncertainly.

"Ham Brooks, an associate of Doc Savage," the voice said. "What about the knife?"

Lion said, "I'll put my purse on the floor."

She did so. At once the elevator doors opened and the young woman stepped out into a modestly decorated hallway, the walls of which were completely blank except for one door, a bronze-colored panel which was labeled, *Clark Savage, Jr.*, in plain letters.

There was another small door at the side of the elevator, and from this a man appeared. He was a lean, thin-waisted man with good shoulders, the wide mouth of an orator, and a high forehead.

Lion pointed at the elevator. "You got an X ray on that thing or something?" she demanded. "How did you know I had the knife?"

"X ray is right," Ham Brooks said.

"*What!*"

Ham said, "We take a few precautions around this place."

A first meeting with Doc Savage, even if he seemed to border on catatonia, was always memorable:

And a moment later, Lion was facing Doc Savage. She knew instantly that this man was Doc Savage. She knew, too, that the magazine article which she had read long ago had not exaggerated as much as she supposed.

The Man of Bronze, the article had called Doc Savage. It was appropriate. Tropical suns had given his skin a bronzed hue that time and civilization probably would never eradicate. There were other impressive things about him—his eyes, for instance. They were strange golden eyes, like pools of flake-gold always stirred by tiny winds. Powerful eyes, with something hypnotic about them.

Only when Doc Savage was close to her did Lion realize his size. He was a giant, but of such symmetrical muscularity that there was nothing abnormal about his appearance; one had to see him standing close to something to which his size could be compared to realize how big he was.

His voice was low, resonant, and gave an impression of controlled power. "You are the young woman who telephoned last night from Missouri."

Lion asked, "How did you know that?" in a startled voice.

The bronze man's flake-gold eyes and metallic features remained inscrutable. He did not explain that his aids had made a recording of her telephone calls—as indeed they recorded all calls to the headquarters—and that he had recognized her voice. "Conjecture," he explained.

The intricacies of Doc's set-up were complex enough to satisfy any James Bond fan:

Because Doc Savage had enemies, and these occasionally watched the skyscraper exits and made trouble, he had arranged a unique and fast method of travel from the eighty-sixth floor establishment to the hangar where he kept his plane. This conveyance was a contraption which Monk called the "go-devil," and other things not so polite. Lion was introduced to the device. She found herself stepping into a cylindrical, bullet-shaped car which was padded, very crowded once all were inside, and which traveled in a shaftlike tube. Doc threw a lever. There was a roaring *whoosh!* and other phenomena.

The other end of the ride was a real eye-opener:

Lion glanced about; her mouth and eyes became round with astonishment. She stood inside a vast building of brick-and-steel construction that looked strong enough for a fortress. There was an assortment of planes ranging from a huge streamlined thing that had speed in every line to a small bug of a ship that had no wings whatever, only windmill blades that probably whirled. All of the planes were amphibian, she noticed; they could operate from land or water. There were boats as well, lying in slips. She saw a small yacht; she stared in astonishment at a peculiar-looking submarine which was equipped with a protective framework of big steel sledlike runners. A submarine for going under the polar ice, she realized suddenly.

"Why—this is amazing!" she exclaimed.

"Doc's hangar and boathouse," Monk explained. "On the Hudson River water front. From the outside, looks like an ordinary brick warehouse."

The financing behind Doc's arsenal was legend. Unaffected by Depression blues, Doc had his own form of banana-republic ju-ju which would have had our modern **C.I.A.** funding experts chewing their checkbooks in envy:

Lion stared at Doc Savage. She had completely revised her opinion of the bronze man.

"All of this must cost a mint of money," she said. "Where does he get all of what it takes?"

Monk grinned. "Oh, he picks up a penny here and there."

"Maybe I'd better tell him I'm broke. I can't pay for all of this."

Monk smiled again. The source of Doc Savage's wealth was a mystery, the solution known only to the bronze man and his five associates. Doc Savage had a fabulous gold hoard deep in the unexplored mountain of a remote Central American republic—a vein of gold that was almost a mother lode, and watched over by descendants of the ancient civilization of Maya. On any seventh day, at high noon, Doc Savage had but to broadcast a few words in the Mayan tongue —a language which they had reason to believe no civilized person other than themselves understood— and the message would be picked up in the lost valley. Days later, a mule train loaded with gold would come out of the jungle. The source of wealth had come to Doc Savage as a result of an unusual adventure; the hoard was his to draw upon only as long as he used the wealth in his strange career of righting wrongs and punishing evildoers.

But Doc was not one to rely solely on technical resources in his fight against evil. His main asset was his constant attention to physical and mental development:

Lion touched Ham's arm and asked, "How does he know where we're going?"

"Doc? I've seen him do this so often that it doesn't surprise me any more. He probably saw a map of Jefferson City somewhere at some time."

Ham shook his head in admiration. "I think Doc puts more time in on memory development than anything else in that daily exercise routine."

"Routine?" Lion was puzzled.

"The aerialists and acrobats with a circus have to practice, don't they?"

"Of course."

"Well, every day since I've known him, Doc has expended at least two hours on what I guess you would call an exercise routine. It's an amazing thing. He has scientific methods of developing all his senses and mental abilities. As you get to know him better, you may be inclined to think he's a little inhuman—but as a matter of fact, he's an example of the degree to which a man can develop himself by concentration and persistence."

No trick, no matter how complicated or homespun, was unknown to him:

Doc went back into the room. He said, "Everyone be as still as possible," and moved over and fastened an ear against the wall to listen. He thought of another and better way to pick up sounds—he drew a pocketknife which he had located on Johnny's plane and brought along, opened the knife, sank the blade deep into the door casing. Then he gripped the handle with his teeth. He knew from experience that he could pick up vibrations—such as footsteps—much more readily in that fashion.

Every small boy dreamed of mastering this one:

The jailer presumed they were all locked in cells, so he had fears about entering the runway. He came in boldly and did not notice Doc until the bronze man's fingers were about his neck.

Doc did not choke him. He exerted pressure with fingertips on strategic nerve centers which produced quick unconsciousness. The man would be out for fifteen or twenty minutes, and eventually reviving, would have nothing more than a slight headache to show for his experience.

His treatment of criminals would have had today's penal reformers shaking their heads in amazement:

After the radio was switched off, Monk looked at Renny and grinned and said, "Bill Larner only knows about half of what Doc has done for him."

The reference was to the fact that Bill Larner, as

a graduate of Doc's criminal-curing "college," had no idea that he had once been a blood-thirsty crook of a type he had been taught to hate while in the institution.

Bill Larner merely thought he was a man who had suffered the loss of his memory in an accident, and had been educated in Doc Savage's institution as an act of kindness on the bronze man's part.

Occasionally the bronze man indulged conjecture in sentences of more than two or three words, but he seemed to have more stamina in matters of physical achievement and scientific thought than in philosophy, as the following discourse would indicate:

He leaned back, half closed his flake-gold eyes, and after a moment indulged in what appeared to be philosophy. "You know, it has often occurred to me to wonder whether the human race might not be fundamentally evil. Otherwise, why should social behavior apparently be controlled by fear?" The bronze man's flake-gold eyes rested on the other. "You do not understand what I mean, do you? Take this situation, for example. The thing could have been a great boon to mankind, but due to the evil texture of certain minds, it is going to be anything but a boon, unless we can stop it."

"What you're saying doesn't make sense to me."

"You'll understand when my associates come back with the prisoners."

The bronze man got up, moved to the door and stood there for awhile.

"Hungry?" he asked.

Nevertheless when all of Doc's faculties were functioning together smoothly and precisely (which was most of the time), he was a marvel of exciting efficiency:

It was one of Kansas City's largest buildings; even in New York City, it would have been rated a skyscraper. There was a bank of eight elevators, all operating, any one of which a visitor might take.

Since the day was rapidly turning into a blizzard, they were using the revolving doors. Sidewalks were crowded. Doc was close to the man—thirty feet or so back—when the fellow entered the revolving door, and all set with what resembled a small rubber ball in his hands.

He threw the ball; it struck in the compartment of the rotating door with the man near his feet. It burst, as it was designed to do, and released a small spray of chemical that splashed on the fellow's shoes and trousers cuffs.

The man glanced down, but the rubber container, having collapsed, resembled a pencil eraser; he shrugged, went on.

It was fortunate, Doc reflected, that he had used a tube of darkening stain on his face and hands, and turned his coat inside out. The coat was lined so that it reversed a different color and cut. Also he had changed the color of his eyes by using the little tinted glass optical caps such as he had employed in disguising Lion Ellison much earlier. He had done this in the taxi.

He walked into the warm lobby of the building and watched the indicater over the elevator. The first stop the cage made was on the sixteenth floor. That helped.

Doc took another cage, rode to the sixteenth, got out and produced a sealed metal canister which looked like a talcum-powder can, and in fact was labeled as such.

He sprinkled powder on the floor in front of the door of the elevator which the long-armed man had taken. Nothing happened, so he took the stairs to the next floor.

He repeated the operation until he reached the topmost floor, and still nothing happened.

Doc leaned against the wall, disgusted and puzzled. The acid which had been in the rubber container was very potent—its vapor, present in unbelievably minute quantities, would cause the normally bluish powder to turn red.

The acid on the man's shoes would leave vapor wherever he walked for a while, and the vapor was heavier than air so that it remained close to the floor. But it hadn't worked.

While Doc was pondering, a rising elevator went past. Went *past*. Something strange about that, because this was supposed to be the top floor.

There was a stairway and a steel door that he had presumed led up to the elevator-machinery housing on the roof.

The door was locked. He started to pick the lock, then became cautious.

He detached a small gadget of wires and tubes which had been affixed inside the lid of the radio. A wire ran from this, and he plugged it into a jack on the radio which utilized only the receiving amplifier. He ran the gadget around the edges of the locked door.

The door was wired with a burglar alarm—one of the most effective types which utilized a circuit continuously charged with a small current which would be broken the moment the door was opened. The gadget had registered presence of the tiny electrical field surrounding the alarm wires.

There was a frost-glazed window at the end of the corridor. Doc opened it, and biting cold wind and cutting snow particles whipped his face. He studied the brick wall, the ornamental coping, with no enthusiasm whatever.

He climbed out and began going up, closing the window behind him. There were hand holds—cracks between the stones into which he could wedge fingertips—and ordinarily climbing would not have been treacherous, if one discounted the fact that to slip was death, and the half-inch width of the fingertip supports.

The cold wind pounded his clothing against his body; it pushed at him, and made a doglike whining around the carved facets of the ornamental coping above. There was ice in some of the cracks where his fingertips had to grip; at first, when his fingers were warm, it was easy to tell when they were resting on ice, but soon the cold and strain made it nerve-shatteringly difficult.

At length he swung over the coping and lay there on a narrow tarred ledge; he had only to get up and clamber over a low wall onto the roof. He was safe now.

There was a penthouse atop the skyscraper.

Some of the trees in the penthouse garden were stunted evergreens; the others were scrawny and naked of leaves. There were flower and plant boxes, the stringy contents looking as dead as bits of binder twine. The snow had drifted over everything.

Doc moved carefully, using a hand to whip out traces of his footprints as best he could.

He did not try to enter the penthouse, feeling that opening a window or door would send a chill betraying draft racing through the place. He found a niche, an angle between two walls, where the snow was deep and a window was convenient.

And now he made use of another accessory of the radio, this one a contrivance no larger than an overcoat button. It was a microphone, equipped with a suction cup which would hold it to a windowpane; wires ran to a small plug which fitted the receiver amplifier jack on the radio. It was an ultrasensitive eavesdropping device.

Doc Savage attached the contrivance very cautiously to a windowpane—he selected a window—which he judged from the proximity of a fireplace was a den or living room—and quickly settled into the deep snow. He used his hands to fill his tracks, then covered himself with snow as best he could.

Within a few minutes, the howling wind would obliterate traces of his coming.

Suffice it to say that if Doc Savage could handle himself as effortlessly as he did in the preliminaries, when the showdown came he would physically subdue the crooks in the twinkling of one strangely gold-flaked eye. And of showdowns there were plenty—under the Earth's surface and in the depths of the sea, in palaces of ice at the North Pole, caverns at the equator, and the jungles of Southeast Asia. He inspired and educated. His readers learned that science could be not just a curiosity, but a formidable tool for the forces of good. He organized a readers' column and awarded honors for club members who did good deeds in the tradition of the Doc Savage code of ethics. Membership was available to all, and the club button, a relief bust of Doc (bronze, of course) was worn proudly by thousands.

Kids of all ages joined together as the ranks of the Pulp Heroes swelled in 1933. They joined the secret societies of *Operator #5* and *Secret Agent "X"* to tackle the forces of subversion. They formed bicycle squadrons in support of *Dusty Ayres and His Battlebirds* and *G-8 and His Battle Aces,* flying with them in the never-ending struggle for peace. As the years went on, astigmatic kids acquired the super-senses of *The Black Bat;* those with acne, the invisibility of *Captain Zero;* and those with overbite changed their facial structure and lisped through the special set of false teeth worn by *The Whisperer.* Their tricks ran the gamut, from the crime-fighting stage-magic employed by *Don Diavolo* and *The Ghost,* to the more speculative stratagem employed to restore failing business by Cash Gorman, *The Wizard.*

Readers rejected all efforts by publishers to foster the popularity of evildoers. Archfiends like *Wu Fang, The Octopus, The Scorpion,* and *Dr. Yen Sin* were shunned like

THE SECRET SENTINEL

ALONG about this time of year, with snow blanketing the ground, people begin thinking about Christmas and carol-singing and giving presents. The aura of "Peace on earth, good-will to men," is pretty much in the air. But it isn't Christmas everywhere. There are places where, instead of the Christmas spirit, lean-faced, keen-eyed men sit hunched over heavy tables covered with maps and campaign plans, wondering if *this* is the year to try to take America or not. Perhaps this year they can unleash the dogs of war, ravage the land of plenty, and make our country the colony of a power beyond the sea. Every day, if you read the newspapers carefully, you can see evidences of their espionage, sabotage, and propaganda. While the nation is lulled by the atmosphere of peace and recovery from the Great Depression, foreign militarists plot to enslave us.

And all the while, a vigilant body of men, the United States Secret Service, is even busier discovering their schemes and making them ineffectual. Constantly alert, ever-watchful, they protect this land of ours. Jimmy Christopher—Operator 5—is just such a person, a prototype of them all. He is ready to make the supreme sacrifice for his country in its hour of need. He is continually at work, out-thinking and out-planning the enemy. And side by side with him are the scores of other sharp-witted operatives.

In exactly the same way, every red-blooded American wants to do his duty by his native land—to protect it from the constant dangers which threaten. For that very reason, The Secret Sentinels of America has been organized. It offers Americans a way to serve their country in time of peace just as they would in time of war.

If you have not enrolled—if you have not as yet received one of these handsome rings, clip the coupon at the bottom of this page, and enlist as a Secret Sentinel of America!

plague by the righteous kids. Yet a rare hero with religious background fared little better: the Himalayan mumbo-jumbo of *The Green Lama* lasted only 14 issues.

In the Negro community both boys and girls could vicariously participate in the crime purge as members of any one of several crusaders' clans. *The Avenger,* for example, was fortunate in having as sidekicks this pair:

Joshua Elijah H. Newton and his pretty wife, Rosabel, usually assume the roles of languid Negro servants, though each is an honor graduate of Tuskeegee Institute. Their keen minds and strong hearts make them invaluable aids to The Avenger's cause.

Pulp Heroes even foretold how the wars of the future were to be fought, and with whom, as did *Dusty Ayres* as early as 1934:

IS AMERICA PREPARED FOR THE NEXT GREAT WAR?

The next war may be ten years from now—it may be tomorrow! The only certain thing—based upon historical facts and knowledge of mankind—is that there will be a war! And the next certain thing is—that it will be fought and won in the air!

WHEN —*ocean flying is made safe by huge seadromes*
—*planes have a speed of five hundred miles an hour*
—*stratosphere rocket ships are a certain thing*

Will we be prepared to carry on our own against the enemy who might attack our borders? You'll find the answers in

THE RED DESTROYER

An amazing novel of the next great war

written by Robert Sidney Bowen

Also several future-war short stories . . . plans for building models of Dusty Ayres' speed plane . . . all complete in

DUSTY AYRES and his BATTLE BIRDS
December issue
On sale Nov. 9

And so having alerted and inspired, broadened and educated, and fulfilled just about every other obligation which could be expected of them by their idolizing fans, the last of the Pulp Heroes faded away in 1953.

The magazines they appeared in have long since disappeared, the crumbling treasures of an exclusive coterie of jealous collectors and university librarians.

Still . . . some dark foggy night . . . you may catch the strange, gold-flaked glance of an almost-familiar stranger, or hear the distant echo of a shuddering, whispered laugh. Take comfort . . . The great Pulp Heroes live on.

BIBLIOGRAPHY

Beaumont, Charles, "The Bloody Pulps". *Playboy Magazine,* Sept. 1962.

Buxton, Frank, and Owen, Bill, *Radio's Golden Age,* Easton Valley Press, 1966.

Chandler, Raymond, *The Simple Art of Murder,* Houghton Mifflin, 1950.

Gibson, Walter, *The Weird Adventures of The Shadow,* Grosset & Dunlap, 1966.

Israel, Fred A., ed., 1897 *Sears Roebuck Catalogue,* Chelsea House, 1968, Preface.

Moskowitz, Sam, ed., *Science-Fiction by Gaslight,* World Publishing Co., 1968.

Moskowitz, Sam, ed., *Under the Moons of Mars,* World Publishing Co., 1970.

Peterson, Theodore, *Magazines in the Twentieth Century,* University of Illinois Press, 1956.

Schlesinger, Arthur M., Jr., "The Business of Crime," Thomas Byrnes, *1886 Professional Criminals of America,* Chelsea House, 1969, Intro.

Shaw, Joseph T., ed., *The Hardboiled Omnibus,* Simon & Schuster, 1946.

Wilkinson, Richard Hill, "Whatever Happened to the Pulps?" *Saturday Review,* Feb. 10, 1962.

The Life History of the United States, Time, Inc., 1964, 12 Vol.

This Fabulous Century, Time, Inc., 1969, 7 Vol.

SUGGESTED READING

The Big Swingers, Robert W. Fenton (Prentice-Hall, 1967). A biography of Edgar Rice Burroughs.

Fiction Factory, Quentin Reynolds (Random House, 1955). A history of Street and Smith Publishing Company.

The Hardboiled Dicks, Ron Goulart, ed. (Sherbourne Press, 1965). Anthology.

Max Brand, Robert Easton (University of Oklahoma Press, 1970). A biography.

Pulp Jungle, Frank Gruber (Sherbourne Press, 1967). Autobiographical reminiscences by one of the better-known Pulp authors.

Pulpwood Editor, Harold Hersey (Frederick A. Stokes, 1938). Autobiographical reminiscences by one of the pioneer Pulp editors.

Zane Grey, Frank Gruber (World Publishing Co., 1970). A biography.

CURRENTLY IN PREPARATION

Voyagers through Infinity, Sam Moskowitz (Holt, Reinhardt, Winston).

Edgar Rice Burroughs, a Biography, Irwin Porges.